SEVERING SANGUINE

A COMPANION BOOK TO THE FALLOCAUST SERIES

BOOK 2

QUIL CARTER

Severing Sanguine Copyright © 2015 by Quil Carter

All rights reserved. No part of this book may be used or reproduced in any manner whatsoever without written permission except in the case of brief quotations em-bodied in critical articles or reviews.

www.quilcarter.com

Cover by Quil Carter

First Edition

978-1508827108

1508827109

This book is dedicated to the boy who hid under the bed.

"We are each our own devil, and we make this world our hell." – Oscar Wilde

PROLOGUE

HE STOOD IN THE CORNER WITH HIS BACK TO THE WALL trying with every ounce of him to make his face appear as neutral as possible. Like a captured wild animal he watched from the shadows with his heartbeat a steady drum for the man to make the first move.

These strange people always made the first move. The ones who had captured him had wasted no time showing off their power – though the man in the shadows had put up a fight.

But now the atmosphere around them was different; an eerie calm that rested badly against his unravelling stoicism. It was unsettling, a soft draw of a well-rosined bow that steadily climbed higher until you automatically felt your teeth start to clench.

"Take a seat, Sanguine," the man in the suit said, breaking the heavy tension in the room, and though Sanguine's face still held its calm the man could hear the boy's pulse jump.

The only move Sanguine made was to press his back up against the wall; his shining reflective eyes fixing on the man sitting in the chair. He didn't take his eyes off of him; if anything he started watching him more intently.

"We're going to get this session over with one way or another, Sanguine. We can either do it with you a spectre in the darkness or you can sit down on the opposite chair," the man said in the same casual voice, though this one held an authoritative edge to it. "I will even allow you to have a cigarette."

Sanguine's head jerked towards the man until he remembered himself.

He forcibly relaxed his body again but there was no masking the want that had appeared in his eyes.

The man on the chair slowly and deliberately reached into his dark blue blazer before pulling out one of those funny blue cigarettes. Sanguine's kryptonite, cigarettes, especially the blue-embered ones, had been Sanguine's only comfort since he was seven years old.

The man held the cigarette by the filter and watched as Sanguine slowly started to inch himself from the darkness.

Sanguine, a man of nineteen years, stepped into the light of the room; though as the light illuminated his features it was obvious that he was no ordinary man.

Sanguine had two deep crimson eyes and straight black hair that fell several inches past his ears; he had a thin, unhealthy face and black circles underneath his eyes; a look that was familiar to anyone who lived in the greywastes.

The man pinched the filter of the cigarette with his fingers and watched as Sanguine slowly sat down; his red eyes going in all directions as he scanned the room for any further threats.

"I am Dr. Mantis Dekker, chimera psychologist and councillor of Skyfall, did Nero inform you of your schedule with me?" Mantis asked, retracting his hand slowly as Sanguine took the cigarette from him. He was about to offer the young man a light but with a flare of smoke Sanguine lit the tip of the cigarette with his finger.

Sanguine took a long inhale of the blue-embered cigarette before breaking his lips away from the filter with a pop. He held it in for a second before letting the silver plumes escape his mouth with a long drawn-out sigh.

Mantis turned the page on one of Sanguine's papers, the red-eyed young man still enjoying the cigarette with his head tilted forwards. His stance and the way he was almost keeled over the smoke suggested that it meant more to him than just a temporary relief from his anxious emotions.

"Do you wish for me to call you Sami? Would that make you more comfortable?" Mantis asked. In lieu of cigarettes Mantis picked up a glass of red wine; he took a small sip of it before setting it down on the black oak side table beside him.

Sanguine, still slumped forward with the cigarette in his mouth, shook his head. "Sanguine is fine," he said in a deep raspy voice; he paused for a moment before adding. "Sami is dead."

Mantis's charcoal grey eyes were fixed on Sanguine and if Sanguine had looked up he would've caught the slight dilation of his pupils. This statement seemed to hold a greater interest on the psychologist.

"Did you kill Sami?"

"He killed himself."

"And…" There was a pause as Mantis turned the page on a thick, stapled stack of paper. "Crow… when was the last time you saw him?"

"He's here right now."

"So right now we can say for certain… you can see him?"

Another silver plume was blown from Sanguine's lips; he nodded slowly and took another drag, already half-finished his cigarette. As his lips broke away this time a row of serrated sharp teeth could be seen.

"That's right," he said in a low voice.

"You don't call yourself Crow though when he comes? It's not quite like you slip into a different skin?"

Sanguine shook his head. "No, it's not like that. I'm – I know I'm Sanguine."

"But you don't quite know who Sanguine is do you? That name was always just what you called yourself inside your head."

"When the other two weren't around… yeah." Sanguine glanced up when he heard movement; he took the ashtray that Mantis was offering him and dashed his cigarette. As he did his eyes flickered around the room and in response he scrunched himself far into the chair he was sitting on.

Mantis nodded and took another drink of wine; when he sat his glass down he picked up a fine-tipped black pen and started writing on the piece of paper he had been looking at.

"Perhaps Sanguine is who you were always meant to be but the trauma of your childhood and adolescence in the greywastes stopped him from becoming more than a blank slate. What do you think of that, Sanguine?" Mantis asked.

Sanguine stared at his cigarette and was silent.

"Could be," Sanguine said after more than a comfortable amount of silence had passed. He then extinguished his cigarette in the ashtray and started looking around again. "I'd like to go now."

Mantis reached into his pocket again and pulled out another cigarette, though this time Sanguine didn't take it.

"No." Sanguine rubbed his nose and swept the room with his gaze again. He shifted nervously in his seat before drawing his knees up; he wrapped his arms around them trying to make himself as small as possible.

Mantis placed the cigarette on the side table. "Sanguine, when you fall into this psychosis – do you black out?"

Sanguine seemed to bristle at this; his mouth pursed and his slender arms clenched his knees tighter to him.

"I'm not that... bad." Sanguine's voice dropped into frigid waters. "I don't forget anything; I just… feel…"

"Liberated? Like being someone else justifies your actions?" Mantis asked. "I found it is a common thing with chimera teenagers to refer to their darker half by another name. It helps them disassociate with what violent acts they are committing."

"I'm not... one of you."

"I am not a chimera, Sanguine." Mantis offered the cigarette to Sanguine again and this time the man took it. "Whereas chimeras are born from what they call their steel mothers I was made immortal after the fact and accepted into this family."

"Why?" Sanguine's eyes rose to greet Mantis's, this fact seemed to catch his attention.

"I helped, and am helping, King Silas properly raise his second generation of chimeras and smooth off some rough edges we have been seeing in their personalities. As a reward for my involvement and my help he granted me immortality and several enhancements. I am now one of King Silas's advisors and I work with all chimeras young and adult."

Sanguine brought the new cigarette up to his mouth and lit it. "They're all fucking crazy."

Mantis smiled and tented his hands; he tapped his index fingers together. "That is debatable. Are we not all a little crazy, Sanguine?"

Sanguine said nothing back; he only put the cigarette back up to his lips to take a long drag. "I wasn't saying I wasn't; I was just saying they –" Sanguine waved his cigarette towards the large oak door that led into Mantis's apartment. "– all are too. I know I'm crazy; I hate myself for it."

"I don't think you're crazy, Sanguine. I think you have a lot of inner turmoil inside of you and a lot of self-hatred. I don't think you want to leave because you're wary of me, I think you want to leave because deep down – you don't think you're worth saving." The entire time Mantis said these words he watched Sanguine's reactions. Sure enough, he witnessed the young chimera's mouth pull down and his fingers tighten around his knees.

"King Silas thinks you're very much worth saving; I do too," he added, prompted by the young chimera's expression.

Sanguine paused; his breath caught in his throat before he regained his composure and shook his head. "No," was all he replied.

Mantis nodded; he wrote more on the paper he was holding before putting the papers down and picking up a manila file folder. He leafed through it and took out a paper with a photo clipped on the corner.

"Sanguine… I want to know about the man Silas, Nero, and Ceph found you with," Mantis said "I'd like you to talk about Jasper."

Like Mantis had just reached over and smacked him in the face, Sanguine visibly recoiled. A silence came over the two of them, but unlike the previous silence this one seemed to set the air around them on fire.

"Don't talk to me about Jasper," Sanguine's raspy voice whispered. His red eyes became as hard as rubies and his right eyebrow started to lightly twitch. Like a snake contorting itself Sanguine started writhing in his spot. His fingers clenched the chair, and his boots scraped against the floor like he was physically trying to get away from someone. All at the mention of Jasper, the entire demeanor of the chimera changed.

"Sanguine… tell me what's happening?" Mantis narrowed his eyes; he raised his hand like he was signalling someone, before he himself rose and stood over Sanguine. "What is happening in your head?"

Sanguine's face twisted in pain; his lips pressed together before his mouth was covered by his hand. He seemed to be clenching his mouth so hard Mantis could see white patches forming around his fingers.

"Sanguine… I'd like you to stay present; can you concentrate on my voice?" Mantis reached a hand out, and as Sanguine bowed his head, hand still clamped over his mouth, he rested the hand on Sanguine's shoulder. Knowing that Sanguine couldn't see him, he glanced behind his shoulder and shook his head at something, though it appeared that only the two of them were in the room.

"Sanguine, what are you seeing?"

"Jasper," Sanguine's raspy voice croaked. Mantis looked down and saw ruby droplets of blood start to fall to the floor, spilling from the fingers Sanguine had grabbing his mouth.

"What did Jasper do to you?" Mantis asked, his tone just lightly urging his words forward. "Is what he did to you the reason you think you're not worthy of help?"

Sanguine shook his head back and forth, more blood dripping red roads down his pale cheeks then onto the grey carpet below.

"Sanguine..."

"Don't ask me about Jasper."

"What did he do to you?"

There was silence.

Mantis stood there, his hand resting gently on Sanguine's shoulder; the red-eyed chimera still looking down with his fingers digging into his own face. The room around them seemed to be plunging into darkness, getting deeper by the second, everything was fading, turning into a slate monotone that repelled all colour.

Sanguine stared at the floor, the voices that were usually only murmurs in his mind now getting louder. They multiplied and spread their forces, seeping into each fold of his brain and digging in to burrow themselves into the sensitive parts of his mind, spreading their cancer in the form of images and feelings that Sanguine had never been able to escape.

They brought with their infection the residue of what had happened to him during his time in the greywastes and as that infection spread and festered in his brain, a new consciousness in him rose from the sepulture of nightmares that was his mind.

Then the change came. The one that Mantis had heard about but had never seen.

The switch that got pulled – where the scared boy hiding under the bed left – and the monster sprung forth.

Sanguine removed his now blood-covered hand from his mouth.

"You ask me... what did he do to me?" Sanguine said in a dry raspy voice.

Mantis didn't bat an eye; he slowly removed his hand from Sanguine's shoulder and took a step back.

"I can still smell his rancid body..."

Mantis watched Sanguine's mouth move, annunciating each word as if each syllable was a diamond on his lips. "I am still being terrorized by the sound of Lyle's skull cracking under the table leg, of Cooper whimpering under my hand."

"What did these boys do to deserve this, Sanguine?" Mantis dropped his voice. "Why did–"

In a movement that happened so quickly Mantis had no time to react, Sanguine jumped up from his chair and grabbed the psychologist by the tie he was wearing; Sanguine yanked him until they were face-to-face and held Mantis there.

Mantis's eyes fixed forward, not a single emotion gracing his face, not even when Sanguine smiled menacingly at him, revealing every single one of his serrated shark-like teeth.

"*Daisy Daisy,*" Sanguine murmured in a singing voice; his red eyes narrowed and his hand raised; he cupped Mantis's chin and tilted his own head back and forth like he was examining him. "*Give me your heart to do.*"

He grinned wider and pressed his face up against Mantis's until their noses were touching. Still Mantis didn't flinch; he watched the chimera intently his movements reduced to only the breath inside of his chest.

"*I'm half-crazy...*" Sanguine sang in a raspy whisper; his eyes closed, "*All for the love... of you.*"

Then, sensing what was about to happen, Mantis raised his hand, in that same instant Sanguine's eyes snapped open as did his mouth.

But Mantis was expecting it; he quickly ducked as the chimera tried to bite his neck and moved behind him.

Sanguine snarled and advanced on Mantis, throwing the chair he had been sitting on to the other side of the room where it crashed into a side table.

In a flash the doors flew open, Nero and his partner Ceph ran into the room and grabbed Sanguine. As expected the chimera struggled, and hard; before they could subdue him both Nero and Ceph got bitten on the arms and shoulders.

Mantis watched calmly as Sanguine screamed, kicking his boots and snapping his head right to left, trying to sink his pointed teeth into anything he could find that was warm. Even the brute chimeras were having trouble subduing the stealthy and slippery Sanguine, who seemed to be able to twist and contort himself like a serpent.

When Sanguine's thrashing started to lessen Mantis walked up to him, the chimera's chest now heaving and his red eyes glassy but staring. The psychologist stopped only inches away from Sanguine and spoke to him calmly.

"We made a lot of progress during our session, Sanguine. I look forward to our next visit."

Sanguine's eyes suddenly shot to Mantis, they were fixed but at the same time Mantis could tell he wasn't seeing what a normal person would.

This chimera is stuck in a mental nightmare; who can escape the thoughts in their head?

Mantis reached a hand up and gently placed it on Sanguine's shoulder, but the moment his skin touched Sanguine's, the boy let out a shrill scream. One so loud Nero jumped, giving the manic chimera the opportunity his psychosis seemed to have been waiting for.

Sanguine ripped his arms free of Nero's strong hold, and with a terrifying grin, he jumped on top of Mantis. The psychologist went tumbling to the floor, Sanguine on top of him. The chimera's teeth bared and his eyes bright with a mania Mantis had never seen before.

And it was the last thing he saw.

BOOK 1

Will You Be My Friend?

CHAPTER 1

Sami

Age 1 & 5

PAULY PRESSED HIS FACE INTO THE SMALL GAP between the boards and looked around the dark cobwebby underbelly of the Sunshine House.

With a snicker Gabe jumped up onto the sun bleached deck and started stamping his feet; immediately Pauly retracted his face and gave Gabe an angry look.

"Asshole! You're going to scare him!" Pauly snapped.

Gabe laughed before jumping up as high as he could jump then deliberately slamming his tattered shoes down onto the deck.

Pauly looked in and saw a sheet of dust fall from the porch onto the greywaste ground. His eyes widened as he saw a flicker of movement.

"He is down there! Get me the stick!" Pauly said excited. He looked around for something he could use but a moment later Gabe handed him a long but thin branch.

"Okay... let's see..." Pauly reached into his pocket and pulled out a lint covered piece of rat jerky; with his tongue peeking out of the corner of his mouth he affixed the jerky onto the end of the stick and slowly threaded it through the hole in the deck. When it was all the way through he pressed his face back into the gap and waved around the thin stick. "Come on little guy, it's food! You gotta be hungry."

Pauly narrowed his eyes; his heart did a small palpitation when he saw a black figure, tucked into the far corners of the porch start to move.

"Okay, be quiet, for serious now..." Pauly whispered. There was a scraping of ground beside him as Gabe kneeled down too and found his own gap to look through.

The boys, only seven, froze in place as the shadow started inching its way towards the stick; it seemed to be crawling on small but sturdy little legs.

"Wow," Gabe whispered in a voice full of awe. Pauly elbowed him in the chest to keep him quiet but the boy's only response to that was to elbow him back.

A small slender little hand appeared in a sliver of light, with nimble fingers the hand grabbed the piece of jerky before the shadow settled on the ground. The two boys heard a small high pitch squeak as the shadow put the entire piece of jerky into his mouth before its hands once again steadied its self on the ground.

"Wow, he's just a baby!" Pauly whispered as the infant's matted black hair became visible in the crack of light. "Go tell Nana!"

"No, I want to see…" Gabe hissed pushing Pauly before pressing his face further into the boards that surrounded the porch.

The infant paused and both boys held their breath; the baby tilted its head towards them and with that, the light illuminated its face.

The boys screamed.

All at once they both jumped to their feet and ran away screaming; the stick laying forgotten, half sticking out of the boards that surrounded the porch.

"What the fuck is all this yelling!" An older woman with a dark complexion, wearing a red dress covered by a soiled apron, appeared in the door way. When the two boys went screaming up the stairs she raised her hand in a threatening manner. "You scream like that and the ravers will come and take you in your sleep. What is all this yelling about?"

Gabe was crying so her eyes were on Pauly whose face was stricken and pale.

"There's a monster under the deck!" Paul stammered. "I saw him this morning… I thought he was a new baby but… but he's a monster, Nan! He had big red eyes and his mouth and face are all bloody!"

Nan smacked Gabe on the side of the head; the boy started wailing holding his ear. "Don't come here and tell me lies, boy. Every time you lie a raver is born, didn't I teach you that?"

"It's true!" Gabe wailed. He turned around and pointed towards the deck of the boys' rooms. "He's under there – he's going to eat us tonight, ain't he?"

Nan rolled her eyes and walked down the steps of the main area of the Sunshine House, a foster and adoption home she had created to care for the greywaste orphans. Behind her both boys trailed, whimpering and sniffing as they nursed injured ears and hurt feelings.

Nan walked up to the deck and kneeled down. She reached into her pocket and pulled out a small flashlight and turned it on.

She swept the small beam under the deck, seeing grey dust and cobwebs, even a few toys that had been small enough to fit through the cracks. She was about to give up when the beam fell onto a little knee.

"Oh... my..." Nan's breath became trapped in her throat; slowly, so she didn't blind the infant, she lowered the beam and traced it over thin little legs and a dirty grey jumper full of holes.

Then, like that of a wild animal, the light bounced and reflected off of its eyes. Nan gasped and pulled the flashlight back.

"See!" Pauly said but with a quick glare from Nan his mouth shut.

"Gabe, get Gill here now," Nan said and looked at Pauly. "Get me some of the jerky. Now, boy; quick like a bunny."

Both boys nodded before turning and running off in opposite directions. Nan grabbed onto one of the boards surrounding the deck and started pulling it off; her face creased with determination.

She had three boards pulled off when the boys came back. Pauly handed her a large piece of rat jerky which she held clenched between her teeth. With the last board laying against the stack she got down onto her stomach and started crawling under the deck.

When Nan started to come closer to the infant she heard a whimper. She took the jerky out of her mouth and started making soothing noises towards the baby.

"Come here, little baby, do you want some food?" Nan held out the piece of dried meat.

There was another whimper before a little hand reached out; Nan retracted her hand just slightly making the baby start to crawl towards here.

"There we go... a little farther," Nan whispered. She started crawling backwards out of the hole in the porch, holding her breath as the small shrouded figure started following her. Though she had seen the light reflect in his eyes in all respects the little infant sounded like a human and a young one at that.

She broke off a bit of the jerky and held out her hand, the fingers took it gently before disappearing into the darkness, gumming sounds could be heard which made her smile. She backed herself out some more until she was out from under the porch. There was murmuring of the people behind her, watching the scene unfold, but they were smart enough to remain quiet.

Then Nan held out both hands in front of her, making a motion that all people made when welcoming an infant to be picked up.

A small baby, no more than a year old, crawled out from under the porch, covered in dust, dirt, and dried blood. It squinted in the sunlight and held a small dirt-caked hand up to its eyes before Nan scooped the baby up.

To everyone's surprise the baby clung to her and whimpered; its lower lip sticking out though the murmurs of surprise were quickly replaced by shocked gasps when the baby opened its crimson red eyes.

Nan patted the baby's head and gently tilted his gaunt sickly face towards her; when she saw the two red eyes still squinting from the sunlight she held onto him tighter and turned around to face the awestruck crowd.

"That's a half-raver!" Gill who did the hunting said. He was a man in his forties with a brown but greying beard and eyes just slightly too close together. "It's best we kill it now, Linda."

"There is no such thing as half-ravers!" Nan snapped at him. She gently stroked the baby's matted black hair. "This baby has no raver blood in it. Look at it, does it look vicious? It's just a baby with red eyes and it's nothing that can be helped."

"It's a monster!" Gabe started to cry again and he only cried harder when Nan reached down and gave him a hard smack on the head.

"It's not and let me never hear those words again," Nan snapped. She swept past everyone and took the little infant, still clinging hard to her, into the main house on her small patch of greywaste land.

She set the baby down on a changing table and started taking off its dirty onesie. Then one of her helpers, a little girl named Missy, started getting a bucket ready for a bath.

"A little boy, what am I going to do with a little boy with red eyes?" Nan smiled at the baby who was looking around the room, his mouth still gumming the jerky he had been given. "Where did you come from, red eyes?"

The baby looked at her as she spoke before reaching a hand up as if wanting to touch her face. She laughed and tickled his tummy.

The baby giggled and threw his hands over his face. He coo'd before turning his head towards a red jar full of clean rags. He stopped and stared at it as if transfixed over the colour.

A half an hour later the baby was in the wash tub, not a single tear down his face even though most greywaster babies hated water. He was looking at everything with an awestruck face and the occasional furrowed brow if he saw something he couldn't make sense of.

"Linda?"

Nan turned around to see Gill at the door; the man was holding a green milk crate.

"The girls found this beside the boys' dorm, out of the way beside the rope swing. I think the baby was dropped off overnight and he crawled out... there's a note with him."

Nan paused; she gave the wash cloth to the baby to distract him and walked over to Gill. She took the note and shook her head. "A note with real words? It's a rarity to find someone who can read this far from Skyfall..." She unfolded the note and started to read it.

My nam is Lydia. Got tetanus, Im dieing. Please lok aftar my Sami. He was my world. Please don't hate him for his eyes hes well beehavd.
Lydia.

"Oh dear..." Nan murmured. She folded up the note and glanced behind her shoulder. "Sami is it? His mother must've loved him. He's thin but he seems to be a sharp boy."

Gill, who couldn't read, just stood there holding the milk crate. Though when his eyes travelled to the baby, he frowned. Sami was chewing on the washcloth his ruby eyes squinted in happiness.

"He seems like just a baby," Gill murmured.

Nan gave him a look, placing the folded up piece of paper into her pocket. "Of course he's just a baby. Look at him. Just like I'm black and you're white, people look different."

"I don't think red eyes occur..."

"It doesn't matter. I don't see a sign in front of Sunshine House that says normal-eyed babies only. He's staying. His mother trusted him to us and I'll be damned if I turn away a helpless infant. We have more than enough help for him. Holly's out of diapers now, he'll be our only one."

Gill's mouth twisted from one side to the other but he nodded finally. He walked over to the baby and patted his head. In response the baby smiled a gummy smile at him but Gill once again frowned "I wonder if this is just a new mutation we're going to see now. God knows what long term effects this radiation is going to have; it's already stunting the number of female live births."

Nan walked back over to Sami and handed him a wooden spoon he was trying to reach. "If this is the worst mutation we see I'll gladly take it. I heard from Coldstone Caravan just last week that Skytech is thinking about releasing their abominations in the cities nearby."

Sami let out a loud squeal; both of them looked down to see the baby wave the spoon in the air, his eyes wide with awe.

"Sometimes I wonder why people even bother having children anymore," Gill muttered with a sigh. "It makes me wonder just what kind of world he's going to grow up in."

"That's not our place to decide; he's here and as I've always said… we'll do our best," Nan said with a smile. She reached over and tickled the side of the baby's cheek making him squawk. "That's all we can do in the Fallocaust."

I ran my finger over the ground making a small rivet in the ashy dirt. I traced it around a black ant before making another rivet around it and another. I did it until there were almost a dozen rings around the unsuspecting black ant.

I stared at the ant as the insect tested the gap in the ground with its feelers before it started to climb into it. With its antennas moving around it started to navigate the many circles and grooves around it.

"And now… the end boss," I whispered. I reached into my pocket and pulled out a small grey lizard. With its tail flapping back and forth I placed the lizard on the far end of the rings and started humming battle music. I hummed the Star Trek one where Kurt has to kill Spot, the ears guy.

The lizard blinked before becoming still as the unaware ant started trying to climb over the third ring of the grooves I made. I grabbed onto the lizard's head gently and turned his face in case he didn't know where the ant was.

Then with a flash of grey movement the lizard charged forward and gobbled the ant up, the sounds of it crunching the shell of the small insect filling my ears. I hated the crunch noise it was always so loud and it made me want to clench my teeth like *ahhhh!*

I smiled and picked up the lizard when he was done chewing.

"You win!" I said, holding the lizard up to my face. I made a goofy face at it and crossed my eyes. The lizard only stared back; I wish they had face expressions.

Suddenly a sharp pain sprung from the back of my head. I yelped and dropped the lizard before holding my hand to my head and turning around. My eyes welled with tears as shithead Pauly and fuckface Gabe started howling with laughter before running away, rocks in both of their hands.

A lump started to rise in my throat I turned and started to run towards the boys but I suddenly stopped and turned back around, just in time to see the lizard escape into a crag of boulders and yellow bushes.

He was gone, my friend had gone back to his home; he didn't want to play with me anymore even though I fed him.

My lips pursed and I made two fists. I whirled around and with a bellow of rage I started chasing the two boys who had ducked beside their dorm rooms.

"You made me drop him! He was my friend!" I couldn't help the tears burning in my eyes as I chased the two older boys. I pivoted and looked around before hearing the dorm room door slam.

Nursing a sore head and an even sorer hurt in my heart, I burst into the room and looked around, my shoulders hunched and my face a blaze of anger.

"The freak is going to get us! Get your freak spray!" Gabe hollered. A moment later Pauly jumped out of a cabinet holding a Super Soaker and started spraying me with it.

And that was it for me. I burst into tears and ran from the dorm room, hiccupping and gasping as I made my way to the main house.

To my whimpering relief Nana was there, always wearing her red dress and usually holding a wooden spoon, not just for her cooking but for whacking any bad kids on the butt with.

"Oh my, what now, Sami?" Nan sighed. She kneeled down and opened her arms and with a sob I ran into them. Caringly she picked me up and rocked me back and forth as I cried on her shoulder.

In between my sobs and gasps I told Nan what happened, taking special emphasis on the fact that they were solely responsible for me losing my new pet lizard. By the time I was finished I had dampened Nan's red dress and had snot running down my face.

Eventually I let Nan put me down; she put on her cooking apron and used it to wipe my nose.

"Sami, you're not a freak." Nan kneeled down and started wiping the ash off of my tear-stained cheek. "Come here, now that you've stopped that bawling you can help me dry some more rat jerky."

That was fun and yum too. I nodded and started helping Nan hang up the dried pieces of meat. When she wasn't looking I snuck some. I liked the thick ones because they were the juiciest and sometimes I licked the blood at the bottom of the bucket we used. I liked doing it in front of the girls because it made them scream and run away and that was funny.

I reached a hand in and grabbed a big red piece and popped it into my mouth. I wanted more so I tried to grab a small piece Nan wouldn't notice but with a quick hand she rapped my finger with her wooden spoon. I squawked and jumped back but because I knew I deserved it I only scrunched my face at her.

Nan gave me her warning eyes and shook her spoon at me.

"He prefers to eat the meat raw."

I turned around and shrunk down as I saw Gill standing beside the back door of the main house. The greywaster hunter was giving me a dirty look, though I was used to it now. Gill was a bad man who sometimes kicked and yelled at me whenever Nan wasn't looking. I had never told Nan though because Gill was a grown-up and if there was one thing I knew for truth it was that grown-ups were always right and they knew what they were doing. I knew he didn't like me but Nan liked me, and she was my Nana and I liked her too.

"It doesn't matter how he eats his food, Gill, as long as he's getting food in him," Nan said with an edge to her voice. I scurried over to her and once again started helping her hang up strips of red flesh and I didn't eat any more of it. The entire backyard of the main house was dedicated to drying rat meat. It was an enclosed area surrounded by a fly net being held up by old wooden boards and a camper van which Spooky the old grey dog lived in. He helped keep the wild animals out and he liked to eat the flies. I ate a fly once but just once.

"Yesterday he was chewing on the corpse bones like a wild animal. He's a little monster not a–"

"Not in front of the boy!"

I jumped; I hated hearing Nana's angry tone. I shrunk away and went to one of the black trees. I leaned against it and I watched with wide eyes as Nan angrily started hanging up the rat strips.

"Linda, we've had almost a hundred orphans and never once did we have one like him," Gill snapped. I cowered down further as the hunter gave me a withering gaze. "He's a bad seed. I watch him when no one's…"

"Get out of here, Gill; I don't want to hear it." Nan's eyes were wide with anger. If it was me making her give the scary eyes I would've gotten a spoon-beating. Just last week Missy spoiled a whole batch of yeast and, boy, she couldn't sit properly yet still.

Gill made a frustrated noise and threw down the rag he had been holding. He stomped inside and slammed the screen door so hard a tile fell off of the roof and made Spooky jump from his nap.

That night I lay in my bed, a small plastic car bed that I had gotten after Josh got typhoid and died, now it was my bed which was high up in a loft room that was all mine. I liked it because I was high above in the heights and I liked that. I also could hear people coming because of the creaking stairs and I liked knowing when people were coming in case I was doing something bad.

Nana came to kiss me good night; she walked around and did an inspection of my room.

"What's that damn smell?"

I shifted around on my bed and shrugged.

"It smells like rotting meat, have you been hiding food again?"

I shook my head back and forth.

"Sami."

I stared at her.

"Sa-*mi*."

My face flushed with embarrassment. I thought she wouldn't notice. I buried my head into my Power Rangers pillow and pointed to behind my dresser.

I heard rustling so I put the pillow over my head and closed my eyes. I heard Nan sigh and the smell get worse.

"Sami, I know this winter we were short on food but you don't need to... to steal bones. You couldn't even eat these bones they'll break your teeth. They're all green now too – oh Sami, they have worms on them." Nan didn't sound angry but she sounded sad and that was worse. I kept my head buried.

"No more hiding bones. I told you this when you hid that rat's entrails... no hiding meat you'll get trideath. Do you want trideath?" Nan lifted up the pillow from my face but I didn't look at her.

I shook my head and stared at my hands. She leaned in and kissed my cheek and I heard her throw the bones out of the window. Out the window meant that Spooky could eat them and that was okay.

Then I perked up when she grabbed Barry, my bear. She wound the dial on his butt and put him beside my dresser. He could play music and it was my favourite song.

Daisy, Daisy
Give me your heart to do.
I'm half-crazy, all for the love of you.
It won't be a stylish marriage,
I can't afford a carriage,
But you'll look so sweet,
Upon a seat,
Of a bicycle built for two.

But I sang it different in my head because marriage was gross and so were girls, and we didn't have bikes here, only in magazines.

"Not like you even deserve that bear's music with those bones I found," Nan said sternly. I shrunk down on my bed and picked up my pillow again.

Nan turned to leave; I watched her go.

"Nana... am I a monster?"

Nan paused and turned around. "I told you not to listen to Gill or the other kids."

I shrugged and grabbed onto my feet; I started pulling on my toes. "Why do they all hate me?"

She was quiet for a moment; I pulled on my big toe and pressed the nail until it hurt.

"Because you look different and sometimes people like picking on different people," Nan explained. She walked over to me and sat down on my car bed; she brushed back my messy black hair. Barry's song was still playing behind us.

"Why do I look different?" I asked.

"That's just how you were born. Just like Pauly and Gabe have green eyes and Missy has blond hair, like me and Richard have black skin but you all have white skin. We're all greywasters and arian humans and that's all that matters, doesn't it?" Nan thought for a second. "All humans taste the same don't they?"

I nodded.

"Then if we all taste the same and inside we're all the same... then why do differences matter? Why does eye colour matter? You'll taste just like the rest of us." As she said this she pinched my side which made me laugh. Nan smiled at this and kissed my cheek.

"You're not a monster, my Sami, and don't let anyone ever tell you that you are. You're a good boy, okay?"

I smiled and nodded and jumped under my covers.

Nana tucked me in but I had something else to ask her.

"Nan, my mom said my name was Sami, right?"

Nan nodded. "That's right, she got sick and passed away and put you in a little green milk crate."

I twisted under my covers; I didn't know why but I felt embarrassed saying it so I hid my head under the covers. "I think my name is Sanguine. I call me Sanguine in my head."

Nan laughed and pulled my covers down. "That's not your name. Your name is Sami just like the note said but you can call yourself anything you want in your head. Just don't ask Nana to call you such a funny name."

Nan tickled my sides so I laughed too. I said good night to her after with *Daisy Daisy* playing in the background.

CHAPTER 2

Sami

Age 6

I PEEKED MY HEAD OUT OF THE DOOR FRAME AND saw that Nan was spreading jam onto rat meat to make it candied. She was busy which was exactly what I wanted! I tiptoed away from the door frame and jumped off of the porch. I ran past Missy and Richard and into Gill's small cabin that was across the street from the boys' dorm.

Gill had left a week ago with some other hunters to make a journey to the borderlands, most particularly a town called Redrock. They were there to fuel up on supplies so we could get through the winter. I had just been walking past his window and not looking in it at all, but I found something I wanted to take a closer look at.

I put my hands on the window frame, the wood old and just waiting to give you a splinter, and the paint cracked like a lake bottom. I pulled the window open and was greeted by the smell of old newspapers and unrinsed cans. Gill always smelled the same way; his cabin smelled like him.

With one last good listen to make sure I was all alone, I crawled in through the window and into the cabin. Immediately I snatched what I wanted and in a flash I was outside of Gill's house and home free. I stuffed the rubber cement into my jacket pocket with the matches and the spray paint and with a grin, and a giddy feeling in my chest, I headed to the outskirts of Sunshine House.

I couldn't hide my smile; the same smile every kid got whenever they were up to no good. I knew I was being bad, and that Nan would paddle my ass if she found out what I was doing, but this was just too thrilling to pass up.

Today was a warm day, with flies buzzing all around me and the grey sun beaming its light down on us. Yesterday I had found an honest-to-goodness sunbeam and I laid in it for an hour before the clouds came and it disappeared. Sunbeams were a rare treat, it wasn't often the sun was strong enough to break through its cloak of dust and ash. Usually Spooky or some of the cats laid in it, and when they were I let them because I think it meant a lot to them to feel sun.

There were no sunbeams today, but I had more on my mind. I sprinted towards an old shack that the kids and me used for a play fort and ran behind it.

They were still there! I wasn't really sure where else they would go, but since I had all of my tools it was important that they were where I had left them.

It was an anthill! I jitterated with excitement and felt like a god as I towered over them. I put my hands on my hips and glared down at my subjects. To show them I was no merciful god, I tapped the side of the hill with my boot.

A couple of the ants stuck to my boot which made me flail. I hated ants! I hated their gross sectioned bodies, their waving antennas. I hated how they walked around like slaves, and I hated how they bit me. I also hated how they crunched when you stepped on them; that put my teeth on edge and made me want to scream. I had a personal vendetta against ants especially black ants, and unfortunately since it was sandy ash here, and we had lots of old buildings, we got ants every summer. Everywhere!

So I was now a god to them, and I was an angry god!

"I banish you to the fires of hell! For I am demon boy!" I exclaimed, trying to keep my voice down. I got out the rubber cement, with a faded blue label and a tip that was covered in gumminess, and sprayed it on the black anthill. I chewed on my cheek with my back teeth, now adult and sharpy.

The subjects didn't care at first but I think the smell started to piss them off. All at once, the thousands of black ants started to move quicker around the anthill. They were one giant swarm of black that almost dazzled my eyes on the backdrop of grey ash and pieces of yellow grass they had gathered for their hill. So tight of a cluster they were like one continuous moving ball, I shuddered at the thought of accidently falling in.

I squirted some more rubber cement onto it before putting it back into my pocket, then I took out the black spray paint and the lighter. I grinned and flicked the flint of the lighter until I wielded a small yellow flame. I held it out and shook the paint a few times before aiming the lighter and the aerosol can for a practice go.

I gasped when a roar of fire erupted from the spray paint combined with the lighter. I stood there for a moment in absolute shock before a nervous giggle reached my lips. I looked around with a cold adrenaline pushing me forward and pointed it to the angry anthill. Then, with a grin, I pressed down on the trigger and shot a spurt of pure yellow and orange flames onto the unsuspecting black ants.

I held it there and watched the anthill start to burn underneath the searing chemical heat. The ants were all running around in every direction, some I could see melting from the flames. They were in a desperate panic, slowly and painfully roasting alive under my own hand. I was a god, and I had condemned them to death for doing nothing more than existing when I had decided they were not worthy of it.

Though as I held the spray paint, a hiss of black coming from the can before becoming the equivalent to a flamethrower, I felt something different. A light inside of me that I didn't understand but felt compelled to foster. There was something about these flames that was giving me a rush of pleasure; it was tickling parts of my body and mind that nothing else did. I didn't know what it was or why it was happening, but I felt an almost inhuman compulsion to make it happen to me again and again.

So I didn't stop. I embraced this electricity illuminating my body and continued to make the flames.

Then a sharp pain. I stopped abruptly and dropped the spray paint can. I shook my hand and looked at it; it was covered in spray paint and my fingers were smoking. I rubbed the aching hand against my jeans before stuffing them in my jacket.

I turned back to my anthill and admired what I had destroyed. I even stepped back as I saw some half-melted ants try to flee their burning home. They were doomed to die a slow death so I didn't squish them myself. The lizards in the rocks or the animals here could eat them, so in a way I was a generous god because I was feeding the other animals too.

I bet I killed thousands today, I said to myself with a smile, squinting under the sting of the smoke and heavy chemicals.

I stuffed both hands into my pockets and enjoyed the charred, burning anthill sending smoke up into the sky. The ants were still churning like little black candles and moving pieces of coal.

Then I looked behind the smoking anthill and realized the wall that the anthill was up against was charred black. I picked up the paint can again and shook it. I tried to spray it onto the wall but the can was only blowing out chemically air now, so I put it in my pocket, made sure I had the lighter, and turned to run away.

"What the fuck are you doing, mutant?"

I froze and looked up with wide eyes.

Pauly and Gabe were both there. Now in their early teens they were big and tall, much bigger than me. I looked at both of them before turning to run away.

Pauly grabbed my arm and I tried to pull it but Gabe grabbed my other. They took my spray paint and my rubber cement and threw it onto the ground.

"That's Gill's shit. You fucking stole from Gill? He already wants your ass for a feast, dumb shit. He's going to beat you to death," Pauly snapped. He shook my arm making my eyes rattle in my head. I tried to pull back but their grips were as tight as Nana's.

"Let me go!" I hollered. "I'll scream for Nan!"

"Ohhh, Nan's pet demon-monkey is going to call for his saviour? And then what?" Gabe walked over to the still smoking anthill and clucked his tongue. "What will Nan say when she hears you almost burned down the shack? You won't be her little Samikins after that, huh?"

This got me. I felt a lump in my throat as I thought of Nan and what she would do to me. Nan would be disappointed and that was the worst feeling. Everyone here hated me because I was a bad kid, but that didn't mean I liked proving to everyone I was bad.

No! They were just stupid ants. I wasn't bad and Gill was an asshole, and he was mean to me, so he deserved it!

Gabe and Pauly started pulling me towards the anthill laughing. I tried to pull my arms away, and even wiggle out of my jacket, but they had me good.

"Eat one and we won't tell Nan. Go on!" They pushed my face into the anthill and held it near. This scared me, I hated ants. I didn't want to be this close to them. I turned my face to the side but they only pushed me further towards the smoking anthill.

"No!" I coughed. The chemicals were making my eyes sting and my nose burn. I coughed again but that only made the now blackened yellow grass blow ash into my face.

"Eat it, mutant!" Gabe taunted. "You shouldn't kill animals and not eat them that's a waste. Go on, demon-monkey, have a bite!"

"Fuck off!" I screamed even though that was a bad word. I yelled as I felt something brush against my cheek before a spasm of desperation and anxiety rippled through me. The thing was moving; there were ants right under my cheek. They were crawling; they were going to bite me!

I burst into tears and I only cried harder when I heard them laughing. I squirmed around desperately, but when I moved my head, I only felt the tickling brushes of feet and antenna on my nose. I huffed out a huge breath from my nose to try and get them away, but that only disturbed more smoking ash.

I began to feel dizziness and nausea. The chemical smoke was choking my breathing and blinding my vision.

Then before I could stop any of it, everything went black. I think I had passed out.

When I woke up Nan was sitting on one of my chairs, a wooden chair with white paint that I painted myself last year. It was the chair Nan sat on when she read me books and told me stories from when she was little. But Nan wasn't smiling like she usually did, when I woke up she was frowning. Nana was already the oldest person I knew and she had wrinkles and her frowns made her wrinkles worse.

My eyes were stinging awful and my face was tight whenever I moved it. I whimpered and Nan looked up and immediately gave me some water.

"Be still. You have some burns on the side of your face and neck, but they'll heal," Nan said quietly. "Drink all the water and rest."

I slurped the water which felt good on my lips and drank the entire glass. I gave her the glass back and lay back down on my bed. I was almost too big for my car bed, but Nan said I could have it until I turned nine and then I would be too big for it.

"Sami..."

I looked up at Nan and pulled my blankets to my chin; she was using her 'talking to' voice with me and I knew I was in for it.

"Pauly and Gabe shouldn't have even grabbed me! If they hadn't followed me no one would know!" I suddenly said. I pulled the blankets over my head so she couldn't see me. "So you shouldn't even know. That means it never happened, and – and my name isn't Sami, my name is Sanguine."

Nan sighed before I felt her try and pull the covers off of my face. "Sami, it isn't that… I had to clear the ash away from your nose and mouth and…" She paused. "Do you realize your adult teeth are growing in differently than the other boys?"

I shrugged but my tongue was running along the gaps where my baby teeth had fallen out. I had four adult teeth in the back and they were pointy and sometimes they pierced my tongue. I liked they were pointy because it made eating the jerky easier and tough meat too. I liked chewing on things with them, because sometimes while they were growing in my mouth itched.

"They're growing in… pointed." Nan said this last part differently than the other parts. "Your two front teeth you just lost last week. They'll…" She sighed and I felt anxious when she lowered her head. I didn't know what I did bad; I thought I was going to get a spanking for stealing from Gill.

She put a hand on my chin and told me to open my mouth. I opened it and her face became sadder as she tilted my chin. "It looks like that's it for you having those two front biting teeth. I can see them starting to peek through. All the same size and pointed as all hell. Oh, what am I going to do, what am I going to do…" She dropped my chin and buried her face in her hands.

"Nana, I'm sorry I stole from Gill," I said and patted her knee. "Don't be sad. I'll put it back where I found it and we can say he ran out and forgot, ran out of the – the rubber cement and the spray paint."

If it wasn't for Gabe and Pauly being nosey and bullying me Nan wouldn't be sad and none of this would've ever happened. I was going to pay them back for this – it all was their fault for making Nana sad.

And now Nan was upset with me. I hated that, it made my stomach hurt and it made me squirm and dig my fingers into my toenails again.

"No, Sami… I'll tell Gill in secret," Nan said quietly. She lifted up her face from her hands and gave me a smile. "I'll think of something, just don't tell any of the boys or the girls about your adult teeth. Can you promise this to Nan?"

I was a bit taken back by this. "Why, Nanny?"

Nan was quiet for a second. "Well, because it's another way you're different, Sami. And I know the older boys give you a hard enough time already. Nana doesn't want to give them more of a reason. Just… tell me if more teeth fall out, okay? And if the boys ask questions just close your mouth and run to me even if it's late at night."

"When's Gill coming back?" I asked

Nan stood, she looked tired. "Gill is going to be slow coming back. It looks like we might have another rough winter. The Ratmeal from Skyfall is delayed and we'll be lucky to have enough food to last us the winter."

I nodded and dug my fingernail further into my toes. I made them hurt until I couldn't take it anymore. The hurt from that was much better than the feelings I had inside about everything that happened. It made me feel better for the moment, but after it was gone I felt rotten inside. Rotten and bad. Especially now that we were going to have to starve again this winter; I would start collecting some more food and bones to last me then, just in case.

Stupid Gabe and stupid Pauly. They started all of this, if they had just minded their own business none of this would've happened.

I stayed in bed for four whole days with only books to keep me happy and I read those so much I could recite them and I proved that to Missy when she came up with my soup and told me I was fibbing. I think she was just saying that so I would tell her the story from the beginning. The story was *Alexander and the Terrible, Horrible, No Good, Very Bad Day*. I felt like Alexander but I don't think he got his face shoved into a burning anthill, and I don't think he was a monster either. Plus one of the bad things he had happen to him was having gum in his hair. If I had gum I would never complain about a single thing for the rest of my life.

And while I was stuck in bed I thought up a plan as to how I was going to pay back Gabe and Pauly for what they had done to me and for upsetting Nan. At first the plan made me giggle and hide under my Power Rangers pillow because it seemed overwhelming, but as the days went on and I went over it again and again, I started to get excited!

On the fourth day Nan said I was well enough to leave my room! I ran all the way downstairs and played nicely the entire day. When no one was looking I started collecting what I would need for my prank on Gabe and Pauly. Missy and her brother Payton usually were the ones who hung out in the front yards but they were helping Nana clean rats for jerky, and since I had been cooped up, I was allowed free play. The other kids were all too small to interfere or see me, baby Pat and three-year-old Ari just toddled around and minded their own business. Everyone else had chores or couldn't walk yet.

By dinner time I was all ready, even the cloth I made for my plan was all ready.

Every time I thought of what was going to happen tonight I was filled with so many prickles, like needles were pricking my skin and each one of them was full of sparks.

Pauly and Gabe shared their own house now since they were teens and Nan said teens do things at night that kids shouldn't see. I wasn't sure what that was, but I think they were smoking. I tried a cigarette that Gabe gave me when I was five and Nan made him howl for it. I liked how it burned though; I tried to smoke the yellow grass once but it wasn't the same.

It was the best thing that Gabe and Pauly had their own house a ways away to stay in, my plan wouldn't work any other way. People would hear them and I'd get spanked and Nan would be mad. I knew Nan would already be mad but I didn't care. This was between me and Pauly and Gabe and it was none of Nan's business.

I was so excited I had to pretend I was sleepy when Missy came up to read to me. It was her turn and Nan was a bit more busy since we had two new babies in the main house. They were both from the same caravan some ravers tried to eat and they cried all the time. Chippy from the East, an old nomad man, found them hanging from light poles wailing with their parents all eaten and stuff. They had tied them up there when the ravers started running towards them. I wonder if they were old enough to see. My mom was named Lydia and she had gotten sick and died, I didn't remember any of that.

Missy left and I dragged my white chair to my window and looked out it. Even though it faced the backyard I could see Nan's light was still on. I had all my supplies in a backpack, except for my plastic container that I had to carry since I didn't want to spill it.

When it was eleven Nan's light turned off, when it was twelve Gabe and Pauly's did too. I waited until two in the morning before I grabbed my navy blue backpack and started to quietly walk down the steps.

Even though I had planned this with a smile on my face, when I walked out of the boys' dorm and into the warm summer night the light approach to my prank slowly slipped away. With the influence of the dark night filling me with awareness and adrenaline, and the reality of what I would get to do tonight, I felt myself become just a bit more serious about it.

This was apparent when I approached Gabe and Pauly's door. Strangely with every step I felt lightness to my movements, and an eagerness that compelled me to do it faster.

I opened the door and sneaked in. I looked around the room and saw Gabe and Pauly both sleeping in their single beds. They were surrounded by old boxes full of comic books they never let me read, and drawings from them trying to draw the characters in those comics. The entire one room cabin was full of things they had collected, some boxes stacked all the way to the ceiling.

I reached into my pocket and was immediately greeted by the smell of sour rope. I had soaked the strips of cloth I had made in water earlier today. I sneaked over as quietly as I could and kneeled down beside Gabe. With my breath trying to quicken in my chest, I tied the first piece of cloth to Gabe's hand before tying it to the bed. Then I did the other one, and then both of his feet.

I had always been what Nana called 'stealthy'. She always said I was sneaking up on her even when I didn't mean to. So that just meant when I really wanted to be stealthy I could sneak around like an invisible man. This was proven to me when I was able to tie both of the boys to the bed rungs without them even waking up.

I took a moment to check every knot to make sure they were secure and dug into my backpack again. I took out my bottle that I had earlier screwed a sprayer on top of. I had gotten it from one of Nan's Windex bottles.

I took out my lighter too and walked up to Gabe.

I held up the bottle to the side of his face, right where they had shoved my face into the burning ants' nest. I squeezed it and sprayed the side of his face, the smell of sour chemicals seeping from the gas bottle and filling the musty-smelling room with my favourite smell in the world: gasoline.

Then Gabe's eyes snapped open but I was ready. As soon as he woke up I slapped a sticky rat trap over his mouth, the sticky side down to muffle his screaming.

Oh no, Gabe was still making noise! I gasped when I heard Pauly wake up in a daze, but, quick as a bunny, I turned around and did the same to him!

The two teens looked at me in shock; a shock which only got worse when they realized I had tied them up. My eyes switched to their glow-in-the-dark mode I called night bright and that made their eyes start to shine white. They were staring at me in surprise, struggling and hollering. They struggled so much I thought the cloth might break, but it didn't.

Without wasting time, I started squirting the side of Pauly's face. He had an ugly face like a rat so a nice burn would be an improvement. I squirted it, hearing another muffled scream come out as it got into his eyes.

I wanted to say something to them; I had planned to say something. I had planned a big speech in my head telling them to not bully me anymore, or call me demon-monkey, but as I watched the two teens struggling and screamin' muffled screams, with their terrified eyes rolling inside of their heads, I found myself silent.

I think I just wanted to watch them. I liked the terror on their faces.

There was a taste on the air tonight, something was different. I found myself almost frozen on the spot, feeling a quiver inside of my chest that pulled me into these dark thoughts that had always been my friends in my head. They whispered things to me that I had once dismissed with a nervous giggle, but now…

Yes, something was different tonight. Not just the chemical sour smell of gasoline, or the relished screams that were muffled on my enemies' lips. A new emotion was rolling through the childish glee I was experiencing, and it was telling me… it was telling me…

I picked up the spray bottle of gasoline, and in a solid movement, I walked to Gabe and started spraying his neck, then his face which brought out shriller screams. Then I moved down and soaked his chest, then I soaked his private area, and then I soaked his knees. When I was done, I turned around and I soaked Pauly too. I even unscrewed the bottle when it was starting to run out, and I sprinkled the rest onto his thrashing body.

I walked back to the middle of the room and turned around, ignoring the sounds of the beds knocking to the floor as they thrashed. *Clunk, clunk, clunk…* hysterical screams, thrashing…

Each one of these screams was making an explosion rock my chest. I wanted to stay here and listen to them scream forever, but I knew eventually they would hear us.

And why watch the opening act forever? Then you would miss the play.

I took out my lighter and lit it, the flame flared so big from the fumes it burned my hand, but I felt nothing. My eyes were fixed on Gabe who was glistening with gasoline and sweat. I walked up to him with a smile big enough for him to see the pointy teeth starting to grow on the front row.

I leaned down, not breaking eye contact, and I… don't know why but I whispered in his ear.

"*Valeo.*"

I lowered the lighter, and before it could even make contact with his skin, he erupted into flames. He was a ball of flames so hot I had to jump back. I backed away until I hit Pauly's bed, unable to take my eyes off of Gabe.

So much fire, Gabe was literally a human fireball. His shape was perfect, still human, and I could still see thrashing arms, but everything else was a beautiful mixture of yellows and oranges. That, with the shrill agonizing screams, made him the most prettiest thing I had ever seen. I wanted to touch it; I wanted a camera to take pictures. Even though Pauly wasn't on fire yet, I couldn't turn away from this scene I had created. I was mesmerized. I was awestruck. I felt a tingling rush through my body that compelled me to do something, but I didn't know what that was so I just stared.

I wish I had more words; I wish I was a poet so I could describe just what I was seeing. I knew for the rest of my life I would never get this beautiful image out of my head. I wished for nothing else but to bottle this feeling inside of me.

Then Gabe's screaming stopped and disappointment darkened the bright thoughts inside of my head. The smell of cooking meat was delicious and it made my mouth water, but I wanted the screams… I needed more…

Pauly.

I turned around, easily ignoring the searing pain going through my own body from the heat of the flames, not just on Gabe, but now crawling up the walls and getting into the boxes. I looked down at him thrashing and shrieking, and lit my lighter again.

This time I pulled off the rat paper, even though I burned my hands more. I backed away towards the door as the open window stopped being able to get rid of all the smoke, and stood in the doorway as Pauly screamed his pain.

And, boy, did he scream. No longer muffled by the rat paper, I enjoyed the music to my ears, even though my own body was hot from just being so near the flames.

I smiled when I saw Gabe was still moving, the ties now burned off of his wrists and feet but his hands were lifting up before falling down. Pauly was thrashing, and after a moment, he rolled himself off of the bed, a fireball in the shape of a human.

There was nothing else in my life that made me happy. I realized this as the flames reached the roof. Fire and screaming I realized were the best things in the world.

"SAMI!"

I whirled around and felt myself get snapped out of my dream-like trance. Nan was running towards me with the older kids following behind. "Sami! Oh god… Sami what did you do!?"

Nan grabbed me and backhanded me across the face, but I didn't cry.

I got mad.

"They burned me! And they made me stay inside for four days!" I yelled. Nan took one step into the burning cabin before she turned around. Her eyes were so wide they were like moons; her face was different too.

I decided to try and reason with her – I didn't want a spanking. "You said this winter we would starve and now we have two more meats for our food," I suddenly said. "It's okay, Nana. We won't starve this winter now. Right, Nana?"

Nan put her hand to her mouth. She looked up at the older kids, all of them, I realized, had began screaming. The summer night was nothing but screaming, and the fire that was now turning the sky a deep red. There were so many big big flames, and I bet they sent sparks to the universe to become stars.

"Nana, do you think fire sparks make stars?" I asked looking up at the sky.

"Nana?"

I looked over and saw Nan staring at me, tears running down her face. I didn't like making Nan mad but I'd take my spanking for this, I didn't mind. I had carried out my prank, and I had seen all this fire and that made me happy.

What a nice evening this ended up being.

CHAPTER 3

Sami

Age 6

IF NOT ALL OF THE KIDS AT SUNSHINE HOUSE HATED me before, they certainly hated me now. In the weeks after I played my prank on Pauly and Gabe I couldn't be anywhere away from Nan. I got rocks thrown at me, and Tomis even threatened me with a knife and was going to cut me before Nan came and screamed at him.

But eventually Nan just put me in my room. She was tired of me being around; I think maybe because I liked to read out loud to myself because I was still learning and it was easier that way.

Maybe she was angry at me too. Everyone was treating me like I was bad, even badder than before because they always teased me anyway.

I stayed in my room for a long time and Missy didn't come up to read to me or bring me food. Nan came to bring me food but sometimes she forgot for an entire day and then it was just a small amount. I asked for more, but I stopped because she slapped me when I asked where Pauly and Gabe's meat was.

So Nan was cross with me which meant no one liked me. I dug my fingernail into my toenail even more until it made me say *Ow*. I kept doing it though to punish myself for everyone hating me. It made me feel better so I did it a lot.

I also chewed on my bed frame and my books because my teeth were itchy itchy. I'd rather have a bone to chew on, something that wouldn't break because I was chewing through the spines of these big fairytale books.

Every day my teeth grew in more, and this morning I lost another two teeth, two of my lower ones which had been loose. I could already see pointed tips poking up over my pink gums. The gums were all red from me chewing and from the teeth growing in; everything ached inside of my mouth. I was just miserable.

That night I heard Gill coming back. I stayed away from the window so he couldn't see me and started to listen.

The voices started out normal but soon they started rising. I heard Gill yell first, then Nan, and soon they were just screaming at each other.

It was scary when adults yelled.

I winded up Barry and held his stomach to my ear. I sang along to his jingle loud enough so I wouldn't hear Gill yelling at Nana. Though behind the musical box I could still hear Nan screaming at him. She kept saying I was just a six-year-old boy and I wasn't evil.

Evil?

Evil people were ravers, the ones with the dark colours in the Disney books, and the people who gave Nan babies who were close to death. I wasn't any of those people though – maybe I was a brand-new kind of evil.

Maybe that was why everyone teased me, because I was evil and bad not because I had different eyes and my teeth were growing in wrong. They just knew I was a bad person before I did and they were just defeating me like the good guys defeated the bad guys in my books and the movies we sometimes watched.

This made me look at the bad people differently. Maybe they didn't want to be bad but everyone else kept telling them they were supposed to be bad, so one day they just decided to go with it. In the Disney books all the bad guys have dark clothes or dark fur but it wasn't their fault they were born that way or that was the clothing they liked to wear. Maybe if Mufasa was nice to Scar and told Scar he could be king on weekends then Scar wouldn't have killed him.

I pressed my right ear into Barry's fur even more when I heard a crash downstairs and then my free hand I pressed my other ear. Barry was on *'I'm half-crazy'* for the second time and I would need to wind him again soon.

Suddenly the door slammed open. I screamed from shock and clutched Barry. Then I screamed from fright as Gill appeared in the doorway with an angry look on his face. I backed up as far away on my bed as I could but he snatched me quickly.

Gill threw me against the wall. I smacked my back against the drywall and it crumbled around me. I lay there stunned but he grabbed me again and started carrying me downstairs.

Nan was screaming and that scared me even more. I kicked and tried to twist around yelling loudly for an older kid since Nan was scared too. Richard would help, he never minded me as much as some of the others.

My head hurt and I was so scared I couldn't stop the tears coming down my face. Gill pulled me out of the boys' dorm with everyone getting up and watching and he took me outside.

Everyone was yelling but it wasn't bad yelling; every one of the kids outside were cheering at Gill. They were egging him on and telling Gill to beat me.

Gill took me into the main house; I almost dropped Barry but I didn't. I held him tight but Gill was holding me tighter. I tried to kick him but he dodged me. He walked me into the kitchen where Nan baked and cooked.

Then in a flash Gill put me down and grabbed my arm. I tried to pull it back away from him but he held it hard. I could smell something hot and I screamed when I realized he was pulling my arm towards a turned on stove element.

It was bright red. I cried and hollered. I tried to yank my arm away; I tried to plead with him *no no no* but he moved my arm closer and closer and I could feel the heat hitting it.

Then a pain I had never felt before. I screamed and smelled the burned skin like with Pauly and Gabe. Right before my eyes closed I could see the smoke bursting from my arm and my wrist and my own fingers outstretched.

Everyone was cheering for him. My arm hurt so badly I thought I was going to die. This must be how much it hurts before you die because I had never felt this way before.

"See how that feels? What do you think those boys went through?" Gill snarled at me.

But then all of a sudden I felt something different. I felt mad; I felt angry. When Gill let me go I was ready; I turned around and bit him on the arm as hard as I could.

He hit me hard on the head and the kids cheered more. I snapped my jaw shut, using all the anger inside of me to bite harder. Then my teeth clipped together, my new ones just growing in and I ripped the meat from his arm.

Nan suddenly was there. She grabbed Gill by the arm to pull him away from me; the meat fell out of my mouth as I warned Nan to watch out but Gill was quick. He hit Nan on the face and she stumbled backwards onto the floor.

I stared in shock holding my bad arm which was screaming in pain. Nan groaned on the floor.

Gill grabbed me again and made me look at him. "Open your mouth." I was too stunned to do anything but stare so he shook me hard.

"Open your mouth!" he bellowed. He turned me towards the stove element and I found my voice again and screamed "NO!"

I opened my mouth and he looked in it and swore.

"His adult teeth are fucking growing in pointed…" Gill dropped me and turned to Nan. "I'm ending this tonight. Something I should have done the moment I saw those eyes."

Nan looked up, her face shocked. "Gill…" But Gill walked past her and went outside.

She looked at me and her face crumpled. When she jumped up and ran towards me I shrunk back scared. Nan grabbed my good arm and Barry, and then she ran with me outside.

But Gill was there and behind him Tomis and Payton were carrying boards with tools. Gill snatched me before I could get more than five steps and held my hands behind my back. I screamed as loud as I could and screamed for Nan. My arm hurt so bad; I knew it was going to fall off. It was unbearable.

Nan grabbed Gill again but this time Gill didn't hit her. He yanked me back hard and started walking me towards one of the bigger black trees I used to climb.

"If you interfere, I'm gone, Linda," Gill told her. "You can starve; I swear on the king you can fucking starve if you're going to house demons."

"I'm not a demon!" I yelled and Gill shook me harder.

I looked at Nan. She was the only adult who helped me and Nan was my Nana… but this time…

… this time she looked away from me.

"Nana?" I whimpered, but Gill pulled me away and started walking me into the greywastes. It was dark but my night bright could see Tomis and Payton with the planks of wood, then the sound of hammering.

"Nana?" I started to get scared but I didn't know what was going on. I just knew I had to get away and I had to thrash. I struggled and started screaming but Gill kept walking me further into the greywastes.

The rest of the kids of Sunshine House were clustered around the porch light in front of the main house. I craned my head just once to look behind me and saw them staring at me. The younger ones looked shocked and some were crying, but a lot of the older ones looked eager and happy.

"Gill... he's just a boy..."

"He's a demon and he'll be treated like one," Gill said angrily. "He burned two boys alive, Linda. How can you be so blind to what he is? His eyes... his teeth... we need to stop these mutations not foster them."

He kept dragging me until I was in front of Tomis and Payton. The two boys were securing the boards, now nailed together, in a small gathering of rocks. I was confused as to why they were there and what they were hammering. I didn't understand what Gill was going to do. Was he going to kill me? Was he going to shoot me?

Then Payton grabbed my hand and then so did Tomis. I kept thrashing as hard as I could, twisting myself and my body back and forth but they grabbed me hard and didn't let go. I looked at Gill and tried to look at Nan but Nan wasn't looking at me.

Why wasn't Nan looking at me?

They held my hands and pulled me up onto the gathering of rocks, beside the boards of wood that were nailed together to make an X. It wasn't until Tomis slammed my hand against one of the boards that I realized what they were going to do.

I started to cry and when I heard the sound of a hammer and a sharp, intense pain in my hands I screamed as loud as I could. So loud my voice broke and I started throwing up.

My hand had a nail sticking out of it, it was leaking blood around the metal and dripping down. Panic was in me so much I felt like I was drowning but suddenly I was frozen I couldn't move.

Another hammer and another stab of pain. My eyes kept filling with tears and the tears stung them. I tried to pull my hands away but I was stuck. I was stuck on the board with nails through my hands and only a small plank underneath my feet.

Gill smacked me across the face twice before he spat on me. Then Payton and Tomis spat on me too and walked behind me towards Sunshine House. I cried and tried to call for Nan but my voice was strangled and whenever I tried I just coughed.

My hands hurt... every time I tried to pull them more pain burst from the nails. I shifted my feet and tried to keep as much weight as I could off of them but all I could do was make them hurt less.

I called for Nan and called for Nan and I said I was sorry... but no one came back for me. I was here all alone with just the greywastes ahead of me and the twisted trees.

No one came for me that night... I stayed in the greywastes my hands throbbing, not just my palms but my entire hand was hurting and all red.

That morning some of the kids from Sunshine House came to look at me. The younger ones looked and ran away and some picked up rocks and threw them. I didn't cry when one hit me but soon all the younger ones were throwing rocks. Even Tracy who was only five; he had a bunch of them he threw until he got bored and went away. Some of the other kids didn't throw rocks but they made faces at me. I think I hated that even more.

I called for Nan again but Nana never came. The people in Sunshine House were too far away, all back in the houses and I couldn't hear them. I only heard when the kids approached and even then none of them would help me get down, even when I said please.

My throat was dry too, when an older kid Roland came to look at me I asked him for some water but he threw a rock and it hit the side of my face. He was Gabe's friend so I don't know what I expected.

I sniffed and wondered when Nan was going to give me water or some food. I had learned my lesson... I wanted to get down.

The blood had dried around my palms and now flies were starting to buzz around the wounds. I wanted to pull my hands right through but the top of the nail I had been nailed with were too big. I tried a few times though but it hurt too much; everything hurt too much.

Why was no one coming to see me? I couldn't look behind me I could only look ahead. Usually when I was in trouble Nan came or Missy came with my food, but everyone was ignoring me now.

The thirst was the worst, even worse than the hurt from my wrists and the hunger. I felt myself desperate for some water, any water at all. The thirst burned my throat like fire, a flame that made my mouth feel like a desert. Even my tongue was raw and dry, it flopped around my mouth like a sandpapery piece of meat.

I called for Nan and called for Nan until my throat hurt too much so I stopped. I even stopped crying because I just didn't have the energy to do it. I just stayed and looked at the grey landscape in front of me and stared.

That night when the sun went down I heard boots behind me. I didn't turn to see who it was, it was probably more kids to laugh and throw rocks at me.

Then I saw a dark-skinned hand. I opened my mouth to say hello to Nana but she put her finger to her lips for me to be quiet.

Nana held some water up to my lips and I drank. It was such a relief on my aching dry mouth. I drank and drank until it was all gone; it was the best thing I had ever tasted.

Then another surprise, Nana had a hammer in her hand. Quietly and gently, she pried the nails out of my hands, and when I fell forward, she took me into her arms.

I whimpered and she held me. She shushed me and kissed my cheek.

"You need to leave, Sami, you need to run away," Nan whispered. Her grip on me tightened and she kissed my head.

I pulled away and shook my head. "I don't want to go."

Nan gently took my shoulder and started walking with me into the dark. I glanced behind me once and saw the lights of Sunshine House far away. They looked so warm and welcoming… I wanted to go back home and go sleep in my car bed.

"Gill's leaving you up here to die, Sami." Nan looked behind her and sucked in a breath. "I got you a bag with Barry inside and some water and jerky. You need to run for Nan."

"Linda!"

I jumped and so did Nan as Gill's booming voice sounded behind us. We both turned around and froze when a shadow could be seen in front of the Sunshine House lights.

Nan grabbed my shoulder and pushed me towards the greywastes. She gave me a pack.

"Where do I go? When can I come back?" I cried. Nan looked behind her again. She was crying and her hands and everything were now shaking.

Gill was looking around; we were in the dark and he was looking for us. My night bright started showing me more of him and I realized he was carrying an axe.

"Go towards where the sun sets, go to the west towards the towns. You can't come back, Sami. You'll do fine, you're a smart smart boy." Nan suddenly let out a sob and hugged me, but Gill heard her crying and he started walking towards us with the axe. In the chaos, kids were looking out the dorm windows and some walked outside behind him, and when they saw that Gill had an axe, I heard some of them cheer. They all wanted me to get axed and they wanted me with the nails in my hands.

Everyone but Nan.

I was bad.

"Run. Go, Sami… run for Nan. I have Barry inside of the bag," Nan sobbed, putting the bag into my arms since my hands hurt too much. She turned me around and gave me a push. I walked a few steps, but everything was so dark I turned around. Everything outside was scary, the kids were scary and Gill was especially scary… Nan was all I had.

"Nana…" I took a step towards her but she shook her head and started walking backwards. Nan blew me a kiss but I was too scared and I didn't catch it.

"Linda!" Gill suddenly bellowed. "I said not to fucking touch him!" I jumped and gasped, and as he came closer and closer, I took one last look at Nan and I ran. I ran into the greywastes with Barry.

CHAPTER 4

Sami

Age 6

I RAN AND RAN WHERE I HAD SEEN THE SUN SET every evening and I didn't stop until I had to throw up.

I looked behind me and saw Sunshine House was nothing but a glowing blue light. It was the only light I could see besides the moon up in the sky. I couldn't hear yelling at all – but I couldn't hear anything.

I wasn't tired though and I could see darker shadows in the distance. I had never been this far away from Sunshine House except when I was a baby and I had a mom, so I wasn't sure if it was a shack or a town. So I decided to walk towards them and maybe there I could sleep until morning.

I bet I wouldn't be able to sleep though; all the stuff happening around me had numbed the pain in my wrists and arm but it was coming back now. It was throbbing and nothing helped. I cried about it at first but eventually the tears stopped. I knew there wouldn't be any water to dunk my burns in like Nan used to do when we had burns. Sunshine House had a well but there weren't any wells here and if there was I didn't know about them.

Eventually I saw that the shadows were abandoned houses. I was too tired and in pain to feel relief about it though. I went inside one of the houses with a half-open door and I started looking around.

Everything was a mess. There was a ripped up couch with all the fluff everywhere and the fluff was covered in dust from the broken plaster and dirt. I checked the kitchen but it was dirty too, and all the appliances were pulled out and thrown around. They were all rusty and spooky-looking; I didn't want to sleep there.

Then I went upstairs and I found a mattress. It was piled and heaped with blankets and the blankets stank but it was warm tonight so I didn't need them. I laid down on the mattress and picked the black skin from my wrist and arm, it was starting to bubble and go redder. It took me a while but I managed to fall asleep in the smelly abandoned house.

When I woke up the sun was shining and my arm was feeling a bit better but when I accidently brushed it against a quilt blanket it yelled at me. I sat up and looked around and almost called for Nan but I remembered where I was.

This wasn't my car bed and I wasn't in the loft above the boys' dorm. I was far away and I couldn't go back or Gill would kill me with the axe.

I wish I was brave like in the Disney books, but I just cried cause I was so lonely. Then I remembered that crying wouldn't do anything but bring ravers, so I got up and started pulling off the blankets from the big ol' mound.

I gasped and jumped back when I pulled the last blanket off. It was a shrively human! He was all black and his eyes were missing and his skin so tight it was like jerky. This gave me an idea and I leaned down and bit his finger but it tasted gross.

Though as I pulled off the rest of the blankets I saw he had pants on and a jacket. I checked his pants and I found a pack of stained cigarettes, a lighter, and a knife holder on his belt. I spent the next long while pulling his belt off of him with the knife. I looped it through my own pants and I think I looked mighty fine.

If I was going to be a greywaster now I had to look the part and I think I did. I had a knife which was on my hip and I had cigarettes though they smelled like the man tasted. I walked downstairs and lit a cigarette so I could stand on the porch and have a morning smoke like Gill always did.

Today I decided I was an adult. Maybe I would say I was fifteen if I met anyone so they wouldn't pick on me or try and eat me.

I lit my cigarette to celebrate my passage into adulthood and took a long inhale. But no sooner than I did, the smoke burned my throat and I was coughing, then I threw up again.

Cigarettes tasted gross but in that grossness I felt my whole body jitter and I felt energy so I kept it in my mouth and looked around the kitchen for any cans.

The merchants and greywasters who would stay with Nan in exchange for food would tell us stories around the fire some nights. They said greywasters survived on human meat and scavenging in abandoned houses. They said there were cans in the houses that were good to eat and houses could keep your ass protected from the greywastes.

I wasn't allowed to say ass but I was an adult now, I bet I could say worse.

"SHIT!" I yelled before clasping my hand over my mouth with a nervous giggle. I expected Nan to come bursting through the door to give me a spanking but then I remembered I was all alone now.

"Shit, shit, shit," I said out loud as I walked into the kitchen and started kicking aside broken dinner plates. I hopped up onto a counter after brushing away some dishes and papers and started looking through the cabinets. "Fuck, shit... piss ass fuckface."

I laughed but sneezed when a puff of sawdust tickled my nose. It looked like radrats had eaten some of the wood around here. I loved killing radrats they were as big as the cats at Sunshine House.

There were packaged plastic things, they had once been inside of boxes but the boxes had dissolved into papery shreds. The plastic inside of the box sat inside of the papery shreds like it was an egg inside of a nest. I opened the plastic but it was yellow rice and I didn't have any water. I put it in my pocket anyway and kept looking.

Nothing above me, though there were rust rings so maybe there had been but it had been scavenged. I checked the underneath and poked my head way in.

I found something! Way in the back behind a pile of sour-smelling rags and a bucket I saw two dented cans. I picked them up and grabbed the bucket too and put it inside. Then I went into the living room to look for books but there weren't any that I could read. I found some black markers though so I saved those and I also saved some fluff so maybe tonight I could have my very own campfire.

Then I stabbed one of the cans with my knife until I got a hole inside of it. I was pleased that inside was mixed vegetables and I ate all of it through the hole. It made my stomach feel gross for a moment since it was a lot of food but I didn't throw up.

I left my abandoned house not soon after and spent the rest of the day scrounging the other houses. I found a couple more cans, some books, and a thin blanket that was pale pink but I didn't care. I loaded everything in my bucket and started walking back to where the sun set every night.

So far my first day of being an adult was a success, though I kept looking in the direction I had came from... back where Nan was. A part of me wondered if maybe Gill wasn't mad anymore and I could go home, but Nan said I couldn't.

I missed Nan. This made my eyes burn and my lip tremble but I didn't cry this time. I felt like a grown-up right then because only babies cried and I wasn't a baby anymore. When the kids at Sunshine House reached adulthood they went off to find their own way. Except for Missy because she was a helper and Richard was Nan's son so he stayed too. Nan told me that they go to the towns where the sun sets and I guess that was where I was heading. I should have been with Nan for another eight years at least but I guess since I was bad I had to leave early.

But since my teeth were growing in all pointy that would make me better able to live out here... but then maybe that meant the towns wouldn't like me.

It was lonely out here but at least I had Barry. I wound up his butt and wedged him inside of the box so he wouldn't fall out. I sang along to Barry's Daisy Daisy song and walked towards the west, seeing grey rocks in the distance and structures that might have been a town but it was too far away to know for sure.

I examined my arm during my walking and I saw that the stove element had left spirals on my arm and wrist. There were three spirals which made a neat design, though it hurt at least it would look cool when it scarred up and stuff.

When I finally reached the town I had looked at it was night time again. I had been walking all day and I didn't even stop to play once. It wasn't much of a town anymore though and there was no one here. There were shops and big building, the biggest I had ever seen. All of the buildings had the glass broken and were streaked with dried black stuff and brown rust. Most of the buildings were also missing huge chunks from their outside paneling showing the wooden beams inside like it was their guts. I was too tired to check all the buildings though so I found one that was once a store and went inside of there to rest and eat. I hoped one of the cans had liquid inside of it, I hadn't had anything to drink since this morning's can which was peas.

I brought out a book and started stabbing the can I was disappointed though because it was something solid. I twisted the knife making the tin pop up and become sharp and jagged and smelled it.

It smelled like meat so it must be dog food. I ate some of it and opened the bag of little noodles to eat.

Though as soon as I popped one in my mouth I spat it out. I looked at the noodle and realized it wasn't a noodle but a yellow pellet. I smelled it and it smelled like chemicals.

I stared at it with my brow furrowed but then it clicked. That place had been chewed on by radrats and there must be a reason they didn't taste this stuff; because it was poison. I brushed my tongue with my fingers and put it back in the bucket. Maybe I could poison animals here and get some food. I could hunt like that until I was big enough to hunt like Gill did.

So far I was doing pretty good, I still didn't have any water though and my throat was parched and dry.

That night I slept in the back of the store on top of some cardboard boxes. My arm didn't hurt anymore but my heart hurt because I missed Nan and Sunshine House, also my throat because I was thirsty and there was no water around here at all.

The next morning I woke up and my throat was screaming for something to drink. All this dust I was breathing in was making it worse too. If I didn't find water I didn't know what I would do. I was days away from Sunshine House now and even if I asked Nan for some water I bet she would chase me away now.

I got up and grabbed my bucket with Barry inside and walked around the store for some food but everything was cleared out. All the shelves were dusty with curly paint that bubbled and blistered and the lights that hung down from the tall ceilings had all fallen or were only hanging from loose wires. Even parts of this store had daylight in them from the holes in the roofs; I could see the dust bits floating around as I passed them.

Then my ears picked up something. I froze and made my hearing go super good and started listening.

Voices? There were people outside now. I felt a shock of excitement go through me but that was quickly replaced by caution. I quietly walked to one of the big windows and peeked my head out of it to see who it was.

There were three greywasters outside. A part of me wanted to go back into the back room and hide but my scratchy throat reminded me that I was thirsty and they must have water. Nan had always been cautious about who she let stay with us, it was always only people Gill knew or merchants. I didn't know who these people were and Nan said most greywasters ate each other when they met unless they were carrying big guns. I didn't have any guns on me and I might be an adult now but I still looked little.

I didn't want to be eaten but I was so thirsty. I watched the three greywasters who were stopping outside of a building I didn't have time to look in. They were all men which wasn't surprising since most greywasters were and they all had guns on them. One person even had a big assault rifle which was on his back. I could smell their sweat and body odour from here and they all had matted dark hair.

Then another one came out.

"Nothing in there – this town's been picked dry." It felt so weird to hear voices, almost jarring, I was used to just hearing Barry's song or me saying swear words out loud.

"I don't want to give up yet, too many good lookin' structures," a tall man with sticking out ears said. "Let's keep going."

"You three can. I want to heat up one of our cans," the one who had come out of the building said. "I'll be in the parking lot of the apartments we passed with the burnt-out cars."

The others agreed and three went off to check out other buildings giving the guy staying behind their bags.

My heart perked up when I heard the swishing of water in one of those bags. I looked closer and saw they were carrying around what looked like a backpack full of water. It was white and all plastic and I could see a spout on the end. It made my throat burn even more and every time I thought about tasting it my body tingled from anticipation.

He had the water so I would follow him. When the others had gone into the next building I started stalking him but not before grabbing my bucket with Barry just in case I had to run. I could move faster with them even if the bucket had two cans still inside; Nan had always said I was sneaky and quick.

And he didn't suspect me at all. I felt so dangerous like I was a carracat stalking his prey. I was only exposed for a few seconds before I found another building to hide behind. I hid behind building after building until finally I hid inside the open entrance of the apartment the greywasters had talked about. The entire roof had collapsed into the third floor and the weight had squished the floors down so they were all compacted. It was not a good place to stay in but there were lots of half-standing walls for me to hide behind and watch my prey!

The greywaster didn't suspect a darn thing. I watched him get out a can and open it with a real can opener before pouring what looked like soup into it. Then he added a bit of water and started making a fire from some black tree sticks that had fallen from some of the trees nearby.

Soon the fire was going and the pot was starting to simmer. It smelled so delicious I wanted it more than anything. On top of that I saw one of the bags had many more cans inside and bags of things too. It looked like these greywasters had food and water and everything, even guns.

I wanted it... I needed it or else I was going to die of thirst.

At the mention of water I swallowed through my dry throat and wished I could move objects with my mind. I would move the white water pack right to my mouth and I'd drink as much as I wanted.

I looked at my own bucket and wondered if they would trade with me like Nan did sometimes, but even if I did trade I would only have one can of food and I'd be thirsty again tomorrow.

This is why people ate each other in the greywastes, because an arian human had enough meat on them to last someone like me for months, and they had blood I could drink too. If I could kill all of them then I could dry the meat like Nan did and eat like a king for an entire year I bet.

Then I paused and looked down at my bucket. I got a dangerous idea, so dangerous and bad it made me put my hand over my mouth to hide my smile.

It would be so bad... but I was bad. If I was evil and bad like everyone said then why couldn't I do bad things? The bad guys in the books always did awful things to get what they wanted and they were always the ones with fancy underground lairs and cool super villain technology.

Okay, Sanguine... I mean Sami. Okay, Sami; you can do this!

I held onto the poison pellets and looked around where I was hiding. All around me were bricks from the half-fallen walls and most were crumbled into nothing. The only other thing was a few boards leaned up against an empty window, that was it.

I picked up a rock and weighed it in my hand. I peeked my head out of the half-fallen wall and spotted an area near the parking lot where there were a bunch of rusted out parked cars. These cars were in even worse shape because a bit of the second-storey wall had fallen onto them making its own roof over the parked vehicles.

I gripped the rock and waited until the greywaster man had his back turned. Then I quickly planned out a good route to the pot which was only about five of me's in length away. Once I was confident I threw the rock as hard as I could towards the rusted out cars and the fallen wall.

The rock pinged against a car roof before pinging again on a wall, and settling between a car and a truck. As the man jerked towards it, I picked up a handful of the poison and watched intently.

The man grabbed his gun and was quiet as he listened; I was quiet too. My heart gave a pitter-patter as he started slowly walking towards the row of cars; his gun out and pointed at the cars.

As soon as he disappeared behind a heap of debris I made my move. I ran on my tippy toes towards the pot and dumped the poison inside, then, without even looking to see if he had seen me, I ran back to the apartment building but this time I went inside so I could hide better.

It was so dark inside of here but my night bright kicked in and I could see better. It smelled too like musty dry. It was so dry that the paint on all the walls had started peeling off like a sunburn and it was flaking on the ground. Even the floor had started warping and I had to watch where I stepped; in some places I started to sink so I ran quickly to the stairs.

The stairs had collapsed in some places but I jumped over it and finally got to the top. I was a bit scared though because some entire floors in the apartments had fallen through and it looked unstable and dangerous. Though I was light and I kept to the edges and didn't touch the middle of the sinking hallway. I pretended it was made out of quick sand and I was Aladdin in the desert. Though instead of trying to get the genie lamp I was waiting for the desert nomads to die.

My hand found the knife I had stolen from the dead man I had slept next to. I was going to have to work fast to make sure their meat didn't rot but if I worked real hard I could jerky them all. Too bad I didn't have any salt but that was just for fancy jerky.

I walked into an apartment with a smashed open door and thankfully this one had a good-looking floor, just a bit of a dip but in that dip was a big television set that must be as heavy as me so if that TV hadn't fallen through I should be good.

I walked in and stepped onto the dirty green carpet. I then shifted myself over a tipped over dresser and a couch that looked like it might've been used as a barricade. I hoped over everything and found a window to look out of.

The greywaster man hadn't seen me! He was back at the pot now smoking a cigarette, though what was weird was that this cigarette had a blue tip to it instead of red. I was even more excited for them to die now, they had magic cigarettes!

Just seeing him smoke that made me want to try one again, even though it made me almost throw up. I think I would have one after for celebration if my plan worked.

So now I waited. I didn't have anything to do so I looked around the apartment and to my surprise there was a kid's room in this apartment! It was a blue room too so it belonged to a boy.

Immediately I found army men, a Conan the Barbarian action figure, and some McDonalds toys so I sat in that room and played Second Cold War which is what Nan said the big war was before King Silas killed everyone. I pretended Conan was King Silas and the army men were the Canadian soldiers and I had a Dr. Robotnick toy from Sonic and I pretended he was the president of the world. He died from being hit in the head by Conan-Silas. I didn't know if that was what happened but I couldn't find any weapons for Conan to hold so now that's what happened.

I kept playing for hours and when I finally remembered I was supposed to watch the greywasters, the sun was way high in the air and shining down through the window now. I quickly put my favourite toys into the bucket and ran into the main area of the apartment.

They were still alive! Ugh! But the soup pot was empty at least and they were all relaxing by the fire talking amongst themselves. I was disappointed but I shouldn't expect the poison to work right away like in movies; at least they all had some. I went back to playing with my toys this time going back and forth to check and see if they had dropped dead yet. Eventually they went out and about to scavenge but I stayed put since they had left their bags stashed behind a debris wall. If they didn't come back by the next morning I'd go corpse hunting I guess. I had a good nose on me.

I played and read until it got dark. Once I made a nice bed for myself and settled in for sleep I checked on the greywasters one more time. They were all back and had some tins lined up on a median; they were all eating and I was disappointed to see they were still healthy. I had put a lot of poison pellets in it and they didn't even look sick. My throat was aching with thirst it felt like it was on fire and I couldn't open a tin because I didn't want to make any noise.

I fell asleep on a bundle of clothes and blankets I had found inside the bedrooms. I didn't like any of these floors so I stuck to the wall closest to the door. I wrapped myself up into a comfortable little nest and tried to ignore the pain inside of my throat.

In the middle of the night I was woken up with a start. It was the sound of gagging, high-pitched gagging. I jumped up and crawled to the window and looked out onto the parking lot.

They were all spread out with pools of wetness around them that looked shiny and purple. I held up my hand to shield my eyes from the fire light since it messed up my night bright and tried to see what was happening to them.

Wow, it was blood! One of the greywasters turned around and had blood streaming from all of his holes. His eyes were bleeding, his nose and mouth, and even his ears. I looked to another one keeled over and saw he even had blood on his pants! He was bleeding out of his butt!

I giggled and held my hands over my mouth. I jumped up and down on the spot; I was so excited, this was so great! My mouth watered just thinking about their warm blood and the real water too. There was still a fire I could make some steaks as I drained their blood into the bucket. I would have to find more buckets too to hold the blood I couldn't drink. This was going to be all night and all day work but I was excited to start right now.

As they all started throwing up blood and writhing and dying like the ants I killed, I went over Nan's recipe in my head: cut off all the fat or it will make it rancid and slice into thin strips, dust with salt if you have it and hang on a rack inside Nan's outside oven made of bricks. Then store in a cool dry place.

I picked up Barry and put him on the windowsill so he could see; I balanced my chin on my hands and grinned as the greywasters started dying; blood dripping from their faces and into the pools of foamy red throw up.

I might like it out here.

When I entered the parking lot everyone was dead or close to being dead. The first thing I did was drink my fill of the water from the white plastic backpack, it tasted so good but I was smart enough to just drink a glass. I didn't want to throw it up and I had blood to drink too.

I emptied my bucket and dragged one of the bodies towards the median they had put their cans on. It was hard work but I got his feet over the median and his upper half, but I wasn't strong enough to get his entire body upside down. I got out my knife and I started sawing through the guy's neck.

It was hard work, a lot harder than it looked like in the movies. I cut and cut and it took me a long time to get the head off but I did. And though the bucket was a bit tilted, I got his bleeding head stump in the bucket to drain.

I looked behind me at the other three and let out a tired sigh. I wanted to jerky all of them but I didn't know if I could before the meat rotted. It was night time and just edging towards the cooler months but once the sun hit I knew I would be screwed.

With a forlorn sigh and a lot of annoyance I gave up on saving all of their blood and just spent the time cutting off everyone's heads so they could drain into the parking lot. Even that was exhausting. I cut off some thigh meat and put it into a thin frying pan one of them had tied to their backpack, and sat down with a glass of blood and one of the blue cigarettes I had seem one of them smoke.

I lit the cigarette and took a small drag, not a big one like I had before that made me cough. I took a small one and smiled as the blue ember lit up.

This smoke tasted a lot smoother than the cigarettes I had found on the dried out man, and it made my head feel dizzy and light. When I was done I dug around and found a different pack of cigarettes, but this one had a red ember and the smoke that came off of it was green.

I smoked that cigarette and suddenly... I got lots of energy.

These smokes must have drugs in them, they were making my heart race and my body jolt around like I had drunken some of the merchant's instant coffee. I took advantage of that and started gathering bricks from the apartment building behind me and making myself an oven out of them for the jerky drying. I worked the entire night smoking cigarettes and taking small breaks to eat and drink. By the time morning was on the horizon I had the first jerky strips in the oven and everyone drained. I knew I wouldn't be able to jerky all of them before they rotted though.

Instead I got a brand-new idea. Since I was lonely and I only had my toys I could make new friends. Before I decided to sleep I moved the three bodies without their heads and propped them up around the fire. I put their heads on their laps so they could watch the fire burn and I even gave them back their cups they had used for drinking water.

When everyone was propped up with their heads in their laps I curled up by the fire and drew a blanket over me. I felt a little less lonely now that I had other people around. If I closed my eyes I could pretend they were the boys in the dorm room or even Nan.

I shut my eyes tight and let the fire warm my face. I settled in for a long nap, my stomach full of water and meat and my body aching and tired from my long night's work. I slept with my new assault rifle beside me with plans to try it out tomorrow, and my brand-new friends watching me sleep.

CHAPTER 5

Cory The Greywaster

CORY WIPED THE SWEAT FROM HIS BROW AND looked around though his eyes were stinging. If he was smart he would just take off the duffle bag on his back and find something to tie over his forehead but he wanted to keep moving until he reached the small shanty town he had spotted in the distance. He needed some basement he could take a nap in, the sun might be grey and on most days, clouded, but it was still searing the greywastes with its heat.

Cory, a man in his early thirties, had been a nomad for over a year now since ravers had killed his family. Now he wandered from place to place doing odd jobs for a bed to sleep in or some food and water to keep him going. He hadn't been to this particular town for over two years but he remembered that though it was in bad shape, it still had adequate shelter and a spring of water in the sewers underneath.

He shielded his eyes before taking a long drink of water; he put the water bottle back into his bag and continued on his long and lonesome journey.

Soon the structures came closer, the lonely apartment buildings still standing high as if they held a false hope that the world would be repaired, and many shops and businesses with their windows boarded up and their contents now gutted to feed the humans still walking the earth. This was the greywastes and this is what it had to offer.

Cory's shuffling movements were the only sound here but he was used to that as he was used to talking to himself when the loneliness took him. Once he had a wife to talk to and a young son he had named Max, now only the ghosts of his old life kept him company and they rarely talked back.

He looked into a rusted out Volvo and scanned the inside for any suitcases or plastic bottles he could salvage but there was nothing; though he didn't expect there to be anything since this place had been run through by greywasters too many times. This shanty town was too close to the big town, Chilko Lake, and only a few miles away from the main road the merchants used to get to Chilko. So though it may not see visitors often it did receive more than the shanty towns and neighbourhoods in the north and east directions. All abandon towns close to blocks or settlements had been almost picked clean of anything in canned form.

Though there was still water. The thought of that made Cory take another drink, he had Dek'ko tablets to make the water drinkable and Iodine pills to back up the radiation the water would undoubtedly be filled with. He was all set and looking forward to spending a couple days out in the open greywastes. Then if he found something worth selling, he could go back to Chilko and drink himself into a blissful stupor for a few days.

There weren't many comforts in the greywastes but one could always count on booze and good drugs and since there wasn't a woman to warm his bed those were the only things Cory had now.

The greywaster visually checked out the structures around him and noticed that several of them had collapsed since he had last been here. The wood seemed oddly preserved in the greywastes but the ones that were built with cheap materials seemed to be starting to crumble now. His grandmother used to tell him stories about what it was like when she was a girl, the radiation had just become tolerable by humans with the public release of the Geigerchip and there were riches everywhere in the greywastes. Thousands left Skyfall to find a free life in the greywastes, though what they found was something much different.

Cory paused as he saw a slumped over figure he hadn't noticed before. His nose twitched as he got closer, smelling a faint whiff of rotting flesh.

A corpse wasn't at all an uncommon thing to find but one that looked like it hadn't been picked or eaten was a small treasure in the greywastes. Corpses meant the possibility of water, better clothing, weapons, cigarettes, and hopefully the right sized shoes.

With a quick glance around he cautiously approached the dead man. He reached into his jacket pockets but was dismayed to see everything was gone.

Almost everything. Cory saw the rotting corpse had a bottle of red juice, possibly Kool-Aid. Though sugar was hard to find to sweeten it even the sour fruity taste was a welcome change from irradiated water.

Cory cracked open the bottle and smelled it. He took a taste of the warm liquid and felt his lips pucker. Yep, that was Kool-Aid alright, cherry flavour though it was sour cherry now. Cory drank it happily and started taking off the man's jacket. His jacket had gotten ripped at the sleeve and back by a scaver he had killed for food a few days ago and this one looked like it was in better condition.

He put the jacket on and zipped it up before stuffing his old one into his backpack. Then he pulled off the man's shoes but was disappointed to see his were in better condition. Still though he could get a bottle of bathtub whisky for the pair so he tied the laces around his backpack and started carrying on down the cracked paved road.

Too bad the dead greywaster was rotten but, well, what are you going to do? If he had only been a day or two earlier he could've had himself a good meal. Hell, if it was winter he would've had months of food he could've kept frozen.

But such is the greywastes.

Cory checked out a few more buildings before stopping to take another drink of the red water. Though to his surprise… he was starting to get a bit dizzy.

The greywaster sat down and wiped his sweaty brow with his jacket sleeve. He blinked hard and took a longer drink, copping up the dizziness to dehydration.

But it started to get worse. Cory slid down the median so he was sitting on the ground and grimaced. He looked around before stumbling to his feet but he wasn't standing for long. A moment later the water bottle fell from his hands and after one more stumbled step – Cory fell to the ground too.

The first thing Cory was aware of when he started to come to was that he had a pounding headache; the second thing was that he was unable to move.

The third was the heavy smell of rot; so strong it seemed to crawl up your nose and ravage one's brain.

Cory opened his eyes and looked around to see where he was but everything was a blur. An anxious chill went through him when he realized he was bound and tethered inside somewhere, though he must still be in the shanty town.

"Hello?" Cory croaked. As his senses started to come back to him the distinct and stifling smell of rot got stronger. He squinted his eyes to focus them but as the room came into view he wished that he had been struck blind.

All around Cory were dead bodies in various stages of decomposition; they had all been propped up against pieces of furniture in a shoddy semicircle focused on the center of a child's bedroom which held different toys. Each one of them was green and black with rot and some even moving with maggots and buzzing with flies. It was a horrific sight which momentarily struck the greywaster dumb.

"Hi!"

Cory jolted and looked to the source of the voice. He was surprised to see a small child with shoulder length black hair in the doorway, wearing sunglasses and a kerchief that covered his mouth. The child couldn't have been older than eight, though children's ages were hard to tell in the greywastes since most were on the verge of starving.

"Why am I bound?" Cory demanded. He looked behind the young boy, his face lined with fear and his eyes wide. "I want to speak with your mother or father; why do they have me tied? Why the fuck are there bodies everywhere?"

The boy put his hands behind his back and shifted from side to side. "Can you read?"

Cory stared at him; he wanted to snap at the boy for dodging his question but he had to remember where he was and that he was bound and unable to move. If the parents were listening in on this conversation they wouldn't take kindly on him scaring the boy.

"I grew up in Blackbay near Skyfall I can read fine…" Cory said slowly; he blew a puff of air to try and get a buzzing fly away from his face. "Now I answered your question, boy; you can answer mine."

The boy jumped up and down and ran past him, stepping on a ripe pair of fingers from one of the corpses which sent an even stronger smell of rot into the air. Cory cringed as the squished fingers started to leak rotting black fluid onto the ground; wondering if he was going to be the next corpse.

"I'd like to speak to your parents," Cory demanded. "I want to know why I was drugged and brought here. Boy? I'm talking to you," Cory raised his voice as the boy with the sunglasses and kerchief over his mouth turned around with a book in his hand.

"I don't have any parents." The boy's tone suddenly became sad. "I'm here alone."

The boy is here alone? Cory looked out the window and from the looks of the structures in the distance he had to be on the second-storey. This gave the greywaster a small shred of hope that he could get out of this alive.

"You drugged that Kool-Aid didn't you?" Cory said slowly.

The boy nodded and laid the small novel down on Cory's lap. Cory struggled to try and see if he could get out of his binds to snatch the kid but he was tied up tight. From the looks of the corpses around them, propped up like he was, no one had been able to break the boy's binds.

"Yeah, I did... someone a few months ago had this drug that made this girl he was travelling with act all sloppy and stupid and then she passed out. He played with me for seven days before he died. The lady choked on her puke and died... she's right there." The boy pointed to a corpse with stringy brown hair and a pink tank top now stained with many layers of putrid liquid.

"P-play with you?" The horror was starting to burrow itself inside of Cory. What had once seemed like a plus having a child be his captor was quickly starting to turn in a different direction. This little boy seemed nuts, and why was his face covered?

The boy nodded. "Sometimes they can't read so they tell me stories. Will you tell me stories?" He laid down on the middle of the dirty carpet where the toys Cory had spotted were, and picked up an action figure. He looked up and though he was wearing sunglasses Cory knew the boy was staring at him.

"How... how long have you been an orphan for?" Cory stammered. "How long have you been here for?"

The boy made his action figure walk over to a toy soldier, who promptly got stomped on by what Cory thought was a Conan the Barbarian figurine. He bashed the soldier a few times before looking towards one of the corpses, a younger-looking man who once had blond hair though it was rancid and matted with rot.

"How long have I been here for, Taylor?"

Cory stared at the kid as he was silent, looking intently at the dead blond-haired one.

"That's right, many many months but I have been an orphan forever," the boy replied, turning his head away from the corpse. It was like he was... pretending they were still alive.

The greywaster could only stare in shock. "And how old are you?"

The boy looked at the blond-haired one again. Cory noticed 'Taylor' was missing his left arm and his thigh looked like it had been carved off in places.

"I am seven."

This kid... he's lost it. Cory's own son had been five when he had been eaten and he knew the boy wouldn't have lasted two nights in the greywastes, but this kid had been alone for months and months?

Cory looked around at the corpses, four of them propped up and all focused towards the center of the room where the boy was laying down. In the depths of his fear and anxiety he felt a flicker of paternal feelings towards the kid. Being a father himself it strummed a different string in his heart to see this kid, obviously mad, all alone out here.

And undoubtedly lonely.

"Have you been... kidnapping greywasters and making them play with you?" Cory asked, his words coming slowly in hopes that the kid would give him an answer.

"Sometimes they don't play and I starve them." The boy's forehead creased as he said this. "Other times I chop off their limbs and make jerky; I have lots of jerky I even found salt on three of my friends." He pointed to another corpse but his eyes were still fixed on his toy. "He's one of the salt-friends. His name is Diaz, the blond one is Taylor, the woman is Nina, and her husband is Charles. What's your name?"

He's referring to them in present tense now... wow.

"Cory..." Cory replied. He tried to make a personal connection with the boy; it might be his only chance. "What's yours?"

"My friends call me Sami; my enemies call me Sanguine," the boy replied. "I've never met a Cory before. I'm glad you can read, maybe after we can play army men."

"If you can untie me, son, I can play with you."

Sami paused and shook his head. He drew his kerchief down slightly and Cory could see a red scar that started down his ear and went zig-zagged to his neck; then he held up his arm and the greywaster could see another patch of red from a less healed scar that still held a flaking scab.

"I let Joshua go to play with me and he chased me around and swung a board at me, then he threatened to fuck me in the ass. I don't know what that means though, do you?"

Cory stared at him; the boy stared back and his forehead creased again.

"Well?"

"I... uh, it means... kill you – he was going to kill you."

"Ohh." Sami nodded. He rested his chin on the dirty carpet and flicked away a beetle larva that had started crawling towards his toys. "That makes sense. I killed him and he's dead outside now so I guess I fucked him in the ass. I killed him by ambushing him. I bit his neck."

"And I won't be any different, will I?" Cory shook his head; he suddenly felt a wave of hopelessness inside of him and if only for a moment he lost his cool. "Well, boy, if you untie me I'll play with you for a while but if I am going to become one of those corpses either way... quite frankly you can go fuck yourself in the ass."

Sami looked up at him and though there was little expression to see on his covered face the creases in his forehead deepened. Cory flinched as the boy stood up and left the room.

"Hey... come back here, you little shithead..." Cory shouted. He started to struggle, trying to pull his hands out of the tight nylon rope. His hands were in front of him but they might've been in outer space, the kid was good with knots.

Sami came back but when Cory saw the large knife in his hand he started trying to push himself backwards with his bound feet. He shouted at Sami as the kid came closer and pulled his tied up hands to his face.

The apartment buildings echoed with his screams when he felt the boy grab his ear and start to saw, a moment later Cory's right ear came off in the kid's grasp. He felt the last strands of skin pull tight before snapping back; his ear now completely severed.

"What the fuck! What the fuck, kid!" Cory screamed. Sami stepped back with the ear in his hand and, as if to taunt him further, he held it up and wiggled it back and forth.

"What the fuck!" Cory was hysterical; his green eyes wide from shock. "You fucking psycho!"

"Are you going to play with me? And read to me? Or do I gotta cut something else off, asshole," Sami snapped, his high tenor voice only adding to his overall psychotic demeanor. This kid was something else; he was a fucking lunatic.

And why was he covering his face?

"Fine! Fine for fuck sakes," Cory said, his face tensing in pain. Blood was pouring out of the deep red gash on the side of his head. "I'll read to you. What the fuck do you want me to read?"

Sami turned around and put the knife and his ear beside one of the ripe and moving corpses. He turned around and pointed to the small novel that had fallen off of Cory's lap during his mutilation. The boy picked it up and re-adjusted it, curiously still the book was being held open by food saver clips

To make it so the book doesn't close. The realization made Cory's chest tighten, this kid had been here for a long time and doing this for just as long it seemed.

The area where Cory's ear had been throbbed with intense pain. With a groan he shifted his legs up so the small novel was on his knees.

He looked at the first few lines and raised an eyebrow. "This novel is about talking mice?"

Sami glared at him. "There are mice, squirrels, voles, and rabbits, and evil foxes, and the good guys live in Redwall Abby in a big forest and the bad guys are pirate rats and foxes. It's the bestest book; don't say anything bad about it."

Cory looked down and closed his eyes for a brief moment. "Whatever, kid. So how far did the last guy get before you killed him?"

Sami kept his stare down, though it would be more intimidating if he didn't have his sunglasses on and the kerchief, a dingy grey, covering his face. Cory decided not to push him and started reading him the mouse book. It would distract him from the intense pain where his ear used to be, the wound felt like it had its own pulse.

While Cory read the kid pulled up a blanket and quietly played with his action figures and other toys, occasionally laughing at funny parts or asking him what a word meant, though most of the time the greywaster didn't know. He had read for about an hour before the kid's head started to droop. Seeing that as a good sign he kept reading until the black-haired boy was still under his blanket, the Conan action figure loose in his small grubby hand.

He might be a fucked up little thing but he was just a kid. Though it doesn't matter in the end; he was a little killer and if I don't get out of here and finish him off, he'll kill me too. Cory pressed his back up against the wall and started to slowly inch himself up the wall to get to his feet; his eyes never leaving the sleeping boy.

Once Cory had stood himself up he turned around and realized he had been tied up to the window. It looked like the boy had made a hole underneath the windowsill and had tethered him around the frame.

Cory's heart sank as he realized that just walking out would be impossible. He gave a small defeated sigh and looked around.

He spotted a knife – it was resting right beside the boy's feet.

Could I reach it... Cory got down on his knees and started inching himself forward. His arms outstretched to try and reach the knife. It was a long knife and it looked sharp; if he could just get it into his hands he could finish the kid off quickly. The kid had made sure he wasn't in slashing distance but he could untie himself and then do it...

Just a bit... closer.

"I knew I couldn't trust you."

Cory jerked his arm and quickly jumped away as Sami threw off his blanket and kicked Cory right in the face. The greywaster swore and put his bound hands up to his nose as it started to drip blood.

"Joshua passed the trust test and he still tried to kill me!" Sami spat; his little fists balled in rage. "And you failed, now I'll never trust you, ever. Stupid greywaster; you're gonna fucking rot!"

"I was just reaching for some water... I... ah –" Cory gritted his teeth together, wracking his brains trying to come up with something better. "I was tucking you in."

The boy kicked him again. "I'm not stupid. I'm going to sleep, and I have my gun with me. I'll show you all my guns tomorrow because I have ten of them and lots of ammo and if you try anything again I'll shoot you. Okay, Cory the greywaster?"

"Sami... come on. Come back and I'll read some more. We can be buds," Cory called before clenching his teeth together. He swore and hit his shoulder against the wall in anger.

Sami turned around and though he had his sunglasses on Cory got the distinct impression the boy was glaring him into the hellfires below.

"You can call me Sanguine, thank you!" Sami spat before angrily stalking out of the bedroom.

"Sanguine... Sanguine?" Cory called before leaning his head against the wall with a sigh.

"What does... extravagant mean?"

"I... I don't know... I–"

"I was talking to Diaz."

Cory turned the page on the book as the boy, now wearing a green kerchief and a baseball cap that was stained with brown, looked over at a brown-haired corpse whose face was starting to slip off of his skull.

The rotting corpse, his eyes now stuffed with moving insects and larva, said nothing back but the boy Sami nodded anyway and continued to draw with some half-broken crayons.

"So what does it mean?" Cory put his damp finger on the book page and slid the paper away from the food saver clip, revealing the start of a new chapter.

"It means... lots of vagants."

Cory looked up at him. "And what's a vagant?"

"Keep reading."

"Give me a drink of water first and I will... my throat is parched and you owe me for telling you where to find that water spring."

Sami, laying on his stomach with his feet kicking up and down, started drawing a circle. "I was doing just fine drinking blood and drinking from the river a mile from here. It was only bad in summer when the river bed dried up. I was doing just fine on my own, just like Nan said I would do fine."

Nan? Cory watched as the kid got up and brought a bottle of muddy brown water up to his lips. He took a generous drink and kept drinking until Sami pulled the bottle away.

"Was Nan your Grandma?" Cory asked. The gash where his ear had been ached and the jerky the boy fed him made his stomach sour; it was almost rotten and the salt did little to kill the taste.

Sami shook his head and laid back down on his stomach in front of his crayons. "Nana was a nice lady who took care of me with a bunch of other kids. She made me leave because Gill was going to chop me up with an axe."

"Chop you with an axe?" Cory repeated in a low tone. The more he spoke to this kid the more his behaviour made sense. "Why?"

Sami kept kicking his legs as he coloured and drew, the dead body of Taylor behind him shifting around under the impact of his boots. "No one liked me especially two boys named Gabe and Pauly. They pushed my face into a burning anthill so I tied them to their beds and lit them on fire."

"Are you fucking serious?" Cory said lowly. He looked around the boy's bedroom, past the semicircle of corpses, with a fresh new determination to get away from this kid. He had been a prisoner of Sami-Sanguine for three days now.

"Yes," Sami said before sneezing onto his paper and crayons. Cory saw a bit of his kerchief rise up; his mouth looked normal enough.

"Why do you always keep your face covered like that?" he asked.

"I don't want to scare you... everyone gets scared and yells and swears at me when they see my face." Sami's voice dropped to a sad level.

This planted another seed of alarm in Cory's chest. "You sound and look normal enough, and from what I can see of your face you don't look deformed. I have seen scarred up kids and even a dwarf once. I don't think you need that face cover."

Sami shook his head back and forth. "That's what Joshua said too and he told me I was a demon."

A demon? Cory tried to look through the sunglasses and through the corners of the kerchief but he had it covered and the sunglasses were pressed right up to his face. He just looked like a normal seven-year-old in need of a bath.

"Look kid... do you want to come with me to Chilko Lake? If you have all of those guns you can sell them in the shops and put in an application to get your own house. You would be safe in a city with water and food and you would have a lot of people to talk to," Cory said, once again trying to reason with him.

"I went there last winter when I was freezing cold and my lighter ran out. I stayed and got a lighter and I wanted to stay longer but they saw me and chased me out with rocks," Sami replied dully. There was a snap as he put too much pressure on one of the crayons, breaking it in half.

This confused Cory even more. What was this kid? Birth defects in the greywastes were nothing new and though you got a few assholes here and there everyone was rather tolerant of deformed people.

Maybe he hadn't gone to the city and this was all in his head. Cory had seen the kid frequently talking to the rotting corpses so that wouldn't be any stretch of the imagination.

"Well, we can always make up a lie, say you have a disease or something..." Cory looked down at the book, being held open by his bound hands. Though the kid had been feeding him the half-rancid jerky and the muddy water he could feel his energy leaving him. His limbs were cramped up and his nose had committed suicide days ago from the overpowering stench of the corpses.

"I don't have a disease, I'm just a bad kid," Sami explained. His tongue poked out of the side of his mouth as he got a red crayon and started colouring something in. "I'm evil, aren't I? You think so too like Gill did, the townspeople did and all my other friends. I'm just a bad person."

Before Cory could say anything back Sami jumped to his feet and lay his crayon drawing onto Cory's lap. The greywaster looked down and wasn't surprised to see a small boy in the center surrounded by what looked like a mom and a dad and... the teddy bear he liked to wind up before bed from the looks of it.

Even the boy was wearing sunglasses and a kerchief over his face.

"Is that you?" Cory motioned down.

Sami nodded. "My mom was named Lydia and she died. I didn't know who my dad was. Barry was given to me by Nana and I drew what I bet my dad looked like."

Another small pang of sympathy, but the pain in his limbs and, especially now, the scabbed over gash where his ear had stifled it rather well. Though Cory wasn't an idiot; he played along and tried another angle.

"I had a son who was five, he got eaten by ravers... why don't we go to Chilko and I'll say you're my boy. I wouldn't mind some company," Cory said to him.

Cory's heart jumped when the kid paused. "You would be my dad?"

I'll be your worshipper just get me out of this disgusting room and give me a chance to escape you. "Sure," Cory said. "I was a father once and you seem like a nice kid. Smart too. Only seven and you read better than I do. Not to mention you survived out here for a long time."

The boy took a step back and looked behind him; still seeming unsure Cory inched his offer further. "Winter will be coming soon... wouldn't it be nice to spend winter in a warm repaired house?"

"I don't trust you," Sami said cautiously. He took a step back. "I trusted Joshua and..."

"Not all greywasters are the same and I was a father that has to count for something. Have I tried to hurt you? I only tried to escape once, and honestly you have four dead bodies circling me, you can't hold that against me. You cut off my damn ear kid," Cory said.

Sami shook his head and grabbed the bear he was always carting around. "No, I'm not... I'm not dumb. I'm going outside to play."

"Wait, kid – *ah fuck*." Cory clenched his teeth as the kid disappeared into the main area of the apartment. It was just him surrounded by corpses now purple, green, and red, and leaking all things foul. He sighed and started trying to wiggle out of his binds again, his wrists now rubbed raw.

CHAPTER 6

Sami

Age 7

  I WALKED INTO WHAT HAD BEEN MY BEDROOM AND put down the hubcap I had been using as a fire pit. Sometimes when I wanted to make jerky I brought the hubcap down to the parking lot and put it into my brick oven but mostly I kept it in the apartment so I could keep myself warm during the cold nights.

  Tonight I had caught a radrat! I gutted and skinned it and now it was resting beside the hubcap just waited to be roasted and eaten with salt.

  My new friend Cory was watching me in silence, his head leaned up against the window frame and his eyes half-open like he was tired. Cory was nice and he didn't yell and try to kill me like my other friends. Though those friends got a whole lot nicer once they died.

  "Good catch, Sami!" Barry said to me, his voice cheerful and happy.

  "That's a big radrat, did you catch that all by yourself?" Taylor asked me.

  "Yes, I did!" I exclaimed. I picked up the rat and held it out for Taylor to see, then I turned around and showed Barry. "I shot it. I'm getting to be a better shot. Cory, I only had to shoot him once and I got him right in the stomach. I've been practicing."

  Cory opened his eyes a bit more and nodded. "That's nice, kid, are you going to give Daddy Cory a bit of that?"

  For the past couple of days he had been saying he could be my dad and now he called himself Daddy Cory. I didn't tell him not to, I kind of liked it. I had never had a dad before, I didn't even know if he was still alive.

  "Yeah, you can have some. Will you tell me a real story tonight? One from when you were a kid maybe?" I asked. I started bundling up pieces of yellow grass as dry as straw and putting them beside some old cloth.

"Sure, I have lots of those…" Cory responded. That made me smile! I lit the fire and moved the hubcap towards Cory so it could be near the window. The smoke would blow out that way though it still got kind of smoky in here until the fire got hot enough.

I set the radrat on one of the oven grates I used for making jerky and laid down on the floor with my toys. Cory had been with me for a week now and he knew the routine, as I played with my toys he told me a story about when he was a kid and he found a warehouse full of candy.

"I looked in the first box with my brother and our jaws hit the floor… inside were bags and bags of all the candy you could ever want." My eyes widened and I looked up at him, he carried on. "Marshmallow strawberries and bananas, Sour Keys and Dino Sours, gummy berries… and even gummy bears."

"Wow!" I said in awe. "What else!?"

"They had snack cakes there too… Twinkies and Dingdongs."

I giggled at the name and said it quietly to myself. "Dingdongs."

"My brother and me ate until we puked and then we ate some more. That was one of the best times in my life," Cory said before chuckling. I saw a sad look come to his face. "We ate him a few winters later after he came down with dysteria. He was a good brother, I miss him a lot."

"I wish I had a brother…" I said. I felt a lump in my throat as I thought of how nice that would be or how nice it would be to see Nana again. "Do you think Nan thinks I'm dead? Maybe she thinks I got dysteria."

Cory shrugged. He stretched his limbs and I heard a few pops as his bones cracked. "Honestly, yes, she probably does think you're dead but that doesn't matter. You have me to keep you company and a dad is better than any brother or any Nan."

He smiled as he said this. I got up and turned the radrat over and looked outside as it started to get dark. I really wanted to untie Cory since he was sore and he complained a lot about having to stick his butt out the window to go to the bathroom but I had trusted Josh and then he tried to fuck me in the ass.

I still think that meant something different… but Cory was an adult so he knew more than me. It was nice that he treated me like any other boy. I liked that he didn't know I had red eyes or my teeth were pointy. Though it was hard to see in the dark with the shades on, my night bright didn't work that well with the sunglasses on.

When the rat was all done and Cory had told me two more stories we both sat and ate our pieces of rat together. Since Cory was nicer than the other ones I gave him a big piece and dusted it with an entire salt packet. He was my friend and I liked his stories.

The rat was nummy. We threw the bones outside and I drank some water and gave him the rest. We had a lot of water now that he told me where to find the water spring though I still drank all of the radrat's blood. I liked the taste.

I curled up with my blanket and Barry and wound his butt. I put Barry beside me and sung Daisy Daisy out loud. Daddy Cory helped sing it but I had to remind him how the words went, sometimes he changed it but I didn't mind. Diaz, Taylor, Nina, and Charles sometimes sang and they knew all the words though.

"Good night, Diaz. Good night, Taylor. Good night, Nina and Charles. Good night, Barry, and good night Cory."

"Good night, Sami," Taylor and Diaz said and a moment later so did Nina and Charles.

"Extra good night, Sami!" Barry said with a laugh. He always had to one up my other friends because he was my best friend.

Cory yawned. "Good night, Sami Sanguine. I hope you burn a lot of bullies in your twisted dreams."

I fell into a deep sleep with my friends all around me.

In the middle of the night I was roused by Cory. He was saying my name over and over again in a hushed voice.

I lifted up my head and quickly adjusted my sunglasses and made sure my kerchief was covering my teeth. "What?" I murmured. I flicked away a couple bugs that had crawled on me and looked over at Cory.

"There are lights in the distance, flood lights... you need to get us out of here, kid," Cory hissed.

A shock went through me which made me jump up to my feet, without thinking I ran over to where Cory was and looked out the window.

He was right! Panic replaced the shock and I found myself gripping the window frame, my teeth chewing on the edge of my cheek until I could taste red. Coming in from the entrance to my town I could see bright bright lights, they were about a hundred me's away maybe a bit more but they were coming closer.

"Stay still and be quiet..." I ducked away from the window and pressed my back against the wall. "They won't check here... they'll–"

"You have that giant brick oven outside and lots of toys and bones, it's obvious someone is here and a small child," Cory hissed at me. "If that's the Legion they will try and find you and then they'll sell you to a slaver or a factory. You need to untie me so we can hide in the sewers, Sami. It's obvious where we are and they're coming right down the street."

What do I do? I grabbed my knife and looked out the window again, my cheek was chewed on even more as I tried to think.

I could... I could trust Daddy Cory. He had been so nice to me this week and told me such good stories.

I decided in that moment I would. I stood over Cory and started untying his feet, then I chopped off the bind that was attached to the window frame.

Cory let out a groan of relief; he slowly stood up and all of his bones were popping as he did. He didn't complain that I wouldn't untie his hands and while he was stretching out his legs I grabbed Barry and got a backpack I had for emergencies. It had some water in it and some jerky and books and a lighter. I put Barry in it and Conan and my Redwall books and I waited for him in the doorway.

"You need to stick by the wall... don't go near the center of the living room or you'll fall right through," I said hurriedly. "We'll go into the sewers near the spring and wait for them to go. Follow me and watch where I step."

"How the fuck did you even get me up here?" Cory murmured behind me.

"You weren't out cold just sloppy like Nina was, it was from the drugs I got," I said putting my backpack over my back. I wish I could have a cigarette so badly but I ran out a month ago. It looked like Cory didn't smoke, he had nothing on him. "Hurry... they'll be coming closer soon!"

I ran, feeling my boots crunch against the fallen plaster of the ceiling. I looked behind me and saw Cory slowly approaching, his boots testing each floorboard carefully before he put his weight on it.

It was like my entire body was made up of pop rocks and firecrackers, I felt like running so badly. Every time I thought of the Legion coming closer the pop rocks and firecrackers exploded and everything was needles on my skin. I didn't like this feeling, I hadn't been this scared for a long time now.

With Cory behind me we crept down the stairs. I had a handgun beside my sheathed knife but my stash of guns was on the fourth floor where only I could find them. This gun had a lot of bullets though at least and I would shoot as many legionary as I could. Legion were friendly with Nana but I wasn't at Sunshine House anymore and the legionaries hated greywasters. They liked harassing them and charging them for stupid things like going down the merchants' road. Diaz had told me a lot of stories about that; he hated the Legion.

I ran through the small lobby and jumped out of a window frame. I looked out and clenched my hands against my sides hard as I saw the lights coming closer. I found my fingers digging hard into my sides and I kept digging them harder and harder until I realized I had made them bleed.

Behind me Cory's footsteps could be heard and his breathing. I reached into my backpack and handed him a flashlight because I knew he couldn't see in the dark.

"Thanks…" Cory said, taking the long metal flashlight from me. "Let's go to the sewers."

I nodded as he flicked on the flashlight and turned to start heading towards the cistern I went down to find my water spring.

Suddenly something hit the back of my head, something hard. I yelped and fell onto the ground, right on the shards of glass. I whimpered, temporarily in a state of confusion; I tried to get up but I got hit in the head again.

My mind shot out of me for a second, I writhed around trying to find where my mind was and found that tears were springing to my eyes. Confusion overwhelmed me, it wasn't until I saw Cory walking away with the flashlight in his hand that I realized he had hit me.

Daddy Cory had hit me in the head.

I looked at him start to walk away and felt tears spring to my eyes. I kneeled on the ground with my head bowed and started to cry. My insides hurt and it made my ears and my head go hot; I felt like how I felt when Nan made me run away. I was losing another friend and what was worse was that he said he would be my dad.

I sniffed and saw that my sunglasses had gotten knocked off but everything was blue-tinged with my night bright so I could see better. I looked down at my bloodied hands and ripped the kerchief off of my face in anger.

The flashlight shined on my back, illuminating my hands and the shards of glass I had landed on. I heard Cory's body shift behind me and his boots crunch.

"Just be lucky I'm not going to kill you; you would slow me down anyway..." Cory said. His voice was low, cold, and angry like Gill's and Joshua's. Adults were always friendly until they had the upper hand again and then they turned mean.

I kept crying; I wiped my eyes. "You promised."

"What?" Cory said lowly.

Anger overtook my body, making my blood boil inside of my veins and making my fists clench even though I could still feel glass. I clenched my jaw tight and let the anger rip through me.

He said he would be my dad!

He said we could go to Chilko Lake!

I stood up and whirled around and with the flashlight shining on me, I opened my mouth to scream as loud as I could.

"YOU SAID YOU WOULD BE MY DAD!"

"HOLY SHIT!" Cory suddenly yelled; his eyes bulging out of his face. He jumped back and dropped the flashlight in his surprise. My face crumpled when I realized he was reacting to my eyes and teeth.

"What the fuck are you?" Cory hollered. He started taking backwards steps towards the door.

I had no answer for that; I was too angry and too hurt. I screamed again as loud as I could, not caring about the legionary coming down the street, and ran at him.

Cory swore and turned around. He managed to get out onto the sidewalk before I charged at him and grabbed onto his jacket. I pulled and pulled it until he whirled around and hit me in the face. I fell backwards but I bounced up like a spring and charged him again.

Though this time Cory grabbed my neck and my arm. I gasped, my eyes wide as he started squeezing my neck, letting go of my arm to start doing it with both hands.

Pressure started building behind my eyes, my head was pounding and going red hot. I gasped and tried to scream but no sound came out. I started to thrash and claw at him but he was gripping me hard.

"Fucking little demon..." Cory muttered. He was staring right at me; his face blazing with rage. "You're not even fucking human are you?"

As my head started to fill to the point of bursting, a hammer knocking against my skull and each pound felt like it was breaking it in half. Darkness filled each hole the hammer made and soon my entire head was dripping black into my vision. I felt my hands drop and my legs give one more desperate thrash before dark pressure was the only thing I knew.

Then a bright light… a bright blinding light.

And gunshots.

I fell to the ground but my body was frozen stiff. Above me I saw lights and Cory's body jerk and jolt as the thunderclaps of gunshots ripped through him. He stood standing for just a moment before he fell to the ground. I saw his hands twitch and frothy blood, bubbly with white foam start to pool around his body. His eyes were staring up and I saw his chest heave just once and his mouth heave too… then he shuddered and fell silent.

"Did you hit the kid?" a female voice sounded.

"No, of course I didn't hit the fucking kid…" a man snapped.

I saw shadows above me but I could only let out a whimper. I wanted to jump up and fly away into the night sky. I didn't want to get sold to a factory or given to slavers. All I wanted was friends to read to me and keep me company. If the Legion took me then Diaz and the others would be worried too.

I closed my eyes as I heard them approach me.

"He's breathing… the dude is dead." The lights were red under my closed eyelids but soon it was dark as the two people loomed over me. My ears were sore and throbbing from the gunshots but I could hear vehicles in the distance. These vehicles sounded big, I had only seen quads and dirt bikes before from the merchants visiting Sunshine House. Was the sound coming from cars?

"Hey, kid… we didn't hit you did we?" the male one said. I felt him tap me with his foot. I kept my eyes closed but shook my head. I wasn't for sure that I wasn't hit but I didn't feel anything on my body.

Arms grabbed me and helped me up. I kept my eyes closed though it was hard with all the activity around me, bright headlights and the low rumbling of vehicles. I could hear more people around too but I wasn't sure how many.

"Open your eyes, we're Skyfall's Legion; we help little kids about to get strangled to death." The man chuckled at his own joke and said to the female one, "He has his eyes shut tight. You know shutting your eyes won't make us go away, right?"

I kept them shut tight. "Can I go?" I said quietly. "I want to go…"

"Was that your dad? Where are your parents?" the man asked, before saying to someone else, "He has to be at least eight or nine. We can get ten bucks if we recruit him. His parents would probably be willing to sell him after such a bad winter last year."

"That's a good idea... where did..."

"What the hell are you two doing?" another female voice boomed. This one made me jump and open my eyes but no one was looking at me they were looking at her.

"We found a kid, General Ellis, and we might've just killed his dad. Dad was trying to strangle the little fucker to death. What do we do with him?" the male voice asked.

I looked at my shoes and saw my hands were dripping blood. I could see the corner of Cory's dead arm too; he had foamy blood all around him. He wasn't my dad or ever had been – like everyone else he had lied.

I closed my eyes again.

"Drop him off in the nearest town, I suppose... why are his eyes closed?"

"Not sure either, maybe he's retarded or something."

"Really..." I felt hands on my chin; she grabbed onto it and gave it a shake. "Open your eyes."

I shook my head and the other two laughed. The angry sounding lady shook my chin even harder. "Open your eyes, boy."

I held my hand up over my mouth and spoke. "You'll kill me if I do... just like everyone else tries to kill me if I do," I said defiantly. I don't know where I got my bravery from, maybe I just didn't like my head being shaken like this.

"No excuses, I said open your damn eyes and put your hand down for fuck sakes," the lady said in a sharp tone. She was getting mad at me – everyone hated me.

I sniffed and lowered my hand before opening my eyes. I looked up and saw the lady come into focus.

She had short black hair and purpely-blue eyes, her face was all serious and she was glaring at me like I was a parasite.

Though something weird happened, when she looked at me she didn't scream or call me a demon – her eyes widened like she was surprised.

"Holy shit..." she whispered. I looked down at my shoes, feeling my body go hot under her intense stare. But a moment later she took my chin, a bit more gentle this time, and lifted it up. Then she pulled on my lower lip and I knew she was looking at my teeth.

"What's your name?"

I swallowed and dug my fingers into my thighs again. "Sami."

She was quiet for a moment, the sounds of the engines seemed lost in the silence.

"Did you call yourself that or did your mother name you Sami? What's your other name, boy?"

I looked up at her, my brow creasing. I didn't know what she meant by that, or how she knew I called myself something else, but I told her what she wanted to know either way.

"Sanguine."

Her face paled; she looked around before her eyes went to one of the legionary who had gotten me. "Get Silas on a remote phone… now. I don't care what he's in the middle of, tell him it's urgent."

She took my hand which made my heart skip. I tried to pull away from her but she tightened her grip. "Come with me, Sanguine."

"No!" I pulled back. "I'm not going with you; I didn't do anything wrong!"

The lady named Ellis kept dragging me, I kept stumbling as I tried unsuccessfully to dig my boots in; she was literally dragging me towards one of the vehicles.

"What happened to your mother?" Ellis asked. She was opening the door of a big giant truck with one hand and pulling me towards it with the other. "Get in."

"My mom's dead, this is my home. Where are you taking me?" I yelled. Ellis grabbed me with both her hands and I started to kick and twist around to try and get free. I only had my emergency backpack on and everything else, all my food and ammo, was in the apartment.

"You're not supposed to be out here alone, child…" Ellis swore and suddenly another pair of hands had me. A big burly man whose arms were huge. "Hold him, Nero. He's a squirmer and he'll run the moment you let him loose. And watch his–"

The man named Nero yelled as I sank my teeth into his hand. I clenched my jaw and kneading my fangs into his skin.

" –watch his teeth."

"You bitch, tell me now do ya? Get the little fucker off of me. Where the fuck is my Taser?" Nero smacked my head but I kept sinking my teeth further and further into his hands until I couldn't bite down anymore. I sat there, his arms still holding me, and started to growl.

"Fuck, he's growling? He's seriously growling? Jack doesn't growl… does he?" I saw a hand in front of my face and a moment later he pinched my nose. I didn't know what he was doing until I realized I couldn't breathe. I unhinged my teeth with a gasp and started coughing.

Nero laughed and grabbed onto my chin. The door closed and a moment later Ellis got in beside Nero. I was horrified when the vehicle started moving.

"I want to go back to my home!" I yelled. "I have my guns there and my food. I spent all year making that place good, you fucks!"

Nero chuckled but Ellis was on her phone and wasn't paying attention to me. I tried to pry myself out of Nero's grasp but he was so strong it was like his arms were metal beams.

"Guns and ammo? He has been doing well for himself... do you have Kingy on the phone yet?" I tried to bite Nero again as he was talking but he was too fast for me. To show he was done with my biting, he put his hand over my mouth.

"Father? We have..." Ellis looked at me and I scowled at her. Her eyes travelled to Nero and she said to him, "Cover his ears. I don't think... you know."

I growled and shook my head as Nero covered my ears with his hands. I took this chance to try and open the car door but Ellis grabbed my free hand and soon my other one was flailing around trying to grab anything I could shred. The angle they had me at was awkward though and there was nothing to grab. I ground my teeth in anger and decided to make as much noise as I could. I didn't want to be taken anywhere, I wanted to go back to my town with my friends and my food and water. This wasn't fair at all.

These people didn't seem to want to hurt me just keep me quiet. Nan had said the Legion was nice most of the time and would give Nan free water filters and radiation juice for us; sometimes they even gave us pieces of candy. Though I had also heard from Cory and the other greywasters that the Legion was bad and would sell me for food or make me into a slave, so I didn't know who to believe.

The Legion did help me because Cory was trying to strangle me to death and they seemed nice now.

I decided to stop squirming not long after. I stayed still and as a reward Nero loosened his grip on me, though his hands were still covering my ears as the mean lady was on the phone.

Then finally he took his hands away and I could hear.

"There he's being good now," Nero said. "See, I'm great with kids. Do you want some candy, Sanguine?"

I furrowed my brow and saw his eyes watching me in the rear view mirror of the truck. A legionary was driving it into the dark. My home was probably way behind now.

"Do you have cigarettes too?" I asked. Both Ellis and Nero laughed a lot at this for some reason.

"No, shithead, just some sweets. You want some or not?" Nero said through his laughs.

"Okay…" I said slowly, then I felt him rustling things in his jacket.

My mouth dropped open when he handed me an entire chocolate bar! This one was blue and white with a Dek'ko label. I ripped into it and started eating it; it was like nothing I'd ever tasted before!

"Take your backpack off and if you don't feel like ripping my arm off again you can sit in the middle of us," Nero said. I looked down and saw that he was wrapping his arm in a piece of rag. I decided to take off my backpack but I kept it on my lap, Barry was in there and the only leftover food and water I had.

Nero shifted me down into my own seat and I sat there savouring the sugary chocolate. I had never had chocolate before only chocolate flavoured hard candy. It coated my mouth in a blanket of creamy sweetness. I loved it.

I smiled as Nero brought out more chocolate bars from his shirt and started opening my bag. I watched him cautiously as he stuffed the chocolate into my bag before, with a laugh, he pulled out Barry.

Fear hit me, I didn't want him to hurt my friend, he was my only friend now. I reached out to grab him and Nero let me take him without argument. He kept putting chocolate and other things in my pack.

"You have a stuffed bear, eh? Who gave that to you?" Nero asked.

"Nan," I said, putting Barry on my lap.

"Nan? Where's Nan?"

"They kicked me out for being bad." Everyone had to ask me where Nan was and it hurt my heart every time I had to say it. I decided to save the follow up question and stated plainly, "I almost got axed to death by Gill because two boys hurt me so I lit them on fire."

The car echoed with Nero's laughter to the point where Ellis told him to shut up because she was on the phone. I smiled though because I had never had someone laugh when I told them I burned two boys alive. I liked Nero.

I looked at Ellis and chewed on my chocolate bar. "Where am I going? It took me forever to get food and water in my town. You can't take me to a town they'll kill me there. Why am I in the car? What did I do wrong? Am I going to be a legionary?"

Ellis at this point got off the phone. I saw she looked mad but I think she always looked mad.

"Silas says if he seems to be doing well for himself... he stays."

Nero said *fuck* and passed me a bottle of brown stuff. I opened it and smelled it before something stung my nose. The surprise of the stinging bubbles made me growl. I think I was just on edge, everything was happening so fast.

"Seriously?" Nero's tone dropped.

"King Silas?" I said in awe. Why did the king care what happened to me?

Ellis nodded and looked at me with a sigh. "We can help him though. Why don't we take him to Little Spring and drop him off there? That has a well and it's full of small game and it also is close to Melchai. Boy, you were saying you've had trouble because of how you look?"

I nodded and held up my palm. It now held a spiral scar that was bright pink. "No one wants to be my friend and if they do it's to trick me. Am I a demon?"

"No, you're not." Ellis's mouth pursed to the side and she looked at Nero. "I think it's too late to find him a family. He seems fine on his own. Are you okay being by yourself?"

I didn't know how to answer that. I liked having people to talk to but I was afraid that if I said no I would have to go to an orphanage or they would make me become a legionary. So I nodded. I wasn't lying anyway, I liked not having to listen to grown-ups and I could always find more greywasters to play with me.

"Why can't I go back to my town?" I said. I started licking the melting chocolate off of my hands. "I was fine there until–"

"Until you decided to get almost strangled to death by that greywaster?" Ellis said, giving me a sharp look. She looked at me like Nan did. She must be a mom or at least a Nan. "We were going to that town for a reason. We've been hearing about people going missing around there... twenty of them. Was that all you?"

I scowled at her. "Why do you care? Why do any of you care?"

"Because you were about a week away from an entire mob from Chilko Lake coming and raiding the town. They would've killed you and eaten you. You're damn lucky we found you first, Sanguine." Ellis glared me down and I looked away from her. I grabbed another chocolate bar and felt

Nero put his hand on my head. I wasn't used to being touched and manhandled so much, it made me squirm. I didn't mind these two but I wanted to go back to my town where my friends were and the rest of my toys.

"We have gear we can give him… we can make him comfy for now," Nero said. He moved his hand back and forth on my head making my head wave around.

"Do you do this for all kids you find?" I asked. I looked out the window but everything was just dark, even my night bright wasn't working properly.

They both paused before Ellis nodded. "Yes, we do for… special kids."

I was special? This made me skeptical. "How am I special?"

"Little fucker asks a lot of questions, eh?" Nero laughed and urged me to take a drink of the brown stuff that burned my nose. I took a drink and coughed, it was full of little bubbles. I held it up and looked at it in awe. It tasted good though.

"Just watch your words," Ellis said. I didn't know what she meant by that. "It doesn't matter why, boy. Just take it and run with it. We're taking you to a place near the plaguelands called Little Spring, you'll be near a town and in a place that doesn't have that many people."

"I want to go back to my home; I liked it there," I said to her. The fact that I was being forced to leave all of my stuff behind was making my fists clench. "I don't want to go to Little Spring. The greywasters always told me the legionary sell people to factories or make them become soldiers."

"The greywasters are all radiation-crazed idiots," Ellis said plainly. "You'll do fine there, we'll give you sunglasses to cover your eyes."

"I already had sunglasses!" I suddenly snapped; my voice started to rise. "And I had my friends there and my toys and my books. I want to go home!"

Ellis shook her head, which made me fume even more. I crossed my arms and kicked my backpack which was resting by my feet.

"You're both a bunch of fucks."

Nero chuckled which made me even more mad. I liked him but I didn't like that he laughed at me. I wasn't a little kid anymore I was almost eight. Why did these two fucks care where I was going to stay? I wanted my home I had worked hard to get everything working good. Cory was dead anyway so he wouldn't be able to hurt me.

Cory… I swallowed down my sadness at thinking of him with a

mouthful of the bubbly drink. He had tricked me. All adults did was lie to you and trick you to get what they want.

What if they were tricking me too? I felt a shock go through me as I started turning over all the information I had received. They said I was special but I knew I wasn't. I was a bad kid, an evil demon and a monster. Nero and Ellis had given me candy and chocolate but I had bit Nero so they might've been trying to keep me quiet.

They were going to kill me… or make me into a legionary. I think they were lying to me because none of this made sense. I had never met an adult who didn't lie to me not even Nana. Nana lied to me because she said I could stay at Sunshine House until I was a grown-up and even then she said I could learn to hunt and stay for the rest of my life.

This realization filled my tummy with angry bugs and those bugs seemed to burst out of my stomach and crawl all over my body. I didn't feel safe here and the more my reality was starting to sink in the more I became anxious to get away.

But Nero was strong and Ellis was quick. If I made a dash and opened the door they would snatch me before my hand even got onto the handle. No, I had to wait… I had to be patient, that's what adults did when they were doing bad things to me. They waited until I trusted them and then they became mean.

I would do the same, I would beat them at their own game.

So I sat patient and drank my bubbly water which Nero said was called pop. While I ate that, I dug into my pack and got one of the other chocolate bars that Nero had given me. I started eating that one too and was amazed to see that this one had crunchy nuts inside and some other sweet gooey stuff. I ate that one and started going for another.

I listened to their conversations too, including Ellis on the phone. She was talking to one of the first legionary who found me and I think she was told about my friends in my bedroom because she mentioned dead bodies out loud and then she mentioned a boy's room. I didn't say anything about it and she didn't ask me about it so I stayed put and ate. Occasionally Nero asked me questions and I answered politely.

"He could use new boots too…" Nero said. He reached down and flicked my boots I wore. "Where did you get those ones?"

"I bought them in Chilko Lake before I got chased out," I said. "I traded my old boots for them."

Then I grimaced and put a hand on my stomach. I had eaten five chocolate bars and drank two bottles of pop in the time I had been in the truck and my stomach was starting...

I lurched and felt hot ooze erupt from my mouth. In an instant Ellis yelled at the driver to stop and just seconds later Nero pulled me out of the big truck and into the summer night. My stomach gave another churn inside of me and I keeled over and started throwing up all the chocolate.

I threw up stream after stream of brown goo and watched it splash against a slab of pavement. I wiped my mouth and looked around and was fascinated to see that we were driving through a big city.

"Nero, since we're already stopped, take him into one of the alleyways to pee. We should re-fuel the truck anyway." Ellis's voice sounded behind me. I looked up and around and saw giant buildings towering over us. So much bigger than my little town's buildings, these ones were massive. They were all intact with barely any crumbling on them at all, though I could see a lot of windows missing but some were still unbroken. Everything was grey and streaked with black and in some places the grey brick had fallen away to show a lighter colour. I wasn't sure what the colour was but in my night bright it was a pale shade of blue.

The city transfixed me and I realized as Nero started walking me towards an alleyway that this place was probably full of things to scavenge. It was an entire city – I could live here like a king.

I think I would like to live here.

CHAPTER 7

Sami

Age 7

I LOOKED AROUND THE CITY AND FELT MY HEART fill with those same insects but this time they weren't bad insects but good ones. They were excited and each way of escape I saw made them buzz around even more. I behaved though and walked down a spooky alleyway with trash bins and went pee.

I could run out of the alleyway and climb up one of the big buildings and hide… but Nero was fast. So I turned around and crossed my arms as Nero lit himself a cigarette.

"I gotta go to the bathroom."

Nero stared at me, his eyes brightening up as he took an inhale of the cigarette. It was a blue-embered one. I hadn't had those in years and I missed them so much but I had to keep focused.

"You just went," he said in a voice that suggested he was talking to a moron.

"No, the other one."

Nero blinked at me and shrugged. "Go nuts."

"I need something to wipe with. My backpack has stuff, get that."

"Jesus fucking christ… okay, wait there." Nero shook his head and turned around. He started walking down the alleyway before calling to Ellis. "The kid needs to take a shit, you handle it, Momma. Kid wants his backpack, maybe that's what he was using those books for."

And I was gone. I turned around and ran as quietly as I could down the alleyway, leaving the headlights and the running vehicle behind me. I ran into the darkness and as the motors in the distance became muffled behind the buildings I felt like I was back in my element.

My night bright illuminated a street in front of me. With tall buildings that framed it and smaller shops that were attached to each other. All of the light poles and electric poles were standing as well but their lights and the electricity had been long dead.

Even the cars didn't look that bad. The cars parked on the side of the road still had bits of paint on them and some even had windows. All places I could duck and hide into if…

"NERO!" I heard Ellis yell. My heart jumped into my throat and I ran across the street into an abandoned park. Then I saw a concrete flight of stairs with a blue railing that led to a half-open door. I looked up as my heartbeat got faster and faster and saw this was a big building that went high up in the air. I sprinted towards it, ran up the stairs and went inside, closing the door behind me.

There was a flight of stairs going up and a grey door with a metal lever to push. I decided to go up the stairs as high as I could possibly go.

The stairs were covered in rubber and I was able to climb up each flight with barely any noise. Every time I hit a new floor I just kept on climbing, ignoring the metal doors around me that could possibly lead to something cool. I would have years to explore this building but I won't get the chance if the legion people found me.

Up and up I went. The higher I went the more I felt safe, this place looked like it hadn't been touched by anyone in a billion years. It smelled like old clothes and how my books smelled when I first opened them to read. I could see lots of stains on the walls too and flakey paint that fell from the walls and crunched under my boots.

Finally I climbed up five flights of stairs. I stopped at another push door and this time I pushed it open. It squeaked on rusty hinges which made me scared that Ellis or Nero would hear but when I stopped and listened and didn't hear anything I let it shut quiet behind me and walked down a hallway.

This was an office building, not an apartment building which meant there wouldn't be any good food I bet, but I could find a store. I walked down the hallway, which had lights hanging from their wires, and found a big room with a bunch of dividers that had computers and desks in each one. None of the computers would work so I left that alone and crossed the grey carpeted floor to where the windows were.

The windows were mostly intact but one was broken so I looked out of it and onto the street below me.

I laughed as I saw two black figures in the alleyway I had come out of. I could tell it was Nero and Ellis from how they were dressed. I bet they were angry at me but I was so small and it was so dark I knew they wouldn't be able to see where I was and no way they could find me.

I was so smart. I could outsmart greywaster adults and now legionary adults! Even one super strong like Nero and all stern like Ellis.

I bet I could outsmart anyone I find, I was just that good. I was just that –

Behind me I heard a crunch. My brow furrowed and I turned around to see what that noise was.

There were more than a dozen people in the corner of the room.

No... not people...

Ravers.

As my heart scrunched inside of my chest. I jumped and started running towards the door I had come from. At my quick movements, or maybe the horror welling in my chest, the ravers gave out a low and long drawn-out moan and I heard their feet start to crunch against the dirty carpet.

I ran down the hallway towards the stairs. I had to blindly trust there weren't any in the stairwell because I didn't know where else to go.

Shock was coursing through me like a lightning bolt had turned my muscles into electricity. With hands that were shaking and feet that felt like jelly I ran down the stairs. In no time their groaning and moaning came closer and soon they were bouncing off of the high walls of the stairwell, pounding against my skull and laying claim to every sense my brain was still able to comprehend.

I was sure my heart was going to burst, explode in my chest like a bomb going off. My mind kept freezing then going super fast but all it was telling me was to run, run, run.

So I ran down the stairs, hearing the ravers thumping behind me and their moaning starting to get louder and louder like they were getting frenzied. Soon as I reached the second flight of stairs I started hearing crashing sounds and I realized they were tripping over each other down the stairs.

I turned on the landing of the second to last flight and felt another wave of horror wash over me as I heard loud banging, so loud it made my ears hurt. I turned towards the metal door on the landing and realized it was pulsing – it being thumped on by the ravers. They were trying to get through, could they smell me?

But... I don't think they were normal greywaster ravers. I turned around and looked at the flight of stairs I had just gone down and saw a long, leathery hand sliding down the white wall. Then the hand seemed to stretch too far for its body because suddenly it fell and stumbled forward.

It was... all dried out and gross-looking. Its eyes were sunken black pits and its teeth shone against my night bright...

I didn't know what the fuck they were –

– and I wasn't staying to find out.

I jumped on the railing leading down the last flight of stairs and slid down to the hallway. With the weird ravers crashing and screaming behind me, filling up the area with their terrifying noise, I ran to the entrance I had ducked into and jumped right off of the concrete stairs.

"NERO!" I screamed. I know I had just ran from them but now there were no other people I wanted to see more. "NERO!?"

I landed on the ground with a thunk and immediately started running towards the road with the cars lined on the ends. I glanced behind me once and screamed when I saw a bunch of them spilling out of the door and jumping down the stairs like I had. They were skinny, with leathery brown skin and their spines were sticking out of their backs like rusted rebar. Their limbs were all longer than a human's should be, like stretched out pieces of jerky. They were so long they almost touched the ground and would have but their legs were big and skinny like tree branches. These monsters looked to be at least four of me tall.

I ran down the sidewalk until I got to the middle of the road. Everything was dark and I couldn't find the alleyway. I looked around desperately and realized with a sink of my heart that I was lost. The headlights and the vehicles were down one of these alleys... I was sure of it.

My body was light, like I had turned into the stuff they put in flying balloons, the stuff was telling me to run and I was running but where was I running to?

I looked behind me again and before I could stop it I let out a scream. I saw three of them hunched over; their dried-out arms hanging down and their legs carrying them towards me in long strides. Their bodies remained still as they walked, just arms hanging loosely down as they reached out a giant leg to step further. The way they walked reminded me of a daddy longlegs spider, one leg up high and down, then another up high and down.

Tears started to fall down my face; every time I looked behind me they were coming closer and closer. They were slower than me but their legs were so long they were easily gaining no matter how fast I went,

"Nero?" I cried. What if they left me behind? What if they gave up on me already and didn't even bother looking for me?

A scream pierced the air but not from me. I turned around and looked as a legionary person came running from behind a building. I was about to shout at him that I was here but as I saw two of the creatures closing in on him from opposite sides my tongue glued itself to the roof of my mouth.

The air around me became frozen, enveloping my body in an icy sheet. I watched, paralyzed, as the man turned his head away from the alley only to run straight into one of the brown skeleton men. I heard the dry sound of sandpaper as he face planted into its chest before falling to the ground.

He looked up and a scream rolled from his mouth. I started taking steps back as one of the tall creatures wrapped its long boney fingers around the legionary's legs and started dragging him down the sidewalk. I could hear the legionary's clothing and body scraping against the pavement.

Then the creatures he had originally been running from reached down and each grabbed onto one side of his shoulders. For a moment they pulled him towards them but the one with the legionary's legs pulled him back with an angry moan. Its small, skull-like head shaking back and forth.

The night air broke with the sounds of moaning and the legionary screaming. I kept taking hurried steps back as I watched them raise the legionary off of the ground and started a tug of war with his body. Two on his shoulders, their long fingers wrapped around his underarms and chest like spider webs, and the other one tugging with its hands on his legs.

Then suddenly the screaming from the legionary shifted to a higher pitch. I watched, stunned, as a red lesion appeared on his torso for just a brief moment before I watched them pull him in half.

Intestines spilled from the gaping holes and I saw his spine twist up and down like a piece of stiff rope, all with a sound like ripping wet cloth. Finally after a tight twist the rest of his spine was pulled from his lower half. Blood spilled onto the ground with the ribbons of guts all falling out of the legionary like a burst pouch of jam.

The creatures started chewing on the man, their white teeth sinking in and gnawing his limbs, tearing out chunks of flesh. I continued to watch in transfixed horror before I heard another bellowing moan behind me.

Snapping out of my fixed vision I turned around and gasped as I saw more closing in on me. I left the legionary to his fate and started running down the most wide open street I could see.

Eventually the darkness ahead of me started to open up and I saw an interaction with two cars tipped over like they were a barrier, behind it in the distance I could see a large store that had a sign that read *Wal-Mart* shrouded in haze and to my right a highway with over four lanes and a divider in the middle. All of this looked wrong, the street we had been on only had two lanes and light poles.

Everything was open, there weren't any good places to hide… they were going to tear me apart like they did that legionary.

I fixed my eyes on the shopping center and tried to make a decision whether I wanted to try to go there. But that was dashed a moment later when I saw what I thought was a car move and shift. I pivoted on my foot and froze for a moment as I watched the black figure start to grow. It became taller and taller until I saw two long arms stretch out followed by two spindled legs.

Tears were welling in my eyes, I looked behind me and saw five of the tall creatures. Their ghostly silhouettes getting closer to me, one long stride at a time.

"Ner-"

"YOU LITTLE FUCKING SHIT!"

I shrieked and almost burst into scared tears as the voice blasted against my ear. I looked over and saw Nero running out from behind an old restaurant and beeline towards me. I was so scared I let him pick me up off of the ground.

"I am going to beat you fucking bloody, you stupid, retarded, fucking cocksucker!" Nero screamed. "Get on my back, NOW!"

I didn't argue. Nero lifted me over his shoulder and I grabbed onto the back of his cape and felt his combat armour underneath. I dug my fingers into the edges of it and held onto him for dear life.

I heard clicking and saw Nero had an assault rifle in his hands. He raised it and shot it down the street. The noise ripped through my ears and made them explode in pain but I had to hold on, I couldn't cover my ears.

I saw one of the creatures fall down before Nero ran across the big road I had seen to my left, I looked and saw the ones I had been running from start to fade into the darkness. I clung on to Nero and crawled onto his shoulders. When I was balanced, my legs on either side of his neck, I got out my own handgun and held it to me.

"Shit, shit, shit!" Nero swore, his voice was sharp and angry. He jumped over a car tire and ran into the parking lot that the small buildings surrounded but a moment later he stopped and started swearing again.

I saw what he was cursing at. I was up higher than him now that I was on his shoulders. All of the lumps I had seen and thought were cars in the parking lot were those same creatures. Each one slowly rising themselves from their sleep, stretching out like a corpse flower trying to reach the grey sun.

I got out my handgun and pointed it, with my tongue sticking out of my mouth I aimed it and shot it off.

Nero jumped before calling me a bunch of names, ending with: "Warn me next time, you little shit fuck!" I said a quick sorry and let him shoot the one that was behind it.

When they fell their limbs started flying through the air like tentacles, writhing and squirming as they let out that low bellowing noise that gave me chills.

"Where are the trucks?" I asked desperately. I grabbed into Nero's head and squeezed my legs together as I saw more of them starting to spill out from behind the buildings and the alleyways around us. There were more and more, walking towards us with their long strides. They looked slow but that was only an illusion, each step they made was four of our normal steps.

"If I knew I'd be running towards them, you fucking retard," Nero snapped. He started sprinting in another direction. "We don't get outside of the fucking vehicles and wander far for a reason. These fucking creatures stay dormant unless you go crashing through their fucking houses, you dumb fuck. I hope you're proud of yourself, you stupid midget."

I deserved that so I didn't say anything. I loaded my gun but before I could aim it at another one, this one peeking up over a store sign, Nero turned and started running in a different direction.

Every time I thought I was only seeing a car it turned out to be one of those creatures coming closer. I squeezed onto Nero even harder and gripped my gun tight.

Nero's own gun started going off, I looked to see where he was shooting and screamed. He had been running by a line of black trees but I realized with a shock that half of them were the creatures.

Then one took a swing at us. I ducked but it hit the back of my head. I tried to scramble off of Nero, terror taking over my senses but before my boots hit the ground the creature grabbed me with both hands and pulled me, a low but loud moan spilling from a mouth that had no lips, only an open black pit surrounded by teeth.

I screamed and thrashed, its fingers were cold and rough, they clenched around my body and enveloped me like I was caught in tree branches. My gun fell to the ground with a clang and shot a random bullet off into the darkness.

A flash of light and several bangs all one after another, in an instant the arms let go of me and I fell to the ground hard. No sooner than I had fallen I felt something pick me up, gloved hands. He grabbed me by my jacket collar and threw me back onto his back.

I clung onto him and saw him retract his arm and throw a punch at another creature. His fist smashed against its brown, hardened cheek throwing it off of its feet in a pile of long awkward limbs. I saw for just a moment a black eye roll around in an almost skeletonized face before it rolled onto its stomach.

Nero tripped. I was thrown off of him landing on my shoulder and the side of my head, stars burst through my vision and my senses but I got them back quickly. The cold night air and the static surrounding us commanded my body to do nothing but stay in its survival mode.

Nero was still for a moment which horrified me. I picked up his gun but it was different than the assault rifle I had had. I pointed it anyway at the three closest I could see and pressed down on the trigger.

The recoil threw me off of my feet and I landed on top of Nero. Two of the raver-like creatures fell down but a third took one last giant step towards me before it swung an arm down. It landed on Nero's leg and the creature grabbed a hold of it.

I snarled as it pulled Nero and bared my teeth at it. It stared at me… its face baked skin and its nose small with two slits for nostrils. It was hairless and I could see pulsing black veins in its skull only making its dark pits for eyes all the more prominent. It was a scary creature but I was evil and I was bad… and I could be scarier!

I coiled myself like a spring and pounced on it from the side. I felt my hands brush tight hardened skin and I clung onto it as hard as I could. As the creature reared back with another low moan I opened my mouth and sunk my teeth into its neck, then I started pulling out chunks of disgusting tasting skin.

When the creature realized what I was doing it reached around to try and grab me, but it could only reach my pant leg. It pulled me until I was only holding on by my hands and mouth, my lower half was completely suspended. I clung for dear life and chewed and chewed as I hit warm flesh.

It bellowed in pain and I heard scratching and groaning behind me. I realized the ones that were creeping up on us had reached me. More hands grabbed me and soon I felt a pain go through my body as another pair of spider-like hands snatched my legs.

I was completely suspended. I looked around wildly and saw that one had my arms and one had my legs. I let out a terrified cry as I realized they –

I shrieked as loud as I could.

– they were trying to pull me in half.

My entire body was searing with pain. I heard them grunt and more pressure coming from my arm and leg sockets. I could hear my bones popping and creaking inside of my head as they pulled and pulled.

I was going to split in half; I was going to split in half.

Then headlights.

Headlights!

Suddenly everything became busy. Gunshots sung around me and I was let go. I fell to the ground and landed on my feet without a word. My eyes wide and my body frozen stiff from shock.

I saw boots and someone pick me up, everything was chaos with the lights and the engines running and so many people yelling and talking. I stared, unable to move or talk; it was like my mind was a thousand miles ahead and my body had no way of catching up to it.

The person who picked me up ran with me, his breathing hard inside of his chest. I was put in the rumbling truck and then doors slammed all around me.

"Is he alive?"

"I don't know; I don't fucking know…"

"Sanguine?"

"Sanguine? Can you hear me?"

My eyes had always been open but it took me a minute to start seeing things. I blinked and saw I was in someone's arms. I looked around and felt my face crumple.

"Shit… I think he's okay. Fuck, Silas would've killed me… he would've literally killed me…" Nero's voice was tense. I felt a hand tap my cheek. "You okay, you little cocksucker?"

I nodded and tried not to cry. I didn't want to cry in front of Nero. I tucked my lip inside of my mouth and heard him chuckle.

"He saved my life, eh? He jumped on one of those celldwellers and chewed through half its neck before it got to him. Did you see it?"

"I just saw them trying to pull the boy in two." That was Ellis. I couldn't lift my head though, I only saw her jacket and a bloody assault rifle in her hand. The truck was moving really fast but I didn't want to look out the window. I could hear the motor revving though.

"That's what I saw too… ten seconds longer and they would've succeeded too. I would've suggested we just say we never found him again but that's just me. We have a couple years before Elish and Perish perfect that brain splicing, after I'm immortal then I would tell him."

I sniffed but I still felt shaken and stunned. I didn't understand what they were talking about or the words they were using, I didn't care either. I was just happy to be in the car again… I wasn't going to try running into abandoned cities anymore and I made a point to avoid them in my future travels.

"How awake does he have to be before I can start beating on him for running?" I felt myself get shaken a bit but I didn't want to move.

"You won't… you were the idiot for turning your back on him. You've had enough experience with young chi… boys to know not to turn your fucking back on them, especially when they know they're in shit. If anything *you* should be apologizing to *him*," Ellis said sharply. I felt a bit better that she wasn't going to spank me or something like Nan did; I think I might be too old for that now but she didn't look like the type of person to care.

"Yeah well, he's a crafty little fucker… it's going to be interesting… when, eventually…"

Ellis was quiet for a second. "You can't keep him."

"Yeah, I know."

I looked up at Nero. "I can go home with you?"

Nero shook his head and chuckled; he ruffled my hair. "Nah, you can't, shithead. That's against the… Legion rules. But I can visit you sometimes, how's that?"

"I don't think…" Ellis was cut off but I don't know why she stopped talking. She sighed instead and I saw her shake her head. "I won't say anything."

"I know you won't, sissy," Nero said and he ruffled my hair again.

"You two are brother and sister?" I asked in awe.

Ellis and Nero both nodded.

"Twins actually," Ellis said. As I looked at her, and then Nero, I wasn't surprised, they both had the same purply-blue eyes and they looked similar. "We have a big family and I'm the only girl."

"I wish I had a family," I said, and then I felt sad. I was going to be alone again but I liked these people. "I don't have any brothers or sisters either. You two are lucky."

"Aww, jeez… that hits you where it hurts, doesn't it?" Nero patted my head. I wanted Nero to be my friend, I think he was too young to be my dad but I wasn't sure. Either way I wanted to stay with him; I liked Nero.

But if he visited me then that was better than nothing. At least he wouldn't disappear like Nan did or die like Cory did. Maybe he would bring me more chocolate and maybe he would teach me to hunt since he did say I saved his life.

The lights in the truck dimmed and my eyes drew me to the only other source of light. Nero lit a blue-embered cigarette with his lighter and I smelled the sweet and pure-smelling smoke coming from his mouth. Behind his cigarette were the headlights now shining on greywaste dirt. I watched the greywastes go by in the beams of the lights and not too soon after, lulled by the conversations between Ellis and Nero… I fell asleep.

"He's such a cute little psychopath." Nero pulled Sanguine's lip down and whistled when he saw a pointed adult tooth poking through. "I think Silas is full of shit for making this kid stay out here."

Ellis looked down at Sanguine, fast asleep and half-lying in Nero's arms. A small smile crept to her face. "You know, you're a murderer, a rapist, a sadist, and an overall deranged fuck… but you sure are a good big brother."

Nero rolled his eyes and took an inhale of his cigarette. "He's a cute kid; boy after my own heart, though he's a bit nuts. But he can move and he can bite."

Ellis shook her head and took the cigarette from Nero. She took a long inhale before handing it back. "We're lucky we found him, at least it seems he was doing alright. But you heard the buzz at the pub in Chilko; they were getting ready to sweep the town and they would've lynched him." Ellis picked up Sanguine's hand and shuddered as she saw the scar, the size and shape of a dime. "The place he was being raised in fucking tried to crucify him. I don't understand Silas's logic; he'll be lucky if he reaches the age for him to come back to the family."

"That's the point, ain't it? If he survives he will have earned his place beside Kingy as his bloodthirsty, insane bodyguard. I'm gonna laugh when it blows up in his face but maybe I can keep him after… he's so adorable. Did you see how he always makes sure that bear is near him? What's with young chimerys and their stuffed animals? Garrett used to flip fucking shit when I tortured his stuffed rabbit," Nero chuckled at the memory, another plume of smoke rolling from his mouth.

"They get it from Father," Ellis said quietly. "I think you're smart to check up on him… I would too but after I step in with the thien force Father is going to be watching me. You at least have free reign of the greywastes and the Legion until Kessler stops pissing in his underwear."

Nero chuckled at this. "Yeah, I will and hopefully Sangy can shut up about it once he comes to Skyfall. I don't give a shit what Silas says, and I gotta obey – but I'm going to make sure he's okay until he comes home. What age did Silas say anyway?"

"Fifteen he said… eight more years." Ellis looked ahead and raised her voice as she addressed the driver. "How long until we're at Little Spring?"

"Another hour, Ma'am," the man replied. "The river is dried out and Commander Heryn tells me he's been sending vehicles through it so that will shave off some time."

"Good," Ellis said. "Father's going to want a full report on this little gem we found. Maybe if we embellish it he'll agree to bringing him home early."

Nero snorted; Sanguine shifted around in his arms so he dropped his voice. "Embellish what? He's gotten scorched, crucified and he was capturing greywasters to force them to talk to him. What the fuck are we embellishing?"

Ellis seemed to weigh this and with a frown she turned her attention to outside. "You're right... I just... I think he's going to see that this is all a mistake. This experiment of his is going to backfire on him I know it. It's hard enough right now to even make chimeras why is he letting this one fend for himself? He's royalty and he doesn't even know it."

Sanguine shifted around and whimpered again but became still when Nero rested a hand on his head. "He will... and I bet he'll be a bigger little bad ass than all of us. He'll be okay... he's been okay so far."

The legion truck's headlights shone against grey sun bleached wood and a covered deck. A rocking chair sat next to a dirty coffee table with the varnish peeling off, and behind it a screen door that led into a two-storey house. All the windows were boarded up with new nails, not the rusted picks one would see in the greywastes, even the boards looked new.

Nero stepped out holding the still sleeping Sanguine. Ellis went in front of him and opened the screen door.

"Start taking the boards off the windows and be quiet about it," Ellis said to the legionary who had been driving them. The entire greywastes became cloaked in silence as the truck engine died, though the headlights remained on.

Nero walked in and Ellis followed with a bluelamp. "I'm going to check and make sure the well is still working. I can see evidence of radrats so he'll be able to eat those," Ellis said.

Nero adjusted his hold on the sleeping child and nodded, glancing behind him at a kitchen covered in plastic, though there was little dust on it, everything seemed intact and in fair condition. "I'll put him in his new bed then I guess. If we want to leave before he wakes up we should hurry."

Ellis turned without a word and left. Nero walked up the single flight of stairs which opened up to a small room with three doors leading off to bedrooms and an unusable bathroom. Though well water could be had in the greywastes indoor plumbing was a benefit only reserved for Skyfall and the surrounding factory towns.

Nero walked into the bigger bedroom, a king size mattress on the floor surrounded by blankets, sheets, and old cloths. All of it smelling heavily of mildew but in the greywastes sense everything had been well-preserved.

Gently he lay Sanguine in the bed and put a blanket over him. Then, with a quick glance behind him, he reached into his jacket pocket and tossed all four packs of his cigarettes onto the bed.

He met Ellis downstairs. "All good?"

Ellis nodded; she was holding Sanguine's backpack in her hand and in another was a jug of water. "Even more signs of radrats; as long as he isn't stupid enough to piss off a carracat this is the best he can hope for. It's northeast enough that he won't meet many greywasters. Even Melchai is scantly populated just the occasional greywaster and merchant. This is the best chance he has."

"Then we might as well fuck off then…" Nero looked around and let out a breath. "Just seems stupid."

"Silas is our king… it doesn't matter."

"Yeah… I know." Nero shrugged and walked out the door, then towards the awaiting legionary vehicle. "I just have a sinking feeling that he's going to regret this."

CHAPTER 8

Sami

Age 8

    THE RADRAT'S WHISKERS STUCK OUT JUST SLIGHTLY from behind the rock. I waited, staying as still as I could, as he started to become braver. At first he only poked out his nose to smell the peanut butter I had smeared on a wooden plank, but then he finally started walking towards it.

    My back bowed until my stomach was almost grazing the ground. I took another step on all fours, my eyes fixed and a growl tickling my throat.

    Then in a flash, as soon as the radrat put a paw on the board, I pounced. In a quick movement I grabbed the rat by the neck and bit down, the taste of greasy fur and dirt filled my mouth but I bit harder and thrashed my head from side to side.

    There was a squeal which made my pulse race from excitement. I thrashed my head and heard a snap then let the dead rat slip from my jaws.

    I picked it up by the tail and started jumping down from the rocky hills I had climbed up to hunt. My house was below these rocks, sheltered from the main road and hidden from anyone who wasn't looking for it. I had been here for six months now though it could have been longer or it could've been shorter… I didn't have a calendar or anything to keep track of time. I just knew it was the middle of winter now.

    Like the greywastes were waiting for me to mention winter, my left boot slipped out from under me, but I caught myself on a ledge of grey rock and managed to remain upright with the rat still in my hand. I jumped down the rest of the way and started walking down the dirt path that led to my backyard.

My backyard was nice though I hadn't been able to find enough bricks to make an outside oven like Nan had. This house was the only structure for miles and the other houses I had scavenged were all made of wood. I had been inside one of them that had a brick fireplace but I had to carry back cans of food and things for my own use so I couldn't carry back the bricks. So instead of making big batches of jerky I could only make small ones inside my stove oven. It wasn't that bad because a bunch of rats lived in the rocks and even some scavers would come.

Though that was summer… it was winter here now and even the rats were starting to get few and far between. I didn't know if the big rats slept during the winter like the urson bears did, but they sure liked to keep hidden in those rocks.

I caught this one though which I was thankful for… this was the first rat I had seen in the last ten days and my canned food was starting to run out. I had to save the jar of peanut butter I found for the rats even though I kept dipping my finger into it.

I quickly cleaned the rat and walked inside of my house, then I put some more wood inside of the stove and started warming myself up. It was freezing cold outside and it was great to be back indoors.

"I caught a rat," I said to Barry and my new friends Zoom and Snappy. They were radrats but I kept their skin and stuffed them with fluff I had gotten from a couch I had found in the basement.

"That's a big rat, good job, Sami!" Barry said in a cheerful voice. I showed him the now skinned rat and smiled at him. He called me Sami even though a lot of the times I called myself Sanguine. Though my friends only called me Sami; my enemies called me Sanguine so I guess that meant I was still my own enemy.

"Thanks, I broke his neck. You can feel his neck flopping to and fro, it's neat." I put the cast iron frying pan on the stove and cut off the lower half of the rat. I kept his tail though because I could use it as bait for the scavers who loved eating radrats. I put it outside near my stack of winter wood since Zoom and Snappy already stank the house up enough as it was. I didn't know how to make them not smell like they did other stuffed animals.

"What are you going to do with the rat? Just pan fry it?" Snappy asked. He was Barry's boyfriend; they were going to get married one day.

"Yeah, I still have salt and I have some pepper too. Remember when I found those salt and pepper shakers a few months ago?" I picked up my flipper and smacked the rat's naked pink skin. Its little paws were still on so I took each one and twisted them off before throwing them near the door. I would make soup with them later but not yet so they could just hang out on the floor.

"*Yes, I went with you,*" Barry responded. He did most of the talking, Zoom and Snappy only talked sometimes. I think Barry was really lonely so I always tried to include him in conversations and give him special attention.

I ran into my kitchen, just a few feet away from my stove in the living room, and started rooting around for my salt and pepper shakers. This kitchen was a small kitchen in a corner with cupboards that were white with wooden knobs. I also had many pull out drawers, though some were missing the drawer part, and linoleum floors. I liked the floors, they were my favourite because in some places the linoleum had peeled back and you could see an entirely different design underneath. What was even more fun was in some places even *that* pattern was peeling back and yet *another* design was underneath that! I laughed for a long time when I realized what I was seeing.

I walked back into the living room with my shakers, a big big living room with two whole couches and a yellow chair with flowers on it. I had my very own lamp but it didn't work and I had accidently smashed it a month ago when a scaver got into the house. I also had a TV but it also didn't work, and lots and lots of bookshelves. The bookshelves were my favourite but they all had adult books on it, big thick novels with boring covers. I still read them though and since there was a dictionary in the books I had learned new words too. I learned what extravagant really meant, and I also learned the word stupendous – that was another word for amazing. I liked learning new words and since we didn't have school anymore I made sure I schooled myself so I didn't grow up stupid. Nana always said we should learn all these things so we can go to Skyfall one day and become bankers. I didn't know what a banker was but it was a hell of a lot better than a greywaster.

One day maybe I could go to Skyfall, when I was all grown up. I think Nero and Ellis had been from Skyfall and that's why they were dressed nice and had those cigarettes. Nero had left me with four whole packs of cigarettes. I still had five cigarettes left. I loved them so much I savoured each and every one. I especially liked how they made my head dizzy and light and made my insides feel all warm and cozy.

Today was a good day today, I decided. I got an entire rat and that would last me for three days but I was still uneasy as to what I would do after that. Ten days had gone by between rats and I only had a can of mushroom soup left to eat and that would only last two days.

It seemed my entire life now was worrying about having enough food. I had water though inside the big well but food was a constant bug in my brain. There were no greywasters here that I could eat, I hadn't had a single taste of human flesh since I had come here and that was the longest in my entire life. I missed the taste but I also missed just how much of it there was. I knew that the time was coming for me to start hunting greywasters again. I remember hearing that there was a big road a few miles from here that eventually led to a town called Melchai. I wanted to pick off a couple greywasters or, if I was lucky, a merchant so I could loot them. But I was sure the merchants would have mercenaries with them, mostly all of them did.

Though going to the town might not be too bad. I still had my sunglasses and if I mumbled people wouldn't be able to see my teeth, they wouldn't know I was evil.

"But the people might try and take your sunglasses away," Barry reminded me.

I nodded and flipped over my frying piece of rat before putting a cover over it. "But then I can just run, right? Or maybe they won't care because I would have money. Nero put two hundred entire dollars in my backpack."

And he did too! That could buy me a lot of food and even a room in a hotel! Like Cory had told me a long time ago I could spend the winter in a hotel room and eat pub food but I think that would be expensive though. I couldn't work in town because eventually they would find out I was a demon.

And it wasn't like they would know for sure I was evil and bad, only I knew that because only I knew me. I could act all sweet and friendly and maybe they would ease up enough for me to be able to run. Though that never happened before and probably wouldn't happen now but I could pretend.

When my dinner was ready I laid on the couch and ate it. While I was eating I told Barry, Zoom, and Snappy about the time Nero and I ran from the long-limbed humans that I heard Nero call celldwellers. Sometimes I had bad nightmares that they were attacking my house but so far so good.

I told them how I bit through one's neck, and how Nero called me a little cocksucker. I knew what that was because Gabe and Pauly told me what cock meant and I thought it was hilarious to call me that.

My three friends all laughed at my jokes and when I was all done eating I put my dishes away in the sink like Nana had taught me and read a bit before bed.

Before bed like I did every night I wound Barry's butt and let him play me *Daisy Daisy*. It helped me not feel so lonely but usually before bed was when I cried. I only cried a little bit though. I wasn't a baby… I was going to be nine next and nine-year-olds didn't cry. I decided as soon as I hit nine I was done crying forever but until then I could a little bit.

Now that I was older though I cried for different things. I cried because I missed Nero even though I only got to know him for a few hours. I also cried because my feelings were still hurt that Daddy Cory tried to kill me…

No, not Daddy Cory just Cory. It was stupid that sometimes I still called him that inside of my head but I think it was a forced habit.

I didn't cry about Nan anymore because I think as I got older I started becoming mad at her. Cory wanted to kill me and Ellis and Nero saved me. Gill wanted to kill me and Nan let him burn me and put the nails through my hands and all she did was cry. It wasn't even that she was a lady either because Ellis was really powerful and she was a lady too.

Stupid Nan… she should've helped me since I was only six and I had just been a kid and helpless. Now that I was eight I was an adult and I could take care of myself and I even had friends now.

The next day was normal and so was the next one after that. It was on day three after I had killed that radrat that I started to get worried about hunting.

I flicked off one of the bugs on Zoom's fur and picked him up. Though as I picked him up his fur started shedding off of his skin. My nose curled and I put him down with a disgusted noise.

"Zoom and Snappy, you stink…" I said with a sigh. I picked them both up so they could go outside and maybe the freezing air would help kill their smell. I didn't like the bugs crawling off of them as much either, but maybe outside they would attract some sort of animals.

I opened the door and placed my two rat friends outside and closed it. I wanted to say I would let them back in but they stank so much maybe they would be outside friends…

Rotting gross smells reached my nose as I walked away from the door. I shuddered and wiped my fingers on a rag I kept by the door. At least Barry still smelled okay though he had blood stains on him and his brown fur was all dusty. Barry might miss his boyfriend though but they could always be pen pals. Maybe if I did go to the…

"Why did you let them outside?"

I paused and looked at Barry.

"What?"

"They're going to be cold outside!" Barry said in an unimpressed voice. Weirdly – his voice sounded clearer than usual. "They'll freeze their asses off, Sami."

Then something happened, something that a part of my brain told me shouldn't be happening… but yet I fully accepted that it was okay.

A young boy my age stepped out from the kitchen. He had curly brown hair the same colour as Barry's and he had bear ears where his real ears should be. The boy looked at me with the same black eyes Barry had and smiled. When he smiled I saw he had teeth just like mine – I had never met someone like me before.

But… he wasn't real…

"They did stink though, didn't they?" He laughed and ran past me towards the door. Barry looked out of it and turned back to me. "Do you think you'll get any snow before spring? We could go sledding outside. We have that hard plastic we found in the attic, right, Sami?"

I looked at him feeling perplexed, then nodded and let out my own laugh. I ran to the window and looked out of it with him. I could picture the black trees we had surrounding the house all covered in a blanket of grey snow, and Barry was right there were a lot of nice sledding places.

"Maybe we can start looking for planks we could use when we go scavenging," Barry suggested. He jumped up and down with his hands still on the windowsill. He was excited and that was making me excited too. "Or the town? Didn't we need to go to the town to get food?"

I nodded and felt my stomach rumbling underneath my jacket. "We ran out of food… I ate the last of the rat this morning and there wasn't too much on it."

Barry tapped his foot against the floor. I laughed as he made a funny face before putting a finger up to his cheek. Then he made a face like he was deep in thought.

"Why don't we go to the town tomorrow? We can bring a bottle of water and all your moneys and you can smoke a cigarette on the way. That sounds fun. Remember when the merchants would tell the kids about rat chips and bread? And ketchup too. We can have pub food with all your money," Barry suggested. He jumped up and down at the thought before doing a cartwheel across the floor.

He was hilarious, I loved Barry as a boy. I wanted him to be with me forever.

I nodded and looked out the window again so I could see the sky. The overcast was all steely grey but there weren't any big black clouds or signs that it was going to rain. We didn't get rain much but for about a month every year it seemed like we had it forever, then after that it only rained sometimes.

"I like that idea... I have my sunglasses so no one will think I'm evil." My backpack was upstairs but I had just seen my sunglasses the other day so I knew they were there.

"Good, they'll put nails in your hands again." Barry looked at me and I saw a flicker in his black eyes. "They'll burn you like Gill did or maybe pull you in half." I scowled at Barry and felt my ears go hot as he put his arms out and pretended he was on a plank like I was when Gill nailed me. "Remember how you cried like a baby? You whined for Nan all night. *Naaan! Naaaan!*"

"Shut up!" I snapped. I turned from Barry and flopped on the couch with my book and brandished it threateningly at him. "I'll throw this right at you."

"I'm sooorrry," Barry said with a long drawn-out sigh. He walked over and flopped onto the couch beside me. His fuzzy ears twitching as a loud pop sounded from the warm fireplace. "What are you reading? Read it out loud to me."

I wouldn't mind that. I was reading The Pawn of Prophecy and it was about sorcerers and it had magic in it so I was having fun reading it. I read out loud to Barry and that helped me ignore the hunger inside of my stomach.

Though by evening that hunger inside of my tummy was eating my guts. I had spent all day playing with Barry or talking to him and that was making me more tired than usual. I didn't even get a chance to hunt either because we were playing Hide 'n Seek and he was a good hider. That took up all my time and once it was dark outside and the bigger radanimals were out there wasn't really anything I could do hunting-wise. My night bright was really good, especially since there wasn't any moon outside right now, but the rocks were slippery from the cold and I didn't want to break an ankle.

When I was bored of reading I played checkers with Barry and I won, then finally I was tired enough to go upstairs and climb into my bed.

"You gotta wind me!" Barry said. He was holding Barry the bear in his hands. He handed it to me with a smile. "I made up a new song though. Wind me up and I'll sing it but it isn't finished yet."

"Okay," I said with a smile. I picked up Barry the bear and wound his butt and set him down beside the edge of the mattress. It wasn't too far down if he fell at least only about six inches.

The jingle came on and Barry cleared his throat. He started to sing:

Sanguine, Sanguine,
Give him your heart to eat,
He's a demon; he'll bite you with his teeth,
You will never see him coming, and soon you will be running,
He'll chase you down; onto the greywaste ground.
And he'll bite you clean in two.

"I am a demon; I don't mind. I need to be scary to be a greywaster," I said to Barry. "I might be a bad kid but that just means adults won't pick on me. I was the one that picked on them… I was doing really well in that town, though Ellis said I was going to get into trouble soon."

"And like the song says, you have your teeth and you have a knife too… you're doing just great and even better now that you made friends with Nero and Ellis," Barry responded.

I clipped my teeth together with a smile, and wound Barry one more time.

Though as he was singing again I realized one of my wiggly teeth was hanging down. I reached my finger inside and pulled on it. A shock of pain went through me but I kept pulling, I didn't mind pain – I even kinda liked it sometimes.

I pulled out my tooth and tilted my head back so the blood would go down my throat. I didn't want to waste it since I liked how I tasted. I looked at my last baby tooth and put it on a little table beside my bed.

"No more baby teeth, that's my last little one," I told Barry. I gave out a long sigh and because I remembered Nan saying it long ago, I threw my hands up in the air like she had and proclaimed: "I'm getting old, Barry! Getting too old for this shit!"

Barry laughed and I laughed too, then I put my head on the pillow and got comfortable. I held Barry and his music box to my chest and wound him one last time before I closed my eyes and started daydreaming about the time in the city when I saw those creatures. Not about the celldwellers though, but when me and Nero were working together to kill them. That was my favourite thing to daydream about, my other one was about finding a warehouse full of blue cigarettes.

The next morning I woke up and when I went downstairs and Barry was waiting for me. He was looking out the window again with a big smile on his face.

"Are we going to town today? I bet you're starving, right?" Barry said. He sounded like he was in a good mood, his mouth was wide open in a grin and I could see all of his shark teeth.

Though I felt nervous about going to the town. My stomach was a big black pit and it was growling and grumbling so loudly it was like it had its own voice box.

"I guess…" I said hesitantly. I looked out the window with Barry and saw that the sky was still grey with the sun cloaked behind the haze. No rain to be seen or any other weather besides the usual. "If we're going we should go early… I don't know how long it will take me to walk there."

"You'll probably get attacked by greywasters and eaten alive." Barry laughed a high-pitched laugh. "They'll eat your eyes since they're demonic and red. Maybe they'll taste like cherries."

I ignored Barry and put my boots on. He only laughed more but afterwards he let me start getting everything ready for my big walk. He was quiet when I put everything in my backpack and quiet still when I closed the door of the house and started walking towards the merchant road I had spotted during my scavenging.

It was cold outside but I bundled up good. I had some gloves but they were almost too small for my hands now. I had gotten them from Sunshine House so they were meant to fit my hands at six years old not so much eight, almost nine. They were all I had though so I made due, even though my fingers had broken through the wool and were now sticking out of the ends.

I jammed my hands into my pockets and started walking, my backpack on my back and my jacket zipped up tight. I didn't have my sunglasses on though, I decided to wait until I saw my first person and then I would. I didn't like the sunglasses that much because it buggered my night bright, making everything dark and weird.

Ahead of me was just a big stretch of nothing, just rocky ground spotted with trees and dark shadows of cars or old signs. There were also some sparse bushes. In the summer the branches sometimes had little dried shoots or were surrounded by yellow grass but they were bare since it was winter. Even the hoppers had gone quiet and a lot of the bugs had disappeared as well. We still got big flies though who didn't mind laying their eggs on my friends.

Snappy and Zoom would stay outside with the bugs. I felt bad but not as bad since Barry had decided to come with me.

I found a stick and played sword fights with Barry as I walked, though the ground was all bumpy in this area so I had to watch where I was going. It was early in the morning and I had a lot of energy, though not much as usual since I wasn't eating.

I eventually just used the stick as a walking stick. I remembered that I should conserve my energy since it would be a long day of walking, and there were some big hills I would have to go up.

In the afternoon I spotted a semi truck that had the front of it burned black. Even though it was slippery with frost I climbed the front of it and got on top of the big part.

It was all dented and had a hole I could fall through so I watched where I stepped. I stood up on top of the large semi and looked around.

My face broke into a smile when I saw smoke in the distance and, not too far from me, the road. I jumped off of the semi without even climbing down and landed on the ground with my boots thunking against the frozen earth. I looked up just to see how far I had jumped without getting hurt at all and felt proud of myself. That was over two me's tall and I was getting pretty tall. I started walking towards the road with a proud and smug grin on my face.

It wasn't just being able to jump down from things without getting hurt, my hearing was getting better too. I had always been faster than the other kids and I could see at night but the older I got the more I was seeing how different I was. And not just my eye colour and my teeth. It just reinforced the fact that I wasn't human and I was a demon or a monster –

but I already knew I was a bad person so it didn't change much.

"You are a really bad person, you should punish yourself…"

I looked at Barry and frowned. I kicked a rock with my boot. "I'm not bad all the time."

Barry laughed at me. He was climbing on top of an old collapsed bridge, I was walking along the river bed because it had dried out years ago. There was an old shopping cart half-covered in mud with a plastic mud flap beside it.

"You should grab this rock…" Barry said. He was grinning big at me and pointing to a large grey rock. "And bash your hand with it… no, your head! Sami – take this rock… and bash your head with it."

I walked over to the rock and picked it up. I tossed it in the air and caught it with my hands.

Well, why not? I didn't hit myself in the head with it but I smacked it against my head just to see how much it would hurt.

And it did hurt. I rubbed my forehead and kept on walking towards the highway road. Barry was quiet after and he let me concentrate on getting to the road. It was up the river bed hill and over a long guard rail that was rusted and twisty and just asking to cut me. So I carefully climbed up the frosty rocks, making double-sure every boot step was secure, and pulled myself up onto the road.

Wow, so many cars… they were lined up almost all the way to where the town and the smoke was. Small little brown pellets placed one after the other until they spread out into the greywastes like a half un-zipped zipper. I guess those cars had tried to flee once they realized they couldn't get into the town or maybe they had been pushed afterwards to make way for the bosen carts. Either way it looked neat and made me excited to check some of the cars for canned food or something I could eat.

But as I walked along the highway I saw almost right away I was shit outta luck, everything was picked clean there wasn't even any padding or anything inside of the vehicles. It had all been ripped out and they were nothing but skeletons of their former selves. I gave up thinking I would find food and drank some water.

Then I lit a cigarette as my reward for walking so long and not stopping to play. I was a pro now and inhaled the smoke. I held it in as long as I could and tried to blow smoke rings.

I still couldn't do it properly but one day I would get it. If I had my own big supply of cigarettes I could smoke every day but I had to ration

Nero's cigarettes like I had to ration food.

I could pick up cigarettes at the town though! This made me excited and I started to walk faster.

There was no one on the road but me, maybe it was because it was winter? I wasn't sure how it worked with merchants but I think we only got a couple of them at Sunshine House when winter was on us. I really wasn't paying attention it just seemed like they were there sometimes and sometimes they weren't.

That just meant it was safer for me.

"You're not safe anywhere," Barry said behind me. I kept on walking since he was using his mean voice or as my thesaurus said: patronizing.

"Eventually your luck will run out, Sami. Or maybe one day you'll realize you don't even deserve to live… you're a bad person and bad people always die at the end of the stories."

My shoulders slumped but I didn't have anything to say back to him. How could I defend myself when I believed what he was saying to me? I knew I was no good and I knew I was the bad guy in the books.

Without realizing it I started clawing my sides with my fingernails. I dug them in hard until the pain was too much but even then I still scratched and dug into my skin. I kept walking towards the wood smoke I could see in the distance, a long row of skeletonized cars behind me.

CHAPTER 9

Sami

Age 8

"WHERE ARE YOUR PARENTS?" THE GUARD HAD THE same skeptical narrow-eyed look that everyone adopted when they saw me all alone out here. A part of me was tempted to say I ate them but I knew that would be a bad idea.

I lowered my head so he couldn't see my teeth. He was standing in front of a big wall made from stacked cars and chain-link fencing, the town and the smoke safely on the other side.

"I don't have parents but I can take good care of myself."

"We don't tolerate beggars."

I scowled at the ground; I wanted to glare at him but I had my sunglasses on. "I have money that's why I'm here, stupid." I knew it wasn't a good idea to call a stranger and an adult stupid but I had been on my own for a long time now and I was tired of people saying I couldn't take care of myself. "I need supplies and a place to stay for a few nights."

I dug into my pockets and picked up one of the fifty dollar bills Nero had given me and waved it around. "See? And I'm armed too so don't try nothin' funny."

The man, an older man with a big grey beard and slanty eyes gave me a look before saying slowly, "I'd paddle my grandkids for speaking like that but I guess if you are an orphan you would need to have a mouth on you. Alright, kid, go on in but I'd watch yourself… we have merchants staying the winter here and as any town we have our shady residents. You'll be looking for the Holi Inn down Read Street. Now Melchai is spread out as you can see. It was founded on a town, the further north you go the less occupied the structures are... it just gets worse further back until it's back into the greywastes. We don't have guards there because it backs the plaguelands... now you know about the plaguelands right?"

I shook my head. I had heard of them mentioned with other areas in the greywastes: the greyrifts, blacksands, borderlands and all of that, but that was about it.

"The plaguelands are where the radiation is too strong for anyone to survive in and no one would even try because of the monsters there. You'll see near the north, if you're ever there, signs that read *Keep out by order of Skytech*. That's not the Legion being assholes, you mind those signs or you'll get radiation poisoning and there won't be enough radjuice to take it out of you. Understand my words, boy?"

"I understand," I said. I had no intentions of ever going that far north, I had no reason to go there. "Can I go in now?"

He nodded again and turned around to open the gate. It was a flimsy gate being kept shut with just a padlock but it was better than what I had in my house. The man opened the gate and I walked inside with a smile on my face, though I kept my mouth closed while I smiled.

Inside Melchai was lots of decaying buildings but ones that had been repaired too. They coexisted with each other standing side by side, some with roofs sinking in like they had become quicksand and others with patch jobs of shingles and sun bleached boards. The structures were spaced out far apart though, like someone had looked down on a big city and decided to cookie cutter Melchai out of it. I could see now why the old man had said further back wasn't as repaired. I could see the buildings in the distance and a lot of them were broken and missing material. I bet the missing material is what had been used to repair this occupied south area.

I walked down a double-lane road and saw there were a lot of people wandering around. A lot of them had guns on their backs but also a lot were just walking casually. They were everywhere, talking and carrying on, going about their day.

For some reason seeing everyone all close together sparked some nervousness inside of my gut. I found myself giving everyone a wide berth and staying out of peoples' line of sight so they wouldn't talk to me. I didn't like so many greywasters being close to me, I almost wanted to go back home so I could be alone again.

That was weird... before I had wanted badly for someone to talk to but now that I was surrounded by many people to talk to me… it was the last thing I wanted.

Maybe I wasn't used to being around so many of them – I jammed my hands into my pockets and lowered my head. I kept walking and only looked up when I passed a building. All of the ones that sold things had signs on the fronts at least, all the other ones were either abandoned or had families living inside of them.

This town smelled like smoke and sweat, it smelled lived-in. At one point I thought maybe I could stay here but now that I saw how many people were around I changed my mind. Barry was enough of a friend for me… though maybe I would meet a friend here.

I followed the main road and finally I saw a big building that had its own court yard, but the grass was long dead and it was just rocky ground now. It did have a big turnaround driveway though with a concrete raised bed in the middle. That raised bed now had garden gnomes in it, all with their faces re-painted to make them smile wider. They were lined up in a circle all facing what looked like a pile of old bones.

That was kinda weird.

I walked past the gnomes and crossed the driveway. It was obvious that it was the Holi Inn because it said Holiday Inn with a big yellow sign but the day part had fallen off so only the outline could be seen.

The building itself was in bad condition but it looked like a part of it had been repaired at least a little. The windows were intact and not broken at all. They also had bluelamps in a few of them, but the siding had fallen off in some places and you could see the naked brick behind it. The brick had no more mortar inside of it just brick on brick with yellow grass sticking out of some places. I guess that was to keep out the draft but I wasn't sure.

The glass doors that most hotels had were all gone and had been boarded up with plywood that looked all swollen and worn out. There was a door though and I opened it and stepped inside.

In front of me was a big lobby with carpet that was clean from the usual gyprock and ash but was still stained and worn down to the mat in some places. There were no people inside of this lobby but I saw some potted plants and a couple couches which faced a television set on a brass cart.

Then I saw movement out of the corner of my eye. I turned and saw a young lady standing behind a desk. She was watching something on a little electronic thing and was smoking a cigarette.

"Hi," I said quietly. I don't think she heard me coming in; her electronic was playing music.

The lady looked up at me and smiled. "Hello, what can I do for you, little man?"

She seemed nice like Nan but her skin was white not dark brown and she wasn't wearing a red dress. I walked up to her feeling more comfortable that it was just her here and not dozens of people like outside. I put my hands behind my back and looked at the ground.

"I'd like a place to stay for two days," I said, and decided to add. "I have money. I'm not a beggar."

She smiled and glanced behind me; I knew she was looking for my parents.

"I don't have any." I decided to save her the question. "I'm just here by myself."

"Really?" The lady didn't seem to like hearing this but she said nothing else to me about it. She just walked to a rack behind her that had little key hooks that held small silver keys. She picked up one and put it on the wooden desk she was sitting behind.

"Okay, well it's two bucks a night so that will be four dollars plus one dollar if you want to use our rain barrel to get clean. Do you want to take a bath?" the lady asked.

"Nah." I shook my head. I was an adult now so I didn't have to take baths if I didn't want to. I hated baths and I hated even more getting wet. I reached into my pocket and looked for a five dollar bill but I only had twenties so I slid that one to her.

She gave me change and I checked to make sure the change was real. Nan showed me how. All the money that was real money here had to be cycled through Skyfall and it got a special stamp that was so hot it melted the outside of the money. The stamp was of a half-cougar half-scorpion creature called a carracat. Though only the second generation looked scorpionish the carracats we had here just had six legs.

The lady chucked. I looked up at her to see what she was laughing about.

"You're like… a dwarf, I swear," she laughed. "How old are you? What's your name?"

She seemed nice so I guess she could be my friend. "I'm Sami and I'm…" I paused and decided to lie. "I'm fifteen."

My face fell as she laughed again; I knew she didn't buy my fib. I should've made it a bit more convincing.

"Okay, Sami, the fifteen-year-old. Your room is on the first floor, the floors above you aren't renovated so don't go wandering anywhere else in this building, alright? I'll charge you extra if you do," the lady said with a smile on her face. She had blond hair like the lady I had killed back in my first town. I wonder how much she would struggle if I tied her up like I did that lady. "There are a few pubs here you can get some food from. Don't have any loud parties now."

I shook my head. "No, I just am here for food and stuff…" I glanced at her electronic and saw it had a screen on it. I pointed to it but I made sure not to touch it. "What's that?"

The blond-haired lady turned it towards me and pressed a button. My eyes widened as the pictures moved like on a television. I hadn't watched TV in years. Our TV at Sunshine House was always breaking but sometimes the merchants that visited let us watch movies on TVs they were trying to sell. They used to set it up for the kids in the main house and put on cartoons.

I watched transfixed and managed to utter, "How much?"

"Sorry kiddo, it's a portable DVD player. It isn't for sale but if it was it would run you a good hundred bucks. Terry runs our general store and he has some TV sets though and there is one in your room."

My mouth dropped open. "For real?" A TV for me to watch for two whole days?

The lady leaned her elbows on the counter and nodded. "Sure, and we have a library of videos you can watch too. Movies and recordings taped from Skyfall TV." She pointed and I looked behind me to see several rows of what I thought were bookshelves full of books. I ran over to them and drooled over all the colourful covers.

I picked out five cartoons and after the lady showed me my room.

My room wasn't as big as my house but it was bigger than my bedroom. It had a double bed and two milk crates that acted as nightstands, each one had a stained table cloth over it. It also had a metal dresser that I think used to be used for tools and a bathroom but it just had a bucket in it with a plastic lid. I had an outhouse at my house right now so I didn't mind that at all, there were lots of rags for toilet paper. I might steal some just for my own use because I was running out of rags back home. Usually greywasters washed their dirty rags after but that was gross

I used mine for fire starter.

There was also a nice carpet in here but there were water stains on it and those places were crusty to step on. It was nice though and had a pretty pattern on it that matched the bedspread, both green and red crosshatches.

When I was settled in I decided to go out for food. With my sunglasses on and my mouth closed tight I went outside and started walking down the main street to find a pub.

It didn't take me long to find one, it was where the most people were. This made me nervous again.

"You'll be okay just don't let them see your eyes or teeth," Barry said. He was walking beside me and I think he was with me because he knew I was scared of being around all these people. "Just get some food and some cigarettes and you can go back to your room and watch The Lion King."

I wanted to do that more than anything. The Lion King was a great movie I watched it once when I was five. I wish I was a prince that had a big giant kingdom but what are you going to do.

"Too bad you're just an evil demon that deserves to die," Barry said nonchalantly. I didn't answer him and walked past the greywasters gathering around the pub.

I walked in and immediately felt a surge of anxiety, enough anxiousness inside of me to really debate turning and going back to my quiet room. The energy was overwhelming and noisy and the voices hurt my ears. The sound was just a low roar of voices broken up by the occasional high octave laugh from a female.

It was dark inside too but my sunglasses made my night bright malfunction. This made me uneasy too because I liked being able to see everything, though now I was just surrounded by darkness and people.

I didn't like it… but I was an adult now and I had to be brave.

So I took a deep breath of stale, smoky air and walked in. There were two gumball machines in front of me full of faded candy and past that a wall which split into two doors. One had people eating and another had people just sitting and drinking. I went to the eating area and found a bar man sitting behind a bar with a bunch of bottles behind him.

I could feel a few people staring at me but I ignored them. I walked past a serving lady and past a dog tied up to a jukebox and put my hands on the counter.

"Can I buy some food?" I asked him.

The greywaster had a cigarette in his mouth, he talked through it. "What do you want?"

I stared at him. I didn't care at this point. "I don't know… what you have. I'm new; I don't live here."

He took his cigarette out of his mouth and gave me the usual skeptical look. He opened his mouth to say what I knew he was going to say so once again I saved him the trouble.

"I don't have parents but I have money and I'll pay for it. I haven't eaten in two days almost I just want something to eat and drink," I said dully. I can't wait until I'm an adult.

The man smiled and shook his head. He dashed his cigarette and nodded behind me. I looked to see what he was nodding towards and as he spoke I spotted a wooden table with two wooden chairs in a corner.

"Sit tight and I'll get you something from the kitchen." The man turned around and disappeared through a doorway that led to a brightly lit place I assumed was the kitchen. I sat down and was sitting quietly when a lady came over.

"Can I get you something to drink?" she asked nicely.

I thought for a second and decided I was going to reinforce my status as an adult, or an almost-adult. "I'd like a bottle of whisky please." I pulled out the dollar that the hotel lady had given to me and handed it to her.

"Is that for your mom or dad?" she chuckled. "You're a bit young."

I sighed and waved my hand at her. "Yeah, yeah, it's for my dad." I was getting tired of this.

The lady said nothing more and she left with my dollar. A few moments later she came back with a bottle of clear liquid and after a few more pleasantries she left.

I opened the bottle and smelled it. Immediately I recoiled, it smelled gross but it always smelled gross. I had smelled Gill's whisky many times and I knew it tasted like battery acid throw up.

Though I had always been curious about it so I took a drink. Immediately I made a noise and stuck out my tongue. How can people drink this stuff? I lit a cigarette to kill the taste and tucked the bottle into a pocket I had inside of my jacket.

"You can't sip it… you need to just take a shot and bear it."

I looked up and saw a man standing near the jukebox, holding a cigarette in his hand.

The man had greasy dark hair that was a bit crinkly and thick eyebrows. He was willowy and was dressed in an old blazer and trousers. Fancy clothes in the old days but these ones showed their age and were ragged. His shoes were also leather loafers but they had foam on the seams like he had patched them with a sealant.

I took out the bottle again and made the liquid tip back and forth. "Maybe on the way home. I don't want to get goofy like Gill did."

The man drew on his cigarette, his eyes fixed on me. "On the way home? I heard you tell the bartender you don't have parents. You live all by yourself in the greywastes?"

I nodded and took another small sip of the whisky, that helped me hide my teeth. I made a face at the taste and that made the man laugh. He seemed friendly enough, relaxed at least.

"Can I sit down with you? I'm visiting this place myself. I'm a merchant and I have a large house on a farm a few miles away." The man smiled and it was a nice smile so I nodded and he sat down.

He looked at me before reaching up to poke my sunglasses. I recoiled away and made sure my mouth was closed. "I need those."

"You're inside though, who wears sunglasses inside? I bet you have nice eyes." The man pulled back his hand though and didn't try and take them from me again.

I decided to try out a new lie I had been working on. "My eyes are really sensitive to light I need them on all the time or it's too bright."

The man nodded and I guess he bought it. Then he reached into a bag he had with him and brought out a similar bottle of whisky. "Want to take a drink with me? Ever clinked a bottle with a friend and said cheers?"

I shook my head and took out my bottle. The man picked up his and nodded at me to do the same.

"You say something you're thankful for and then you say *cheers* and clink the bottle with a friend," the man explained. "What are you thankful for?"

I thought for a second and smiled with my mouth closed. "I have a TV in my hotel room and I'm going to watch The Lion King tonight and eat for the first time in days. I'm thankful for that."

The man raised his bottle and clinked it with mine. "Cheers!" he said and I said it too but I mumbled it to hide my teeth. It was dark in here but I didn't want to take chances.

"I'm thankful for finding a new friend," he responded. We clinked bottles again and said cheers.

"What's your name? My name's Jasper," Jasper said. He took a drink from his bottle and I took a drink too but I still made a face and Jasper still laughed at that face. It was a nice laugh though not a making-fun-of-me laugh.

"I'm..." I paused and decided in that moment he could know me by my friend name not my enemy name. "I'm Sami."

"Jasper..."

I looked up and saw the bartender man walking out the door, he was holding a cloth bag full of what I think was my food. It smelled really good; I could smell human meat.

Jasper turned around and for a fleeting moment, just a tiny one, I saw his eyes darken like he was mad about seeing the bartender, but in an instant it was gone and he smiled at him. "Good evening, Gordon."

Gordon the bartender put my bag of food on the table and I started getting out my money.

"Can I help you with something?" Gordon asked. His tone was dark and I think I might've done something to make him mad. I hope he wasn't mad he had to get me my food himself, or maybe he had seen my teeth? I had been extra careful.

"Nope, was just leaving."

"Home?"

"I was planning on it," Jasper said crisply.

Gordon nodded and took the money I handed him. He handed me my change back and skidded Jasper's whisky back towards him.

Then he gave me a hard look. "Off you go, boy. You have no business being in a bar unless you're ordering food and you have your food."

I cowered and nodded, wondering what I did to make the man angry. I wanted to say goodbye to Jasper but he was glaring at Gordon. That made me a bit more comfortable with him because it showed me he knew Gordon was being mean to me for no reason.

I left even though talking to Jasper made me forget about all the people around me. I got my food and ran all the way back to my hotel room keeping to the side of the road so I could avoid everyone and their stupid questions.

When I got home I opened up my bag of food and squealed from happiness when I saw it was full of shredded human meat and warm cracker-like bread. There was also some fried canned corn in another container and even a handful of pre-Fallocaust hard candies! I would go back and tell Gordon thank you for giving me some candy. I had eaten Nero's chocolate bars real quick so this was the first sugary good stuff I had had in months.

But I would eat it slow since sugar made me throw up in Nero and Ellis's car and that was the reason I was almost killed by celldwellers.

All the food helped me forget about the incident with Jasper and Gordon. I grabbed a candy piece, put the movie on, lit a cigarette, and relaxed in my bed with The Lion King playing on the TV and a pile of food in my lap.

The cigarette made me drowsy and since it was nice and warm in here with the small heater that came with the room I found myself getting too sleepy to stay awake. I snuffed out my cigarette halfway through and decided it was time to have a good rest. My stomach was all full of delicious food and one of the candies. I knew tonight was going to be out like a light.

Though in the middle of the night I was woken up by yelling. I got up and yawned and put my ear against the door. When it was too muffled I opened the door just a little and tried to listen better.

"If you don't get the fuck out of here I will get one of the guards to escort you out, Jasper."

Jasper? What was he doing here?

"He invited me to come and visit him."

"Bullshit. It's fucking 1 am… I'm giving you one more fucking warning and if I catch you trying to sneak around my hotel you'll lose a hand."

"He asked me to…"

"NOW!"

I jumped as the angry man yelled that. I closed the door really quiet and snuck back into bed. I wonder who Jasper knew in here and why the man was getting so angry at him. I was tempted to poke my head out and wave to Jasper but I decided the other man sounded way too angry. I didn't want to get kicked out at 1 am if I did I'd freeze to death.

I burrowed back into my blankets and ate some shredded meat which I had resting on one of the milk crate night tables. It was quiet outside again and a few minutes later the main light turned off and I could only see a faint glow underneath my doorway.

Poor Jasper. If the person had told him to come and visit I didn't see why it was the other guy's business but maybe the hotel had a curfew like Sunshine House did. Well, whatever, it was over now. Jasper would just have to go and visit him in the morning I guess, if he was still in town.

I closed my eyes and grabbed Barry, I wound his butt and made him sing the Daisy song to me, though like he had been doing lately he sang his version in my head, the one where I bit them in half in the end. I liked that one better.

I fell asleep with everything quiet, Barry held to my chest.

The next morning I woke up feeling nervous about having to go outside and buy my supplies. I kind of wanted to stay in my hotel room and watch movies all day but I wasn't here to watch movies and I needed stuff so I didn't keep starving. There were so many people outside though and I didn't want to be around them, it made me anxious.

But the sooner I got this over with the sooner I could go home. So I put Barry in my backpack and put on my sunglasses and ventured out into the cold day.

And it was cold too. There was a layer of frost on everything and the people outside were blowing their own smokes from their breath.

That reminded me though. I reached into my pocket and lit a cigarette for comfort. I took a moment and stood beside an old white van that was sitting outside of a mechanics shop and let the smoke hit me.

When I was feeling nice and dizzy-warm I walked quietly and unassumingly through the main part of town until I found the general store.

The man inside was busy chatting with what looked like a merchant since he was dressed for greywastes and not town. So I started looking at the rows of pre-Fallocaust, scavenged, and Dek'ko items, and started putting what I needed on the wooden counter that the store man was standing behind. I had never ever had anything from Dek'ko before so I grabbed a can of Good Boy and some antiseptic in case I ever got hurt.

They had some canned food most of it mystery and some cracker things called tact that I recognized from my pub food. They were cheap and had vitamins according to the package so I grabbed a case of that and some water purification droplets.

While I was doing this I noticed everyone had stopped talking. I looked up and around and realized the merchant and the store owner were staring at me.

When they realized I was looking back they started acting casual and going back to their conversation, something about a new supply of meth coming in.

I put my hand on my face just to make sure I was still wearing my sunglasses and picked up a bag of marshmallow candies for a treat.

"What's wrong with your eyes, kid?"

Anxiety shot through me like a loaded gun had gone off. I looked at him and immediately felt my pulse rise. I didn't know how he saw my eyes but they had.

"I... I got an eye infection when I was little and blood bled into them," I stammered. I quickly reached into my pocket and grabbed my handful of money. "How – how much?"

The merchant looked grumpy but he counted up all of my items. I started putting them quickly into my backpack though I needed an extra bag for the box of tact.

"Twenty-two," the merchant said in a voice that was as sharp as a razor. I quickly paid and turned around to walk out the door.

"And what the fuck is wrong with your teeth?" the man called. "Are you half raver or something?"

"No," I said and quickly walked out the door. My heart was beating up against my chest like a battering ram, each hammer urging me towards the gate to the greywastes. Without going back to the hotel room I started down the road to leave Melchai. I had another day paid for in that hotel but there was no way I was going back. I had been nailed to wooden boards, hit with rocks, and chased out of places before and I knew the warning signs. I knew I had to go.

My eyes burned but I was almost nine so I yelled at my tears inside of my own mind and made them go back into my eyes. I squinted hard and kept to the shadows of the streets, my head hung low and my lips pursed tight.

Though the tears wouldn't listen to me, they felt cold on my face as I ran towards the gate and to my humiliation Barry started taunting me.

"Demon-monkey!" Barry laughed. He was running beside me his fluffy bear ears pressed against his head like he was a mad cat. "Bad Sami, you can't be around people. You even hate being around lots of people now, that just means you don't belong anywhere near humans. You have no family, no friends and the only people who do like you left you behind or kicked you out!"

Barry laughed his high, cackling laugh before he tripped me and made me fall onto the ground.

I landed on my face and burst into tears. I cried harder when I realized my sunglasses had flown off of my face. They skidded along the cracked pavement and came to a stop.

I got up, my palms scratched up and my nose bleeding. I picked up my sunglasses and covered up my eyes as quickly as I could. Though I could feel their eyes on me, all of them even the ones I only saw inside of my head.

"He has fucking red eyes…" I heard someone gasp. I didn't even look to see who it was I just picked up my bag of tact and kept running towards the gate.

I opened it without waiting for the old gatekeeper man to talk to me and kept running until I hit the old road with the rows of cars. I could hear yelling behind me but I wasn't sure what they were saying and I wasn't going to wait and find out. I was never going back there again.

I was never going to another town ever. I was alone and, like Barry said… I couldn't be around people anymore.

When I had ran for an hour I leaned against an old station wagon and cried. Eventually it was hard to stand with all my crying so I sat down beside a deflated tire. I grabbed Barry the bear and held him hard and sobbed into his fur.

"At least I'm still your friend," Barry whispered inside of my head. I nodded and clutched him tight to me.

"I love you, Barry," I sniffed. "You're my only friend, never leave me."

"I won't ever leave you," Barry said back. "I am here to help you, that's why you should always listen to me."

I nodded because Barry had never told me anything that wasn't true. He even made up songs about me and he was always there before I went to sleep and after. Sometimes he fell off the bed in the middle of the night but that was my fault.

"I have an idea… something that will make you feel better."

I looked up and saw Barry the boy looking at me with a toothy smile. He was never afraid of showing his teeth.

He looked different though… his ears were still flat against his head and his hair was starting to turn black and that was pressed against his head too.

"What is it?" I whimpered, wiping my nose with my jacket sleeve.

Barry pointed to my knife on the side of my belt. "Pain makes the inside pain not hurt, Sami. You should cut your arm a little bit, cut your arm and I promise you – you'll feel better."

I looked at Barry and saw his black eyes were wide and staring unblinking at me; his grin big and showing me his pointed teeth. My eyes travelled down to the black handle of my knife sticking out of my belt, always ready to help me.

They just want to help me.

I took the knife out of its holder –

– and held it to my arm.

CHAPTER 10

Sami

Age 8

I DIDN'T THINK I WOULD FEEL THIS MUCH RELIEF TO be back in my home but I did. My entire body seemed to sink into the couch as I laid on it for just a moment to enjoy being back where I was alone.

My greywaster clothes were still on me and my backpack had been thrown down beside the door. I didn't even stop to get a drink of water I just curled up on the couch with Barry and closed my eyes.

Everything was so tranquil now, like pressing pause on an action movie. The town was the movie, all chaotic with lots of people talking and clustering around each other, busy and overwhelming. It filled my tum with more of those angry insects, the ones that liked to fill my insides with nervousness and anxiety.

And having darkness around me as I closed my eyes was even better. I could already feel my heartbeat slowing down though that might also be because I ran a lot of the way here. My breathing was still quick and my throat dry but I could drink as much water as I could once I got up off of the couch.

I was never going to leave this house, this was where I belonged and I would just have to hunt for more rats to feed myself or look for greywasters to eat. Since spring would be here soon I could build a jerky oven and I would only need one greywaster to feed me for months and months. That was all I needed to be happy; I didn't want any people.

Well… maybe Nero and Ellis.

My lips tightened as I thought of them and I let out a whimper into

Barry's fur.

"You miss them so much don't you?" Barry asked quietly. His paw was over the slash in my arm which was stinging and hurting now that I wasn't running anymore.

I nodded. "They were nice to me and they let me stay in their house. Nero said he would visit me and it's been over half a year."

"He probably forgot about you," was Barry's reply.

I didn't believe Barry but I knew if I said it out loud he might get mad at me, so I stayed quiet. Nero and me had fled from those celldwellers and even though it was my fault I attracted them, Nero seemed to have liked spending time with me. And he gave me all those cigarettes too and chocolate. Ellis seemed nice near the end too, at least before I fell asleep.

I didn't even get to say goodbye to them; they put me in my new room and left me with some new boots and some supplies. Though I wasn't mad at them for not saying goodbye. I liked this place a lot better than my old town. It had a well and a backyard that backed a big mound of rocks and it was out of sight from almost all angles so it was safe too.

They had done a lot more for me than stupid Nan and a hell of a lot more than Cory or the other people. In the end though I had to do everything for myself.

I wish I had a mom and a dad.

"But your mom died and your dad was a raver," Barry said beside me, his voice was light and amused. I felt him pat my shoulder. "But that's okay, you'll always have me."

"Yeah," I said quietly. I stayed lying down for a few more minutes before I got up and started unpacking all of my stuff.

I glanced down at my arm and saw the blood had started to dry around it. I took this chance to practice my bandaging skills and I put on some antiseptic and wrapped it in a long strip of pillowcase I had been slowly ripping for toilet paper. I bound my arm with it and tied it together.

I admired my handiwork and pressed down on the cut just to make it hurt a bit more. Barry was right the pain did take my mind off of my bad experience in Melchai; Barry seemed to always be right.

That night I didn't sleep well. I kept getting up and looking out the window afraid that the townspeople were going to find me. They sounded really upset when they noticed my red eyes and the store owner had seen my teeth.

What if they came with guns to shoot me... because I was a demon boy.

"Then you need to act like a demon and shoot them back," Barry mumbled behind me. He sounded half-asleep.

"I only have my handgun..." I said slowly and sighed. "My good guns are probably still in my little town, I think it would take a long time for someone to find them."

My eyes scanned the blue-tinged wasteland, all dark and spooky with the black trees rising up from the grey dirt like big gnarled hands. I saw nothing out there but an expanse of vast emptiness not even a radrat or a chipped bird.

Nothing... it was just me.

In the end... it had always just been me.

I didn't notice the tears falling from my face until it was too late. I turned away from the window and held onto Barry and once again cried into him. I felt frustrated because I was so lonely. I was lonely and I would never have any friends or any family because I looked funny and I was evil.

Even the bad people in books and movies had friends. Scar had his hyenas in The Lion King, and Jafar had Iago. Every evil person had their sidekick but I didn't have anyone but Barry and Barry was mean to me sometimes.

And what was worse was that even when I was walking down the road I got anxious being around so many people so I couldn't make a friend even if I wanted.

I was all alone and that felt like a giant boot was stepping on my heart. It made me not even want to live anymore because all my life was, was being lonely, worrying about starving, and getting chased out of towns because I was a monster.

I wish Nan had let Gill kill me. I wish Ellis and Nero had let Cory kill me and, and... and I wish my mom Lydia hadn't given me to Sunshine House and I just died with her.

My life was a big pile of shit and I hated it so much it made my teeth clench together and my legs want to kick and thrash. Though what was the point...? I'd just waste energy and I need that to hunt and scavenge.

There was nothing I could do but fall asleep and hope that I'd have a better day tomorrow.

The winter sun was shining through my window and right onto my face. I opened my eyes and told the sun to piss off but, of course, Mr. Sun didn't listen.

Eventually I dragged my butt out of bed and peed out the window because it was just easier that way, and walked myself downstairs to eat some of the food I had bought.

The tact was what I was most interested in. I had heard a lot about it before. It was a cracker type of bread that was supposed to be full of all the vitamins and nutrients you needed to not die. It didn't taste that great though but half of the case I bought contained sweet tact which, like its name suggested, was more sweet and tasty to eat.

As I ate my piece of tact I looked at the wrapper. The wrapper was see-through with blue edges and blue and white lettering. Like everything Dek'ko it had its name on the front and the slogan 'We care at Dek'ko', and on this one it had a picture of a cartoon puppy with the tact in its mouth.

Dek'ko was the only business that still makes food after the world ended, the other company was called Skytech and they were the ones that made the carracats but also things like vaccines and technology stuff. Another big thing was the Legion but they were military not a company and I kind of liked them more now since I found out Nero and Ellis were a part of the Legion. Even though I had heard bad things I decided this was my opinion.

I lit my fire with the tact half in my mouth and took a sip of my whisky just because I was feeling adult. When I was all warmed up and fed I wandered outside to gather some firewood from the big woodshed and stacked it all inside so I wouldn't have to go into the cold anymore. Since I had food I saw no need to go out and freeze my butt off so today would be an inside day.

I spent the entire day reading The Pawn of Prophecy and I wrote down every word I didn't understand and looked it up. Though since it was a fantasy book a lot of the words weren't real words which was confusing at first but I got the hang of it. After I was bored of reading I drew some pictures with my old crayons and when I was bored of that still I decided to write myself math problems to try and solve. I had found a calculator in one of the nightstands and that was fun to play with. I would type in equations and try and figure out what each sign meant. I was just starting to learn what X meant.

That night I went to bed not feeling as sad, Barry was being nice and we even played legionary together. I was the legionary and he was the greywaster Cory. I beat him with a stick until I made him cry mercy.

As was my usual routine I piled myself up with blankets and closed my eyes, listening to Daisy Daisy though I now sung my own version in my head. When his music box wound down everything was quiet and I drifted off to sleep.

When I woke up the next morning I was confused, for a moment I thought I was back in Sunshine House with Nan and the kids she took in. The noises were the same... the stove crackling and the good smells, food smells. I didn't understand what I was hearing or smelling but it was comforting all the same. For a few moments I even closed my eyes again in anticipation to wait until Nan sent someone up to get me.

Then with a wash of cold dread my mind started to catch up with my daydreaming and I realized I was hearing someone downstairs.

Nero and Ellis had come back to visit me! I jumped up from my bed with Barry and ran into the living room.

I stopped dead in my tracks and stared.

"Hey, Sami," Jasper greeted me. He had a smile on his face but I still took a step back. My feet felt like lead though and one step back was all I could manage.

"Hi..." I said slowly. I looked to the door and saw that a new big duffle bag was there and his boots. He was in my living room minding something on the stove only wearing his pants and a sweater, not dressed for outside at all. "Why are you in my home?"

Jasper's eyes brightened; his face creasing under his pleasant smile. "I felt horrible that you left town so quickly, especially after those assholes made you feel bad because of your eye colour." I gasped realizing I didn't have my sunglasses on, I turned to run but Jasper said quickly.

"I had a brother who had eyes like yours, Sami..." Jasper called after me. I stopped halfway down the hall. "He had teeth like yours too. Pointed teeth Terry said? I'm not like them... I don't care."

He... he didn't care? I stopped and turned around, Jasper was looking right at me, at my real eyes and real teeth. He wasn't scared of me and he wasn't throwing things at me or calling me a demon.

"Really? Someone like me?" I said quietly. I looked right at him to try and see if he was fibbing but Jasper just looked back at me with the same friendly attitude.

He nodded before waving me over. "Yeah, he lives back on my farm.

His name's Tristan. I thought maybe you'd want to meet him since you seemed a bit sad."

"How old is he?" I asked eagerly.

Please be my age, please be my age.

"He's ten years old."

I smiled but put my hand over my mouth just because I didn't want to show off all my teeth. This made me so happy though, I felt like running around the house.

"Could you bring him here next time? Can I play with him?" I asked. All of my nervousness over this man had disappeared with the excitement of having a boy like me to play with. He would be my first real true friend besides Barry. And maybe he would become an even bigger friend than Barry since Barry was mean sometimes.

"Well, I was thinking I could spend the day here and we could both go back to my farm tomorrow morning. I have a three-wheeler so it would only take a day to get there. I brought some food for you too and some toys. Want to see?" Jasper slid the cast iron frying pan off of my stove and put it on the kitchen counter.

I frowned though because I had just gotten back to my place and I didn't want to be on the road again, but Jasper was an adult and I didn't want to make him cross with me. If I made him mad he might not let me be friends with Tristan.

Jasper didn't wait for my answer. He walked over to his duffle bag and unzipped it, his crinkly black hair falling over his face. I think he had greeny brown eyes but I wasn't sure, they certainly weren't red like mine. I wonder why his brother had red eyes and he didn't.

"Wow!" I gasped as I saw what Jasper was pulling out of his bag. It was the same electronic that the lady at the Holi Inn had had! The one that played the cartoons on a little screen.

I ran over excited but felt my brow furrow as I got a closer look at it. "This was the one the lady had… she said she wasn't going to sell it."

Jasper handed it to me and I took it from him like it was made of glass. I laid it carefully on my cluttered dining table and opened it up. The screen was small but it looked so high tech, I had never seen anything like it. It was like space age!

"I'm a merchant, remember? I traded some of my supply for it so you could finish watching those cartoons you left behind," Jasper said behind me. "Do you like it? I found The Lion King on DVD too and another one you had in there – Aladdin, I think."

He bought all this for me? I turned around and gave him a skeptical look. "Why did you buy this for me? You don't know who I am."

"Sure I know who you are… Sami from the pub. We said cheers twice, right? We're friends now, aren't we?" Jasper laughed. He had really bad teeth.

I still looked at him skeptical. He carried on, "I brought that portable DVD player and you can say thank you by letting me stay here tonight. That's how friendship works doesn't it? You do nice things for each other?"

I shifted around feeling a bit nervous about it. "I shouldn't have people I don't know in my house…"

"But you do know me." Jasper smiled but then his smile turned to a frown. "Well, it would be dark before I get home… but I can leave right now. I might run out of gas if I travel too fast and the urson and carracats don't hibernate…"

I kept shifting. I felt hot in the ears and it dripped down to my face like burning sludge. Everything on me was burning and I felt uncomfortable.

"I just thought we could be friends, but I guess that was stupid of me…"

"No…" I said hastily. I felt awful for making him cross with me already. He had come all the way here with a present for me. I'd never gotten a present before. "You… I just need to ask Barry."

Jasper gave me a funny look. "Wait… you have someone else here?" His eyes looked sharply towards the hallway and I saw his mouth purse.

I shook my head and held up Barry by his paw. "No, he's my friend."

"Oh… ohhh… hah, alright," Jasper chuckled. He scratched his short beard and nodded. "Go ahead, it's all up to Barry then."

The greywaster smiled a warm smile and patted me on the shoulder. "Maybe we can watch one of those movies or something. I brought candy too. You can't tell me you don't like candy, I know you do."

Candy too? I looked over at Barry.

Barry's fuzzy brown ears were sticking up and his black eyes were wide but bright and friendly. When he saw me looking at him, he grinned and nodded his head.

"He sounds great, Sami. Be his friend."

I looked away, still feeling uncomfortable in my spot. I kind of wanted him to go away right now and maybe come back another time when I had some notice… but I didn't want him to get eaten by carracats or else I wouldn't have any friends to talk to besides Barry.

And he seemed to want to be my friend, unlike Cory and the other greywasters who I had to force to be my friends, or Nero and Ellis who left soon after.

So maybe I was being mean for my hesitation…

"Barry says it's okay," I replied in a small voice.

"Great," said Jasper. He walked over to me and ruffled my hair, then he pressed the button on the portable DVD player. "I fried up some arian meat I have. Want to eat some with me?"

My eyes transfixed onto the screen as it lit up with a bright blue light that hurt my eyes. I nodded dumbly with my eyes glued to the screen and heard Jasper take out dishes.

We sat on the couch together with our food and the DVD player on the coffee table in front of us. The arian steak tasted fresh and great. I'd have to ask Jasper later who he got it from but maybe he got it from Melchai.

Halfway through the movie I realized something though. "How did you know where I lived?" I asked confused. No one knew I was here but Nero and Ellis.

"Oh I guess it was just luck and a couple places where I saw blood spots," Jasper said, his voice was always so cheerful. I never sounded that happy, I didn't have much to be happy about. "Did you hurt yourself?"

I nodded and drew my sleeve back so he could see my bandaged arm. There was a bit of brown blood that had soaked through and I needed to change it.

Jasper sucked in a breath and ran a caring hand over it. "Poor boy, did someone do that to you?"

I shook my head and drew my sleeve back. I grabbed a piece of soft caramel candy. "I did it to myself because I'm a bad person."

"You… cut yourself?" Jasper gave me another funny look.

I nodded. "I'm evil, that's why I don't have any friends."

"Is it because of your eyes?"

"It's because I burned two people alive and I killed a lot of greywasters," I said darkly. Then I stood up a bit straighter when I realized he was a greywaster. "But… you're my friend so I won't hurt you."

"But... you're only... what, ten?"

"I'm almost nine, on the first warm day of spring I'm nine, Nana says." I shrugged and started playing with a hole the blanket I had over me. "I've been living by myself since I was six."

"Wow, it's a big surprise that you're still alive... it's pretty harsh out there." Jasper popped a piece of meat into his mouth. "It's not like people really adopt kids anymore, they have enough trouble feeding the ones they have. I guess it was even worse with your eyes and teeth, eh?"

"I don't really want to talk about that..." I looked back at the portable DVD player and watched Timon and Pumbaa sing. "Want to play legionary later?"

"Sure," Jasper said. "We can do whatever you want."

Whatever I want? That made me look forward to the rest of the day... maybe Jasper was going to be my first real non-Barry friend. I didn't even have to tie him up and make him stay for him to play with me. That meant he wouldn't die too and we could be friends and visit each other all the time.

After the movie was done we played legionaries and greywasters, and he was the greywaster and I shot him soooo many times. Jasper was a great friend to have and super nice too. He let me play whatever I wanted with him.

We played the entire day but Jasper had to stop a few times to rest because like Nan he said he was *gettin' old* I asked him how old he was and he said he was thirty-five which wasn't as old as Nan but still ancient.

We even shared a smoke and that was a big deal since they were some of my blue-embered ones. He said he hadn't seen one in years and that they're only available in Skyfall. They're called Blueleaf and there was a chemical in the tobacco leafs to make them glow blue. He also said they had other cigarettes that were laced with drugs and those cigarettes had funny-coloured smoke. I had smoked one with green smoke once and when I told Jasper that he laughed and said it was laced with cocaine. He found that really funny for some reason, I was more interested in the fact that he said he had a lot of different cigarettes on his farm!

That night I fell asleep happy, which was the first time I had been happy in a long time. I didn't cry once because I was lonely because I wasn't lonely. I had a friend now and tomorrow I was going to meet a boy my age that had teeth and eyes like me. It was like Jasper had been sent by the universe to be my friend. Maybe it was to make up for all the bad stuff that happened to me. My life was finally looking up and I hoped from now on everything would be okay.

Maybe Jasper and Tristan could even be my family. That... that made me squirm in my bed with a big smile on my face and it made me hug Barry even more. I was so excited for tomorrow! I couldn't wait to go to the farm.

And on top of Tristan being there he had cigarettes I could try, and he even said he had whisky that tasted better than the whisky I had on me, and lots of cartoons and kid's books for me to read. That place sounded like a fun paradise.

I was right in the middle of having a good dream. I was a legionary with a huge assault rifle and I was shooting greywasters that were popping up from the rocks behind my house. I was tall and all grown up and when I laughed it was in an adult tone. It was a great dream and I was mad when something woke me up from it.

I opened my eyes just a little bit and saw that it was still dark outside but I felt the hair on my neck prickle like there was someone in the room with me. This had happened before so I shut my eyes again feeling a spark of fear in me.

Then my ears started to adjust to the sounds of the room and of outside and, oddly... I heard something strange. It was heavy breathing and a strange sound like someone was smacking their hand against their skin. I didn't know if I was still dreaming or if it was my imagination but I was too scared to look. I pulled my covers over my head and for a moment my ears were filled with the sounds of my blankets rustling and not the strange smacking noise.

Once my ears started to adjust again I listened for the noise but it was gone. There was no more noises around me so maybe it had been in my head.

When I woke up the next morning everything was normal. I didn't even remember the noise for the first little while but when I did it didn't seem as spooky now that it was daylight. I shrugged it off as me just being half-asleep and ran into the living room to say hi to Jasper.

And Jasper was still here! I was almost scared he was going to disappear the next morning like Nero and Ellis had when I had woken up but he was here. He had slept on the couch since my second bedroom was full of firewood and bugs.

"Good morning!" I said happily. Jasper looked at me and smiled. He pushed some cold arian meat towards me and I saw he was putting the portable DVD player in his duffle bag. It made me feel good that when he looked at me he didn't cringe like some people who saw my eyes and teeth.

"Morning, Mr. Sami, are you all ready to go to the farm?" Jasper asked. I saw in his duffle bag some bottles of water. I had forgotten to pack water, my backpack was all full of my toys and some tact crackers. I only brought four though since I wasn't planning on staying more than a day or so. I didn't want to be far from home for long since Nero did say he would visit me and I'd feel bad if I missed him.

"Yeah, I'm all ready... everything is packed," I said with a nod. I looked around the house to make sure there was nothing else I needed. I wouldn't even bother to light the fire, it would just be a waste of wood.

"Good, let's go then," Jasper said and got up. He looked around. "You know... it looks like this place is pretty maintained. Did you just find it?"

"Nope." I started heading towards the door. "My friends let me stay here. They're legionary and we fought celldwellers together and I watched a man being pulled in half."

Jasper was quiet behind me, I turned around with my hand on the doorknob and saw he was giving me another funny look.

"Gotcha," Jasper said with a chuckle and he went out the door with me.

I ran all the way to the trike and started running my hand along the smooth metal. It was painted grey with indoor paint that was already starting to chip.

"Can I drive it?" I asked eagerly.

"Maybe on the way back," Jasper said. "There are some nice riding areas on my farm, it's all flat ground and you can ride it around there too. How about that?"

"Really!" I squealed. I bounced around and jumped onto the trike. "Let's go! Let's go!"

"Okay, okay!" Jasper got on behind me and turned it on. The motor roared to life and made me feel a bit nervous for a moment. I looked to my side at a half-fallen fence and, behind that, all the rocks, and briefly wanted to go back inside. I was a bit nervous being away from home but I reminded myself that Jasper was my friend and there was another friend waiting for me.

I would be back soon anyway... I wouldn't be gone for long.

Everything would be alright.

Still though when the trike started to move and my house was getting far behind me I started to squirm in my seat. My eyes started to burn so I looked ahead and made the wind dry them.

Thankfully Jasper couldn't see. I didn't want him to tease me or anything or think that I didn't want to meet Tristan. It would hurt his feelings and he already got sad when I had implied I didn't want him inside of my house without giving me notice.

He – he would bring me back soon enough and I was an adult now – I could take care of myself.

And Barry had said he was okay… so…

So everything would be alright.

It was a long trike ride… a long long trike ride. We were off-road mostly and sometimes Jasper even had us both get off so he could get the trike up steep places. The terrain was all rocky and in some places there were hidden concrete dividers or rough crumbly concrete that Jasper said was from fallen buildings.

We stopped to rest but Jasper didn't play with me, he just ate and drank some of his whisky. I played a bit with a black tree I could climb, I climbed to the very top to see if I could see the farm but Jasper said it was still quite a ways away. This would take a long time to walk so I was happy he had the three-wheeler.

I ran around and 'burned off some energy' as Jasper put it and we were on the road again.

I was starting to get tired of the trike. By the afternoon, and once evening was starting to creep in, my body was squirming and my imagination was my only entertainment.

Barry was good entertainment – he could fly now. At first he could only jump really high up in the air but soon he had black wings. He was starting to look like one of those lost boys that you saw in Peter Pan. Barry flew around carefree, laughing and having a great time. He was so fun to watch and more entertaining than the barren greywastes.

Finally. FINALLY! Jasper pointed out a small blur in the distance and said that was his farm. I jumped up and down in my seat and squealed from happiness. I wanted to jump right off of the trike and run all the way there because my entire body was bursting with energy and I hadn't moved much all day. I stayed still though and behaved, but I looked at every structure we drove past. First we drove past a couple old-looking houses that Jasper said were dangerous and I shouldn't go inside and then we drove past a big big red farm house with the roof that had new wood on it. The wood looked raw and still had peach colouring in it so I looked at that until it disappeared from view. Jasper said that was where he created the stuff he sold to merchants, a drug called meth. I noticed before it disappeared that it had a lock on it and Jasper said that was to keep greywasters out, though he said none ever came but it doesn't hurt to be cautious.

Suddenly I saw a flash of black and something rise into the air. I looked at it and didn't think I was seeing real things until I heard Jasper laugh.

"That's one of my crows," Jasper explained. "I got mating pairs from a merchant Skyfaller a few years back with Geigerchips. I put the chips in their offspring and let them go. There are crows everywhere here."

"Wow!" I exclaimed. I had seen a couple birds around that Nan had said must've been escaped greywaster pets but never a big black crow! I kept watching it until I saw it land on a wooden plank with a yellow sign on it.

Oh, I remember the old man in Melchai mentioning these signs! The triangle ones that said: *Stay out by order of Skytech.* That meant the plaguelands were close to here! I watched the crow flap its wings and I was thrilled as all hell when it cawed! I cawed back and Jasper laughed at that. That made me happy, I liked making people laugh.

Then I noticed something weird, behind that farm house I could see darker ground like it had recently been dug up. It looked like a grave from the size of it. I had helped Nan dig a few graves when we had some of the kids die.

I pointed to it and Jasper didn't even wait for me to ask.

"That was just a friend of mine who died," Jasper explained. "He died a couple months ago and I buried his bones."

That made me feel sad, maybe that was why Jasper had decided to come and visit me in my house. He was lonely too.

"How did he die?" I asked.

"He got an infection inside of him and it poisoned his insides," he replied sadly. "I miss him a lot; his name was Lenny."

Poor Lenny. I looked at the grave and saw Barry flying over it. He landed beside it and looked down at the mound of dirt.

Barry kicked the dirt with his foot before looking back at me with a smile. Then, without a word, he jumped high up into the sky and flew away. It was like he knew something about that grave that I didn't... I wasn't sure what.

Jasper parked the trike inside of an open shed. There were two right beside each other. One half-filled with firewood and scraps from old buildings, and the other one had boxes and an area in the middle for the trike. He wheeled it in and I stood there looking around the farm.

His farm house had one floor in it and windows that were dusty and old. It had a porch with an overhang and a worn railing that was wiggly and slumping in some places. The wood was patched in some areas with the same peachy-yellow wood I had seen on the barn's roof, and what wasn't patched had been painted with the same peely indoor paint his trike had.

I walked over to the house and peeked in, then looked down and realized he must have a basement. But weirdly the windows to the basement had been boarded and those boards were held in by big big nails. I tapped it with my foot and it was stiff as rock; it didn't move an inch.

I looked around and stuffed my hands into my pockets. Everything was flat except for a hill in the distance that was covered in trees and the broken-up buildings we had driven past. I could also see some old rusty farm equipment that I might like to play on but that was about it... there really wasn't much here.

But Tristan was here! I smiled and put on my backpack from the back of the trike and waited for Jasper to be done putting it away in the shed. I looked around for my new friend but I couldn't hear anything.

Jasper took the keys out of the trike and put them in his pocket. When he turned around he was smirking, and with the same smirk he walked right past me.

"Can I meet Tristan now?" I said eagerly. I had so many questions for him, like if he had people hate him because of how he looked. I also wanted to ask him how to keep from biting his own tongue since I had to teach myself to not do that, though sometimes I did by accident and I took a little chunk out.

"Sure, he's probably asleep in his room..." Jasper took out his bottle of whisky and drank it. I followed him as he walked inside of his house.

His house was a pigsty... but I didn't say anything about it.

Everything was dirty and it smelled like rotting food and beer; it kind of smelled like Gill's house. I curled my nose since he wasn't looking – he needed a Nan to help him clean everything.

I walked past a big pile of milk crates with junk inside of them and even saw an arian arm sawed off of its body. It smelled awful, he should throw that out.

And more body parts too... I ran my finger along a severed foot that had a box lying on top of it. It was laying there forgotten and I could see a couple maggots wiggling around.

"You need to throw that stuff out," I said, finally not able to hold back my comments. He was an adult and he should know by now that meat would go rotted if you left it out for too long.

"Yeah, I was away for quite a few days... I'll get to it tonight. Gross, I know." Jasper's voice was a bit quicker than it usually was. I craned my ears and also could hear his heart racing. He was nervous about something... maybe he was afraid I wouldn't like Tristan?

"He's down in the basement where his room is... just down these stairs." Jasper pointed to a set of stairs. I looked down them and suddenly I felt nervous. Those stairs looked spooky and they led into more darkness. I could only see a bit of concrete with black stains on them.

I hesitated and took a step back.

"You can wake him up... he's just a bit shy but he'll be happy to see you. Go on, you first," Jasper said, giving my back a small push towards the stairs. "Go on."

My feet seemed glued. I jammed my hands into my pockets and looked at the ground. I felt scared and the fear was paralyzing my body. Suddenly I just wanted to go home back to my house. Why did I go all the way here? I should have stayed home...

"Go on, Sami... you came all this way. Don't you want to meet Tristan?" Jasper urged me with his hand. His voice was pressing against my brain like each word weighed a hundred pounds. "I spent a lot of fuel... don't you even want to say hi?"

"I... I don't know..." I whispered. I took a small step forward towards the stairs. My head was starting to fill with heat and it was making my ears deafen with a static sound. I didn't want to go down there... but I didn't want to make Jasper mad.

"Go on... you don't want to hurt his feelings do you? I thought since you have the same abnormalities as him you'd be more understanding of that…"

"I… I don't…" I stammered and took a step down the stairs. Everything seemed scary at that moment and my eyes started to burn again. I realized too that my hands were trembling and my teeth were biting down so hard on my cheek I started tasting blood.

"Go on, Sami," Jasper urged. "Don't hurt his feelings now."

I didn't want to make anyone mad. I didn't want to lose my friends… especially a boy my age. So I took another step and then another, feeling the temperature drop as I descended down below ground level.

With my heart thrashing against my chest, my boots stepped onto the concrete. Jasper right behind me. I put my fingers on the door frame and peeked inside.

My brow furrowed as I looked around, there was nothing down here but an unfinished basement with a mattress in the corner. I turned around to tell Jasper this but suddenly he roughly pushed me inside.

I stumbled and fell with a shocked yell. I jumped to my feet and whirled around to yell at him when suddenly the door slammed.

"Jasper?" I called. I ran to the door and tried to open it but I felt a click as he locked it. "Jasper?"

"Jasper?" I burst into tears and started banging on the door and trying to force it open but it was locked. It was locked.

It was fucking locked.

CHAPTER 11

Sami

Age 8

  I SAT ON THE DIRTY MATTRESS AND STARED AT THE door, my knees drawn up to my chest and my arms wrapped around them. I think I was stunned but I wasn't sure, I just knew I couldn't move and my throat was too raw to yell anymore.

  This room was dark, only small slits of light leaking through the boarded up basement window which laid across the dirty concrete floor like landing strips. Besides that there was no light switch for the single bulb above my head and no open window I could get through or look through.

  And it was cold, but I couldn't pull the single blanket I had over my body because what I saw underneath it disturbed me so much I covered it again. It was blood, streaks of blood and droplets of it all over the dirty mattress. There was more blood than grey fabric and just looking at it made my heart jump into my throat. I didn't want to know why there was blood there, or why there were dried blood stains on the floors and spray on the wall.

  He was going to kill me.

  My arms tightened over my legs and stared at the door, seeing a streak of blood just several feet from me on the concrete wall. I knew there was more blood on the walls and probably by the door but I hadn't gotten up to look. I hadn't done anything but stare at that door.

  This was a place where he killed stupid kids like me… it had to be. Kids without parents that were stupid enough to go alone with a man they barely knew.

But he had said he would be my friend…

He said Tristan was down here – but now I knew there never was a Tristan.

Just like I never had a friend.

A part of me wanted to walk up to the door and hammer on it, but I knew there was no use. I had been down here for two days now and he hadn't come at all to any of my yelling. Even when I told him I wouldn't run away I couldn't hear anything.

Luckily I had my backpack and inside of it I had a couple bottles of water, tact, and some of the hard candies I had gotten. They were almost all gone but I had learned how to ration everything. Jasper knew I had this with me which must be why he hadn't come.

Though what was the point in eating when he was going to murder me? Murder and eat me and bury me near that freshly dug grave I had seen on the way here.

My eyes closed and I tried to put myself back on that trike, though this time in my head Barry flew over to Jasper and bit his face off. I pushed him off of the trike and rode it all the way back home. I never went with anyone I didn't know again and I was safe forever.

Then Nero and Ellis would come and visit me and maybe if I asked really nice and was on my best behaviour they would let me join the Legion. Because at least the Legion was safe, safer than being locked in this basement.

No, no one was going to come with me… I was alone here and I was fucked.

I reached over and grabbed Barry. I wound him up and let him play his song for me. His Daisy sound echoed off of the basement rafters and filled the entire room with his music. It was my only comfort, I had smoked all of my cigarettes over the last couple days just because I had nothing else to do and they helped calm me down.

Now I didn't even have that… I was alone.

I glanced down at my arms and looked at them. They were covered in red lesions and had blood crusted on them, drying into the wounds and creating small red fissures. I didn't realize I was doing it until I had already drawn blood but I had started digging my fingernails into my arms. Though now I was doing it on purpose.

"Because it makes you feel better… doesn't it?" Barry whispered into my ear. His voice was sad and full of pity. I don't know what I would do without Barry.

I nodded and started picking the dried blood off of my skin. It flaked off and fell into the darkness never to be seen again. I went to work cleaning my wounds with my fingernails though in the end I found myself tearing off each and every scab to make them bleed again.

There was nothing inside of me that cared, I scraped and picked and when enough little rubies formed droplets on my skin I licked it with my tongue and picked the skin some more.

The next day I got creative. I sat in front of one of the concrete walls and started painting with my own blood. I liked licking it off of me but this kept me busy for longer. I would dip my finger into my wounds and paint whatever images were inside my head at the time. Mostly it was Barry since he had been the only one in here to keep me company.

I drew him and coloured in the areas where he was brown and left the areas he was white as just bare concrete. I drew his fluffy bear ears and his black eyes, and carefully I put blood on my fingernail and used that to paint his teeth. I couldn't finger-paint that since my fingers were too big and you needed precision to draw the pointed teeth.

While I was drawing I looked over at Barry to make sure I got him right. He was staring at me with his huge black eyes wide; his mouth opened in a big grin that showed off his pointy teeth. Whenever I saw Barry now he was smiling at me like that. I wasn't sure whether he was trying to be encouraging or if he was laughing at me. It depended on the day whether he was nice Barry or not.

Barry was looking normal again so that was good. He still had curly brown hair but his fuzzy ears were perked up and not flat against his head. He was my bear once again and that was comforting especially at night. Barry would still play me the Daisy song and I found myself playing it a lot just to hear something besides my own heartbeat or the blood going through my body. He was a good companion to have and if it wasn't for his ideas I wouldn't know that cutting myself helps.

"Barry, Barry, give me your heart to do!" I sang to him after I was bored of painting on the walls. *"I'm half-crazy, all for the love of yooouuuu."*

Barry laughed and he grabbed a table leg that was laying in a corner. I didn't mention to him that it looked like it had blood on it because I didn't want him to drop it in disgust. So I looked around and found the broken chair it had come from and twisted a table leg off for myself. Barry and I played together for a while but then since I wasn't eating too much I laid back down in bed and decided to rest for a while.

Though instead of resting I cried for a bit. I was almost nine and I knew I shouldn't cry but I was scared. I didn't know if Jasper was going to kill me or what he wanted from me. And even though I wanted him to come and tell me what I did wrong – I also didn't want to see him.

Jasper had said he would be my friend... and once again I was tricked.

So that night when the slits of light from the windows had disappeared I made a solemn promise to myself that I would never trust another person ever again. No adults or kids or anyone. Everyone I trusted besides Ellis and Nero had ended up betraying me one way or another. Even Nan had by not stopping Gill from nailing me to the planks. Adults were mean and all they wanted was to trick you... I would have been okay in the greywastes if I was just smart enough to not trust anyone.

It was my fault, I was stupid.

I was stupid. I was evil. I was a demon, and I was bad.

Maybe I deserved this? Maybe Jasper had put me in here because I was a monster and all monsters belonged locked up.

In the middle of the night I heard the door open.

I looked up and froze from fright when the light switch turned on. All of a sudden I felt like a wild animal. I backed up as far as I could until my back hit the wall and stared at him in horror.

Jasper was standing in the doorway, dressed in around-the-house clothes like he hadn't gone to sleep yet. He was staring at me without an expression on his face, a cigarette in his hand.

"I want to go home," I said in a small voice. Immediately my eyes started to well. I was so scared I couldn't move. Each small movement Jasper made filled my body with horror to the point where small noises were escaping from my lips.

"This is your home now..." Jasper said in a voice that held nothing in it. No emotion, no anger, it was empty. It was a voice made out of blank paper with nothing on it.

I whimpered and shook my head. My body tensed and I pressed my back further against the wall as he took a step closer to me.

I wanted to be brave... where was the boy who poisoned the greywasters? Who jumped on the celldweller? I was a coward and too terrified to do anything when he walked up to my bed and took my arm.

"Come with me..." Jasper said.

"Where?" I yelled, tears sprang from my eyes and my entire body started to tremble. He started pulling me towards the door. My feet automatically stepped one in front of the other. I was too much in shock for me to do anything but walk with him.

Jasper dragged me up the stairs. I managed to try and pull away from him several times but he jerked my arm every time I did.

Though when I was on the surface, in the smelly main area of his house I got a burst of energy. I tried to pull my arm away with all my might and I almost managed to slip away but he grabbed me hard and squeezed my arm.

"YOU'RE GOING TO DO AS I SAY!" Jasper suddenly yelled at me. I stared at him in shock, no one had yelled at me like that in years. It stunned me and it made me forget to breathe.

Jasper pulled me outside, outside in the fresh air. I looked around into the darkness and saw there was only one light in the greywastes besides the porch light. A lamp that was shining down on what looked like an outside shower.

"What are you doing?" I whimpered.

"You're having a shower, get in and clean yourself," Jasper demanded. Immediately he started taking my jacket off.

I was confused and still stunned. I let him remove my jacket and then my shirt. He stripped me down to absolutely nothing and took a step back.

He wasn't holding me anymore, no one was holding me… but I was completely naked and already the frozen air around us was making me shiver.

I stood there with my arms around myself, sniffing again and again as my nose started to run. I looked around wondering what I was supposed to do now and noticed Jasper was staring at me.

He was looking at me like how an animal looks at meat. I didn't understand why but it made me uncomfortable and immediately my hands covered up my private parts. My lips pursed and my eyes burned.

"Nice… very nice…" Jasper kept staring, then finally he seemed to snap out of whatever state he was in. He walked past me and opened up the door to the shower, then turned on a tap making cold water come out. "Get in there and clean yourself off." I saw him secure the door with a bungee cord so it was still open.

"Close… close the door…" I said in a small voice.

Jasper didn't answer. He just reached up and turned the porch light off, making me clean myself in only the dim light by the shower. He stepped into the greywastes night and I heard clothes rustling. I ignored it and started soaking myself with water and then grabbed a bar of soap. It had been almost two years since I cleaned myself and I know I needed a bath badly. Nan would only let me go without baths in the summer time. During the rainy season she made me bathe once a week to make up for it.

I squeezed some shampoo into my hair and smelled the flowery smell of the bottle. I closed my eyes and tried to lather it into my greasy black hair, it was so long now it was almost touching my shoulders. I didn't feel like cutting it and I had no adult to force me to cut it so I just let it grow.

I probably was filthy and I probably did smell I –

– there was that noise again…

What was it?

I stopped and tried to wash the soap out of my eyes.

It was that noise I had heard before I left with Jasper, the one in the middle of the night. I opened my eyes but closed them as they stung from the soap. I tried to rinse them just to see what the noise was when I heard Jasper grunt, grunt like how Gill grunted when he was moving something heavy.

I opened my eyes when they were finally free of soap and looked out into the greywastes darkness.

What I saw confused me and the only way I knew how to express that confusion was to look away and pretend I didn't see it. My ears burned and my face was red hot, I didn't know what he was doing… or why he was doing it… or why he was watching me while he did it.

I didn't think I would wish to be back in the basement but now I wanted to be back there more than ever. I closed my eyes and tried to put my head near the shower hose so I didn't have to hear it anymore but that only made my mind listen to it more.

Grunting, weird sounds, heavy breathing, and Jasper… and Jasper… I didn't know what he was doing, I just knew he wasn't supposed to be doing it with me near him.

I turned away from what was happening and washed myself as quickly as possible. I ignored the grunting noise even when it started to get louder.

Then Jasper was behind me, the sound of the water had muffled any warning I could have had of him approaching. I looked behind me and stared in shock. He was entirely naked. I had never seen a naked adult before and it made me start to cry.

I just wanted to go home, and if not home, I just wanted to go back into the basement.

Jasper grabbed my hand and turned the water off. Though this time fear was filling me with the need to run. I tried to pull my hand away from his but even though it was wet and slippery I couldn't break from his grasp. He had his hand tight around my wrist and he wasn't letting go.

Jasper pulled me back into the house and because I didn't know what else to do and I was freezing cold and naked, I screamed for help. For anyone, even if it was a greywaster, even if it was Gill, or a bad man like Cory who would eventually try and kill me. I didn't care, I just needed an adult to help me kill Jasper so he would stop doing…

I… I didn't know what he was doing. I didn't know why he was naked or why I was, I just knew the panic rolling through me was telling me I had to prevent him from doing it.

"What are you doing!" I screamed. He pulled me through his trash-filled apartment and started dragging me down the stairs. "Fucking let–"

He was pulling me too roughly and I tripped over the stairs. I fell on top of him and he let go of my hand.

Immediately I jumped up and started running up the stairs but my fleeting moment of freedom was short lived. Jasper grabbed my ankle and threw me off-balance.

My face landed hard on the steps and blood filled my mouth. I took in a gasping breath and felt his cold, rough hands pull me up by the shoulders before dragging me back to the basement.

Jasper threw me onto the bed and I edged to the back wall expecting him to leave me alone. I pulled the blanket over me and put a hand over my mouth to try and stem the blood.

Jasper was looking at me, naked with everything exposed and swollen-looking. I sniffed and waited for him to leave me alone but he just stood there, staring at me.

Then Jasper walked over to the foot of my bed and he picked up Barry and tried to hand him to me. When I wouldn't take him Jasper wound him up and put him at the foot of the bed.

I heard Barry's song, and I felt Jasper's hands on me. Cold and uncomfortable, going places they shouldn't go.

I screamed at him and kicked. Jasper hit me again and I fell back on the bed with a cry.

His hands were everywhere. I whimpered and asked him to stop.
But he didn't stop.

    Barry was looking down at me, his eyes were wide and his body frozen solid. He was looking at me in shock. I could see his jaw tight and his hands kneading his sides.

"Barry?" I whimpered. I couldn't move. My entire body was raw and painful and I had stayed where Jasper left me. A heap of meat and in unbearable pain; he had left me to rot where I lay.

My insides were empty, everything was draining out of me like the wetness I could feel whenever I moved my body. Jasper ripped a hole in me and now everything was leaking out, though Barry was here... at least Barry was here.

I tightened my arms around me and let out a low cry. Everything inside of me was hollow and empty, I felt disgusting and gross and I wanted to go use the shower again but Jasper had left. I wanted to try the door but I couldn't move. My backside hurt so much and my hands from him slamming them when I tried to scratch him.

I wanted to get clean... no, I just wanted someone here to stay with me. Just be beside me so I could cry and maybe give me a hug.

I missed hugs.

"Barry?" I said to him again. Barry wasn't saying anything; he was just staring at me in horror. A look of surprise and terror on a face that was once always smiling.

Barry had watched everything.

"I... I'm sorry but..." Barry whispered. He looked behind him towards the door, before his eyes shot back to me. "I don't... this isn't what I... I signed up for."

Tears started to well in my eyes, a deeper pang of loneliness went through me as he started walking towards the door.

"Barry? Don't leave me," I whimpered. "I'm sorry."

Barry looked down and he picked something up off of the floor. He had in his hands the gun, the handgun I had left at home many miles away.

I sniffed and tried to get up but a vicious pain tore through my backside and I collapsed back onto the bed again. "Will you shoot Jasper for me?"

Barry looked at the gun, before putting it into his mouth. His fuzzy ears pressed back against his head. He looked at the ceiling before closing his eyes.

And he blew his brains out.

"No!" I shrieked. I jumped up from the bed and ran over to him. I crouched down in front of my dying friend.

His head was a ruin of blood and brains. The left side of his skull was missing and his left eye was out of its socket and staring into nothing. Blood was running and soaking into the concrete, joining the other brown stains.

"BARRY!" I screamed at the top of my lungs. I jumped to my feet even though it hurt more than anything and grabbed onto my hair. "BARRY!" I pulled my hair until it hurt and I grabbed onto more so I could pull harder.

Pain helped; Barry always said pain would help.

Pain will help.

I looked around but I didn't have a knife anymore. I looked with my eyes wide for something I could hurt myself with and grabbed the leg of the chair Barry and I had played legionary with.

"Kid… what the fuck is…" Jasper was at the door. I could hear surprise or maybe confusion in his words.

I turned around with the table leg in my hands. Jasper took a step back with his face creased and his hands hovering by a knife he had on his belt.

"Barry's dead! Barry's dead!" I screamed. I held onto the table leg and swung it up, and it hit me in the face.

"Shit!" Jasper ran and ripped the table leg out of my hand. I screamed and tried to grab it from him. When he wouldn't give it back to me I closed my eyes and screamed. I screamed and screamed at the top of my lungs and felt my legs give out from under me.

I felt nothing and heard nothing but my own voice ringing inside of my head. When I opened my eyes I saw the door closing and the table leg gone.

I stood up and ran towards the door and kicked it, kicked it until my toes became bloody. It left small prints against the brown and black stains that painted the door with the torment this basement did little to conceal.

Then a single thought crept into my mind, a mad thought but in my own turmoil it was the most sober one I had. I rose to my feet and picked up the other table leg and turned to the bed.

I saw Sami laying on the bed. A small boy with tangled black hair, welling red eyes and a mouth pursed and bloody. He was laying there whimpering, naked with blood smudges on his backside.

I walked over to this boy and stared at him, stared at the pure creature that had so innocently caught himself in the web of the most depraved of spiders. A poor little soul who had no idea just what awaited him in the future.

Sami, Sami, give me your heart to chew.
You're now fully crazy, your mind is finally through.
I left you torn to ribbons, you really should've listened
Now you are dead, I'll smash your head.
And Sanguine will step on through.

I raised the table leg and swung it down on the boy's head and, like Barry behind me, I painted the walls with his blood and brains and left him nothing but the shell of the boy he once was. He didn't even struggle – he didn't beg for mercy. He let me kill him and as the thick, copper smell of blood filled the small musty basement I knew he wanted this just as much as I wanted to do it.

Tonight was the night, a night where I had to perform the necessary evil.

I had killed Sami.

Sami was dead.

CHAPTER 12

Sanguine

Age 8

WHEN THE DOOR OPENED DAYS LATER, I LOOKED UP and saw Jasper step inside my musty, dark basement. Though he didn't command me to get on my hands and knees or stay on my back, this time Jasper had a bottle of water in his hand.

I shrunk back when he took a step closer to me and looked away.

"I have water for you," Jasper said. His voice sounded odd, high strung, and as I looked at him a bit closer I saw his pupils were dilated.

And he smelled weird... like chemicals.

"Come here and take it," Jasper urged. I saw his hands were trembling and there was something glassy and shiny tucked behind his ear.

I didn't answer him, it was probably a trick to get me to do things to him, like last night. He had promised me food but he would only give it to me if I did things to him I didn't want to do. I said no and he said I wouldn't have food until I did.

My tact was gone and everything in my bag but I still didn't do what he wanted.

Jasper shrugged and closed the door, he put the bottle beside the bed and sat on my mattress. I watched him, an unsteady, off-kilter feeling rolling through my body. I was confused and I didn't know what he wanted from me today. It was usually at night that he did his thing to me and I could still see light coming through the boarded up window.

Then he reached behind his ear and withdrew a glass tube with a bulge on the end. He put a clear rock inside of it that he got out of his pocket and lit it with a lighter. He inhaled it like he was smoking a cigarette and blew the chemical smoke out of his mouth.

My nose wrinkled but I still said nothing and I still didn't reach for the water. What Jasper wanted with me I didn't know and I wasn't going to ask. Though he had no issue getting what he wanted out of me I still was worried that if I planted the idea into his mind he would do it.

"Do you know what I saw while I was patrolling my farm, Sami?"

I looked at him, in my own desperate sadness I was surprised at how rushed and fast paced his voice was. The shock continued when he got up and started pacing around my basement.

"My name is Sanguine," I said quietly to him. "I killed Sami."

Jasper ignored me, he walked over to the small cracks of light in the boards on the windows and peeked outside.

"I saw the carcass of a greywaster, picked apart by my crows. I think it was a warning, Sami, a warning to me from the Legion," Jasper carried on. I saw his hazel eyes, still dilated and wide, staring out the window and shifting around as he looked for something. I didn't know what though.

"They send me these signals, small little signs that they know I will pick up on. Only I am smart enough to figure out their signs. The dead greywaster as a distinct message that they know I have you."

I looked up. "They know you have me?" Does that... does that mean Nero and Ellis would come?

"They know what I've been doing; they know who I've killed. They've been putting cameras on the crows and sending them to perch on my railing. They're putting cameras in the fucking crows now, can you believe it?" Jasper shook his head. He stared out the window for a moment longer before tearing himself away. Though he only started pacing around my room again, his mouth pursed and his staring eyes wide with concern.

Cameras on the crows? Does that mean if I see one they'll send the image of me to the Legion? If I saw the crows enough maybe eventually Nero and Ellis would see me.

"First the dead greywaster and now all these crows turning against me. My own crows, Sami. My own crows turning against me and letting them put cameras on their bodies. I think the cameras are inside their mouths. They're only visible for a split second as they caw." Jasper's voice was a speeding train; he wasn't talking the way he normally did.

Then he turned and looked at me. "Drink your water. I'm going to... I'm not going to kill you, Sami. I only killed Lenny by accident, I was too rough... he ended up torn inside, and it rotted his insides. I ate his body but I didn't find any cameras on him."

Jasper's eyes narrowed and his head jerked back to look at me.

"Take off your clothes!" he suddenly snapped. He threw his glass pipe onto the bed and stalked over to me.

I scrunched back and whimpered. "But it's not night..."

"Now!" Jasper barked; his mouth smelled like the chemicals. "You have a camera on you, don't you, you little shit?"

"NO!" I yelled. I didn't have a camera on me; if I did and the Legion saw that I was down here, Nero and Ellis would've rescued me.

"Prove it!" Jasper's booming voice sent a shock through me, it seized my bravery and dissolved it to nothing. I got up and took off my jacket and then my faded blue shirt. Then my pants fell to the ground.

But he didn't make me take off my underwear. He put an unlit cigarette into his mouth and started squeezing and touching my body; he even made me open my mouth to look inside and then my ears and under my arms.

When Jasper was happy he stepped back and lit his cigarette. "You're clean... nothing on you. Figures, no one really cared about you did they?"

His words cut to the quick and I felt my head lower. My eyes burned and I shook my head because he was right – no one did care about me.

Jasper took another hit of his pipe and looked out the window again. A small billow of yellowy smoke falling from his mouth as he checked the outside for something... cameras maybe, or the Legion.

"They have this place surrounded at night, sometimes I can hear their vehicles," Jasper commented. "My own crows... selling me out. They can talk, you know – they can talk. If it's not the Legion harassing me it's the damn townspeople in Melchai. All of them, always watching me, always stalking my steps, telling me to keep away from their little boys. Most don't care though because only I can create this stuff. The town doesn't care because if they lose me they lose the goods. A few of them even gave me tips on where to find boys in exchange for a few rocks – I had a man sell me his own son. Drugs talk, Sami, never forget... drugs talk."

"Okay," I said quietly. Finally my thirst got the best of me and I reached over and grabbed the bottle of water. I unscrewed it and took a drink as Jasper continued to ramble. I had been drinking my own blood to help me get rid of the burning in my throat but all of that drinking was starting to make me feel dizzy when I stood up.

Jasper looked at me and swept his gaze up and down my body. "Once I can trust you I'm going to start making you check the crows. I know you'll try and run now and let me tell you, Sami. If you try and run the alarms will go off and I'll find you right away."

His words stunned me. I lowered the bottle. "Alarms?"

Jasper nodded and quickly walked back to the window again, sweat was starting to bead off of his forehead. "That's right. I have invisible sensors here, if you try and leave I'll know. So it's your job to catch the crows. I want you to catch them and check their mouths then you can let them fly away."

Suddenly he whirled around and glared angrily at me. I gasped and shifted further into the brick wall. "Don't you dare fucking eat my crows," he said threateningly. "That's what you were thinking wasn't it? WASN'T IT!"

"NO!" I yelled shaking my head. "I won't – I won't hurt the crows. I won't hurt the crows."

"Good!" Jasper snapped. He paced around for several more minutes until he took another hit from what I realized must be drugs. I wasn't sure what drugs though, but I guessed it was the drugs that he sold to the town. Drugs were the reason why he was able to get little boys like me, because the town wanted them. I forgot the drugs name though, or if he had even told me.

"I'll send you out… not now. No, not now…" Jasper dropped his voice and sat down on my mattress, only to get up again and walk around. All he did was pace, it was making my head hurt and I just wanted him to leave me alone. If he wasn't going to do the gross thing when why was he here?

Just as soon as he came he disappeared and re-appeared a half an hour later with a portion of arian steak. I was starving so I ate it quickly. I hadn't eaten fresh meat in a really long time but it was hard to savour it when I was swallowing it whole almost.

I was still hungry though. I looked at him and was tempted to ask for more but he was looking out the window again.

"Can I go outside?" I asked quietly. I sniffed and tried to sit on the edge of the bed but my bottom was too sore. I sat on the side and used my hand to prop myself up.

"No – no, not yet… I think… I think I see Legion out there," Jasper murmured. My heart jumped as he said this and I ran to the other boarded up window to peek outside, just to see if I could see them too.

But there was nothing. I didn't understand what he was saying or what he was seeing and it frustrated me that I didn't. I limped back to the mattress and curled up on it. I threw the blanket over top of me and waited for him to leave.

I hated Jasper but I was scared of him too. I was scared he was going to do that thing to me again; he had done it three times already and it hurt. I hated having him so close to me, I hated how he breathed on me and groaned on my ear. And I hated digging out of me the stuff that he left behind.

I also hated that I got stunned whenever he did it now. I wanted so badly to bite him and kick him like the first time, but now when he was doing it I laid there and stared at the ceiling. Going inside of my head and finding fun things to think about like Nero and me on adventures.

All the times I should have been biting and being an evil demon I was just laying there and thinking about my friends.

And Barry… I thought about Barry a lot and how he died, and how Sami died too.

Everyone was dead, I was just Sanguine now… I had always been Sanguine. It was Jasper that made me kill Sami and now that he was out of the way I was just Sanguine.

Defeated, sad Sanguine.

Jasper left sometime later, leaving his gross chemical smell behind. I got up and dug out my thesaurus and my dictionary and read it a bit. Maybe if I caught crows for him he would find me some books to read.

My thoughts travelled to the words he was saying and inside I felt a sting dig into my heart. I wanted so badly to believe his words, that the Legion knew he had me and his crows had cameras… but I think he was just crazy. I didn't see anything out there and…

I got up and peeked out the small slit between the board and the window frame. I saw a black blur in the distance and knew it was Jasper. He was walking around free and without anyone coming to kill him so I knew the Legion wasn't there or sending him messages either.

Looking outside through the window and into the fresh air made me more sad, so I turned away and laid down again. I had slept a lot this week and I think I would sleep some more.

As I fell asleep I dug my fingernails into my skin, flexing them until I felt wet beneath my nails. I clenched them harder and let the pain numb what I was feeling inside, the dirty feelings, the sad feelings; pain was my only medication, one I would never have to worry about running out of.

Two weeks later

"If you go past the fence, the alert will go off," Jasper reminded me. I walked behind him and went up the stairs slowly, my legs cramped and sore and my bottom aching. It was hard to walk and running wasn't even on my mind because I knew I wouldn't get far. It was flat land everywhere and I could barely walk as it was. I didn't know how I was supposed to catch crows.

"I won't," I said in a hushed voice. I didn't want to make him mad. I wanted to go outside for a little bit at least to have some fresh air on me.

We walked outside and I took a deep breath of the cold air. I squinted my eyes as the light stung them and started looking around my surroundings. Immediately I crossed my arms and felt sad. I wanted to go back to my house; I wanted to go to my home.

"When can I go home?" I asked Jasper in the same small voice. I sniffed and felt my eyes burn.

"You belong to me now, you can't go home," Jasper said back. He gave me an icy look and walked past me, his head turning back and forth.

"You don't own me…" I said slowly. I walked behind him and swallowed the bitterness in my mouth, it sat in my stomach and made me feel queasy. "You just kidnapped me… you don't own me at all. When can I go home?"

"How old are you?" Jasper said with the same icy look.

"I'm almost nine," I said quietly. I shrunk under his gaze and inside I felt shame at my submissive state. I don't know where the demon went… I felt like a wimp – I was a wimp. I don't know what he did to me, what he took from me, but I had no fight inside of me anymore.

I was an easy target and I gave myself up to him as soon as he did that stuff to me. I didn't feel right after that; I didn't feel right after Barry and Sami died. Inside of me just felt like puzzle pieces that no longer fit together, pieces that didn't even come from the same box.

"You're just a kid, and you're a kid with no parents. So I own you."

I sniffed. "Can I leave when I'm grown up?"

"Depends on if you do everything I ask of you. Just like what you need to do to get food and water, if you're good you'll get benefits." As if he was expecting this speech he threw me a tact cracker. I caught it and took a small bite. "But if you're bad, I'll leave you in there until you starve, got it?"

I looked down at the cracker, my fingers were all caked with blood.

"I thought you wanted to be my friend."

Jasper was quiet for a moment. I didn't look up, I just stared at the blood pushed underneath my fingernails. It was dried all over me and had helped form the scabs on my arms.

"We are friends, Sami. That's why I'm not going to kill you... because we're friends."

I looked over where the barn was and saw the mound of dirt, darker than the ground around it. That was where Lenny was buried.

"How many other boys are buried there," I suddenly asked. I gripped my arm with my fingers again and started feeling the scabs break underneath my skin and then a sticky feeling.

"Seven," Jasper replied.

"Did you kill all of them?" I dug my nails in deeper. I pressed my fingers in and kneaded the flesh as deep as I could.

"Yes, eventually they either die... or they get too old." Jasper's voice dropped. "Now go catch those fucking crows. I'm going to have a smoke."

"Okay..." I said and took a step forward.

Though as soon as I was in the empty pasture ground I felt a pulse of fear throb inside of me like a blister. I took a step back and made a nervous noise in my throat, inside was stuffy but it was dark and enclosed and... and I kind of liked that.

Out here was... open and it was making me nervous.

But nothing was going to hurt me outside... inside was different, inside was where Jasper would hurt me. So I walked into the pasture, covered in a thin coating of yellow grass with twists of old farm equipment sticking out of the ground. There were a few crows sitting on the fence and a couple further on sitting on the Skytech signs.

I dug my hands into my pockets and wished I had asked for a cigarette. I started slowly walking towards the crows, wondering to myself if I was still as fast as I used to be.

I didn't feel like catching the stupid crows because I thought Jasper was stupid to think the Legion was after him. If the Legion was after him the Legion would come in and shoot the place up not waste time giving him signals. Jasper was crazy and I was his prisoner now. I was an entire day's trike ride from my house and I didn't even know the way.

I was so stupid; I was such an idiot.

I deserved everything that happened to me. I let Jasper do those gross things to me and in turn Barry shot himself in the head.

The crows looked at me and one ruffled its feathers before it started to peck at the ground. I had never been this close to such big birds before and I realized for the first time how pretty their wings were.

And – I gasped and slowly got down on my knees to get a closer look.

They all had red eyes like me.

I reached into my pocket and got out my tact. At the same time the crows, five of them, all turned to me and watched the cracker with their deep red eyes.

I broke off a piece and threw it in the middle of them. A bigger one stepped in and ate the piece so I threw another.

"You guys don't have cameras in your mouths..." I whispered to them. I sat down and crossed my legs and started throwing them small chunks of the cracker bread. "You're just normal birds. I have never seen a crow before, just some robins and pigeons."

They hopped towards me and I let out a laugh as the big one hopped over and tried to snatch my tact away. At first I was startled at my own laugh, I hadn't heard it in so long it sounded alien to me.

"Go on get!" a crow suddenly said.

My mouth dropped open, I put my hand over my mouth to hide the smile. I had forgotten that Jasper had mentioned they could talk. He had been high and rambling it and it completely went over my head.

"Go on get?" I said with a smile. I bet Jasper yells that at them and that's why they pick it up. "How about... Sanguine! Sanguine!"

The crow tilted its head at me before it tried to pick the tact out of my hand again. I let it pick a few times trying to say my name as often as I could so it would stick.

"Go on get!" the crow said to me, then another one said from a few feet away.

"Come here, crow!"

"No, say *Hello, Sanguine*!" I said. "*Hello, Sanguine*!"

The crow kept picking at my hand so finally I gave in and broke off a piece. I put it in my hand and saw the big crow cock its head back and forth before pecking at my skin.

It hurt but like my own self-inflicted pain I liked it. I tucked the cracker further into my hand and left him peck at it, soon the others followed and all of them started pecking at my hand.

"Come here, crow... come here, crow," one said behind me.

When I pulled away my hand was all bloody. I threw a bit more crumbs to the crows and started licking my hand free of blood. Now my hand was hurting and that helped distract from the pain in other places. Barry might be dead but I had learned a lot from him.

"Do you guys want to be my friends?" I said to them. Unlike humans, animals won't trick you or kidnap you; they're honest. Even the ones who wanted to kill you, at least they were straightforward about it. They made their intentions known, good or bad.

"Friends, friends, friends," I repeated, maybe I could get them to say that. "Hello, Sanguine! Friends, friends!"

The crows hopped around me, tilting their heads back and forth. Their feathers were so beautiful like they had been painted on with a paintbrush. It made me want to paint their wings on the concrete wall. Though I don't think I could ever get it right, but maybe if I practiced really hard...

I didn't have Barry the bear with me, he was in my basement so I couldn't wind him, but I felt like singing to the crows. So I sung them the Daisy song in between trying to teach them words, and let them hop around me. Sometimes they pecked at the ground for seeds other times they just flew around.

Soon a lot of them were surrounding me, even the ones that had been balancing on the Skytech signs came. I smiled and tried to say more words to them, and while I did that I threw them more pieces of tact. Unlike with people I felt good having these animals near, flying around and being close. They were like me, though they didn't have sharp teeth.

I looked down at my bloodied hand.

But they did have sharp beaks.

"Sami?"

I jumped up to my feet and jammed the rest of my tact into my mouth so he couldn't take it away from me. All around me were the sounds of wings beating the air as the crows flew away.

"I didn't see any cameras..." I said hastily, chewing as fast as I could.

By the time Jasper reached me the tact was all gone and so were the crows.

I took a step back but, to my shock, Jasper raised a hand and hit me right across the face. I fell onto the ground and choked when he kicked me right in the stomach. I gasped as the wind got knocked out of me and grimaced in pain.

"Go on get!"

Jasper looked at me, his hazel eyes blazing and his mouth tight. I could smell the rage radiating off of him. I scrambled to my feet and cowered down shaking my head.

"I didn't... I–"

"I heard you fucking talking to them!" Jasper roared. "Are you talking into the microphones? Huh? Are you a legion spy, you little shit?"

He was high again, I could see it in his eyes and in his movements. Jasper got paranoid when he was smoking from that pipe; he would spend hours and hours in my basement rambling about people being after him. He would make me agree with him and tell him all of this theories were correct even if they weren't.

"Well?" He leaned down and smacked me on the head. I choked and coughed, spitting blood onto the yellow grass. I could hear the crows behind me talking and cawing.

"No!" I sputtered. "I gave them some of my tact. I just wanted to make a friend. B-Barry killed himself, Barry died. S-Sami died."

"You gave them your fucking food? Am I feeding you too much?" Jasper snarled. He grabbed me by my tangled up hair and jerked me up to my feet. "Fine, no food! How's that? No more food. No more crows!"

No more food? And no more crows? The scream I let out stole the air from my lungs but this wasn't a scream of pain or a scream of fear... I felt inside of me a burst of anger so explosive it was like bomb of black matter ripping apart my chest. I whirled around and pounced onto Jasper and clamped my mouth over his upper arm. I sunk my teeth in and thrashed my head back and forth.

"Rip out his flesh, Sami," a new voice echoed in my head. This voice was deep and raspy, the voice of an adult not a young voice like Barry. It had an edge of dominance to it that told me I had no choice but to obey. Though I didn't need a choice, I wanted to bite him, I wanted to cause Jasper pain. To pay him back for the pain he was causing me and the gross things he was doing to me at night.

My mouth filled with blood and I started chewing, taking in and swallowing pieces of flesh as bright light after bright light shot through my skull in tandem with the physical blows I could feel from Jasper's fist. He punched me and punched me right in the head until the daylight around me became a sickening hot haze.

I fell to the ground and felt the grass underneath my skin. The crows' cawing echoed and with every echo the sounds of their wings stirring up the radiated air around them.

It was cold… but the ground smelled of copper. I saw through my hazy eyes Jasper's shoes, and the crimson droplets of blood from his chewed up arm.

Then that as well faded into nothing and all I could hear was my own heart pumping blood to my brain… and the crows singing around me.

"Come here, crow. Come here, crow."

CHAPTER 13

Nero

NERO ZIPPED UP HIS CARGO VEST AND CRACKED HIS knuckles. "Alright, grab the handle and on three, we lift."

Ceph's tongue stuck out of the corner of his mouth as Nero started to count down, on three he tucked his tongue back in and started lifting up the large crate of water. Both their faces strained but a moment later the wooden crate started to lift off of the ground.

With a grunt they slid it onto the Falconer plane, the sound of wood scraping metal filled the plane as Nero pushed it into a corner with the other crates.

"You said he has a well… why does he need water?" Ceph wiped his brow and started handing him much lighter crates. These ones he knew were filled with non-perishable food and essential items like clothing, weapons, and even a small generator.

"This is fancy vitamin water or some shit, I don't know; it's supposed to make him not be a runt forever," Nero explained. He glanced past him as he saw his twin sister Ellis walk through the hanger doors. A newborn baby sleeping on a sling that was wrapped around her chest.

"Hey, sissy, how's baby Drakey?" Nero jumped down and walked up to his sister. He raised his pointer finger and started waving it around.

"Don't you dare I just got him to go to sleep," Ellis said in a threatening tone, but no sooner than she had said that Nero, acting like his finger was a torpedo, lowered his finger and poked the baby in his chubby cheek, making missile noises while he did.

The baby opened his dark orange eyes and let out a muffled grunt before closing his eyes again.

"Aww... stupid well-behaved baby." Nero tickled his cheek and grinned at Ellis though she was giving him an iced glare.

"What!"

"Unless you want to take him into the greywastes let him sleep... though he's the easiest newborn I've ever taken care of. He's barely whimpered since I got him," Ellis said glancing down at the boy's blond head. "I almost tossed Ceph out the window twice, he wouldn't shut up."

"Hey!" Ceph called, popping his head out from behind the crates. "I was hungry!"

"And I was tired of giving you twenty bottles a day," Ellis called to him. "You were such a fat baby too, covered in rolls."

Ceph sniffed, his nose up in the air, but he said nothing else. Like Nero, Ceph was what the family called a 'brute chimera'. Standing almost six and a half feet tall with auburn hair, and a burly, muscular body, he was a sight to behold even though he was only fifteen years old.

"At least he eventually learned to be quiet," Ellis muttered before looking at Nero with a sigh. "I wish I could go with you... I really want to see how much he's grown. He would be eleven years old now, wouldn't he?"

Nero nodded. "Almost, Garrett checked his records and his birthday is at the end of March, so yeah."

"Silas gave us our orders," Ellis said with a sigh. "Did you put in some videos for him? And those books?"

Nero nodded as he turned around. He jumped back onto the plane and kicked a wooden crate with his boot. "I raided Apollo and Artemis's collection. I think he might be getting too big to watch The Little Mermaid but Garrett still fucking watches that movie so maybe he ain't. Anyway, I put in some older shit, Batman, Jim Carrey crap, and some Skyfall VHS's of some actual TV shows. Any other ideas?"

"Hey, you're not giving that little shit my Ace Ventura movies are you?" Ceph suddenly spoke up. He started opening the crate but Nero slammed a hand down on it. Ceph retracted his hand with a yelp and started sucking on his fingers. The Hawaiian shirt he was wearing plus his wavy cowlick suggested to anyone who knew those movies that he was quite the fan.

"We have like fifty of them we've found, he can fucking have one of each for fuck sakes," Nero said with an eye roll. "Okay, turn the plane on,

I ain't fucking driving today. So, sissy? Can you think of anything else to send to the little bugger? Any sissy wisdom?"

Ellis's mouth twisted to the side. "How long are you planning on visiting him for?"

Nero shrugged. "Couple o' days? I wanted to teach him how to use our bush masters properly. He should be tall enough now that the recoil won't knock him on his ass."

Ellis walked over to the plane and put her hand on the sliding door. "If... he has a lot of stories to tell about people bothering him, why don't you move him into the mansion?"

Both Nero and Ceph froze at this, both of them stared at Ellis with a surprised expression on their faces.

Sensing their hesitation Ellis continued, "He only has a few more years until Silas will bring him back to Skyfall. If he's as slippery and sneaky as his engineering suggests... he can stay in a back wing and keep quiet. I just... it's dangerous out there and it's just getting worse. Right now we have pockets of greywasters, but as the towns they're building these settlements on run out of canned food they're going to start spreading out. I just don't want anyone fucking with him, he's still just a little boy."

Nero let out a gruff laugh. "You've become such a mommy over the years."

Ellis narrowed her eyes at him. "You're a lot worse than I am. Well, get out of here and don't get yourself killed not when we're so close to becoming immortal."

"Yeah, wouldn't that be a kick in the balls, eh?" Nero brought out his cigarette tin and put an unlit smoke in his mouth. "Alright, we're gonna piss off. See you in a few days. Bye bye, Drakey! Be a good little cocksucker now." Nero leaned down and poked the baby in the face one more time.

The tiny, orange-eyed baby opened his eyes and looked around, and as his face started to crumple and become tomato-red Nero laughed and closed the sliding door.

Ceph got into the co-pilot's chair and chuckled with Nero when the sound of an upset newborn filled the hanger outside the door.

Soon the Falconer was up in the air and flying over the greywastes. Nero was sitting with his boots up on the dash of the plane with a blue-embered cigarette lit in his mouth.

"Here smoke this… Garrett gave this to me as a trial pack. These are supposed to be like half-opiate or something, a lot better than the Blueleafs we are selling now," Nero said. He gave the cigarette to Ceph before immediately lighting another one himself. "It has china white in it, fuck I shouldn't have left my bag at home. Though I was getting tired of it killing my sex drive."

"No kidding, I was surprised when you only wanted to cum once last night," Ceph remarked with an almost patronizing smirk. He took the cigarette and put it in his mouth. "They need to invent a drug that makes you all warm fuzzy like heroin but also makes you still want to fuck. Though I guess all good things have their downside."

"I'll get on Garrett, he loves getting pounded by me. I'll just withhold it from him until he promises to start working on it. We need more sciencey chimeras already. Right now we just have Eli and Gare-Gare and they're doing chimera crap for Silas, too busy to make good drugs," Nero said. He looked out the window and looked down to observe the block they were flying over. Sure enough, he could see several people the size of ants watching the plane go by.

Nero waved at them. "Apolly-wolly and Art are supposed to run culture and Dek'ko; I ain't got no use for that unless they're planning on bringing Butterfingers back to the world. What did they want Jack for? Can Jack invent us drugs?"

Ceph laughed at this. "Jack isn't into science he just likes his art and writing. Valen is pretty useless since he didn't develop for shit, but at least you have Rio. His surrogate parents are saying he's smart as shit but the fucker's only eleven. Sounds like you're pretty S.O.L until the new batch gets born. Silas will probably have a few more science ones now that he's mastered typecasting us."

"True," Nero said. "Maybe we can get him to start accepting orders. He's already mastered fucking up our eye colour and crafting our appearances. Why should he get all the fun? I'm going to order my own little chimera one day. Then I won't have to keep sticking my cock up your ass all the time."

"And Garrett's and Silas's too, and the younger second gens we have coming up!" Ceph said with a smirk on his face. His dark green eyes sparkled and that smirk turned into a grin. "You know… I can autopilot and we can take half an hour to ourselves on these seats. I'd still be able to keep an eye on where we're going."

A frustrated noise filled the Falconer's cockpit. Nero took a long inhale of his cigarette and glanced behind him.

Ceph kept his smile and to further his offer he pressed the autopilot on the plane and unzipped his pants. He took his penis out and waved it around though in more of a lewd manner than an inviting one.

"Nah, I want to see Sangy, maybe on the way back." Nero waved a dismissive hand, then lowered his cigarette towards Ceph's penis making the brute chimera squawk and shift away from the blue ember.

"But now I'm horny!" Ceph whined. "Come on, you have me addicted now. You've been drooling over me and waiting for me to turn fifteen and now you're going to pass up plane sex? Come on, Nero, fuck me!"

That was a brute chimera in his teens for you. Horny as all hell to the point where they came knocking on your apartment door at two am with a full salute eight and a half inch hard on and a desperation in their eyes that told you they were ready to go to the streets and find an unsuspecting nightwalker to pin down and fuck.

Which Nero did in his youth… and still does.

This gave Nero an idea; he chuckled to himself at the evilness about it. "Maybe on the way back… I'll take you to one of those blocks and let you choose a pretty one for us to take into the plane. Pass him between the two of us for a few rounds and make him shriek and squeal under our cocks. Would you like that, Cepherus?"

Ceph looked at him, his green eyes wide and his mouth slightly open. Below him his hardening penis was in his hands which was now flexing behind the head.

"R-really?" Ceph sputtered, his breath catching in his throat.

"Sure… grab him on the way back from the store… drag him into the plane as he screams and cries and I'll rip his pants off exposing that firm white little ass…" Nero was laughing inside of his head as Ceph groaned and shut his eyes. His fingers now running slowly up and down the shaft of his dick.

"I'll spit in my hand and prep his ass for you, then grab your cock and put it to his tight hole. You can slam that dick right into him and before he even has a chance to gasp you'll start riding him hard as his screams echo throughout the plane," Nero went on with a grin dripping self-satisfaction. He loved riling the new teens up.

"Oh fuck you, Nero," Ceph groaned, his hand now picking up speed as it stroked a large and thick penis. "You... fuck, stop taunting me." The auburn-haired chimera opened his eyes and did a quick check to make sure the plane was flying correctly before dropping his pants and putting one knee on the co-pilot's chair. "Come on, don't be a cunt. Stick it in me already."

Nero unzipped his own pants and pulled out an equally large member, already rock hard and begging for some place to be. He got up and immediately started teasing Ceph's hole with his finger.

Ceph's ass immediately rose up higher, at the realization Nero might actually take him up on that offer he leaned over and put his hands on the windowsill of the Falconer and braced himself.

"Quick," Nero said as his finger stretched out the tight opening in preparation. "I am not fucking giving you wine and candles, brother." He raised a hand and smacked Ceph's ass then grabbed it. He positioned himself and tauntingly pressed his large cock against Ceph's opening. "I'm fucking you and I'm sitting back down and if you dare cum on my leather seats I will rub your nose in it, got it?"

Ceph let out a gasp; Nero could feel the young chimera's hole tighten in anticipation. "Y-yeah, fuck... I don't care, just ride me hard."

A smirk graced Nero's lips, accentuated more by the lust pouring from the man's eyes. He spat on his hand and rubbed it on the head before, with a well-aimed push, he broke himself into Ceph.

Ceph cried out and stuck his ass out further. Nero sunk into him slowly and after giving the window of the Falconer a glance and then the controls to make sure he wasn't about to literally fuck him to death (via plane crash) he grabbed Ceph's hips; as the young chimera let out a gasping cry, Nero started to roughly ride him.

"Oh hear him cry, you like that, puppy?" Nero leaned down and licked Ceph's neck, his hips slamming into Ceph's backside as Ceph grabbed onto the windowsill to keep himself from falling over. If he didn't have his knee resting on the seat of the plane he might just have fallen over with the power behind Nero's quick and rapid thrusts.

Ceph groaned and tempted fate. He leaned his forehead against the side window of the plane to steady himself and let his right hand disappear between his legs.

"Fuck..." Ceph started stroking himself, listening to every gasping groan that came from Nero's lips. "That's the spot... fuck, you're like a tank. No wonder you're Silas's favourite."

"Oh, always," Nero growled into his ear. He kept his pace, continuing to glance at the main window of the Falconer, just to make sure everything was going good.

What a crappy place to fuck, overrated like shower sex... but well, you gotta drain the brute chimera teens often or else they'll just go off and start raping every pretty face with a cock. I know this because I was one and it was the most bullshit thing in the world that I had to wait until fifteen for Silas to finally let me loose on his ass. Not to mention the thrill of finally getting hammered by my king. He might look slight and tawny but holy-fucking-shit.

Garrett cried during his first time and Elish was catatonic... me? I think I cried from happiness.

Soon, sooner than Nero would have liked but they *were* hundreds of feet up in the air, he felt the tension gathering in his groin. He picked up the sound of his moans to give Ceph the hint he was close and saw the chimera teen's hand start to pick up its momentum. With another minute of heavy fucking and a chorus of loud groans Nero came inside of him and just moments later he heard Ceph's groans move to a higher octave.

The young man's body tensed up, Nero reached down to finish him off and Ceph quickly grabbed a rag they always kept in arm's reach. With a few rapid strokes, thick spurts of cum started to shoot onto the rag.

Nero leaned his head against the back of Ceph's neck, heavily panting into the chimera teen as Ceph himself tried to catch his breath. After giving themselves a few moments for recovery Nero separated their bodies.

"There, now shut up and fly the plane." Nero grabbed the cum soaked rag. He folded it to find a non cummed-on spot and started drying himself off. He tossed the rag to Ceph as he pulled up his pants and sat down.

Ceph had a grin on him a mile wide. He sat back on the plane and gave out a loud embellished sigh. "Thanks, bruddah, there's a bit of charm in a quickie so high up in the air. How close are we to Sharky's house?"

Sharky... I'll have to remember that one. "He's way near the plaguelands, we have a few more hours to go. I might take a nap." Nero yawned and put his feet back up again, soon the sounds of flint were heard and blue-embers erupting from both of their mouths. "He'll be thrilled as shit to see me. Little bugger liked me a lot once he trusted us."

"Sounds like a cute thing, is he all calm and zen like Jack?" Ceph asked.

"Nah, he's a little shit just like you were. Silas says he's the first stealth chimera as he calls them. Long, wiry, silent as all hell and sneaky as fuck. If this boy survives the greywastes Silas says his little stealth experiment was a success but I dunno... I think it's bullshit. You can be all quick-witted and stealthy as you want but it only takes one asshole to decide he wants to fuck with a kid. Si-guy won't listen to me though because he doesn't give a shit. We can make another Sanguine he keeps saying, we can clone him all exact but I don't know... I liked the kid, not a clone of the kid."

When Nero looked at Ceph he saw the hints of a smirk on his face. Nero glared at him and pointed his cigarette at him. "You got something to say?"

"Nothing new, just the same shit Garrett and Ellis always say when you're not around. We just find it adorable you love your little brothers so much. You're so protective of all of them."

"Bah, don't give me that... it's just... I dunno. I guess..." Nero shrugged. "Kids are different than adults, they don't BS you until they get older and I like it. Plus Ellis, Elish, Garrett, and me had to raise all you second gen assholes and you do grow attached to 'em."

Ceph remained silent which was probably the best considering Nero still had a short temper on him, especially when some of his weaknesses were being pointed out. The subject changed not soon after and several hours later Nero was pointing out the little grey blur that was Sanguine's house.

"Well it hasn't burned down... that's what I was worried about the most," Nero said through the cigarette being pinched between his teeth. "I bet right about now he's wondering what the fuck is going on. Lower the Falconer, bro, just don't look at him funny he's a bit sensitive to how he looks, he's a little girl like that."

Ceph laughed and soon Nero could feel the odd pull on his body as the plane descended down onto the greywaste ground.

Nero couldn't help the excitement he was feeling. He quickly got up as soon as the plane touched down and opened the door.

Well, he didn't come out to greet them but maybe that was good. It wasn't like Sanguine would be expecting Nero to come via plane. He was probably terrified and hiding in his bedroom with piss running down his leg.

A flow of cigarette smoke came out of his mouth and disappeared into the air. He looked around the two-storey house, empty and dark, and took a step towards it.

"Sanguine? It's Nero, come out you little cocksucker, I have shit for you," Nero called. He dashed his cigarette and started walking down the faint trail leading to the porch. Though as he walked past the half-fallen fence and the sparse tuffs of yellow grass he started feeling a small spur of nervousness dig into his chest.

Ceph was behind him, Nero didn't even realize he had stopped walking towards the entrance. He had frozen in place as his eyes fixed on the door.

It was partially open… with a small dune of greyash piling up in the entrance.

"Nero… are… are you sure this is the house? It doesn't look like anyone has been here for years," Ceph said in a dropped tone, a tone that eased the words gently as if afraid of what impact they might have.

The spur dug in further. Wordlessly Nero walked up the steps and opened the door.

Everything looks… normal.

"It doesn't look like there was any sign of a struggle… maybe he just left? Greywasters wander, right? Maybe the well dried up or…" Ceph stopped talking as soon as Nero raised his hand. The black-haired chimera's brow knitted as he looked over every inch of the kitchen before walking into the living room.

Though Nero prided himself on being the picture of brute masculinity, which included steering away from any emotions, he felt a sting inside of his heart when he saw an unfinished crayon drawing on a dusty table. He picked it up and looked at it.

A picture of a giant spider and two people?

No. Nero felt a tightness in his chest.

That was a celldweller and the other two are me and him... little fucker gave himself red eyes and me purple with blue coloured on top.

He folded the piece of paper and put it in his jacket.

When his eyes fell on the next thing his heart dropped.

It was an entire box of tact crackers…

And there were only about five missing from the box of twenty-four.

"I – I don't think he just took off…" Nero's throat felt dry, he tried to swallow it down but felt himself reaching into his jacket pocket for his flask of vodka. He took a long drink and turned around to find Ceph.

The mood had been light and happy on the plane, and now the tension was so thick in this house it could be cut with a dull knife. Nero spotted Ceph looking into the bedroom and he realized then the boy could very well have died in one of those rooms.

"No smell though," he said answering his own thoughts out loud. "Though it has been three years... we would still smell something if he had died."

Ceph nodded and looked in the second bedroom. "The covers are messed up but no one has died here or even been here. I'm sure he just–"

"No one travelling would leave nineteen tact crackers behind," Nero said dully and promptly took another drink. "And he would've brought his books... wait..."

Nero walked back to the box of tact crackers and pulled one out. He checked the *created on* date.

An angry and frustrated bellow flew from Nero's lips as he read the date. Unable to hold his emotions back any longer he tossed the package against the wall and kicked the box.

"Those fucking tact bars were made the fucking same winter we brought him here," Nero whirled around and snapped. Ceph visibly flinched. "Those fucking crackers don't last two months on the shelf before they're bought they... they... fuck." Nero put a hand on his forehead and another bellow echoed off of the ceiling. "I think... I think he disappeared a few months after we left him. Ceph, these... these... where is he?"

Ceph stood there awkwardly. "Want to try Melchai?"

Nero let out a breath and nodded. "Yeah... yeah, let's go."

They took the plane there and not a word was spoken between the two. In less than twenty minutes from leaving the house they were parking the Falconer in the middle of an abandoned park in the sparsely populated north area of Melchai.

Nero and Ceph both got out, their bush masters in their hands and their capes swaying behind them. During the short flight they had both changed into clothing fitting their status. No longer in jeans and a t-shirt like they had on previous the two brute chimeras were wearing fitted leather pants, black combat armour, and a black cape trimmed with blue.

Nero walked ahead and Ceph trailed behind him as was his status. Leaving the emotions behind in Sanguine's abandoned house Nero was the embodiment of the words 'don't fuck with'. His face was menacing and his walk strong, and as the two of them walked confidently down the main road of Melchai they were already starting to draw a crowd.

"We want every single shop owner to come out here right now," Nero barked, sweeping the gathering crowd with his burning glare. "I am Prince Nero Sebastian Dekker, third born of King Silas Dekker and the leader and ruler of the Legion. I don't suggest you dawdle, now piss off!"

At this command several of the greywasters ran off, the other ones still standing, gawking at the Imperial Commander of the Legion. Each one undoubtedly wondering just why Nero was there.

Nero stood with his arms crossed, his gun now clipped to the holder he had on his back. Ceph was in a similar stance, his face hard as rock and his green eyes sharp enough to cut glass.

Several minutes passed and three store keepers came out, each one giving Nero surprised and scared looks. If the Legion was in town it was bad enough, but if the leader of the Legion was in town and specifically requesting you – you were fucked.

Nero didn't waste time. "A little boy came here sometime during the winter or early spring three years ago and bought a box of tact possibly more shit. He was a little eight-year-old boy with black hair, red eyes and pointed teeth. Which one of you fucks sold the tact to him?"

It was easy to see which one it was, his face paled and his heartbeat jolted.

Nero narrowed his eyes and made the 'come here' gesture with his finger. The older man took a step forward and drew in a deep breath.

"It was me, he bought other supplies and left."

Another shop keep glared at him. "And he left quickly too – all thanks to the assholes who were harassing him like a bunch of fucking buzzards."

The merchant turned around quickly. "You were one of them, fuckface! Don't sell us out, you were doing it too."

"Enough!" Nero roared, his jaw hurt from clenching it so hard. "Did he ever come back?"

The two merchants shook their heads no. The first one spoke, "No, just that one time. He was wearing sunglasses and would only talk to the ground. Apparently while he was leaving in a hurry he tripped and his sunglasses fell off his face. Everyone started hounding him as being a half-raver and the boy left in tears… he never came back after."

Nero grinded his teeth. He badly wanted to murder all three of those merchants for their statements but besides bombing the entire town he knew there wasn't much he could do.

"The boy is missing," Nero said to them. "If anyone sees him, they're to find the first legionary they see. There is a reward for his safe return." He paused and narrowed his eyes. "And if I ever hear of anyone treating him below anything than a prince I will personally twist off their fucking heads. Got it?"

The merchants nodded dumbly and around them the crowd started to buzz. Nero turned around with nothing more to say to the residents of Melchai and started walking back towards the plane.

"What now?" Ceph said quietly when they were high up in the air.

Nero looked out the window, his eyes heavy and his throat dry.

"Now I look for him," Nero said in an voice void of emotion. "Until Silas tells me I can't."

Ceph was quiet… and though his own self-preservation urged him not to he found the words coming to his lips. "What if he's dead?"

I think he's dead, Nero whispered to himself. He tried to remind himself that there was no sign of a struggle, no blood, no tossed over boxes or gunshots in the walls. No squatters in their house or any sign that he had been overpowered.

There are no sure signs he's alive; just a few puzzle pieces missing to confirm to me he's dead.

No, he can't be dead… he – he's a tough kid.

But he's just a kid.

"I'll find his body then…" Nero replied. "Even if it takes me seventy years – I won't stop looking for him. I'll spend all the free time I have out here until I find him."

CHAPTER 14

Sanguine

Age 13

I RUBBED MY FINGER AGAINST THE WOUND IN MY arm before putting it back onto the cold concrete. I brushed it back and forth to colour in the dark areas, then carefully scraped my fingernails against it to make feathers.

When I was done I stood up to admire my handiwork and because I had no one to ask if they liked it, I turned around and sat back on my bed.

Like was my routine I sat with my legs crossed, staring at the door and going over every detail of its shape, size, and state. Over the years it had gotten dirty with both blood stains and my dirty feet when I kicked it, though eventually I washed it off.

Today there was a footprint on it outlined with blood, each line making a straight print that would eventually flake and slough off onto the ground. I had kicked that print myself, no particular reason why, I had just gotten angry. Sometimes I got so angry I trashed my entire room but perhaps that was me just doing a small service for myself... a dirty room meant I could clean it and sometimes it was nice to burn the energy.

Though mostly I just sat and stared at that door, my mind taking me everywhere and at the same time... nowhere.

Sometimes I talked to the crows.

Sometimes they talked back.

"Hello, Sanguine. Hello, Sanguine."

"Come here, crow."

The crows were the only voices I heard outside of my own head. The people I had once known, their faces were lost on me now. Throughout the years locked in this basement I had violated and tainted their appearances and personalities until they were nothing but snarling monsters in my mind. It seemed that whatever my mind touched would eventually become polluted so I tried to steer clear of those thoughts.

Nero, once a picture of strength and a much needed role model, was no one to me now. A man without a face, without a voice, without a presence. He sunk into the outskirts of my mind and stayed there with other such people: His twin sister Ellis, Cory, Gill, and Nan. They were no one to me now but when my sewage-covered being traced over their fading memories I knew that had not always been the case.

I was no one and yet I felt like a thousand different people stirred in an overflowing pot. Sometimes I was angry and sometimes I was okay, sometimes I stared at that door for days on end and other times I just slept.

And why did I stare at that door?

The only break in my monotonous life.

When Jasper decided he wanted to fuck me.

Yes, I knew what it was now. If I didn't know then the porn movies he forced me to learn from explained it simple enough. He was pressing upon my once pure and fragile body the sexual needs of the most perverse of men. For his half an hour of dominating me was much more important than the innocence of one small child. Children were worth nothing in the greywastes, they were just toys and victims unless they had the wits about them to not trust anyone… or luckier still, they had parents.

I had neither wits nor parents, though when I was that innocent child I wished for both.

I laughed at my own mental ramblings. Innocent? I was never innocent, as soon as I was big enough I was killing things whether it was ants, radrats, or two boys who decided to pick on a demon. I may be a lot of things, but I was never innocent.

Maybe that was why I look like this.

"Crow? Crow?"

I looked over before rising to my feet. I peeked through the small gap in the window board and saw three crows outside. Occasionally they would come and talk to me through that opening. I taught them new words to entertain myself.

"Hello, Sanguine," I said to them my voice a dry rasp. "No food for you."

"Hello, Sanguine."

I nodded and broke my eye away from the space between the board. The light bothered my eyes now and the crows preferred to look inside the basement rather than at me anyway. So I sat back down on the bed and stared at the door.

My eyes mentally traced each area of the frame and I stayed there cross-legged and stared as I most often did. I stared at it until Jasper came the following day, sometime in the evening I wasn't sure.

After he fucked me he sat on the edge of the bed with a cigarette. I said nothing and stared at the wall again.

"I have water for you." Jasper looked over at me. I had sucked his dick without complaint and that earned me either water or food. "Do you want it?"

I saw the red ember rise to his mouth and brighten. He was naked and there was a smudge of blood on his lower back where I had clawed him. I did it to relieve stress and he had stopped trying to get me to stop years ago. His entire back was covered in scars now, though so was mine. Funny though, mine were all self-inflicted – would you believe Jasper rarely beat me anymore? Besides a knock or a punch here or there when he was high or I had ticked him off, I had stopped fighting long ago.

Sanguine had no fight in him, he was no powerful demon. Even though I was taller now and parts of me were starting to change, I was more submissive and useless than I had been at eight years old.

I was nothing.

My solemn thoughts made my eyes travel over at Barry, now just a bear.

Though he had always been just a bear. I think the hardest part of getting older was realizing that.

"Sami?"

My body flinched when I saw Jasper snap his fingers in front of my face. I looked over at him.

"Sanguine." My voice was getting deeper too, though the times I heard my own voice was few and far between. I rarely spoke; I had no reason to talk except to speak to the crows. Jasper wanted to either fuck me or ramble on about the Legion he was still sure was after him. He didn't need me to talk back just agree with him.

"I already said I'm not calling you that," Jasper said. He handed me the cigarette and I took a hit of it. He was a bit nicer after he had gotten off. As the routine went, he would disappear then come back high as a fucking kite and rambling about whatever paranoia he had that day.

"Sami's dead," I said for the millionth time.

Jasper made a noise and took the cigarette back. I wanted food, not water. He hadn't brought me food in three days and though I was used to the raw, gnawing ache that only starvation brought to you, I still didn't like it.

"I told you it doesn't work like that. You can't just say you're dead and still be here. You can't pretend you're another person," Jasper said annoyed. "You're Sami, and you always will be."

I brought out a small piece of spring I had twisted off of my mattress and started scraping it against my scabbed and scarred arms. "I was never Sami; my name was always Sanguine," I said in the same flat monotone tone that was my voice now. Even when he beat on me and fucked me I no longer screamed. I never showed any emotions anymore. I was just... a walking corpse. Dead inside and just waiting for my body to get the memo.

I forget when I had died. I think perhaps it was the first time he had skewered me.

"Whatever, you crazy fuck." Jasper got up and peeked out the window. The hole where I saw the crows was one I had made myself out of a piece of metal. I had twisted it out of one of the mattress springs. Jasper had beat me for making it but he let it remain because he could look outside better too.

Jasper narrowed his eyes before taking the glass pipe from behind his ear. "The crows are multiplying. The Legion is releasing more and more, half of them I know are robots, the other half... I'm not sure. I think my original crows are training them on how to spy on me. All they do now is talk, they're learning new words too."

The flint on the lighter sparked, producing a small orange flame. I watched the flame and wished I had my own lighter. I enjoyed feeling pain and seeing blood but I missed the feeling of burning heat. The only time I could burn myself was when Jasper took me to the main floor to sit beside the fire and that was only on the coldest days.

I raised my hand and looked at the silver spiral scars, from a time long ago when Gill had held my hand against the stove element.

What would I tell that boy if I saw him now?

Kill yourself. Throw yourself onto the flames with Gabe and Pauly.

"Sami? Have you noticed anything different with them?" Jasper asked. He started pacing around the basement again, stepping over the bloody blankets I piled onto myself during the winter. Then he kicked aside the table legs I used whenever I felt like smashing myself in the face.

I glanced up at him, the stiff piece of wire still in my hand. "No, they're all the same."

"Are they talking to you? What do they say?"

Hello, Sanguine.

"They just say what you tell them… *go on get*, all of that."

The crows were my only friends. I would sit behind a rusty tractor and feed them and teach them to speak. Only when I could hear him approaching did I pretend I was chasing them around.

He caught on though – I hadn't been outside in four years because of that, even going to the main level made me nervous and short of breath… so they came to me now.

I preferred to stay inside of this basement, a basement which I had come to call my own. Jasper could come and go as he pleased but I saw this area as my own personal cave. A cave that held the little possessions I owned: a dictionary, thesaurus, my plastic bottle, my piece of wire, and whatever books Jasper brought me to read.

Jasper hadn't cared about me reading but when I started to become quiet… when I started to be able to stare at the door for days on end he started bringing me books he had bought from Melchai. I read them and he brought them back and exchanged them for others. I loved my books and thought of them all the time, especially when he was on top of me.

"I want to go again." Jasper extinguished his cigarette.

I looked up from my carving of my skin and put the metal wire down. Without complaint I got on my back and let him hold back my legs.

When he was finished he pulled himself out. I shifted away from him to lay on my side and maybe go to sleep when he put a hand beside my groin.

He never touched me or did anything but fuck me so it made me recoil and pull away.

"You're starting to get hair." Jasper's voice was bitter. "It's getting bigger too I see." He grabbed my scarred up arms but they were so full of half-healed and scabbed flesh there was barely any normal skin for hair to grow. So he looked at my legs, still scarred but not as bad.

"Leg hair… and your voice is cracking. Great, I was hoping I had at least another year before you became spoiled." Jasper pushed my leg away with disgust and got up.

I was becoming an adult and he hated it. Jasper liked fucking little kids but unfortunately little kids grew up.

Then those kids got buried by the barn.

"Can I get some food?" I asked him dully. I picked up the wire and pierced it roughly into my skin, when that pain wasn't enough I started to drag it back and forth. Immediately the relief started numbing the disgust I felt after he used my body. Once he left I would dig my fingers into myself to draw out his cum, that usually tore me worse than he did but I had to get it out one way or another.

Jasper slammed the door behind him and I turned over to go to sleep but he came back a few minutes later.

"Get on your back."

Again? I grudgingly threw the blanket off of me and stared at him. I realized he was holding tweezers.

He brought out a flashlight and shone it right on my private parts. He swore when he saw the black strands of pubic hair, now fully illuminated in the light. He got up and smacked me right across the face.

So it was my fault I was becoming an adult? I didn't fight him, I let him hit me a second time and didn't move when he started ripping the hair out of my groin with vicious rough pulls. It hurt, each tuff of black hair sent sharp jabs of pain to my brain.

Though... I found my eyes closing as he plucked the hair from me, only wincing as my entire area became hot to the touch and burning from the pain. The more he did it the less I found myself not liking it, pain was my friend and I enjoyed the feeling it gave me.

"What the... stop that!"

I opened my eyes at Jasper's strangled and high tone, I opened them up just in time for him to smack me so hard my head snapped back and hit the concrete.

He got up and threw the tweezers at my face. I didn't know what he was angry about. I looked down and saw nothing but small droplets of blood and random tuffs of thin black hair.

No, something felt different. I reached down and put my hand on my lower area and saw my penis was getting stiff, something that happened in the mornings occasionally but I always ignored it.

Jasper hit me a third time, this time his hand was balled into a fist.

When I realized he wasn't going to stop I put my hands over my face and tried to shield myself from his blows.

But he was angry at me and it took me a moment to realize why… he was angry I had gotten half-stiff… like he got before he fucked me.

Jasper was angry he made me that way… or maybe he was angry I was old enough now to have that happen from his touch.

I don't see why. I had no desire to do what he did to me. I just ignored it. That part of my body didn't even feel like it belonged to me, none of that area was mine it was his and I had no business doing anything with it.

Anyway, it was… disgusting, everything he did to me was disgusting. I wasn't going to be one of those men on the porn movies he showed me who touched himself and made noise. I was an object to him and that was just how it had been and always would be. I wasn't having sex with him, I've never had sex with him… he just did what he came for and I didn't fight it anymore.

I had fought… the first time… fuck, had I ever fought.

But he overpowered me… an eight-year-old had no chance against a full-grown man.

So he kept beating me, his breathing heavy under his rage and his blows sound and with a good amount of force. I stared at the concrete wall as his hits, now just numbing thumps against my raw skin, hit their mark. Blood sprinkled on the concrete to match the other designs my own masochism had painted. I had quite the murals over these concrete walls, even the floor was my canvas.

By the time he was tired, my eyes were stinging from the blood, and my mouth was so full I had to spit onto my blanket just to be able to breathe.

"If that ever happens again… I'm cutting it off," Jasper panted, exhausted from beating me. I heard him get up and walk away. "I'm going to Melchai."

"You didn't bring me any food…" I rasped. "It's been three days."

The door slammed.

To help distract myself from the gnawing discomfort inside of my stomach I painted crows on the walls. I had run out of room about two years into my imprisonment here so I had started washing some of my paintings away with saliva. I had kept a couple paintings from when I was little but I was much better at it now.

I hummed to myself as I used the stiff wire as a quill and slowly and methodically painted the feathers on the crow. I sung one of the only songs I knew, *Daisy Daisy*, a song that had been with me since the beginning.

I glanced over at Barry, laying on his side beside my pillow. I hadn't wound him since Jasper used to give him to me to stop me from crying too hard when he fucked me. The sound of his musical box made my throat tight and I broke into a sweat. I was sad I had that association now but it was what it was. Maybe that was why my mind made him blow his brains out.

And bludgeon Sami.

My gut growled. I looked down at my stomach, so empty that it sunk in. My ribs and bones were sticking out of me, thin outlines of bones that tried to push through my skin like they themselves were trying to escape from me. Everything on my body was pencil thin though I hadn't looked at myself in a mirror in over five years, I knew my face must look ghastly though but... it wasn't like anyone saw me anyway.

I was hungry... really hungry. Jasper had gone to Melchai yesterday so now it was day four of me not having any food whatsoever. Even painting was starting to make me feel faint, so I laid down on my bed and tried to get some sleep.

The next day Jasper didn't come back... and the day after he didn't come back either.

Today was a bad day for me, today I wasn't in a good space.

Weak and unable to move I lay in bed staring at the blood paintings of my crows that I had made. Though I had been strong enough to withstand starvation he had never left me without food for this long. This was day six and even my water was starting to run dry, all of my resources were disappearing.

I reached over and grabbed the water bottle with shaky hands. I brought it up to my lips and drank the warm liquid down. It was hot outside today and my basement was stifling. It was going to be fall soon and once spring came again I would be fourteen years old. I was a teenager now though something told me I wouldn't live to see my voice stop cracking. If Jasper's anger and frustration over me growing hair was any testament it was that my days were numbered.

Who cares.

I put the bottle down and closed my eyes, though I didn't see the bright colours or the detailed adventures with Nero anymore. I only saw the black feathers of the crows that I was too weak to talk to, and behind that just darkness. My good memories had faded into the abyss and with them my hopes for a life that wasn't this. Sanguine was depression encompassed, sometimes I wish I hadn't killed Sami.

Sami had fight in him; he had the arrogance of a child who still had hopes and dreams. A child who didn't know just how unfair life was… I wish I still had that outlook on life. Now… it was what it was.

Sanguine, Sanguine… give me your heart to eat.

My eyes opened slowly and I looked around the dark room, wondering where that voice had come from. I swear I had heard it… I know I had.

I blinked the crusted sleep from my eyes and, to my shock, my eyes immediately focused on a man.

A different man, this was no man that I had ever seen before or would ever expect to be here. He had brushed back black hair, burning red eyes and a grin as wide as the Cheshire cat's. His teeth were pointed and he was dressed in a black long coat.

This man couldn't be real…

"Who are you?" I asked him cautiously. I sniffed and tried to move around.

"I am Crow," he replied.

"Rip out his flesh, Sami,"

There were so many things I forgot over the years but there was one thing that always lingered in my mind. One thing that I had copped up to insanity or my dire need to finally break free from my submissive chains – and that thing was that dry and raspy voice I had heard that first time in the farmer's field. The voice that commanded and gave me the tools to finally fight back against Jasper.

That voice had disappeared as quickly as it came, and I had never heard him again.

The man named Crow kneeled down with the same grin on his face and I saw his eyes take me in with a glimmer of desire.

"You're not real," I said to him dully. I sniffed and with all my remaining strength I rolled over so I wasn't facing him anymore. Barry had never existed and he was dead now and, like Barry, Crow would eventually die too. Though now I was old enough to know Barry had always been in my mind.

The room was silent so I closed my eyes. Though as I tried to force my brain to accept sleep I felt the hair on the back of my neck prickle.

I opened my eyes and let out a small gasp of shock.

Crow was laying down beside me, his back pressed against the concrete wall. He was looking at me with his blood-red eyes glistening and his mouth still spread in a smile that showed off his serrated pointed teeth.

"I have no friends, and you are not my friend," I said to him. Though to my shame saying those words made the space behind my eyes burn. "I am alone; I have always been alone."

Crow shook his head and raised a hand, then gently brushed it against my cheek. I could hear his dry breathing near my ear. Inhale and exhale, sucking in the musty air of the basement.

"No, *mihi*, you're not alone." Crow's voice, dry but at the same time smooth, wrapped itself around my heart like a cold ribbon. Out of loneliness or perhaps just desperate sadness I found myself drawn to his words. "My little thing… my poor poor Sanguine. You are not alone, no."

I looked at him and so badly wanted to pull away.

Sensing my hesitation his smile faded until his lips pursed.

Then his eyes squinted under his closed mouth smile; he leaned forward and kissed my forehead. I could feel the pressure against my skin.

"Are you hungry?" he asked gently, running his cold fingers up my chin and down the side of my neck.

"Yeah," I said, my voice rising several octaves at his touch. I didn't feel nervous having Crow touch me it… it almost felt natural.

Crow nodded and kissed my forehead again. He started to sit up and as he did he put a hand on my shoulder directing me to sit up too. Though I was weak and it was difficult, I pulled myself up to the sitting position.

Still naked from Jasper's last time with me I sat cross-legged in front of Crow and watched him.

The man put his hands up to my face. He leaned in and kissed me before, oddly, he put the soft underneath of his forearm to my mouth.

"Eat."

I looked at him puzzled and shook my head. Crow only squinted his eyes like a content cat and urged me towards his arm.

"Eat, Sanguine."

Hesitation froze me but the gnawing hunger inside urged me to open my mouth. I put my lips over the flesh of his arm and looked up at him.

Crow nodded and petted my hair back. "That's right, sink your teeth in, eat enough to sustain you. He will not kill you, my beautiful *amor*... my mihi so sad in his basement. Eat and grow your strength."

I looked down at the arm and started to bite down, as soon as I tasted the coppery blood a groan fell unbidden from my lips. The flesh was ambrosia and the blood the life that I needed to sustain me. Suddenly, unable to hold myself back, I bit as hard as I could and ripped a chunk of flesh from Crow's arm.

Meat... fresh arian meat, still warm. My body trembled as the sweet meat kissed my lips, letting rush after rush of pure ecstasy take me as its willing hostage. In a fleeting moment the atmosphere of the room had been transformed, from my dark depression to a brilliant light all centered around the food I was devouring like a starved animal.

I took out the chunk and devoured it. My mind was telling me to savour it but my mouth was chewing and swallowing without care. Instincts taking over me and tossing aside any human need to prolong the pleasure. Getting it inside of my stomach was more important.

When I was finished I so dearly wanted more but Crow's arm was bleeding heavily and I could see I had chewed off a big piece of his arm flesh. Instead he pushed my head down onto the wound and I fixed my mouth over it and started to drink.

My throat burned with desire. I leaned down to take in more and as I shifted I realized some of that burning was coming from my groin area. It was stiff again, the blood and the flesh I was devouring was doing more to me than I had expected.

But I didn't care. I closed my eyes and drank the coppery elixir of life and let myself slip into the delirium that came hand-in-hand with isolation, starvation, and almost six years of abuse could bring.

"That's it, drink..." Crow whispered. I felt his hand on my head gently pet my hair back. I relaxed under his touch, something I knew I would now do only for him. "Get your strength back – he will not kill you. We will not let him."

He already killed me... I said to myself, sucking on the shredded wound of his arm like he was my pacifier.

"Then we shall resurrect you."

I opened my eyes and looked at him and he tilted his head to the side. Crow leaned in and kissed my forehead.

The door behind me opened.

My neck jerked towards the dirty white door and I saw Jasper step through. I hadn't even heard him come in, I had been in this daze for longer than I...

"What the ever-loving... fuck..." Jasper stopped dead in his tracks. He was travel worn and covered in ash, his goggles resting on top of his head. He wasn't looking at me though, he was looking at... at...

I looked down as the haze started to drip from my mind like water rolling off of the windowsill.

My mind refused to acknowledge what I was seeing.

A large chunk of flesh was missing from the underside of my forearm, the thinnest layer of yellow fat before a crater of red, still bleeding muscle. The blood was so dark compared to the pink meat, already it was pooling in the crater and spilling out the sides like an overflowing lake.

I had eaten my own flesh, not Crows.

"You... you fucking crazy..." Jasper's tone dropped and he took a step towards me before he paused and looked behind him. "You... you need to get a hold of yourself, kid."

My flesh, my blood... it was Crow's and yet it was mine and because of this in my own lingering madness I lowered my head and snapped my jaws back over the wound. I tore another bite away from my flesh and when Jasper ran over to me... I growled at him.

"You would do best to stay back," I said in a low raspy voice. "I am rather hungry."

Jasper took another step towards me and I hissed; my mouth full of warm meat and the nutrients from the food I'd already devoured filling my body with a rush of energy.

This time Jasper didn't come closer, he just stared at me. I wonder what he was thinking, I wondered what he was going to do.

I wondered if he would dare come closer to us.

"Can I meet him?"

Shock hit me like a splash of cold water. I looked behind Jasper and saw small little fingers grasping the door frame.

No...

"Jasper? I can hear him... can I meet him?"

Jasper started at me and his lips tightened. He turned around and picked up one of the dirty, bloody blankets and threw it over my injured arm. I was too busy staring at those soft, nimble little fingers to do anything else.

Horror gripped me and not even Crow on my shoulders could mask the foreboding, terrible feelings that were being stirred up in my chest.

"Yes… come in here, boy." Jasper's tone changed. It changed like a switch, the same one I had seen flick on and off. The one that made him sound cheerful. The façade of the happy depraved monster, who wore a mask on his face that held so many people underneath it.

The paranoid meth addict.

The friendly man who wanted to be my friend.

The child molester.

I wonder if he even knew who he really was anymore. And I wondered in that moment if I even knew who I was, or if I had ever been someone in the first place. I don't think I had ever gotten a chance to be the person I was supposed to be. I was just an empty shell that men filled with different things. Sometimes betrayal, sometimes hatred, sometimes cum.

A little boy with sandy blond hair stepped through the door. He had a look of fear on his face as his eyes swept the room.

I swallowed down the bile in my throat when I saw the rubbed chafe marks of what I knew had been a slave collar around his neck. Nan got those boys and girls sometimes, from friendly and rich greywasters who bought these child slaves out of pity though had no intentions of raising them. We got them in various states of health, sometimes they thrived, other times they wilted like a picked flower and died with Nan holding their hands.

The boy looked at me and I saw the shock on his face. Immediately when he saw my eyes his face crumpled and he started to cry.

"It's okay, he's not a monster though he looks like one. Why don't you go in and introduce yourself?"

Don't do it, little one, he will slam the door and you'll be stuck in here. Then soon – possibly even tonight, you will get the worst surprise you could ever have and after that… after that you will cry yourself to sleep.

That will be the last time you cry though, that might just be the last emotion you feel.

The little boy hesitated but when he saw me he smiled shyly and stepped inside on little boots that wouldn't have even fit my feet when I came here.

Jasper slowly got behind the boy as the boy stepped further into my basement. The kid, unaware of what was going on walked over to me, but his smile turned to a frown when he saw the blood all over my lips. Then he looked around and I think then he realized just what my paintings all around him were made of.

The boy started to cry and with that... the door slammed and Jasper was gone.

"What's your name?"

An hour after Jasper had left the boy's tears had been reduced to whimpering. He was sitting in the corner of the room, as far away from me as he could get. Like I had been when I first came here his arms were wrapped around drawn up knees. I could only see the blond hair falling over his face, the rest was buried in his knees.

"Cooper." He sniffed and rubbed his eyes.

"My name is Sanguine," I said to him. I withdrew my arm from the blanket though the blanket had fused itself with the wound from my own drying blood. I peeled it off and started wrapping the gaping hole in my arm with some old rags.

"Were you a slave?" I asked as I buttoned up the jeans Jasper had given me a few months ago. The first time I had seen Jasper naked I cried from the shock of it. I had only disregarded my clothes because I had been too weak to change after Jasper left, now the two bites of flesh in my stomach had given me a small burst of energy and the first thing I wanted to do was have clothes on again.

Cooper sniffed and shook his head. "No, Mama said she would come right back for me... she doesn't know where I am."

I picked up Barry the bear and made his fuzzy arms move up and down. "Oh yeah? Did Mama leave you with a man after he paid her money?"

Cooper was quiet for a moment. "That... that was just money he said he owed her."

Because you were sold into slavery, my little friend. "Oh, I see," I said in a bitter voice. "Then what? Did that man give you to Jasper?"

Cooper's head nodded, still buried into the space between his knees. I got up on shaky legs and stumbled over to the boy. When he saw I was coming closer he shrunk back but I saw his eyes widen a bit when he noticed I was holding Barry.

I leaned down and handed it to him. "His name is Barry... if you're here long enough he might just become real and talk to you."

"Really?" Cooper said in a hushed awe. He hugged him to his chest and I heard him whimper again. "He's soft."

I got down on my knees and watched the little boy run his fingers through Barry's matted fur. Soft and innocent. I wonder if I looked the same way when I came here, though I was never innocent like him.

"How old are you?" I asked.

"Six."

My eyes closed. I got up and turned from him and found myself wiping my hand down my face. I could feel crusted blood on my lips rub off, falling to the ground with the other blood I had shed over the years.

I sat down on the bed unable to say much else and watched him start to play with Barry. Putting the stuffed bear onto his knees and making his arms go up and down like I had just been doing.

He seemed unsuited for this place. I belonged down here. I was the celldweller now in all respects. A monster to be kept in the basement to be used for my master's own pleasure. This was my oasis, my home, and my sanctuary and a place in which I felt safe.

This little blond boy... his skin porcelain smooth like his slave owner had deliberately made him as beautiful and desirable as he could. He seemed to me a slab of opal in a coal mine, shining its brightness for no one to see but the very thing that would eventually make him as black and colourless as the others.

It made me nauseas, it made sour rise up in my throat and every time I tried to swallow it down it only rose higher and higher.

"Are you okay?" The boy looked up from his games with Barry; his eyes were brown. Such a fragile chocolate brown, like rich earth before the Fallocaust made the greywastes

"No," I told him. "I'm not okay. I have not been okay for a long time."

My eyes fell to the window with the small slits of light that streaked across the floor, one of these lights falling over the boy's small boots. Little boots caked in greywaste ash, with patches made out of old car tires on the bottoms. They moved back and forth as he bounced the bear on his knees.

Will you scream like I screamed...? Will you eventually just lay on your back and take it because you evicted your own mind from the tormenting storm inside of your head? What will you see? I saw Nero, a man who once said he would come and see me, I saw him and we went on wonderful adventures together.

I wonder if you will come back less of a person each time. I wonder if you will feel a piece of yourself break away every time his breathing started to get quicker and his thrusts start to become more forceful. Will you realize your own mind is slipping like I did in my fleeting moments of lucidity? Or are you too young to hear the swan song playing in your head.

Though mostly... I wonder if he is going to do it here where he broke me for the first time. Because that would mean I will be forced to watch, forced to be in the same room as him as he breaks this fragile porcelain doll in front of me.

I thought I had been trapped in a nightmare for almost six years, but it looks like my terrors were just beginning.

"Maybe we can be friends," Cooper said. He didn't look up as he tossed Barry up in the air and caught him.

A raspy laugh escaped from my throat and my head started to fill with a dizzy heat.

Once I would've given everything – everything – for a friend like this boy.

"Come here... with Barry. I would like to show you something he can do," I said to him quietly. A lump of emotion rose in my throat, an emotion I hadn't felt in a long time and had once thought dead. I patted the area of the bed beside me and once again tried to swallow the sadness down.

He would be my friend. I knew this because I would be the only comfort he would have after Jasper fucked him for the first time. I would be the one comforting him, maybe even holding him like Nero had held me when I had fallen asleep on his lap.

I could be his Nero and he could be what kept me on the plains of sanity.

Your first real friend, Sanguine. Here he is... your first real friend. Now you won't have to suffer alone, you can suffer together and help each other heal from what Jasper would do to both of you.

Your first real friend and, like in the Disney movies, best friends did whatever they had to do for each other. Through thick and thin that was what real friendship was about.

"Sure… I'll be your friend, Cooper," I said to him. I took Barry from him and for a moment I looked down at the stuffed animal.

Will I teach you to cut yourself to relieve the pain and stress? Will I teach you to eat your own flesh?

Will I teach you how to dig out his cum? Will I teach you how to claw his back to help release the anxiety steaming and rising from your frozen blood?

What will I teach my new friend? What kind of friend will I be?

I looked at Cooper and handed him back Barry, then reached to his back and started to wind his music box.

Cooper let me put him on my lap, easily with a trust that no little boy in the greywastes should have. Then, with my arm on his thigh, I released Barry's music box and watched the boy's face brighten as he started to play his song.

The music made my lips pull down, each strike of the notes stabbing my heart in places so scarred I had once thought no more emotions would penetrate. I tightened my hold on the boy's thigh and both of us listened to the music play, chord by chord.

When the song was half-finished my hand slipped from his thigh and I held it over his mouth and nose.

Barry fell to the ground as the boy jumped and squirmed but I easily held his arms down and pressed my hand further into his face.

The little boy let out a muffled cry and I found myself having to close my eyes. I shut them tight as my grip remained true and for the first time in many years I felt tears running down my face.

"Shh… shhh…"

He struggled but he was no fighter, soon, with one last desperate thrash, his arms went limp and fell to his sides. Cooper's entire body became loose in my arms and when I heard his heart give one last desperate beat I let out a cry and held him tight to my chest.

I sobbed into him, such desperate congested sobs I heard them echoing off of the high rafters of the basement. With every ounce of my strength, of my very being, I held that little boy to me and clenched my teeth until blood filled my mouth. Then, as my agony reached its peak, I screamed so loud and held him so tight I felt the boy's bones break underneath my iron grip.

I will be your friend.

I will be your friend.

And I will do what any good friend would've done.

Jasper stormed into the room holding something black in his hand. When he saw me and when he saw the dead little boy in my arms he ran towards me with his fists swinging.

"What the fuck did you do!" Jasper yelled. His eyes were wide and his teeth clenched over an sneering lips. He hit me across the face and tried to take the boy from my arms.

"Don't you fucking touch him!" Crow snarled through me. I felt my mind mentally stepping back as this dry raspy voice suddenly sprang from my own weak and cracking tones. "You will never fucking touch him. You'll never touch another fucking kid again!"

Jasper hit me again with a closed fist and as the bright lights flashed in my head I saw my own self take one last step into the darkness.

And for the first time in my life I felt my hold on my own mind tear away like two pieces of detaching Velcro. Leaving a trail of swarming birds and insects, this dark and menacing creature ripped me from my own battered and bruised mental state and took full control.

I put Cooper down on the bed and rose to standing, trails of blood leaking down the sides of my face like rivers on a map. In a flash I tackled Jasper to the ground and bared my shark-like teeth at this man who had kept me prisoner.

I snapped my mouth over Jasper's neck but in a flash Jasper put his arm out to stop me from making friends with the soft flesh so welcoming to my teeth. I responded by clamping my mouth shut over the arm and snapping my head back, holding in my jaws the white and red flesh that was me and Crow's reward.

Though I was older now, and taller, I was still only thirteen years old. Jasper, with all his strength, pushed me off of him and grabbed the black object that had fallen from his hands.

I flew backwards but in a flash I was back on my feet. A deep growl rose from my throat as my eyes watched for the man's next move.

Jasper was panting, staring at me with a surprised but angry look on his face. I stared back, with Crow's energy still charging through me.

"Enjoy it, that will be the last piece of me you ever get, Sami," Jasper said out of breath. He was holding his arm as it dripped onto the ground.

I lunged at him again; my jaws snapping. Jasper flinched but remained steady in his stance. He looked down at Cooper and his eyes blazed.

"I was going to let you fuck him too," Jasper said with a lewd laugh. "Just to see the turmoil on your face when his little body makes you cum. Next boy I bring home I suggest you–"

The scream of rage ripped through the dead and stagnant atmosphere of the room, and though anyone would see Jasper was waiting for just that, I was too disgusted at the mere thought to see for myself that it was just a trick. With the animalistic shriek on my lips, I ran towards Jasper, my arms outstretched and my teeth bared.

There was a clicking and a snap of static, and before I realized what the device was that Jasper was holding, I was on the floor screaming, electricity ripping and perforating my veins to the point where I thought I was going to die.

I remembered nothing else.

Another electric shock and another, by the time Jasper was done using the taser the boy was passed out cold, his red eyes glassy and staring off into nothing and his fingers twitching beside the dead corpse of the little slave Cooper.

Jasper spat on him and gave him a kick in the side, pursing his lips as the desire to kill him right there taunted him.

But he still needed someone to fuck, and someone to talk to.

Jasper went to the door and walked up the stairs, passing the piles of garbage and half-eaten body parts – and went to the barn to find his chains.

That boy will never see daylight – he will never look out that window again. He will be chained like the animal he is and will be fucked like one too.

CHAPTER 15

Sanguine

Age 13

MY NECK WAS CHAFFED AND SORE FROM TRYING TO get myself out of the metal collar on my neck. I couldn't see how bad it was only that it was hot to the touch. In some areas it was rough and scabbed but in other areas it was leaking fluid and as sensitive as a busted open blister. It hurt to the point where I couldn't move my neck at all, so I just sat on the edge of my bed and stared at the door.

Oh the colours I saw when I stared at that door, the images that went through my head. Sometimes I felt like I was floating in water, though I didn't know how to swim; other times it felt like I was flying in the air… even though Jasper had clipped my wings.

Mostly I saw nothing because even my imagination had retreated inside of my mind after the horrific act I had done just two weeks ago. There was nothing to see, nothing to hear, just darkness laid on top of darkness, a thousand and one strips of fine black carbon to which no light could penetrate.

Though there had never been any light.

My mind faded to black but I became aware when Jasper handcuffed my hands and legs and urged me to get up.

"Come on… we're going outside." Jasper's voice sounded like he was underwater. It was a thin, wobbly voice and it took awhile to reach the back alley in my brain where I was hiding.

"Sami?"

Finally I looked up at him. He was staring at me with my neck chain in his hand, cold metal was felt on my wrists and legs and I looked down to see the chains. Everything was chains and darkness, there wasn't much else anymore, inside and out.

"Sami?"

He roughly smacked the side of my cheek and I blinked away the last of my inner delirium.

"What?" I rasped.

"Pick up the boy rotting in the corner and come up the stairs."

I looked over and was reminded of the smell of rot so heavy in the air it seemed to physically weigh me down. Tinged with blue I saw the corpse of Cooper, green now, and surrounded by brown stain.

Without complaint I got up and took a step. My legs buckled underneath me from not walking or standing in weeks.

I held up my hand and steadied myself by the boarded up window, and took a moment to get my balance.

I saw that even the cracks of the window had been boarded. I had no light whatsoever, not even the little slivers that streaked across the dirty, stained floors. Everything was in darkness but… but I had already known that. Perhaps my awareness was having trouble catching up with the world still turning around me.

Life was going on outside of this basement and yet I felt like I was stuck in an eternity of limbo.

My next jolt of awareness came when I reached the top of the stairs. It was the smell that brought me back, leading me to look down and see the small boy I had in my arms.

He was so light… and he was missing his eyes, his cheeks… he was missing large chunks of him that made him look more like a zombie than a little blond-haired child.

I think someone had been eating him – I don't know if it was me or Jasper.

Maybe both.

Yes, look at all those bits missing, he did indeed look like a zombie. Though in all respects the zombie was me – I was the dead one, even in death Cooper was more alive than I had ever been.

I froze at the top of the stairs and looked around, shocked as I realized I was on the surface… I hadn't been above ground in years.

Immediately I felt apprehension. I turned to walk back down the stairs when Jasper grabbed my arm.

"No, outside… you're burying him. You killed him, you bury him,"

Jasper said in a biting tone. "Are you telling me you're scared of being outside?"

I looked around the filthy house, stacks of boxes with old appliances sticking out, worn-out furniture and counters covered in garbage. In the kitchen I saw a leg of a rat, its skin leathery brown but for the fat poking out of the sever marks. I wasn't hungry; I wouldn't eat that I don't think.

"Sami?" Jasper made a frustrated noise. "Are you even still in there? You're a fucking wreck… go outside. Go on, I'm having a hit."

I shuffled over to the door but stopped again. It was dusk but the dark blue hues were still too bright for me. I wasn't used to not seeing the world without the night bright I had had since I was born.

Everything was so… open.

Vast without walls or boundaries.

It made me anxious, I once again turned to go back to the basement.

And again Jasper grabbed my arm and pulled me towards the open door to the outside world.

My breathing started to catch in my throat and desperation sunk into every crevice of my mind, unravelling the tight coils of my brain and exposing the soft membranes to the cold greywastes air. I didn't want cold air… I wanted my closed-in basement.

"Go!" Jasper snapped. I heard a lighter flick and the smell of the meth as he took a hit. "Hurry up, he fucking stinks."

"Basement…" I whispered.

"No!" Jasper pushed my back, my chains clinked around as I stumbled forward. "Go!"

I was a broken man and this was proven to both Jasper and me when I took a step forward and walked onto the porch. Swallowing down the anxieties screaming and shredding my damaged mind I walked onto the greywastes ground and tried not to look at the open world, now so threatening it made me wish for the white door to stare at.

So I looked at the ground, hearing nothing but my own desperate breathing and the crows in the distance.

My crows?

I looked and saw them tinted in a ghostly white, their red eyes now bright stars that had fallen from the inky heavens above me. Beautiful twinkling stars.

I started walking towards them, this rotting body still in my arms. My chains chimed and rattled as I shuffled over past the opening in the fence.

"Sami?" Jasper called but I kept walking towards my crows.

I got down on my knees, for a moment the crows hopped away from me but as they prepared themselves to fly away... they started to come back.

My crows surrounded me, tilting their heads back and forth, wondering if I had food for them. All I had was Cooper, the boy in my arms, dead and long gone.

"Come here, Crow."

My arm outstretched to touch them. "Hello, Sanguine," I whispered.

"Hello, Sanguine," one said.

Red eyes, black feathers... just like Crow. The Crow who talked in that dry, raspy voice.

And me, just like me. They would be my friends; they were only animals but yet they were all I ever had.

"Come here, Crow."

"SAMI!" Jasper snapped.

I looked up at the sky and saw stars peeking through the grey haze above us. One day I would grow wings and fly from here... though perhaps not.

I was a celldweller hiding from those who would hurt me and unfortunately – the entire planet wished I was dead.

Everyone except the crows.

The sound of a shovel striking dirt filled the night air around me. I looked and saw Jasper driving it into the ground.

"Start digging," he commanded. "Put the boy down."

I looked back at the crows and wished I could ask them what it was like to be able to fly. But I was defeated and had been broken, so I put Cooper down for the crows to watch over and took the shovel from Jasper.

Jasper's movements were twitching and his eyes jutting off in different directions. He sat on a stained, old lawn chair as I started to dig and drank from a flask in his jacket.

He watched me dig and then he started to talk, rapid speech that said everything and nothing at the same time. Rambling words of legion soldiers, crows with cameras, and the belief that the world was after him.

"The Legion has been nosing around Melchai, nosing around the area for the past year," Jasper said taking another drink. "They stay on the edge of my property. I saw claw marks on my fence an acre away. Near the bones of that greywaster I found when I first brought you."

I kept digging and I didn't answer him back, but every few minutes I had to stop and rest. I had no energy, no strength. I was grey skin stretched over brittle bones.

After a while though he stopped rambling on about the Legion and turned to talking about me.

"You're growing quickly," he commented darkly. "Too quickly for me. I bet you feel like a big man now that your cock is bigger than mine, eh?"

"No," I said back. The hole I was digging was almost up to my waist, though I still had to make it wider.

"Yeah, I know that. You're beaten down, the perfect slave. Shark teeth, blood-red eyes, and handsome as all fuck but inside your brain you're just a mental piece of shit."

"I know," I replied. I dug the shovel in again and threw the dirt over my back. I glanced to my side and saw the crows were pecking at Cooper but I let them. That was the only food I had to offer them.

"You know you should thank me for taking care of you. The people of Melchai would've found you with torches lit and crucified you on the spot."

I paused and stared at the hole I was digging, half grey ash but underneath I was seeing bits of brown soil. His words meant more to me than he thought – I had never told him what Gill had done to me. Maybe he had seen the scars on my palms?

"Thank you," I said dully, not knowing what else to say. Jasper laughed at this and started pacing around the field, his flask rarely leaving the tight seal of his lips.

"Why should I keep you alive, Sami?" Jasper suddenly said.

I looked at him and saw he was looking down at Cooper's corpse. "You killed a cute, pure little boy I paid a hundred and fifty dollars for."

My eyes once again fell to the hole I was digging, and I wondered if this hole was meant for me all along.

Then I heard a click.

I turned around and stared down the barrel of a rifle.

"Well, Sami? Why don't I just kill you right now?" I could smell the whisky on his breath and the overpowering stink of meth. Though that was all that I felt, I felt nothing else.

And perhaps that was my answer.

"Because you know I want you to," I said to him and I turned around and went back to my digging.

Jasper stabbed the back of my head with the barrel of the gun. I had to steady myself on the ground to keep myself from falling down. He hit me again, twice, and a third time until I had to stay hunched over to keep steady. Satisfied with whatever point he was trying to prove Jasper growled before spitting in the hole I was in.

But he didn't shoot me; he just yelled at the crows and sat back down.

And I kept digging.

Then there was a scraping of the chair and a light caught the corner of my vision. I looked over towards the barn, where Lenny was buried, and saw two pairs of headlights coming down the dusty greywastes, in the same direction I had come from.

Jasper swore. "Get out of the hole!" he snapped but as soon as he said that he swore again and said instead, "No, get into it. Lay down and don't say a fucking word, there ain't time to hide you. DO IT!"

Obediently, or perhaps I was too tired to argue, I lay down in the hole and curled myself up with an indifferent feeling. It felt nice to be laying down some place dark so I closed my eyes and enjoyed the sensation of being closed off in something.

Though as soon as he started putting dirt on me I got nervous.

And on its heels a feeling I didn't think someone like me could feel: claustrophobic.

"Shut up! I'll dig you out when they fucking leave, just brush it from your nose and stay still," Jasper hissed when he noticed my breathing start to quicken.

"Basement…" I said in a broken voice. I blew air out of my nose to clear the dirt from my nostrils as more cold dirt started piling on me.

It was going in my ears… it was going in my eyes. I shut my eyes tight and put my hands over my head, shielding myself from the worst of the dirt and giving me a big enough gap that I could still draw in breath.

"Shh!" Jasper hissed again then suddenly a slew of curse words fell from his lips. "That's the fucking Legion. I told you, didn't I tell you!? They'll kill me and then kill you so shut up."

"Put the shovel down!" a muffled voice suddenly called. I tried to shift and move but the layer of dirt around me was thicker than I thought. My bottom half was paralyzed and all I could move were my hands, but no, I couldn't move my hands because every time I did more dirt fell on my face making my claustrophobia even worse.

Then one last pile of dirt on my head and the voices were nothing but muffled vibrations to me. I couldn't hear if I wanted to and it wasn't just from the cold dirt on top of me, it was because my breathing was bordering on hyperventilating and my mind circling around an anxiety attack.

With my eyes closed I tried to push myself out of my body. Fly away with the crows, fly away to the stars with my friends.

No... I didn't need friends.

The uncomfortable feeling of being closed in was starting to drive me mad but the voices only continued. So desperately did I want to burst out of this grave just to get a breath of fresh air but I couldn't... I couldn't do it. I stayed absolutely still as Jasper got interrogated by the Legion for reasons I didn't know.

I just wanted to go back to my basement, back to my cave, where I could be closed-in and safe on my bed staring at the door.

Not here... not with other people.

"Sanguine..." I heard Crow suddenly whisper. In my mind I found his smiling face.

"Yeah?" I whimpered to him.

"Sit up."

"I can't."

"Why?" Crow whispered to me.

"I can't move," I said to him and that was the truth. Something was keeping me down, something was preventing me from sitting up and letting the Legion know I was here. I didn't know exactly what it was – I think I just wanted to sit in my basement in the quiet and I knew if I sat up I wouldn't get that. That Jasper would bury me the rest of the way if I disobeyed him.

Or maybe it was none of those things – maybe it was the hope lost, the submission that was now my being, maybe it was my sadness.

Maybe it was because I was a scared coward and I didn't want anything to change around me anymore. I had had enough change.

I just wanted my basement... I just want to go home.

"Sanguine... sit up."

"I can't... I can't move."

When Jasper finally grabbed my tangled black hair and pulled me up off of the grave I was in full panic attack. I had breathed in enough dirt to make my mouth dry and raw, and every breath I was inhaling was filling my lungs with ash.

He let me be as I tried to catch my breath, my eyes so wide my eyeballs hurt and my hands clenched over my neck and head. With every sharp inhale my mind tried to clamp onto reality but it was like grasping onto broken ice after you've already fallen in. I kept slipping back into panic induced delirium and madness.

"Get a hold of yourself..." Jasper snapped and he smacked me upside the head. "Get out, I'm putting the boy in."

My chest burned, my mouth open and sucking at the air. I managed to weakly crawl out and I collapsed beside the grave.

Jasper left me on the ground clawing for breath and picked up Cooper. He put him in and started burying him. I stayed laying, coughing and breathing, and trying to get a hold of my head.

"Basement?" I hated the weak cry that rolled out of my mouth, a weak susurration with no pride to give strength to the words. Just weakness, just submission.

"Please?" I whined.

Jasper turned around. I realized the visit by the Legion had spooked him. He stared at me for a moment and I saw the apprehension; it was painted in bright colours all over his gaunt face.

What did the Legion want?

What did the Legion want, Jasper?

"Yeah, go... go back inside, I'll finish with him," Jasper said slowly. "Go on, you're allowed.

I nodded and stumbled to my feet, chains still binding me though nothing compared to the chains that bound me internally. Without another word I turned... and went back to my basement.

CHAPTER 16

Sanguine

Age 19

Every year I used to say to myself – it can't get any worse than this.
And every year I am proven wrong.
As each summer brings the stifling heat; I find myself wishing for winter.
But when the heat turns into the biting cold that turns my fingertips blue.
I wish only for the grey sun that I can no longer see.
Sometimes I wonder if the world outside of this basement has ended,
And if I could break these chains, I would be free,
But then I remember the devil still has be bound and chained,
And that devil is me.

SOMETIMES MY THOUGHTS WOULD RACE A MILE A minute, like a wound up car spinning in circles until it eventually slowed down and became still. Other times I had no solid thoughts, just images or past events that would surface like a hand brushing back the toxic film on stagnant water… curious to see what lies underneath but once you saw the brown sludge you would only wish for the film to cover it once again.

All I had were my thoughts now – because I was chained by the neck to an anchor coming from the wall behind my bed. I was chained and unable to see anything but the tinged-blue darkness that my eyes had grown accustomed to. The slit between the window frame and the boards had been covered, the hole I had made in the middle of the board had been filled and I was nothing but a celldwelling monster that hid from even the bluelamp Jasper carried when he wanted to fuck me. I saw no more crows. I had no more friends not even the birds.

Jasper didn't come down here to ramble about legionaries spying on him anymore, because he was more afraid of me when he was high. He only came down to have sex with me, usually when the boys he had upstairs were too injured from his appetite or perhaps when one died.

Sometimes I would hear him dragging their bodies over the greywaste dirt outside my window, sometimes, if I listened carefully, I could hear his shovel strike the ground with a metallic clank – but mostly I heard nothing but the own conversations in my head.

Crow was my only company.

I looked beside me and saw him staring at me. He sits on the edge of my bed with that Cheshire smile on his face and his eyes squinting like the happy cat I hadn't seen since my childhood. He would sit there for days without speaking and stare at me with that glaring smile. He always wore his long coat though sometimes he dressed in colourful shirts and pants. I don't know why, perhaps I was just experimenting with this demon who lived inside of my head.

My only friend.

I remember I almost had another friend at one time.

But I killed him.

Cooper would've been eleven years old.

I am nineteen… I am a man now though I am a man in appearance only, inside I feel like an animal most days or the walking corpse of a young boy who had never been shown how to die.

My only friend was this demon sitting on the edge of my bed, watching me and watching me, though most of the time I didn't engage him… because he rarely had kind things to say.

Crow wanted me to keep fighting Jasper. Crow wanted me to bite, scream, and stop letting him fuck me so easily.

My eyes rose to the cobwebbed rafters of the ceiling as I heard one of the boys upstairs scream, followed by Jasper's muffled yell back.

But I had no fight left in me, it was only in the throes of the most painful or mind fucking turmoil did Crow join himself with me and actually fight back.

I had never been strong… not even when I was a child. I had a weak mind filled with a need to be loved and talked to. That was my weakness, and unfortunately it was what had ended me up here.

I had been in this basement for eleven years now.

Eleven years.

Another scream above me and I wondered if I would hear another body get dragged across the ground but I only heard whimpering in tandem with the speed of Jasper's thrusts. I knew the rhythm, if it wasn't stuck inside of my head, whirling around like that wound up car, it was in my dreams.

Sometimes he brought them down here, just to torture me. Because he knew there was little else that drew me into madness. When he brought them down I closed my eyes and clawed my ears until they bled, but I could still hear their crying before they faded out and went into their own minds.

I didn't know their names but I knew there were three of them. A little one that was six with black hair, and two blond-haired brothers that would hold the victim's hands for them. I didn't want to learn their names. I think if that last step was made to humanize them to me I might just bite my wrists until the blood shot to the other side of the room.

My eyes stared at the door as I heard Jasper and the boys above me. Then slowly my eyes closed and I felt my fingers break away from my present thoughts. I slipped inside my head to find the only oasis I had and I stayed there.

Sometimes I stayed there for days, until thirst and hunger brought me back. I would close my eyes and I wouldn't sleep… but I wouldn't move, talk, or do anything but stare at that door. That was usually when Jasper would come to throw the scraps of food at me and the bottle of water… that was the time he would fuck me too.

Always on my hands and knees now; he didn't trust his face near mine anymore. He never knew when Crow would come and make me strong.

The next thing my mind comprehended was the very thing I had been thinking about. My awareness came to me with the painful pressure in my backside, and Jasper's familiar groans as he pounded himself into me.

I was grown now… I had pubic hair, a beard unless he shaved it to make me look younger, long willowy limbs with leg hair, underarm hair, and a dick bigger than his. But even though I was nineteen I had absolutely no desire to do any of the things he did. I had never touched it except to go to pee in the bucket I had beside my bed. There was no part of me that wanted anything to do with sex… sex was disgusting and that was all there was to it.

My eyes were fixed on my filthy grey pillow now, not washed once in those eleven years. I could see my tangled black hair flying back and forth as Jasper thrusted into me. I didn't struggle unless I had already been torn open and it hurt more. I think perhaps I knew that if he got off on me… he might leave the kids upstairs alone.

Jasper moaned and I felt his body tighten up as he started to cum. I grimaced at this part and waited for it to be over.

Then he pulled out and I got down on my back, the sounds of chains around me. Immediately I started digging his cum out of me with my fingers.

Jasper lit a cigarette and sat on the edge of the bed. Crow only inches away from him, no longer smiling and no longer staring at me. He glared at Jasper with his red eyes burning suns, urging me with desperate sadism to lunge and attack him.

No… I can't do that. He locked the door behind him and if I killed Jasper now the boys upstairs would starve to death and so would I.

This was my life – I had accepted that years ago.

I waited for him to leave but he continued to sit there smoking his cigarette, filling the disgusting unclean basement I had been inside with the rancid smell of cigarettes. It was better than the meth smell though it lingered longer.

Jasper reached into his pocket and tossed me a piece of meat. I picked it up and though it was covered in dirt and lint I ate it.

It was tender and soft, melting in my mouth. "Did one of the boys die?" I asked knowing this meat had come from a child not an adult.

"A new one, you never met her," Jasper replied quietly. He had gotten older too, his curly black hair had more than its fair share of silver threads in it and the lines in his face had gotten deeper. The meth had also done him no favours, half of his teeth were gone and the other half were rimmed with black and surrounded by gums that always looked sore.

"Her?"

Jasper chuckled and shook his head. "Short hair, dressed in overalls, it wasn't a pleasant surprise when I undressed her for the first time. I went to Melchai and found the slaver's route and I broke his jaw and took my meth back and a hundred dollars for my troubles. What use do I have for a little girl? Her bones are feeding the crows."

I had no emotions left to feel badly for her, only a foolish wish I had been born a girl just so he would've killed me right away too.

"Did she die pure?"

Jasper nodded and I was glad for at least that... Cooper did too, and once you came to Jasper's farm, that was the only good outcome you could hope for. Die before he fucked you and made you into an impure monster. Maybe I don't wish I was born a girl... maybe I just wish I stayed a kid forever so he would stop bringing other little boys home.

Or put them close enough to me that I could kill them... though I had only been able to do that once. Jasper kept the kids out of me and Crow's reach now.

At the mention of his name Crow's glaring scowl at Jasper faded, he looked at me and smiled and ran a hand down my leg.

"Is he going to leave soon?" Crow asked.

"I think so," I replied.

Jasper glanced back at me but he knew I was talking to Crow; he knew all about Crow.

Jasper said nothing to me and continued smoking his cigarette.

"Would you have fucked her?" Jasper suddenly asked.

"No," I said back.

"I always wondered what your preference would be. Boy or girl?"

"Neither."

Jasper laughed and got up. "Everyone is attracted to at least one, sometimes both. Though I guess you'll never know... I always assumed one day you would ask for some time with one of my boys but you seemed to have skipped that stage of being a teenager. I was fucking any man or boy that I could have at nineteen."

My teeth clenched, even the thought of having sex... even with an adult made me feel sick. I might have control of absolutely nothing but I had control over who I stuck my dick inside and I knew it would be no one – ever.

I wouldn't... I couldn't do it and I never would. I would never be like Jasper no matter how old I got.

I don't know what Jasper was waiting for, perhaps it was just the tightening of my jaw but he got up and let me finish off his cigarette.

My lips sealed the still wet tip of the smoke and I inhaled it into my lungs. My lungs were bad and I had trouble taking deep breaths some days, especially the cold days, but I still took every cigarette he gave me. Even if he made me suck his dick for them, I did it because cigarettes were the only comfort I had now.

And at that silent admission Jasper took two more cigarettes from his tin and turned around on the bed. He spread his legs, exposing his greasy pubic hair and unwashed skin. I knew what he wanted so I turned around too and lowered my head. I took the disgusting piece of flesh into my mouth and paid the price needed to be paid for the cigarettes.

Then he tossed me a lighter after I had finished him off.

"Be careful with it," Jasper said as I stared at the lighter in awe. It had been so long since I had had a lighter, I felt a shock of almost giddiness go through me.

"I'll come back for it later. I'm going to Melchai tomorrow, I need supplies."

I lit the cigarette and wiped his cum off of my shoulder and neck. He didn't make me take it into my mouth which was one of the few things I was thankful for. I inhaled the smoke to get his filthy dick's taste out of my mouth and started playing with the lighter.

I reached down and put ol' Barry beside me to watch. Barry the boy might've died long ago with Sami but I still loved that bear. He was the only thing in this world I loved.

I singed the sides of the blanket with my lighter and burned off the imbedded strands of hair that had worked their way into the smelly synthetic cotton. I enjoyed the smell, a different smell from must, age, and the piss and shit in the bucket beside my bed.

The flame was beautiful but it stung my eyes with such a brilliant and blinding elegance I knew for sure if I ever did go outside again I would be blinded by the grey sun. It was transfixing almost and I found myself not letting go of the red trigger.

As the lighter got more hot I ran it along my palms, illuminating the silver scars of when Gill crucified me years ago and when he had held my hand to the stove element. All of these scars were like small stories imprinted on my skin, most of them I wished to forget. Though like the stories of my past were printed in black my brain couldn't help but memorize every word.

My forearms told my worst stories, my legs did as well… and my groin.

There was no skin on my arms that didn't have scars on it, every inch leading all the way to my shoulders were covered in silver, pink or a mixture of both. The only parts that remained pure were the areas I couldn't reach and even some of those places were damaged. When I made Jasper mad he would beat me and a few times he even wielded a stick just to break the skin on my body easier.

I ran the flame over the scarred mosaic that was my forearms and singed them. I found myself holding the lighter on the scar tissue, even when the warm burn turned into searing pain I still held the flame there.

And I watched it; I watched the skin start to constrict just slightly before it started to blacken and break. The smell of burning flesh reaching my nostrils and soon the black and red was sizzling.

I felt every throb of pain but what instinctual commands my brain had for my hand to pull the flame away from my skin had been numbed from my own miswired brain. I held it there and watched soberly as the lighter burned my arm, and not just my arm, the trigger on the lighter was also becoming hot.

But I kept it there, I kept it there and ignored the stiffness between my legs. The pain, like I had been taught years ago, was a relief to me. Whereas so many other people avoided pain above everything else, I had come to rely on it as my own personal coping mechanism.

Fire, beautiful, alluring... its kiss was warmth and it attracted everything from humans to insects, but get too close to it and oh my friend... it will destroy you.

I live for that destruction.

When the flame went out I closed my eyes and focused my mind onto the burning pain in my arm. Though I saw nothing but darkness through my eyelids I could feel the pain like it was a small orb of light on my arm. I crawled into that brilliant incandescence and I lay there with it, it comforted me and held my hand like no one had done in years.

After the lighter had cooled down, I lit it again and started burning the sides of the mattress, watching with fascination as it melted before turning black. I liked that the flames made my night vision go away because it seemed like for the past eleven years it rarely left me. Only when Jasper was in with the bluelamp, and when that happened I didn't want to see normally.

The little boys upstairs thumped and bumped around like little boys do. Sometimes I could hear them playing with one another and that sent a small flicker of emotion to my chest. I no longer felt happy, relieved or even sad... so all I could describe it as is just feeling *something*, something different than the null and void that was me now.

I wish when I was a little boy I'd had a friend. A friend that I didn't have to kill or one that didn't want to kill me. Though those dreams were long dead, like my dreams that one day someone would come here and find me. I didn't even think of that now, it wasn't in the vocabulary of my head. This was all I knew and not once in the past seven years did I imagine being out in the daylight. The only things I missed out there were my crows and...

I looked over at Crow, grinning at me with his eyes squinted.

... and I had my own crow now anyway.

I heard Jasper leave the next morning to get the newest boy he was going to abuse. I could hear the boys upstairs talking to him and even one of them say goodbye. Though when he left I could hear the distinct sound of chains rattling and I knew they were locked and secure.

Or so I thought... the day after Jasper left I started hearing little voices coming from the stairs behind my white door. I was inside of my own head flying around the world with Crow, visiting the fantasy books I had read and becoming one with the characters. The sounds of them trying the door handle brought me back.

"It's unlocked... go on. Do it!"

"No... Jasper says he'll kill us."

"He's chained up, he can't reach us. Wasn't he chained when Jasper brought you down here?"

"Yeah... but..."

"We dared you, Juni, you don't have a choice."

The door handle turned again, and a moment later, it opened. A little black-haired boy peeked through, one with dirt stained on his face and tangly black hair like mine was.

When he saw me he gasped and quickly retracted his head.

"I saw him!"

I was a sideshow now I guess. Well, I was a monster after all.

One of the blond-haired ones peeked through the door to get his own look at me and, like the one named Juni, he withdrew his head and said in a hushed voice, "He looked right at me."

Well maybe I could use this for my own advantage. "Will one of you bring me some books? Perhaps a candle I can read by?" My voice was so dry I could barely speak, it sounded like two pieces of sandpaper rubbing together.

The three boys exchanged surprised quips and the blond-haired one looked through the door again. "You can speak?"

I nodded but I wanted new books to read more than I wanted to talk to them. Even though it had happened years ago, I still relived the moment I had killed Cooper regularly. These little boys... I didn't know what to make of them because I...

I so dearly wanted to murder them.

My eyes closed and I shook my head. I tried to push those thoughts out of my mind. They knew not to come near me. I just wanted some books.

"Yes, will you bring me some books to read?"

More quiet discussions.

"Jasper says if we go near him he'll kill us..."

"You can throw them onto my bed, you'll not be in grabbing range," I said to them. "Jasper hasn't given me anything new to read in years."

Juni got his first wave of bravery and walked through the door. The little boy about Cooper's age had his hands behind his back.

"Books and candles?" He turned around and looked at me.

I nodded. "It would be appreciated, yes." Though I didn't need a candle to read, I wanted something more efficient for when I wanted to burn myself.

Juni disappeared out the doorm and as he pattered up the steps, the two blond ones poked their heads out and stared at me like the carnival attraction I was.

"Why are your eyes red?" one of them asked, perhaps only seven or eight... the age I was at the time I was taken.

I had been so small. How did Jasper not tear these little boys in two? How had he not done it to me?

"Because Jasper made me bleed so much... the blood went into my eyes," I said to him, then looked past him to the other ones. "Jasper hasn't chained you?"

The two boys shook their heads. "No, why would he?"

I stared at them. "You're bought as slaves?"

They nodded.

I wouldn't argue with that logic, perhaps knowing they were slaves were what was best. I had been free, I had tasted freedom, and look what imprisonment and constant abuse had done to me?

"Are you a slave?" the younger of the boys asked.

I shook my head no.

"What are you then?"

"A monster," I replied blandly. Beside me Crow laughed at this. I looked over at him smiling at me, laughing sometimes for reasons I didn't know.

"You are so much more than a monster, *mihi*," Crow said quietly. He crawled onto the bed and kissed my forehead.

"No," I said with a shake of my head. "I know what I am."

"Who's he talking to?"

"Jasper says he's crazy and talks to make-believe people."

Crow kissed my forehead again and I closed my eyes. I let my friend slowly draw his fingers down my arm, and relaxed under his touch.

I heard little footsteps on the stairs but I tuned them out and let Crow run his tongue down to the side of my neck. His soft growls in my ear sounding almost like a content cat purring.

Though as soon as I felt the stiffness again I pulled back and opened my eyes.

Those same eyes widened when I saw Juni right in front of me, in grabbing distance. He was holding in his hand a little white stick candle and a fat novel without the cover.

In grabbing distance…

Crow wanted him; he whispered at me to snatch him and eat him raw.

But I pushed my nefarious urges away and stared back at him.

Juni held the items out to me; his face holding no expression but I saw a flicker of fear inside of his eyes.

Trusting me completely he let me gently take the book and the candle out of his hand before taking a step back.

"Thank you," I said to him quietly.

"You're welcome, Mr. Sanguine," Juni said back and smiled at me, then he walked out the white door.

The boys left me alone after that, I could hear them banging around upstairs. I occupied myself finding things to burn, though with the metal collar around my neck and the anchor secure on the wall, there really wasn't much to use. Just the mattress, blankets, the edge of my bathroom bucket, Barry, the candle…

I picked up the candle and started flicking the lighter to light it.

My brow furrowed as nothing but sparks came. I shook the lighter and held it to my ear before tossing it up in the air a few times.

I sighed. I think it was out. I flicked it a few more times before turning it upside down. I ran my thumb raw trying to flick it.

Flick flick

Flick

Nothing... meh.

Though something odd was happening... my fingers were getting warm, and not just from the raw burning that was a result from spinning that flint wheel. They felt like I had held matches to them but I hadn't.

"Make them burn more."

I looked over at Crow who was smiling at me. He reached over and grabbed my hands and started pinching my fingers. "Make them burn more, Sanguine."

Make them burn more? I couldn't do that. I let Crow play with my fingers, taking each dirty, twig-like digit into his hand to roll them around his own cold fingers.

Then I heard Jasper's voice and the sounds of the kids greeting him. I scowled at this and felt a jab in my gut. I'd had a couple days free of being fucked or hearing the kids scream – I'd enjoyed it.

My mood darkened and I turned away from the boarded up window I couldn't see out of anyway. I looked back at Crow and pursed my lips as I saw him start to lick and suck on my fingers.

"None of that, not even from you," I said. I tried to withdraw my fingers but I felt them frozen in Crow's mouth.

No, not frozen – they were getting hotter.

My eyes fixed on him, fanning the flames of awe inside of my chest as I watched his mouth move up and down on each finger, sending heat into the tips of whatever digit was between his lips. When he withdrew his mouth and went to the next finger the heat was still there.

They were burning... like they were on fire.

When he moved to my left hand I raised my right and wiggled my fingers back and forth. Then, as if in a trance, I picked up the half-smoked cigarette I had left from blowing Jasper and pinched it between my fingers.

There was no explanation for what happened next...

With a puff of smoke and the smell of burning tobacco... a small flame burst from the cigarette, followed by a red ember,

Riding on the same awe now mixed in with incomprehensible shock I dropped the cigarette and stared at my fingers.

They weren't smoking but there was ash on the tips. I lowered my hand down to the blankets and focused my mind to try and make it happen again.

Smoke started to erupt from my fingers and soon I saw the faint flicker of light around the tips. I quickly recoiled my hand and to my own shock... I laughed.

Though the laugh was more like the cross between a dry gasp and a cough, I don't think I knew how to laugh anymore.

"What's so funny?"

My hands snapped back and I kicked the covers away from the now distinct burn mark. I glanced over at Jasper in the door way.

"Nothing," I rasped.

I heard him sniff and I knew I was in for it. "What the fuck were you burning? I told you to be careful with that..."

Then he paused and I heard footsteps come closer. I looked at the wall and only looked towards him when I saw his hand pick something up.

Shit, it was the candle stick.

Jasper smacked me on the head, once... then twice. "How the fuck did you get this?" He hit me again, making my ears ring and my eyes temporarily blur. I squinted them and held my head but again he hit me, this time making me bite my tongue.

"Found it..." I said.

Jasper growled and with one last hit, this one making me sway to the point where I had to hold myself up, I heard him call the boys downstairs.

I spat blood on the bed and glared at Jasper. The chain on my neck rattled as I tried to back as far away from him as I could.

Though my head was swimming so badly I didn't make it far before I had to stop and try and get my mind to go back into my head. Jasper's punches were nothing to fuck with, he always hit me right in the head and it shot the consciousness out of me. Add that to my already weak state, I was starting to feel my mind dip into darkness.

The boys walked downstairs. Juni poked his head through first... looking terrified.

"Who fucking gave him a candle stick?" Jasper barked. "Where's Lyle and Levi?"

"B-behind me... I..." Juni grabbed onto the door frame and stared at the ground. "I gave it to him, Jasper."

Juni yelped as Jasper flung the candle stick at him; it connected with the boy's forehead making his head snap back. The little boy stumbled a few paces before he slid down to the ground, sobs coming from his lowered face.

I started to growl. Jasper heard me and whirled around, this time punching me in the face with a well-aimed blow.

And I lost it.

With a snarl of rage I lunged at Jasper, but he was quick and he knew how far my chain went. My captor, my abuser, and my rapist jerked back before turning around and laughing right in my face.

I swung my arms trying so badly to get at him but I just barely grazed him. He was only a half-fucking-inch from my face and I couldn't get him. Crow and I couldn't get him.

"Make it a fair fight!" I suddenly snarled, feeling Crow's bravery inside of me again. I was so frustrated I thought I was going to explode. "Make it a fair fight, Jasper! Unchain us!"

Jasper laughed which infuriated me more. I pulled as hard as I could on the chain around my neck and screamed so loudly it was all that I could hear, all I could feel. My own manic and crazed voice boomed throughout the basement and sunk into my bones. I was losing it, I think I was…

I was finally losing it.

"Come closer!" I screamed, tears starting welling in my eyes. I was so frustrated, so angry. I don't know what set me off, whether I had reached my point and I was finally fighting back – or if it was seeing Juni hurt for doing something I asked of him. "Come closer, you fucking coward!"

Jasper's laugh pierced me, his laugh felt more like rape than the very act itself. Jasper got almost nose to nose with me and sneered. "You fucking animal, look at you. You're nothing but a useless, fucking monster. I should get a reward for chaining you like the demon-dog you are. Who are you today, you pathetic lunatic. Crow? Sami? Are we Sanguine today? Who's the one I fuck, huh? Did you name him? Because I just call him my little bitch."

"FUCK YOU!" I shrieked, more tears spilling from my face. "Fuck you!" I tried to swing at him again but I only got air.

"Stay by the door, boys," Jasper said, turning around. I looked behind him and saw three pairs of eyes staring at us, shocked and stunned.

Jasper walked over and picked up one of the wooden table legs, one I had played with as a child and hit myself with as a teen. I ground my teeth and glared at him as he smacked the wooden leg against his hand and shook his head at me.

He turned to the boys. "This is what happens if you disobey me – this is what happens if you piss me off."

Suddenly Jasper whirled around and swung the table leg. It hit me right across the face, filling my mouth with blood and knocking out most of my senses.

Desperately I tried to grab onto my quickly unravelling mind so I could fight back, but my world was crashing around me. My head felt like a thunderstorm, everything was roaring, everything was loud

I felt another hit, this time on my shoulder.

My mouth was open as the blood poured out. I took in a sharp inhale to try and fill my lungs but only breathed in my own blood and saliva. The world was fading into dark around me, darkness and the smell of copper – old friends of mine.

Then I saw Jasper trip – no, he didn't trip – as Jasper fell on top of me I saw little hands on Jasper's back. I looked and saw a flash of blond for a split second before my mind shot back to me.

I was weak but having Jasper in reach awakened the person stirring inside and around me. Like a crocodile feeling prey brush its jaws Crow came. Crow came and filled me with the energy and drive I needed to fight back.

Crow looked on as I grabbed Jasper's shoulder and sank my teeth into the fleshy part of his underarm. I clawed and held onto his jacket and thrashed as much as I could. Like an animal I threw my head back and forth as I growled through my locked teeth, trying to take as much of him as I could.

I tore the flesh away and went back for more, needing more… needing every inch of his body near me so I could eat him alive, and I would. I would devour him; I would destroy him. I would… I could… I…

Without me realizing what he was doing, Jasper slipped out of his jacket, the one I had been grabbing onto. I threw it aside and lunged at him again, his strip of chewed skin dropping from my open mouth, but he was already out of reach.

Then to my horror he picked up the wooden table leg and turned around.

The three boys gasped and tried to run up the stairs but Jasper chased them. He grabbed one of the blond ones and yanked him back and swung him so far he skidded across the dirty floor and slammed into the wall by the window.

"No, no it wasn't him, it was me!" one of them screamed. The older one ran back down the stairs, tears streaming down his face. "I did it, it was me!"

Jasper's eyes were blazing; his chest heaving up and down. He was in an insane rage I had never seen him in before.

Jasper glared at the boy and brandished the wooden table leg at him. "You did it, huh? You think you're brave? This is what happens to brave boys."

"NO!" I screamed as Jasper swung the table leg up over his head and with all of his force, he struck the younger of the boys. It hit the side of his face, dislocating his jaw and smashing his gums to the point where I saw the fissure open inside of his mouth.

A roaring filled my head, a burning deep inside that drew me into desperate insanity. I screamed. I lunged at him. I clawed the air as Jasper lifted up the table leg again and smashed it down on the boy's head, opening up the fragile skull just above the ear, spraying blood all over the concrete wall, him, me, and the little boy's older brother.

The violent emotions boiled me alive. And the frustration of being the chained beast that I was, was driving me further and further to the brink. With Crow egging me on I threw myself against the chain again and again as Jasper beat on the boy's now dead body, all for the pure pleasure of hearing his older brother scream and cry.

Again… I lunged… and again. I lunged and lunged until the breath left my throat and the screams became manic howls. I tore at nothing and achieved nothing. I was helpless – I was helpless.

Jasper, panting from the effort of murdering the young boy, looked at me and sneered his face like he was smelling something awful.

"Juni, start helping me bring the box down I have strapped to the trike," Jasper said darkly, glaring me down with a smug look. The same expression any coward had when they were looking at a dangerous, but chained, animal. "I think Sami has had enough freedom."

I growled at him; I didn't turn my burning gaze away.

Jasper looked behind him. "Juni!" he snapped.

Levi was crying by the door frame but he wasn't moving… and Juni wasn't there either.

"Juni!" Jasper screamed, his voice insane with anger. He made a frustrated noise before turning back to me.

He swung the table leg hard, cracking me right over the side of the head.

And I blacked out.

When I woke up, I was inside of a box and I could barely move.
It was locked with several air holes beside where my head was laying.
It was dark and I was trapped, in complete mind-numbing darkness.
All alone.
All alone in what I knew was my coffin.
With *Daisy Daisy* playing beside one of the air holes.
Over and over
Over again.

CHAPTER 17

Nero

NERO STEPPED INTO THE REMAINS OF WHAT USED TO be a mall and placed a large spotted cat, about the size of a small cougar, onto the ground.

The cat, a crossbreed of a serval and an ocelot called a kitner, smelled the air; its striped tail swishing behind it. It flexed its big bat-like ears and looked behind it for its signal.

"Search for Sanguine," Nero said to it, a cigar in his mouth and travelling goggles on his head. With a fleeting glance at the big cat he leaned up against a row of dusty payphones and took a long inhale of his cigar.

This mall was in good condition, the roof was solid and the only debris on the floor was the push paneling from the roof and a few broken florescent lights. Though everything was covered in dust, it was undisturbed dust, suggesting that no one had been here since the Fallocaust.

But that was expected, Nero was so far north he was rubbing shoulders with the plaguelands and this place had only recently became safe enough for humans.

He dashed the cigar ash onto the ground, before he started walking around the vast and open building. Shops lined the walls on the first floor, and behind a kiosk full of brittle papers and old cell phone cases, he saw a double escalator that led to a second floor with even more shops and kiosks. There were even the remains of a fountain though it was stained black now and had an old pay-per-use massage chair in it.

Nero walked over to the chair and made it upright. He sat in it with a sigh and leaned back.

He saw Ceph looking in an old video game store, his own cigar hanging from his mouth.

Over the last seven years that boy, now very much a man, had become his significant other and now the greywastes weren't the same without his auburn-haired partner by his side.

"You look so stressed, puppy," Ceph said, his voice held sympathetic tones that he used only on his partner.

Nero shrugged and glanced over at the kitner cat, named Pickles by young Drake, and saw the spotted cat slip quietly into one of the mall shops. He said nothing but the expression on his face told Ceph volumes.

Ceph walked over with a smile, and caringly rubbed Nero's shoulders.

"Every year… I see your shoulders slump more and your hope slip…"

"You're seeing things. My hope hasn't fucking 'slipped', stop talking like Elish," Nero said annoyed. He got up and roughly tossed the massage chair back on its side, then stalked over to an old Kodak store. He started roughly rooting through it.

"Nuuky…" Ceph sighed, calling Nero the nickname that was his and only his, and also a nickname Ceph didn't dare use with any of their brothers around. "It's been eleven years…"

"We talked about this already, shut up and help me look. If you're not going to help me look, go wait in the fucking plane," Nero snapped. He picked up an old camera before throwing it onto the ground. After sneezing from the dust he stalked over to the back room and started kicking around boxes with his feet, looking for any sign that someone had stayed there.

Even if I find evidence that is years old… it'll be something.

It will be something.

Why can't I find something?

"He's dead, babe."

Nero whirled around and balled his fist. He was tempted to punch Ceph in the mouth, but he had been trying to control himself around his boyfriend since breaking his jaw last year.

So instead Nero threw a few more cameras at the wall.

"Just keep looking, okay?" Nero chucked an old camera lens at the mall windows, though the windows had broken under a warped frame so it flew right through, eventually landing beside the cell phone case kiosk. "I take one damn month a year to look for him, I'm not asking the world."

"I know," Ceph said quietly. "I'm sorry… I just hate seeing you like this. Every year I'm watching you get more and more sad during these trips. I don't fucking like it, okay?"

Nero walked out of the Kodak shop and was about to look into an Orange Julius restaurant but Pickles was already coming out of it so there was no use. The kitner knew Sanguine's scent and he would tell them if Sanguine had been here.

"He's a chimera… he's alive," Nero said in a firm tone. "He's just… I don't know, the greywastes are big. He's probably shut up in a house with five hot guys getting his cock polished every night."

Ceph chuckled and rubbed Nero's shoulder. "I can't believe the little tiger would be nineteen now."

"*Is* nineteen," Nero corrected. "He *is* nineteen…"

"Yeah, Nuuky, he is nineteen," Ceph said with a sad smile, though behind that smile there was still the churning oceans of doubt. Like their master King Silas, like Elish, Ellis, everyone who knew about Sanguine there was no longer a hope that the red-eyed chimera was alive. King Silas had even started talking about making a new clone of him though he had smartly decided to not mention this around Nero.

Nero had been encased in concrete for three months four years ago for attacking Silas during a heated argument about Sanguine. Nero had lost it on him like he did every few years over his decision to send the boy into the greywastes. Finally it escalated to the point where Nero laid a punch right to the side of the king's head, killing him. And for his punishment Nero spent the next several months in cold isolation.

It was worth it, Nero said darkly to himself. *I am loyal to my king but like all of us – sometimes things had to be said and sometimes they had to be said with fists.*

After an hour Nero copped this mall up to time wasted. He walked out into the greywastes with Ceph behind him and Pickles sniffing an old concrete planter, now just a shell full of greyash. They walked towards the Falconer parked beside a shopping cart coral, kicking rocks for the cat as they did.

When they were up in the air Nero pulled out an old worn piece of paper and carefully unfolded it.

He smirked at the drawing of him and Sanguine with the celldwellers. He had kept it in his wallet for eleven years now. It was dog-eared and faded but it was still his connection to the little red-eyed brat he had grown attached to.

I had only known him for a few hours but... but he was family. He might fade into the background for eleven months out of the year but once a year – once 1 year I took time off and looked for him for the entire month.

Since no one else was fucking looking.

And Nero was immortal now, forever stuck at thirty-three, he could look for the next seventy years if he wanted to.

I'll stop looking when he's died of old age... how's that?

"Well we have a couple more days but this day is at an end, want to stop at Melchai for a drink?" Ceph asked. He was flying the plane high over the greywastes, the darkness falling on the both of them.

"Yeah, they have a great meth supply there too..." Nero mumbled. "I think I need to get high tonight and fuck you for a few hours. I've just been on edge all day."

"Really? I couldn't tell."

Nero gave him a dirty look but Ceph only smiled at him back, before leaning in and puckering his lips.

Then the young chimera closed his eyes and made a pursing sound in such a comical way Nero had to hide the smile.

What an ass... well, he's my ass. Nero grudgingly leaned towards his boyfriend and kissed him before smacking his cheek with his hand. "Now fly the plane, dipshit."

Ceph smiled smugly and gave Nero a grin and a wink. "Wanna kidnap us a nice perky little teen and give him some post-traumatic stress?"

Nero laughed at this and shook his head. "We'll see what the meth does to me. I might just send you out to get us a boy though, rough-fucking screaming fifteen year olds is a good stress reliever, isn't it?"

Ceph nodded vigorously. "Fuck, I don't think anything will top fucking Ares and Siris though. How old are they now?"

"Almost eleven, we have over four years before we can start stalking their footsteps. I'd die if we can break them in but something tells me Silas would have my head if we took twin virgins from him. Though if I know our family they're probably going to break each other in first. Apollo and Artemis were pros with each other before Silas even got a taste of them."

"Those two are so hot!" Ceph groaned. "We should call 'em over when we get home. Why don't we fuck them more often!?"

Nero snorted. "We can fuck them whenever you want, puppy. I'll bring you anyone you know that. Well, except Elish… you've seen him at our family gatherings, he never bottoms. He'll fuck all of us once he's got some ressin in him but I think he only lets Silas top him and that's only cause he has to."

"Yeah, but you have before right?"

"Before the stick up his ass stopped me."

Ceph burst out laughing to the point where Nero wondered if he should take control of the plane. Though eventually the auburn-haired chimera gathered himself, however he had to wipe several tears from his face.

He had become quite the handsome guy that was for sure. Cepherus Dekker had grown out of his Hawaiian shirts and cowlicks (buzz cut now) and usually dressed in a normal t-shirt and cargos like Nero did. With his burly, muscular body and a firm, square face, he was every inch a brute chimera, but had retained his teenager-like attitude which Nero found refreshing.

Ceph wasn't trying to be someone he wasn't. He never tried to be tough and he never tried to hide what he was feeling. In the Legion it seemed everyone was putting on a show of being a hardass, but Ceph was just Ceph and perhaps that's what had caught Nero's eye.

And his full acceptance and encouragement of ravaging teenagers, even if that involved kidnap and rape, didn't hurt either. He was a wonderful little sadist with a bloodthirsty streak that made Nero's cock throb. Though they only had eyes for each other there was an agreement that if the opportunity presented itself, have a good time with it and if you can… bring some home for daddy.

They landed the plane in the same abandoned park they always used and walked out with Pickles on a leash to keep him from eating the residents' dogs. Though instead of drawing a crowd and demanding where Sanguine was they walked through with only a few sideways glances from the newcomers. For a month every year they spent their nights in Melchai or some of the other surrounding blocks and free towns. They knew the mayor and the important residents and they expected them every year now. Nero spent money on hookers when kidnapping a twink was too much effort, plus they bought all their supplies and alcohol from the shops and bars, so they were treated like the royalty they were when they were in town.

Nero glanced over and saw a small boy with black hair rooting through a trashcan.

He's Sangy's age when I first saw him, Nero said to himself. The skinny boy with dirt on his face and an obvious wound on his forehead was a sight to be seen, obviously half-starved and in need of a good meal.

But he wasn't Sanguine, he was just another grubby greywaster kid, so Nero moved on.

Though he noticed the kid was watching him. Nero glanced over and gave the boy a hard look.

"Got something to say, son?" Nero asked in a cold and authoritative tone.

The boy flinched at Nero's words before shaking his head and disappearing behind the house he was scrounging in front of.

Nero and Ceph, with Pickles behind them, went into the bar and ordered themselves a bottle of vodka each and a pitcher of greywaste beer. Greywaste beer tasted like dog piss mixed with cat piss but it was better than nothing and it got the job done. The two of them settled in with their alcohol and sent the waiter to the restaurant area for some rat meat sandwiches and a half-case of Dunkaroos they saw advertised.

"I've never had Dunkaroos. What are they?" Ceph cocked an eyebrow.

Nero chuckled. "They must've found a box in a building or something. It's just cookies with icing for dipping. I'm sure the icing tastes like stale shit but that's all they have here… whatever they scavenged that week."

Ceph looked intrigued, and when the six packs of Dunkaroos came he looked downright mesmerized.

"We have to make Apollo invent these again," Ceph said, tearing off the top of the blue package. He looked down at the cookies and the container of white icing with rainbow bits and his eyes lit up.

Nero smiled though he tried to hide it. He watched his boyfriend eagerly dip the cookie into the icing and pop it into his mouth.

Ceph beamed. "This shit is good! Let's force Miky to make us some of this. I mean that little ball buster can make cookies and icings cupcakes so let's combine the two? We'll call 'em Cepharoos."

The laugh became a suppressed chuckle. Nero took a cookie and popped it into his mouth. "Alright, puppy. We'll harass Apollo once we get home and make him invent Cepharoos… you fucking wing nut."

"Fucking sweet," Ceph said through a mouthful of cookies. In a classic chimera manner he washed the cookies down with a shot of vodka and shook his head with a satisfied gasp as it disappeared down his throat.

"No beggars inside here. Get lost, kid."

Nero and Ceph looked towards the voice and saw the bartender giving the doorway to the pub an annoyed look. They craned their heads farther and saw the same black-haired boy standing awkwardly beside a jukebox.

"I'm… I'm not a beggar…" the boy said in a small voice.

"You got money on you?"

"No…"

"Then you're a fucking beggar, now get lost before I call the warden," the bartender said angrily.

Nero went back to his beer when behind him the little voice said, "I need to talk to the legionaries."

Nero and Ceph exchanged glances before they both turned to the kid.

"Maybe he wants to become a legionary?" Ceph said with a bemused tone.

"They pay so they don't have to deal with grubby–"

"Let him in, Dorian. Hey, fucker, you wanna Dunkaroo?" Ceph called out. Nero turned around and gave him a look but Ceph only smiled, shaking a Dunkaroo container at the kid like he was tempting a cat with the treat bag.

Dorian the bartender stepped back with a soured look and the kid shyly walked over to them. As soon as he saw the Dunkaroo pack he ripped it open and started shovelling the cookies in his mouth.

"Jeez, he's starving… he's not even eating the icing." Ceph chewed on his rat meat burger. "What do you need, kid? You wanna be a legionary too?"

The kid didn't answer them and though Nero would've clapped him upside the head for not answering a legionary's question he realized that the kid was on the verge of starving to death and his brain was probably still in instinct mode.

Finally when he was done the crackers he put the plastic container down, breathing heavily since it seemed he had forgotten to breathe while eating. He looked up at the two of them and cowered down.

With a swallow, he shifted his feet. "I need help… please, I… I need help."

Nero took a drink of his beer before tearing off a piece of his rat burger for the kid. The small boy eagerly ate it in one swallow like he was a fucking duck.

"With what? I'm the Imperial General of the Legion and this is my partner and second-in-command, if some fucking dude smacked you around that's a bit below our duty," Nero said. He didn't have that much patience. It had been a long day and he just wanted to do some drugs and hammer a tight ass for a few hours. Not feed starving boys, and the possibly of having to play big brother.

"There's a man… northwest of here, he murdered a little boy right in front of me and he's killed others. He has a monster chained in his basement and he's starving the monster, and he's… he's doing bad things to all of us," the boy said in a small voice. "My friend Levi, he – he's in there, back there with him."

Nero stared at him and shrugged. The kid's face fell.

"Look, it's been a long day, kid. Just be happy you got out of there alive, your friend is probably dead there anyway," Nero said. "That's the greywastes, buddy, friends die and they die a lot."

The boy's large eyes stared at Nero and he could see them glisten. "He's going to lock Levi downstairs with the monster. He says Sanguine's already killed–"

Nero didn't hear the rest of the boy's words, his ears had succumb to a roaring noise that filled his entire brain with a hot red haze. With automatic movements he grabbed Pickles' leash, took the kid by the shoulder, and started leading him outside.

"He has a monster in his basement?" Nero's voice was twisted. He couldn't believe what had just come out of the kid's mouth. Did he hear it right? What if he had misheard… he had already had a few shots of vodka.

"Yeah," the boy said. "Are you going to help Levi?"

"This monster… is he a monster because he has red eyes and pointed teeth?" Nero asked. Ceph was jogging in front of them with the plane's keys in his hand; he had said nothing to Nero, he knew not to talk to him right now.

When the kid nodded Nero felt his face go hot. Without a word he picked the kid up and started running down the street towards where they had parked the plane.

"Call Silas," Nero yelled to Ceph but as his boyfriend turned around he saw he was already on his remote phone.

They jumped onto the plane and Nero set the kid down on the co-pilot's chair. He leaned back as Ceph put the keys into the ignition before starting the plane, keeping one ear open to listen to his boyfriend's conversation with their king.

While Ceph was talking they rose higher into the air, the black-haired kid looking out the window in shocked awe, seeing the twinkling lights of Melchai become smaller and smaller.

"What direction? Where's he?" Nero demanded. "What gate did you come in from?"

"South, the south gate..." the boy stuttered; he looked stunned but that wasn't important. "It took me a week to walk here... it's been two weeks since I was there, no one will help me."

"South gate..." Nero murmured. "We had the Legion check the south years ago..." What would one week walking be compared to a Falconer?

"I need more details, kid. Where's his house?" Nero asked harshly, making the boy's eyes widen. Though he didn't care, if the kid was scared he would have to deal with it.

"It's a farm. It's all out in the open but I passed an Esso gas station and I passed a big white truck that had red spray paint on it..." the boy replied.

Nero's jaw tightened, all of this was well and fine but they were flying a plane and the greywastes were swallowed up in darkness below them.

"Okay, Silas is still overseeing the repairs on Cardinalhall. We're lucking out he's bringing the Charger plane," Ceph said, handing the remote phone back to Nero. "He's already got a location from the Falconer's tracking chip and he says to land now and he'll find us."

Nero's hands clenched on the throttle of the Falconer and he swore under his breath. "I don't want to fucking wait for Silas, I want to go now."

Ceph put a hand on his shoulder; they all felt the Falconer start to descend. "The Charger's fast and it has the night vision and heat sensors on it. We couldn't find the house in this darkness. Cardinalhall isn't too far away anyway, I doubt he'll take more than half an hour."

"He... he just bought some bosen," the boy said suddenly. "He bought two of them. He has a meth making place inside of his barn and he uses that money to buy us and the big cows."

Ceph snapped his fingers. "That's it, that's how we'll find them. The bosen will show up on the heat sensor scope."

"Lots of greywasters around here have bosen…"

"Yeah, but if we know there are only two…"

Tension and frustration was starting to eat Nero piece by piece, there were so many things that had to go right tonight and even more things that depended on either shoddy information or the memory of a kid. He felt like lashing out and finding something to shoot, but he had to remain calm.

So Nero landed the plane and lit an opiate cigarette, no one spoke as he took deep inhales.

The lights of the Falconer shone onto the greywaste ground, to his left Nero could see the outline of a store and some parked cars now shells from the elements. Everything else was darkness, not even his night vision helped him; as soon as artificial light got to a certain point his enhanced sight switched off.

Finally they heard the Charger plane overhead. Nero grabbed the boy's arm and the kitner, and all four of them walked out of the Falconer and into the night air.

The Charger's engine slayed the dead tranquility of the greywastes, filling everyone's ears with a roaring noise so loud Nero felt the boy cling to his hip. He looked down at the little black-haired boy and made a face of annoyance, though it was endearing in a way so he put a hand on the kid's head.

The lights inside turned on as soon as the plane touched the greywastes. Nero opened the door and was met with Silas and a legionary solider.

Silas's face was stern; he was in king mode. He looked behind him and nodded at the legionary who immediately got off the plane and onto the Falconer.

Nero handed him Pickles' leash and turned to Silas.

"We're all going together," Silas said authoritatively, before his eyes travelled down to the boy. "What's your name?"

"Juni," the boy replied in a small voice that was barely audible over the planes' engines.

"And you're sure? Lying to the king is punishable by death… you say his name is Sanguine? He has red eyes and pointed teeth?" Silas asked him.

The boy nodded, still clinging to Nero with weak but determined little hands.

Silas's face darkened and the lines only deepened when he made eye contact with Nero.

"He's been locked in a man's basement," Nero said, trying to mask the coldness his own voice was carrying. The wounds he had been nursing for years over Silas's decisions regarding Sanguine were slowly being torn open.

"Then let us get him, love." Silas smiled before turning around and re-boarding the plane, leaving Nero to seethe by himself.

He turned to Ceph, looking to him for some emotional backup, but his boyfriend's smiling face offered little in the way of sympathies. Ceph was just happy that they had found Sanguine but Nero couldn't get past the conditions the boy seemed to have been staying in.

That was a thought for another day though, first things first they actually had to find the boy. So Nero, with Juni's shoulder in his hand, got onto the Charger plane with Ceph and soon they were in the air heading northwest.

In front of the control panel was a seven inch television screen showing the greywastes below them. Everything that had heat showed up like a brilliant light and the objects grey shadows. Right off the bat Nero could see orbs of radrats and croaches, and as they drove over a small neighbourhood, he even saw a hunting carracat with her kittens.

Juni was leaning beside Silas's chair and was staring intently at the screen, everyone was quiet as the boy looked, holding their breath for the moment the kid saw something he recognized.

"I walked past that!" the boy exclaimed after five minutes of flying. "That's the Esso, just keep going straight from the back of the building, I walked to the back of the building keep going straight."

Kids give such shit instructions. Nero's eyes narrowed. He sat on the edge of the co-pilot's chair and wiped his hands down his face.

Then a cigarette popped into his vision, already lit, he took it with a muttered thanks to Ceph and started immediately smoking it.

"You're probably the first little boy in all of the greywastes to fly in this plane, son," Nero said to Juni. "Bet you can't wait to tell your family that, eh?"

Juni looked surprised that Nero was talking to him. "Levi will get to fly too. He's my only family."

"You're a slave, right?" Nero asked.

Juni nodded. "I wasn't born a slave though. Jasper killed my daddy when Dad was trying to steal his meth. He took me after. Levi's a born-slave though."

"No other family?"

Juni shook his head.

Past him, Silas smiled. While he pressed several buttons on the Charger's screen he said to the boy, "I am your owner now, young one. If you are indeed partly responsible for bringing us to my beloved little creation you will be well-rewarded with a good life. Would you like to live in royalty?"

Juni looked like he didn't know how to answer that question. "In Skyfall?"

Though before Silas could answer, the boy pointed to the screen. "That… that's Jasper's barn. See? See there? His house is… there it is, that's his house, that's Jasper's house."

"Ceph… start loading us up some guns." Silas's tone suddenly dropped, like a hot ember landing in cold arctic waters Nero could see the bright fire inside of his king switch to a cold, emotionless, slab of ice.

There were no more light conversations and no more questions. Nero got up and walked to the back of the plane, and started loading their assault rifles.

"Okay, little man," Ceph said when the plane was starting to land. "We're going to keep the plane on and you're going to be the pilot until we get back, alright?"

Juni's eyes widened and his face paled in a way that suggested he was taking Ceph more seriously than he should.

"You're going to take this handgun and protect this plane from the bad guys… but don't fucking step a foot outta this plane or we'll leave your little ass behind, gotcha?" Ceph handed the boy the handgun, the boy's wrist buckled under the weight.

Nero helped Ceph strap on his combat armour, though his boyfriend growled at him when he put on the helmet. But unlike Nero, Ceph wasn't immortal, so his complaining was in vain.

"Ready, Kingsly?" Nero called as they all piled outside. By now the air was full of electricity, an invisible current that every chimera could feel brush up against their skin.

"I want him alive."

Nero looked to his side and saw Silas's face, cold as granite but his eyes were bright. He looked over at Nero and nodded. "Don't kill him, love. That will be too easy, are we understood?"

Nero nodded and so did Ceph, and with that the three of them started walking towards the house.

There was a middle-aged man with curly black hair standing on the porch, but the moment he saw King Silas, Nero, and Ceph he turned and ran back inside.

"Get him, Ceph!" Nero barked and on that command Ceph's heavy boots could be heard even over the plane's engine. The brute chimera jumped onto the porch and immediately went inside. Nero and Silas quickly followed.

Nero's nose wrinkled as soon as he stepped inside the disgusting house, it smelled like putrid meat and garbage. His eyes scanned the first floor of the house, hearing the man's yelling and swearing coming from one of the back rooms.

Then they both saw the stairs, cautiously and with their guns out, they walked down the concrete stairs, leading to a white door with a thick metal padlock on it. But the padlock was without its lock so they pushed the door open and peeked inside.

The smell seemed to sodomize Nero's nostrils, it smelled of rotting blood, human waste, and it looked like something out of a horror movie. The walls were covered in paintings of birds that, from the looks of it, were painted with blood, and the floors were covered in trash and even more blood stains.

There a dirty mattress in the corner too, also stained with blood with barely any white showing and behind it a short but thick chain anchored to the concrete wall.

But where was Sanguine?

"Boy?" Silas suddenly said. Nero looked to the corner of the room and was surprised to see a little blond boy, completely naked, sitting beside a long wooden box with a bear in his lap.

"That's Sanguine's fucking bear!" Nero's voice caught in his throat. He walked over to the boy who had already started backing himself up into the corner of the room.

"We're here to rescue you... Levi?" Silas's tone shifted to the same one he used when he was talking to one of the chimera children. The delicate and almost encouraging tones that seemed to resonate with the younger ones.

The boy's eyes widened with a look of disbelief; he shifted back further and clutched the bear to his chest. "No one rescues us… I'm just… just a slave." His face crumpled and he looked past Nero and Silas. They looked behind them too and saw the decomposing remains of who Nero knew must be his little brother.

"Where's Sanguine?" Nero asked him, getting down on one knee and clipping his cape off of his back.

Levi pointed to the long box and let Nero put the cape around him. "I played him the song a lot, he's in the box… Jasper says he's to die in there but I fed him a little."

Nero looked at the wooden box that resembled more of a coffin and grabbed onto the edge of it. He got a good hold and wrenched it up.

The sounds of nails scraping against wood could be heard, mixed in with the shouting and screaming upstairs, but when Nero saw Sanguine in the box all the noises that were around him disappeared.

Sanguine wasn't Sanguine anymore.

The critically malnourished man was crumpled up in himself, staring blankly at the side of the box. He was so skinny his scarred arms looked like broomstick handles, and his face gaunt and hollow to such an unbelievable level he looked like the photos the media took when the Second Cold War was at its worst, right before Silas ended the world. The sunken faces of skeletons that still held breath, but were alive in an organic sense only. And it looked like this little boy, once so full of life, was in a similar state.

And his injuries… Sanguine was covered in bruises of all colours, and the chafe marks around his neck were so worn in he looked like a stray dog with an embedded collar, his neck was nothing but a strip of scabbed brown skin that moved from the insects feeding on it.

He was bad, Sanguine was really bad.

"I hope you're proud of yourself," Nero whispered, his grip on the side of the wooden coffin tightening. "You fucking monster."

Nero saw Silas's lower lip tighten for just a moment, before he reached down and tried to put a hand on Sanguine's boney grey shoulder.

"Sanguine?" Silas whispered. "Get up, Sanguine."

Sanguine
Age 19

"Get up, Sanguine."

I was floating in water; I was surrounded by bright lights that flashed and waved around me like someone was twirling around a bluelamp. They stayed with me even when I opened my eyes, as did the voices of the men I saw in my delirium.

Though when I felt a hand on my shoulder my senses attempted to reach the parts of my brain not yet suspended in time-freezing madness. I found myself blinking and trying to move my head.

"I don't think he can move... can you pick him up?" one of them said.

Who were these... these people? Why are there people here?

I looked at them, my eyes feeling like two pieces of brittle paper, I attempted to blink again but there was no moisture to soothe them. Everything was dry and tight, and everything hurt.

Hands grabbed my shoulder and tried to tuck themselves under my body, inside of me Crow demanded that I thrash and bite, to stop Jasper from fucking me again but I was too weak – I had nothing left.

They talked in hushed voices... but no, this was nothing but another daydream and soon I would be flying again, swimming in waterless oceans and chasing the lights that came and went with each passing delusion.

That was my life, the end of my life as I waited for the Grim Reaper to remember that I was still alive. That he had failed at killing me those other times – but perhaps, perhaps... he would finally succeed.

I was in someone's arms. I saw clothing on him so much different than Jasper's greasy jacket and jeans.

"Who is he?" I asked Crow.

"I don't know, but I don't like it," Crow responded. "They're carrying you up the stairs; they're carrying you to the surface."

"Why? I am a celldweller..."

"I know."

"He's mumbling to himself."

"He has friends in his head."
Levi?

The door frame passed and the garbage-strewn main level was around me. My awareness was starting to trickle back but my mind was slow. Like I was walking through oil, it took a long time for my brain to process what was happening to me.

Then I saw him.

Jasper.

Jasper was on his knees, blood streaming down his nose and mouth. He was staring at me with such awed-hatred, I was surprised at the energy behind his look. Jasper had always seen me as nothing more than his sex slave, why was he angry at me? I didn't… I didn't…

Where are they taking me?

Where are they taking me?

I want to go back to my basement… I want to go…

"Let me down…" I rasped. "We need to go back, we need to go… basement?"

"No, you're never going there again," a voice said firmly. "Ceph, stay with him and we'll order the Falconer back around. I don't want that piece of shit travelling in the same plane as us."

Plane?

"NO!" I suddenly yelled. I started to try and thrash my body around but the person holding me locked his grip. "LET US GO!"

"Us?" a voice said curiously. "He said us…"

Desperation flooded my damaged brain, drowning out all the senses that told me to stay still and let them bring me out of this prison. The thought of having to go outside, out of my basement, filled me with such an anxiety it trumped all of my reasoning.

I started struggling and hard, and in that struggling I felt my only friend start to back my movements. Like Crow was breathing life into a dead corpse, he filled me with energy and poured fuel on the rage this situation brought with it.

"Holy shit." The man holding me dropped me as I whirled around and sunk my teeth into his shoulder. I landed on the floor and snarled at these men who were trying to take me away from my basement, my oasis, my only safe place. I took a step back, looking in all directions but as I looked around my mind became so confused and overwhelmed. I didn't know what direction I was supposed to go in.

"He's... what's going on with him?" a blond-haired one dressed in combat armour yelled at Jasper. When Jasper didn't answer a big man behind him kicked him in the back.

"He goes into these trances," Jasper coughed, blood sprinkled onto the garbage on the floor. I backed away and tried to find the stairs to the basement but I just saw old couches, the kitchen, half-eaten body parts...

"He flips out. He's mental... he has people inside his head he talks to. He's fucking crazy, I've been protecting the greywastes from him. I haven't done anything wrong," Jasper snapped.

In my anger I roughly shoved a pile of boxes down to the floor and bared my teeth at all of them. "Let me go!" I snarled. "I will eat every single fucking one of you, let me go back to my home!"

They were staring at me, closing in on me... I took another step back and felt my back hit one of Jasper's broken stoves. A low growl resonated from my throat and I continued to bare my teeth at them.

"Sanguine... Sami? Sami?" a man, muscular and thick with short black hair and odd purple-blue eyes, said to me. I looked at him and tried to glare him down but he wouldn't look away.

"Sami is dead!" I snapped at him.

"Sanguine... do you recognize me?" The man took a step closer to me and reached into his pocket. He pulled out a sheet of paper and started unfolding it.

"Remember Nero? Ellis and I set you up in a house... we battled celldwellers... I've come to get you, buddy." Nero's tone was kind, reassuring. It didn't fit the situation, I didn't understand it.

But what was he saying? My brain was a whirlpool of confusion, a toxic brown soup that bubbled and swirled so I couldn't focus my thoughts.

I had to focus... we have to listen, Crow.

'I trust no one,' Crow growled inside of my head. *'Rip out his fucking throat, Sanguine. They want to take you outside, they want to take you away from your home.'*

My head lowered in a challenge, but as it lowered I saw the piece of paper the man was holding out to me.

I remember that...

The entire room fell into a deafening but heavy silence as I reached out and took the piece of paper. I looked down and saw a crayon drawing, of two people and a human monster with long legs and arms.

I stared at it, and with my eyes going over every detail, I remembered when I sat down by a coffee table and drew it. I remember choosing carefully the colour combination for Nero's unique eyes.

Drawing my adventures with me and Nero. Adventures I would create and make up inside of my head when Jasper was on top of me. Memories I would replay again and again until it became too painful for me to remember the brief moments when I had friends.

"Nero?" my voice came out dead but it was my voice. As the realization came to me, the truth came to me.

"Yeah, buddy… it's Nero. I know you don't understand but… we're… we're your family and we've come to take you home," Nero said slowly. "You're one of us."

I looked at him, then behind him to the blond-haired man, and then to the other muscular person who had Jasper.

Jasper was staring at Nero in horror.

Nero took a step closer to me but I still flinched away. He took the paper out of my hand gently and turned to Silas.

"Let's get him out of here, now, this shithole will just make him worse."

I shook my head and wrapped my arms around my chest. "Basement…" I murmured.

"No, bro, you're not going to that pit. Come on, we're going to take you to Skyfall."

Skyfall?

I looked at Nero… Crow was behind him smiling at me. He shook his head no, and I knew…

"We're not going anywhere with you."

In a flash I grabbed onto Nero's combat armour and tried to bite him, but the man was quick. He stepped back with a startled yell and grabbed my tangled hair before jerking my head back. I snapped at the air and tried to claw him with my hands but before I knew it the other muscular one was there holding me back.

I screamed from rage as the two of them started dragging me towards the door. I kicked and thrashed, twisting my body and trying desperately to grab anything that I could draw blood from.

No, no, I don't want to go outside. I want to go back into my basement.

"Let go of me!" I screamed. I tripped, unable to keep up with their quick steps, but they kept dragging me towards something loud and noisy. Horror washed through me when I realized it was some sort of vehicle. "Let me go!" I demanded.

When I saw the plane my breath started getting short, the ball of anxiety already growing inside of my chest reached critical and I felt myself completely losing my mind.

'Fight! Fight! Fight!' Crow taunted, his raspy voice scraping against my mind. *'FIGHT!'*

There was nothing I remember after that but people restraining me, the two strong ones, and the sounds of the little boys' crying. I thrashed with every ounce of me and made as much noise as I possibly could. I was desperate, desperate to go back to my basement where it was safe.

But it wouldn't even be the basement it would be the fucking box.

Do you want to go back into the box?

NO! I screamed inside of my head. *I want to sit on the mattress, I don't care if I'm chained just BRING ME BACK!*

"Silas, he's going to kill himself spending this much energy, you gotta do something!" one of them yelled. I felt metal underneath my feet and a door slam but I was too inside of my head to realize they had brought me onto the plane.

'LET US GO!' Crow screamed inside of my head. *'LET US GO! FIGHT THEM! FIGHT THEM!'*

"Shhh… be still, little thing." I felt breath against my ear and the presence of the blond one.

"LET ME GO!" I shrieked.

"SILAS!" Nero snapped.

That was the last thing I remember – there was nothing after that but calm, soothing darkness.

BOOK 2

These Voices In My Head

CHAPTER 18

WHERE AM I? I ONLY KNEW I WAS HUDDLED AT THE back of the plane, engine noises all around me that rattled my bones. I had wedged myself in between two crates and there I stayed as these strangers stood around me.

"He's so scared…" I heard the blond one whisper. "I cannot silence his mind again without dying but I don't believe he will lash out again."

I stared at a metal bench, a few feet away Nero was smoking a cigarette, one of the ones with the blue ember. I saw him nod and offer the cigarette to the one with the buzz cut, though neither of them looked at me.

It had been so long since I had seen an adult besides Jasper, it was overwhelming in a way how big they were. Taller than me and three times as wide. They had a build on them like they were bodyguards.

I remember Nero being big; it had made me feel safe with him.

"Do you want a cigarette, Sangy? It'll relax you." Nero's eyes met mine for just a second before I quickly looked away and drew up the blanket they had given me.

"We're flying over Skyfall now… Want to come look?" Ceph asked cheerfully.

I didn't answer but I heard Nero say to him, "It'll stress him out I think, all those lights in the middle of the night… I don't know, but you remember those rabbits having all those heart attacks from stress? I bet his heart is even weaker than theirs."

"Yes, I want him kept in darkness," the blond-haired one replied. I shrunk back as he casually strolled up to me; his own cigarette in his hand. "Do you know who I am, Sanguine?"

I watched his every movement, every liquid movement of his feet and hands, how he seemed to glide instead of walk. I could... barely walk.

"No," I rasped, still feeling that soothing cloud over my head. This man had done it to me with a narrowing of his eyes. He had abilities in him I used to read about in my fantasy books, the one with sorcerers, but I knew they didn't really exist.

Though red-eyed, shark-teethed humans didn't either, so maybe my own views on reality shouldn't be so iron clad.

"I'm King Silas Dekker, the immortal king of the Fallocaust, and the one who ended the world," Silas said to me with a small smile. I tried to hide my amazement but it showed on my face.

"Why did you take me from my home?" I said to him.

Silas drew a hand up but when I shrunk back he lowered it. "We are *bringing* you home, Sanguine. You are not who you think you are... you are no monster to be kept in a basement. Love – you are a chimera, my chimera, and my creation. You are royalty."

My already fuzzy mind blanked under his words. All I found myself doing was staring at him in disbelief as my head tried frantically to process this information.

Was he lying?

Crow whispered that he was, but I found no reason for the King of the Fallocaust to lie to me. There was nothing I had to give him and nothing he wanted from me but...

How can that be true? How can I be a chimera? I didn't even know what a chimera was, only that they were engineered by Silas to help him run Skyfall and the greywastes.

I was one of them?

"Is that why I look different?" I asked him before jumping when I saw a flash of light reflect opposite of the plane's window. I didn't like light, it made my chest tighten, it made me want to give in to Crow.

No, I had to hold on...

Silas nodded. "Yes, that is exactly why you look different, and why you always knew your name was Sanguine. I created you to look exactly how you look. You're no monster, Sanguine, you're a genetic marvel."

I was no genetic marvel...

I was a monster; I did deserve to be locked up. I knew myself better than them and I knew what I was capable of – what Crow was capable of.

But still those words... what Silas was saying to me...

"You created me... does that mean you're my owner?" I found myself asking.

"Not in the way this Jasper person was no," Silas said slowly. "Though I am your king and master, my chimeras are free to live their lives. Once you have healed mentally and emotionally... you can find out just what you want out of life. Doesn't that sound nice?"

He kept edging his head into my vision even though I was trying to move my gaze away from him. I shook my head and said quietly, "I want my basement. I want... I want..."

"Darkness? Tell me, Sanguine... when was the last time you saw the sun?"

I knew when that was. "I fed crows... I was eight."

"Eleven years." I saw Silas frown out of the corner of my eye. "You have not been outside since you were eight?"

"Once I was let out at night to dig a grave for a boy... I was twelve or thirteen. It was dark; I didn't like it..." I said, before turning away further. "I would like to stop answering questions."

"We're landing right now anyway," Nero called from the front of the plane. "How do you want to handle this, Kingy? Do you want him in Alegria?"

Silas slowly stood up. "Yes, summon Kirrel and we will bring him to my hospital wing. I want him to have medical attention as soon as possible."

When I looked towards the front of the plane I saw Levi and Juni huddled in a corner with Nero's cape over them. Looking wide eyed at everything but they... they were smiling.

Juni saw me looking at him and he waved at me. Levi looked too and also waved.

"We're going to Skyfall, Sanguine," Juni said in a hushed but excited voice. "They say we're going to live with chimeras, real chimeras! We won't have to see Jasper ever again."

Juni seemed happy with this but I was pensive. I didn't trust any of it... I just wanted to go where I felt safe. Right now I was out in the open amongst strangers, I didn't know them and I didn't trust them.

At least the boys would be safe – that was something I was relieved about.

But then again at their age I trusted whomever was nice to me, maybe they were making the same mistake I did?

I closed my eyes and with that I slipped back into myself. I don't know what this state was called but it was more like a walking zombie state than anything. My eyes were still open, I was still breathing and could follow instructions... but besides that I wasn't responsive. I was deep inside of my head where my own mental barriers could keep me safe.

Yes, my eyes closed. On my mattress with... with... Barry.

Wait, where was Barry?

"Barry?"

I opened my eyes, heavy and full of sand and my mouth parched and dry. There was a weariness in me that suggested I had been asleep for a long time but... but where was I?

Immediately my eyes widened, even though the room was dimly lit it seared my eyeballs and filled them with fire. And not only that... I was connected to things, wires and machines that hummed and beeped, each noise hammering itself against my skull.

"Okay, he's aware... shit, shit... um..."

My head jerked towards the voice and I saw another adult, this one with thinning black hair and a trimmed beard. He was reaching over to a machine and rapidly pressing buttons.

I tried to jerk my arms up and was horrified to see I was restrained. The moment I realized I was tied down, I went into panic mode and felt my destructive other half start to skim the surface of my previously calmed state.

"Let me go!" I shouted. The man paled before running out of the room, I took this opportunity to try and slip my hands underneath the belts that were securing my wrists. I frantically scanned the room trying to figure out where I was.

It was a hospital room and I was connected to machines. What were these machines doing? It was too bright in here; it was too open. I saw a window to my left that had the blinds closed but I could see daylight trying to shine its way into the room I was in.

No, no, no, everything was wrong here... everything was wrong.

"Run," Crow murmured to me in my head. *"Run and find some place safe."*

Victory. My skinny wrists slipped out of the binds and I jumped off of the bed. I tried to run out the door but I felt a sting of pain followed by the sounds of the machines crashing around me. I looked behind me alarmed and saw them falling to the floor, the wires connecting me getting ripped out of my skin and chest.

Panic claimed any reasoning I might've had, and trumped the small defeated voice inside of me that was telling me it was okay, that things were different outside of the basement, but my frantic mind was having none of it. I ripped off the last of the wires, ignoring the blood shooting out of the punctures in my skin, and ran out of the room.

"Sanguine… wait!" I looked and saw four people running down the hall, none of which I recognized. My instincts kicked in and I turned and ran in the opposite direction.

Hospitals in movies were huge but this hallway looked like the hallway of a normal building. It had sculptures and bright paintings, its lights were still dim and not cold like the bluelamps. Everything was different, nothing was like how it was in movies or books. I didn't understand what backwards place I was in.

My head whipped around until I saw a door. I opened it up and ran through it and was horrified to see I was in a storage room.

But it was dark… it was dark and it was quiet.

I ran past stacks of boxes, more paintings, and objects I couldn't discern in my racing mind. I took a chance and hid behind an old couch that had another couch laying face down on top of it, making a perfect cave in between.

And it was perfect, as soon as I crawled into it I felt the tension entrapping me start to give.

I took in a deep breath and backed away further inside my cave, cushions below me and all around me. It was comfortable and cautiously relaxing.

And it was dark, enclosed and dark…

I closed my eyes and curled up inside of it and waited for their voices to come nearer.

They didn't come though and as I waited I found the exhaustion catching up with me. Though I was on edge, and my mind was an over-revving engine, I felt my eyelids start to droop, before I knew it I had fallen asleep in my couch cave.

"Well, you look like the cutest little thing all curled up in that couch."

I opened my eyes and jumped from surprise as I saw Silas staring at me.

I hissed at him and backed away further; he laughed at this which I didn't like at all.

"Sanguine, I have a wonderful place for you... it is dark, quiet, and no one will bother you there... unlike here, which usually has someone going in and out. Would you like to go there?" Silas asked.

"Leave me be," I said to him. "Don't put any wires in me... no wires."

"You're dehydrated, malnourished, injured, and worse... we've had you sleeping for days, little love. But don't you feel better now just a bit?"

"No."

I saw him lift something up.

It was Barry.

My eyes fixed on my old bear. I could smell the basement of Jasper's house on him. I outstretched my arm and took it from him and put him under my chin.

"Levi made sure to bring it. Did your mother give him to you?" Silas asked.

"I don't want to talk to you," I said slowly. I inhaled Barry's smell, of rotting carcasses and stale water and felt myself back in the basement where everything always stayed the same.

"Look, Sanguine..." Silas sighed. "You can't stay in this couch fort forever. You need to get your strength back up. You're a shell right now and we cannot rebuild you if you're hiding in the darkness for the rest of your life."

"I don't need..." Why would I even finish that sentence if I knew it was a lie? "I'm fine."

"No, you're not... I have already made plans for your re-emergence. I have arranged therapy sessions for you, regular doctor's appointments to monitor your health... nothing too overwhelming, not at first. Most of your family doesn't even know you're alive. *I* didn't even know you were alive."

I looked up over Barry's fur. "I don't understand."

Silas was quiet for a moment. "For our second generation of chimeras I decided to give several of them to surrogate families. Your mother was hand-selected by me to be your–"

"She wasn't my mother," I said bluntly. "Didn't you say I was engineered?"

Silas nodded. "Yes, but she would've been your surrogate parent. How old were you when she died?"

"One."

Silas flinched at this and murmured, "I see."

He regained himself a moment later though. "Nero and Ellis told me they had found you. Did you know Nero came to visit you with supplies several years later and you were gone? After looking–"

"You looked for me?" I asked.

Silas nodded. "Yes, love. Every year Nero looked for you, though as time went on we all thought you had died. Once a year for an entire month that determined man set off to comb the greywastes for any sign of you – but there was never a shred of a clue that pointed to anything but death."

So that was why Nero and Ellis were so friendly towards me, why they gave me that house to stay in. They had wanted me to stay safe, and I would've been safe if I just... if I had never met Jasper.

Jasper... below the surface of my skin I could feel bugs crawling. I started clawing at my arms, my teeth finding my lips to chew on.

"Sanguine... you're drawing blood," Silas said slowly. He made a motion to reach out and touch my arms but when I recoiled back he stopped. I looked down though and saw my fingernails embedded in the thick scar tissue. I scraped the nails back and felt relief under the pain.

Pain solves everything. Right, Barry?

"Did you inflict the injuries that caused those scars?" Silas asked.

"Most me... some him."

"Jasper?"

My heart froze again, the ice started to form around it, encasing and protecting it from the images and feelings that man's name brought with it.

Was he alive? I didn't want to know.

"What did Jasper do to you, Sanguine? What did he want you for?"

I could feel the blood drain from my face, unbidden I choked as my brain forgot to remind me to breath.

"Don't ask me about Jasper," I rasped. "I will play along with this, but don't – don't ever ask me about him."

Silas looked at me. A man with blond hair cut right below his ears, wavy and styled above groomed eyebrows. A man who had never lived in despair, a man who had never sucked dick for food and water.

I froze at my own words and stared in horror at my now heavily bleeding arms. I backed up further into the couch and suddenly… this cave wasn't a sanctuary. It was trapping me; it was making it so I couldn't escape. King… King Silas was blocking the only exit.

I looked around wildly, my breathing becoming short.

"Sanguine, it's alright. It's just–"

I reared up, feeling the bottom of the couch above me press against my back. I lifted it up and let it fall to the side, and as it did I tried to jump over it.

But my legs were weak. I fell onto the ground, and when the cold floor smacked against my face, all of my rage, fear, and frustration came flooding back to me.

Crow snapped, like a temporarily misplaced puzzle piece he came back and made himself right at home.

And that was it, everything else was a flurry of gnashing teeth, thrashing bodies, and King Silas yelling at someone named Elish to come and help him.

There was only darkness after that.

CHAPTER 19

"I REALLY DON'T THINK THE BOY IS READY FOR HIS own room," Elish said in a cold tone. I knew from the first time I laid eyes on him that he didn't like me, but I don't think any of them liked me. "I do hope you plan on installing chains."

I rubbed my still scabbed and aching neck, and backed myself up against the wall of this weird-smelling room. It was painted dark purple and there were paintings in black frames, everything had a dark feeling to it and it smelled… strange.

I didn't like it, though at least the colours were dark – I didn't like bright colours.

I pressed my back against the wall and slid down to the ground before wedging myself as far into the corner as I could. I watched the men in what was supposed to be my new bedroom.

"He's fine. Kirrel has him rather sedated and I'm learning his signals," Silas replied. He turned on a table lamp that had a thick shade over it. I squinted and tried to press my back further into the wall. I almost hoped I could melt into it, disappear into some solid mass where no one could hear me or see me.

My head felt funny… the shot the man with the beard gave me was leaving my mind nothing but fuzzy static. I felt calm though… oddly calm.

Crow was not calm. He didn't like being drugged; he didn't like this bitter liquid they had put into our veins.

"This is your very own bedroom, Sanguine." This King of the World gave me a smile. He walked over to a king-size bed and straightened out a corner of it. "Come over here and feel this fabric. I picked out purple and grey but I can change it out for any colour you wish."

I didn't look at him; I was unsure of this man. He seemed kind but I felt an unease with him, with all of them. Especially the man with short blond hair who had come rushing into the room when Crow was just about to bite Silas's face. He had purple eyes, a strange colour like mine, and his voice was as cold as ice.

Crow and I had come so close to being left alone, then Elish had to ruin it with his weird electrical touch.

Like I could make my fingers burn…

"He's inside his head again."
"Yes, but he answers when you call his name."

"Come here, Sanguine," Silas called. I looked over at him and saw he was patting the bed in an encouraging manner.

I didn't take my gaze off of him; my brain was already filling me with the adrenaline needed to make a desperate escape. There was nothing about this situation that felt okay, not a single thing I could take comfort in but Barry. I wanted my greywastes. I wanted my basement where I could hide in the darkness. Where there were no other people, just me and Crow.

I want that silence. Where's my white door I can look at… where are my concrete walls I can paint? It was strange here… and the blinds made me uncomfortable.

It made Crow uncomfortable, he was just under my skin barely breaking the surface tension.

But he would; he would.

"Sanguine?" Silas's voice sounded again. My eyes which had become unfocused snapped to him again. I watched his movements and started sweeping the room for anyone else to be wary of. "Look at that, Elish. He's scared out of his mind; look at his eyes flickering back and forth. Nero mentioned that as well; he's always looking for threats."

I glared at the two of them, but they only stared right back at me. Unable to keep their gaze, I looked to the black side table instead.

Silas had normal green eyes but Elish's were odd like mine. A lot of them had strange-coloured eyes. I had seen oddities and strange mannerisms too. They were crazy like me... crazy like me.

I was only half-crazy, like the Daisy Daisy song.

"There is certainly a myriad of mental issues on this one," Elish commented. I wrapped my hands over my chest and pulled my knees up; my teeth found my bottom lip and I started to chew through the already heavily-scarred skin.

"I don't suggest we ever put another baby in the greywastes; I don't know if Mantis will have the skills to curb this one's issues. We had an exuberant amount of problems with second gen and those were with children raised with us, or close by in Skyland or Nyx."

Silas's mouth pulled to the side. "Yes, this one did not go as planned. I would have never suspected these mental issues. I will never tell him but Nero was right," he sighed. "Well, at least Ares and Siris reportedly are doing well in Moros."

"Ares and Siris are borderline retarded," Elish replied coolly. "There's not enough mental for there to be an issue."

Silas laughed at this which made me automatically be on guard, but he only patted the chimera with the short blond hair on the shoulder. I glared at Silas when he looked at me again but he only shook his head with a cluck of his tongue.

"He'll get used to us."

"Having a crazy greywaster-chimera with a seven-year-old boy running around is not a smart combination," Elish replied with eyes still analyzing me.

"Of course it isn't. Drakey will be staying with Garrett and Tom for a few months. They're getting too cozy with each other for my liking and Drakonius will keep them on their toes."

"The boy can stay with me as well. He learns bad habits from Garrett, and Garrett lets him get away with too much."

Silas smiled at this. "Of course, love."

Elish left not soon after that which I liked, all of these people around me was making my heart race. I wanted to be left alone in this moment, alone and some place small where I could be by myself. I wasn't used to this – any of this – and it was starting to give me that anxious churning in my gut; the one that made my breath short.

Silas left for a moment to show Elish out. I took that chance to try the rectangle window that was beside my bed. I tried to open it since it was getting dark outside but the mechanisms were strange. All the windows in the greywastes were rusted shut or missing altogether. We'd had several at Sunshine House and Jasper's were intact, but the window in my basement had thick boards over it.

Now I was in the only surviving city after the Fallocaust. A place that I had only heard of from the people who I had been around since my earliest memories.

Skyfall, the city on an island in the west greywastes. I had remembered the tales, of electricity all the time and hot water that came out of the tap. I remember them saying there was pre-Fallocaust food and they were creating new food all the time. There was a police force, and cars, and streets, and…

I traced my hand over the window and rested it against the cold glass. I looked out and onto the city that spread to every inch of my vision, all bathed in night vision blue. Skyscrapers in various states of disrepair but it looked like they were actively repairing them. Several of the towering buildings I could see were trapped in metal cages with the workers crawling on and around them like ants in their anthills, even though it was night.

I tried to swallow through the anxiety this gave me but it seemed nothing more than a scab that my mind kept picking. It was an itch and whenever I saw these new things in front of me I felt my own mind neurotically scratch it.

I just wanted some place quiet… some place safe.

"Sanguine?"

I looked up and saw Silas in the reflection of the window; he was in the doorway holding something in his hands. I smelled the air and turned around at the strange scent.

"Come with me to the living room," Silas said in a calmed voice. "I have coffee, have you ever had it before?"

I backed up against the window feeling my hands tense around the frame. I looked around for a place to escape, feeling his words start to add fuel to the growing apprehension that seemed rooted in my soul. This strange king made me on edge. I disliked that he was friendly because I knew, like Jasper, that it was only a mask. All men wear masks; it isn't until they're comfortable with their control over you that they let them slip from their faces. Only then can you see the darkness that each one carries in their hearts. All hearts are dark; some men are just better at cloaking their most sickening transgressions.

When will I see your mask slip off, Silas Dekker?
King of the World.

"Come on, it's just the two of us…" Silas took a step closer towards me and it was then the apprehension flared, ignited by the fuel already pooling inside of me. I took a chance, and crouched down and slid under the bed. I backed my body up to the corner and watched his feet with narrowed eyes.

I wasn't going anywhere and whoever was foolish enough to touch me would see my own mask slip off. I still had my teeth; I still had my weapons.

Silas's feet, black loafers, pattered over to me and he kneeled down. When he poked his face down my instincts kicked in… I hissed at him.

Silas chuckled, every time I tried to threaten him he laughed which infuriated me. A growl rumbled in me, and in response, he put the steaming cup down on the edge of the bed and sat down.

"I was amused and a bit worried the first time I heard you growl. Did you know you are the first? Not even my Jack has gotten angry enough with me to growl. I might use your genes for our future chimeras, I am rather impressed with how you look physically – the mental part we'll work on." Silas slid the coffee cup further towards me. "Out of all of your brothers we altered your genetic makeup the most. I did things to you that made me wonder if I was doing the right thing but I'm happy with my results. You are a chimera unlike your brothers, Sanguine, and I think we will be spending a lot of time together."

"I don't want any of this. I don't want to be a chimera," I said in a low voice. I looked at the coffee cup and restrained myself from tossing it right back at him. I could take the guy; he was shorter than me by several inches and slight. His blond hair was styled and wavy and his face porcelain smooth; he was used to being taken care of. I bet he knew nothing of the greywastes. I could destroy him and I would if he came near me.

Silas chuckled again and I heard him sip his coffee. "Well, there isn't much of a choice there, Sanguine. You're a chimera through and through, my successful experiment."

"I'm an experiment?" I didn't like how this made me feel, it weighted on me in a way that suggested it was going to bother me for the rest of my life.

"No, love, no," Silas murmured. "You're so much more than that.

You are perfection, everything about you… Oh I wish I could look at every inch of you."

I started to growl again, the hair on the back of my neck prickled. I didn't like what he was implying… I didn't like those words. I didn't like… No, I would never let that happen again.

"I don't mean it in that way, Sanguine."

I backed away further, my feet now crunched against the corner of the wall.

He seemed to be reading my mind. "When you create art, do you not enjoy gazing upon it? You are a piece of art, Sanguine; from your ruby-red eyes to your serrated teeth. Tell me, would you like to meet someone like you?"

I was quiet. I looked past the coffee mug and saw him set down his own mug with a soft clinking noise. My mind argued with itself whether to answer or not but I decided to throw chance to the wind.

"Who's like me?" I asked quietly.

"He's a chimera your age, exactly your age actually. His name is Jack and he has teeth like yours and eyes as black as an eclipse. Jack is currently attending college. Would you like to meet him one day?" Silas asked. His voice was continually rising. Jasper would do the same trick, talk to me like that to gain my trust but then he kidnapped me and I was never free again.

Jasper had also fooled me into believing he had someone like me. I remember that boy who never existed; I remember Tristin.

"No," I replied.

Silas took another drink of his coffee. "You're going to just stay under the bed forever then?"

I shifted around and rubbed my nose as it started to run. The person who took care of this place needed to dust underneath the bed; it was making my nose itch. "In the greywastes we don't think that far ahead."

"True." Silas rose to his feet and I saw him dust his pants. "I encourage you to come and join me. Would you like a cigarette?"

Silas got down on his knees and he pulled out a cigarette from a tin, without using it as a bargaining tool like Jasper had, he slid it towards me and then slid me a lighter.

I stared at it resting beside the coffee and drew my hands up to my chest. I let out another growl for good measure. I wanted to show him I wasn't scared, even though the hammering in my heart was telling me that

I was.

"I have dealt with my fair share of frightened cats, Sanguine. We have all of eternity to fix what the greywastes broke; you can take your time." And with that he rose and walked out of the bedroom; he even closed the door behind him.

When I was sure he was gone I crawled out from under the bed and stood up. The new clothes they had dressed me in were covered in dust but it was normal dust not the ash I was used to. Like Silas had done, I dusted them off and sat on the bed with the cigarette.

I ignored the shaking in my hands and smoked the beautiful silver smoke into my lungs.

King Silas left me alone for the rest of the evening. I heard several other voices come and go, male voices with strong tones so they must've been chimeras. I stayed in my bedroom and explored it. I found clothes that I didn't like, new and without a tear or a rip to them. I was still wearing a white t-shirt and cloth pants they had given me when I first came here. I assumed my greywaster clothes had probably been torched. This place smelled fresh and springy; my clothes were not welcome here.

The television I was enchanted with. I turned it on and when an image appeared right away I tried to extract the tape in the disc player but there was none in the tray. This was a television station which was fascinating. I turned it a few channels until I found cartoons. I hadn't watched cartoons in years and I had a lot of catching up to do. So I watched it and it kept my buzzing and overactive mind from taking me to places I didn't want to go.

Eventually though I started to get hungry. I had been starved half to death at Jasper's and I had no intentions of starving here. King Silas, Nero, and the others were all healthy with well-toned arms and perfect bodies. All of them ate well so there must be food somewhere.

I opened the door and looked out, and when I saw it was dark I slipped into the main area of this big apartment and started quietly walking towards the kitchen.

The crisp vision I had always enjoyed at night coated everything in a cold blue glow. Like the LED lights we had in the bluelamps, it helped me plan every movement I made to make the least amount of noise.

Cautiously, I crossed the large dining room and felt my bare feet hit carpet. My ears were so focused towards any noise I felt them start to fill with static. I pushed it down with the apprehension inside of me and made my way towards a separate room which held the kitchen and most likely – a fridge.

I stepped onto the wooden flooring of the kitchen and tested it for any squeaking or noise – but it was silent.

Then my nose twitched, I looked up and took in the kitchen in for the first time.

It was so big, with dark wooden cabinets and stainless steel appliances. The counter tops looked like the marble floors in the lobby of this skyscraper and there were so many knives and utensils with no rust.

I swept the room with my gaze and stood there in a state of awe, everything was so clean with no dust and no age. It looked so unworldly I couldn't believe Jasper's disgusting house was in the same dimension as this place. It was foreign to me, and though I knew I was in reality, it made my gut quiver and my pulse race. I felt uncomfortable and I wanted to leave.

But I had smelled something... what did I smell? I followed the smells and spotted something covered in a dome of thin metal. I walked over and lifted up the metal plastic and felt a wave of dizziness.

I was a real chicken. It was half-eaten but it was there and there were other things too. I opened up another metal sheet wrapped thing and found vegetables.

A rush came through me. I picked up the chicken and stacked the other metal-wrapped things on top of it and ran to my bedroom. I stashed the food under my bed and on tip-toes I ran back out and opened the fridge.

Another rush. I was so excited as I gazed upon all of this food that my hands started trembling. No one who'd never been starved would understand the feeling you got when you found more food than you thought you could eat. All of it was just sitting here, unguarded, there was no Jasper to come out and beat me, I could eat it right now.

I started taking things from the fridge, a bottle of soda pop, a container full of something red and white, maybe spaghetti, a foam packaging filled with noodles and vegetables. I took all of it back to my room and hid it all. I hid some in my closet and under the bed, in my dresser drawers and behind the night table. I stashed all of it before, once again, going back for more.

Then I found it.

I found it.

I stared at the entire cake, a white cake with pink flowers, for a brief moment before I plunged a hand into it and brought it up to my mouth.

As soon as the sugar hit my tongue the darkness around me and the apprehension about being out in the open disappeared. I took the cake, some more noodles from a foam container and some pieces of chicken, and sat down on the floor. I surrounded myself with the food and started eating it as fast as I could. My mouth was never empty, I couldn't get enough of it. I had never in my life tasted anything as good as fucking cake and my survival-mode mind wasn't letting me stop eating. Every time I told myself to stop my fingers were reaching in to grab another handful of the delicious cake or grabbing at another piece of fried meat.

Then suddenly I felt a hand on my shoulder and my world turned dark again.

Out of surprise and fear – my mind snapped.

It was like a dark shroud coated me, hugging every inch of my body and becoming a second skin. A dark covering that, once affixed onto me, became my master. I was nothing but a puppet on strings to it – and the longer I was in Skyfall the less awareness I had when it came.

I whirled around and snarled, and in a flash before my mind could calm down I attacked the person who had made the mistake of sneaking up on me and Crow.

I grabbed his left shoulder and dug my fingers into his flesh, then sank my teeth into the victim's neck and bit down.

'BITE! BITE! BITE!' Crow snarled, commanding my movements like the puppet I was. *'DO IT!'* he yelled, his voice so loud it hurt my head. *'KILL HIM!'*

My serrated teeth clamped down and I waited for the rush of blood to coat my mouth, but as I adjusted my jaw I realized in my crazed state that it didn't feel right.

Stars sprung into my vision as I felt a blow on my head. In response I tightened my grip as the flesh I'd bitten into jerked back. I realized, as another light but forceful smack hit the side of my face, that the person had been faster than us. I'd bitten not a neck, but an arm.

I thrashed with a snarl and whipped my head to the side. I heard a loud voice telling me to stop, and telling me he didn't want to hit me harder.

But I couldn't stop – Crow didn't want me to stop.

If I stopped Crow would be angry at me.

And I didn't want to make him mad.

'BITE! BITE!' Crow screamed, he was manic, out of control. I couldn't disobey him.

Then light… light; the light was too bright.

'Shut it off!' Crow snarled.

But I maintained my stance and looked around, feeling dazed and dazzled by the bright lights above us.

Then I saw movement.

Nero was there, naked, and Silas in nothing but a robe. I held the piece of flesh I had ripped from Silas's arm and looked around frantically, still stunned by the lights.

"Sanguine, Sanguine… it's okay, calm down." Silas held up his hands in a *calm down* manner. One of his arms held a laceration that went down to the bone; it was dripping blood onto the wooden floor. Everyone was closing in on us, everyone was there, even Ceph, the boyfriend of Nero, was in the background beside the light switch.

Too many people, too many people. I bared my teeth at them, looking and looking for a dark place I could hide in. They were on all sides, me and Crow were trapped. Crow told me we had to escape, we had to run.

"Do we have any sedatives handy?" Nero asked as he glanced over at Silas. I glared the chimera down, my neck aching from the continuous growl that was vibrating in my throat.

"No – more – drugs!" I yelled grabbing my tangled hair. "You won't drug us; you won't drug us!"

Oddly, this made Silas's eyes brighten. "Us?" he whispered.

He reached out a hand as if wanted to touch me, his eye were intense. "Look at that, Nero. He's insane, fully in psychosis. I bet he doesn't even…" Like a cork popping under pressure I crouched down, and in a fluid steady motion I cleared the counter island in front of me and knocked Silas to the ground. This time I hit my mark. I sunk my teeth into Silas's neck.

Then a different shroud covered my mind, one that brought with it a soothing melody that drew out of me the remaining wisps of reason I had managed to hide from the demon below the surface. The colourless darkness captured the ravaging anger and in its cold embrace it calmed the beast. Then, the moment the monster inside of me let its guard down… it snatched away our consciousness and plunged me into darkness.

CHAPTER 20

I SAW A HAND APPEAR, IT WAS HOLDING IN ITS gentle grasp a piece of fresh bread with a spread of white, solid grease-type stuff on top of it. I could also smell something that had sugar in it, but I wasn't sure just what that was. He hadn't slid it to me yet.

I took it and quickly popped it into my mouth then waited for the next bit of food to be handed to me.

I was under my bed again, where I had been for several days now, not too sure how many. I had woken up in my bedroom with no new wounds on me but still my mind told me I was unsafe. My safety was where it was dark and where no one could reach me and that oasis had been found underneath the large, four poster bed King Silas had in this room.

Three times a day Silas came to feed me and bring me things to drink. Then he would slowly feed me, I guess to make sure I didn't wolf it down like I did several days ago.

To my own disdain they had quickly discovered my food stash and I got the joy of watching Silas and several sengils remove all of my hidden, stashed food.

My back was aching from the awkward position I was in underneath the bed. I was on my stomach but whenever Silas came to feed me I scrunched myself against the wall and watched him with a growl inside of my throat. I didn't trust him, but there was a spark of excitement inside of me whenever he came. I never knew what sort of food he was going to bring and that drew on my survival instincts.

Though it was bland food.

"I'm sorry about only giving you bread and margarine. You'll throw up if I give you rich things. You don't remember but you threw up for hours after we dimmed your mind when you were going food crazy that night in the kitchen," Silas said as if reading my mind. He handed me another torn piece of bread, this time with a shred of half-raw meat on it.

I tried to snatch it but he pulled away.

"You've had five pieces so you're not famished anymore. Can you please take it nicely from my hands?" Silas said in a half-amused voice. "Show me you know you're not going to starve anymore. I would appreciate it."

I paused and swallowed the growl that was crawling up my throat. I could only see his black pants and his elbows which were leaning against his lap. I could picture King Silas watching the edge of the bed with his chin resting on his hands. Though I wasn't sure that was what he was doing.

A fresh wave of wonderful smells reached my nostrils as he tore something else in half out of sight. I watched with anticipation wondering what it was, trying to force my nose to recognize the smell but I had never smelled anything like it.

Then his hand appeared again and I saw it was a disk-shaped bakery thing with black chips inside of it.

I went to snatch it but Silas once again pulled his hand back.

I growled a warning, and reached my hand out further trying to find where he was stashing this food but to my own anger he laughed at me.

"Just take it nicely! Is that so much to ask? You don't need to have a growl about it, my god," Silas chuckled. "Take it nicely from my hand and you can have two."

I suppose that wasn't too much to ask. He had been patient with me living under a bed in his apartment. So I relented and retracted my hand and waited patiently.

When the bakery thing came back into view I fought down my survival instincts and gently took it from his grasp. Though as soon as I had it I crammed all of it into my mouth and started to chew.

Whatever this food was it was made by the hands of a god. It was sweet, but it was a less-potent kind and the texture was amazing. It melted inside of my mouth and flooded the inside of it in a lake of sweetness. Immediately my brain commanded me to find more and I reached my hand out in hopes of getting the other half.

"That's a chocolate chip cookie and you can thank my grandson who has a sweet tooth larger than me."

I blinked and gave him (or his crossed legs anyway) a confused look. "But you're..." This made absolutely no sense to me. Everything I had heard about King Silas, all the conversations I had eavesdropped on, had led me to the confirmation that King Silas was gay. All of his chimeras, me included, were gay and that he had been gay since well… forever.

"You have real kids?" I asked quietly. I pulled my hand back and was happy when he slid me the other half of the cookie. It disappeared quickly inside of my mouth.

"Like a biological child created with a female? Of course not. That's… ew," Silas said with a laugh and I found myself smiling at that comment. "You've met her before, my daughter is Ellis. My lovely Ellis Arwen Dekker. She was an unexpected twin from Nero, and we assumed she would be male so we kept the twin. Though she split soon enough from Nero that she missed out on the Y chromosome and here I was with a female chimera. I could've aborted her but, well, I was curious. I raised her as a daughter and she gave me a grandchild four years ago. Knight is a half-chimera, half-arian and he loves his cookies."

I swallowed down the cookie and rested my chin on my arms. "She was kind to me when I met her as a child. Does she know you found me?"

"She has been wanting to see you since you came," Silas explained. "Nero more so. He wants to talk to you in a more… calm setting. Not so much when you're in those states." He paused. "I have not told my other chimeras about you, Sanguine. Only my first generation and Ceph know you've been found. It would be overwhelming for you. We are close-nit to a probably unhealthy level but that just means our family ties are strong. They treated you well when they saw you?"

Even though he couldn't see me I nodded before sneezing. It was dusty under here and my nose didn't like it. "Nero and Ellis were my first alive friends," I replied. "They're… they didn't care I was a monster. They only wanted to help me be safe…"

I was puzzled when I heard him sigh. I stared at my hands and started going over every scar I had on them. I think I had memorized every one of them by now. I spent a lot of time staring at my hands.

"They knew I was your chimera…" I said in a small voice. "Nero knew –"

"– that you two were brothers? Yes, Sanguine, he did," Silas said back.

"Why did it take eleven years to find me?"

The silence that descended on the room weighed heavily on the both of us. It centered on my shoulders and pressed down with a weight that told me I would've been brought to my knees if I was standing. And like a physical weight, with every passing moment the pressure only gathered until I found myself unable to stand the silence.

"Was I a failure?" I asked.

"No!"

I jumped under the sharpness of his voice. Immediately I backed away from the edge of the bed until my feet hit the back wall. I crushed myself against it and watched him intently.

I saw him shift around. "You're no failure and you never were," Silas replied in an odd tone. I couldn't put my finger on his mood, I just knew I was uncomfortable with it. "You're perfection and now that you're in our family you'll soon reach your potential. We'll build you up, repair you, and make you better than you ever were before. Sanguine, you're a chimera, a Dekker, a prince. Don't let anyone ever tell you otherwise, not even your own self-degredating thoughts. Do you understand me?"

"He's wrong."

My eyes shot to my left, to the far corner of the wall.

Crow was laying on his side, with a hand resting on his hip and the other one holding up his head. He was giving me a wide smile that showed every single one of his pointed teeth. The look he was giving me was dripping transgressions and nefarious, dark thoughts. In every way he looked like a sinister monster under the bed but… so was I.

We were one of the same. We always had been.

"Do you really think so?" I asked Crow. "He's… being kind to us."

Crow's shining red eyes narrowed, and he glanced over to the edge of the bed where Silas was sitting. He stared at him for a moment, still and silent, before I saw his hand grip his thigh. "How can you be this 'perfection' when the family abandoned you in the greywastes without even checking in on you? No, he's fooling you. There must be something that he wants, perhaps you should find out what he wants."

I looked at the crossed legs, and then the crumbs that were all that remained of the cookie Silas had given me. "He has everything. What could he possibly want from me? I have nothing to give him."

"How is that a good thing? It means we now have to watch out for everything," Crow said. I saw his mouth twitch. "Has there ever been anyone in your life who only wanted to help you because they just wanted to help you? Even Nero and Ellis only helped you because they knew you were their sibling. No, beware of him, mihi. Life has taught you that. Life has taught you to be on your guard. Everyone wants something from you, even if it's just your body. Don't forget what Jasper taught you."

I stared at him, feeling sadness swell inside of my throat. "I will," I said slowly. "I… will."

"Sanguine?"

I looked and saw Silas's legs shifting, then another piece of cookie appeared, being held gently in Silas's grasp. "Can you see Crow when he speaks to you…? Or is he just a voice inside of your head?"

Running on the unease that Crow had filled me with, I hesitated to answer, but with the cookie in my sights I couldn't resist. I took it gently from his hand before replying, "I see him. He's in the far corner under the bed with me."

"What does he look like?"

I didn't see any harm in answering this so I glanced over at Crow and got a good look at him. "He has long black hair that is shiny and clean. He wears black and red, usually a leather jacket and black pants. He… looks like me, his eyes are red and he smiles all the time. But I don't smile."

"Does he tell you to do bad things?"

"They're not bad things," I replied. "He tells me how I can help myself deal with… my situation."

Another piece of cookie was held out for me. I took it carefully and ate it. I didn't like feeling like I was being rewarded for talking to him like I was some sort of dog, but I ignored it.

But in truth, though I didn't trust King Silas and had no plans to start, I hadn't had a conversation with an adult in a long time, not since I was a child.

Jasper… Jasper didn't count. The only time we had conversations was when he was on meth and that was pretty much like talking to a child.

Silas paused for a moment. "I would love to talk to you further. I have had the sengils cover all of our windows since I know you dislike sunlight right now and it is only the two of us. Will you join me in the living room?"

I shifted away and shook my head. "No."

"Come on, Sanguine… must I bribe you with more cookies and cakes? You know my second born, Garrett, is coming later with a wonderful gift for you. He's very non-threatening and a kind man... will you receive it?"

A gift? This drew up an interest in me, but what if it was a trick? A way to get me out from under the bed to... to...

King Silas had been nothing but kind and patient with me. Not only did he look past my food hoarding and the mess I made in the kitchen, he had been personally feeding me and trying to ease me out from under the bed. Though time had made everything soft about my personality worn leather, I still recognized kindness when I saw it.

Though the thought of coming out from under the bed made my hands clench and my breath become short. I was nervous about it, but if he said the windows were covered...

I took in a deep breath and looked at Crow for help. Barry had told me to go with Jasper but Crow wasn't Barry. Crow erred on the side of caution and if things went sour I had my teeth. King Silas might bring with him a presence of being superior and put together but physically I was taller than him and he had no pointed teeth.

When Crow gave me a small nod I turned back to where Silas was sitting and drew in a long breath. One that only fanned the flames of anxiety smouldering inside of my gut and threatening to tear open the wounds that every other man who had taken advantage of me had left.

"Okay," I said quietly.

Silas's pulse jumped... I had made him happy. I watched as he shifted away from the bed and rose to his feet.

I waited until he was by the door on the other side of the room before I crawled out from under the bed. Immediately I folded my arms over my chest and started analyzing the room. Making sure no one was hiding from me, waiting to ambush me or something worse.

My gaze only shifted back to Silas when I heard him take a sharp inhale. I looked at the blond king quizzically and realized his mouth was pursed and his jaw tight. There was also a glimmer in his eyes, a light but obvious look of sadness when he looked at my body.

"Those scars..." Silas whispered. Immediately I put my arms behind my back, making sure the sleeves were drawn down as far as they could. "You're trying to kill your greatest enemy aren't you?"

I looked away from him and took Barry. I wanted him to go with me to the living room. I had nothing to say back to Silas so I didn't reply to his observation. I knew what he meant: that I was my greatest enemy and since he knew and I knew… why say anything?

"And you're just so thin. You're going to be spoiled and pampered for a very long time, my red-eyed beauty. I'll make up for the life you have led so far," Silas said in a tone full of sadness and regret. I saw a sad smile draw from his thin lips but it only seemed to make him look more solemn. There was something to that man… a heaviness like he was carrying the weight of the world on his shoulders.

As that thought crossed my mind, I realized he was.

I stood there and looked at Barry's dirty, matted head and didn't say anything back. There was nothing really I could say so I stood there until he made the first move.

And that first move was him turning around, making predictable slow movements.

He opened the bedroom door and walked into the dark, dimly lit living room. Slowly I followed him, ignoring the temptation to turn around and duck back under the bed.

I walked into the decorated living room, with the clean fabric furniture and the stained wood desks, coffee tables, and other furniture I didn't know the name of. I looked around it to make sure no one was hiding in a corner or behind the curtains and, to appease my paranoia, I listened as well.

But it seemed like it really was just King Silas and me. So I walked into the area of the living room where the couches were. There were two of them, and a wingchair, surrounding a large television set.

I stood there. I looked longingly at all the bookshelves that he had and mentally picked out several I wanted to investigate when I had the chance.

"Sit down, lovely," Silas said. I saw him walking towards the kitchen out of the corner of my eye so I decided to follow him with my gaze. I disliked turning my back on people. "Make yourself comfortable."

Comfortable? I looked down at the couch I was nearest. Dark brown with what looked like a soft texture. There were no stains, it was pure and without a single blemish. It was new, or at least refurbished.

I wondered if this couch had ever been abandoned in a house alone. I wonder if it ever felt sad like the other couches in the greywastes when the roof started to leak onto it, or the radrats started to come. Knowing there was nothing they could do to escape the fates that time would eventually bestow on them. They were frozen where their masters had left them, forgotten and cold and at the mercy of time.

And when time was your only god, there were no happy endings.

But not this couch... this one had been lucky.

"I don't want to," I said slowly as Silas poured some hot water into two mugs.

Silas glanced over to me with a puzzled look. "Why? You may stand but you don't have much strength to you. Your heart is weak, I can hear it."

"I'm dirty... it's clean. I don't want to contaminate it," I replied honestly. "It would make it unhappy."

The king smiled faintly and started walking towards me with two cups of tea. They smelled neat and I found myself anticipating what it would taste like. The coffee had tasted wonderful but it made my hands shake.

"Love, the couch doesn't have feel-" He paused and I saw him glance at Barry. Then to my confusion he didn't finish that sentence, only started saying something else. "Well, would you like to have a long bath later? I have a tub that five people can fit into in my personal bathroom."

A bath? I took the tea from Silas but he didn't sit down, instead he walked down the hall and I heard one of the closets open. He came back a moment later with a red fuzzy blanket with swirling gold patterns. He threw it over the couch and gave me a smile before motioning for me to sit.

I suppose a blanket could be washed. My sad blankets were still in the basement forgotten. I wonder if they had ever seen daylight.

I sat down on the couch. It was just as comfortable as it looked. I settled in with my tea and drew my knees up to my chest. "I haven't had a bath since... since I was eight," I said. "How old am I now? Nan says my birthday is in the spring."

"You're going to be twenty in March," Silas said. He grabbed a box of something before he sat down on the couch beside me. He then opened the box and handed it to me. To my happiness the inside were filled with cookies. A blue and white Dek'ko package with black cookies with white in the middle. I tested one out on my teeth before diving in.

Silas made a noise and I looked at him.

"Slowly, love."

I looked over at Crow who was checking out the paintings on the walls. He could tell I was watching him though, he immediately looked over.

"Slow eating..." Crow said with a nod. "You don't want to throw up, mihi."

I nodded and took out two cookies before closing the box to keep them fresh. Silas nodded at this, looking content and grabbed a cookie for himself. I wanted them all for myself. I wanted to hide them in my closet or perhaps the space behind the dresser. My instincts practically screamed for it, but I pushed my own will ahead of my survival instincts and only started eating the two cookies I already had.

"Now, I know we're at the beginning of your recovery and I want to tell you what I would like to have happen," Silas said.

This piqued my interest. Though in the greywastes we never really planned our futures; we weren't sure we would even have one. I didn't know what was going to happen to me or what their plans were for me in the first place.

I had been a greywaster boy and all I knew how to do was survive. I think it might take me a while before I learned how to do anything else.

Silas took a sip of tea and so did I. It burned my mouth but I enjoyed the pain.

"As I said before... no one knows you're here except for my first generation of chimeras and Ceph. You've met Elish, Nero, and Ellis and the man you're going to meet soon is named Garrett. You have eight other brothers around your age: Jack who is like you, Valen, Rio, Ludo, Felix, Ceph who you've briefly met, and the twins Apollo and Artemis. All of them, except Ceph, attend my college my first born runs: the College of Skytech, and avoiding them will be rather easy. I don't want them to know you're here until you've had some time to heal. I feel it would be too much for you."

I nodded at this, overwhelmed by the information but still receptive to it. "I don't want a lot of people around."

Silas held his tea mug in his hands. "I understand. You've been alone for most of your life, haven't you?"

That question made my shoulders slump. I looked down at the cookie, with jagged little bite marks and said quietly, "Even when I was with Nan, I was alone. The other kids didn't like me, just Nana. When I was exiled... I was all alone." I looked over at Crow. I almost smiled as he picked up a purple flower that was resting in a ceramic vase and smelled it. "Until Barry came, and when Barry died... Crow came. For a long time... it was just me and him."

"Perhaps... since you're with your family... you won't have a need for Crow," Silas said lightly.

My eyes shot back to King Silas, I narrowed them. "Crow is my best friend. I won't abandon him just because you finally decided to come find me. Crow was there for me when Jasper left me to starve." My voice started to rise. "Crow was there for–"

"*Shhh- shh.*" Silas made a soothing noise. "I'm sorry. I understand… Crow was your only friend when you were locked away. It's insulting for me to insinuate that you could so easily toss him aside when he has been the only constant thing in your life. I understand, Sanguine. I apologize. Okay?"

I tried to hide the surprise on my face. I fully expected an argument to start, or for him to transform into this cruel king I had thought he was deep down. There was nothing inside of my mind that had expected him to not only understand but to apologize. He wasn't what I was expecting… almost the opposite.

"I… accept your apology," I said, pulling up the old manners I had learned long ago in Sunshine House. I hadn't had to use manners in longer than I could remember.

Silas seemed happy with this. He grabbed another cookie from the bag and took a bite out of it. "You'll be living with me and my sengil Kinny. I do have our family coming by to visit, plus we get together at least once a week for dinner, and once a month for a party; birthday parties or some excuse for a celebration," Silas explained. "During this time, I am to assume you have no problem being in your bedroom or the entertainment room?"

I nodded. "I like that."

"You'll also, I hope, be open to doctor's visits. You're extremely malnourished and your body requires more than an average arian since you have genetic enhancements. Other than that, I just want you to… figure out what it is you want," Silas said.

Figure out what I want? I swallowed this down and answered dryly, "Figure out what I want is in the same league as asking me what my future plans are. Why can't you understand… I never thought I had a future. There was no… dreams, no desires… I'm a walking corpse. I have nothing, I am a shell. He stole…"

I paused.

He stole all of that from me.

"He?" Silas dropped his tone. "Jasper?"

I visibly recoiled and felt the veins nestled under my skin contract. My muscles froze and the breath got sucked from my throat making me visibly gag.

"He's going to ask you about Jasper," Crow said behind me. I heard the clicking of his high heel boots as he walked over from the paintings he was examining. "He'll force you to tell him that Jasper was fucking you down there the entire time. You realize that don't you? They all are so eager to know just who Jasper was."

I glanced over my shoulder before tucking my knees up tighter to my chest. "I mentioned it first. He's only… wondering what I was speaking of."

Crow walked in front of the couch and leaned against the back of it. He had the flower in his hand which he brought up to his nose.

Then he gave me a closed mouth smile, one that made his eyes squint. "And if you tell him you don't want to speak about Jasper. What then? Do you believe he will stop?"

"Yes," I replied. I looked over at Silas who was watching me with a confused look on his face. Jasper looked at me the same way when I talked to Crow in front of him, though I knew it was because only I could see my friend.

When Silas saw me looking back at him he smiled, though there was no lightness in his eyes. "We don't need to speak about him. Why don't we continue to make plans? Give you a reason to be excited about your future."

Crow made a disgruntled noise. He walked behind me, the flower still in his hand, looking cross. Silas had just proven Crow wrong and I knew my friend didn't like this. I wasn't sure if he disliked Silas or not. Sometimes Crow liked people – sometimes he didn't.

I took another drink of tea and wondered what I could say to Silas so he would leave me alone with his penchant for wanting me to have a future. Right now the thought of doing things filled me with apprehension. I wanted to go back to my bedroom or even the basement. If Jasper wasn't there anymore I could stay there alone with my crows.

My crows. I frowned as I thought about them. I would miss them but at least they didn't have Jasper to yell at them anymore.

"We found a lot of books in your old house and in that basement," Silas said. "So you know how to read and your vocabulary is impeccable. Would you like to attend school?"

I shook my head vigorously, so vigorously Silas chuckled.

"How about school at home? Elish is the Dean of the college, Garrett and your brother Perish also teach. Why don't we get them to make you some work books? You can learn about Science, English, Math from your bedroom, and I can grade them or one of the others. Just warning you though, love, you're going to be awful at math but no worries. Unless I specifically engineer them to be able to do it, all of us are horrid at it."

"School?" I said slowly and nodded. "I would like that."

This thrilled him. "I'll make the calls tonight then."

I stared down at my tea and took another drink of it. I liked mint. I had once been scavenging in an old gas station and I had come across mint gum. It was dry and it sucked all of the saliva out of my mouth but I remember loving the minty flavour.

"If there is anything I can do to make you more comfortable," Silas said. "We will make your recovery–"

Terror ripped through me as there was a sudden loud noise coming from the double doors that led to the hallway. I looked over in fear at the loud knocking and in an instant my brain clicked back to survival-mode.

With Silas rapidly trying to calm me I jumped to my feet, my tea spilling onto the floor. Another loud bang soon sounded, followed by a man's happy voice. I jumped over the couch and ran as quickly as I could back to my bedroom. Without stopping I slid under my bed, a deep growl vibrating against my Adam's apple.

"Garrett!" I heard Silas roar. He sounded angry at the man but my mind was too high-strung and in a panic to think much of it. I backed to the far end of the bed and watched the bedroom door with fixed eyes.

The growl only intensified when the door opened and I saw a pair of polished leather shoes step into the bedroom.

"Oh, I just want to see what he looks like!" the man I knew was Garrett said. "I won't be long."

Then there was a pause and everything went quiet around me.

"Oh my god... Silas, you're right... he growls – oh my god, that is fucking precious!" The noisy man got down on his knees and poked his head underneath the bed.

He was a man with spiky black hair, three earrings in each ear and a trimmed goatee. This one had normal green eyes, not some of the odd colours I had seen and been told about.

"Wow... okay, I can see what you mean. I won't fuck with that. He looks like he's going to rip my bloody face off. Hello, Sanguine! I got you a present, would you like to see?"

I hissed at him and continued to growl, suddenly I didn't like that I was being cornered. But from the looks of him I would win any fight he wanted to start... though he didn't seem like the type.

"Garrett, will you get away from him?" Silas said in a voice dripping annoyance. "You're going to make him worse. I just fucking got him out from under the damn bed!"

"Oh, just wait, you big grump."

Then the oddest thing in the world happened, something that I didn't expect or even think was possible. Garrett reached up to grab something... and proceeded to put a black kitten down in front of him.

"There you go, growly. I got you this as a present. Well, Silas and I did. Don't tell me you hate kittens, I won't believe you." Garrett pushed the tiny little kitten towards me and chuckled. "He growls and hisses too – well, not yet, but some of them do. Do you like him, Sanguine?"

The small kitten looked at me and I looked back at the kitten. The cats at Sunshine House had all been fixed older cats that Nan got money from the Legion to look after; I had never seen such a small one before.

Immediately the growl left my throat and, intrigued, I reached over and took the kitten and brought him up to my face. No sooner had I done that the kitten started to purr and arch its back to rub against my face.

"He's purring! Look at that, love at first sight. No matter how bloodthirsty and tyrannical, you give a chimera a kitten and he's a happy clam forever. See, Si, I know what I'm doing," Garrett said smugly. "Your chimeras love kittens."

"At least you didn't bring one of those wild ones Ceph is raising," Silas said with a chuckle. "I can hear him purring from here."

I drummed my fingers against the floor, making the kitten bat them with an enthusiastic paw. I almost smiled as he pounced and bounced over the excitement of drumming fingers. I liked him already.

I glanced past the kitten at the shiny shoes and tried to gauge how I felt about this man.

Garrett didn't seem threatening, though he was loud but I had to get used to loud. So I shifted myself out from under the bed, the kitten held in my right arm. It was hard to do, my body seemed to pull me towards the dark corners of the room where I knew I was safe, but I overruled my own emotions.

"Oh, hello!" Garrett's voice was singing when they saw me emerge. I stood up and backed up all the way to the wall and held the kitten to my chest as he purred.

"Hello," I said, quietly looking at the floor. "Thank you for... kitten."

"Think of a nice name for him," Garrett said cheerfully. "I am Garrett, second born of the first generation, and the man who helped create you!"

He created me? I looked at him suspiciously and noticed Garrett was staring at me intently, looking over every detail of my face and mostly... my mouth. It was obvious he wanted to take a better look at me but I could only be pushed so far... I didn't want him near me.

"Alright, you had a good look. Come back into the living room, Sanguine. I have another surprise for you. He will be here soon, is that right Garrett?" Silas said and started pulling on Garrett's blazer collar. Garrett gave an embellished sigh and turned around to walk out of the bedroom.

"That's right. He's just finishing his appointment with Kirrel. Poor kid isn't in the greatest of health just like our Sanguine," Garrett explained.

I followed the two of them out into the living room and saw another man I had never seen before opening up a sack of sand.

The young man with blond hair cut short looked up at me and smiled.

"Hello, I'm Tom, Garrett's sengil. I'll be out of here in a second just setting up the litter box so Shorty there doesn't crap in the apartment. Are you liking it here?" Tom walked towards me with his hand out. I took a cautious step back and stared at him.

Tom stood there with his hand extended, until Garrett found him and gently directed him away from me.

Having one person in the house was tolerable but having three was making my insides squirm, so I found a chair in the corner of the new apartment and sat down with the new kitten.

"Sanguine, are you okay?" Silas said as he snapped his fingers and pointed to the door outside. Obediently Tom set the litter tray down and left the apartment without another word.

I looked at Silas before shaking my head no.

"Would you like some Xanax to keep you calm? You seemed to like it at the hospital," Silas said before reaching into his pocket.

I held out my hand. I had enjoyed being on Xanax. It made the motor that was constantly revving inside of my chest slow down.

I swallowed it and Silas smiled before turning back around as Garrett spoke.

"So are you still loading him up on Xanax, love?" I heard him ask from the kitchen. I heard a bag getting moved around but obviously the sound meant more to the kitten. My new friend started trying to scramble off of my lap, but a moment later Garrett came over to me and handed me a plastic container.

"It has been vital for him," Silas said. "I haven't seen a panic attack yet but at this point I would be more than happy if that was all we have to deal with." Silas sighed. I didn't think I liked them talking about me like I wasn't there.

"Well, we have tons at least. He's skinny. Fuck, is he ever skinny."

I opened up the container and saw little brown squares that smelled interesting. I popped one into my mouth and it didn't taste bad. I ate a few more as the kitten started to sniff and rub up against the rim of the plastic.

"No, no, those are cat treats, dear. Not for chimeras," Garrett said gently. He took the container away from me and shook a few into his palm. The kitten started eating then hungrily. I took one before the kitten could eat it and ate it myself. They tasted pretty good, I didn't see why the kitten couldn't share.

"Sanguine, come sit on the couch." Silas walked over to me with another kind smile. "We have a visitor coming in a moment but you know this one so don't be apprehensive."

"I know this one?" I said quietly. I tried to think of who it could be as I sat down. I wanted to ask if it was Nan but I didn't. For all I knew Nan was dead.

I sat down and wrapped the red blanket around myself. I nestled into it and moved to the far corner of the couch and tried to make myself comfortable.

The two sat down. Silas with that same odd, kind smile and Garrett… he wasn't hiding his fascination with me.

I let Garrett pick me apart with his eyes and burrowed myself into the blankets. Garrett and Silas chatted freely about me though it wasn't anything offensive. They spoke of my medical issues which I knew I had and also with the diet they had been feeding me.

When the next knock came on the door I froze but remained sitting in my blankets. Garrett rose to his feet and walked towards the door, his earrings sparkling in the faint light coming from the fireplace.

It was warm and cozy tonight. I don't think I would ever take being comfortable and warm for granted. Most of the time in Jasper's basement I was either freezing cold or almost dying from heat stroke because of the lack of proper ventilation in that basement.

The memories still stained my skin and made me clasp my arms with my clenched fingers. I locked my jaw and stared at the red of the blanket, wishing the Xanax would kick in so I didn't have to suffer through the memories my masochistic mind was more than willing to torment me with.

Though curiosity was a demon on my shoulders, so I watched intently as the door opened, wondering just who this person I supposedly knew was.

A small boy stepped through with a shy smile on his face. A little boy with newly cut and brushed black hair, wearing a grey batman t-shirt and green pants.

"Juni?" I said, feeling my mouth go dry. Immediately Juni looked towards the living room and his face brightened.

"Hi, Sanguine!" Juni said happily. He put his hands behind his back and walked towards me, but he hesitated and stopped halfway there. "Are you okay?"

He was cautious, and he had a reason to be cautious. Juni had seen me as the maniac tied to the dirty mattress. The boy didn't know who I was.

Not like I even knew who I was...

"Yeah," I said sitting up so I wasn't slouching as much in the couch. "I'm feeling a bit more in this world. Are they treating you well?"

Juni smiled and nodded vigorously. He walked the rest of the way, with a bravery inside of him that reminded me of me.

As I said that thought though, I realized that, as a child, most bravery was stupidity. In all respects he shouldn't trust me, or anyone, but perhaps I was drawing from my own experiences.

"Garrett... can I tell him?" Juni said eagerly, rubbing his hands together and almost bouncing down on the spot.

"Of course!" Garrett said with a laugh. He put a hand on Juni's back and directed him into the front of the couch where the coffee table was.

"I'm going to be adopted!" Juni said excitedly. "King Silas says I can stay here. He says because I was so brave to find Nero and Ceph... I can be a Dekker. I'm Juni Dekker now. Can I get red eyes too? Can I get sharp teeth too?"

My eyes widened. I looked over at Silas who was looking proud of himself. When we made eye contact he nodded and took another drink of his tea. "Juni found Nero and Ceph in Melchai, Sanguine. Juni told them about *him* and told Nero a red-eyed man was locked in the basement. Of course Nero knew immediately who you were. Sanguine, did Nero ever tell you what he did every year?"

Beside me I saw Juni take a seat on the wingchair, leaning back with his little feet off of the ground. Both stick thin legs happily wiggling up and down to show his contentment. That little boy seemed happy as can be. He seemed to be taking these changes a lot better than me.

I shook my head and dug my fingers into my skin. "I… I haven't spoken to Nero. I wasn't really myself when I saw him in the kitchen." My throat tightened as I tried to swallow down the apprehension. I couldn't pinpoint why but I was getting nervous, perhaps I needed another Xanax. I don't think I liked them speaking about the basement.

Juni… Juni knew what was happening because he had had it done to him. From what I remember in that monotonous hell Levi and Lyle had come, followed by Juni. I think Juni had only been there for six months, possibly ten. I don't remember; I could only tell there was someone different by their screams when Jasper was on them.

I looked at Juni as Silas said something back to me, but I my ears were elsewhere. I didn't pick up a single thing Silas was saying. My eyes were fixed on that small boy, that small, happy little child, who had seemed to have bounced back already.

What if he told… what if he told…

"Sanguine?"

I jumped as I felt Silas's hand on my knee. I looked over at him and blinked, realizing with embarrassment they had been trying to get my attention for a while.

"Are you okay?" Silas said lightly. "Is this too much for you?"

Is it?

I shook my head. I was face-to-face with a boy who had been through the same abuse I had. I didn't want to appear weak in front of Juni. I just… didn't.

"I'm fine," I said slowly and looked back down at the blankets. I took in a deep breath and started to count them as the three chatted happily.

"I remembered that there was a gas station," Juni said. I could tell he was chewing on something. I glanced over and saw he was eating from a different box of cookies. "I told Mr. Nero that and I got to fly in that big plane. The bartender guy almost told me to piss off too, but they let me speak to them. I liked those two, one gave me Dunkaroos but he called them something different."

Then Juni paused. "I'm happy Levi is being adopted too. He's so sad about Lyle…"

"Lyle?" I heard Garrett ask.

I sunk further into the blankets and started counting the small threads I could see. My ears started to burn.

"He's going to tell them," Crow suddenly said behind me. "He's young. He doesn't realize how dangerous it is to admit what happened to him. You should tell him to keep his mouth shut."

"I'm not going to do that," I said darkly to Crow. "I won't scare him."

"Lyle was Levi's little brother. We played cars a lot. Jasper beat him to death because we gave Sanguine things we weren't supposed to."

"What things? Did Jasper keep you down there too?"

Stop saying his name.

"He's going to tell them." Crow's voice suddenly dropped down to the depths of darkness. I saw lines appear in his face as he scowled but in a flash the scowl turned into a snarl and I saw him gripping the couch.

I gripped my arm hard.

"Sanguine, he's going to fucking tell him!" Crow's voice rose. Then, instead of sounding behind me, his voice went back inside my head. The same piercing, loud voice that hurt my brain.

'Sanguine! He's going to tell them Jasper was fucking all of you!'
'Sanguine! SANGUINE!'

'STOP HIM!' Crow's essence pressed on me, stifled and smothered me with a determination that told me he wasn't going to leave me alone until I did it. *'STOP HIM, YOU FUCKING WEAK BITCH'*

'STOP HIM, SANGUINE – STOP HIM, SANGUINE! NOW, NOW, NOW!'

"No," I heard Juni say. "Jasper kept us above ground because he said Sanguine was dangerous and because it was easier for him when he wanted his time–"

'ATTACK HIM! SHUT HIM UP! SHUT HIM UP!'

"SHUT UP!" I suddenly roared. In an instant I was back on my feet, a snarl escaping from my mouth though when it drew sound it was more a cross between a scream and a roar. I jumped across the coffee table to get to Juni but I felt myself get pulled back.

"SHUT UP!" I shrieked again. I fell backwards on the couch and started clawing and digging my fingers into the scarred flesh of my arm. On all sides of me I saw movement, the hands that had pulled me back still grabbing me. Juni was staring in horror; his dark eyes wide and his gaunt face stricken with terror.

"Don't you say a fucking word!" I yelled as they pulled me away. I could feel wet from my arms as I clawed and clawed. I kept grinding and twisting my nails into the skin to try and draw as much pain as I could but the adrenaline was stopping me from reaching my threshold. I needed more pain.

No, no, I had to shut the kid up. "Don't you ever tell them!" I yelled, my voice breaking; a sob came to my lips. "Do you understand me? Don't you ever tell him what happened!"

Juni nodded before Garrett picked him up and sprinted with him towards the door. Silas grabbing and pulling my arm, talking soothingly to me but I heard nothing but the roaring of my own blood rushing behind my eyes. Taking with it the seeds of calm that the evening had tried to plant inside of me.

I didn't like his arms on me. No one was going to touch me again. So I yanked my arms away from Silas and brought them back to the now wet and sticky skin. Bumpy and warm and with the texture of ground rat meat.

"Sanguine…" Silas said calmly. "Lovely, stop hurting yourself. It's okay, he's gone."

"It's not okay!" I whirled around and yelled. Though I got no recoil of fear, I didn't even get a glimmer of apprehension. King Silas was cold and calm; his face neutral and his movements planned and steady.

"Shhh… it is." Silas's voice dripped honey; sweet and reassuring. I scanned his face for deception but all I saw was the calm and control. "It's okay. He's gone, everyone is gone and it's just…"

Suddenly a spurt of red shot from my wrists. I watched it shoot like a fountain from the deep gouge I had made in the soft veiny area of my arm and splatter against one of the paintings Crow had been looking at earlier. Another spurt came soon after and as I stared blankly at it, my pulse gave another beat and with it, another spurt.

Silas swore and clasped my wrists. "You hit a vein. My poor sick boy…" he said those words quicker than his usual controlled tone but I was too stunned at the power behind the squirts of blood. I said nothing back.

I pulled my wrist away from Silas's hand, and because he was now busy grabbing what I knew was a phone in his pocket, I got my arm free and immediately brought my bloodied wrist to my mouth. Seeing, before it disappeared from my eye sight, the deep shredded gouge I had made.

The blood squirted into my mouth and I swallowed it. As Silas spoke hurriedly on the phone I took a step back from him, drinking my own blood, the excess dripping down my chin, making crimson droplets on the grey carpet.

The kitten came with his tail in the air as I tried to swallow the stream of blood shooting into my mouth. He smelled the ruby puddles and I saw a pink little tongue stick out to lap it.

I took a step away from him and stumbled, my head suddenly going dizzy and my body filling with the feeling like I was being drawn up into the heavens.

Then my legs wobbled before they gave in to the haze – and I fell to the ground.

CHAPTER 21

KIRREL PUT THE CT SCAN ON THE BRIGHT LIGHT BOX and dimmed the lights in the room. He motioned Silas over and let him take a good look at the scan of Sanguine's brain.

Silas was quiet as his eyes analyzed the x-ray, seeing more in the light blues, blacks, and greys than even Kirrel himself.

"Brain damage," Silas said simply. His eyes narrowed as the force of his own words sunk into him. "Look at all those dark areas on the edges, the grey matter is reduced, and his thalamus…"

Kirrel nodded, the light box illuminating every line in his face. "It could've been worse. From what I can see in this scan he's only this high-functioning because he spent the first six years of his life with who he calls Nan. If he was in that basement from birth he would be feral and mentally retarded."

Silas's eyes jutted back and forth as he stared at the scan. "Schizophrenia? Multiple personalities? What is it? He speaks to this Crow like he is a physical person. He described him to me."

Another figure, hidden in shadows, stepped forward. Elish crossed his arms and, like the other two, he looked at the scan.

"I would hesitate labelling him, Silas," Elish said. He was wearing a blue dress shirt with a matching tie, and an open black blazer. "Mental illness was often mislabelled before the Fallocaust and with Sanguine being a chimera, I fear if we put a label on his illness we might end up with more problems than solutions. We don't want to assume he has symptoms he does not."

Though there may be dozens of emotions passing through King Silas's head, none of them showed on his face.

"I agree…" Silas said slowly. "And unfortunately Skytech just doesn't have the doctors yet to diagnose problems. Have you run all of this past Mantis? He's our only skilled psychologist."

"Yes, Kirrel has forwarded Mantis everything we have on Sanguine right now," Elish said. "He is interested in sitting down with Sanguine. You said earlier Sanguine lashed out on the little boy they found with him?"

There was a rustling behind Elish as Kirrel put up another scan onto the light box. This one of a left side view of Sanguine's brain.

"He was fine, well, as fine as he could be, until the boy started mentioning Jasper. I see nothing odd about that but what he was saying to the boy sparked my interest. He was commanding him to say nothing else about what went on in that basement and the little boy has clammed-up about it ever since," Silas responded.

"And Jasper? Where is he?" Elish asked.

A frozen air entered the room as Elish said those words. Silas's face became overcast and for a moment no one spoke.

"He's being held on the Dead Islands." The tone that came from Silas's lips was a cold stream. A trickle of ice that froze everything it came in contact with. In the dark corners Kirrel visibly flinched.

"You can ask him what he did," Elish replied.

Silas was silent again, his lips disappearing into his mouth.

"No, call it insanity if you will but I would rather it come from Sanguine when he is ready."

Silas's green eyes shot to Elish as Elish chuckled. Then with a glare that could peel fresh paint he said acerbically, "Do you have something to say, *gelus vir*?"

Elish shook his head slowly before saying in his own cold tones, "The guilt is too much for you right now, isn't it?"

Kirrel swallowed beside Elish before a stream of light spilled into the room, it was promptly followed by the soft latching of the door to outside – Kirrel had made a swift exit.

The middle-aged man had first been a sengil before becoming a doctor – he knew when it was time to leave.

"You may be my golden boy but I would still watch your mouth…"

The blond-haired chimera gave him a glance, going over every line in his king's face. He knew his moods, he knew his emotions. Elish knew his master more than anyone else on the planet and he prided himself in that.

"I think you know very well what happened in that basement and why Jasper had three little boys and a teenager that had been with him since he himself was a little boy. You just want to stay in denial for as long as you can," Elish said. "That is your reality and I understand it as I understand you."

When Elish went to put a hand on Silas's shoulder the king jerked it away. He gave Elish a dangerous look. "I feel no guilt over what happened and what you're implying never happened either. He was some stupid meth-addicted malinger-sadist who needed... who just wanted some fucking company."

"Occam's Razor, love."

"Shut up!" Silas suddenly snapped. He stalked over to the lights and flicked them on. He glared at Elish, his eyes green fire and his eyebrow twitching. "Don't you dare even bring it voice. Nothing like that ever happened to him and will never happen to any of my chimeras."

Then Silas turned around and made a motion to go to the door... but he paused.

"We won't label him with an illness but I need a plan on how we can repair his mind before his immortality."

"His mind could repair itself during his first resurrection..." Elish's voice trailed.

"Or it could not," Silas countered. "We don't know enough about it yet. What if his brain doesn't see the damage as something that needed to be repaired? We now have... at least four years to repair him as best as we can, until his brain stops growing."

Once again the king paused. He turned around and looked at his first born. "You would be proud of me, love." Silas chuckled dryly. "You wouldn't recognize me when I interact with him. I have never been this patient and kind with one of my chimeras."

Elish put a hand on Silas's shoulder and this time the king didn't jerk himself away from the touch. With that small gesture, all the permission Elish needed, he rubbed it in a caring manner.

"You feel guilty, Silas," Elish said. "And that is not a bad thing. You'll be able to help Sanguine better with that guilt."

"I have nothing to feel guilty about," Silas said, opening the door to the white and blue hallways of the College of Skytech. "I put him in the greywastes so he could come back and be my bodyguard. And with the greywasters starting to cause trouble in Irontowers I have every reason for needing one right now. Though he's a ruin as of this moment, it is only laying the foundation down for the man he will become."

"Do you really believe that?"

Silas walked through the doors and made his way down the hallway. Various Skyfallers were roaming the halls, most young men and women with textbooks and binders in their arms.

"It's a fact," Silas said darkly. "I know my chimeras and I know…"

He was quiet.

"They're stronger than that. Sanguine is stronger than that. He'll be fine – he'll be more than fine."

Elish said nothing, but his mouth was pulling in a frown. There were some things he could discuss with his king but in the same breath so many things he knew he couldn't. It would be fruitless to try and make Silas realize that Sanguine was a lot sicker than all of them knew. To even try to explain that to the king would be the equivalent to yelling at a brick wall.

So instead of taunting the cobra, Elish decided to be his support instead.

"I am sure Sanguine will turn out just fine, Master."

Silas pursed his lips but said nothing else. The cloud of dark energy forever gathering over his head. Elish could practically taste it in the air. Silas was troubled, though how troubled he was Elish didn't know.

Denial was a powerful and crippling thing.

"What will happen when King Silas finally admits to himself that Jasper was a pedophile? The fallout from that will be great. At least I'll be near enough to help him when his reality comes crashing down on him. I'll be his rock and no one else," Elish thought to himself. *"He will never forgive himself for what he let Sanguine be exposed to. This will be interesting."*

The two of them took the elevator to the second floor and walked into Elish's office, an office adjacent to the large classroom where he taught Science. Everything from Genetic Science to Physics. He was also Dean of the college and ran the entire college with the help of his brothers Perish and Garrett.

"Though his reading level is that of an adult, I assume his basic education is slim to nothing." Elish started gathering binders and stacking them on his office desk. A pandemically-organized oak desk with no personal items on it besides a photo of Silas holding Elish when he was three years old, and one of the entire family taken just last year. Both photos in simple black frames.

"Eventually I want him to start coming to the college once he passes elementary school," Silas said. "By then he should be confident with going outside and the rest of the family will have been told he's still alive. I want him in college. I want him to have a normal life like the rest of the second generation."

"I don't think…" But Elish stopped himself. He had a class to teach at the top of the hour and the last thing he needed was a bruise to show off to his students. Or even worse, for them to hear King Silas verbally lashing him for second-guessing his decisions. "Whatever it is he wants to do, the family will provide it for him."

That was what Silas wanted to hear. Silas got the binders and tucked them under his arm. "I was homeschooled, I can tutor him myself. I think right now he needs to bond himself to someone and that person has to be me. It might take a lot of painkillers and Xanax but I'll keep myself calm around him. Be a dear and come over tonight. I need to let out all the tension this chimera has been building inside of me."

"Of course," Elish replied, tucking another binder underneath Silas's arm. "Are you off to see Ellis now?"

Silas shook his head no. "I'm going back to him. He's being watched over by Kinny right now but he was staring off into space when I left him. He'll do that for hours on end, just stare at the wall. He barely blinks."

"Kinny?" Elish said with a hint of surprise in his voice. "You left a small sengil with him?"

Silas gave a wave and a scoff and at this Elish smirked. "He's just a sengil. We have a hundred orphans at Edgeview right now and half of them will turn out to be gay. If he kills him we can replace him."

Yes, King Silas's sympathies rarely stretched past his family. Elish opened the door leading outside of his office and was about to step through it when he suddenly was face-to-face with a young man. A man that Elish knew as his younger brother, Jack. With short silver hair, ebony black eyes, and a thin but soft face. He was a handsome chimera, though his clothing and style choice usually detracted from that in Elish's view. Jack dressed in a more gothic-style, complete with black eyeliner, a total of nine earrings in his ears, and to set himself apart from his family: a pair of black rimmed glasses.

"Is there something you need before class, Jack?" Elish asked in an unimpressed voice.

The young man's eyes widened as Elish said those words. In a way that suggested he was hesitant to say what he had come there to say. In response Elish raised an eyebrow and crossed his arms.

Jack's black eyes shot past Elish and he paled further when he saw King Silas standing behind him, the binders still tucked under his arm.

"It's nothing," Jack stammered. He swallowed hard and turned around to make a quick exit, the nerve that he must've hastily gathered quickly leaving him as he was confronted with both the King of the World and the Dean of the College of Skytech.

There was a shuffling of chains and metal on metal as Jack tried to walk away. The chains hanging off of his tight jeans (women's, to Elish's further distaste), shifting and tinkling together.

"Jack?" Elish called in a flat voice. "Is this it for your issue? Because I am giving you one chance to tell me. If you think you can go back and forth and waste my time with your cowardice I would think differently. One chance."

The young man immediately froze, as if Elish's words had encased him in ice. Slowly he turned around, looking stricken with nerves like he was being faced with the prospect of torture.

Jack raised his arm and scratched the back of his neck. He let out a long breath and glanced up at Elish and Silas.

With one last look he gathered his nerves and walked into Elish's office, closing the door behind him.

"You're going to fucking yell at me for this…" Jack said slowly.

"The King and Prince of Skyfall have no reason to yell," Elish responded coldly. "Now hurry up, Jack. Classes are starting soon."

A silence fell over the three of them as two pairs of eyes locked on Jack's. Nervously the chimera further itched the back of his neck before saying in a subdued and quiet voice, "Valen's been harassing me… him and his stupid gang."

Elish and Silas both gave him flat looks. The tips of Jack's ears went red and soon his gaze dropped to the floor and there it stayed.

"You're wasting my time because your brother is picking on you?" Elish said in a condescending tone. "Because your brother who's a year younger than you – is picking on you with his group of polo-shirt-wearing sluts? A couple of who are chimeras?"

"They call me names…" Jack's voice was barely audible; his shoulders slumped. "He's been threatening to gang rape me…"

One wouldn't believe that Elish's face could become colder than its natural state but at Jack's mumbled admission ice could practically be seen forming in the lines of his frown.

Then Silas stepped in front of Jack and gave him a small smile. Though this was no reassuring smile or even one of kindness; it was unimpressed and almost patronizing.

"Jack," Silas said. He raised a hand and stroked the young man's cheek before removing the black rimmed glasses that Silas knew, above everyone else, he didn't need.

Jack said nothing back. His ears reddened further as he stood face-to-face with his king and creator.

"Smile," Silas commanded, still holding the same patronizing smirk.

Jack sighed, trying to ignore the wave of embarrassment that was ravaging the bravery he never had. He knew what Silas wanted and why he wanted it, so he relented and smiled.

And in that smile held two rows of snow-white teeth, each one serrated and sharpened to a point.

The king nodded before lightly brushing the balls of his fingers over the genetically engineered teeth. Then he leaned in and gave Jack a kiss on the corner of his mouth.

"Do you know what you are, love?" Silas said in a hushed whisper. He put the slightest amount of pressure on Jack's cheek, directing the young chimera to look at him.

"A chimera?" Jack mumbled.

Elish gave an irritated sigh in the background but Silas only nodded. "Yes, lovely one, but not just that… you are a stealth chimera, *my* stealth chimera. You have weapons for teeth, agility like none other. Your body is perfect for quiet movements and your reflexes sharper than any of your brothers. Jack, why is my beautiful silver fox letting Valen get the best of him?"

Jack looked at his king, then behind him where Elish was giving them both an impatient look. These men were men that Jack respected like no one else. Silas, his king and master, and Elish, the man who helped raised him. Both of them were so strong, so in control. And though they both radiated elegance and dignity – there was an aura about them that told everyone in the room to be on guard.

And to be wary... because they were as dangerous as they were beautiful.

Jack's mouth twitched as Silas continued to stroke his cheek. "I'm not quick like you, King Silas. When they confront me I tighten up. I stall. My mouth turns to mush and I just want to get away from them as quickly as I can. I don't... I don't have that bloodthirst that our family has. I'm a horrible chimera."

"No," Silas said shaking his head. "You're not. You know very well you will receive no discipline if you kill Valen's arian gang members. All I ask is you do not fatally injure your brothers."

"I won't... I can't..."

"Stand up for yourself, Jack. You're a chimera. You're a Dekker. You rank higher than Valen, Ludo, Rio, and Felix, and they're only bullying you because you let them," Silas said.

Then above them a series of chimes sounded on the loudspeaker signalling that classes would start in five minutes.

Silas glanced up and so did Jack and Elish.

"You will receive no protection from me," Silas said, slipping his hand away from Jack's cheek. "It would be an embarrassment if I had to come to the rescue of someone who is supposed to be one of my most lethal," Silas said.

Elish frowned. "It looks like for the next batch we will have to make adjustments. This chimera is obviously a failure."

Jack's shoulders slumped.

Silas clucked at Elish. "We should be happy that he hasn't had to be used. Besides the chaos in Irontowers we've had quite a few years of peace. He'll grow into his own. Won't you, Jack?"

"Yes, Master," Jack said. When Silas handed him back his glasses he made the motion to put them back on his face, but at Silas's narrowed look he shifted uncomfortably and put them into his jacket pocket instead. "Thank you for taking the time out of your day to – to help me. I'll be going to class now. I will see you for Sunday dinner, Master?"

Silas nodded and patted Jack's shoulder. He turned Jack around and started walking him to the door.

"Yes, love. Learn lots now."

"I will..." Jack said with a sigh and the door closed behind him.

There was no mistaking the look of disappointment on Silas's face when he turned around. But as soon as he saw the equally negative expression gracing Elish's cold features he seemed to back pedal on his emotions.

"Don't start with me," Silas said bitterly.

Elish gave him an apathetic look before absentmindedly organizing his notes for today's lecture. "I'm just saying... we're having an exuberant amount of problems with your stealth chimeras."

"We only have two," Silas said flatly.

Elish glanced up as he put a folder in his briefcase. "One of them chewed a hole through his wrists last week and spends half his time hiding under his bed growling at people. The other is a cowardly oddball who weeps whenever a tree gets cut down or a bird flies into a window."

"He isn't that bad."

"He cried when the willow tree got struck by lightning."

"He likes nature!"

Elish sighed and shook his head; there was a clicking snap as he locked his briefcase.

"When you were little, Elish, I thought I had failed with you." Silas's tone suddenly dropped.

Elish paused and like Silas had been waiting for that chink in his armour he took a swing and hit his mark. "You were worse than Jack. Or is that why you're so hard on him? You had anxiety attacks as a child over how much Nero tormented you. Even Garrett stood up for himself more than you, and why did he? Because I protected you and sheltered you, and I left Garrett to fend for himself."

Elish ignored him and put a hand on the door handle, though he wasn't quick enough, another blow came swiftly.

"You were worse than he was, golden boy," Silas said.

Unable to stand it any longer Elish whirled around.

"I am practically your clone, Silas," Elish said sharply. "Jack is not. You fucked up the Chimera D's genetics so badly they're unable to function in normal society. Don't compare my genetics to his. I was able to overcome my issues because I am an arian with chimera enhancements. These stealth chimeras are barely human and now we're suffering the consequences of their maturity. And not just those chimeras, half of the second generation are failures."

"Remember your place, Elish," Silas said, each word becoming more and more hostile. "Don't throw me a paper tiger to rip apart. This isn't about his genetics; it's about his personality and his need to grow a pair. This has nothing to do with our problems with the second generation. This problem is an issue with Jack and nothing more."

"And what about the chimera you brought home a broken, traumatized shell?" Elish said, his hand testing the handle of the door, wishing he could open it and leave, but he knew better. "Your second stealth chimera?"

"Sanguine's problems are due to being in the greywastes and locked in a room for over eleven years. It has nothing to do with his genetics," Silas snapped.

"Yes, it does. Because his genetics kept him alive. Which is why we now have to deal with a schizophrenic mad man who's been sexually abused since he was–"

Silas slapped Elish right across the face.

Elish's eyes hardened and his lips pursed tight, but he said nothing as Silas glared at him, the king's chest heaving up and down.

"Get out of here," Silas said in a harsh grating whisper. "And you can forget about coming over. Get the fuck out of my sight."

Elish glared back before turning away and opening the door. "Gladly," he growled, before disappearing out the door.

Silas gave an approved nod to the two thiens who were guarding the door to his apartment.

"Were there any noises inside?" Silas asked them.

The two thiens shook their heads. "No, my king," the one on the left said. "Everything has been quiet inside and no one has come or gone."

Well, that's a plus, Silas thought to himself. *No blood curdling screams. No Kinny trying to flee from the gnashing teeth of the monster under the bed. Perhaps I can trust Sanguine to be left alone for several hours – though he seems like the type of man to snap on a hair trigger so perhaps I shouldn't become lax.*

The doors opened and Silas walked inside the dimly lit apartment, still shrouded in darkness from the black curtains on the windows. Immediately he was greeted by Kinny who still had all of his parts. And even more surprising he seemed calm and collected, not a single hint of terror on his face.

"Everything went well?" Silas asked as the auburn-haired sengil took his coat. Beside him, as always, was a glass of bloodwine and steaming mug of tea. Kinny knew what Silas wanted when he came home after being gone for a couple hours. Though since Elish wasn't coming over tonight Kinny may be used for other things, unless he decided to call one of his other chimeras.

Perhaps I should summon Valen. He sounds like he needs a good fucking for picking on Jack.

Kinny paused and Silas saw his mouth press. Immediately the king took a step away and gave Kinny a dangerous look.

"My apologies, Master," Kinny said. He was a very soft spoken sengil with the face of a cherub. A young man of twenty-one who had been Silas's personal sengil since the retirement of Kirrel six years ago.

The sengil dropped his voice, "He snapped out of his trance about an hour ago. Immediately he seemed stressed out and anxious and he started hiding food in his bedroom again. I hope you will understand… I let him do it out of fear that if I stopped him he may start hurting himself or worse."

Though the prospect of having to once again gut Sanguine's bedroom was annoying, the sengil did have a point. So Silas gave him a nod of dismissal and left the relieved Kinny to finish whatever duties he had been doing previous.

With the glass of wine in hand Silas walked over to Sanguine's closed bedroom door and put his hand on the handle. He opened it and walked inside the completely pitch black bedroom.

A growl immediately sounded, like Silas had just hit a trip wire.

"It's just me and I'm alone," Silas said. He closed the door and a moment later his night vision started to focus his eyes. Right away he could smell the food that Sanguine was hiding. Cookies mostly from the scent, and last night's dinner had made its way into the bedroom as well.

Arian meat spaghetti with bosen cheese on top. Well, I suppose we have another day before it becomes spoiled, though less since – Silas looked around – *he has the heat cranked right up. It's like a sauna in here.*

The growling stopped and this made the king hopeful… if only a bit.

He sat down on the floor and reached into his pocket. Silas pulled out a bag of potato chips he had gotten from the college vending machine and held it under the bed.

Though knowing what was about to happen he quickly pulled it back. Sure enough, he heard the scraping of nails on the floor as Sanguine tried, unsuccessfully, to snatch it.

"Nicely," Silas said sternly. "How many times must I tell you you're not going to starve? Try these, if you would like more then please join me in the living room."

"No," Sanguine's raspy voice said.

Well of course. I suppose he's already had his fill of food if Kinny was giving him free access to the fridge.

"How about you sit on the bed?" Silas said, trying his hand at negotiating. He had been a wonderful negotiator when the first and second generation were small. Though negotiations turned to demands once they hit their teen years but Sanguine was a bit... different.

Yes, that's the word for it.

There was a pause under the bed and for several seconds the sounds of their heartbeats and steady breathing were all that could be heard in the room.

Then the sounds of shuffling and shifting clothing. Silas stood back and soon Sanguine emerged.

Every time Silas saw him after being away he was taken aback with how ill the boy looked. His limbs were like grey broomstick handles and his face a skeleton that still had its skin. His hair was unhealthy and unbrushed, straw-like strands of black hair like he had a pile of hay on top of his head.

And those scars – Silas looked down at Sanguine's arms absentmindedly, but winced when he saw fresh cuts in his new chimera's skin.

Though the king bit down the comment on his lips and smiled instead.

Patience... you told yourself this year you would practice patience and now you must. Yelling at him will do nothing. You can't fuck this one up. The entire family, well the first generation anyway, is watching you. If you fuck up Sanguine you will suffer Elish's smug fucking look for the next three hundred years. Show them you're the calm leader you know you are and handle this with grace, Silas Dekker.

And I will.

Silas watched Sanguine sit on the bed and slowly, without any sharp movements, he sat at the head of the bed with him with his legs stretched out in front. Sanguine sat cross-legged beside him, surprisingly close, and held out his hand for the chip bag.

As Silas handed it to him he noticed something in Sanguine's hand, a small piece of sharp metal.

Silas motioned to it. "Are you using that to hurt yourself?"

Immediately Sanguine became flustered. He hid the piece of wire underneath his pillow and mumbled a small denial.

"Are you sure?" Silas asked.

"What does it matter?" Sanguine murmured. He took a nibble of a chip and weighed the flavour, before grabbing the bag like it had suddenly become the most important thing on earth. Though as he made the motion to duck back under the bed, oddly, he thought better of it and re-crossed his legs. Though that didn't stop him from starting to shovel the chips into his mouth.

"Because if it is… I would rather you use that than a knife," Silas replied.

Sanguine looked at him and swallowed the chips in his mouth. "I like the wire better because it hurts more without so much mess."

This sparked curiosity inside Silas. He decided to press him, if only to peek inside of that tormented mind. It may be fruitless but perhaps there was a method to this madness.

"So… you enjoy the pain not necessarily the gore?" Silas asked.

Sanguine nodded and Silas felt his heart jump. He slowed it and held out his hand to Sanguine.

After a pause, which Silas was sure was an inner debate going on inside of Sanguine's head, the red-eyed chimera reached into the bag and laid a chip onto Silas's hand. With a nod of appreciation and a small thank you Silas ate it.

Silas slid a hand under the pillow and grabbed the piece of wire and held out his hand. He traced the sharpened point over his pale, flawless skin – before digging the wire into it and, with a fair deal of pressure, dragged it across his skin.

The crunching of potato chips stopped. Silas looked up and saw Sanguine staring at Silas's hand with his red eyes wide with surprise and shock, the chip bag forgotten in his left hand.

Silas looked down at the inch long cut, before moving to the top of his wrist. With Sanguine watching, he dragged it across his skin, with a little less pressure but still enough to draw a red line.

Though as he dragged the wire, the line started to weave and curve, until Silas had made a beautiful design complete with a spiral. It looked like a long twisted string of ivy, the little ruby blood droplets gathering in the wound making it look like little roses.

Silas handed Sanguine the wire. "Even in the clutches of the most destructive agony... you can find beauty," Silas said, watching as Sanguine moved the bloodied wire around his hand. "Start with that. Make me a beautiful picture, Sanguine. Make me something out of that pain. Will you do that for me?"

Sanguine looked down at the wire, a perplexed but curious look in his eyes. Without a word he put the wire to his already scarred hands and arms and started pulling the thin piece of metal over his rough skin.

"I liked to draw crows," Sanguine said in a subdued voice. "I drew them on the concrete walls. I drew them over and over... I think I got good at it."

He drew crows... Silas watched as Sanguine started to draw what he realized was the head of the bird before he started to draw the curved body.

"Why crows?" Silas asked lightly. He weighed the emotion inside of the room, and deduced that it was calm and quiet enough for him to start trying to press Sanguine for information. He seemed to have succeeded in making Sanguine feel safe, at least tonight.

There is an odd feeling in the air... he does seem calmer. I wonder if the masochism is the key? Unfortunate but if I can make them non-fatal injuries we can make his skin perfect once I make him immortal.

"Outside the basement he had crows as pets," Sanguine explained. "Big crows with red eyes like mine. They spoke too. The few times I was allowed outside when I was younger they would surround me and speak. *Hello, Sanguine. Go on get! Come here, crow.* They spoke with me and I spoke back."

Red-eyed crows that speak? Silas tried to hide the surprise on his face. He knew what crows Sanguine was speaking of. They were genetically created crows that Perish had made, though more ravens than crows to be honest. They were an attempt to add more birds to the city. They had released several breeding pairs years ago but they were never seen again.

That man must've bought some of them from a merchant in one of the harbours. Where they had found Sanguine was literally on the other end of the greywastes, it would take months of travel for a merchant.

"And they were your friends?" Silas asked.

Sanguine nodded. "My only friends until Cooper... though Cooper is dead. Please don't ask about him."

"I won't," Silas whispered. He lightly traced his fingers over the bleeding arm seeing the image of the crow starting to take shape. It was standing like the hieroglyphs that the Egyptians used to draw, wings folded and stick-like legs steady. Silas thought Sanguine would stop after but instead he started to make little incisions that Silas realized were his bird feathers.

"Do you miss them?" Silas asked. He took in a small breath and started to focus his mind on the chaotic hive that was Sanguine's brain.

The young chimera nodded again and his jaw locked. He showed no sign that he was aware of what Silas was doing to him which made the king happy. Elish could tell now when he was trying to calm his mind and Garrett was starting to become aware also.

"They're going to die without him there to feed them, but birds aren't stupid. Perhaps they will go to Melchai," Sanguine said.

Perhaps... Silas thought to himself. He looked at his fingers, tipped with Sanguine's blood, and brought them up to his lips.

"No, he won't," Sanguine suddenly said. Silas looked at him, tasting the silky, copper blood as it taunted his mind. Every one of his creations had what tasted like the blood of gods inside of their veins. Silas could never get enough of that taste and Sanguine's blood was no different.

Then something fascinating happened. Sanguine looked up from his masochism and looked to his side, towards one of the purple painted walls. He fixed his eyes on the wall and to Silas's further surprise, his pupils actually dilated at the invisible thing he was seeing.

He really does see him... his brain really does see Crow.

"He's been kind so far," Sanguine said slowly. "I think he knows what not to ask about. He has respected that so far."

Well, he may be talking to a demon who only exists inside of his mind, but at least he's saying good things about me...

Sanguine's brow knitted and he turned away from the wall, though a moment later he viciously dug the wire into his arm and started to roughly pull and rip at his skin.

Silas cringed, debating whether to stop him. "Sanguine... you don't need to... be that rough."

Sanguine shook his head, his arm shaking under the force of his masochism. He clenched his teeth and made a noise before cutting a rather thick slice in his arm. When the wound was open and bleeding he stopped and let out a relieved breath.

Then something occurred to Silas. The king in that moment realized that Crow had most likely been the one to tell him to do that.

"Why do you listen to him?" Silas asked in the same casual light voice. Seeing a faint opportunity he gently took the wire from Sanguine's grasp and started rubbing the blood away from his wound with his fingers.

"Because he knows what's best for me," Sanguine answered. He held his arm out to Silas as if inviting him to continue to touch his blood. Silas obliged and started bringing his fingers back and forth to his mouth, gathering the small trickle as it spilled over his skin like an overflowing basin.

When Sanguine gave him a curious look Silas smiled.

"We enjoy each other's taste," Silas said, holding out his own arm, giving Sanguine an invitation. "You have certain things in your engineering that you cannot escape. I can help you be the best person you can be."

Sanguine cautiously ran his finger over Silas's wound and tasted it. Obviously impressed he gathered more. The sound of him sucking his fingers filled the room.

"I like it... I'm glad that's normal," Sanguine said. He laid down on the bed and took in a deep breath. Silas was happy to see his eyes were starting to relax, and though he glanced at the wall where Crow was, he didn't address him. "Is liking pain normal?"

Silas smiled. "Sometimes we do – on certain occasions."

Sanguine fell silent for a moment, his red eyes not as petrified and his jaw finally becoming loose. To further confirm the young man's relaxed state he held up his injured arm to Silas and handed him the wire.

Inside Silas breathed a sigh of relief. Usually when he was using the abilities inside of his brain, it was to shut off his chimeras' minds, calming them into dark oblivion if they became enraged or hostile. He had done it to Sanguine several times.

But today he decided to calm his chimera a different way. A soft flow of static, a relaxing higher octave of sound that would be the kiss of bliss to the troubled chaotic mind of the man in front of him.

"Will you draw that design on my arm?" Sanguine asked quietly.

The king glanced down at the injured arm. The picture of a crow smeared with blood though the lines were still holding those crimson rubies. It looked like a rubbing of a cave painting, light smears of red though the outlines shone through, showing off every scarlet line and every carved feather.

He wants me to touch him? Though he was over two hundred years old this drew up a restriction in his throat. As it stood Sanguine was the only chimera of age that he hadn't been intimate with. And though he was the picture of self-control, there was something about touching Sanguine… cutting Sanguine, that brought a tight heat to all the wrong places.

But he couldn't resist. Silas took the piece of wire and rested Sanguine's hand on one of his crossed legs. He took a deep breath to try and vanquish the quivering inside of his body and picked up Sanguine's hand.

Silas traced the rough skin and tried to keep his breath steady. Then he started to slowly cut the young chimera's skin.

He shuddered as he saw the first droplets of blood start to gather.

But if Silas thought that this was as far as his self-control would have to go he was gravely mistaken. As he cut a beautiful swirling, almost floral design into Sanguine's skin, the chimera closed his eyes and let out the smallest moan.

He likes it… he really likes it. Silas's insides clenched, constricting tightly around his stomach and filling the cavity of his body with a burning tension that was almost painful. In the areas of his mind where he kept his most vile transgressions, he danced with the idea of going further. Of either increasing the pain or trying to switch it to something sexual, but he had to have restraint.

Sanguine moaned softly again; his eyes still closed and his hand relaxed. His heart was pounding though, like he was in the middle of intense foreplay. This did nothing to stop the hardness Silas could feel below, on the contrary, it was driving his mind crazy.

He drew the wire over Sanguine's skin, making small patterns of vines and swirls like a delicate henna tattoo. In all respects it was a beautiful work of art.

"There…" Silas whispered. "Beauty in pain."

Sanguine's eyes opened. Soft discs of the deepest red, like a crimson sea so full of emotions, both good and bad. He was the most relaxed and content that Silas had seen him since his arrival. It filled Silas with hope for his future, though as the purple sheets showed off their blood droplets he had to remind himself just what he had had to do to get Sanguine into this state. Not only just cutting him – but his own mind soothing those open blisters that Sanguine wore on his sleeve.

"I liked that," Sanguine whispered. He put his arm down and stared at the wall, blinking slowly in a disconnected state, the smell of blood filling the entire bedroom and still sinking itself into Silas's body.

The king smiled and put the piece of wire down. A small act, a small smile, but underneath his surface his heart was racing, and below his dick was rock hard and throbbing. It was aching to feel the tightness around it, begging for the chance to draw out more noises from this mysterious creation he had finally found.

And I could take him, right now. I am the King of the World I could take him every day if I wanted.

And do I ever want to…

Not soon after he realized his hands were starting to tremble, matching the shaking inside of his chest as his lust desperately tried to convince him to take Sanguine right now. To lean in and kiss him, to stroke that pale skin, to peel off his clothing and see just what he had to offer his king. The desires inside of King Silas boiled him alive and left him with such a want he found himself raising a hand to touch Sanguine's cheek.

But he pulled back, and to prove to himself that he was in control, he shifted off of the bed.

"I will leave you to rest, love." Silas's voice cracked under his dry mouth. He swallowed and forced the smile to remain on his face. "Sleep… sleep well."

He turned around and started for the door, though when he put his hand on the door knob he heard a faint voice sounding from the bed.

"Thank you," Sanguine whispered.

Silas closed his eyes and nodded. "You're… welcome."

And with that, he quickly left, closing the door behind him. Immediately he spotted Kinny watching television with the kitten on his lap.

"You," Silas said breathlessly. "Remove your clothing and come with me to the bedroom."

CHAPTER 22

SILAS WAS RIGHT… I DID HATE MATH. I ACTUALLY hated everything there was to do with math. I didn't understand anything more complex than what the X symbol did, the one I had learned on the calculator as a kid, and even then I didn't understand why carrying numbers made everything suddenly work. It was stupid.

"Why don't you just outlaw this?" I said bitterly as I dropped the lead pencil onto my work book. "You hate it; you say all of my brothers except for the science chimeras and intelligence ones can't do it. So just make it illegal already."

Silas laughed, his face beaming with a smile that seemed to come from Puck himself. He picked up the pencil and started filling out the question I had been stuck on, upside-down. I knew he wasn't purposely being smug but it still made me give him a flat look.

"It wouldn't be the first time I made something I hated illegal," Silas replied. Then he pointed to a nine he had written down. "See… twenty-three times fifteen… you put the one over the three…"

"Long division is stupid… when do I need to long divide in life?" I muttered, but I tried to follow the steps.

Silas ignored me. "So then we now turn the two into a three… times that by five and we have fifteen."

I grunted. Silas carried on, still holding his stupid smile. "On the second row we times the one by twenty-three and with our two rows what do we do?"

I sighed and rested my cheek onto my hand. "We plus it."

"We add it together, that's right... now I know you can add so what is one hundred and fifteen times two hundred and thirty?"

My eyes looked at the numbers and I took the pencil from him. This wasn't as hard as the other problems in the workbook so I took a moment to do the math on my fingers and started writing down numbers.

"Three hundred and forty-five," I said out loud, then looked at King Silas to see if I was right or not.

I disliked admitting it but there was a flicker of pride welled inside of my chest when Silas nodded his approval. "Correct! See? Long division isn't hard. The other stuff is complicated but we don't really teach trigonometry or any of that unless you're taking the course at the college. So in a way you are lucky. I haven't made math illegal but the complicated stuff isn't in the school system. There *is* really no need for it."

I guess that was better than nothing. "So you say that you made illegal certain things you didn't like..." I glanced up and visibly flinched when Kinny appeared beside me. I was in the living room with Silas and though it was only the three of us Kinny was extremely quiet. He appeared beside you at random moments seemingly out of nowhere. It still gave me a start though he always looked apologetic when he did.

Kinny put a bowl of chips down beside my workbook which I immediately dug into. Silas grabbed one and ate it politely but I still couldn't help cramming them into my mouth.

The king chuckled, as if the answer amused him and, sure enough, it was a rather amusing answer. "Before the Fallocaust... Disney started churning out horrible sequel after horrible sequel of some of the world's most beloved movies. A selfish cash grab. The Little Mermaid, Tarzan, The Hunchback of Notre Dame... almost everything. Horrible low budget movies with barely any thought put into it. The Lion King was even worse... oh don't get me started on that horrible sequel." Silas took another chip and nibbled off a bite. "But since they made so many I have never found all of them of course, and I don't... per se, *punish* my people for watching them. I just have a huge bounty of forty dollars per movie to encourage people to hand them over to the authorities. I wish to not taint a nice Disney legacy so... we burn them after we get them. I have some elites who've gotten rich finding boxes and boxes of these movies in the greywastes. I enjoyed the smell of boiling plastic when I light them on fire."

"That's a lot of money," I said trying to finish the last problem in my work sheet. It was long division again but I think I could do it since I had an example of one right there. "All of you have so much money."

"You do too," Silas responded. I gave him a skeptical look and at that he reached into his pocket and handed me a card. "We just put the system in about ten years ago. Our first digital way of paying for items, just like they had before the Fallocaust. If you give this card to anyone in Skyfall they'll charge it to us at a discount and give you the item."

My mouth twitched as I took the strange, shiny black piece of plastic. I glanced at it and saw raised numbers and letters in gold writing.

Sanguine Sasha Dekker. Over the last week I had learned my middle name was Sasha like most of the second generation. King Silas says we were named after a friend of his before he ended the world. I wondered if he had killed him but I hadn't asked.

"I don't go out though…" I said in a subdued voice. I looked back down and wrote a number I thought was right.

Silas waited until I was done my math problem before he spoke. "Would you like to go outside?"

I shook my head no. Even the light that sometimes streamed into the dark apartment, mostly when the kitten was playing with the curtains or he found a fly trying to get outside, made me uncomfortable.

"You know you'll have to go out sometime, lovely boy," Silas said but still I shook my head. I was just starting to get used to being in the living room without my mind constantly having me on guard. Outside there were… too many people, too much light, and too much noise.

I tried to explain this to him, and though I was mumbling and tripping over my words he seemed to understand what I was saying. He could hear really well. He had the enhancements I had learned were unique solely to chimeras. My sharp eyesight plus night bright… well, night vision as they called it, plus my hearing. All of these had come from my genetic engineering.

"Well, you'll have to go outside to receive a gift I was able to get for you," Silas said and at this I looked up at him.

I gave him a curious look. By now I was used to his bribes, usually said in a singy voice, with every word coming out of his mouth like it was coated in glitter.

I wrote down the last number in my math work and handed him the paper. "You can't bribe me to do everything…" I said with a frown. "I'm not a cat where you can shake a treat bag and I come running."

"And how else do I get you to do things?" Silas smirked, his eyes scanning my work before he took a red pen that he had tucked behind his ear. "Asking doesn't wield any results. How am I supposed to coax you into your family?"

I thought for a second as he graded my paper. I grabbed another chip and was proud of myself that I had left some in the bowl while I had this conversation. I hadn't eaten and eaten until it was all gone.

"Let me do it on my own?"

Silas snorted and I gave him an angry glare. He caught it and smiled at me. Then with a wave of his hand he said, "If I let you do it at your pace you would still be hiding under that bed and I fully believe we would be celebrating your seventieth birthday under there too. Why can't we just make it a mutual thing? If you promise not to shoot me down every time I ask you to make a step, we can meet in the middle."

"I don't like outside," I said flatly. "There is nothing for me out there but people who can hurt me, and activity, noise, and busy things that I dislike. Tell me what awaits me outside that is so important I see? I've seen the sun; I've seen what arians look like. No thanks."

"You can see Stadium!" Kinny suddenly said. He was behind Silas with a statue of an Eskimo man on his lap. He was polishing it with a rag. "That would be exciting!"

"Stadium?" I asked and looked to gauge Silas's reaction. He made no facial expression though he just continued grading my paper. "What's Stadium?"

Silas was using the red marker a lot but I ignored that. "Stadium is a way that the royal family makes money, plus gets rid of condemned criminals," he explained. "Every Saturday we bring out that week's convicts who have been convicted and sentenced to death. Rapists, murderers, terrorists, you know, bad people. We put them in front of Nero and give them a knife or some small weapon and Nero with nothing. If the convict kills Nero we set him free, though odds are the crowd is treated to a gladiator-type fight to the death which is amusing. We also have entertainment usually from your brothers. We bring out the lions and cougars, wolves and other pre-Fallocaust animals to do tricks, and we have contests between the chimeras to show off their strength or intelligence. We will also show off any new babies. It's a wonderful show and promotes community and culture. It also helps remind the Skyfallers that the Dekker family is in charge and just as powerful as they think."

Condemned criminals? Though this Stadium thing piqued my interest the part about bringing out the convicts churned my gut. I had a question on my lips, one I wanted to ask so badly it seemed to coat my mouth in embers… but I couldn't form the words. I couldn't ask…

So I looked down at the work book, and stared at it. Pursing my lips and forcing down the question that was searing my insides.

My saviour came in the form of a knock on the door. A light knock so I knew it must either be Garrett or Elish. With a jump in my heart I got up to run to my bedroom but paused when Silas cleared his throat.

To my surprise he pointed to a corner of the living room with no lamps or any light near it. I looked over and realized it was a large structure covered in blankets, with a small dark hole leading inside.

"Garrett and I made that for you last night, love. It's safe and protected. Hide in there not under that bed. You'll destroy your back, and this way you can watch who comes and goes," Silas said rising to his feet. He gave Kinny a nod to answer the door.

I gave Silas a suspicious look, but I had been here for almost two weeks now and not once did he make a move to harm me. So I quickly walked to the little home-made cave and ducked inside.

I was content to see that inside was a foamy mattress and lots of pillows and blankets. I crouched down at the back of the den (an old cage it looked like but I wasn't offended by that) making myself as out-of-sight as I could and watched the sengil answer the door.

It was Elish. I disliked Elish because of his cold, patronizing voice but he was predictable when it came to his movements, voice, and personality. He might be a jerk but he was the same jerk every time he came so I was okay with that.

I didn't move though, but I managed to swallow down the growl that was vibrating in my throat.

Then a little boy appeared in the door way too. He looked to be about seven or eight with thick curly blond hair and as he looked around I noticed he had orange eyes as well. I had been told about the youngest chimera in the family. His name was Drakonius, or Drake for short.

As Elish and Silas started making conversation I saw Drake's eyes sweep the room. Though as soon as they fixed on my new den he paused and suddenly grinned.

"Play fort!" Drake suddenly exclaimed, and at full speed he started running at me.

I bristled and immediately tensed as the boy started speeding towards me like a little blond freight train, and I wasn't the only one. Elish and Silas both turned around at the same time, yelling an enthusiastic NO! in unison.

But as the little boy with a huge smile peeled towards me, I mentally berated myself and forced down the growl. In a split second I reversed my thinking and destroyed the part of my mind that felt threatened. Instead I shifted away from the entrance of the cave to give him room.

Drake stopped, Silas and Elish still running towards him, and when he saw me… to my surprise, he grinned and poked his head in.

"HI!" he said in a cheerful voice.

"Hello," I said back. The boy squealed, though as he lifted a little boot to come into my cave two sets of hands grabbed him and pulled him back. The shock of the suddenness of the grab making Drake scream in fright.

Elish yanked Drake back, and to my anger he gave the crying child a hard smack upside the head. Drake started wailing.

And I started to growl.

"Stop your pathetic whining. I told you beforehand to stay with me while we see the king!" Elish snapped. "You can wait outside the door now and think about why you decided to disobey a direct order."

"Fuckface!" Drake suddenly screamed and at that Elish dealt him a harder smack.

As Drake's face crumpled and went red, I felt a blackness descend on my vision. A dark curtain that disrupted the normal impulses of my brain like I had been cloaked in a veil. In my radiating anger at Elish hitting Drake I heard Crow in my mind.

'Attack. Attack. Attack.'

"I can't! I can't attack him!"

"ATTACK!" Crow demanded. He started saying it again and again in my head and when I shook my head his voice only got louder and more painful.

I clenched my teeth and closed my eyes, Crow still screaming inside of my head.

Screaming and demanding. I had to do it. I had to go it.

'Attack. Attack. Attack! Protect Drake! You didn't protect the little boys. FUCKING COWARD!'

'ATTACK! ATTACK! ATTACK!'

I jumped out of the den and lunged at Elish, tumbling with him to the floor. Elish swore as he landed hard, and made the motion to throw me off of him but I was too quick. Without hesitation the man who ruled the darkness in my mind opened my mouth and sunk my teeth into Elish's throat, feeling the taste of chimera blood mixed in with my own saliva.

'Bite! Bite!' Crow's own raspy voice demanded in my head. His painful commands had switched to a dry hiss. A slippery demand that was almost taunting. *'Bite! Bite him! We'll kill him!'*

Then an electric percussion tore through me. I gasped, my teeth automatically unhinging, and screamed as I was electrocuted on top of the blond chimera. Ripping current after ripping current slicing my veins like my blood had turned into electricity.

I rolled off of him with a groan but though my mind was still writhing on the floor my body was already righting itself. I went back in for a second bite but instead Elish smacked me across the face, and soon after another pair of arms, ones that belonged to Silas, grabbed me.

I screamed my rage and tried to yank my limbs away from Silas. Thrashing and screaming, kicking my feet up in the air, trying everything I could to get loose. Crow demanded more blood, he wanted me to kill him. He wanted me to pay him back for hurting that young boy.

'Revenge for fucking you, pay him back for tricking you into coming to the farm. Rip him, tear him. Why should he be in the Dead Islands still alive? We have to get him! We have to pay him back for everything he did to us!'

The caustic demands of Crow ravaged my mind, making a burning come to my face that threatened to spill every emotion I had onto the carpeted floor below me. Inside I felt a new insanity, an insanity in the forms of demand after demand to do something to this blond man, pay him back for things I knew he hadn't done to me.

I tried to tell Crow this but he wouldn't listen. He was trying with every force of energy he could to get me closer to Elish. Everything in his mental power to unleash himself, on not only the tall blond chimera, but the entire world.

"Sanguine…" Silas suddenly whispered into my ear. "Why are you so upset?"

"He hit the little boy… he hit the little boy!" I snarled. "He was just a fucking kid!"

Silas continued to make soothing noises, though the only thing calm about him was his voice. His hands still held my own in an iron-like grip. He was strong, incredibly strong.

"You're angry because Elish hit Drake?" Silas said quietly to me. "You don't like seeing him hurt, do you?"

I nodded. I saw the images of Jasper get drawn up inside the theatres of my mind. Video images of him hitting me when I was outside with the crows. When he had let me out to look for video cameras in their mouths.

"Drake's fine," Silas said calmly. "Elish loves Drake. He takes him for months sometimes. Drake isn't being hurt."

"He's crying!" I yelled, and I realized that the little boy was. I turned my head and my eyes focused on source of the noise.

Drake was on the couch hiding under my red blanket; soft, scared crying coming out from underneath the fabric. He sounded terrified.

"That's because you scared him," Silas said in a calm voice. "He's only scared because you're being scary."

And at this admission, Crow took a step back. I could feel a caution inside of him though, but, feeling a bravery I had only recently acquired, I pushed down this psychosis I had fallen into and tried to get my mind back.

Silas loosened his grip. I ignored the look of ice from Elish and pulled my arms away from Silas. I looked towards the bundle underneath the red blankets and took a step towards it, but felt Silas put a hand on my shoulder.

"I want to show you something…" Silas said slowly. "The surprise I told you about earlier. Would you like to see it?"

I took a step away from him and crossed my arms tightly over my chest. Suddenly I felt cold inside, like Crow's presence was an iceberg imbedded between my ribs. I sniffed, hearing Drake still whimpering under the blanket, and nodded.

"Where do you think he's taking us?" I asked Crow as Silas led me by the shoulder towards the edge of the living room.

Crow, now beside the tall archway leading to the kitchen, gave Silas a skeptical look. He still had some of Elish's blood on his lips.

"I'm not sure but I suppose we can let him lead us," Crow replied in a low voice full of mistrust. "You trust this one, yes?"

"Yeah," I replied quietly.

My nerves were lost when I realized Silas was leading me to the sliding door. It was light outside; I could see the sun underneath the curtains. I didn't want to be outside.

"No…" I stammered. "I don't want to go out." I tried to stiffen my legs but with a light pull I stumbled forward, my breath catching in my throat as I did.

Silas let go of my hand but I was too petrified to run back to the den. Instead I watched as he drew the curtain and peaked outside, a stream of light piercing the dark room, making my eyes automatically squint.

I shielded them and turned away as more light flooded the room. My heart hammered in my chest, two continuous thumps like the muscle was trying to escape out of my rib cage.

Unable to stand it any longer, I closed my eyes and started walking towards my cave. Needing the shelter of darkness, and the security of an enclosed space. Somewhere where there were no people, no one but me and Crow. I had to get away from this – this was too much.

"Hello, Sanguine."

My consciousness seemed to shoot out of me as those words reached my ears. Suddenly the apartment melted away from me, the sounds, smells, the tension. Everything dripped down to the floor like melting plastic and pooled underneath my feet.

I must be back at Jasper's – how can I be hearing…

"Come here, crow."

I opened my eyes and slowly turned around. I forced my eyes to remain open under the stinging sunlight and I covered the short distance to the sliding glass door.

They were watching me. Silas was only several steps from my body, but I saw nothing of him or Elish, or their presence. My focus was on the door and the blurs starting to take shape in the glaring, brilliant sunlight.

I opened the sliding glass door, and felt the stinging of air on my face, but it was pleasant and warm. It seemed to caress my face in its heat, and in that warmth I was reminded of the sunny days of Sunshine House. Or my summers in the shanty town. When I would run around, free and untamed, enjoying the sun on my face and the air in my lungs.

Yes, fresh air. Air that seemed to coat my lungs in cold water. I didn't feel scared as I breathed in and out, and that urged me into taking my first step outside.

Then a flutter of wings, and the sounds of nails against a metal railing. As my eyes adjusted I looked around and was greeted by well over a dozen crows. All of them perched on either the railing or the patio furniture, watching me with ruffled feathers and bobbing heads.

I took another step forward, my mouth open in shock and my heart pounding. They were here... my friends were here. How did they get here?

I held out my hand, and to my inner joy one of the crows jumped onto my wrist. Then, like they were taking their cues from the leader, other ones started hopping over. Soon another one jumped onto my arm, and then one on my shoulder. With a flutter of feathers and a few caws, six of the crows landed on my body and perched on me with a casual comfort that told me they knew who I was.

And that they had missed me.

"Hello, Sanguine."

"Do you want food?"

Then something strange happened. Something that hadn't happened to me in a long time.

I smiled, my mouth open and everything. It had been so long since I had smiled I almost didn't know what to do with myself. I was so happy, so giddy inside I thought I was going to explode. During the eleven years of my captivity, the only permanent, flesh and blood friends I had ever had had been the crows. They'd never left me unlike my family; they'd always been there to keep me company.

"Hello, Sanguine!" one of them said.

"Hello, friends," I said to them, still smiling. "You came a long way... would you like some food?"

"Do you want food?"

My smile widened and I looked behind me. "Did you bring them?"

In the doorway Silas stood, his face holding a smile like mine and a content glint in his eyes that told me everything he was feeling was genuine. He stepped onto the balcony, making the crows around me bob up and down and caw at him.

Silas nodded. "Yes, I did. They're yours now, Sanguine. We'll let them live a spoiled life here and we can let them multiply and in time... all of Skyfall will be full of them."

He had done this? Never in my life had I felt appreciation for another human being. No one had ever done something nice for me to make me experience that emotion. I knew the basics of it but had never felt that pull towards someone.

But I was feeling it now. I was feeling it towards King Silas. A man who had created me, and when I had returned home… had shown me more patience and kindness than I had ever experienced in my nineteen years.

"Thank you," I said to him and to make him happy I smiled again, my eyes squinting like Crow's did whenever he smiled. "My king."

Silas beamed at this and walked over to me. I flinched as he raised a hand and put it to my cheek, but I didn't back away.

"The smile I see on your face is something I will remember until time ceases to go forward," Silas said to me. There was that sparkle in his brilliant forest-green eyes, a lightness to them that attracted my own vision immediately. "Thank you, for letting me see it."

He stroked my cheek with a touch that was like that of a feather. Softly stroking and feeling my prickly beard. It wasn't bad and I no longer felt the need to get away from it. I felt calmed by it almost.

"Can I come and look, please?"

Our gazes broke. We both turned around as the sound of a little boy's pleas reached our ears. Sure enough, Drake was standing in the door frame of the window, Elish in the background with his arms crossed and a cold expression on his face.

Silas turned back to me. "They're your crows, love."

I knelt down and motioned Drake to come over. I was happy to see that he had stopped crying, though his eyes were red and I could see the tear stains on his rosy cheeks.

"Yes, come here." I bent my elbow, so my hand was resting beside my heart, the leader crow perched on my forearm, watching the boy as he slowly walked towards us. The birds seemed content with him being close to them. They cocked their heads back and forth and hopped around me. The ones on the railing continuing to scratch their claws on the metal.

Drake smiled and walked over to the lead crow with a bravery only a child could have. The little boy, with curly blond hair and big orange eyes, smiled and outstretched a hand.

One of the crows hopped off of my shoulder, walked down my arm and then jumped onto Drake's outstretched hand. He flapped his wings and at this Drake's face broke into an even wider smile.

"I love birdies!" he giggled and held up his hand. "Like the kittens and puppies…" Drake turned around and looked at Elish and I realized he was speaking to him. "We are gentle to animals. Right, Master Elish?"

Elish, still inside the apartment looking at us, nodded stiffly. "That's correct."

Drake turned back to me, and made the motion to say more, when one of the crows pecked at one of his spiral curls and tugged on it. The boy burst into giggles and shook his head, his head of curls shaking back and forth, encouraging the bird to do it again.

But as he did this, my smile faded and soon my lips disappeared into my mouth.

He was so young... look at this boy. He was – fuck, he was my age.

I was on my own at this age. Nan made me leave Sunshine House when I was this small? I didn't even realize how young I was at the time. I just did what I had to do to survive. No wonder Cory and the others were so shocked that I was an orphan rogue.

Jasper...

Jasper must've thought he had won the lottery.

My lips pursed, and my face tensed.

"Why are you sad?" Drake suddenly said, noticing the expression on my face. "You have so many bird friends."

I held up a hand and touched the side of Drake's face gently, the area behind my eyes started to burn. Before I could stop myself or think better of it, I found myself saying:

"You're so... little."

I pulled my hand back immediately but the damage inside of me had already been done. Crow started stirring inside of me, and I could see him out of the corner of my eye. Though he said nothing his presence brought with it a new wave of suspicious. Ones that I knew were unfounded but what had happened to me at Jasper's farm left me no room for assumptions. My trust of strangers had been shattered over and over again, and my experiences with people had made me suspicious of everyone.

There was no default trust. That trust had been bled out of me.

Children were honest. Children didn't know deception outside of white lies. Though Silas had treated me well, I had seen Elish hit Drake and –

I didn't want to think of my family in this way – but as I looked at that small boy, this fragile creature, this empty vessel. I had to have that confirmation that this royal family I belonged to weren't hiding any caustic beliefs behind their crowns.

"I'm little!?" Drake said aghast. "I'm eight soon! I'm not little. Master Silas says I'll be taller than him."

I looked at his face and scanned it. Though as I did I realized that even after everything that had happened to me I still smiled and played. So perhaps only direct questions would wield me the answers Crow and I needed to hear.

"Do they hit you often, Drake?"

Drake shrugged, and absentmindedly rubbed his head, where Elish had struck him, but as the crow pecked his arm he snorted and lowered it.

"Sometimes I get spankings for being bad. One spank for every year I was born. I'm almost eight and soon I'll get eight spanks with the spoon."

I nodded slowly. "Where?"

"On my butt!" Drake laughed. "Usually, or if there isn't a spoon or I'm running I just get thwacks. Thwacks are... are... Garrett says thwacks are like spankings-on-the-go and they thwack me wherever. You know, they're for when there ain't no spoons."

"*Are* no spoons," Elish corrected him from inside the apartment.

Relief flooded through me and I nodded, smiling at Drake's joke even though my stomach was full of poison over what I had to ask next.

"My Nan did the same to me..." I said, and swallowed hard. "Is that all they do to you? Do they hurt you in any other way?"

Drake shook his head and at that my entire body started to relax. "I got a spanking and sent to bed without dinner just two nights ago. Did you know what I did? I called Garrett a fuckface. He was being a fuckface too. I like that word."

I held up my hand as another crow started trying to hop onto Drake. I put it on his shoulder and we both watched as the crow jumped over to him and gave a caw.

"Hello, Sanguine."

"Are you happy here? You love your family?" I asked Drake.

Drake nodded vigorously; his tongue sticking out as he did. "I love Master Silas and I love Master Elish, and Garrett, and Mrs. Ellis, and Knight, and I love Jack, and I love Nero, and I love Ceph. I love everybody! I even love *you*." Then another crow jumped onto his arm. Drake outstretched both his limbs and started walking around, stiff like he was pretending to be a robot.

"I am a chimera of the future! I am half-crow, half-boy!" At his movements the crows flew off of his shoulders and landed on the railing. Drake laughed and jumped up and down. "I'm going to get them food!" He ran back inside without another word.

I got up, feeling the crows tighten their claws around the fabric of my clothing as they tried to keep steady. I watched the little boy go into the apartment and looked over at Silas.

The king was looking at me, with a strange expression on his face. It was a mixture of pride, but at the same time guilt. Two emotions that seemed strange together but they seemed to swirl perfectly on this king's face.

Though as soon as Silas saw I was looking at him they disappeared, and his kind smile was brought forth. Content and beaming, without the hints of sad feelings that I had seen previous.

"Did you get the reassurances you needed, love?" Silas said quietly.

I felt embarrassed at being directly called out, but I nodded. Silas sat on one of the patio chairs, one with a grey cushion on it, and motioned for me to do the same. The vast expanse of cityscape in front of me was making me nervous. The cityscape stretched on for miles before I could see a grey ocean. I had never seen the ocean before and it made me nervous more than it impressed me. So I turned away from it, pretended it didn't exist, and sat beside Silas in the sunshine.

"Yes," I said quietly.

"We're a good family, Sanguine," Silas responded. "We love our children and we give them the best childhoods as we can. A lot of love, education, and guidance."

I wish this made me happy. I wished I had the strength to push past the feeling burning my contentment alive. But I either wasn't that strong of a person... or the wound was still too raw.

"And yet you sent one of your children away to fend for himself," I responded bitterly. "I suppose it didn't matter did it?" I looked at Silas and saw a pull on his mouth, but it didn't stop me from saying what I knew I had to say. "You could always just create another one."

Unable to swallow down the sadness this brought to me, I got up. And without another word, I walked back into the apartment... and crawled back to my den.

CHAPTER 23

"COME ON… IT'S BEEN MORE THAN ENOUGH TIME. You need a bath."

I shook my head and pulled my sweatshirt hoody over my head. Silas made a sound through his teeth and I saw him cross his arms out of the corner of my eye.

Today marked me being in Alegria for two months, I was slowly starting to put weight on and Silas and Kinny had both told me I was starting to get some colour back to my face. I couldn't tell because I hadn't shaved in months and months and my hair was tangled, knotted and sticking out in all directions.

"Sanguine, lovely… could you at least brush your teeth?"

"No!" I shook my head again and this time drew on my draw strings so the hoody closed around my face. I didn't care how I looked. I was comfortable with clothes on, and every fiber in my being wanted me to stay in clothes, as many clothes as I could put on myself.

Silas sighed and I saw him sit down on the edge of my bed. The bed was made because I had slept underneath it. I was starting to have terrible nightmares and I felt better if I woke up under the bed during those times. Everything seemed manageable if I was in an enclosed space, I wasn't sure why.

"Why not? Don't you think you would feel better? Washing all that grime off of you from that basement?" Silas asked.

It would make me feel better… I think it would anyway, but I oddly felt comfortable with the grime on me. I like being dirty and disgusting…

no one would stay near me if I smelled horrible and I was ugly.

"I like being this way…" I mumbled.

Silas, of course, didn't like this answer. "But underneath that layer of dirt lays an Adonis of a chimera. I want to see what you would look like at your best and I know it would make you feel better."

I was quiet. A moment later Silas got up and left the room and I thought that was the end of it. But a moment later he came back and put a toothbrush into my lowered gaze.

"Do this for me at least. Just brush your teeth and I'll leave you in your eleven years of filth," Silas said in a flat tone. I knew he wasn't happy but I didn't expect him to understand how I felt. He never had anything like what I had gone through happen to him. How could he understand?

I stared at the toothbrush and as I held it Silas unscrewed a tube of toothpaste and put a bit on the brush. Immediately I brought it to my mouth and licked the toothpaste off. I ate it and held out my hand for some more. I enjoyed the flavour of mint and I liked that it was gooey.

The king sighed and then he chuckled. "I can't stay mad at you. Eating toothpaste, what an idiot." He put some more on the brush. "Brush your teeth with this, you know how to do that don't you?"

Nan made us brush our teeth, we used old toothbrushes where the bristles had fanned out and there was barely any brushing, more polishing. I knew how to do it.

I smelled the toothpaste and wanted to eat it again, but if this was the worst thing he was going to make me do I took it. So I got up and started brushing my teeth and made my way to the bathroom. These bristles were stiff and I liked the colour of my toothbrush; it was red.

"Good man!" Silas praised. "Keep your teeth healthy. One day I'll take you to Irontowers and let you loose on the stupid rebels."

I stopped mid-brush and spat into the sink. "I heard you talk about that before… what's going on there?" I started brushing again. I liked the bubbles. I may not be oppose to doing this more often.

"Some disgruntled Skyfallers who were too lazy or cowardly to make it past a huge city we have twenty or so miles from the coast," Silas explained. I saw him appear in the mirror. He leaned against the doorframe and watched me continue to brush my teeth. "They've taken residence in the town, which has a water supply and an old military bases and barricades, and have joined forces with some radhead greywasters.

They tried to bomb one of our factories six months ago. We've always had rebels but these ones seem to be getting too brave for my liking."

"Why don't you just go in there and kill them?" I asked through the toothbrush in my mouth. I finished off my teeth and started brushing my tongue and the inside of my cheeks.

"We can't quite yet," Silas said with a frown. "Garrett, who is currently in charge of relations with the Skyfallers, has an idea we're putting into motion. He's decided we're smart to make the rebels look bad before we kill them. If we just go in there and shoot them all, more will crop up thinking of themselves as some sort of martyrs. We don't want martyrs. So we're currently using the underground media to make them look bad. After public opinion shifts, we're going to capture them."

"That sounds smart," I said. "What's the underground media?"

"What it sounds like," Silas responded. He walked with me back to the living room and on the table I was pleased to see things coated in chocolate. Though when I advanced towards it Silas picked it up and started walking with me to the patio. I was okay with going outside but not in the sunlight. I enjoyed the warmth on my face but the brightness made me uneasy and so did the cityscape. The idea that thousands of people were in those buildings was rather daunting, I didn't like thinking about it.

When we sat down he continued, "The underground media is something we set up when Skyfall was in its infancy. We have SNN, the Skyfall News Network and they have the UFM the Underground Free Media. The Skyfallers believe it's chimera-free media where they are free to bash us if needed or whine about our policies. Unfortunately for them – we control that too." Silas chuckled as he said this, he seemed pleased with himself. "We have our loyal court in the underground media system planting what we want them to plant and printing what we want them to print. Harmless things but awful enough for them to get their rocks off hating us. Rapes, murders, unfair taxation, rigged Stadium matches, and bullshit like that."

"Sounds complicated," I said. "You should just kill everyone involved and kill anyone else that decides to be terrorists against the family." My brow furrowed. "They should be scared of all of us."

Silas smirked at this and my furrowed brow deepened. He picked up a piece of chocolate and handed it to me. I took a bite and realized they were filled with a brown gooey liquid, so I grabbed one more, one in each hand, and started filling my mouth with sugary goodness. Well, so much for having a freshly brushed mouth.

"It's politics and history. Nothing good ever happened to monarchs who decided to rule with dictatorship-type domination. Especially after the Fallocaust where we have media, free will, and the technology to fight back. It's easier to keep them in a guarded happiness, but at the same time, obedient and scared of us. It's a balance we need to achieve, though the Skyfallers are mostly idiots who have no idea how good they have it. It only takes one crazed lunatic with a bomb strapped to his chest to start inciting a rebellion."

"You're right," I said. "They don't know how good they have it. The greywastes are awful. We're free but… people suffer a lot." I thought back to my own childhood and immediately felt like I had swallowed a rock. "It's horrible out there… what are the rebels trying to achieve?"

"They want chimeras out of power, they want democracy." Silas frowned. "Which is incredibly stupid, but like I said if we go in there guns ablaze it will only prove them right."

Then he smiled and handed me another chocolate. "I have a wonderful idea, lovely. Would you like to hear it?"

I gave him a skeptical, narrow-eyed look which made him smile wider. "If you can be brave… and we can do it tomorrow night even if you wish. But I would like to invite you to our military base in Skyfall. Nero and Ceph spend most of their days there and they would be ecstatic to see you. I want a greywaster perspective on the rebels, perhaps you can come up with some ideas as to how we can take care of them with the Skyfallers not getting up in arms. Would you do this for me, Sanguine? Your first request as my newest addition to the family?"

His words hit me and immediately anxiety simmered deep inside of me. I had been here for two months now; perhaps it was time for me to touch the ground.

Though I knew my mind, and I could already feel Crow churn inside of me. He didn't like it but not enough to stop me, just enough to breathe caution.

"We could go at night?" I asked cautiously. "Would it just be the four of us? No one else?"

"Yes, your other brothers don't know you're alive and I want to keep it that way a while longer." Silas nodded.

I mulled it over in my mind while I chewed on the sticky chocolate.

The taste of mint and freshness quickly disappearing from my mouth as it was replaced with sugar. I liked the taste of sugar more than toothpaste, though toothpaste did have its perks.

"You'll have on dark sunglasses so the legionaries don't recognize you as a chimera. The windows in our car will be tinted too, sweetness. You wouldn't see anything but dark until Legion Base."

I could do this, and when I told Silas that I saw him smile big and clap his hands together. It made me happy to make him happy… ever since he started cutting me last month, and allowing me to use the wire to relieve stress, I had become more drawn towards the king.

Silas had been nothing but kind and patient towards me but I knew he treated his chimeras differently than the Skyfallers and the greywasters. I had been around greywasters and they were all a bunch of idiots.

The rest of the evening passed without anything bad happening. Silas went out for his Sunday chimera dinner and I stayed in with Kinny and he ordered us meatball subs which was my new favourite food now. I ate two and spent the rest of the night on the couch watching TV and doing my school work.

I fell asleep on top of the bed but as usual I woke up underneath it. I brushed my teeth, trying to make it into a habit and went on with my day. Most of the time I was alone still, since Silas had king things to do but TV was good company and so was Kinny. I didn't mind that sengil, he was silent and he was considerate too. He even warned me when he was going to vacuum so I could hide in my bedroom with Jett, the name I decided on for the kitten.

Jett and I didn't like vacuums.

"Can I at least brush your hair?"

"No."

Silas glared at me and slapped the top of the hairbrush against the palm of his hand. I smirked at him as he did this. "Nan used to threaten me with spankings the same way. Too bad I'm taller than you, I'll smack you right back."

We were both in his bedroom. I was picking out sweatshirts and pants for me to wear and Silas was primping himself with the bathroom door open.

Silas gave me a look like he wanted to accept my challenge. Then, as I put on a black sweatshirts with an old logo on it, I popped my head out of the top of it to see Silas hovering the brush over my head.

"No!" I protested and threw my hoody back over my head. "Stop trying to preen me. I like me this way."

"Why!" Silas said in an aghast tone. "Why do you like being filthy!? It's baffling me and two months later I'm starting to play with the idea of giving you water wings and pushing you into the pool."

I stared at him in awe. "Water wings? Wings made of water?"

Kinny laughed behind me. I turned around and gave him a glare.

Though to my horror Silas saw this as an opportunity and put the brush in my hair. I jerked back and gave him a push before stealing the brush out of his hand.

I smacked him on the head with it. "Bad King."

Silas gaped at me for a moment. "You brazen shit! Look at you…" Though as he made a motion to grab the brush I held it up over his head. I was about half a head taller than him and I took full advantage of it.

Silas reached his hand up and jumped. I held the brush up higher and tried to suppress a laugh.

But to my surprise Silas decided to play dirty. He jabbed me right in the stomach making me keel forward with a squawk, then he snatched the brush and as I turned to run away he smacked my shoulders.

Then a laugh escaped my lips. Enjoying the light and playful mood I hadn't experienced in years and years, Silas chased me around the apartment trying to hit me with the brush.

I really thought that being chased would make Crow upset. That it would spark something inside of my head that would switch my mind to panic mode. But I was fine, and the realization that I was fine made me laugh even more. I think I had finally found someone that I trusted.

Silas was hitting me on the shoulders with the brush, both of us laughing, when we heard a throat clear. Silas stopped and so did I, and we both looked towards the door to see Elish standing there. He was looking on with an unimpressed expression on his stern face, dressed in a white cape, a dress shirt, and grey trousers underneath.

"Hello, *gelus vir*," Silas said happily. "Did you see him laugh? Doesn't he have a wonderful laugh, love?"

Elish didn't look at me; he held the door to outside open as Kinny ran towards Silas with his shoes and cape.

"Yes, splendid," Elish replied back blandly. "I'm glad he laughs at being beaten now, instead of screaming and growling. It will do well once his novelty wears off."

My head hung low; suddenly I didn't feel like going anywhere.

"Elish." Silas's biting voice sliced through my defeated emotions. I glanced up to see the king with his back to me, and Elish with a stone-cold expression on his face.

"My apologies," Elish responded, his tone not changing. "It's... been a long day. Sanguine, will you accept my apology for my rude comment?"

I looked up at my oldest brother and stared at him, taken aback by his swift apology. Perhaps that was just King Silas's rule, I wasn't sure. I certainly wasn't going to not accept it; it was time for me to learn the rules.

"Yes, thank you," I said quietly, and once again I pulled my hoody over my head and drew the strings. "Can I have my sunglasses, Silas?"

"Sure, sweet one," Silas said. Kinny was draping Silas's cape over him. It was a beautiful cape, black with dark blue trim and a design of a carracat symbol on the back. It looked expensive, just like Elish's did. I guess going out in public he had to look kingy. He certainly didn't look kingy when he was eating Fruit Loops in his underwear like he was this morning.

Everything became dark with the sunglasses on. Sunglasses didn't trigger my night vision so this was the darkest my world had ever been. I liked it. So once Silas was preened and primped and I was concealed under my sweater hoody and sunglasses, we made our way to the lobby.

I didn't see much, I kept my head down and my mouth closed. The next thing I knew we were all in the back of a black car, heading towards the military base.

"You made sure none of the other boys are at the base?" I heard Silas ask Elish.

"They're all in school. Jack and Valen only have military training on Fridays now. Drake is playing with Zhou's daughters and he's been doing well with not mentioning Sanguine to the others," Elish replied. "The only chimeras there are Nero and Ceph. The legionaries know not to ask questions."

"Good," Silas said.

The rest of the trip the two of them talked about monarch things, stuff I didn't understand. I stared at my feet instead and half-listened. Apparently another skyscraper was undergoing renovations and that was costing a lot of money, and also that Silas was holding an open forum next month. That was when he listened to his chimeras and top peoples' requests for things. He did it twice a year. I thought of something I might want to request but all I secretly wanted was different foods I had seen on the television. I had always wished that donuts still existed.

"Do donuts still exist?" I suddenly asked out loud.

"Do not interrupt the king," Elish snapped.

I slunk down and mumbled an apology. He reminded me of Nan sometimes, but Nan usually slapped us upside the head. I think Elish would if he could get away with it.

Though to my surprise Silas answered without chastising me. "Yes, they do. One of the first things that Skytech did after its creation was to figure out and manufacture yeast. Now it's readily available to the people of Skyfall through Dek'ko. So since we have yeast, we have donuts, bread, cinnamon buns, a lot of your favourite foods."

I nodded. "Thanks for answering." And I went back to staring at my feet. I would have to think of something else to ask for during the forum then.

When the car stopped we all filed out. We were in front of a giant gate which immediately opened for us. I glanced up once and saw a concrete building in front of us with no windows. It was two-storeys tall and a huge emblem of the carracat sigil was painted on the front of the building. Over the emblem were the words *Skyfall Legion Base*. Around that building was flat pavement but further on I saw smaller one-storey buildings and large vehicles all surrounded by a concrete fence topped with barbwire.

Quickly we were ushered inside, but not before I heard someone calling to us.

I looked but King Silas grabbed my arm. I caught a glimpse though before the man disappeared behind the concrete walls. He was holding a camera and was shouting Silas and Elish's name.

"Underground media?" Silas murmured.

"Want me to stop him?" Elish asked under his breath. I let Silas pull me towards the door.

"No, Sanguine's completely covered; they won't know who he is. Let them speculate all they want."

"It could get back to the younger boys… they read the UFM."

"It won't."

The doors shut behind me but Silas still had his hand firmly clenched on my arm. We were in a grey painted welcoming room with legionary soldiers everywhere. One at each door and three of them at the entrance. There was also a small reception desk that was being occupied by a huge man with a weathered face and one with narrow eyes.

As soon as everyone saw Silas they stood at attention and got down on one knee. Silas nodded at them in approval and we walked down the hallway. I was behind Silas but in front of Elish, and I could see everyone looking at me. I guess I was an odd person to see with Elish and Silas all dressed and regal-looking. I was a worm walking beside birds of paradise.

"Sangy!"

I jumped and looked up. Immediately a small smile pulled on my lips as I saw Nero's beaming face poking out of a door. He was grinning from ear to ear and he looked excited to see me.

"You're looking sane! Kinda…" Nero laughed. Then I heard Silas made a warning noise.

"Don't startle him; he's still getting used to being outside. Low voices, no quick movements," Silas said sternly.

Nero laughed again and I stepped out of the room. "Sangy, I'm giving you ten seconds to brace your manic-self for a hug. Okay?"

My smile widened and I looked at the floor as I shrugged my shoulders. "It's okay, you can." I had only seen Nero briefly since he had rescued me, only when I was shovelling food into my mouth. I had missed him. He had taken up a lot of space in my dreams while I was at Jasper's farm.

Nero came close to me and I just stood there bracing myself and my mind for it. As soon as he was close enough Nero wrapped his arms around me and squeezed me hard. Then he lifted me right up off of the ground and crushed my body against his.

When he was done he set me down, my entire body aching. I think I knew what someone felt like now while they were being squeezed to death by a boa constrictor.

Nero put a hand on my hoody-covered head before giving me a loud kiss on the cheek. "You're home, puppy-wuppy. I'm so fucking happy you're home and doing good. Is the ol' man treating you good?"

Ol' man? I think he meant Silas, I think he was over two hundred years old. So I nodded and said faintly, "He's been extremely nice to me. Thanks for… for everything."

A strange look passed on Nero's face. He put a hand on my shoulder and shook his head. "Bro… my life is like… made now because I found you. You got no idea what guilt can do to someone, how much it fucks with them. I'll feel guilty though until I see you at your prime. I'm just happy we pulled you out of that shit hole. So fucking happy, little bro."

I nodded and tried to hold my smile. "You were my first friend... I thought of you a lot in there."

Nero made an *aww'ing* sound and hugged me again. "Aw, man... fuck, Sanguine. Fuck, fuck... I'm so sorry I didn't find you sooner."

"You still looked though," I said to him. "Which is a lot more than anyone else has ever done for me."

I wasn't expecting that to get a reaction, but to my side I heard Silas's pulse jump for just a few moments, before it slowed down. I guess without realizing it I had just personally attacked Silas. I wouldn't apologize because it was true.

Nero nodded and shook my shoulder, before turning to the king. "He was a hilarious little fucker when he was little. Loved to bite too. When can we introduce him to the family, Kingles?"

Everyone walked to the doorway that Nero had come out of, Nero with his arm around my shoulder hugging me close to him. Crow wasn't nervous having Nero around. Crow might not have been with me when I had met Nero and Ellis, but he knew him from my thoughts.

"Seriously..." Nero dropped his voice, Silas and Elish had walked ahead of us, into what looked like a meeting room. They were talking to each other. "You're being treated well?"

I nodded. "Silas has been really nice to me."

"Good," Nero said quietly. "He can be a bit of a twit, but he's great, okay? He loves you, and we love you, and me and you are going to be best friends, ya hear?"

"We already are," I said back. "At least in my mind we always have been."

"Good man!" Nero praised and squeezed me to him. "Now come and listen to us be military masterminds. We have to kill some rebels!" Then he raised his voice. "Right, Kingy? Can we kill the fucking rebels yet?"

Silas glanced behind his shoulder and waved us both over. "The time is coming soon, *bellua*. What are the new reports coming in? What's the UFM saying?"

Nero and I both walked over. The room had a large marble table in the center of it surrounded by clean chairs with curved wooden armrests. On the wall furthest to me was a projector and surrounding that were lots of framed pictures of military things and medals too.

"UFM is working smoothly. Valentine, as you probably heard, slit the throat of some Nyxian asshole and our UFM writers are playing on that right now. The rebels are still second story though, and they're still singing their praises. Oniks is still doing what we told her, not holding back the chimera bashing but the stories are getting dry. It's the same ol' same ol' and it's not shifting public opinion. We need to think of something massive to report, some way to make them hate the rebels." Nero picked up a black laptop that was resting on the marble table and plugged it into the projector.

I saw an aerial view of what looked like a large city, I assumed that was Irontowers, it had several red marks on it. "This is where we know the rebels are. We know where their military supply are coming from and also where they got those vehicles. We know their movements too, after we got some of our top military into their circle. We have everything ready for an attack, Silas. We just need your orders," Nero said.

But Silas only shook his head. "No, not without our hook. We need the public to want to destroy them, Nero. Believe me, I saw the same thing play out during the war. We have to get the public on our side or people who normally would be compliant will start to turn. Trust me."

Nero made a noise before clicking the touchpad on the computers. "You might think differently after this report. Right now, the last UFM issue anyway, they're on about the sengils again. We had Rich go over to Edgeview; he's started eyeing up some potential sengils. Oniks didn't see it as important enough to squash so it was printed. The rebels and their supporters are starting to complain that we're taking orphans and as they say… 'forcing them to be sex slaves'."

"Are they now?" Silas murmured.

"Is that true?" I suddenly said, my heart seemed to send a pulse of cold water through my veins. "Are sengils sex slaves? You said Juni is going to…"

"Shh, shush, love, no," Silas reassured. "Sengils are orphans who would otherwise be stuck in the filthy slums if they weren't taken and trained under our hand. Straight sengils work in the kitchens or other places and the ones who like men are given to chimeras. They're never forced to do anything sexual, but as time goes on…"

"… and we are all pretty hot shit," Nero said beside me.

"If it happens, it happens naturally, and no chimera gets a sengil until the sengil is fifteen," Silas finished. "We treat those little orphans better than most elites. It's like winning the lottery for them."

I was skeptical but Kinny looked happy to be a sengil. I was planning on asking him if he was alright with it though.

"No one is going to mistreat Juni or Levi?"

"Of course not and especially not Juni, he saved you."

"Okay," I responded and with a nod, they continued.

Nero switched to another file on the computer. This one was a copy of the newspaper they were talking about. I saw a lot of highlighting on it.

"Speak for the children! When are we going to start standing up for those with the weakest voice? The sex slaves of chimeras, or as they call them: sengils," I read out loud.

The cold ice that was pumping through my body from thinking that the chimeras were using the sengils in such a way, turned into anger over the headline. I felt a sudden rage come over my body at these people accusing my new family of such a thing.

"They're not even telling the truth," Nero said bitterly. "They think we pull these fucking kids out at seven and make them sengils then. They have another eight years of training and living life before we even get them. It's bullshit propaganda but it's shit like this that Oniks says we have to let through."

Silas's face darkened. "This won't help the opinion on us, but I refuse to let the public into our private lives. Our lives are not on display, and we won't give out more information just because of a stupid article. I refuse."

Nero nodded as looked down at the laptop screen, his fingers drumming against the plastic case. "It definitely isn't helping, that's for sure, because it has too much truth mixed in with the misinformation. Right now is a bad time for it to be printed too, Rich says we need four boys since Loren, Kinny, and Wyatt will age out in eight years and we'll need more sengils for second gen. And you just know they're going to get more support once it's realized we just took four more."

I looked at the screen and found my mind starting to grind its gears together. I lightly scanned over the article and matched it up with the rebels in Irontowers.

Right now my family's biggest problems were the rebels and how to switch public opinion without making the chimeras and the king look bad. If I was king I would just bomb Irontowers and be done with it, but I guess if Silas had been around since before the war… he knew more about this than me. That fascinated me in a way. That King Silas was so smart he knew that public opinion was important. Like he said he had to keep the public happy, but also slightly uneasy and cautious so they would be obedient.

There were two news sources SNN and the UFM, both they controlled.

As Silas and Nero continued talking I thought this over, staring mostly at the marble table as my mind mulled through it. Sometime during the conversations I saw Nero's boyfriend Ceph who gave me a clap on the shoulder, but I was inside of my head trying to help my family.

Though my mind was constantly being interrupted by the sticky tendrils of my own past thoughts. As I tried to think of things I kept going back to Jasper. I kept seeing his face in front of mine. I could never shake him…

How could those assholes say my family was like him? Even if it was just an inflammatory article it made my blood boil over. Jasper was a pervert, not them. Jasper was the fucking greywaster asshole who kidnapped kids and forced them to…

"I got it," I suddenly said, looking up.

All eyes turned to me and but this time I didn't shrink under their gaze. I looked at Nero, Ceph, Silas, and Elish's inquisitive faces and looked right back at them.

"I know what you should do," I said again. "How… how you can sway the public."

Elish didn't seem interested but the other three were watching me with intense eyes.

"Tell us, love." Silas urged me forward with just a slight push of his words. "What is it?"

I took in a deep breath, as quickly as it came my bravery disappeared, but I forced my mental self forward and with a push, I shoved him into the front of my mind.

Melchai townspeople didn't care, they wanted their meth supply. But normal people, the city people –

"You need the public opinion to shift, right?" I said, and swallowed. "And you have people in Irontowers that work for you, right?"

Silas nodded. "We have people in the Underground Media and people in Irontowers."

"Have Rich take some orphans…" I said slowly. "Hide them for a while, so no one can see them, and have one or more of the kids turn up in Irontowers. Make our informant give them ratty clothes, and photograph them looking injured or even tied up... but... but don't actually hurt them just make it a set up. Send that to the UFM and tell them the rebels have half a dozen children in their possession, both as sex slaves or even child soldiers. You could even twist it that these were children previously adopted that were found in Irontowers. The article was just them covering for their misdeeds and we can have proof. We have insiders so we can get more proof on them than they could on us."

Silas's eyes widened and Nero whistled. Elish was less than amused though.

"They would never print that," he said acerbically.

"Then get Oniks to wear a wire, or a camera, like on TV," I said quickly. "Because that would discredit the UFM in the process. Free media means free media right? Not anti-chimera, pro-rebel media. If they don't print it, we have it documented that they refused to print it even with thorough documentation, and we can either expose them to the public or blackmail them into printing it. If you want to support the rebels you're now supporting child molesters, simple as that." I took in another deep breath.

Silas looked at me and I saw his head nod slightly. "He's right. People are stupid, we know this. They don't understand us explaining how our policies benefit them or why we have such strict rules. They're idiots and all they understand is less money and less free will. What they do understand is the basic human emotion of empathy, especially empathy over children. I already have the Law of Fifteen and that is one policy I have never been criticized for." Silas looked at Elish, the blond-haired man still didn't look happy, but Silas obviously didn't care. "We can pin it that this is one of the policies that the rebels want to change and our proof would be in the Underground Media, and once it starts to leak... the SNN can pretend to pick it up. Elish, this is genius. The plan needs some fine tuning but... this is perfect."

Nero made an impressed noise and shook his head. Then he turned to Silas and pointed a finger at me. "You better give this nucky a present. He knows the human mind. He might be a bit batty but I would watch out, Kingly, he's smart as fuck."

My heart almost burst inside of my chest as Silas looked at me with a proud expression on his face. There was so much pride inside of me I thought I would explode. This was another feeling I had never felt before and I literally felt like I was floating.

I had made King Silas, and Nero, proud. I had never made anyone proud before. I was included, I was helping my family.

"He is. He's really going to fit in well with this family." Silas seemed to be radiating pride and Nero was too. I dropped my gaze, too embarrassed to keep it, or maybe I just didn't want them to see how happy I was.

"Elish says your novelty will wear off," Crow murmured beside me. "So don't get too smug, mihi."

I glanced over at Crow; he was leaning against the wall with a smile on his face.

"But I made them happy," I said to him. "I like making them happy."

Crow's black eyes jutted over to where the three were standing. "Your novelty is going to wear off and you'll see they'll be just like the others. You're still a monster, you're still bad. You will always be worthless. You don't deserve this life, you don't deserve pride. You're nothing but Jasper's slut; you're a whore, a damaged, insane whore."

'WHORE!'

'YOU'RE A WHORE, SANGUINE!'

'FUCKING DEMON-EYED, WHORE.'

Not even Nana wanted you.

Daddy Cory hated you.

Even Barry killed himself.

"Shut the fuck up!" I suddenly screamed. Crow laughed and pushed himself away from the wall with his hands. He stepped towards me and tried to glare me down but I turned away and looked at the carpet.

"Daisy, Daisy… give me your heart to fuck. You're such a little bitch, you're Jasper's little slut."

"Not here. I'm not that here," I said through my clenched teeth. "I'm better here."

"You'll always be a demon, you're best on your back and screamin'… Oh Sanguine, so full of sin, with Jasper's cum in you."

"Shut up!" I shrieked.

"Love?"

I jumped and as I jumped I screamed from fright as Silas touched my shoulder. I looked at Silas, my mouth open and gasping, beads of sweat running down my face.

"Sanguine..." Silas said his forehead creased in concern. "What's Crow telling you?"

It took a moment for my mind to start trickling back. I stared at the floor for a few more moments trying to catch my breath, before I looked up at Silas.

"I can't say," I panted. "Nothing good..."

Silas's eyes narrowed. He looked to the wall, where Crow had been before saying slowly, "You say he's your friend and he protects you. Why does he torment you sometimes?"

I shrugged, when I realized everyone was staring at me I shrunk down feeling embarrassed. "Friends torment friends sometimes." I wiped my nose and pushed my sunglasses further onto my face.

"Friends don't..." Silas paused when I got down on my knees and got under the large marble table. I shifted some chairs back and immediately felt relief some place closed in.

"Well, alright..." Silas said. I could hear Nero and Ceph chuckle by the laptop and the projector. "We'll let him be then. Okay, let's look at the other articles in the UFM and see if there is anything else we should be monitoring..."

CHAPTER 24

THE WHITE DOOR OPENED, AND A SLIVER OF LIGHT appeared that got larger and larger until it illuminated the filthy bed that I had been sitting on for almost half of my life.

I recoiled from the light and moved my body until my back was pressed up against the wall. Chains rattled around, and the anchor behind me dug its frozen fingers into my back. Those senses meant nothing to me though; I was too scared to pay attention to physical stimulus. My eyes were fixed on that door waiting for Jasper's face to appear.

"You know what I like about this?" I jumped and let out a startled yelp as Jasper's all-too-familiar voice hissed in my ear. So close to me I could smell his breath, rancid from years and years of smoking meth.

A dark chuckle before I felt him grab my ass and clench it. I tried to scream but I realized my entire body was paralyzed. I couldn't move and I realized that he knew I was locked in place.

"What I like most about this… is that now that you've had a break from me… you will be even tighter. Now that you're back, you have a fresh energy about you. You'll fight more; you won't just go inside of your head and escape. Perhaps I'll let you go back to Skyfall more often. Though it's too bad you're older, I wish you were still seven like Drake… I really do."

Despair trickled down my body, starting at my head and raining down like someone had poured a bucket of acid on top of my head. I felt my shoulders shake, my head drop as the realization came over me that I was still in that basement. I had never been rescued; I had never been to

Skyfall. I wasn't a chimera, of course I wasn't, I was just a demon-monkey and I deserved to be caged. Just like Crow had said to me last week at the base.

I was a whore, just Jasper's whore.

I deserved to be caged. I couldn't be trusted around people. That's why the people in Melchai wanted to get rid of me, that's why they let Jasper take me. Even though I had heard… I had heard the man at the hotel tell Jasper to leave when he had tried to sneak into my bedroom. And the bartender had known as well. He had acted like they'd known.

All of Melchai had known, but their meth supply was more important.

The Skyfallers might care about children being used in such a way, but the greywasters didn't. They were just a bunch of selfish savages.

Then, like there had been a snap of electricity, my entire body jolted. Darkness filled my vision and the only sounds I could hear was the pounding of my own heart. Alarmed, I shot up in bed and looked around, the tinges of blue starting to form as my night vision kicked in.

'Jasper's in your bedroom,' Crow warned. His voice was a low growl, he sounded threatened and I immediately became even more on edge. *'He's in your bedroom.'*

'He's in your bedroom!' Crow said in a more forceful tone. Like his words were sharp barbs I could feel them digging into my skin. I knew by now if I didn't do something he would keep yelling at me until I did.

I leapt off of my bed, and jumped away from it in case he was hiding under it. My hands shaking from fear and my chest so tight my breathing was laboured. I was gasping for air like a fish but my chest was so constricted I couldn't take in a full inhale.

My hand rested against my lungs. I ignored the shortness of breath, my panicked and anxiety-filled mind urging me to check every dark corner of the bedroom. My physical health didn't matter; I had to find where Jasper was hiding.

With the sounds of my quickened breathing filling the room I looked under the bed, then I looked in the closet and even behind the curtains still shielding my window. I looked twice before I started to pace my bedroom, still trying to catch my breath.

I was too anxious though; my mind was two speeding trains, each trying to determine who was going to crash first. They barrelled along with no regard for my mental state, sending dark thought after dark thought to torment me, all in quick succession.

One after another.

Of Jasper fucking me, both as an adult and a child.

Of when he killed Lyle – and when I killed Cooper.

That basement. That basement… I could smell it. Why can I smell it?

I looked around desperately and a whine escaped my lips. I had to get out of this room, it smelled like my basement. That meant Jasper had to be here, I knew it.

I walked out of my bedroom and started pacing the dark living room. It was completely dark save for a few lights that belonged to Silas's electronics. I walked up and down the halls and through the kitchen before I started checking the closets and spare bedrooms for any sign of Jasper.

Wave after wave of panic, and they weren't stopping. Every time I checked a new location and found he wasn't there, the warnings in my head only grew louder. Telling me with grim certainty that this only meant that Jasper was getting smarter. That not only did he know how to get inside, but he was also going to hide until I let my guard down.

He always did that… he used to come when I was sleeping. He used to stand over my bed and watch me, even if I woke up he was there. I could smell him. I could smell him so I closed my eyes and pretended to be asleep even though as the other senses left me I could hear his pounding heart.

Sometimes it sped up… sometimes I heard his ragged breathing… sometimes I even felt stuff drip onto me. Though when that happened I was thankful, because he would leave after.

Where are you hiding… Another whine escaped my clenching teeth, barely audible over my breathing. I looked in the bathroom and drew back the black shower curtain, before walking back down the grey-carpeted floors and going back into the living room.

Then the sound of a door unlatching.

"Sanguine, love?" Silas's voice broke my lucid turmoil like a lamp lit in an abandoned building. "What's wrong?"

Like my body was a tightened rubber band I snapped towards him and shrunk back. Suddenly Crow was whispering to me that Jasper was in his room.

He's in Silas's room… he's in Silas's room…

I started walking towards Silas's room and towards Silas. There was nothing else inside of this disturbed hive of thoughts but to check his room and find Jasper.

"Sanguine?" Silas said confused. I pushed the door open and walked inside.

The bed was empty...

I dropped to my knees and looked under the bed but there was nothing there. I got up and tried to pull the closet open but then Silas's hand grasped mine. "Sanguine... what are you doing?"

I looked down at his hand and though I had been talking inside of my head and talking to Crow I realized I had said nothing to King Silas.

Slowly my hands travelled to my face. The silver discs on my palms and on my left hand: the spiral scars of the stove element. Jasper hadn't done that to me... but he had done worse.

"Jasper..." I mumbled. I pushed his hands away and opened the closet. Inside were suites and clothing, stacked boxes, and sex toys which my mind ignored.

"Jasper?" Silas said under his breath. He gently closed the closet door and took my hand. "You think Jasper is inside this apartment? No, love, the thiens guard our doors and we're at the very top apartment of a rather large skyscraper. It's impossible. Jasper is miles of land and ocean away; he's on the islands."

I shook my head and started clawing and pressing my nails into my skin. I walked out of Silas's room and decided to walk towards the balcony. Silas followed behind me and when he realized I wanted to go outside he stopped.

Confused, I glanced back to see what I had caught myself on, not realizing he had still held my hand.

I pulled it but Silas shook his head, his tussled blond hair shifting back and forth. "No, you're not going outside in a half-asleep state."

"I have too!" I said sharply. I sucked in a breath, saying those words left my lungs empty and I started wheezing, my shoulders shaking. "I have to look!"

"Sanguine!" Silas said sharply but I pulled my hand away and glared at him.

I took a threatening step towards him, feeling real, undiluted anger in my blood that, in my state, drew the growl to my throat. "I HAVE too!"

Silas grabbed my hand, but there was no Crow inside to advise me or tell me to attack him. I wasn't sure why, and I didn't care. All that mattered was going outside to see if Jasper was there.

Before I knew it Silas led me to the couch, he sat down and pulled my hand until I sat down too.

Then as I jerked away from him I felt his hand on my head – and all of a sudden a biting, electric pain that ripped through my chest, pooling inside of my head before spreading like oil, throughout my body.

I gasped and let out a cry, and as it dissipated my chest loosened… and suddenly I could breath.

"There… now, close your eyes," Silas whispered, and running on the adrenaline caused by the jolt of pain, I closed my eyes.

Another percussion, like his fingertips were small hypodermic needles filled with an electric, burning current. I opened my mouth and groaned again, before the centralized pain started moving across my skin.

It was… I liked it. It was like I was tasting a drug, a beautiful agonizing drug that carried on its heels an intense release of pressure. It made my head light, my shoulders light; it was like what happened when I cut myself.

When he retracted his hand my breathing slowed and, like when he was cutting me, I relaxed and sunk into the comfort. Feeling the paranoia that Jasper was in my apartment start to trickle down the gutters of my brain, leaving only reality in its wake.

"Pain brings your mind back… I bet if we measured those endorphins they would be off the charts," Silas said in a low but soothing tone. "My little masochist. My little *crucio*."

I took in a deep breath and let it out slowly. "Crucio?"

His lips spread in a smile and he lightly ran his burning, electrified touch over my cheek. "Latin, lovely. It means my tormented, my tortured soul. *Cruciantur animae*. All my loves are born with certain words in their heads. It's…" he smiled thinly. "I was trying to plant language, like I plant enhancements but the technology isn't quite there. But I realized as the first generation started learning to speak they held onto an understanding of some words."

I stared at him, still in a half-dreamy state. The pain was even stronger than the Xanax; I don't believe I had ever felt so relaxed. I didn't want to move, I didn't want to lose this feeling. So as time continued on forward, an hour possibly more, I spent the time in his vision and he spent his time in mine.

"You're so… beautiful," Silas whispered after more than an hour had passed. "Do you like it here?"

I nodded in my dazed state, holding dear to my chest these fleeting moments of contentment. I had felt this odd comfort before; it seemed to happen whenever Silas was near me.

It made me... it... it drew me to him. I wanted to get closer to him but I didn't understand why. It was like he had a warm hand around my head, stroking and petting the blistered, rotting emotions festering inside of me.

"Can I kiss you, Sanguine?"

My eyes focused back on him, and immediately my heart started to speed up.

Kiss me? He wanted to kiss me? I had never kissed someone before... ever. I had only seen it on the television, I didn't even know how. Or if it was a good idea.

But Silas had been so kind to me... so patient.

I had made him proud with my suggestion back at the Legion Base. I had liked him even more after that.

Butterflies and nervousness flooded me, a tight clench inside of me that felt like hands made of iron wrapping themselves around my heart. But in the same breath, in the same inhale of warm air and calming thoughts, a curiosity inside of me spiked. A want that rested in the small area of my being where my curiosity still lived.

I nodded and, without hesitating, he gently slipped his hand behind my head and leaned down.

Our lips locked and I felt him try to ease my own lips open. I closed my eyes and took his direction and let him take me in.

He broke away but he hovered his face only an inch away from mine. With my eyes still closed I felt his warm breath against my cheek, until his lips pressed against mine once again. This time with a bit more force and eagerness. He put a slight amount of pressure on the back of my head, and before I realized what he was doing, he tried to slip his tongue into my mouth.

I let him, my head starting to go light to the point where I felt dizzy. The warmth inside of my head intensified, and quickly it spread over my body.

Acting on impulse I met my tongue with his, and this only intensified the feeling that was starting to permeate my body. It was like pure alcohol sinking into meat, it soaked and pooled inside of my bones, inside of my gut...

No, it was pooling lower.

Our lips were locked together, our tongues joined and slipping into each other's mouths. I found myself starting to breathe heavier again as my mouth became pre-occupied, riding every wave of tension as it seared me like a white hot brand.

Then I made the mistake of shifting my body. As soon as I moved I realized that the tight burning I had been feeling had been solely focused to my groin. I was hard; it was throbbing and rigid, pulsing inside of my underwear to an uncomfortable level.

I pulled away with a gasp, and looked down.

"It's okay…" Silas whispered.

I stared at it, and all of a sudden the heat boiling my insides turned to the coldest of winters. Like a frozen comet I fell back to earth, back to this world, and back to the nightmare that was my life.

Horror claimed me then, horror over what was happening to my body. I was getting hard, I was hard and when it got hard it wanted sex. Just like Jasper got before he fucked me.

"I can take care of that…" Silas said in a low and seductive tone. "No need to be anxious. It'll feel good, I promise. You've never done anything like this before, have you?"

I jumped up off of the couch. Silas immediately sat up, looking surprised at my sudden action.

For a moment I was frozen, frozen in a state of limbo. The terror, embarrassment, and sickening feeling inside of me was so thick I swear I could see it coming off of my body. It was so many emotions combined into one horrible feeling and at that moment I just… I had to get away from this feeling. I had to escape this situation.

My eyes started searching every inch of the living room and I could feel pain on my arms as I clenched and clawed them.

This wasn't good. This wasn't good. These feelings were bad; it meant I was a pervert like Jasper. I was going to turn into Jasper. Why was it getting stiff? I had enjoyed the kiss so why was this happening to me?

I was confused, I didn't know what I was talking about and I knew I didn't. I knew something was happening inside of me but all it was telling me was that I was some sort of pervert. Some sort of… of…

'I told you, you will always be Jasper's whore.'

'You're broken. You're broken, demon-monkey.'

'What's worse though is now you want it. Your body wants sex.'

'I bet you liked it the entire time. I bet you really liked Jasper fucking you. Remember that time you got hard when he was yanking out your pubic hair?'

'I do.'

'I DO!'

Silas got up and I took a step back, the constriction in my rib cage making me start to pant.

"Sanguine..." Silas whispered curiously. "You're in turmoil. Why?"

Then he took another step towards me, and I took another step away from him. My movements quick and my skin crawling with insects that burrowed in and out.

"Sanguine... you know I'm not going to hurt you, right? I understand you're... you must be confused." Silas's brow furrowed and I saw him sigh. "You're... I'm sorry. You must not even know what the hell is going on. Of course you wouldn't, you were down there for so long."

He glanced at me. "When they're eleven we tend to sit them down with me and Elish and we explain how things work... do you want me to explain what's happening with–"

"I know what's happening!" I suddenly screamed. I put my hand on my unbrushed, messy hair and clenched it. My teeth ground. "I know what's happening! I'm a pervert, there's something wrong with me."

Though I was deep in my own inner misery, I saw Silas's face pale and his hands drop. As I looked around the dark apartment, I could see Silas staring at me, a blank expression on his face like he was an android and his mind had been wiped.

A low whine sounded from my throat and I looked around desperately. I don't know what I was looking for. I didn't know what I wanted. Down there was already starting to return to normal, so what more was I looking for?

I just wanted this feeling to go away. I wanted to become a different person, someone who didn't have Jasper's rotten breath always an inch away from my face. The only thing I wanted out of life was to just be left alone in peace.

But I was in peace now... if you took away all of what was wrong with me I was in a safe area. Alegria, this skyscraper, was a safe place to be with guards by the door... I was living with the king for fuck sakes.

But the king had started to want something in return for his hospitality. Was that it? I knew he had sex with the others; I had been ambushed by Nero and Ceph when I had gotten into the fridge.

I looked at Silas who was quickly walking towards me.

"Calm down… we don't need to do anything," Silas said. "Take a deep breath, I'll get the wire and make some designs on your arm. Would you like that?"

My eye watched him like they were motion sensors. I could see his mouth moving. I could hear the words though they sounded far away, too far for me to make proper sense of them.

Then I felt his hand touch my shoulder and with a recoil of horror I snapped away.

Though my mind didn't let me stop at just flinching away, I had to make him stop being… being near me. I had to make him stop saying words. I had to stop him, stop him from making me feel this way.

Without thinking I raised my hands, and not knowing just what I was doing or how I was doing it, I raised my hands and pressed them against Silas's face.

And I made them burn.

I made them burn like the inferno that was eating my internal body alive.

A burst of burnt-smelling smoke erupted from King Silas's face, and soon after a scream of pain. In my shock I retracted, not realizing what I had just done. I looked at Silas's face, two raw, red patches in the shapes of my clenched hands appearing where his smooth, porcelain skin used to be.

I looked down at my hands and saw they had a layer of Silas's skin on them.

My entire body started to shake. I gagged on the bile rising up from my stomach and almost threw up from sheer horror.

"I'm sorry!" I said, half-choking, half-gagging on my own words. "I'm sorry! Please forgive me I didn't… I didn't mean to…"

Silas was on his knees, his hands over his face. I could see papery skin in between his fingers, some charred and black but most of it almost opaque. His own hands were trembling, but I could see he was trying to take deep breaths. He was trying to push himself past the pain. I had done the same thing.

"It's okay…" Silas said in a raspy voice. He pulled his hands away and let out a breath as more skin pulled away, the raw and tender flesh underneath the seared skin was bright red. And the smell. Fuck, the smell… burning corpses. I knew that smell.

"Sanguine, love…" Silas looked up at me. I put my own trembling hand over my mouth as I saw I had seared both of his eyes. I could see wrinkles in the whites of his eyes, they were burnt. "Get Elish… it will be just fine. Just, be a dear, get Elish… now."

I stared at him dumbly.

"Now, Sanguine!" Silas said in a sharper voice.

The edge in his tones snapped me out of my stupor. I nodded, suppressing another gag, and ran out of the doors and into the hall.

"Hey… are you allowed out?" one of the thiens asked. His voice was full of hesitation but I also sensed apprehension.

"Yes," I said before heading to the stairwell. I pushed open the door and started quickly walking down the stairs, two by two.

Everything inside of me had frozen in a state of animation. My brain was frozen, as was my emotions. I was on autopilot, I could panic later. I just had to get King Silas help.

'He's going to kill you after,' Crow growled.

I pushed him from my mind, though he was always the fly buzzing around my head. I ignored him though and walked down the two flights of stairs. Then I went through a door with a metal two and a six above it and found the double doors that had the main apartment behind it.

I knocked on it lightly at first but I realized it was still early morning so I knocked harder.

A sleepy sengil answered me, but as soon as he saw me I saw his face pale.

"Silas needs Elish," I said to him, talking sucked the breath out of my lungs. I clawed my arms more. "Silas needs Elish, now."

The sengil paled further. He turned around, looking at the closed bedroom, and turned back to me.

"Okay," the young man said nervously. He half-shut the door and I stood there staring at the ground. I wanted more than anything to escape right now.

"Silas is going to kill you," Crow taunted, his voice no longer in my head. Like he so often did he went from being a voice in my head to a physical person behind me.

I whimpered and shook my head. Had I really screwed all of this up? I hadn't meant to hurt him.

"Monster, monster, monster." Crow's voice was singy and taunting. "You hurt everyone you who likes you. You can't be trusted around people. That's why all you have is me."

I scrunched my shoulders and tightened my arms around my chest. "I know…" I said slowly. "I know he's going to be angry at me."

"You fuck up everything good that has ever happened to you," Crow said. "Which is why you belong in a cage. Which is why you can never have friends."

He continued, "You can't even let someone who likes you, touch you. You'll never have a real relationship, a real friend, or a real family."

"I just need more time to recover…" I whimpered.

"Either way, it will be different from now on," Crow said.

"Who are you speaking to?" I jumped and let out a gasp as the door swung open. Elish was staring at me, his purple eyes frozen slabs and his short blond hair messed up. "What does Silas want?"

"He needs you…" I said to him, staring at the carpet underneath my loafer-type shoes Silas had given me for indoors. "I – I…"

Do I say it?

"Say it," Crow suddenly snapped. "Say it, say it, say it, say it."

SAY IT SAY IT SAY IT.

"I accidently burned him. I think I blinded him."

No expression on Elish's face, not even a faint tightening of his jaw. The chimera immediately walked past me and disappeared into the stairwell. No second glances, no pulling my arm to go with him, he just walked away.

"Would you like to come in?" the sleepy sengil asked. "We have a guest room."

I shook my head, that was the last thing I wanted was to be in Elish's apartment. I knew he would beat me for hurting the king, and once Silas recovered he would beat me as well.

But where was I supposed to go? I couldn't go back to the apartment – I just couldn't.

"I'm going to…" I said quietly. It was summer, it was warm… maybe I could go on the roof? "I'm going to go… walk around, clear my head."

The sengil gave me a skeptical look but he nodded. I think he didn't have the authority to tell me what to do.

I didn't know where I was supposed to go but my feet took me towards the elevator. I think maybe I would go to the roof… or I would go to a storage room and find a couch I could make into a cave. Some place that was dark where I could process what just happened. I needed some place to hide… until they killed me for hurting Silas.

Or would they? Silas said he wasn't angry but how could he not be?

When I was in the elevator I looked at all of the buttons. There were twenty-seven floors, then the roof and the lobby though that was listed as floor one. There was also a basement but I knew they would look there first.

I was about to press the button for the roof when the elevator gave a pull. My heart leapt and shot to my throat as the elevator started to bring me some place downstairs.

I tried to push the button for the roof but it wasn't overriding its other command. I gritted my teeth, trying to force down my anxiety and angrily slammed my hand against the keypad, lighting up all of the buttons.

It still wasn't stopping. The floor numbers were changing rapidly and soon I was in single digits and then… I was on the lobby floor.

With an anxious thrum inside of my chest and my body pressed against the wall, I braced myself for who was going to greet me.

The door opened and I felt a growl but it disappeared when I became face-to-face with Garrett.

"Ohh… hey… gotta… gottsa job as an elevaty attendernat, eh? Good… good man!" Garrett slurred.

A very drunk Garrett.

He stumbled into the elevator, needing to support himself with a hand pressed against the wall. He reeked of alcohol and smelly cologne and was completely blitzed.

Garrett looked at me with glassy eyes. "Floor… floor… what's, what's Apolly and Arty's floor? Take me to… Arry and… Party's… take me to the party floor."

I stared at him, before I turned around and looked towards the lobby. A fancy lobby with a fountain in the middle that was sculpted to look like a carracat. There were even those persian carpets on the floors, the ones that rich people in movies had.

And beyond that were glass windows, reinforced with bulletproof glass, and two doors leading outside, both guarded by thiens.

I… I think I wanted to go outside. I think I needed… time away.

Or maybe I was scared of seeing Silas after what I had done to him. Maybe I was too full of shame and hatred for myself. For not being able to control myself.

I just was scared of turning into Jasper.

That's all.

My eyes travelled back to Garrett, just in time to see him slide to the floor. A crumpled mess of chimera, dressed in a black suit and a crooked red tie.

Then I saw he was wearing shiny black shoes. Beautiful shoes that looked like they had never touched greywaste ash.

I started untying them, and as I did I slid out of my loafers.

"Can you tell King Silas I'm sorry, and I'll be going away for a few days?" I said to Garrett as I pulled his shoes off and started lacing them on my own feet. I quickly realized I didn't know how to tie shoes though so I just made several knots.

Garrett's glassy eyes didn't move, but his head made a twitching motion like he was trying to make it look up at me, he wasn't doing a good job though.

"Party floor?" Garrett said in an asking voice. "Polly-wolly... Ah- Artemis... floor?"

"Ah, sure," I said and put my loafers onto his feet. "Just tell Silas I'll be back. I just need a bit of... time by myself."

"Okay, we'll p-parthy some other time, it's s-sokay."

The elevator would stop on every floor because of me mashing the buttons, so I let Garrett be on the elevator carpet and walked down the lobby towards the door.

I glanced behind me once as the doors closed. Though the guilt overwhelmed me, and the incident that sparked my outburst was still glaring in my mind, I felt an odd sense of calm.

Perhaps even the most insane had their moments of peace. Or maybe my emotions had finally burnt out; the flames had been ravaging me for quite a while.

When I opened one of the glass doors to outside I paused. Feeling the early morning air on my burning face. It was a small comfort, but the cold air did feel nice against the flames.

"Would you like me to call you a driver, Master Dekker?"

I jumped and looked to my left to see a thien, dressed in black with a red trim. He had an assault rifle on his back, and a bullet proof jacket that I think was combat armour.

"No..." I said hurriedly. "I just... need to be by myself."

I looked around, though I had no hoody to pull over my head. I was unshaven, with twisted, oily black hair, I was a wreck with no clothing to bundle myself in.

So I wrapped my arms around myself and gave the thien a mumbled goodbye. Then I walked off into Skyland, leaving Alegria, the king I had injured, and my family, off in the distance.

CHAPTER 25

THE SUN WAS STARTING TO RISE, AND WITH IT MY own anxiety was rising as well. People were starting to crawl out of their buildings. Some holding hot cups of liquid, dressed in suits and ties, and others putting out food carts that carried on its heels some wonderful smells.

It was strange to be inside such a huge city that actually had people living inside of it. The only big city I had ever been in was the one with the celldwellers and it had been entirely abandoned for good reason. Skyfall had the same tall buildings, broken up by double-lane roads, but everything had been repaired or was in the state of being repaired. There was washed brick, intact windows, and most of the buildings had a peaceful cold glow from the hanging lamps inside. Not even bluelamps but real LED lights that were attached to wires that snaked through the building's interior. No extension cords here, it was like the cities on the television.

Though the wear was still apparent. The pavement was patched to the point where it was equally dark, new pavement and light, cracked pavement. The cars that were on the road were rusty and some missing windshields entirely.

Though most of the Fallocaust could be seen on the buildings in the distance, the ones in the other districts. I had seen this from my view on the patio. Hundreds of ruined buildings, some of them half-collapsed or in such a state it seemed like the only thing holding them up was the collective will of those who lived underneath them. They were buildings that wouldn't be able to be renovated, but, from the looks of it, were in the process of being scrapped and salvaged. Their bodies would be dismantled and taken apart, only to be used to repair the other structures. It was like the greywasters in a way: we eat one another so their meat doesn't go to waste.

I turned my attention away from a man with a food cart talking to another man in a truck that had Dek'ko farms on the side, and went inside a building I had eyed up from half a block away. They advertised apartments and that was exactly what I had been looking for.

Immediately my anxiety rose. The inside of the building was like the entrance to Alegria but, of course, not at all as elegant. It was just an open room with chairs and tables to one side, and a reception desk on the other. There were inside plants too that were a beautiful shade of green.

Before I could stop myself I walked over to one of the plants and touched a leaf. The leaf was the shape of the club on a deck of cards and was not only green, but the inside part of the leaf was a lighter shade of green.

I pulled on a leaf and popped it into my mouth, though as soon as I bit down a sour, unpleasant taste filled my mouth so I spat it out onto the pot of dirt.

"Hey!" a man suddenly called. "Bums aren't allowed in Skyland. Get out before I call the thiens and don't eat my fucking—"

As soon as I looked over to him the man, a balding man with glasses, froze in a state of shock. I flushed, embarrassed over my appearance, and looked at the ground.

"Are you... are you a chimera?" the man suddenly stammered, before to my amusement he dropped to one knee and bowed until his nose touched the ground. "I'm extremely sorry, young prince. I didn't recognize you, please forgive me. Take the plant home, it would be my honour, it was my grandmother's."

I stared at him and pulled off another leaf, even though I had spat the last one out. I nibbled on the edges, the taste a little less potent now.

"Do you have apartments?" I asked, not knowing what to say to him bowing to me, and even less: what to say to him calling me a young prince.

The man slowly got to his feet, his limbs stiff from old age, then adjusted his glasses which had become ajar on his face. "Oh, yes, of course we do!"

I nodded and took out my black card. As he gave me a confused look I handed it to him. "One apartment, please."

The man glanced down at it, and the confusion he had on his face only got more apparent. "One... you want to buy an apartment?"

I nodded. "I need to move into it right now."

"Right... now?"

I nodded again.

The man went behind the counter and put my black card on the table. He then clicked a few times on a big computer before glancing at my card.

"Well, Master Sanguine... I have two apartments for sale right now. One has a family that will be living in it until it sells but the last one, a two bedroom, is for sale. Would you like to go see it?"

I shook my head. "No." I thought back to some of the choice places I had spent my childhood. I had pretty low standards. "Does it have furniture?"

"Yes, we currently have furniture in it for showings. We usually include furniture for an extra cost but..." He shifted nervously before wiping his creased forehead. "If you promise not to tell our king I called you a bum, I'll throw it in for free."

I was finding all of this strange and odd until I remembered something that King Silas had told me. That the Skyfallers were subservient to us, and rather terrified of us too. He had said I could walk up to anyone and ask them for something that they had and they had to give it to me.

I was a prince... that was a hard rock to swallow. I wonder what Nana would say if she found out I was a prince. I wonder what Gill would say.

Or even Jasper.

What would Jasper think of this? I wonder if he would be surprised I was talking to people on my own and that I was outside in the city.

"Okay, I won't," I said to him and I saw a visible look of relief on his face. I guess insulting a chimera was a pretty harsh offence. He was sweating bullets and seemed just as anxious as I felt all the time.

"There are some papers for you to fill out..." the man said slowly. "The deed and all of that..."

"Not now," I said to him. "I just would like the key. In a couple days, three or four perhaps. I need time to get myself back."

I burned the king's face. I knew he was immortal but... I didn't know how it worked.

The man nodded slowly and pulled open a drawer. He started rooting through it, shifting around papers before he produced a key with a leather circle as a keychain. He slid it over and I took it.

"I'll get one of the housekeepers to bring you back your card and the invoice in a few days, nothing will be charged until you sign the forms," the man said. "My name is Jan. I own this building. We would be… honoured to have a Dekker living with us."

"Okay," I said looking at my new key. I brought it up to my nose and smelled it before testing it out on my teeth. "Tell housekeeping man to knock and wait for me to answer… tell him to… announce himself and make sure he's alone."

"Sure… no problem," the man said in a voice that told me he probably thought I was crazy. That was okay, I didn't care what they thought. Silas says they were below me.

I had never had anyone below me before.

Without another word I walked to the elevator and looked down at my keys. They had 401 on it and I assumed that was my room number.

So I pressed four and hoped that no one else would be in the elevator, but at this point I was tired and mentally exhausted from the night's events so maybe I could be too fatigued to care.

I hope Silas was okay and out of pain… he had been so nice to me and what had I done in return? I would apologize in a few days – after I got some time to myself.

The plain elevator took me up several levels until it opened to a white painted hall with a floor made out of light-coloured wood. Unlike Alegria there were no sculptures and paintings, no hanging lights or anything but something that I think may be a smoke detector.

I put my key in the lock and opened it, and was immediately pleased with my surroundings.

Never in my life had I ever had a real place to live. I had had shelters, like the apartment in the shanty town or the abandoned buildings I stayed in, but never a real home. Even the room at King Silas's, I never felt like it belonged to me, it was Silas's and I was a guest there.

But this… I had a blue fabric couch pressed against the wall which faced a medium size television, a wooden coffee table, and side tables on either side. I also had two standing lamps with see-through bulbs, a big dresser-type thing with lots of drawers, paintings on the walls, and I even had throw pillows. All of this was on a blue carpet, and even the walls were an off bluey-greeny colour.

I also had a kitchen now, though I wouldn't trust myself to use it. And as I walked around I found two closets and a bathroom with pink walls and a pink rug-thing on the toilet lid. I liked the colour pink, it was bright and not threatening like some other colours I've seen here.

Then I walked into my two bedrooms, both of which had comforters of a mixed pattern of gold and red designs. I decided on the bigger one to be my bedroom.

To show myself just how far I had come and just how brave I was, I opened up the blinds of a sliding glass door that took up half of the far wall. I looked outside at my view of the green park and enjoyed the scenery. Even with all the other feelings inside of me – I was kind of proud of what I did. And if Silas kicked me out of Alegria, I would have a place to stay.

I made sure the door was locked and locked well. Then, just to make sure I was safe, I dragged my couch and pushed it against the door, and even got creative and leaned my new silverware against the door so if someone did try to push through it would come crashing to the ground and it would alert me. It might not be much but it was good enough, so I slipped under my covers and quickly fell asleep.

I slept for a long time, longer than I usually slept. Though I was used to sleeping whenever I could. At Jasper's I was either sleeping or staring at the white door, so I was used to being inactive. This was different though; this was a deep, restful sleep, with the cautious confidence that no one was going to bother me. Even if they were looking for me they wouldn't know where I was.

But when I woke up I found myself not wanting to get out of bed. There was something that was keeping me inside of this safe bedroom. I was drawn to the warm comfortable nest like a magnet to shavings so I stayed in there for quite a while either daydreaming inside of my head or having quick cat naps throughout the day. Even better when I was reminded that I had a television in my room. I quickly found the cartoon channel so when I wasn't napping I was watching cartoons or rerun shows.

I stayed away from the Skyfall News Network, or SNN. I didn't know if Silas was going to announce that I was missing and I wanted to avoid the stress if he was. I was happy in my cave and… I would see him soon. I would apologize and tell him I just needed a break. I wasn't sure how long I had bought this apartment for, and I would eventually have to return.

The next several days were my own, and I cherished every one of them. In that time I had realized the phone in the apartment could be used to call the desk, and I used that opportunity to call in any food I decided I wanted that day. Suiting to my chimera status they brought it and left it outside of my door. I was getting used to being a chimera and a prince.

The morning of the fourth day I think, there was a small knock on the door, immediately followed by a male voice. "Housekeeping here. I have your papers and everything." Then a pause. "It's just one person... just me."

I got out of bed and looked around for my cloth pants. I had taken them off sometime during the last day and had been nestled in bed with just my underwear and a t-shirt. So I put my pants on and walked towards the door.

"One... second..." I said to the door. I pulled away my couch but that made the silverware come crashing to the ground. I jumped at the noise and kicked the silverware into a pile, before opening the door.

Immediately a young man around my own age flinched before stammering an apology. My ears burned with embarrassment over his reaction. I hated meeting new people, they always reacted the same. I hated myself even more for being different. All of the sengils and my family were used to seeing different-looking people... everyone outside of Alegria were not.

"I'm sorry..." the housekeeper gasped before, like Jan had, he started to get flustered. "Really... really sorry..."

"It's okay," I said in a small voice before walking towards the living room, my head hung low. "I'm used to it."

The housekeeper followed me inside, and I heard the door click behind him. He was tall, almost as tall as me, with dark brown hair that had blond streaks in it, and blue eyes. He wasn't threatening so I didn't mind him in the apartment with me. I hadn't spoken to anyone in days, and though I wasn't lonely... it was nice to have a conversation with someone.

"What's your name?" I asked him as I sat down. I only had one couch, no chairs so he sat on the other end of the couch holding in his hand a couple of papers and a pen. He was dressed well, in a shirt that said the apartment building's name (Skylanding) and pressed black pants. He smelled nice as well – I was sure I smelled awful.

I pushed down the further embarrassment over that. I was starting to feel self-conscious about my appearance. I had a beard and tangled black hair, I was still extremely thin and gaunt and my clothes were dirty. I think the more comfortable I got in Skyfall the more I was starting to feel ashamed about my appearance.

Silas had been on me constantly about cleaning myself… maybe it was time. I was alone here so I could be naked without feeling scared.

The housekeeper didn't seem to care, or if he did he didn't voice it. "My name is Kass. You're…" He got that stricken look again. "I'm sorry I don't want to insult you over trying to pronounce it."

"Sang-win," I replied back. I took the papers from him and started looking at them. I was good at reading but they used complicated words that I didn't know, and said confusing things I didn't understand. I assumed if they were trying to rip me off I could kill them since I was a prince, so I signed the papers. Though admittedly I had to look at the card to see how to spell my own name properly.

"Sanguine…" Kass repeated. He cleared his throat and I heard his heartbeat speed up. "Um, does your family… know you're here?"

"Are you allowed to ask these sorts of questions?" I asked plainly, and he flinched again.

"No…" he said and pointed to a place I had forgotten to sign. "Just… there too."

He was quiet for a moment as I signed, but I realized quickly he was still squirming in his spot like he had to pee. I looked over at him as I handed the paper back and gave him a look.

"You're a mess, why?" I asked. Did I really look that bad?

Kass's blue eyes flickered up to mine, his pupils were small, little black specks lost in a sea of blue; I even saw hints of green. He wasn't that bad-looking, though the streaks in his dyed hair were rather weird.

"Ah… Jan told me to ask you if the king was looking for you…" Kass said slowly. "He's worried because we could… all be forced into Stadium if King Silas finds out we're harbouring an escaped… an escaped chimera."

I blinked as my brain processed this information. I didn't think I would be putting anyone in danger. I just wanted a couple days by myself.

"If… if I don't come down with an answer he's threatened to fire me." Kass's voice was slow and cautious. "This… I, ah… do you… are you new here? I'm sorry, Master Sanguine, but you showing up here and buying an apartment is… strange. And it's making the workers and Mr.

Jan extremely nervous. You must understand... if you make King Silas mad, or Master Elish or the others... you die. Simple as that. You die."

You die? I guess that was... understandable. The family had to keep the Skyfallers in line and if they were hiding something from the king that was grounds for treason or something. I felt badly for that but... King Silas liked me, if I asked him not to kill the workers he would.

"I am new here," I said rather stiffly. "I am from the greywastes. I've only been here for a few months."

Kass's stricken face only got more apprehensive. "So... you don't know how the family works do you?"

I shook my head. "No, I know how they work. You obey the king and the family or you die. I know how that works... but I'm in the family so you have to obey me, right?"

"Technically... but... Jan..."

"I'll be gone in a few days... I'm not here permanently," I said with a shrug. "I just needed a couple more days... then I want to go back and apologize to King Silas. So you can tell Jan that."

But this seemed to make Kass pale even more. "A-apologize?"

My mouth twisted to the side, but I decided to exercise my authority and not tell him what I had done. Instead I had a better idea, something that made my insides quiver.

"I have an order for you..." I said, testing the waters on my authority when it came to the Skyfallers.

Kass looked at me, but I couldn't read his expression well. "Order?"

I nodded slowly. Since I had hurt King Silas and had fled from Alegria, I decided maybe I should do something nice for Silas once I came back. Not just because I was worried he would be angry, even if he said he wasn't before, but because I wanted to make him happy.

"I want to look good..." I said. "Can you help me look good?"

I wasn't expecting a big grin but that's exactly what I got.

Kass looked me up and down with a beaming face, before he tapped his chin with his finger. "I can make you look good... I can make you look *very* good. What do you want? Hair? Clothes? Soap? You need soap, lots of soap, that's for sure."

I nodded and slid my black card over to him. Kass stared at it like I had just handed him the chalice of life.

"Buy what you think I will need... but if there is any odd charges..." I gave him a look and at that look Kass chuckled dryly.

"You think I would steal from a chimera? One day, when you're all established and killing random Skyfallers like the others, you'll realize how stupid it is to even think I'd do that." He took the black card and started running his fingers over it. "They'll think I'm stealing from you though… you might want to come with me."

My head couldn't shake back and forth any faster. "No, no, I'm not going outside. Just tell them you're my sengil, I'm sure it will be fine."

Kass didn't seem to be happy about this but that was too bad. No way I was going to go out in broad daylight with lots of people around, least of all talking to the store clerks, and having all of them flipping out because of my eyes and teeth. And further more they would know right away I was a chimera and that might leak back to Silas. I didn't want to see him yet.

I didn't know how he was now. I assumed since he was immortal he would have some process they went through to heal his face. Though I never learned how that worked obviously. Nan and Gill had just known King Silas and some of the chimeras were immortal and could heal themselves somehow.

"What are your measurements, do you know?" Kass asked. He reached over and pulled on my t-shirt and glanced at the tag. "Small… well, I guess that's obvious. I'll get you some nice clothes that should fit. Do you have a style? You kinda seem more like… rock star, gothic, punk."

I stared, I didn't know what any of those words meant and I think Kass realized that because everything else he just wrote on the back of the folder he had kept the deeds in.

"Want me to get you some food too?" Kass asked after he had stood up to leave. "You look like you've missed about fifteen hundred meals."

"Sure," I said. "I like meatball subs and I like cheesecake."

"Who doesn't?" Kass said and slipped his shoes back on. "I'll be back in a few hours." And with that my new delivery boy left the apartment.

I locked the door behind him, and walked into my bathroom, my very pink bathroom. I looked at the tub and sighed.

Admittedly, I spent about fifteen minutes just staring at the tub, trying to find this bravery that seemed to be coming in spurts. I haven't had a bath in years and even then it was in a river. Never in my life had I had one with hot water.

I turned on the tap and ran my finger under the water. Then I picked up one of the bottles of soap that was resting on a white wire rack that hung from the showerhead and smelled it.

Then I drank some, but spat that out into the collecting bath water. It smelled like fruit and perfume but it tasted just as bad as those plant leaves I had eaten.

Eventually I figured out how to plug the drain so the water would stop draining out and after squeezing a little bit of everything into the tub I got in and sat down.

So there I sat in my hot, bubbly water. I sighed and breathed in the fragrant steam and tried to relax. No one was going to find me here, no one was going to hurt me here – I just kept having to remind myself of that.

I held up my hands, my fingernails chewed short and my skin rough and covered in scars and cuts. Then I lifted up my leg and saw that that was even worse, though I got a glimpse at my groin and immediately lowered it. Even seeing it made me nervous, so I got out of the tub and grabbed my underwear.

"Okay… scrubbing time," I sighed and picked up a scrubby, rough mit-thingy and started getting to work on my body. I had to get this done before Kass knocked on my door because I knew if he did, Crow would flip out and he had been acting like a huge asshole lately.

After trying to scrub off the layers and layers of dirt, I took a break and soaked in the hot water, just to loosen up the other grime. Then, with lots of scraping and scrubbing and more soap, I got the important parts of me clean, or as clean as I could get them. I decided to leave my hair for Kass, since I had no idea how to do that and I didn't even want to try.

When I was done I drained the tub and put on a robe coat thing that was fluffy and also pink. Then I laid down on the bed and took another nap. I liked naps, a lot.

I woke up in the worst possible way, to banging on my door. I jumped to my feet; my entire body tensed as if anticipating the world ending again, and tightly did up my bathrobe. I debated getting my clothes but the robe actually covered more of me than my shoddy nightclothes had.

I walked to the door with a yawn, eagerly looking forward to finding out just what Kass had bought for me. It was like having my first Christmas in a way. I was going to have lots of little presents to open.

Though when I opened the door… it wasn't who I expected at all.

Nero stared down at me, his indigo eyes burrowing into me with such an unimpressed look it made my head drop in embarrassment and shame.

Though as I took a step back and mumbled and apology I realized he had Kass by the neck, standing just off of the doorway.

"You should be sorry!" Nero suddenly said loudly, though when I flinched he lowered his voice. "Kingy's been having kittens over this, and then I get an emergency call from fucking Peterson saying some asshole is in Skyland hitting five shops in an hour using Sanguine Dekker's new black card? After he's been gone for five days? Do you have any fucking idea how worried I was that some dude had slit your fucking throat?"

Nero stalked into the apartment. Kass stumbling behind him, rubbing the nape of his neck. I took another step back until my back hit the corner of the fridge.

"I just…" I stammered, but Nero whirled around and gave me a hard look.

"What? You just what, Sangy? Where's your fucking logic? You run away, make it three whole fucking blocks, and decide it would be a fine idea to buy a fucking two hundred thousand dollar condo? You knew we would know where to find you. You suck at running away, fucking dumbshit," Nero snapped.

I stared at the floor before walking towards my bedroom.

"Don't you even hide under that fucking bed! I'm not done being pissed at you!" Nero called angrily.

I ducked into my room but I was horrified when I realized the bed I had been sleeping on had no under-the-bed, only wooden drawers attached to the bed frame.

Quickly I turned around to go back out into the living room, but Nero was already in the doorway, still looking angry.

Nero glanced behind him. "You can piss off. You got off easy this time."

Soon after there was a slam of the door and all attention was on me again.

"Why, Sanguine?" Nero asked coldly.

My eyes travelled around the room, looking for any place I could hide myself, any dark corner, but I was out and exposed. This didn't sit well with me or Crow, but I knew since it was just Nero – I was on my own.

I shrugged and shook my head, before sitting on the bed.

"Why did you leave?" Nero asked again. "And why did you hurt Silas? I know you don't fucking know how he usually is, but he is being unworldly and uncharacteristically kind to you. Why the fuck would you take advantage of that? You don't know how good you have it, do you?"

My face burned. I could feel the humiliation and shame smouldering under my skin. It was searing me so badly I was surprised smoke wasn't seeping out of my pores.

"I can't... tell you..." I said slowly, wiping my nose though it was more from stress than anything.

Nero paused but I didn't look up. I just stared at my bare feet, now clean and pale.

When he spoke, his voice had gone softer. "Tell me what? There's something to tell?" He was quiet again. "We're friends and brothers – you can tell me anything."

Slowly I looked up at him. Nero's arms were still crossed but he looked a little less pissed at me now. There was still trust left in me to trust Nero... I think out of everyone in my life he was the most worthy of being trusted. I wasn't sure if that was smart but... I didn't want him to be angry at me, or at least angry at me for the wrong reasons.

"He kissed me and I didn't like that I liked it," I said quietly.

Nero gave me a look of pure confusion, before he narrowed his eyes and spread out his hands. "That's it? No asterisk at the end where he tries to savagely rape you or something? That's it?"

Rape me? I choked on the sharp intake of breath and closed my robe around me tighter. My heart raced at even the mention of something like that. Automatically I tried to pull my robe even tighter around me, but it was stretched to the point where I was worried it was going to rip. Instead I grabbed a pillow and held it on my lap and clutched it for dear life.

"Oh no..." Nero moaned and he swore. I glanced up to see him wiping a hand down his face. "Silas tried to get with you, didn't he? You fried his face and took off... I get it. You've been raped before, haven't you? Well that makes..."

Suddenly Nero stopped and I saw the exact moment he remembered just how long I had been in Jasper's basement.

"Don't tell anyone..." I said in a cracked voice. My own terror over Nero realizing who Jasper was had sucked all of the liquid from my mouth and throat. "Please."

Nero's lips disappeared into his mouth.

"I think the entire family... except Elish... is in denial about it... about why Jasper had you three in there," Nero said. He walked over and sat beside me on the bed. "Silas is really really in denial about it and I'm worried about how much he's going to fly off the handle when he finally accepts it." I felt him put an arm around me before he pulled me close to him. "So he wanted to get with you and you just kinda lost it?"

I shook my head, probably to Nero's surprise. "I didn't like how it made me feel."

"Bad?"

"No… I liked it. I'm a pervert just like Jasper…" I said, the burning returning to my face, especially my ears. I don't know what was coming over me, but suddenly I just wanted to tell him everything. This secret had been festering inside of me for so long and the rot from it was starting to leak further into the life I was living now. Maybe it was time to tell someone I trusted.

"Because you liked him doing shit to you? What did he do?"

"Kiss me."

Nero was quiet for several moments. "That's it?"

I nodded.

"That's as far as he took it?"

I nodded again. "He stopped when I became uncomfortable."

"He *stopped* when you asked? He actually fucking *stopped*?"

"Yeah."

More silence.

"And you still blinded him and burned a hole in his face?"

"I didn't like how it made me feel…" I said again.

Nero let out a whistle and squeezed my side tighter into his. "Okay, well I'm not Mantis, but you kinda burned your bridge with him, so let me try and crack this, okay?"

"Okay," I said in a low voice. I just wanted to crawl somewhere and hide, but at the same time I think I did want to have this conversation.

'Share the infection?' Crow mused in my head. *'Give him a little bit of that putrid rot you carry on your shoulders.'*

"You say you didn't like how it made you feel. So it made you uncomfortable because it reminded you of being in the basement?"

I shook my head no. "I didn't like… that it was doing things to my body."

"OHHH!" I jumped as Nero said that loudly, then to my further embarrassment he laughed.

"I fucking get it now. You didn't like that you liked it and you panicked didn't you? Oh my god, I think I get it now – he made you horny and you flipped shit, didn't you? You panicked and I know why... because you felt shitty for liking something sexual."

"Can you not say it so bluntly?" I murmured. "You're making me even more uncomfortable."

"It's Nero, dumbass. I'm your older brother... it's my job to make you uncomfortable." But then he sighed and I saw him reach into his pocket. He pulled out something brown, liquor obviously, and put the bottle to his lips.

Another sigh, and he pursed the inner corners of his eyes with his fingers. "I can't believe we left you just to have that happen..." He swallowed another mouthful of liquor. "You gotta understand... Silas just wanted us to leave you in a town. Ellis and I did as much as we could under his nose. We were even going to hide you in Cardinalhall Mansion when we came back three years later."

He looked at me. "I'm sorry."

I held out my hand and he gave me the bottle. I took a drink, trying not to wince at the taste. It was rum, which was better than the whisky I used to be able to smell on Jasper.

"Look, bro, so it doesn't come as a shock when you see it..." Nero began. "King Silas can be a huge, controlling, manipulative, fucking insane, jealous, psychopath... he's kind of nuts sometimes. He's being really, weirdly kind to you and it's because he feels guilty as fuck over what happened to you and he hasn't felt the feeling of guilt in quite a while. But just know: he does love you, all of us do, more than anyone will ever love you. Silas isn't perfect, okay? He jumps on all of us as soon as we turn fifteen, so jumping on you isn't odd or anything... it's kinda cool he backed off right away."

I tipped the rum bottle back and forth and took another drink. "I know... I think I know anyway. I heard things from the merchants growing up. I just assumed he treated his family different."

"And he does," Nero said with a nod. He took the bottle back and tucked it back into his pocket. "But just... shit, Sanguine. Don't hate him when you start to see the protective covering peel off. Don't be scared. Silas is... kinda manic. He's suffered a lot, and he's kinda messed in the head like you sometimes."

Then another silence filled the room. "Maybe that's why he likes you?" Nero suddenly said, then shrugged it off. "Anyway... less about the king, more about you. You do know you're in for a lifetime of torment if you flip out every time your cock gets hard, right?"

I groaned and put the pillow over my head. "Stop being so blunt…"

Nero pulled the pillow away and lightly smacked me in the face with it. "Someone needs to be blunt with you. If we all dance around it you'll never feel better. Look, bright eyes… I'm not even going to go there when it comes to this Jasper shit. It'll just piss me off and make you go into that crazy-Sanguine-psychosis and I don't want that. So…" He dug into his pocket and got the rum bottle out again, then to my surprise… he also got out a tin of cigarettes.

He shifted away from me and laid the rum bottle on the bed, then the tin of smokes which he opened, displaying over twenty perfect cigarettes all on top of each other.

"This is simple shit because I'm a simple guy…" Nero took out a cigarette and put it to his lips. "Jasper got you when you were a tyke… Jasper is the cigarette tin." Nero pointed. "And you're the rum bottle."

I looked at him like he had just gone crazy but he seemed to have a method behind this odd madness.

Nero took all the cigarettes from the Jasper tin and started surrounding the Sanguine rum bottle with cigarettes. "Jasper messed you up big time. Now you have all this fucked up baggage. You're scared all the time when you shouldn't be, you have this Crow dude screaming at you and talking to you, you have an incredibly messed up view of sex." Each time he made a statement another cigarette surrounded the bottle. "All of this Jasper did to you, all of your weirdness. Well, some of it is being a chimera but that's normal to you so it doesn't count. Anyway, see what you're looking at? All of this shit you're dealing with… is stuff Jasper did. This is all Jasper stink surrounding you."

Nero then flicked the empty tin onto the ground. It landed with a rattled clank. "Now Jasper is gone… but look at that, honey-beans, you're still surrounded by his shit. Now you're in Skyfall with your family but… look at all this Jasper residue you still have in you. That's Jasper still… what you need to realize, kiddo…"

Nero lifted up the rum bottle and swept the cigarettes away. "That's not who you are. You need to get rid of all those cigarettes and just be a rum bottle. Jasper's gone, and you need to realize… you're okay."

Then he smiled and shook the bottle back and forth. "You're okay, brother. Seriously, you're a sweet little fucker who can thankfully still feel emotions. You're not as lost as you think or as messed up as you think.

You just need to listen to your heart – and not the voices in your head."

It was an odd visual display... but I understood what he was talking about. I wish it was just that easy, to push the essence of Jasper away, but–

"I was with him longer than I was alive," I said in a quiet voice. I stared at the rum bottle as the little bubbles rose to the surface. "What being around him, locked in that basement, did to me... those cigarettes are me now. If you strip every part of Jasper away... there isn't much of me left."

"That's okay," Nero said, he gave me an encouraging smile. "That's just fine. We can rebuild you, baby. We have the technology."

I chuckled at his stupid quote, and that made him smile wider.

"You can still laugh, you can still love, and you have some hilarious quirks like that squirrel-food thing and the Crow dude... but you're okay. One day you'll be banging all of us and you'll look back at this moment like... why the fuck didn't I stick my cock inside of Nero that day in the Skylander condo."

My heart jumped and I held my hands over my head. "No, not ever... I could never do that."

"Oh, you will..." Nero smirked. "There isn't a chimera past fifteen I haven't had sex with besides you. Same goes for every single one of us, even Elish. It's like how we reinforce our family bonds. It's not weird for us, it's normal and eventually it will be normal for you too."

I shook my head back and forth. "No... not me."

"That's the Jasper stink talking... not the nineteen-year-old chimera. You're in your prime right now, you should be having at least two of us between your sheets every night," Nero said with a shake of his head. "Throw that cigarette away already; it doesn't belong near the Sanguine rum bottle. Look... you trust me right?"

I nodded but shifted around nervously. I didn't like where this was heading, and I was wondering how much more of this conversation I could take before my anxiety overshadowed my need to talk about some of the things rotting inside of me.

"Good..."

My body spasmed from shock as Nero started taking his boots off. Immediately I got up and tried leaving the room.

"Oh, fucking sit down... I promise I won't touch you," Nero said in such an indifferent voice it... actually made my anxiety go down. He wasn't… tense or nervous. That resonated with me, because it meant he was casual about all of this. I liked casual more than… more than… the lust I had felt in Silas when he kissed me.

And myself.

I slowly turned around. My eyes widened when I saw he was slipping his cargo pants off.

"What are you doing?" I said alarmed. "You gotta tell me or else Crow's going to command me to rip your face off…"

"I'm going to make you hard," Nero said with a coy, almost boyish smirk. "And you're going to sit there with that hard cock and not be freaked out about it. It's normal and you're going to deal with it until you realize it's normal."

I put a hand over my mouth, feeling my entire body flush with dizziness.

"Have you ever seen another dude aroused? Besides him?"

With my hand over my mouth I shook my head.

The smirk got wider. He honestly didn't care… he wasn't like Silas, he wasn't throwing himself at me. Nero didn't want me like Silas did at all. He either wanted to fuck with me… or he wanted to help me.

But how was this helping? Why was…

I swallowed and almost choked on my own shock when he pulled down his underwear and separated his legs. He was baring it all at me, sitting on my bed.

His dick was huge… even soft it was long and thick. I had never in my life seen one so large, not even in that movie I saw.

Nero chuckled and I knew he was laughing at my reaction. "I've seen that look before, though that's when the poor guys know they're going to have to take it. You have a huge one too you know. We all do, but yours isn't as big as mine. I'm the biggest, thank-you-very-much."

I couldn't talk; I stared at it before my eyes slowly travelled up to Nero's face. "What are you going to do? You won't…"

"I'm – not – going – to – touch – you," Nero said again, slowly and deliberately annunciating every word. "Just… watch, and hell, I know you won't… but if you want to touch it, get a feel for it… by all means."

Nero put one arm behind him to help prop himself up, and the other started pulling and rubbing his dick. All I could do was stare, but I found the breath quickly leaving my throat.

I wanted to tell him to stop. I wanted to turn around and run out of the apartment and go back to Alegria – but as I watched that giant, thick dick start to harden, suddenly all my mind demanded was for me to keep watching him.

His eyes closed for a moment and a growled curse word rolled from his lips. As it stiffened and got rigid, he ran his hand down to the shaft and grabbed the base, before removing his hand altogether.

It stood at full salute, with a round, well-defined pink head, connected to a thick shaft that had a small blue vein. His pubic hair was trimmed and neatly groomed and his testicles big, oval-shaped, and shifting around as he rubbed his inner thigh.

When I tried to swallow, I found that my throat was parched, and as I started to become aware of my body again, I confirmed to myself that I was indeed liking this... because I was hard as rock. I was... so hard it was aching inside of my underwear.

"Have you ever..." Nero opened one eye. He started running his index finger and middle finger over the shaft, before twirling the digits around the head. "... cum before?"

I swallowed again and shook my head.

Nero groaned and tugged on the head. "Oh fuck, you're killing me. Not once? You've never jerked off once?"

"No..." I croaked. "I hate my body, I hate my–"

"You just haven't been properly introduced," Nero said cutting me off. I saw a twitch in the side of his mouth. "How can you hate something you've never tried? Sex isn't what you experienced, that's rape, Sangy. Sex is different than rape and jerking off is different than both of those. No wonder you're so fucking tense... you would be a lot more relaxed if you busted yourself for the first time."

I tried to squeeze my legs together, in a feeble attempt to make the hardness in my dick go away, but it wasn't working, mostly because I couldn't take my eyes off of Nero's penis. I had never felt this pull towards another man, ever. With Jasper I looked upon him with disgust, but for the first time...

I think I wanted to do something with him.

Nero closed his eyes and groaned. He started rapidly moving his hand back and forth over his dick, his other hand now unbuttoning the white shirt he had been wearing.

Like I was walking on air, I took the two steps towards him, and in an act I saw in myself as pure insane bravery... I held out my hand and put it over his.

Nero stopped and opened his eyes. The atmosphere inside of the room thick and heavy but also quiet, and it was in that silence that I heard his pulse jump in excitement.

I drew my hand down and gently took the piece of flesh into my grasp. It was hot to the touch, and I could feel the blood rushing through it, and as I gave it its first stroke, I felt it twitch.

Nero said nothing, but his breathing was ragged. For the first time, consensually, I started running my hand up and down the thick shaft, until I found a good rhythm.

My heart was pounding, the dizziness that had taken hold of my mind making me see spheres of white and red in front of my eyes. A part of me felt like I was going to pass out, but another part of me, a large part of me… was enjoying every moment of this.

"You don't have to…" Nero gasped, before he let out a groan. "But if you want to open that robe. I would worship you."

I didn't even care to ask for reassurances that he wouldn't touch me. Without protest I undid the ties on my pink robe and let it drop onto the bed.

Nero let out a long groan. "You are huge, I knew it. Fuck, look at that beautiful thing."

I shook my head; I didn't want to look at it. I just wanted to keep touching Nero, not do something that might kill the warm tense feeling I was enjoying. It felt like an inflatable trying to expand in a glass jar, it was so tense, so… tight. It felt like it wanted to break, or explode.

Nero watched my groin with his eyes half-open and glassy. I mostly watched my own hand going up and down on him, putting a slight amount of pressure to my grip as his moans started to become more close together.

"F-faster…" Nero gasped. He leaned back on the bed and spread his legs. "Work it good, puppy. Fuck, squeeze it a bit more – yeah, like that. Holy shit."

I bit the edge of my tongue as I obeyed his request. I couldn't believe I was doing this, and I couldn't believe I was doing it naked.

But I wasn't scared; I wasn't in fear of him forcing me into something more… I was okay. I really was okay.

Nero let out another loud moan, he started clawing the side of his thigh, then his eyes shut tight. "Faster… fuck, fuck, I'm going to cum. Faster, fuck!" I moaned myself from sheer lust and started to speed up, watching his face as it scrunched up like he was in pain. His mouth open, drawing in the thick sexual tension overloading this room.

I was going to make Nero cum – oh my god, I was going to make him cum. Me. I was doing this to my hero.

Surging with hormones, a lust I had never felt before, and more, I sped up. I put a knee on the bed so I was almost kneeling and leaned over him. My hand rapidly going up and down on his dick as Nero moaned and grasped his thigh and the comforter he was laying on.

Then, with a loud cry, Nero let his head fall back onto the bed. He twisted his body and gasped. I looked down and saw a thick spurt of cum shoot out of his dick, followed by another long string of opaque and white. I sped up for several more seconds, the cum coating my hand, before I slowed down and massaged the thick shaft, easing out each milky spurt.

And there was a lot of it; it completely covered my hand and his short, black pubic hair. I even saw several glistening beads on his chest and collarbone.

"Fuck!" Nero groaned and put a hand over his face. "Oh, fuck, that's the best cum I've had in a year. Oh my god…" He looked up and swore, he was staring at my dick.

I removed my hand and brought it up to my nose. Curious of how Nero tasted, I stuck out my tongue and licked some of it off.

"… you want to kill me don't you?" Nero moaned. "Fuck, Sanguine."

I moved the cum around in my mouth. "You taste pretty good," I said, and I found myself smirking. Then I licked up some more, making sure he could see it on my tongue. "Does that really turn you on?"

Nero nodded, and his gaze dropped again.

He nodded towards my dick. "Look at yours; you have precum dripping down the tip, right down the slit."

I pushed down the anxiety that brought. I killed the bees buzzing dangerously around my uneasiness at seeing myself hard, and glanced down.

Oh, wow, I was big. I had never realized it before. Like Nero had stated, it was long when it was hard, and though it wasn't as thick as Nero's dick it still had a good width to it. I hadn't seen many to compare but I knew for sure I was bigger than average.

And he was right about the precum… I had never heard that term before but it was obvious what it was in just the word. There was a bead of it that was forming on the tip, and another one that was slowly making its way down the slit, to the bottom part of the pink, mushroom-shaped head.

I touched the tip of my finger to the slit of my dick and gathered the drop of precum.

Then I held it out to Nero.

He took in a shuddered breath, before he grabbed my hand and put it up to his mouth. I felt his warm tongue wrap around my finger, before he gave it a few sucks, creating a suction with his mouth.

When he broke away, he took in another ragged breath of air and shook his head. "You're going to kill me... you're so fucking hot and you don't even know it."

I smiled, feeling a bit coy, and shrugged.

"Do you want to do something with it?" Nero asked nodding towards my dick. "Whatever you want, honey. I can take care of that for you, or you can take a cold shower – you tell me."

I looked down, and I was curious as to how it would feel. From how Nero sounded, and looked, it looked like it felt good... maybe a bit painful since he looked like he was in pain and almost sounded like it.

But...

I think... I think I wanted to see if Nero would actually let me not do anything. I wanted to test him and see if he could stop himself. Nero and Silas were the two men I trusted, and I wanted to confirm to myself and Crow... he wouldn't force me into anything.

I pulled my robe back over my naked body and shook my head. "Not today... I think I want to wait."

Nero let out a disappointed whine. "You're killing me, sweetness, killing me." But then he slapped his knees with his hands and sat up. "We got work to do anyway."

He motioned once again towards my groin. "You're at least going to let me trim that, right? Trim that, get that hair on your head lookin' fine. You already bathed which is wonderful. Come on, we're going to make you look pretty, you hot, fucking piece of work. One day though, Sanguine."

Then he winked at me. "I'll have you."

I smiled and felt my cheeks redden. "Yeah, one day." I leaned over and kissed his cheek, before I pinched it with my fingers. "One day, amor."

CHAPTER 26

"WOW," NERO WHISPERED. THE LOOK HE WAS GIVING me was like a carracat eyeing up a biigo in its prime. I didn't mind that wolfish grin, on the contrary, I was starting to enjoy making him feel this way. "You... you don't even know. Wow."

I had just stepped out of the bathroom, wearing the brand-new clothes that Kass had bought for me. And though I was feeling rather good about myself, I was currently sporting a beet-red face over what Nero had done to both my clothing and my appearance.

I had on a tight, long-sleeved black shirt with some silver designs on the front that ran down the sleeves, and just as tight fitting black jeans with a chain going from one loop to the other. I also was wearing the shoes I had stolen from Garrett and new white socks.

But Nero was looking at my head, which brought a further burn to my cheeks, one that told me I was blushing. He was looking at my newly cut hair, no longer a rat's nest on top of my head; it was now brushed and trimmed. All of this done by Nero himself, a talent I would've never thought my brother would have.

He hadn't cut too much off; my newly washed black hair now touched my cheek bone and smelled like flowers.

I... really looked like a different person, and I felt like a different person too.

A rush of nerves got to me. I looked away and smiled, before waving a hand at Nero. "Stop wowing at me, you're embarrassing me enough as it is."

He laughed before grabbing my shoulders and pushing me into the bathroom. I saw his huge grin reflecting in the mirror and beside him... a man I only recognized from his pointed teeth and crimson eyes.

I did look... so different. I looked like a human – not so much a monster anymore.

Though when I tried to smile I saw my teeth and I still disliked that. So I did something I had seen Crow do many times before: I smiled with my mouth closed, the rise in my cheeks making my eyes squint.

Maybe... maybe I did look kinda nice.

"You look like a chimera, a real prince chimera," Nero commented, shaking my shoulders. "You just look good enough to eat, god damn. Are you ready to go say hi to Silas? I got the ping that he woke up this morning. Usually after he wakes up he takes a day off and hangs out in the apartment to catch up on what he's missed."

I stared back at this strange person and saw he was indeed blushing. I smiled and turned away embarrassed before shaking my head no.

Nero laughed and my world once again became distorted as Nero shook me back and forth even harder. "You're so shy! Oh my god, you're so shy over how you look. Puppy, you're not a monster locked up anymore, you're a prince. Say it: I'm prince hot shit – I'm Prince Sanguine."

"I am... Prince Sanguine," I said to the mirror before I saw myself smirk. "I feel like an idiot."

Nero kissed my cheek, I let out a snort. I don't think I had been in this good of a mood since... since...

I don't really remember.

I rubbed my slobbered on cheek with my hand and let Nero flick my hair around with the hairbrush. Then we started heading towards the door, it was broad daylight but I was okay. I felt safe with Nero, and Crow had been quiet all day. I was okay today and I was going to prove it to everyone.

"Isn't Ceph going to be mad we... did that?" I asked when we were in the elevator.

Nero snorted like that was the most dumbest thing he'd ever heard. "That's not really how this family works, pickles. At least not with most of us. Think of it like this though, since Cephy really is my main man: as a family, we fuck around with each other, but I go home to him. Does that make sense?"

I thought of it for a second and nodded. "So we're allowed to have relationships with other chimeras? What about non-chimeras?"

Nero let me walk out first. I gave Jan a wave, and though the old, bald-headed man was giving the both of us equally terrified looks he managed a wave and a nervous smile. I don't think Jan was going to miss me, but I might come back sometime though Nero said we wouldn't be buying the condo since we apparently had a whole bunch all around Skyfall and mansions in the greywastes. That was a bit disappointing but I left a note for Kass that he could come to Alegria and say hi anytime he liked.

I doubted I would ever hear from him again though.

"Yeah, we are free to date who we want," Nero said with a nod. "Though if it starts to get serious you'll have to make sure it's okay with Kingy. He has a wicked ass jealous streak so you gotta make sure he's okay with it."

He chuckled, though I saw a pull on his lip. "He can get a bit crazy but... ah, he loves us."

"All of us."

Alegria

Silas's face was neutral, though the same couldn't be said for his eyes. The twin emeralds were burning with green fire as they glared down at the whimpering man at his feet.

The man, half in shadow, was on his knees, his head bowed and his forehead touching the ground. He was choking through sobs; his shoulders shaking under his grief.

"After all these years and you really think your pleading will do something?" Silas said in a low growl, his black and silver cape swaying back and forth behind him as he paced. "You think this display of weakness will get me, the man who ended the world, to show you mercy?"

King Silas smirked and walked a circle around the whimpering man, his gaze only briefly shifting to the corner of the large room, where a young blond man was kneeling with a stream of blood running down his pale face. The young man seemed to be in a daze, his eyes glazed and staring off into space, and his mouth slacked.

Silas slowly got down on one knee, and petted the man's spiky dark hair back. "You must not know me well, Garrett."

A small whimper broke the tension that was plaguing the room the three of them were in. Then the man in front of the king looked up, tears staining his eyes.

"Why, Silas?" Garrett said in a thin voice. "You said I could have a sengil…"

Silas lifted up Garrett's chin with a gloved hand, and gently stroked his second born's skin in a deceptively caring way.

"Yes, and I told you not to fall for him, didn't I? Did you think you could hide it from me? That you two had become more than just sengil and master? Do your brothers really have to rat you out to me? Has our relationship deteriorated that much?" Silas whispered, each word slipping out of his mouth in such an odd casual way it made Garrett's heart palpitate.

Garrett looked over at Tom. The sengils eyes were glazed over, barely aware of what was going on around him.

Garrett let out a desperate moan and shook his head. "I was scared."

Silas's hand retracted, and his eyes narrowed. "Scared? Of what?"

Then Garrett's face tensed, his lips pursed until the ridges of them started to turn white. Finally, not able to hold back he jerked his chin away from Silas's hand and rose to his feet. "Of what? What kind of question is that!?" Garrett said, his voice carrying a vein of anger. A small glimpse into the rage that Silas knew he was holding back with every shred of his self-control. "You know of what! Because I was scared of this." Garrett's right hand swept the room. "Of all of this! Of you killing him because I love him!"

Silas let out an amused breath. "You don't love him… you're too immature to love anything and no chimera of mine will be with some worthless sengil."

"He's not worthless!" Garrett suddenly screamed, before dropping to his knees. He lowered his head again before slowly shaking it back and forth. "He's not worthless… he – he understands me; he listens to me. He treats me kinder than any of you! You've never loved me; I was just your fucking disappointment, your second daughter as you always love to say. And now you're pissed because I found someone that loves me for me?" Garrett shot to his feet again, his shoulders shaking and his hands clenched into tight fists. "It's not fair!" Garrett took in a deep breath, a bead of sweat running down his forehead.

Not a single emotion crossed Silas's face as Garrett's heated words reached his ears. He brushed them off with an amused look before he picked up a 10mm that had been resting beside him on a side table.

Slowly he walked around Garrett, rapping the tip of the gun against his face-up palm. "So because you have yet to earn your place in the family, you decide to lower yourself to doting on the slaves... interesting indeed. You have an odd approach to winning my respect, Garrett Sebastian, a very odd approach."

Silas casually turned his back to Garrett and started walking towards the cowering sengil in the corner of the room. Shadows devouring almost his entire body but the side of his face and his arm.

Tom stared at the king, his face holding stricken horror and his body language reflecting that of a rodent beholding a cat. He cowered into his corner and started hyperventilating.

"Who told you?" Garrett demanded, his voice cracking. "Who told you about me and Tom?"

Silas spun the barrel of the gun before pressing back the safety. He closed one eye and stuck his tongue out of the corner of his mouth as he pointed it towards the sengil.

"You know better," Silas murmured before lowering the gun. "Just as I never tell my chimeras when you tattletale on them, I will show them the same respect, *savis*."

Then Silas sheathed the gun and turned around. In an odd display of his indifference to Garrett's turmoil he clapped his hands together and grinned. "I have a wonderful idea. I propose a game!"

Garrett's tear-streaked face blanched to a sickly white. With a groan he put his hand back over his mouth and shook his head no. Garrett knew just what King Silas's games involved, only eight years ago he had front row seats to Silas's game for Ellis and her husband Stellen, one that almost killed the man.

But they had won... and they could be together now, Garrett thought to himself, but as his stinging eyes travelled to Tom his heart gave a painful lurch. Tom was a sengil, a meek, polite, small sengil. He couldn't endure any games, he didn't have the strength in him, the mental strength most of all. Stellen had been a legionary soldier and he had barely survived.

"A game?" Garrett whimpered and let out a sob. "Of what... M-master?"

Silas drew the gun and tapped the tip against his cheek, then he smiled. The smile on his face filled Garrett with nothing but more anxiety, and at this point he was surprised he hadn't had a nervous breakdown.

"I think we need to toughen Tom up, don't you?" Silas said with a grin. "I think if he is going to be a part of this family – he needs a bit more life experience!"

Garrett's face fell, but he didn't say anything.

"He needs to go out into the world, Garrett. He needs to see what life is like beyond that luxury apartment I put you in. So I think–" Silas twirled the gun and caught it. "–I'll be sending him into the greywastes. I'll be putting a parachute on him and pushing him out of a plane. If he can make it home... he's yours. Though that being said, I will be a long walk – I think I'll put him in Melchai. On the other side of the greywastes."

"No!" Garrett suddenly sobbed. He started crawling over to Silas on all fours, his head lowered in a submissive stance. When he got to Silas's shining leather shoes put his hands on them and grabbed clutched them. "He won't survive and you know he won't. Sanguine barely survived there and he's a chimera. You train our sengils at seven to be meek and obedient... he'll never..."

Several teardrops fell onto Silas's shoes, making even blacker specks against the new leather that pooled until they ran down the silver stitches and onto the floor.

Then in an act of even further self-degradation and humiliation, Garrett kissed his shoes and hugged his feet. "I'm throwing myself at your mercy... please, Master, please. Forgive me for not telling you, forgive me for being scared. Tom won't survive in the greywastes, and he's only four years from being released as a sengil. I'll wait four years to carry on my relationship with him, I'll end it now. Just give me a chance to prove to you I can do this right, please."

A shuddered breath and another kiss to Silas's shoes. "He won't survive in the greywastes; it would be cruel to send him there."

Silas stared down at him in cold indifference, the 10mm still in his hand and the black and silver robe he was wearing just lightly brushing against Garrett's discoloured, tear-stained face.

"A chance to prove yourself to me, that is what you want?" Silas murmured. He lowered the tip of the gun and directed Garrett's face upwards. He stared down at it, his eyes narrowed.

Garrett nodded. "Just a chance… please, love, it's too dangerous in the greywastes for a sengil. It would be cruel to send him there."

A rush of relief washed over Garrett's face as Silas slowly nodded.

The king smiled. He removed his foot from Garrett's grovelling and pulled the gun away from his chin. "You're right, Garrett. You always have been my voice of reason. It would be cruel to send a sengil into the greywastes."

And in a quick, solid movement, one that happened so quickly Garrett barely had time to scream – Silas turned around and shot Tom in the head.

Garrett screamed, his hands going up to his face in horror as Tom's head snapped back. A large, black hole appearing on Tom's forehead before the sengil's head slumped over. Immediately blood started pouring out of the gunshot wound, it spilled onto the floor, sounding like water spout draining on a rainy day.

Garrett got up and ran to Tom, but with a click of the gun Garrett stopped only a foot away from him and fell to his knees in his own grief.

"Tommy…" Garrett moaned. He reached out a hand before, in his grief, he let out a loud, heartwrenching scream and slammed a fist onto the ground.

"Tommy baby… I'm sorry."

Behind him, Silas wiped the blood specks off of the gun with his sleeve, before casually twirling it in the air again. Not even the slightest hint of emotion on his face, only the cold, staring eyes of an immortal being that had ended the entire world.

"Four years to prove it to me," Silas said casually, though his voice was barely audible over Garrett's hysterical screaming. "Four years and you may bring to me any man you fancy, whether you've been together for four years or four days, and during that time I will decide whether you're mature enough to handle a relationship."

Silas lowered a hand and rested it on Garrett's shoulder, but as soon as he touched Garrett's clammy, sweat-soaked shirt the chimera whirled around.

"Fuck you!" Garrett suddenly snapped. "Fuck you, Silas. You're only acting this way because Sanguine ran away!" he shrieked, before getting up on shaking feet.

"You were happy until that stupid fuck-up took off and you're only taking this out on me!" he continued to shriek. His face was red with anger and his eyes holding tears that slid down his face with every tremor inside of his body. "I've always been your whipping boy. Well go ahead! You fucking bully. I fucking hate you. I will always hate you. FUCK YOU! No wonder Sky killed himself! Anyone who's around you eventually wants to kill –"

Silas raised the gun and shot Garrett in the head, in the same spot he had shot Tom. Though unlike before when the king had remained cold and calm, there was a noticeable tightness to his face and his eyes had gone dark. The casual, slippery mood he had found himself in had disappeared, and instead all that remained was a darkness the king knew all too well.

Silas lowered his arm and shot Garrett four more times in the head, blowing out both of his eyes and his jaw.

"Dismember him," Silas said, though at first glance it had appeared that only he was in the room. "I want him gone for at least two months."

Then a man with short blond hair and purple eyes stepped out from the shadows and into the light.

"Yes, Master," Elish responded, before gently taking Silas's gun out of his hand.

Then the blond-haired man smiled faintly and brushed a caring hand over Silas's blood-speckled face. "He said awful things to you, love. You know grief was speaking those words, not him, right?"

Silas's mouth pursed; he shook his head. "He's right though… and you know he's right."

Elish shushed him, before slowly drawing King Silas's into his arms. "It shouldn't have even been mentioned. Forget what he said." Elish kissed the top of Silas's head, and smelled the beautiful perfume of his wavy golden hair. "He's paid for his disobedience."

"Yes," Silas said with a sigh. He pulled back and gently kissed Elish on the lips. "I'm pleased you told me about them. You are my golden boy."

Elish smirked and brushed Silas's hair back. "I will always be, Master." He kissed his forehead again, but as Silas raised his head Elish knew he wanted more. So he cupped Silas's cheek into his hand and sensually kissed him.

"Warm my bed tonight?" Silas whispered, and at this request he let Elish put his arms around him. "It's lonely in that damn apartment. I miss my monster under the bed."

Elish's face suddenly hardened, though in their shared embrace Silas couldn't see it. The blond chimera's eyes narrowed in vexation, though he knew better than to show it in his words. "I know you miss, Sanguine. He'll be home soon." The look on Elish's face though suggested that he would be more than happy for the newest member of the family to stay missing.

I dislike sharing my king's attention. I've always been his favourite and I am not going to have that change, Elish thought to himself. *It's my right to be beside him, to be king, and no one else's.*

"I can't even send out a proper search party," Silas said quietly. "Just Ellis's thiens and well... Garrett *was* looking. Mostly it's just Nero..." He sighed long and hard before pulling away from Elish. "I don't think he'll be ready to meet the family in time for his twentieth birthday, maybe not even when he's twenty-one. At least I know... he will be okay. I just... I'm worried about him."

"He should've been thankful for the kindness you've shown him," Elish responded. He sheathed Silas's gun and they both started walking out of the dark room, now soaked with the smell of fresh blood.

"He is, I know he is... I just..." Silas's brow furrowed but suddenly his pocket started to ring and vibrate.

Silas dug out his remote phone, and squinted as Elish opened the doors to the large lobby that was floor fifteen in Alegria. A floor that many chimeras had come to dread their time in.

"It's Nero..." Silas mumbled before putting the phone up to his ear. "Hello, lovely."

Silas's eyes suddenly widened, but at that physical reaction Elish's only narrowed.

"I'll be right there..." Silas said in a rasp before turning to Elish.

"He found him..." Silas said, his throat tightening. There was no jumping up and down, no happy cries or hugs. Silas only nodded to himself before putting the remote phone back into his pocket. "He's safe – Nero even says he has... a surprise for me."

"Odd," Elish responded coldly. It would be obvious to anyone that Elish was less than pleased at this information but Silas seemed too distracted to notice. "I'll call Jack and tell him he has bodies to collect. Did you still want me tonight?"

Silas shook his head, and at this admission, the lines on Elish's stormy face only deepened "Not with him back so soon... we will reschedule, or perhaps I will sneak away once he sleeps. I am in desperate need of release, especially if Sanguine is around."

Elish stood rigid but said nothing.

Silas made a motion to embrace him and Elish let him. The king kissed his lips before patting his cheek. "I will see you soon, golden boy. I'll let you know how he is."

Elish made no move to even pretend he cared. Instead he bid his king goodbye and headed to the stairwell.

It was a long ride on the elevator up to floor twenty-seven, the entire time Silas was standing completely still, watching the red numbers above the door steadily rise. Though his mind was not as still and neither was his heartbeat.

I want to strangle him, wrap my fingers around that fragile, nimble neck, but I can't. I want to beat him until he screams and promises to never run away, but I can't.

I can't scare him, I can't traumatize him – I have to do this right.

Admittedly, it won't be that hard to push down my inner desires to punish him for making me worry so much... because I did miss him and I do love him already.

The elevator doors opened and Silas was faced with the long hallway leading to the double oak doors of his personal apartment. As always it was guarded by two thiens with bushmasters, ready to shoot anyone dumb enough to try and get into the monarch's apartment.

"Are Nero and Sanguine inside?" Silas asked as he walked up to the two combat armor-clad men.

The one on the right nodded. "Yes, King Silas. They're both inside and waiting for you."

Silas nodded, not letting a single expression show on his face. He opened the doors and stepped inside.

Nero was leaning against the bar with a drink in his hand. Immediately a smirk creased the corner of his face when he saw Silas. He put a finger up to his lips and used his pointer finger to make the 'come here' motion.

Silas looked into Sanguine's open bedroom door. "Where is he?"

Nero chuckled. "Kinny is just bandaging his arms; he's really nervous about seeing you and clawed himself up a bit. You're lucky, Kingy. He really is sorry for hurting you, it was kinda cute actually."

"He's okay though? Did he get hurt?" Silas asked.

Nero shook his head. "Nah, he tried to buy a two hundred thousand dollar apartment but besides that he did pretty well. Slept most of the time and bullied some housekeeper into buying him some clothes and grooming supplies. I think he's finally had enough of smelling and looking like a homeless person."

Those words meant more to Silas than Nero knew. Many years ago he had been in the same place mentally as Sanguine had. Feeling disgusting inside, a stagnant pool with a thick film of putrid rot. When you feel worthless in your core, you just stop caring about how you look on the outside.

"Good..." Silas whispered and took a drink from the cup of wine Nero was holding. He put it down and turned towards the open bedroom door... just in time to see Sanguine step out.

And though he was an immortal king, a man who rarely showed an emotion he didn't mean to show – Silas's face lit up into a smile.

Sanguine was beautiful, and any other words wouldn't do the man justice. His hair was shining in the sunlight coming in from the wall-to-wall windows, his eyes bright and his pale skin milky smooth and fragrant. He was dressed in new clothes that fit his slim physique perfectly, and was standing tall and confident... something Silas had never seen before.

"Sanguine," Silas said, the breath leaving his throat. He reached up and gently put his hand on Sanguine's cheek. "You look... perfect."

Silas saw a redness come to the tips of Sanguine's slightly pointed ears, before travelling down and bringing out the blush in his cheeks. Such a stark contrast to his white skin.

Then to Silas's absolute shock, Sanguine got down on one knee and bowed.

"I'm deeply sorry for hurting you, King Silas, and for running away. I needed some time by myself, and during that time... I found my confidence and my courage. Can you forgive me, Master?"

Silas's eyes widened. He looked over at Nero, who was a grinning hyena in the corner, and then back at Sanguine's bowed head.

It was like a different man had walked into his apartment. That week away from him and the apartment had seemed to have done him well.

Silas rested a hand on top of Sanguine's head. "You are forgiven, love. You may rise."

Sanguine stood up, his thin face holding in its warmth a small smile.

Unable to help himself Silas drew the young man in, and gently kissed him.

His lips were soft, not tense like he was during their first kiss a week ago, and his mouth minty and pleasant. Silas gently separated Sanguine's lips with his own and together they kissed deeply.

They only pulled apart when Nero let out a rather girlish squeal.

Silas looked over to his third born, a flat and rather unimpressed look.

"Sorry, sorry," Nero laughed and waved. "It's just cute that's all. I hope I get a promotion for this, Kingles."

With a gentle caress Silas stroked Sanguine's jaw line until he got to the young chimera's chin. Then he pinched that very chin and shook it. "You can have him, Nero."

Sanguine might not know what those words meant, but Nero did. The brute chimera's face dropped, and his mouth with it. He looked at his king in a combined mixture of shock and awe, and for a moment it seemed he was unable to speak

"R-really?"

Silas turned his head, his hand still holding Sanguine's chin and nodded. "Yes, for everything you have done from the beginning with Sanguine, and for bringing him home now. You may have Ceph with my blessing. He's yours, bellua."

Nero's bottom lip tightened before, in classic Nero fashion, he laughed it off with a wave, a huge grin on his face. "I'll break the news to him tonight. I might just marry that asshole."

Sanguine looked at Nero. "Is that what you were telling me about? You have permission now?"

With Sanguine's head turned Silas gave Nero a dangerous look, a look that Nero knew meant that he had to sugar coat and butter up whatever he was going to say next.

But Nero didn't even have time to open his mouth. Sanguine suddenly withdrew himself from Silas's touch and gently took the king's hand. "You have blood all over your sleeves… are you okay?"

Nero knew better than to speak, and for that Silas was grateful. Nero had been the one to tell Garrett that he and Tom were to have a meeting with their king, and he most likely knew how it had ended.

"Yes, lovely, I'm just fine, just a bloody nose," Silas said sweetly, brushing Sanguine's shiny hair back. Each lock seemed crafted from the hands of a god; he was stunning. "I was worried about you. You didn't get into any trouble?"

Sanguine shook his head. "No, everything went well. The workers at Skylanding were kind to me; please don't punish them for letting me stay there. I was worried you might."

"Never," Silas said, though he was mentally crossing it off of his list now. He was planning on imprisoning everyone who had seen Sanguine without telling a thien or going to the precinct, but now that wasn't going to be a possibility. "If they treated you well, we will leave them unscathed."

"Now." Silas clapped his hands together, though when he realized his cuffs were sprinkled with still damp blood he withdrew them as quickly as he could. "You'll be coming with me down to Kirrel's. I want to make sure you're still healthy. Come with me, lovely, and think of something nice for us to have for dinner."

But Sanguine's brow suddenly creased, and Silas tried to hide the annoyance at the young chimera noticing the blood on his cuffs. However as Sanguine's nose twitched Silas knew it was much worse than just that.

"Gunpowder too..." Sanguine said quizzically. "Why are you lying?"

"Sangy..." Nero laughed nervously. "You can't really ask boss man questions like that. It's king business and we're just his lowly subjects."

Sanguine's lips pulled and Silas saw his fingers start to grip his arm. "Okay, my apologies."

Silas forced a smile. "Just king business as Nero said. Come love, let's get you some food."

CHAPTER 27

I WAS STARING AT THE WHITE DOOR AGAIN. IN THE end it seemed I was always staring at that white door. The one with blood streaks on the doorknob and the splashes of blood over the frame. So many different ways that blood wound up on that door. From beating on me, from Jasper's hands when he got it on his fingers, or even from me when I wanted to paint my crows.

In my own trance I watched that door, because time no longer affected me during these states. That was why days and days could pass with me staring forward in this trance. Only coming-to when Jasper would snap his fingers in front of my face to feed or water me... or when I felt the pressure against my ass.

Then the doorknob turned and a small beam of light shone into this dungeon I had been trapped in. A dirty hiking boot stepped through, followed by stained jeans and a grey t-shirt that had been patched with different scavenged articles of clothing.

And finally it was followed by his face. A gaunt face, with eyes sunken in so far it was like he was a skeleton with a voice. All of this below stringy, unkempt curly black hair which he sometimes tied back to keep me from grabbing it during the rape.

Jasper. I'm too scared to ask how you are. It has been five months now and I'm still terrified of the question. Though I think when you boil it down – I'm more afraid of the answer.

"Do you know I'm a chimera?" I asked him while I got down on my back and separated my legs. I must still be young if I'm on my back. As soon as I got too big for him to physically handle he had me chained, so hands and knees only.

"Does it matter?" Jasper said in a hoarse voice. I gasped when I felt the pressure between my legs. I could already hear Crow calling me to come fly with him over the city. He's telling me Nero will be there too.

"It doesn't matter because your ass feels the same, and that's all I care about," Jasper said with a grunt. His hand raised and he picked up Barry. "And you'll take my cum the same, demon-monkey."

Then Jasper wound Barry's butt, and put it near my head. I turned my face towards Barry's furry stomach and made his song fill my eardrums.

Now I don't have to hear the grunting; now I don't have to hear his heavy breathing.

Just Daisy, Daisy.

No...

Sanguine, Sanguine.
Give me your body please,
You might be a chimera, but you'll never escape me.
I'm always on your shoulders, and even when you're older.
You'll be all mine, I control your mind.
In the clutches of insanity

I woke up with a rattled cry, and immediately felt a hand on my arm. Though my half-asleep, nightmare-infested mind was unable to process the touch as anything but threatening, so I found myself jumping out of bed with a manic snarl, falling backwards onto the floor.

"Hey... it's okay," Silas's voice sounded.

I squinted, trying to adjust my eyes to night vision, and saw his silhouette start to come into view. My body was shaking from the nightmare I had, and it was hard to keep my breathing steady. I tried to get up but as I looked down I saw my arms covered in shining blood. I had clawed myself in my sleep.

Silas sat down on the edge of my bed. I could smell fresh cleaned laundry and realized he was dressed in clothing for outside, even though it felt like it was still night.

"You were grunting and tossing in your sleep," Silas said. "And it looks like you hurt yourself again. Would you like some Xanax?"

I shook my head, even though I enjoyed how it made me feel. "I was dreaming of…" I paused as I saw Crow standing in the doorway, giving me a hard look. He hadn't been happy with me since I had come back from running away. Every time I saw him I felt like there was a deep chasm in my stomach. He was angry because I had been ignoring him when he tried to talk to me – I wasn't meaning to hurt his feelings I just didn't like how he insulted me. It was just a small break from Crow… I would play with him soon.

"Jasper?" Silas said.

I shrunk down; my lips disappeared into my mouth. I nodded and Silas made a sympathetic noise. "Unfortunately, lovely, I need to go to Cardinalhall or I would stay with you until you fell asleep." He brushed back my hair and smiled. "I would fight that man every time he dare infiltrate your dreams."

My body was drawn towards his touch, not only had I gotten used to it… I was starting to enjoy his soft hands. I felt safe when Silas was near me, and for once in my life… I was feeling valued and loved.

In a place where I belonged.

"Why do you have to go there?" I asked as Silas got up and disappeared into the living room. He came back a minute later holding two blue pills and a glass of water.

"We're putting your plan into motion, lovely boy," Silas explained, and at that admission I smiled before taking the two pills, just to make him happy.

"You're going to take care of the children, right?" I asked cautiously. Above everything else I wanted to make sure the kids didn't get scared.

"Of course, they're already prepared and are excited to do some acting. We told the little things they're going to be movie stars," Silas said, and he took the water glass from me once I swallowed the pills. "After we're done with the photos everything else can happen without me, but I need to watch over the process to make sure it's believable. You'll be asleep for the entire time with the amount of Xanax I gave you, and it will hopefully be without nightmares."

I laid back down in bed and chuckled when Silas gave me Barry and drew my blankets up over me. "I'm not a child, you know."

Silas laughed with me, and just to be an ass I suspected, he started tucking me in. "I can still baby you, and you can just deal with it, smartass." Then he pinched my cheeks. I snorted and made a motion to bite his hand.

"Sleep well, love. Think of something fun we can do tonight, perhaps have dinner outside on the rooftop? It's going to be a beautiful day and we can bring some extra bread for your crows."

I smiled and nodded, feeling incredibly stupid as he tucked my blankets into me, but also doted on which was kind of nice.

My body was anxious and my mind racing after Silas left, but soon the Xanax kicked in and I was lulled back into a deep and restful sleep. Not a single nightmare dare defy the king's orders, even in my subconscious. So I actually stayed asleep and remained as such.

Though when the black veil started to draw back from my dreams an unusual sound could be heard. A sound that was two drum beats being beaten simultaneously one after another like they were making their own rhythm.

I opened my eyes to see what it was and realized I was listening to a heartbeat. I turned my head and saw King Silas fast asleep beside me on his side, smelling of greywastes and covered in a thin cloak of dusted grey. It looked like he was so tired he hadn't even had time to change.

Something else was perplexing me too. I looked down and saw he had his hand on my chest and his face almost touching my shoulder. This was odd and I wasn't sure how I felt about it, I just knew it wasn't making me anxious.

Maybe I... I might like it...

So I moved my body so I was closer to him, but no sooner had I done that did he open his eyes, and blinked slowly at me. The sandman was still in him though, he was half-asleep.

Silas's hand drew down my side and he pulled me closer to him until his body was pressed against mine. I felt him let out a long breath that was followed by a sigh.

"Stay still, that's an order from your king," Silas murmured. "You're warm, and soft, and I've had a long night."

"I don't mind," I said, enchanted with the fact that I did indeed not mind. "This isn't as scary as I thought it would be."

Silas laughed lightly, his eyes were still closed. "You thought cuddling was scary? Weird boy." He yawned and fell silent again and I stayed still to let him continue his nap. I enjoyed having an excuse to be still and in bed. I always felt lazy when I spent days watching television like I had done in the condo apartment.

So I closed my eyes too and listened to Silas's breathing and his heartbeat. I was even able to tell when he started falling back asleep. And when he had I felt shy but also warmly content to have him near me.

I think I might be… developing feelings for him.

Crow snorted when this thought appeared in my head. I looked over at him and saw that he was perching on top of a big piece of furniture that my clothing was kept in. I forgot the name but it was a large cabinet.

"What?" I said to him in a low voice.

Crow shrugged and started flicking his nails like he was picking dirt out of them. "You're exposing yourself to more hurt. The moment you let your guard down is the moment you get burned again."

His red eyes lifted from looking at his nails and I saw an eyebrow rise. "All pretty and dolled up, ready to flaunt your body and throw yourself at the king. You look like a whore now, and above that you rarely listen to me anymore. Are you starting to think you don't need me?"

A sting pricked my heart at his words. Crow had been my oldest friend. "No, never," I said. "It feels nice to start to trust people again, and it makes me feel good to be around Silas."

Crow snorted again, his face dripping with a patronizing sneer. He shook his head though and said nothing else, a few moments later it was apparent why.

Without even hearing anyone come into the apartment, I saw my bedroom door slowly open.

Automatically I growled but I swallowed it when I saw it was Elish. Cold, intimidating, towering Elish… but also predictable. Only his words held bite, physically he wasn't a huge threat.

Though, to my shock, I saw an intense look of distaste come to his face when he saw the scene that was right in front of him. I didn't understand it; because Silas had made it clear the entire family was used to him being touchy and physical with them. Why was Elish not happy that Silas was sleeping next to me?

"Is he asleep?" Elish asked in a tone that matched the displeasure on his face. His strong jaw was locked and his purple eyes narrow slits.

I nodded, and my mouth moved to explain that I had woken up like this, but I realized I didn't owe him anything. Silas was the king of the entire world and if he chose to sleep next to me then I was honoured to be beside him.

"I bet you think you're special to him, hm?" Elish asked coldly.

Taken aback I stared at him, not knowing what to say to that.

"Lying next to you, so fast asleep. Spending all his days and evenings schooling you, coaxing you from cowering under the bed like a feral cat, patiently urging you into the daylight like the rabies-riddled vampire bat you are."

I stared at him.

"Don't get used to it, or perhaps you should... because I will enjoy the look on your face when you realize that the king who sleeps slung over your body... is not the king who rules the world," Elish said, continuing his verbal assault. "You are his new toy. Even though the only reason he plays with such defective, damaged goods is because he feels guilty for breaking it in the first place. Do not get used to this treatment, Sanguine. King Silas quickly grows tired of broken toys. Your novelty is going to wear off, and soon, so prepare yourself."

Crow was a black shadow behind this chimera who radiated white and silver. And though these contrasting men could be no different, the hostile glint in their eyes made them almost appear as twins.

My eyes travelled from Crow's to Elish's and back, though as a thousand retorts moved swiftly on my tongue not one of them made it to voice. I seemed too stunned to form a proper response.

Elish turned to leave.

"How do you know?" I suddenly asked.

My oldest brother slowly turned around and I saw his hand clenching the handle of the door. I decided to press my words forward and ask again.

"How – do – you – know?" I repeated. "I thought I was the first abandoned chimera to come back. The first *broken toy*. So how do you know?"

I was looking at Crow, but when my other-half glanced down at Elish's arm I looked there, and saw the exact moment Elish's hands tightened against the golden door handle.

Then I realized it.

"Because it happened to you?" I dropped my voice, but I was unable to hide the amusement on it. The prospect made my heart flutter and though I didn't want to admit it – a smugness soon followed, a sense of pride or perhaps satisfaction.

In spite of my own personality, in spite of my own cowardice that I still had… I smirked.

"I would watch your words," Elish responded coolly. His back was still turned to me, and his head lowered. "You will only get one warning."

"You made no attempt to watch yours," I responded back in my own harsh tone. I felt a swell of anger jolt through my body and there was no part in me that wanted to take this chimera's talking without defending myself. "Whatever he wants from me… I'm fine with it. He's my king and as you can see… right now he is quite content under my arm."

I watched perplexed as Elish's shoulders started shaking, and his head remained bowed. It appeared like he was under grief, like perhaps he was crying. I didn't think such an emotion was possible on someone like Elish. Was he really that affected over my words? Did Silas really hurt him?

Then Elish turned around.

And I realized, he hadn't been crying – he had been laughing.

"You delusional fool…" Elish whispered through a smile. "You weak, insane creature… he's going to destroy you. He will utterly, unrequitedly, destroy you."

Without another word, Elish left, closing the door behind him. I glared at the door before, even though Elish couldn't see me, I drew Silas closer to me and turned my head so my forehead was against his.

Several minutes later a remote phone in the living room rang.

Like a spring Silas woke up, which I found odd because though Elish and I were trying to keep our voices down I had assumed if anything that would have woken him up. But then again back with Jasper I would sleep through Jasper talking to me, yet if I heard one of my crows outside I woke right up.

"Get the phone, lovely," Silas murmured. "Kinny's not home."

"E-Elish is in the living room…" I stammered, realizing that Elish could very well be up to something right now. "Do you want me to still…"

"Elish?" Silas opened his eyes and glanced at the living room door. "He must want to speak about what happened. You may sleep more or join me." The king rose and stretched, before walking to the door and opening it.

Silas disappeared into the living room and I heard their exchanged greetings. Suspicious of this I followed King Silas.

Elish handed the phone to Silas and gave me a look of disinterest, like he didn't just verbally thrash me in the bedroom. I walked to the couch and grabbed my red blanket before curling up on the soft fabric.

I glared at Elish as Silas started talking on the phone.

But this polished, radiant-looking chimera didn't meet my glare. There was not a single expression out of place that would suggest we had just exchanged scathing words. It frustrated me, if I was going to have a new enemy I would rather he show the same hostility back to me.

"Really?" Silas's voice made my gaze turn. "This moment?" He pulled the phone away from his ear and looked at Elish. "Perish had a breakthrough?"

Elish nodded but my eyes narrowed.

"I just spoke with him," Elish said. "He has a baby that is in its second trimester. The laboratory in Kreig suffered a greyout and the steel mother was offline for five minutes but the baby still lives."

The phone slipped out of Silas's hands and landed on the floor with a thud. When he turned to Elish I saw a look of shock on his face. It filled his eyes to the point where I could see the emotion radiating off of them.

"He... he might have a... a born immortal?" Silas whispered. "Which one?"

"I believe it was the baby you decided to name Adler," Elish responded. "Reaver was the child that died last year at four months, and another Adler and a Linnix died at two months. We already have several embryos of each of your chosen names ready for our next round of tries."

Silas put a hand to his mouth and nodded with eyes fixed forward. "I wanted my love to be named Reaver but I will take any of the names I assigned the born immortal embryos at this moment. Elish... I need to go to Kreig."

A tremor of terror ripped up my spine. I looked over at Elish but I might as well of been invisible to him.

What was he planning? I wasn't an idiot, I had learned the games of men years ago and I knew, as sure as I could see Crow staring at me from the open bedroom door, that Elish was up to something.

"I'll take on duties as king, Master Silas," Elish said with a confident nod. "I'll talk to Kessler and see about you getting a ride to Kreig now."

"Good, do it," Silas responded. "I want to make sure Perish isn't going to do anything to jeopardize that baby..." Then I saw a smile break his lips. "My life would be complete again if I could... if I could get my Sky back."

Elish smiled thinly.

Then, before Elish turned and left the apartment, I saw the mask slip from his face. For a brief moment the chimera's eyes met mine, and in them I could see the smug look of satisfaction.

I glared at him, before speaking out loud. "Master Silas?"

"Yes, *crucio*?" Silas said in a haste. He had picked up the phone but I assumed the man named Perish wasn't on the other end anymore because he put it into his pocket.

"Can I come too?" I asked.

To my surprise Silas's lips pulled. "No, not this time. I won't be gone for long. If this baby is what I'm looking for I'll be bringing the steel mother to the apartment so I can watch over him. I will only be gone for two days, perhaps three."

I couldn't come? Elish's eyes broke from mine as if he knew this would happen. He left without a word, leaving me on the couch feeling exactly what I am sure he wanted me to feel.

"You'll be bringing the baby here?" I asked, leaning my head against the back of the couch as he started running around packing things. I remembered what a steel mother was from my first and only counselling session with Mantis. I had come from one myself.

Silas nodded. I glanced to my side and saw Kinny coming in with a laundry basket, the kitten bouncing behind him trying to swipe at what looked like the belt of a robe.

"Kinny, pack me," Silas said hastily. "I'm leaving for several days, help pack and get to the plane."

"Kinny gets to go but I don't?" I said. I was trying not to whine but Elish's sinister motives were forefront in my mind. "Why?"

"Kinny is staying to look after you."

"Why can't I come though?"

Silas pursed his lips and to my surprise the smile that he had seemed forced. "Because I need… to not have to worry about you doing something. I won't be long."

"Do something?" I asked with a frown. "Like what?"

Silas gave me a sharp look. "I have other things on my mind and I don't have the time to sit you down and point out the destruction you have caused while being here. Or have the fun conversation about what could possibly go wrong with not only you but that delusion you converse with inside of your head. Now enough of this, and I will tolerate no more whining."

I felt like he had just hit me with a sledgehammer. I stared in shock as his hurtful words stabbed me and the affection I had held for the king. Each painful octave skinning me alive, with no care whatsoever to how they made me feel.

Silas turned from me and started ordering around Kinny. Leaving me on the couch, stunned and offended... and wondering if Elish was right, that my novelty had just worn off.

The humiliation set in not soon after. I rose to my feet feeling flushed and embarrassed over his scathing dismissal of me, and crawled into my den in the far corner of the living room. I curled up with my blanket and stared at the wire fencing of my cage. I knew then that I wasn't going to come out for anything. I was too hurt and much too embarrassed.

After an hour went by I saw King Silas kneel in front of my den. "Are you going to come out and say goodbye to me?"

"No," I said flatly.

Silas sighed before rising to his feet. "Well, when I come back perhaps you'll be done pouting. I suppose that is better than you destroying the apartment or killing Kinny. Behave yourself and while I'm gone: Elish is king and in charge."

I stared at his feet, feeling a nervous churn inside of my gut. *Elish was king?*

"Can't Nero be king?" I asked from inside my den.

Silas chuckled like this was the most absurd thing to be asked in the history of the world. "Of course not. If Elish mistreats you, you may stay with Nero but you are forbidden from running away, understand? You will not run away like you did before. That is a direct order."

I just wanted him to leave me alone and stop treating me like a damn child. His patronizing tone rivalled Elish's – or perhaps Elish's rivalled his.

"Okay," I responded, and after a brief goodbye, King Silas was gone.

I sighed and since Silas was gone and only Kinny and Jett remained I laid down on the couch and distracted myself with school work.

"Master Sanguine..." Kinny's voice trailed as I reached for another cream-filled donut. I gave him a look that dared him to tell me I had had enough donuts because I knew that's where his voice was leading.

"You've had eight," Kinny said cautiously. "You already threw up twice from eating too much, you don't need more..."

"Since I threw up, my stomach is empty," I said to him acerbically. "So that means I have room for more."

Kinny kneaded his hands, and his thin bottom lip turned a shade of white as his tooth pressed down on it. "That's not healthy..."

"Do I look like someone who cares about being healthy?" I snapped, making the sengil shrink down. I let out a breath of air through my nose, and started eating my ninth donut. Kinny left me alone after that.

These donuts had been brought by an elite who I didn't care about, probably wanting to curry the king's favour while he was safely away in the greywastes. All of the elites that had come to visit Silas over the last several months usually came in pale and looking like they had been stricken with some sort of sickness. They were stressed out and shaky at having to have a personal summons by the king, so obviously they had fucked up one way or another. Either way it wasn't my concern, they brought food and the more I lingered in this apartment... the more I ate.

And at that mental admission I reached and grabbed a square of fudge and shoved it into my mouth. Glaring at Kinny the entire time, daring him with my eyes to say something about it.

Kinny sighed and grabbed a square of fudge for himself. "King Silas will be home tonight, at least you listen to him."

I grunted and went back to watching the television. I hadn't touched my school work since the hours after Silas had left me and felt little desire to do it.

"I wonder if there has been a fat chimera?" Crow mused. The entire time I had been eating he had been sitting at the opposite end of the table, watching me with his chin cradled in his hands. "Sanguine the fat chimera. Look how stealthy he is as he wheezes from the exhaustion of climbing a set of stairs!" Crow chuckled.

I threw my piece of fudge at him which he ducked. "No one asked you," I said, though I put my half-eaten donut down. My clothing was getting tight but that was supposed to happen. I had only weighed ninety-seven pounds when I had come here, and I was at one hundred and fifteen now. Silas says I had to be at least a hundred and fifty to be healthy according to my height (I was six foot two apparently), but I didn't think I wanted to weigh that much, even though Silas said it would be muscle.

"What was that?" Kinny asked from the kitchen.

"I was talking to Crow," I called back picked up the donut again even though I had just decided I wouldn't eat it. I brought it to the window and started looking out at the cityscape.

Four days had passed since King Silas had gone into the greywastes. In that time I had done nothing but eat, watch television, and argue with Crow. For the most part Kinny stayed out of my hair, it was only when I really started screaming and fighting with Crow that he got nervous and called in a thien to sit with him. I didn't know what the thien was supposed to do if I did attack Kinny and I don't think he did either, but whatever made him feel better.

I had been in a foul mood and eating had helped distract me from my own thoughts. My mind kept turning over Elish's dark omens and with every turn they contaminated my brain with their acidic words. I found myself more and more worried that Elish had planned to get King Silas away from me and that was building on a rather thick foundation of paranoia.

Everything about that blond chimera set me on edge. And it wasn't only that I believed he was trying to get Silas away from me so he could do something to me, but also the stern warning that the king would get bored of me once my novelty wore off. I had so many things to worry about now it was hard to focus on just one.

Though it looked like I didn't have to worry about Elish planning something. King Silas was going to be home in several hours, and I hadn't seen Elish since Silas had made him temporary king. Maybe the phone call was just a coincidence and I was looking into it too much.

I winced and looked down, realizing I was clawing my arm again. Inside of my head Crow whispered at me to dig my nails in deeper and get a good chunk out. I did it, only because if I didn't he would bug me until I did. Though sometimes I could fight off his pushed words, like when he was egging me on to hurt Kinny. If it was just self-masochism though I gave him what he wanted, at least I was only hurting myself that way.

"Though it would be interesting to find out just how Kinny's blood tastes," Crow said with a vile lick of his lips. "Chimeras have a different flavour to them. I wonder if sengils do too?"

I shrugged and brought the rest of my donut to the living room couch. It was five o'clock and that meant Three's Company was on the Vintage Channel.

I was just starting to get settled in for a couple hours of television with Jett on my lap, when there was a sudden banging on the door. Before

Kinny could even get two steps towards the door to answer it, it opened.

Garrett, Elish, Nero, and Ellis all walked through.

I blinked, confused as to why they were all here, and made a jolt towards running towards my den.

"Stay here, Sami," Ellis suddenly said.

I froze, like her words were an ice ray, I froze. The first person besides Jasper who had called me Sami in… in years. I had been a Sami for so long but in my head and to my family I was only Sanguine.

I slowly turned around and faced my only sister, and King Silas's daughter.

Ellis was taller and older now. She was beautiful as ladies go, with black hair cut to ears length like Elish's and blue-purple eyes like her twin brother. Though the expression on her face wasn't that beautiful – she looked pissed off.

"What did I do?" I stammered, backing away from them until my back hit the grand piano Silas had in the far right-hand side of the apartment. I grabbed onto the smooth wood and gave them all cautious, nervous looks.

"Nothing," Garrett said in a calmed voice. "It's nothing you did… nothing at all." Garrett let out a long breath, but he was the only one who looked like he was trying to remain calm. Elish, Ellis, and Nero looked angry. I could see their jaws were locked and their stances rigid.

"Silas's plane got shot down," Nero said darkly. "He's toasted, literally charred. They were flying over Irontowers, he and several legionary, and they fucking had a rocket launcher and lucky aim."

"He – he's dead?" My head felt light, my hand went to my mouth and I had to steady myself against the piano. Though as I felt the world around me start to smother me alive, I was reminded that King Silas was an immortal. This wouldn't be permanent… but still. "How long will he be… be dead for?"

"It's what we call a level five," Nero explained. He crossed his arms over his combat armour. I could smell the charred meat on him; he must've handled Silas's body. "Meaning his body is almost a complete loss. Sorry, chickadee, Silas is going to be gone for at least four to five months."

Four to five… months? The lightheadedness came back to me and I sat down on the wooden piano bench. I stared at the ground; my emotions solid on the outside but inside I felt a coldness in my blood.

I was too stunned to speak. I only stared at my black loafers wondering just what was going to happen. I really liked Silas.

You know… I was starting to really really like him.

"We are keeping it quiet that Silas was on the plane, until we have to tell the public," Nero said as I looked blankly at my shoes, lost and unable to make my tongue move.

Nero continued, "So we're going ahead with the plan you suggested. Until Silas wakes up Elish will be king and–"

Elish will be king.

Elish will be king.

I shot up from the piano bench, tempted to throw the piece of furniture to the other side of the room. "You did this!" I suddenly yelled. I stalked up to Elish but immediately Nero stepped in front of him and held out his hands to calm me down.

"He fucking shot the plane down!" I snarled. Another wave of dizziness came over me, but this one brought on its heels a red haze of anger. I could almost feel Crow feeding on it. "Elish did this! He killed King Silas on purpose!"

When I tried to push Nero aside, my friend and brother grabbed my arm and held me back. Elish only glared at me, his purple eyes hard and intimidating, but showing no window into any underhanded thoughts.

Of course they didn't, Elish wouldn't let it show not even on his face.

"Puppy, that's ridiculous…" Nero said, a moment later Garrett was grabbing my other shoulder. I didn't realize it until they both had put some force behind their movements that I was trying to push them away.

I shoved my shoulders but the two were like spiders clinging to my arms and back. "No, it's not. He's jealous because King Silas likes me. He found Silas and me asleep in my bedroom and he was pissed off. And now King Silas is suddenly fucking dead? That's bullshit! Elish did this!"

Elish shook his head slowly and waved a dismissive hand, before turning around. "I'm not even going to waste my breath defending myself against such stupid allegations. Keep your mind on your madness and don't embarrass yourself further."

I growled when I felt Nero patting my shoulders, before rubbing them in a soothing manner. "Sweety-pie, there is no way in a billion hells that Elish would do that to King Silas, or even possible. We only have a few plants in Irontowers and they answer to either Kingy or me at the Legion. I know you're upset but King Silas will be back in a few months and he'll be happy as a clam to see your improvements."

I kept growling at Elish's turned his back; he was sifting through a briefcase though I didn't know why.

"He's right, Sanguine," Ellis said calmly. "Eventually you'll learn just how misguided that accusation is. We're all not looking forward to picking up King Silas's slack, least of all Elish. He has a college to run, and being king is going to give us all a lot of late nights."

I felt like I was in a room with blind people. How could they not see that Elish had done this? This was all his stupid plan to get me away from King Silas and vice versa.

"Isn't it true?" I suddenly snapped to Crow. "It's true isn't it?"

Crow was beside Garrett, running a finger up and down the small creases in Garrett's black suit. He nodded and said casually, "Without a doubt. He knows Silas loves you. You should defend Silas against him. Perhaps Silas needs your–"

"Don't listen to him, Sami," Nero suddenly barked.

Nero suddenly clasped his hands over my head, the sound of his gloves filling my ears and blocking out Crow's response. I thrashed but Nero only pressed harder and I realized he was deliberately trying to make it so I couldn't hear Crow.

The black shroud of anger coated my body and sunk in through the layer of skin. I snarled from frustration and rage and tried to break free from their binds but they had me held tight. I tried my best to keep myself together under their imprisoning grip but soon panic started flaring up inside of my mind like activated landmines.

The next several minutes were lost on me. I only knew that some time in the moments after the panic started my mind had had enough with being restrained, and my emotions had had enough of… everything. With the pain from losing King Silas reigning inside of me and the anger at Elish boiling over, I launched into a blind madness. And after that, there was nothing but fog, boiling anger, and finally… darkness.

When I became conscious again I was lying on the couch, the summer sun shining red through my closed eyelids. I slowly opened them and a blurry shadow started to form out of the corner of my eye.

I blinked away the sleep, and held my hand to my head as a headache made itself known. I grimaced under the throbbing pressure and squinted to make out the figure.

To my distaste and anger it was Elish, and beside him was Nero.

"Why is he here?" I said lowly. Elish was typing something on his laptop and Nero was going through folders, both of them sitting on the couch surrounded by documents and loose papers.

As soon as he saw I was awake Elish got up. "I'll be back," Elish said and left the apartment.

Once Elish was gone, Nero looked up at me and smiled. "How are you feeling, baby boy? A little more with it?"

I glared at him but his smile only widened, and with that he got to his feet and plopped down on the couch beside me. I grumbled my annoyance when Nero put his arm around me and pulled me close to him.

"I remember when you were just a little squidgen," Nero said playfully. I growled louder as he positioned me on his lap and wrapped both arms around me. He squeezed me to him and kissed my cheek. "You bit me and I plugged your nose. My cute little Sami-Wammy. Who's my cute, binky-winky?"

I glared at him and he kissed me again.

"Who's my cute, binky-winky?"

"I'm nineteen, Nero," I snapped. "Stop treating me like a child."

Nero smirked and squeezed me to him. "I know you're not, but I love you bunches and I hate seeing you flip out like that. I wish I could just love you and hold you forever."

I grunted but when he blew a raspberry on my cheek I grinned and soon let out a laugh.

"Made you laugh, now you can't be mad. Hah!" Nero sang his victory and gave me another hug. "Really though, puppy. Everything is okay. What happened with Silas sucks but he's been dead before, all us immortals have. Elish is a good king, and really, he would never hurt Kingy. He's fucking in love with Silas."

Which is why he killed Silas, I said in my head, but I didn't voice it. I appreciated Nero being so friendly towards me and making the effort to make me laugh. Never in my life did I think I would have brothers, and now not only did I have dozens of them – I had Nero who really did act like a goofy older brother.

So I decided not to push him, because like everyone I knew if I continued to be a grumbling ass he would lose patience with me. I missed Silas already though. I missed his presence and his protection and it was going to be hard to live the next four to five months without him.

I sighed and stared at my socked feet. "What am I going to do now?

Silas was… he was always here. I really liked Silas… we were, you know, getting close."

"I know, hun. We all love Silas and I'm happy you're starting to open that little heart of yours, but this will be a good opportunity to take a step outside of Alegria and start experiencing new things." Nero cleared his throat at this and was silent for a moment.

When he talked I saw a smirk on his face. "Look, brosy. I don't know how you'll take the news… but Elish has been talking with us first generation and we have a plan for you. It will be scary for you at first but we all think it would be the best step for you. Since we're worried you're going to regress back to being a monster-under-the-bed if it's just you and Kinny alone in the apartment."

Immediately I tensed up, but the attention turned to the white figure coming back into the apartment. I looked over at Elish as he came in holding his briefcase in his hand.

I slid off of Nero's lap, just because I felt stupid sitting there with someone like Elish watching, and cautiously watched the blond-haired chimera sit on the chair beside the couch.

"Have you talked to him about our plan?" Elish asked in an even tone. There was a series of clicks as Elish opened up his briefcase on the coffee table.

"I was just about to," Nero said, and though I had slid off of him I felt his hand on my back.

"Go ahead then. I gather he will take the news easier if it is you telling him," Elish said.

Another snap of unease shot through my body.

"We want you to go to college," Nero said patting my back. "You're smart, and we think you're ready to be out in public. We want you to start attending the College of Skytech. A couple classes at first and then we can bump you up to some selective classes, whatever your passion is."

I looked at him in alarm and my throat became parched and dry. "C-college?" I stammered. "You want me to go to college?"

Nero nodded with a supportive smile and grabbed my hand. He squeezed it and I saw pride and confidence in his eyes. The look weighed heavily on my shoulders and I felt them slump. Nero wanted too much from me, and though I hated disappointing him – I didn't know if this was something I could do.

I sighed. "I don't know if I can… I can do that…" Then my already dry throat tightened and the reality of what that would entitle fell on me. "I can't go out looking like this… I'll scare people. They'll hate me. I'm a fucking monster to everyone who isn't a chimera. I can't handle that."

And then another thought. "And Silas wanted me hidden from everyone but the first generation, Ceph, and Drake, right?"

It was like Elish was waiting for this very realization. He pulled out a plastic box with hinges and handed it to me.

I opened it up and raised an eyebrow. Inside were colour contacts, brown ones to be exact.

"Brown is the only colour that will not change your eye colour to an odd tone. You will be going to the college under the pseudonym Samuel Landon Fallon, or Sami if you prefer. A factory boy, or perhaps a greywaster, who got a scholarship. You won't know me or Garrett and we will not know you," Elish explained, then he handed me another box and with that my next question was answered.

Inside that box were fake teeth, ones that looked like they could slip right under my pointed teeth. The realization I had something to hide my teeth and eyes filled me with a rush of excitement, one that almost trumped the terror of having to go to college.

"You're also going to be staying in the apartment you previously tried to purchase," Elish went on. "Kass the housekeeper and Jan the manager have already been warned that you will be going disguised and if they value their lives and the lives of their families they are going to be silent about it. The apartment is only a block away from campus. Are you understanding everything I am saying to you, Sanguine?"

I nodded slowly and started slipping the blunt, flat-edged teeth over my pointed ones. I adjusted my jaw and clipped my teeth together as I tried to push them in. "I understand…" I said slowly. "Are you sure Silas would want this?"

Elish nodded and I wondered if he would outwardly warn me again that Silas was going to soon get bored of me and my actions. But Nero was there and, sure enough, Elish steered clear of anything that might tip Nero off that he hated me.

"I would think Silas would be thrilled to see you attending college and becoming a use to this family, instead of being a poltergeist under the bed," Elish said casually. Well, I suppose he still had to get his bitten words in. "Do you not think so? Perhaps you can use this opportunity the same way you used fleeing after you blinded him and seared his face. Use your freedom to find confidence and become a chimera, don't you agree?"

Did I agree? I didn't like Elish, and I was sure he was somehow behind Silas's plane being shot down, but I had no proof and he had direct control over how the next five months of my life would go. Honestly the prospect of going to college was starting to excite me, and the prospect that everyone would think I was a normal person sealed that excitement.

I had never been a normal arian before. I had always looked like a monster.

Maybe... this would be something great. How could it not be great?

I picked up another white tooth and slipped it over my front pointed teeth. They must have had my dental records on file because they knew I didn't have two front biting teeth like normal arians. I just had three small pointed ones. This particular tooth was wide enough to slip over two instead of one.

"I agree," I said finally and I felt Nero sigh before rubbing my back supportively. "I'll do it... if I can just be normal and look normal. I've never looked like everyone else before."

Elish smiled thinly and put his laptop into his briefcase then, with a click, he closed it.

He rose and so did I to be polite, and when he held his hand out to shake mine... I took it too.

"Then welcome to the College of Skytech, Samuel Fallon. I think you will find it a quite rewarding place to be."

CHAPTER 28

MY APPEARANCE HAD BEEN AN ALBATROSS AROUND my neck since I could remember. Even when I was a baby the other children were either scared of me or they hated and made fun of me. Then as I grew up it became not only a source of teasing and being left out of things... but it became a danger to my life. I was enemy number one to Gill and when I was out on my own, surviving in the greywastes, I was chased out of town with the threats of being shot or chopped up for food.

I had never asked to look like this. I had never wanted to have pointed teeth and blood-red eyes. And even though I was accepted and loved in this family – I still wish I looked different. It would be nice to meet a person and shake their hand without seeing that flicker of apprehension, or nervousness. The knowledge that before you even had a chance to open your mouth they've already judged you; they were already afraid of you.

Normal people didn't know how lucky they had it. I would never just be Sanguine; I would always be a monster.

Until today.

I smiled, but even though the initial smile was just to see my new teeth, as soon as I saw the white, normal human teeth I smiled even wider. Then to my own surprise a laugh broke through and I just stood in front of the door to the college laughing at my own reflection.

My brown eyes were light and full of happiness and I didn't even care that there were five people surrounding me, going in and out of the building, I wasn't scared of them. I had no reason to be scared of anyone! I was completely normal and no one knew I was a chimera and no one knew underneath those contacts and veneers... I was hiding red eyes and teeth that resembled a shark's.

Though on the same note Nero had given me a big pill bottle full of blue Xanax pills and I was currently taking several of them a day. I might be happy to be going to my first day of school today but Crow was still an anxious dark cloud inside of my head. He wasn't loud when I was on Xanax and most often I didn't even see him in the physical world. Crow didn't like that and he was angry once I got off of them but I knew he understood. I needed him quiet for school because I didn't want everyone to think I was crazy, especially since they didn't know I was a chimera. So every day before school I would make sure I had a good amount of Xanax in my system just so school would keep being fun.

I glanced behind me at a lady with glasses who was giving me a bizarre look, and said a cheerful hello before walking through the automatic doors into the College of Skytech.

A week had gone by since Elish had given me the news that I was CoS's newest student. In that time Elish's sengil Loren, and Kinny (who apparently were dating which I thought was cute) were let loose on my apartment and now on top of the furniture that was included in the price, I had it stocked full of food, clothing, a brand-new big television and gaming systems and even a bushmaster assault rifle that Nero included just in case I felt like 'showing someone what's what'. The apartment looked wonderful; they even painted it though that meant I no longer had a pink bathroom. The bathroom had been painted a rich brown and the counters shiny black, and it was full of soap and other things to make me look nice.

Last night Nero had dropped off my school supplies too and had given me a remote phone that I could use to reach him. I wasn't supposed to use it at the college though since only chimeras, sengils, and cicaros got remote phones and it would look suspicious. Nero had said that six of my brothers were going to CoS and I didn't know what they looked like. Nero said only a few of them had different colour eyes and hair, the others appeared normal.

I dug out my school schedule from my pocket and looked at it, my backpack on my back full of brand-new textbooks and a binder that zipped up. Last night I had organized everything and had made special sections for every subject I was taking. I had two subjects today and most days but my Friday's were free.

"Psychology... with Professor Mantis Dekker," I mumbled. "Well, I hope he has forgiven me for injuring him during that therapy session."

I looked at a split in the hallway. I had three possible directions I could go in. A white sign was posted in front of a vending machine full of food but I didn't recognize what the abbreviations meant. Though I decided to take a guess that Psy was Psychology and 101 was posted beside my schedule so I'm assuming that was the right place to be. If not... maybe today I would just pretend that was the right classroom.

After Psychology I had introduction to English with Elish. Elish had told me that would be something I would be good at. He said I also would be sharing most classes with the chimera brother that had pointed teeth like me, a man named Jack. The prospect of seeing him filled my stomach full of insects but my identity was hidden safely behind colour contacts and veneers so I knew I could handle it. I hoped once my generation and the others realized that Sami Fallon was really Sanguine Dekker they wouldn't be angry with me, but then again it wasn't like this was my idea or my doing. Silas had wanted me to stay hidden until I was more prepared to be integrated into the family and if there was one thing I had learned since coming into this family... it was that no one questioned King Silas's decisions, least of all the second generation.

My other classes were something called 4-point Science, World History, Sociology and something called FSS which was Fallocaust Survival Studies. I don't know why Elish chose that class for me, I had survived just fine in the greywastes and I didn't need a class to teach me anything. Maybe eventually I would be a professor for that class, that would be –

In a flash my entire body smacked against something hard. I looked up from my schedule just as my feet got swept out from underneath me and fell right on my ass, the schedule flying out of my hand and my backpack, which had been slung over my left shoulder, slamming onto the ground.

There was a crash in front of me and a rustling of books, one of which slid over to me. "Fucking watch it, dumb shit!" an angry male voice snapped.

I grabbed the book and quickly jumped to my feet, and at the same speed the angry person who I had slammed into did the same.

I knew immediately it was a chimera. Just my luck.

The young man was my age, and had large, bubblegum pink eyes that were framed by wavy matching pink hair, though I could tell from his shaped blond eyebrows that his hair was dyed. He had a thin, triangle-shaped face and small ears adorned with over half a dozen rainbow earrings. He was handsome, clean-shaven, and had the face of a model but currently he was giving me a pissed off sneer.

The man snatched the book I had picked up for him out of my hand and gave me sweep of his gaze.

"Watch where you're going," he said angrily and tucked the book under his arm. Then he narrowed his eyes at me and for a second time, swept his pink eyes over my body. "You're new here?"

I stared at him; he was such a… brilliant shade of pink, every part of him. Even his clothing was bright colours that were dazzling to stare at. Besides his pink hair and eyes and his rainbow earrings, he was dressed in a pink plaid button down, open with a tight-fitting purple shirt, and pink jeans that hugged his body with a purple belt speckled with rhinestones. He even had bracelets on his wrists, and a rainbow beaded necklace. And his shoes were pink high-tops with spiral laces.

My brother was weird.

"Yeah, I am…" I said, nervously clawing my thighs, though it was hard to get any pain into my system since I was wearing black jeans, not as tight-fitting as this new brother but they… as Nero said 'made me look hot as shit'. "I'm…"

I stopped when the pink brother held up a hand. "I don't care who you are, you should only be concerned with who *I am*. I'm Valentine Dekker, or Valen. I'm a chimera. You would do well to know that. I'm a part of the royal family of Skyfall, so remember that next time you decide not to watch where you're going."

Before I could even form a response, or get angry at the rude attitude I had gotten, Valen stormed past me in a huff.

I turned and watched him go, and though I was ticked at this rude and rather arrogant introduction I didn't know what to say or what to do about it. It wasn't like I could tell him I was also a chimera… I would pay him back for his attitude one day. I might be new and maybe it had taken me months to become comfortable around people… but I was a chimera and a strong chimera. I wasn't going to let anyone walk over me ever again.

Ignoring the several students that had been watching our interaction, I picked up my fallen backpack and headed towards where the arrow was pointing me. Sure enough, I found my Psychology class.

The room was half full of students murmuring to themselves and immediately I felt a jolt of anxiety go through me. There were about fifteen men and several women sitting at desks facing a whiteboard that said *Psychology 101*. Not just students either, there were people of all ages exchanging notes, looking at textbooks and even a couple of them staring at laptops. Elish said I would be assigned a laptop but I would have to wait if I wanted a newer one and not a 'brick' as he called it. Newer though just meant that it had been created closer to the Fallocaust. I don't think the technology was there to actually create laptops yet.

I scanned the room but I didn't see anyone with different colour eyes or hair, and I didn't see anyone who matched what Jack looked like in my head. So I quickly walked through the rows of desks and found one in the back.

The nerves quickly turned into giddiness as I faced the whiteboard. I couldn't believe I was actually in a real life classroom about to learn real things. What would Nan think of me now? Would Silas be proud of me too? I was far away from the safety of being under a bed, and I would be lying if I said I wasn't extremely proud of myself.

As I waited for Professor Mantis to come into the room I busied myself organizing my binder and my pens, taking some time to read the posters of old men's faces with inspirational quotes underneath. The classroom reminded me a lot of the ones I saw in movies. White walls and posters, and a television that was attached to the ceiling, the only thing that was interesting to look at was Mantis's desk which was metal and had a nice leather chair on it I would've loved to sit in.

I organized my pens by colour at first, but then I decided to organize them by alphabetical name. I had a blue pen for writing and a mechanical pencil and a sharpener, and then I had a red marker which was similar to the one Silas marked my math work with, a yellow highlighter, and then a brown eraser for mistakes. I wasn't great at writing yet but I was improving, my skills were mostly focused on reading. I was excellent at reading.

I was too busy organizing things to realize the class had filled up with people. Though to my embarrassment I realized that not only was no one sitting beside me, the only person in the back row was four seats away and he was overweight and kind of looked like Chris Farley.

My shoulders slumped. I guess even though I looked normal I was still going to be a pariah. The classroom was full, every single seat except for the four empty ones between me and the bigger gentlemen. At least, if there was any silver lining, this would calm my anxieties with being close to people. Even being in the back of the classroom was good because it meant I wouldn't have to worry about people sneaking up behind me.

There was a click of a door closing. I looked to the front of the room and saw Mantis Dekker enter, dressed in a suit and dark blue tie and shoes that shined under the florescent lights above us. He was looking nice, though I saw a red scar on his cheek from where Crow had bit him. I wonder if I should apologize for that…

To my fascination the entire buzzing room got dead quiet as soon as Mantis put his briefcase down on his desk. Every buzzing noise, every murmur of voices, was stifled so quickly it was like I had suddenly gone deaf.

The clicking of the latches filled my ears, and I could hear every paper he picked up out of that leather case. My chimera hearing did the sudden shift in atmosphere no favours either, because as Mantis took out a leather-bound notebook and a long black object that looked like a pointer, I was assaulted by the sounds of almost two dozen hearts around me pick up to a rapid thrumming pace.

"Welcome–"

To my humiliation I jumped and let out a surprised gasp as Mantis spoke. My hearing had been so tuned into what he was doing the sudden loud voice felt like a firecracker going off inside of my head.

Everyone turned to look at me and an intense rush of heat completely took over my body. I murmured an apology and pulled my hoody up over my head. I almost didn't wear my new black and red hoody to school today due to the nice weather but now it was as valuable as air to me. I did up the pull strings on it and stared at my binder until, to my relief, Mantis started talking again.

"Welcome back, I hope everyone enjoyed their weekend. We have a lot to cover today and as a reminder: exams are in September and those who pass will be welcomed to Advanced Psychology which will be starting in December. Those who have missed most of this semester –" Mantis looked right at me and I shrunk down even more. "Can take the exam and if they can prove they're capable of handling the work, will also be welcome to attend my class."

I wasn't sure if I was going to pass that. I didn't even know what degree I was supposed to be getting or if I was even supposed to be getting one. Elish had only wanted me to start being social and learning more things. Expanding my knowledge or stuff like that. Maybe next time I saw him I would ask what the end goal was supposed to be... I wonder what Valen, my new brother, was taking? He wasn't in this class which was a relief.

Mantis told us to open our textbooks and after that he started going over the text. I got out my new yellow highlighter and started highlighting the things he was talking about. We were studying an experiment that was performed hundreds of years ago that involved a baby monkey. The experiment was about whether the monkey only liked its mom because it could feed him, or if he liked his mom because she was a source of protection and comfort. That was an easy one to figure out; I think I knew how it ended.

Then there was another click of the door leading outside. I looked up from my highlighting and saw a thin young man, who also had a hoody over his head, standing in the door way. He had a glow of red around his cheeks that suggested he was embarrassed. Well, I guess I wasn't the only one humiliating myself today.

"S-sorry I'm late..." the young man stammered in a voice that was small but overflowing with submission. I couldn't get a good look at him, his face was partially covered with the hoody and his hands jammed into his pockets. I could see he had on blue jeans with tears in the knees and a silver chain that looped around a black belt. His hoody was a nice shade of blue with silver swirly designs. I liked the designs; they reminded me of the ones King Silas used to carve into my arm.

Mantis stopped and I saw the professor give him an absolutely scathing look. "Take your seat and don't interrupt me further," he said in an icy tone that rivalled Elish's.

I saw the young man nod before he lowered his head and clutch his binder and books to his chest, then without another word he walked through the rows of desks.

Then I got a good look at him...

And to further add to my ongoing embarrassment and humiliation, my heart skipped.

He was... he was beautiful.

The young man had shining silver hair that fell over large eyes so black they seemed to suck in the light of the room. His face was thin, his lips full, and his nose small, all of this on a backdrop of milky white skin that didn't have a single flaw on it.

Then he made eye contact with me, and quickly I looked away and pretended I was busy highlighting things. I heard the chair scraping beside me and then him sitting down, and as I heard his binder unzip I smelled the faint and pleasant aroma of peppermint mixed in with something I could only describe as sugar or candy.

I could hear Mantis giving his lecture but my mind was swimming and my heart rapidly beating. I didn't know what was happening to me but I felt like I had been picked up and held by my feet then shaken. My thoughts were a mess; my breathing and my heart were a mess... what was happening to me?

This was kind of like how I felt when King Silas had kissed me. Did that mean... did that mean I might like this guy? That was incredibly stupid I had only known him for about sixty seconds.

My ears burned. It wasn't until ten minutes had passed that I gathered up the nerve to look over at him.

He had his hoody drawn down now, and his silver hair was falling over ears adorned with black crystal earrings embedded in polished silver. He was looking at his binder but he wasn't highlighting like I was... he was drawing something on a blank piece of paper.

I craned my neck and saw he was drawing a tree with his lead pencil, and a good one at that. It had a thick trunk full of knots and burls and long branches that he was just starting to draw the leaves on. We didn't have trees like that in the greywastes. The blacktrees didn't get leaves, or at least not the ones I had seen. Merchants at Sunshine House used to say that further north some of the old trees got leaves but the kind we had here were pine-type trees that didn't grow anything but sharp needles that got into your shoes.

Without realizing it I found all of my attention drawn to the young man's art work. In a hypnotic way he was dragging the lead pencil over the snowy white paper, in such feathered, light movements it made me envious of his grace. He seemed like a delicate angel in both his appearance and his movements.

I wished for talent like his. I could only draw crows and that was nothing but chicken scratch compared to his flawless movements.

Maybe he could teach me how to draw...

Suddenly the young man turned his head to look at me. Through a spasm of terror I quickly looked away and distracted myself highlighting something. I hadn't been paying that much attention to what Mantis was talking about though but I knew that wasn't the point.

"*And as time went on the baby monkey in cage B was found to have extreme emotional problems. It was fearful of the researchers and would scream and hide in the back of the cage when they attempted to handle it...*"

The man with the silver hair was still staring at me. I tried to shake off the heat covering my face but as the seconds dragged on I found myself unable to handle it. He wouldn't go back to his drawing and I didn't know what I was supposed to do.

I looked up at the doorway leading to the hallway outside. I played with the idea of dropping everything and making a break for it but that would cause more people to stare at me and I had had about enough of that today. And even if I did run away I would only have to come back again for my Thursday class, unless I was planning on giving up college altogether.

I swallowed hard and started paying deep attention to my textbook, highlighting everything that Mantis told us to highlight, and to distract myself further, I took the notes so detailed they had come word-for-word out of Mantis's mouth. If this young man was going to stare at me for the rest of the semester I would probably be at the top of my class.

Finally, after assigning us an end-of-term essay about our choice of topic, class was dismissed and we were free to go. I glanced up as the rows of people started putting their binders and textbooks away and tried to draw up on my confidence to get out of this seat and go to my next class.

To my relief the young man got up first, I watched his back as he left.

He has really nice curves...

I heard Crow chuckle inside of my head which flustered me. So I got my things and tried to leave the classroom as quickly as...

"Sami." I froze in place like Mantis's voice was the freeze ray of a super villain. Then slowly I turned around and looked at him.

The silver-haired man was standing right beside him. Struck dumb I gaped at the two of them, my mouth twisted into a knot with not a single answer inside of my head. All I could do was stare and I knew I looked like an idiot.

Mantis smiled at me, with a shine inside of his steel-grey eyes that hinted to an amusement I didn't appreciate. I knew Mantis didn't care for me and I was hoping he hadn't noticed the man with silver hair staring at me, and I hoped even more he didn't have Silas's penchant for deriving joy in other people's discomfort.

"Have you thought about what your end-of-year group assignment is going to be, Sami?" Mantis asked casually. The young man beside him was shifting around, a hand scratching up and down his arm like he was nervous. Though I saw that he was holding a red piece of paper in his hand and I wondered if that was the source of his unease.

I shook my head and glanced at my textbook as if hoping it would help me.

'What about the baby monkeys?' Crow suggested.

"The… baby monkeys," I blurted, taking Crow's help and running with it. Though as I thought of what Mantis was saying I realized this probably would be the best project anyway. "I… I think I would do good at that, from experience."

The silver-haired man looked at me with a spark of new interest; Mantis only nodded and then took the red slip of paper from the young man's hands. "Yes, I was actually hoping you would choose Harry Harlow's experiment. I think you would do wonderful studying the effects of social isolation." Mantis took the pen cap off of the pen he was holding with his teeth and signed the red slip for the young man.

"Have you thought of a partner yet?" Mantis asked.

I stared at him, Mantis waited several seconds for me to respond before saying lightly, "I did say you could pair up as long as your work reflects that of two people." Then to my horror he looked over at the young man. "Perhaps having someone else's grade as a responsibility will encourage you to come to class and actually be on time, Jack?"

Jack?

I looked over at the silver-haired man in absolute shock, to the point where my mouth dropped open. Sure enough, as he spoke… I saw…

I saw he had pointed teeth like me… exactly like me…

"You want me to… partner with him?" Jack said surprised. He looked over at me, or what was left of me anyway. I believe I had melted into a pool of nauseas sickness. I felt so queasy I was sure… I was sure…

I stumbled back and held out my hand to steady myself. I managed to grab hold of the desk but it offered nothing but a solid thing to focus on as the room spun around me like I was on a carnival ride. I tried to close my eyes in a desperate attempt to find reprieve from this spin-cycle Mantis had inadvertently put me on but it only made the bile rise up my throat.

"Sami are you... okay?" I felt a cold hand on my forehead. I could see his tie and his blazer but everything else was going shiny, shiny and swirly and...

Like a dormant volcano announcing its re-emergence into the world... I suddenly threw up.

Right on Mantis's shoes.

I clasped my hand over my mouth to stop the vomit from spilling out but it was no use. I gagged again and another stream of puke shot from my mouth and splattered onto the grey carpet below.

Humiliated and horrified, I turned and ran out of the room as quickly as I could, ignoring Mantis behind me calling my name.

I ran down the hallway which was thankfully empty, to further hammer in what was now the most embarrassing moment of my life I suddenly heard none other than Jack call to me. Though facing my brother, the man who had teeth like me, who I had shared a steel mother with, was the last thing on my mind.

I needed some place dark to hide in... I looked around the hallway but only saw lit up classrooms. I took a turn to find the exit to at least lead me to outside, but I found something better.

I opened the door of a janitor's closet and when I saw enclosed darkness, I took it. I closed the door behind me and crouched down into the pitch black, smelling cleaning chemicals and the stale damp smell of an air-dried mop, and closed my eyes. Though not before drawing my hoody even farther over my head.

That was it... I was never going to be able to show my face in public again. There was no way I could ever face Jack over what had just happened. I was going to have to leave the family, go back to the greywastes... no, they might find me. I was going to have to leave the planet and go live on Mars. There was no way I could see them, my entire life was over.

My eyes burned. I wiped them with my sleeve and in that moment I had never hated myself more. I felt so angry I opened my eyes and looked for anything I could hurt myself with.

"*Yes, you know what to do,*" Crow said in a silent hiss. "*You know what will make you feel better. Just like when your sunglasses fell off in Melchai and everyone saw your eyes. Hurt yourself to feel better – that's your only reprieve.*"

I sniffed and nodded. "Why did that have to happen? I'm never going to be able to face Mantis or Jack." I felt a prickle of relief as I found an exacto knife resting beside a plastic container of bleach. I took it and slid the yellow lever until I saw a shine of metal. I rolled up my sleeves and started pressing the blade into my arm.

'Because you can't be around people,' Crow hissed. I couldn't see him, the room was too small, but his voice was crystal clear inside of my head. So clear I was surprised it didn't echo. *'You might be a chimera but you'll always be socially inept. Just like the baby monkey without a mother – you'll never be normal. No matter your new clothes, your college classes, or your family you will always be fucked up. Just look what happened to the monkey without its mom? No happy ending there and you will have no happy ending either.'*

His words crushed me, but perhaps the only reason they had so much power over me was because I saw truth in every syllable. Even psychology wasn't on my side; I was always going to be broken. You could fix up the exterior of a house all you want, but once you stepped inside you would see the gouges in the walls, the wires hanging from the ceilings, you would see the mould, the destruction, the sadness, and the abandonment.

I would always be broken. And to prove to myself just how broken I was I slid the knife over my already scarred skin and watched the pale white split in half like an unzipped zipper. The yellow bubbles of fat were my reward and the blood that started to frame the pockets, my relief.

My face twisted in misery and pain. I let out an anguished cry and threw the knife up against the metal door… then I buried my face into my drawn-up knees and sobbed.

I cried for a long time. Lost in misery and self-hatred, I let my pain take me by the neck and throw me into the deepest chasms of my mind. The dark places where Crow was born from and fed from. The areas where Jasper's presence still lingered, and still left trails of slime behind it that glowed a brilliance that rivalled the sun.

Why would I even think I could manage going to college? I couldn't even handle knowing that silver-haired man was Jack. I threw up on Mantis's damn shoes from the shock of it, how could I handle school?

'You can't,' Crow hissed inside of my head. *'How many times must it be made obvious? You can't handle being in public; you're not even human. You belong in Jasper's basement away from people.'*

I shook my head and whimpered, feeling lower than greywaste dirt. "I was doing well. King Silas said it, Nero said it... I can go outside now. I was doing great until... until this..."

And... and it wasn't that bad was it? At least I didn't hurt anyone... I just threw up from... from surprise.

But as I said that Crow let out a loud and cruel guffaw inside of my head. He seemed angry at me mentally downplaying what had happened. He didn't want me to try and put it into perspective; I knew he wanted me to hate myself. Crow was supposed to be my friend but whenever I showed improvement he turned into a cruel asshole.

'You threw up because you realized the boy you are developing a crush on was revealed to be your chimera brother. What happens if he likes you back? What happens if something else sets you off and you end up hurting him? Everyone who ever went near you ended up getting hurt. You strangled and killed Cooper. Lyle died because the boys brought you things you asked for. Even Nan is probably dead now. I bet Gill beat her to death after he found out she let you go...'

"No," I sobbed, feeling anger temporarily overshadow my agony. "Nana's still alive, and it's not everyone. Nero is fine, and King Silas will come back. I fucking have friends, Crow. I have family. And maybe Jack wants to be my friend too. And if he does he'll be fine also." I looked up and clenched my teeth. I couldn't see him but inside of my head I was glaring daggers into him. "I'm fucking getting tired of you always putting me down, always making me feel like shit. Friends don't fucking do that."

Crow growled. *'You don't want to make me mad, boy. You don't want me to be your enemy.'*

"You already act like my enemy!" I yelled. I stood up, and in my anger, I grabbed the metal rack containing the janitorial equipment and slammed it against the wall, making its contents rain down on me and come crashing to the floor. "It wasn't that bad... I'm... I'm fine. I'll tell Jack I just have a bug. I can handle fucking college and I can handle life."

'You're nothing but a demon –'

"I AM A CHIMERA!" I shrieked, picking up the bottle of bleach and throwing it against the wall. It smashed and a spout of bleach erupted from the top and sprayed onto a wooden handled mop. "I am Sanguine Sasha Dekker, a chimera and a prince! And I will be damned if I'll regress to a piece of shit under the bed just because I got nervous. And you won't tell me otherwise. Fuck you, Crow!"

I thought it was adrenaline coursing through me, coating my veins in a hum of electricity and energy, but as I said those words to Crow I realized it wasn't adrenaline… it was relief. It was liberation.

I closed my eyes and took in a deep breath of the bleach-smelling air. Then I squared my shoulders. In the backdrop of my mind, behind the black velvet curtains, I could see my old friend's red eyes blazing; his pale skin shining with the silver light of the moon. I could see this friend who had emerged from the stagnant pool of suffering, glaring at me with such a look of hatred I found myself almost stepping back.

But I was brave, so I lifted up my chin.

'Kill yourself,' Crow whispered to me calmly. 'Kill yourself.'

I stared at him. In defiance I locked my eyes with his and I didn't look away.

"No," I whispered.

'Kill yourself, Sami,' Crow urged. And as if our heated argument had never happened, he smiled at me, his eyes squinting under his closed-mouth grin. 'Kill yourself, Sami.'

'Kill yourself. Kill yourself. You're nothing, Sami. You're nothing.'

'So kill yourself, Sami.'

'You're nothing, and if you think you can get rid of me, you're wrong. I'll always be there; I take many forms. I will always be the demon on your shoulder and you will crumble under my weight.'

I shook my head, what he was saying not only confused me – but it made me uncomfortable as well. I didn't like this sudden switch in attitude. It didn't make sense to me, but at the same time… I didn't want it to make sense.

"I'm not going to do what you tell me anymore," I said simply.

'SAMI!" Crow's voice started to rise. 'SAMI! SAMI! JASPER'S LITTLE WHORE BOY, SAMI!'

I put my hands over my ears and shook my head. "I'm not listening to you."

'HE FUCKED YOU, SAMI!' Crow started screaming, his voice hammering against my skull like his words were a battering ram. Each knock making me wince and cry out. 'AND NERO FUCKS TO THE THOUGHT. YOU'RE NOTHING, SAMI.'

'SAMI! YOU'RE NOTHING SAMI!' Crow shrieked in a high-pitched hysterical tone. I screamed with him and started grabbing my ears, wanting to do anything to stop him from yelling at me.

"I'm not listening to you!" I yelled back. I snapped my eyes open, tasting copper inside of my mouth. I hadn't realized I was biting the inside of my cheek. "I'm tired of listening to you! You're not good for me. Maybe you used to be, but you're not anymore. Leave me alone!"

'Kill yourself, you fucking whore!' Crow taunted, another wave of pain. *'Relieve the pain, Sami! JUST LIKE I –'*

"NO!" I screamed so loudly my voice broke. I keeled over hacking and found myself once again throwing up on the ground. Crow's taunting and continuous voice ringing like the bell towers of hell. "NO!"

I had to get him to stop. I had to escape from him. But how can I escape from a voice inside of my head? I had nowhere to go, and no one to help me fight. I was trapped with him both inside of this room and inside the cage I had always been locked in inside my head.

In my desperation I opened my eyes and saw the metal door leading to outside. With Crow's voice booming and commanding my thoughts I reached out and grabbed the handle.

I turned it, the light of the hallway slaying the darkness of the room and the deep bottomless chasms that was my own consciousness. I opened it wide but as I took a step to walk through… I saw Jack standing in front of the doorway, a look of absolute shock on his face.

And as I looked at my brother, and my brother looked back at me, Crow's voice disappeared like someone had pressed mute. Without even an echo, the booming, commanding, and authoritative voice was vanquished into oblivion and all that was left was a silence so weighted it was almost louder than the voice of the demon inside of my head.

The ongoing assault of mortification that seemed as ingrained into my existence as my breath continued. Quickly I ran past Jack, my bleeding arm clutched to my sweater, and ran towards the first exit sign I saw. Thankfully he didn't call to me but in the end that really wouldn't have changed anything.

With a loud clang I pushed the lever of the door and a blow of cold air reached my face. As my new sneakers hit the pavement I realized that it was raining, completely out of season for the Fallocaust. In a matter of hours the content day had turned stormy. It was like the weather was reflecting the change in my emotions since coming here, from light and happy to once again falling into turmoil.

As such is the life of Sanguine Dekker.

Holding my arm and pressing the split-open wound together I crossed the parking lot and headed for an alleyway that promised me darkness and shelter from my thoughts and the storm gathering above me. The smell of freshly wet pavement filling my nose and making friends with the overwhelming aroma of chimera blood. The greywastes had their own particular smell when it rained after so many months of dry, and it seemed the paved streets of Skyfall also had their own.

I stopped and let several cars pass me by until I ran across the road, knowing full well I probably looked like a mad man with my arm so bloody and open. In the greywastes I would have found an abandoned building to hide in until my wounds healed but now I was in a busy city surrounding by thousands of people. It was harder now to find a quiet place to hide myself but at least I had alleyways and eventually… my apartment.

Then I tripped. With a surprised yelp my face met the pavement. What made it worse was that my arm was tucked up into the sleeve of my injured arm so I wasn't even able to break my own fall. My face smashed against the wet surface and stars burst through my vision on impact.

My lungs filled with cold air as I gasped from surprise. I rolled onto my back and groaned, before opening up my eyes and seeing the steel-grey sky above me, raining drops of water falling onto my face.

Then red stung my eyes. I blinked away the blood and stumbled to my feet with a groan. My face throbbing with pain, my nose especially.

I wiped my face with my sleeve and looked down to see it shining and bright, the dark red patterns on the sleeve now a deeper shade of crimson from the stains of my own blood.

With a hand pressed against the rough brick of the alleyway, I staggered on for any cover I could manage.

I sniffed and tried to hold my wet sleeve to my nose. As I tried to stem the flow I looked down and saw my pants covered in dirt.

And just to seal in the weather mimicking my stormy mood I heard a rumble of thunder above, and what was left of the grey sun become dimmer under the gathering black clouds.

A part of me wanted to apologize to Crow because once again I was alone and he had always been there for me when I was alone. But even in my state I knew that wasn't an option. Crow would offer me no comfort, only taunting words, and I was better off alone than with that stagnant swamp of negativity.

I pushed on, walking past dented trashcans and a rusted box spring of a bed leaning against graffiti-painted brick. Then I stumbled out of the alleyway and saw I was heading down a road that separated the backyards of Skyland apartments. A dirt road with tall fences on either side, and further on, an abandoned parking lot with an old basketball hoop.

It wasn't much but it was empty, so I continued to walk in the rain, my hand clenched around my arm and my head lowered to the ground. Blood was now freely running down my nose, possibly my head, but I was mostly ashamed of the tears.

I sniffed again and winced as a jolt of pain went up my nasal cavity. Without realizing where I was going I walked to the abandoned parking lot, shivering now from the cold rain falling from the heavens, and I sat down beside the basketball hoop.

Alone, without Crow's taunting beside me, I drew my knees to my chest and wrapped my arms around them, my entire left arm soaked and leaking rosy droplets of rain-washed blood onto the cracked pavement. I felt like staying here until I froze to death and died.

I wish Silas was here… he would've made it all better. Silas always made me smile; he was the best king that had ever existed. I only wish I could grow up to be half the man he was.

My heart ached from missing him and it had only been a week since I had learned he had died. I still had another four months at least of not seeing him and that seemed like three lifetimes away.

I whimpered buried my face into my knees and choked back the tears. A thousand derisive thoughts stinging me like little demons wielding swords. What I would do to turn back time and be that little baby again. The red-eyed infant in Lydia's arms. If my adoptive mother had lived she would've taken care of me and loved me. Nana had even shown me the note when I was little and feeling bad after not being included in a baseball game. She had said my mother loved me and had told Nan not to hate me for looking different, that I was a good boy.

Suddenly I heard an odd pattering noise, like the rain was falling against something plastic or paper. I opened my eyes and slowly looked up, and to my surprise I saw blue jeans. My gaze shot up and I jumped from surprise as I saw Jack standing only inches away from me –

– holding an umbrella over my head.

CHAPTER 29

I LOOKED AT HIM, SHOCKED AND SURPRISED, AND MY mouth turned to absolute mush. All I could do was stare at him, my eyes wide with surprise. He stared back at me, with no apparent expression on his face. He only held the black umbrella over my head, letting the rain fall onto his shining silver hair.

I couldn't make words, I couldn't say anything. So desperately did I want to apologize, or get up and run but I was frozen. It was like his crystal-like black eyes had paralyzed me within his vision, and there I would stay until he decided to release me.

Then he smiled, and as his full lips split I saw small pointed teeth inside their inlets. And unlike how everyone reacted to me when I smiled, I didn't look back shocked and I didn't turn away. I was still sealed where he left me, so still I only stared.

"The weather this morning warned we would have a storm…" Jack said. His voice sounding like a delicate ringing bell. He had a soft voice, friendly and welcoming. "I may be the only man in Skyfall to have an umbrella today… I thought perhaps you needed it more than I."

Talk, Sanguine… I urged myself. I stared back dumbly before I forced my lips to move, to say something.

"Thank you," I managed to say before breaking my gaze of those beautiful onyx eyes. I looked at my wet shoes, speckled in blood and covered in mud.

"It doesn't look like you're having a good day…" Jack said. "Mantis says you have problems with anxiety and – and some other issues."

There was a pause before he hastily said, "I know that's none of my business… I just, I brought it up because I wanted to say it's okay."

It's not okay... but I just nodded and wiped my nose with my sleeve. "I'd say I've had better days but... today hasn't been that good."

There was movement. I looked up again and saw an outstretched hand. "My name is Jack."

I held out my blanched, rain-washed hand and took his. I realized as I opened my mouth that I badly wanted to tell him my name was Sanguine, that I was his brother, but I had my orders and I had to respect King Silas. "Sami... I'm – I'm from the greywastes. I just moved here."

"Sami?" Jack smiled, then he pulled on my hand. I knew what he was trying to do so I let him help pull me up. Though as soon as I stood up I put my hands back into my pockets and stared at the ground, seeing my rosy blood swirl around several loose cigarette butts, before falling down a drain only a foot away from me.

"That's a lovely name. Sami." Jack looked around and I witnessed his smile turn slightly shy. "Want to play hooky with me? My oldest brother Elish has been on me about skipping classes but I'll suffer his wrath. Want to come to my apartment and get warm? I share it with a couple of my brothers but Rio won't be home for a few hours and Felix is at his boyfriends."

Apartment? King Silas had said all of the chimeras lived in Alegria... I don't think it would be a good idea for me to go back there. Especially if Drake was wandering around. He had been told to keep his mouth shut but then again he was only a kid.

I shook my head. "I have my own place... I would... kind of..."

"Of course," Jack said. "I bet the last thing you want is to go some place that isn't your own. Sorry. I'm trying to get a major in psychology and I should know that about anxiety. Where do you live?"

"S-Skylanding," I stammered, though as I stammered I realized the broken up word was more because of my shivering than nervousness. I was starting to get really cold. Jack sensed this and we both started to walk faster, making a beeline for the road that would lead me to my new apartment. One I had barely broken in.

Jack whistled and gave me an impressed nod. "Those are expensive –" I knew that part, Nero had told me and so had King Silas. "– did your family win the lottery or something?"

You are my family... you're my brother. We shared a steel mother. You're just like me...

I wanted to tell him, so badly did I want to tell him.

But I only shook my head, and told him what Elish had told me to tell everyone. "King Silas found me in the greywastes, near – near a factory town, and from the goodness of – of his own heart he decided to put me through college. He saw potential in me…" I paused before adding. "I don't see what he saw, but I'm thankful for the opportunity to go to college and make something of myself."

Jack jerked his head back to show his surprise at that explanation. I was hoping that King Silas perhaps had done this before but the expression on Jack's face suggested otherwise. Though like all of the chimeras I had met he didn't provide any voice or details to his surprise.

"That was kind of him…" Jack said. He was walking side by side with me, holding the umbrella over both of our heads though he was still getting rained on. I was enjoying having him close to me; he smelled nice and I felt warm inside of my chest at the fact that he was near. His presence was warm, and though his eyes were as black as the dark side of the moon they seemed to slay the darkness that had been eating me alive.

Even thinking of how content he made me brought a blush to my cheeks. I think I was developing a crush on him. I would have to talk to Nero about it and ask him if that was okay. I know our family was odd, and that being with one of our brothers was acceptable – but I still wanted advice from my best friend.

We both crossed the street, me visibly limping from my bad fall and constantly wiping the blood running from my nose. Along the way Jack had given me a kerchief he had kept in his pocket, and by the time I got into the lobby of Skylanding the once green kerchief was now stained with purple.

Jan looked at me and, like always, he looked at me the same way a person looked at a dropping atomic bomb. I guess it was even more of a shock to him that two chimeras were in his apartment building now. At least he knew to keep quiet with my origins.

"I have never been inside of this place," Jack said kindly as he closed the umbrella in the elevator. "My apartment is several blocks from here on the seventh floor, it still has a nice view though but I hate sharing. I just like being by myself. Do you have roommates?"

I shook my head, my teeth chattering hard and my arms tightly wrapped around my sweater. Jack wasn't shivering at all, not even a little bit. "No, it – it's just me. I have a kitten though, his name is Jett."

Jack gave me a sympathetic cluck and made the motion to wipe the wetness from my face but he thought better of it and pulled back. I guess even with normal teeth and eyes I still gave off the impression of someone who didn't enjoy human contact. I was getting better though.

"You're going to catch a cold or pneumonia..." Jack said. "Why were you out there anyway? Why didn't you just go home?"

I shrugged, before almost falling down as the elevator gave a hard lurch. Jack held out a hand to steady me but once again retracted it.

"You don't have to come in if you don't want..." I said when we both stepped into the hallway. "I appreciate it but – I... I don't really know you and you don't know me."

Except only the latter was really true, I did know who he was.

Jack let me step ahead of him. I started limping towards my apartment.

"You don't... know who I am?"

I stopped and turned around. My heart fell to my feet at the prospect that he actually did know who I was and I was making a fool out of myself.

Though I decided to keep my cards and err on the side of caution. I shook my head and brought out my apartment key. "No... no, I'm... I'm new."

"Oh." Jack's brow furrowed. I saw a single drop of water run down the side of his cheek before dripping down onto the carpet. He then raised an arm and scratched the back of my neck. "I thought you would... you didn't comment on my hair or my teeth."

Fuck! I chastised myself in my head and gritted my teeth. They ground together a lot better than they did when they were pointed. Which was good, I had a lot of vexation in me in that moment.

"I didn't want to be rude," I stammered. Obviously I was no stranger to the reactions I got when people saw my teeth and my eyes. I should've at least pretended to be curious. "It's no one's business but yours." I think I was voicing out loud what I wished other peoples' thoughts were when they saw me.

Jack laughed lightly and shrugged. I blushed and opened the apartment door before stepping inside. Immediately I was greeted by a rush of heat. I always kept the heat cranked up and today I was even more glad I did that.

"Well... I'm Jack Dekker." He put a light emphasis on *Dekker*. "I'm a chimera. I'm genetically engineered to have teeth like this, black eyes, and silver hair."

I nodded. "Oh alright," I said. I didn't know what else to say. "Would you like some coffee or tea? I have ChiCola as well."

There was a heavy pause behind me after I asked this question. I was looking at my white cabinets waiting for his answer but when I was only met with silence I turned around.

Jack was giving me a confused look. I stared back, and kept staring at him.

"I usually get a reaction when I tell people I'm a chimera…" Jack chuckled. He seemed confused but also a bit embarrassed himself. "They usually start acting all weird, scared too."

The realization once again crossed my mind that I was handling this in an improper way, but I was too far into it now to start acting surprised.

"I don't care… or does it change anything? Am I supposed to bow or something?" I asked. I pulled a mug from my cabinet and turned on the water. He never answered me and since I was wet and frozen, a mug of tea would be nice.

"No…" Jack said. I heard rustling as he took off his jacket and shoes. "It's just new that's all. The people of Skyfall fear chimeras and… and I expected the same from you."

"You're not that scary… I was raised in the greywastes. I've seen scary," I said, and put our now full cups of warm water into the microwave.

Suddenly I think Jack remembered that I was soaking wet, injured, and shivering. He quickly walked over and held out his arms before moving his fingers as if requesting something from me. I looked at him in confusion not sure what it was he wanted.

"Your sweatshirt," Jack said, reading my mind. "I know my way around a kitchen. We're short of sengils right now so I'm pretty much my apartment's sengil. Get some warm clothes on and bring a blanket back from the bedroom for you to get into. I'm also training under our family's physician Kirrel, though it doesn't take a doctor to know you have to get into something dry."

I smiled and took my sweatshirt off, closing my eyes in case one of my contacts popped out. I was lucky they hadn't flown out when I had wiped out on the wet pavement. I needed to be careful right now.

"You're studying under a doctor, plus you want to be a psychologist… you just want to be everything, huh?" I asked. I tossed my wet sweater into my laundry corner, just a space between a tall wooden case that Nero had put my bushmaster in and the wall. Kass was instructed to get my laundry every Monday and Thursday.

"One day I'll be made immortal, so I have time to learn everything," Jack said proudly. "I love psychology and am studying everything I can. All of our first generation are incredibly smart and they are always learning and expanding their knowledge. I want to make the family proud just like they have."

I took a moment to find some warm clothes in my bedroom. I chose fleecy pants that Nero had gotten for me that had Simpsons characters on a background of yellow, and a long sleeve t-shirt that was made from soft cotton. Then I grabbed another fleecy blanket and came back into the main area of the apartment. Jack was already sitting on my couch with his mug of tea, mine right beside his. I guess he wanted us to sit together on the couch. That filled my stomach with nervous butterflies but I was also eager for the challenge. I was doing so well with being social with someone and a part of me wanted to push the envelope.

So I sat down beside Jack and a moment later Jett, who was getting long and lanky, jumped up and started playing with one of Jack's belt chains.

"What's your job?" I asked Jack. The tea was warming my insides up already. This tea had been a gift from Elish, apparently he loved tea. "Aren't most of you created for a specific purpose?"

Jack nodded, clasping the purple mug with both hands. "Yes, though some of our jobs are more important than others. King Silas started experimenting with type-casting chimeras. The first generation is kind of normal in a way, they're all hyper-intelligent and they hold the typical chimera enhancements, but us second generation were genetically engineered for purposes while the first generation was just created to help run Skyfall and keep Silas company."

When he saw I was listening to him intently, he smiled shyly and continued. "The second generation is called the second since we're a new and improved type of chimera. Officially I am the oldest second gen, but there was Ceph, Perish, Apollo, and Artemis who are also grouped into the second gen but those four were born before us and don't have the improvements that the real second gen have. Not only am I the oldest of the actual second generation, the ones of us all born at the same time, but I'm also the first and only stealth chimera."

He was wrong about that, but, of course, I didn't say anything.

"I'm engineered to be incredibly stealthy as my name suggests, and intelligent. We're tall, long, and willowy, excellent grip strength, and we can do well in fights. There is also a type called a brute chimera which was modelled after Nero. Ceph is a brute chimera and so is Felix, and we have two brute chimeras in Moros named Ares and Siris but they're only eleven. Then there are science chimeras that would be Rio, and intelligence that would be the twins Artemis and Apollo." Then Jack's mouth pursed and moved to the side. "Then there is Valen, who isn't anything. He was apparently made as a Valentines present which is why he has pink eyes. He's supposed to be King Silas's cicaro but Silas finds him annoying so Valen's decided to just be a piece of shit, that's his fucking role."

Jack suddenly looked up from his tea mug, and I saw the tips of his ears turn red. "I'm... I'm sorry, that was completely uncalled for. Valen and I... ah, sorry. That was rude of me."

"I had the pleasure of meeting Valen..." I said slowly and I found myself scowling at the thought. "He isn't really that nice of a person..."

"You met him?" Jack asked surprised.

I nodded slowly and took another drink, before telling him about my literal run-in with Valentine Dekker. And as I told the story my temperature started to rise again. The fact that that little shithead was just a cluster of rudeness just made me angry.

"He has issues..." Jack said darkly, before he smiled. His smile immediately dismissed my own negative mood. "We don't have to talk about that asshole. He's just mad that Silas doesn't want him. The king rarely ever summons him to his bed, whereas he has me at least once every two weeks."

Now it was my turn to go red. I busied myself by drumming my fingers on the fabric of the couch to get Jett to pounce on them. "Oh yeah..." I mumbled.

"Ah, sorry..." Jack sighed. "It's kind of... we all want King Silas to like us, especially since there are so many in the second generation and the first gen loves flaunting how special they are. It must be weird hearing about those types of things... do you have a... boyfriend or girlfriend?"

Girlfriend? I shuddered at the thought. "No, I don't have a *boyfriend*, and I've never had one." I put emphasis on boyfriend. "I'm such a mess I don't think I could handle something like that. I'm just kinda getting used to being out in public. I spent quite a few months just staying inside and a lot of that time hiding under the bed."

Jack laughed lightly; his laugh was so pure and just... undiluted. It seemed like I should be paying him to hear it.

"You're funny," he said with a smile, but as he looked at me his smile faded and I think he realized that I wasn't joking about hiding under the bed.

I coughed into my hand and busied myself taking a drink of tea. I wracked my brains to try and think of some conversation but my mind was stalling. The silence quickly started to eat me alive though, so I grabbed the remote and turned on the television.

Cartoons were on and that was good. I curled up with my tea and Jett made himself comfortable on the blankets. We didn't talk much after, not very much at all. At first it made me uncomfortable and I felt like a bad host... but Jack didn't seem to mind.

Though two hours into us watching television again, I was starting to feel uncomfortable and antsy. I got up once to use the bathroom and then again to make tea.

When I got up a third time to get some pop, then offered him chips for the fourth time I think Jack had enough.

"Do you want me to leave?" Jack asked.

I paused, my hand outstretched to grab a glass for the pop. I retracted my hand and nervously itched my prickly skin. "N-no..."

"You just seem really uncomfortable..." Jack said. "If you want me to go home just tell me, it's okay. I just kind of like hanging out with you."

He was liking this? "But... we're not really talking," I said slowly. "I was sure you must think I'm boring or something..."

I scowled at him as he laughed. Though I still liked his laugh I didn't like it as much when it was directed at me.

"Why do you think we need to talk to hangout? Why can't we just enjoy each other's company and presence? I never understand why people think we have to sit around shooting the shit and making small talk for it to be a fun time," Jack said with a smile. "My brothers are all the same way. It's always so noisy at home. They have to talk and drink and be loud. I usually hide in my room to escape them, though they usually drag me out at some point in time. Isn't it nice to just... I mean, isn't this nice?"

His statement caught me completely off-guard. I was just trying to do what I thought you were supposed to do when you had company. Whenever Silas had a chimera over they were always talking about work or their personal lives, they were always chatting and having a good time. Then once I went into my bedroom and Silas thought I was asleep they would move to Silas's bedroom. And even though it was supposed to be soundproof I always heard a few groans.

In truth… I agreed with everything that Jack said, and I liked his idea of hanging out. It helped my anxiety to have that pressure off of me. He was my first real guest after all, well except Kass and he was different, Nero was different too he made himself at home everywhere.

"You're right…" I said.

I wished I could explain better that I would be more comfortable in silence too. I grabbed the ChiCola and turned around, but suddenly an assaulting jolt of pain went up my arm and I dropped the can onto the ground. I swore and tried to pull my sweater away from my sleeve but another painful jab shot through my arm as I did.

My cut arm, the blood had dried and fused itself to my clothing and moving it had ripped the fabric from the wound. I swore again and grabbed a towel as a fresh trickle of blood started dripping onto the floor.

"Oh my god." Jack shot to his feet. "I forgot about your arm. Oh fuck, I'm so sorry. I'm such a forgetful prick. I'm so sorry, you've been fucking sitting there with your arm split open for hours. What's wrong with you?"

Jack ran over towards me, the quick movements making my heart palpitate in my chest. Jack grabbed the towel and tried to squeeze the split open wound back together but after realizing it was going to split right back open he gave up and instead started rooting through his backpack.

I held my arm. "It's… it's okay. I can stitch it up somehow."

"No, I'm taking you to Kirrel so he can stitch it. He's our chimera doctor and he'll have antibiotics so it doesn't get infected," Jack said hastily. Horror ripped through me when I realized he had a remote phone in his hand.

Shit, he was going to call Kirrel… did Kirrel know that I was in disguise? The horror started turning into outright terror, and my head started to go light. I stumbled back feeling absolutely sick and tried to mumble an excuse. I couldn't blow my cover, Silas would kill me and Jack would hate me for lying to him.

"Hey, Nero?" I heard Jack say.

My mouth dropped open; the dizzying heat that had started at my ears quickly dropped down my face and started pooling behind my eyes. As Jack's mouth moved up and down as he talked to Nero, his eyes wide and his free hand moving while he talked, the world started to spin.

I groaned and put a hand on my head, my chest lurched and I gagged from the stress alone. Then I made the mistake of trying to take a step away from the wall I was using to support myself... and with a single gasp I fell to the floor.

When I woke up I was on my bed, the heat was cranked up and the kitten was stretched out beside me on the red blanket. I listened and tried to pick up any sounds in the living room but to my surprise it was quiet.

Though I felt bad for disturbing the kitten, I got up off of the bed and made my way to the living room.

It was empty... but immediately my eyes fell to a note written on the back of a piece of paper.

Kirrel came and bandaged your arm. You were in and out of it and Nero insisted we leave you be. Sorry if I stressed you out. See you in school. Jack

Sorry if he stressed me out? It was because Silas wanted me to stay hidden from this family that was stressing me out. And he said see me in school? I didn't want to go back to school.

I knew I would have to though.

With a groan I put the note down and flopped down onto the couch. I reached to grab the remote when, to my shock... the toilet flushed.

My instincts immediately brought me to my feet and even though I knew it was silly my eyes drew to the bushmaster resting on its pegs inside of the wooden cabinet. But as the door opened and Nero walked out wiping his hands on his cargo pants my anxiety dissipated and my heartbeat started to calm. Maybe I had watched Pulp Fiction one too many times.

"Hey, I thought I heard you rummaging around. Sorry I probably gave your toilet nightmares, the sengils made enough pot roasts last night to feed an army, I ate an entire roast. I brought you some and put it in your fridge," Nero said with a long stretch. Then he walked over and put a hand on my forehead. "How are you feeling? I never knew someone could stress themselves out that much. Threw up in Mantis's shoes, eh?"

I flushed and nodded, then grabbed him and myself a ChiCola. The cracking of soda cans sounded and I sat down on the couch.

"It was going well until I realized the man I was sitting next to was my brother," I said grimly. "I wish you guys would've at least showed me pictures or something."

Nero, of course, thought this was hilarious. He clapped his hands together and shook his head. "Nah, where would the fun be in that? I wanted to see the expression on your face. What do you think of our Jacky? He's a complete oddball but he's one of the nicer chimeras in the family. He must get that from Garrett. Dresses like a girl though. I don't know what's with chimeras and skinny jeans. All of the second generation are little fashion icons right now. I'm glad Kingy is starting to have more control over the media, it's starting to get out of hand."

Nero flopped down on my couch and started scratching himself, before holding out a hand for the ChiCola I was handing him.

"He thinks I'm crazy..." I said slowly. I looked down at the can of pop and flushed. "I had a bad breakdown in a janitor's closet... I told Crow to get lost because I was tired of him making me feel bad. I don't know how much Jack heard but I know he heard me fighting with him."

Nero was in the middle of drinking from his pop can but I saw his purply-blue eyes widen. When the can broke away from his mouth he grinned. "You really told the head demon to shove it?"

I nodded grimly, and at this he let out a loud holler before thrusting his can into mine to make cheers. "That's amazing, puppy. Look at you! I'm so proud of you I could give you a hand job."

I groaned and at this I felt him ruffle my hair. "You're fine, Sangy. You're doing more than fine, you're doing amazing. Silas is going to be thrilled when he wakes back up. Though you seem pretty interested in what Jack thinks of you... do you like him? You know we have an attraction for each other, right? It's in our blood so don't feel weird about it. Especially since you two are so close in the genetics, you're probably meant to be together."

Nero never cared about embarrassing me; I think he thrived on it. I knew my brother and best friend's humour though and I appreciated him trying to lighten the mood, even if I was in emotional agony.

"Do you like him?"

I shrugged.

"Do you like him?" Nero asked again. I could hear the glee in his words as he pushed them forward.

"Kinda."

Nero squealed. My brute chimera, probably two hundred and fifty pound, all muscle brother squealed and ruffled my hair again.

"Sangy loves Jacky! Oh, please, please tell me how your first night grinding goes. Oh, promise me! That's completely unfair though, I wanted to be the first one to make you cum. I always had something for being guys' firsts."

Halfway through saying this I couldn't take it anymore. I picked up a red throw pillow and covered my face with it, knowing there was no under-the-bed for me to flee to. Not that Nero would let me get far, and even if I managed to hide he had a rather booming voice.

Though as he laughed at my misery, I decided to take advantage of the fact that he was here and that he knew Jack. Fighting my greater instincts to hide behind anything I could, I lowered the pillow and looked at Nero.

"Can you give me advice? How do I make him... not think I'm crazy? And... what do I do next?" I asked, then added, "Seriously... can we be serious?"

The corners of Nero's eyes pinched as he gave me a beaming smile. "Yeah, I guess I can be serious. Jack probably thinks you're a bit batty –"

My heart sunk.

"– but chimeras are batty, unfortunately you can't even fondle the idea of telling Jack until Kingly comes back. I think you should seriously just be yourself."

Be myself? "I don't really like myself that much," I said flatly. "I was more hoping you would tell me how to not be myself."

Nero laughed. "He'll figure out who you are sooner or later. Jack is weird. He loves art, he loves poetry, emotional music, and he loves animals. Why don't you ask him to draw pictures with you or some shit? You know, be sappy and stupid together."

I mulled this over and I was happy with that advice. "Maybe tomorrow I'll invite him over to draw things."

"There you go!" Nero praised. "You're going to college tomorrow, right? Take some Xanax and sit by him in class."

The last thing I wanted to do was go to college, but I would do it.

So I nodded and with a long sigh I leaned over to get a pack of cigarettes Nero had thrown onto the coffee table. I took one out and lit it with my fingers, and tried to figure out something special I could do to impress my new crush.

CHAPTER 30

I PEEKED MY HEAD THROUGH THE DOOR AND quickly swept the occupied hallway. I thought I would be lucky in the fact that I would only have to look for a silver head but to my dismay what Nero said was true: the chimeras were fashion icons and more than several roaming students had silver hair styled almost exactly like Jack's.

And pink hair too. I sighed and called myself an idiot for being so hell-bent on sneaking to my English class without Jack seeing me, and Valen too. It wasn't like I wasn't going to see him when I got to English with Professor Elish. I would just feel more comfortable if I saw him while I was already sitting down and settled. So at least I could give him the option of not having to sit beside me.

I knew I was overthinking all of this, but I just had to do things my way. Crow had been silent since our fight in the janitor's closet so I didn't have him to offer me advice. Though it wasn't like he had been giving me good advice lately.

Probably looking like an idiot I sprinted towards the classroom across from Elish's office and ducked inside. I was a full five minutes early and I was thankful that Jack had a bad habit of being late for class.

Quickly I ran in and gave a sigh of relief. I eyed the back row where I knew I would be sitting and started walking towards my new seat.

"Early, are we?"

Like a cat getting tapped on the back when it was stalking something, I sprung up into the air. I turned around and felt my heart jump to my throat as I saw Elish sitting behind his desk with a red pen in his hand and a stack of papers in front of him.

"Y-yes…" I said, before my mood started to edge towards foul. I still believed Elish had purposely told the rebels in Irontowers about the king being on the plane. Just to get Silas and me away from each other.

"Take your seat then," Elish said. "Since you are entering college in the middle of the school year I am going to be assigning you a tutor."

A tutor? As was my nature I immediately felt hesitant over this idea. Elish seemed to have sensed it.

"You will find your tutor to be quite understanding and patient." I saw a glint in his eye that made my own narrow. And what he said next told me why.

"I was thinking since you've already made friends with Jack... that he would be a wonderful tutor for you."

Jack? My narrowed eyes widened, but then I felt the familiar sting of humiliation. "So he told you what happened yesterday?"

"He comes over for chess every few days, and regales me with tales of his life at college while we play," Elish responded. "He had quite the story to tell. Of course, he has no idea why you were yelling at things in that custodial closet, but he did say you were quite the interesting, though disturbed, person."

I frowned. "I bet you liked hearing that."

Elish tented his hands. "It was interesting hearing how those who do not know your origins perceive you. Though that is irrelevant. Jack will be your new tutor, though do try and stop yourself and your demon shadow from murdering him. King Silas wouldn't be happy once he wakes."

"And how is he?" I had to ask. I didn't know anything about how immortals recovered. I wish I could see him. "Is he healing okay?"

Elish nodded and handed me a folder that was tied off with a piece of red thread. "Yes, three and a half months would be my guess. It's hard to tell what internal organs the resurrection will decide can be kept and which will be expelled. There are so many different factors in immortal healing it is always hard to pinpoint."

"Jack said he was going to become immortal..." I said taking the folder from him, and as I said that a new thought entered my head. "Is Silas going to make me immortal?"

"Most likely," Elish said, and though I knew he was trying to hide it I could catch the derisive tone. Though I ignored it in favour of the realization that this brought.

I was going to be made immortal? Meaning I would live forever in this family? Thousands of years? I swallowed at the thought; the prospect that I wasn't going to die was rather daunting.

"I would try not to think about it," Elish said, obviously reading my mind. "It's an overwhelming thought, but you must understand that Silas has deep issues with loss. Seeing other people, his friends before the Fallocaust and a partner he had, die in front of him... deeply wounded Silas. It would be in Silas's best interest that you just let him do what he wants. It's easier that way."

It was strange to see Elish showing a caring, more empathetic side, but I guess if he was in love with King Silas, maybe it was harder for him to be the cold and dead inside chimera I knew that he was. Or perhaps he was just trying to trick me again.

Or maybe all of this was in my head and I was well on my way to driving myself crazy with these conspiracy theories.

A tone coming from the loudspeaker suddenly sounded, telling me and all of the other students that class was going to start soon. So I tucked my folders underneath my arm and with a polite goodbye I took my seat in the back of the class.

People started filing in soon after, none of them sitting beside me which I had come to expect. It didn't wound me internally as much as it did during Psychology because I wanted the space open so Jack could choose to sit beside me if he wanted.

I eagerly watched the door, feeling jolt after jolt of anticipation rock my chest as the timer on the television ticked down to zero. He had two minutes to get here... then one...

My insides exploded when I saw the feathery silver hair of Jack, but in an instant the feeling of adrenaline was replaced by shock when I saw that my chimera brother was sporting a nasty bruise on his right cheek.

Jack's eyes immediately travelled to the back of the room, and he smiled shyly when he saw me. More fireworks went off inside of me as he walked past the other desks and took a seat right where I was hoping he would. I looked over and gave him an equally shy smile back.

"Are you okay?" I asked, motioning to my face.

Jack flushed and nodded, rubbing his cheek where the sore wound was. "I'm fine, just had a disagreement with a road sign. I didn't quite see it coming."

I smirked at the thought. "Poor guy, I hope you'll be more careful," I said, before adding. "Elish talked to me just now about you tutoring me."

Thankfully Jack nodded like he had already been briefed on this idea. "Elish has already given me all the work you're supposed to catch up on.

I'm busy with my chimera duties tonight but how about tomorrow after school?"

"Sure," I said. Then with a cleared throat our attention was directed to Elish standing beside a projector.

Elish was a good professor, even though I was still extremely suspicious of him. He was teaching us the works of Hemmingway, Poe, and even the unfinished works of Rowling. I was hoping he would assign us a book to read but maybe that would come later. I would be a lucky chimera if he assigned one of the books I had read dozens of times in Jasper's basement. Now that would be a treat, I would be the one tutoring Jack then.

Though as I paid attention to the inner message of 'The Raven' I noticed that Jack was doodling on his paper again. A part of me wanted to nudge him and tell him he should be paying attention but instead I turned the page and started to draw my own doodle on a clean, lined piece of paper. I drew one of the only things I knew how to draw: a celldweller.

This time when Jack started looking at me I looked back. I saw him raise one of his silver eyebrows at me. "That's one fucked up-looking creature."

I opened my mouth to start the story about me and Nero's adventure but clamped it realizing that was an incredibly dumb idea. Instead I decided to tell one of many white lies.

"When I was little I found a city full of them…" I said and searched Jack's face. I would think he would know what his, I mean *our*, family was depositing into the bigger cities. "Long limbs, baked-brown skin. They tore their victims in half–"

I watched in amusement as his mouth dropped open. "You were in a city with celldwellers? And you survived?"

I smiled proudly and Jack gave me an impressed nod. "You sound like a real badass for surviving out there. I'd love to hear stories one day."

"I'd love to tell them," I said back, feeling almost giddy. I think he liked me back. Maybe I would have my first boyfriend soon? The thought alone made me almost want to throw up, but it was kind of an excited throw up. Silas would be so impressed with me.

The rest of the lesson passed by quickly, and the next class I had which was Science taught by my brother Perish. He was supposed to be in our generation but like Jack had mentioned he looked older, around Ceph's age. He was incredible smart but a bit quirky. I liked that though, I was rather quirky myself.

Or that was a nice way of putting it.

The next night had me waiting at home to see Jack for my first tutoring lesson. Though I was disappointed that I hadn't seen him in Psychology today but I assumed he had some chimera duties to take care of.

I had everything already laid out on my coffee table for him to arrive. I even had the pens arranged by colour and the assignments I was supposed to complete put into individual folders that were neatly labelled and also colour coded. Then I made us both glasses of ChiCola, no ice in Jack's, and also laid out an assortment of chocolate and cured meats and cheeses in case he got hungry. I had to shoo Jett away from the food more than once, and finally distracted my cat with a can of *Alex's Choice* rat meat by Dek'ko.

When it was almost time for Jack to arrive I sat down on my couch and watched the clock, but soon that became frustratingly boring so I got up and started pacing. My heart was picking up its pace and pattering inside of my chest every time I thought about the time we were about to spend together.

I grinned a mile wide when there was a small knock on the door. I forced it down to a small smile to try and not give off the impression I was completely insane, and walked towards the door.

Jack looked absolutely beautiful.

He was dressed in a black button-down that seemed to shine under the hallway lights, and had a silver chain around his neck. When he smiled I saw that he was wearing crystal black earrings and those black framed glasses that I knew he didn't need.

"You're here," I said shyly. I took a step back smelling the faint aroma of shampoo mixed in with a slight hint of cologne. He smelled so good; it made me want to be even closer to him.

Jack laughed lightly, his laughter still sounding like a ringing bell. As he stepped in I saw he was holding something, food from the smell of it, and he had his satchel slung over his left shoulder.

"I'm really sorry I'm late," Jack said. To my dismay I noticed as he walked to the kitchen to put the bag of food on the table that he was limping.

I frowned but he didn't notice, he kept talking as he dug out some plastic containers out of his bag. "I got some food from the sengils and my brothers Nero and Ceph just brought several large boxes of packaged food back from the greywastes. They found an untouched food bank, can you believe it?" Jack turned around looking happy, but when he saw the expression on my face it faded.

"What's wrong?" he asked, though he was shifting from one foot to another so I knew he knew what was wrong.

"You're limping…" I said slowly, "and that bruise from yesterday… are you okay?"

Jack laughed nervously and waved his hand in a dismissive manner. "I'm a klutz, alright? I just tripped last night and didn't feel it until this morning. I just made it worse with all the running around I was doing last night. I had to go into the greywastes and bring back Nero's body, from the same food bank I just mentioned."

I frowned as his words sunk in. Jack, as always, noticed and gave me an animated groan. The comical look on his face as he did that made me smile slightly. Grabbing onto it like it was his hook Jack did it again, and topped it off with a goofy face. I laughed and shook my head.

"Stop being so caring. I live with uncaring chimeras, you should be telling me to walk it off like Elish, or shut the hell up and walk it off like Nero," Jack said sticking his tongue out at me. "I'm just fine. I've had a lot worse."

I grabbed the food and brought it to the coffee table to join all of the other food I had laid out. "Okay, I just… I want to make sure everyone is being nice to you, that's all," I said with a half shoulder shrug. When Jack grunted his dismissal of my caring words I smiled wider, I didn't want to voice it out loud for fear of making him regress but I was enjoying him being so relaxed when it was just us. It was like underneath that layer of meek, polite chimera he was really funny and animated.

"Jett! No!" I said with a hiss as I walked towards the coffee table. My black cat had been taking full advantage of my turned back and had been eating a piece of my cured meats.

"He's a smart one," Jack laughed. "You got him from King Silas didn't you? We had been fostering street kittens to teach my little brother Drake about caring for animals. A black one vanished a few months ago, is that him?"

"It sure is," I said cheerfully. I decided to pick my white lies; it wouldn't be out of the realm of possibility for Silas to give me a kitten. He had already given me a scholarship and housing as far as Jack was concerned. "He was a housewarming present. King Silas sure does love his cats."

I sat down with my binder and tried to clear a spot, but it looked like we had enough food to feed the entire Legion. I heard Jack laugh behind me and he sat down too. A warm electric feeling rushed through my blood at him sitting right beside me.

"He sure does, we all do. We love dogs too but there is just something about cats." Jack picked up Jett and made him sit on his lap like a person. Jett flattened his ears for a second but as soon as Jack started massaging his shoulder blades with his thumbs he started to settle in and purr. "We have ten cats in the skyscraper right now; they go to whomever they feel like though some stay with their original owners. Elish has an old grey cat named Dave, can you believe it? Dave!"

I snored at the thought of Elish calling a cat Dave. I had never met that cat before. "Why Dave?"

Jack reached over and picked up a piece of cheese for Jett and held it as my cat started to sniff it with his nose. "He would never admit it but Garrett says it's because he would feel stupid yelling at something with a name like Whiskers or Fluffy. So he gives them people names. I've heard him call him David when he was cross with him. I had to leave the room to keep from laughing. It was kind of cute."

Something amusing occurred to me. "So you have arian humans with names like Artemis, Apollo, Cepherus… but you name your cats Dave? Interesting."

Jack's eyebrows rose like this had only just occurred to him. "Well, I lucked out, though I'm not sure who I was named after. Some of us have names of roman gods or rulers; others are named after pets Silas owned before the Fallocaust, or just names he likes. How about you, how did you get the name Sami? It's short for Samuel, right?"

In truth it wasn't, or if it was my adoptive mother didn't mention it in the note, but Elish says my name on the records was Samuel Landon Fallon so I guess it was now. So I nodded and started making myself a sandwich out of the crackers and cheese. "I was orphaned young," I replied. "But it's supposed to be short for Samuel; everyone has always just called me Sami though." I popped it into my mouth, the entire thing, and started flipping through our textbook, assuming Jack would want to get started.

School work seemed to be the last thing on his mind though. Jack leaned back on the couch with Jett, a piece of cured meat and cheese in his hand. "What was it like?" he asked quizzically, then immediately he backtracked. "You don't need to talk about it if… you know, if it's difficult or anything. I know I'm a chimera but you don't have to hesitate when telling me to shut up and stop being nosey." I saw his grip on the cat get harder like he was tense. "Honestly, just forget I'm a chimera. I'm – ah… I just Jack."

His entire face went beet red as I burst out laughing. Jack pursed his lips together and hit me hard on the shoulder. "Don't you dare even…"

"I just Jack," I said, mimicking the voice of Tarzan. "You Sami, I Jack."

"Shut up!" Jack hit me again, his smile filling my heart up with joy. Jett jumped off of him, and that freed his other hand enough to continue his assault. "I'm a chimera now, never mind what I said. And as a chimera I am ordering you to never mention that again! My tongue tied up for a second!"

"Okay, okay! I bow to you, chimera." I grinned and Jack lowered his hands. The way he was looking at me, this shy, half-smile on his face, and the glow of red on his cheeks… it made my heart skip.

For a moment I just stared at him, my chest was like a vacuum, sucking the air out of the room and pooling it inside of me to the point of bursting. He was something else, like a divine god that took in, and kept for himself, all the light in the room.

I looked at him, with his silver hair gleaming against the lights, his ivory face without a single blemish, his soft jaw line, and pink lips, and committed it to memory.

Then I realized to my embarrassment, I was staring right at him, for longer than was polite. I coughed and looked away, realizing as I did that Jack had been staring at me in the same way.

He – he had been staring at me the same way.

I tucked my hair behind my ear and glanced up at Jack. He was now staring at the cat, the blush on his cheeks all the brighter as the silence entered the room. Jack had said before that he never minded silence between two people but I had a feeling this wasn't one of those times.

Though in a way I wished it would stay quiet, because the moment that had passed between me and Jack had taken my breath away and had left me desperate for more. It was like I had sipped ambrosia from the golden chalice, a sweet taste that awakened every drop of dopamine in my brain.

In the back of my mind, as the warmth swept through me, I wondered if this crush was developing into something more. And I also wondered if I would be fortunate enough for Jack to be feeling the same.

"Do… do you want a drink or something?" Jack suddenly asked. I looked up and saw that the shyness on Jack's face had amplified since our gaze had broken.

I considered this and nodded slightly. "Yeah, that would be great."

The quickness of Jack jumping up from the chair made me flinch. I once again tried to flip the textbook to the pages we were supposed to read to each other.

Jack came back holding a bottle of rum and poured generous amounts into the ChiCola I had made us previous. The both of us downed half of our glasses in one gulp. I think that act spoke more to our mutual need to loosen up than words ever could.

I put the textbook on my lap, and when Jack didn't raise any objections or change the subject I brought out my highlighter and started reading off the pages we were supposed to cover. It was still about the baby monkeys though we were taking extra notes since this was supposed to be our group project.

We both settled in, thanks to the alcohol, and together we took turns reading as the other one made notes. We discussed together the moral conflicts we had with such a study and how differently we would do the studies now. Jack had even told me that before the Fallocaust studies like this were banned due to the cruelty, but now after the Fallocaust Silas had allowed certain studies like this to take place, citing that the scientific benefit outweighed screwing up a couple rats here or there.

"Do you have monkeys still alive?" I asked before draining my glass. I was on my third drink but I thought that was pretty good for it being three hours into our studying. I was feeling warm between the ears and my tongue was loose but I was enjoying it.

Jack shook his head; he was half a glass ahead of me and had become even more chatty and open since the alcohol had started to flow. "No, no monkeys, we experiment on convicts or rats. But we have quite a few pre-Fallocaust animals still alive! Mostly on the Dead Islands or the outlands, the rest of Skyfall Island that is inaccessible to the greywasters or Skyfallers."

I cringed when he said Dead Islands, for obvious reasons… Jasper was there. "Why doesn't he release them?"

Jack smiled, the same smile he gave me whenever I asked a stupid question. "They would die; even if they were Geigerchiped the radanimals are just too strong. So we release some of them on the islands so they cannot escape and others we keep in institutions, kind of like… zoos. We have Skyfallers tour there to help pay for their upkeep too. The animals we do think can survive we have released but for the most part we just keep them so we have them around. The animals we haven't brought back yet we have the DNA for too. One day Silas says he's going to bring back tigers. Can you imagine? We have lions, cougars, bobcats, servals, ocelots, but we don't have tigers, cheetahs, or leopards. We have their genetic material though."

I leaned my head back on the couch; I was half-laying on it with one foot on the cushions and the other on the carpet. I held out my glass and nodded at Jack to refill it with some more rum. "Well, I'm glad you don't have monkeys, I never liked them," I said with a smirk.

Jack raised an eyebrow. "Why?"

My lips loosened further under the alcohol. "I had a friend once who used to call me demon-monkey in the greywastes. So maybe I'm a bit bias to not liking them."

Jack frowned; he pulled back the bottle before pouring himself some. "That's horrible. I'll kick him in the groin if I ever see him."

"He's dead," I said before I could stop himself. "He killed himself when we were both locked up and–"

As much as the drink was lubing my lips I still stopped myself before I jumped right into the pit I had so eagerly been digging myself. I mumbled an apology before distracting myself further with the alcohol.

Another silence fell on the both of us. I swirled the ice cubes around, my fingers leaving a trail of see-through on the foggy, dew-covered glass. I took yet another drink.

"Why… did Silas bring you… here?" Jack asked slowly. He was nudging his words towards me with such a caution it was like he was pushing a baby bird out of the nest for the first time.

"Sometimes I wonder that myself…" I said back. "He found me – he found me locked in the basement of a meth head, and he took pity on me."

I heard Jack swear under his breath, and his pulse start to speed up. I only looked into my glass, counting the carbonated bubbles as they shifted around the brown liquid.

"Are – are you okay now?" Jack stammered. "You seem…"

"Messed up?" I said with a dry laugh. "Fucked in the head?"

"No!" Jack said. I was surprised that he sounded almost angry at my own self-derisive comments. "Not at all. You seem… I don't know what you seem. I just… I'm happy he brought you to Skyfall." Then silence.

"I like you, you know?" His voice was barely audible, even with my enhanced hearing.

I looked up, and at the same time Jack's already ivory face paled. I don't think he had expected me to hear that.

I searched inside of myself and felt the faint vein of bravery I had been calling upon for the last several months, without breaking eye contact I pursed my lips before saying quietly, "Me too."

Our eyes didn't break from the gaze they had both fallen into, a peaceful, comfortable silence that was a far cry from the awkward tension I was used to feeling when I stumbled into the deep black oceans that were his eyes. Together we stayed in each other's sights, until my eyes broke as I felt his hand slip into mine.

I stared down at it, and relying on that same vessel of bravery, I took it and squeezed it. "So… I'm not the only one feeling it, huh?" I said, wondering just what was in that liquor to make me speak so freely. Maybe I was just comfortable around him.

"No…" Jack said quietly. "The first time I saw you, I knew you were different. I don't know how… maybe it's because you're from the greywastes, or maybe it's because I know you've lived a different life than anyone else I've ever met. But I would be lying if I said I didn't feel drawn to you." He laughed lightly, the nervousness clinging to every octave. "I heard of this happening between chimeras, this attraction, but not greywasters…" He squeezed my hand back.

But then Jack pulled his hand back, like a door to the cold winter had opened, all of the warmth got sucked out of the room.

"I'm… I'm so sorry," he stammered. "I'm being creepy. I'm being really creepy…"

Jack rose to his feet; he reached for his jacket but stumbled, forgetting his sore knee.

I quickly jumped to my feet and helped steady him. His pulse was racing and his heart was hammering like twin drum beats. He took his jacket from me and started limping towards the door.

Unable to help myself, or perhaps I was just tired of dancing around the feelings I could feel growing inside of me, I grabbed Jack's shoulder and pulled him back.

"I'm not letting you do this," I said. "You're not creepy... I'm not letting you ruin this by being... by being..." I didn't know what he was being, so I said to the first thing that came to my head. "By being stupid."

Jack flushed and stared at the ground; he had a white-knuckle grip on his jacket. "I've only known you for a couple days..."

"So? It's not like we're going to get married tomorrow," I said flatly. "Stop making this a bigger deal than it is." It sounded like I was saying this to the old me, not Jack.

I saw his full, pink lips disappear into his mouth, before his tongue nervously licked them. "You're right... I'm sorry. I tend to overthink everything. Even so... I should speak with Elish about this."

It wasn't like Elish was going to care, but I had to pretend I didn't know how they worked. I would do that, I would tell as many little white lies as I could. I just wanted to...

I just wanted to...

Did I even know what I was trying to do? I had just been annoyed at Jack backtracking and pulling himself back, what was I trying to do? Did I want to date him?

My mind took me back to the conversation between me and Nero. He had wanted me to go for it, and he was second-in-command with Elish being king. Nero knew a lot of things I didn't and he knew Jack better than I did. Nero had wanted me to go for it and I was going to use my best friend's wisdom to be the chimera I was supposed to be.

"Ask permission then, but don't make it into something it's not," I said. "We can take it slow like I said. I just..." The edges of my heart melted when I saw just how small Jack looked in that moment. He seemed so innocent, meek, and tiny in my own shadow. Even with his sharp teeth and onyx black eyes he was a bird in my hands. I never realized it but... if we did have a relationship eventually, I was going to be the dominant partner, not him.

The prospect fascinated and intrigued me, and it gave me the confidence to say what I said next. "I just want to see what happens. I know we just met... I'm not stupid, this shit takes time. Why don't we... go out for dinner sometime?"

With a shy look that made the blush come out in his cheeks Jack nodded slowly, and when I handed him his drink back he took it gently and swirled its contents. "Okay... I would like that, as long as you'll let me make sure it's okay with the brothers in charge of me. I don't want to get you into trouble."

I smiled when Jack put his jacket down and together we walked back into the living room.

We both sat down and I picked up my glass too. I was both surprised and proud of myself for how I handled that. I had come a long way from being the chimera hiding under the bed, and an even longer way from being the boy chained to the bed.

I could do it though. As I took in Jack's beautiful face, seeing my potentially new boyfriend in an entirely different light, I felt a swell of responsibility go through me. If I was going to be the dominant one, it would be me taking care of Jack, it would be me protecting him from everyone. And I would do it. I would spend my entire life making sure he was happy, and that no harm would come to him.

And when it was time to tell him I was a chimera... he would know for certain that we were really meant to be.

"To dinner with a new friend then." I raised my glass.

Jack looked at me. I could see a thousand unspoken thoughts passing through that gaze, though what they were would remain a mystery to me.

"To a new friend," Jack said with a shy smile, and clinked my glass against his. "Cheers."

CHAPTER 31

"OHH, DOESN'T HE JUST LOOK SO FANCY!" NERO gushed. He was standing beside one of the black cars that the chimeras were driven around in, several snowflakes falling around him. He was dressed in a suit and tie because he was going to be my driver. It was him insisting it, not me; I think he just wanted to be a fly on the wall while I went on my very first date.

"That's me, all me," Kass said rubbing his hands together to keep them warm. "I bet it didn't take nearly as much soap to clean him this time. He had three inches of grime on his entire body."

Nero's mouth raised in a smirk, even though it was dark outside his white teeth seemed to glow. "Oh, I remember. I remember that day real well. I was the one who did his hair after I made you piss off. Remember what happened after that, Sangy-Wangy?"

My cheeks burned. He was talking about the first handjob I had given him. Even at night sometimes I thought about it to the point where I got hard down there, but I still had refused to do anything to it. I wasn't quite comfortable with the idea, even if my body sometimes ached for me to touch it. Fantasizing was one thing but actually doing what Nero and me did? No way!

"He's blushing!" Nero said his singy voice making plumes of vapour from the cold. "Do you think he's going to break in Jack tonight? You can if you want. I'm sure he wouldn't care."

Nero winked but the reward for his quips was only a glare from me. He chuckled and opened the car door for me with an over embellished bow. I got in and turned to Kass.

"Thanks for helping me get ready... Nero, can you give him a ride home once you drop me off? It's already dark out and his apartment is five blocks away."

"Whatever you want, puppy. He's a cool kid, tight ass too." The door slammed on my scowling face. As Nero got into the driver's side of the car I wondered to myself if he was joking or not. He seemed to love having threesomes with Ceph, and telling me about it after, so I didn't put it past him.

"Elish has made reservations for you at his favourite place. Some pretentious yahoo-fuck restaurant that pays a piss-load of money for fresh ingredients. Just watch out for the media, Silas has started approving cooking shows, not just the olden day ones but today ones, so it's no stranger to cameras. Anyway, it's a stupid place but I guess it's right up your alley for dating and woo'ing your future husband." Nero paused as I groaned, before saying. "I was getting somewhere with this... give me a moment."

I put a hand up to my face and groaned again. "You're high aren't you?"

"When am I not?" Nero said with an absurd laugh that suggested it would've been more of a surprise if he wasn't high. "Oh, right. The media has already been kicked out and threatened by Elish himself. So if you see anybody with cameras tell Jack, he's gotten the same briefing from Elish that there isn't to be any media on this. It's bad enough the family can't know you're here but it'll be even more difficult to explain it to the public once Sami Fallon comes out as Sanguine Dekker, okay?"

I nodded, glancing out the window, though there wasn't much to see it was completely dark and the tinted windows only made it worse. "No media, okay. Um..." I furrowed my brow. "Can I borrow some money?"

The entire car echoed with Nero laughter. Thankfully he was able to get it together enough to turn down another road. "Money?" Nero snorted. "We're chimeras we don't need–"

"I'm not though," I said in my own defence. "And I'm going to be – you know – I want to make a good impression. On the television the man always pays for things... and well, I know we're both men but–"

"Ohhh..." Nero nodded. "I understand now. You gotta be the manly man and everything. That's kinda dumb though, you're not really going to be the dominant one. You two are kinda just going to be equal subs."

I glared at him, and my glaring only intensified when Nero gave me a shit-eater grin through the rear-view mirror. "You're not really the dominant type, Sanguine, and having thoughts like that is kinda stupid and old fashion. If you want to be the dominant one you're better off taking him as a cicaro which Silas would never allow. It doesn't work like that pre-Fallocaust, not like how it works in books or movies, especially when you're dealing with chimeras. It's best to throw out all those old fashioned notions and just enjoy the other person." Nero then paused. "That goes for sex too. A lot of dominant guys think it makes them less manly to let another guy fuck them, but that's just dumb and you're missing out on a lot of fun experiences if you have that mentality. Please don't fall into that trap, I fucking hate guys who think like that. I love pinning 'em down and giving 'em what for, but yeah, bro, don't be one of them."

"I don't think I would mind…" I said honestly. "I'm not really into any of those types of things yet."

"Still!?" Nero sighed. "Please tell me you've at least rubbed one out by now?" I saw his head shake before I got a glare from the mirror. His royal blue eyes were reflecting against the bright lights of the buildings, it looked like we were heading into a really populated place of Skyland. The street lamps were all lit up and the stores were too. We had some stores where I lived but a lot of it was still in development.

"I just…" I sighed and slumped back in my seat. "It feels gross to think about…" When Nero let out a loud angry groan I tried to backtrack, "I know it's stupid but… I associate all of it with… *him*. I know it sounds retarded but it's like if I enjoy it… I'll have enjoyed everything he did to me."

I expected Nero to laugh at me, or toss a couple insults my way but instead I saw his jaw tighten and his eyes deflect away from the rear-view mirror. It was quiet between the two of us for a solid minute, though it seemed like a lot longer.

"I'm not Mantis. I'm not Elish… I'm not smart," Nero finally said, his tone was low and serious. "Just please try and make an effort to kick that idea out of your head, okay? You'll have to do it eventually, man. If you want it to be me. Seriously. I'd be gentle as fuck. I might have an expert-level size dick but with some easing we could make it work, and if you want to take my ass to town I'd let you do whatever you wanted."

I slunk down in my seat at his stern expression. It was weird to see Nero being serious and it made me uncomfortable since this was a topic he had rarely been serious about. Though since he was being sincere with me I had to reciprocate.

So I nodded. "I think when I am ready… it'll be with you. I trust you more than anyone else in the world. You've…" I looked at my feet. "I mean it when I said it before. While I was down there, when he was doing those things to me, when I went inside my head, you were there waiting for me, waiting to take me on an adventure until it was over."

"Shit, Sanguine…" Nero whispered. "If I wasn't engaged to Ceph I'd marry you in a second. You know that, right?"

I smiled, and I would never admit it out loud but his words had flattered me. Though the thought of having Nero as a husband made me tired just thinking about it. Plus I would demand he not sleep with anyone else, and if he did I'd chew his face to ribbons so maybe it wouldn't work. Nero seemed to love having sex with all his brothers but I understood that was just his way of showing affection.

"Okay, I'm going to pull into the restaurant," Nero said, before looking at me through the mirror. "I've been driving in circles for a few minutes now. I didn't want to ruin our important discussion. All ready for your first date, puppy-wups?"

My smile widened and I nodded. "Yeah, I'm all ready. Thanks for… everything. I hope this goes well. I really like him, and it seems he likes me too."

The car turned and I looked out the window to see we were pulling into a detached building in a large parking lot, though there were only several cars parked in the spots. Most Skyfallers couldn't afford cars, and they were still rare even in Skyland which only housed the elites.

The building itself was brightly lit with Christmas lights and even had its own sign. The sign though looked like a bunch of old pre-Fallocaust signs welded together. It was called Red King, and it looked like the Red from a Red Lobster sign and the King from an old Burger King sign, but above it there was also a brightly lit M from a McDonalds except it was turned to its side so it resembled more of an E. Even though it was rather patch-worked it was still impressive, and as I stepped out into the winter air and the wonderful smells and low playing music sounded, I was even more impressed.

I dug my hands into my pockets, and admired the bright Christmas lights that trimmed the entire building, the roof included. Everything on it looked newly repaired with building material that almost matched but not quite. Even the porch (with Christmas lights twisted around the railings) had a lot of newer boards in it.

"He's waiting inside," Nero said clapping me on the back. "He has the phone if anything goes wrong but it won't. Order a lot of food and don't ask who's paying, the monarchy is paying. Just fucking have a good time, pup, you seriously deserve it. Call when you wanna go home. I'm going to drop Kass off and do some Legion work with Cephy until pick-up."

Suddenly I felt the blood drain from my face. I couldn't believe it but standing in front of that restaurant had made all of this a reality. I was nervous; I couldn't believe I was nervous!

"Okay." I managed to nod. I took a step towards the restaurant and inhaled a deep breath of cold air. "Have fun with work… wish me luck."

I felt his lips on my cheek. "Good luck." Then he gave me a smack on my butt. "Go get 'em, tiger."

I decided to ignore that, and the urge I had to kick him right in his own backside, and headed towards the restaurant. Trying to ignore the dizziness on my heels and the nervousness steadily forming a lump inside of my throat.

It was just a date with Jack, and you've already spent a lot of time with him. You'll be fine. It's just a date.

Your very first date…

And though Crow was gone, there was still a derisive little voice in the back of my head that told me, one way or another, that I was going to screw this up. I ignored it, I was good at ignoring these voices now, and walked up the steps and opened the door.

It was entirely empty…

The restaurant walls were made out of logs like you would see on a log cabin, with paintings hanging up that had matching black frames. There were plants on the windowsills and giant ones in big brass planter pots, all surrounding over two dozen tables with white tablecloths and black leather chairs. It looked peaceful inside, extenuated by the recessed lighting in the ceilings and the candles lit on the tables.

But still… it was empty.

"Hey…"

I sprung up in the air and heard a soft laugh. I quickly looked towards the voice and saw a shadow standing beside a fish tank. I don't know how I hadn't seen him when I had walked in. I guess my mind had expected to see him sitting beside a table.

"H-hi," I stammered. I wish I had brought something to give him, chocolates or something like in the movies, but I had nothing on me.

Jack stepped out of the shadows and I felt my breath get taken away when I saw him. He was dressed in what looked like a cross between a jacket and a blazer, with long sleeves that had silver cuffs. The jacket-blazer also had shining buttons going up the middle of it, all the way to a collar that held a silver chain. He was all…

"You're all sparkly," I said before realizing that was a stupid thing to say. I swore at myself internally and bit my lip as punishment. "W-want to… sit down?"

Thankfully Jack ignored my comment. He brushed his silver hair behind his ear and nodded, looking so shy and nervous it made my heart swell. I was just as scared as he was, but there was something inside of me that wanted to protect him. Nero said it was old fashion for me to act like how the straight men do in movies but I still wanted to be the one to guard him. I wanted to be his rock, even if I was still too messed up to be my own rock.

"We have a private room… Elish made sure this place was empty but I knew you would feel more comfortable some place closed off." My temperature rose as he took my hand and started leading me through the main area of the restaurant, weaving between the leather chairs and table cloths so white I just had to run my free hand over them as we walked.

"The family is really thrilled about this. I'm surprised. I was expecting them to raise an issue considering you're new and a –" I knew he was going to say greywaster, but he stopped himself. Probably realizing it would be rude to bring up. "Well, Elish likes to keep tabs on everyone and I was worried since there isn't a record on you he would raise an objection but he…"

Jack's voice trailed and inside I was laughing hard at his confusion. "He seemed happy for us to be on this date and even called and made special arrangements for us."

Jack pushed open another wooden door and we walked inside a small area about eight by nine with a table and a blue booth on the left hand side. Behind the booth was a big map of what used to be Vancouver Island, now Skyfall. It looked all green and blue. I liked the colours.

"Did you like… save Ceph's life or something?" Jack asked as we both sat down. Still not able to help myself I started smoothing out the tablecloth, it was amazingly white.

I shook my head. "King Silas just really seemed to like me…"

"I see that," Jack said. We both glanced up as a young man with gelled blond hair wearing a waiter's outfit came in and silently started filling our glasses with something that might be wine. Then he gently set down burgundy leather-bound menus and slipped out, all without saying a single word.

Once he left Jack continued, "Silas I can see… he has these… whimsies about men he finds, but Elish? Elish doesn't like anyone; he doesn't even like me that much. It's baffling. I don't understand why everyone likes you."

I gave him a flat look and I bore witness to Jack's cheeks turning bright red.

"You know what I mean…"

I did know what he meant but I still crossed my arms and sniffed, deliberately turning my head away from him.

Jack hit my arm before pushing my menu towards me. "My family is weird but Elish is really predictable. He won't give you the time of day unless you're first generation or King Silas. I love him but he's just… Elish, I guess." Jack then shrugged and picked up the menu. "If I try and piece it all together my mind might explode though so let's order food."

I opened up the menu and was greeted by about a dozen things I didn't recognize. What the hell was:

"Spanik-ko-peeta?" I raised an eyebrow at Jack.

"It's really good!" Jack said with a pointy-toothed smile. "It's spinach and creamed bosen cheese and they make this flaky crust and deep fry it…"

I laughed incredulously. "I was raised on half-rotten rat jerky, and raw meat that came from Jasper's pockets. You order. I have no idea what any of this stuff is. Surprise me."

Jack seemed perfectly okay with this. He spent the next ten minutes rattling off what each dish was and then carried on about how it was grown in a skyscraper in Skyland specifically designed for growing produce. They even had special LED-type lights that could act like sunlight and irrigation systems that went up the walls. I didn't understand most of what he was saying but Jack seemed so excited to tell me all of these things I let him ramble on and on about it.

The kid sure did love to talk.

The quiet waiter came back and took our orders. Jack ordered us the spinach thing and breaded turkey bites. I learned a lot about turkeys in the time that it took for the food to come. Perish was supposedly genetically engineering the turkeys to be twice as big to the point where they couldn't stand on their own anymore. So they were engineering them to have bigger, thicker legs.

After talking my ear off about giant turkeys Jack started going on about our brothers.

"Felix is a total asshole. Rio is okay, but he's a part of Valen's gang. They all torment me relentlessly, Valen especially. Ceph I love though," Jack laughed lightly. "You don't have any brothers?"

I shook my head.

"But you mentioned someone before. A friend? He…" Then Jack cut himself off, maybe remembering as he said those words that I had mentioned that my only friend had killed himself.

I slunk down and kept shaking my head back and forth. "Barry was his name. He wasn't a real person…" I said slowly. I wiped my hands down my face, feeling spring after spring of anxiety start to sprout from my body. "Neither was Crow, my other friend. They were… friends inside of my head."

A tight cord started to wrap around my chest, I felt it tighten as the realization started dawning on me that I was probably coming off as completely nuts. But Jack already knew I was nuts so what was the use? I had impaled myself with enough swords so what was one more?

"I told you I got… I got problems," I said glancing up at Jack. He was looking at me with a grave and serious expression on his face.

The silence that descended seemed to have its own noise; it was static to my ears and a rushing behind my eyes. I turned away from his grave expression and wished I was anywhere else but here.

Then the food came, though the door opening made me flinch and jump in my seat. The boy with the gelled hair smiled at us but still said nothing but he was holding a pad in his hand.

As Jack quickly ordered our main course I stared down at the golden, flakey pastries and the small breaded nuggets of meat surrounded by green things. I poked one with my hand before picking it up and tasted it.

My mind went wild.

Immediately I started grabbing the small appetizers with both hands, before realizing Jack was staring at me a bit bewildered. I looked at him, two spinach things and two turkey balls in each hand, and felt my face go hot.

"Sorry…" I said hastily. I clenched my own teeth and smacked myself in my mind. Old habits die hard – but I also knew it was the stress brought on by that horrible silence.

"I'm still kinda feral. So, um, tell me about Ludo? You mentioned he was one of your brothers too?" I stammered, praying he would just take my offer of distraction and go for it.

Jack looked like he was going to question further my odd food hoarding, but he was the polite guy I knew he was so he decided to ignore it. "Well, Ludo is a total drug fiend. He's a slut too – I don't care for him. He has sex with anything with a penis." Jack smiled, gently picking up a turkey bite. With the polite manners of royalty he carefully bit it in half and waited until he had swallowed the morsel before continuing on.

"Not just the usual drug user either, because we all do drugs, but he's a complete lowlife addict but he's also incredibly smart and kind of functions better on drugs. He works with Perish a lot, and Rio does too though he's still in college," Jack explained. "He uses his drugs to get guys which is just gross, but I can't say anything…"

I didn't like him already. I swallowed the flaky spinach thing. My mind spiraling as its greasy goodness coated my mouth and lit up my taste buds. Once again I slipped back into survival mode and snatched another one.

I let out a long breath and put it down, mumbling another apology.

"Are you okay?" Jack finally asked. He tensed up before shifting his body like he was uncomfortable. "Is this too much for you? If it is, it's completely okay. I understand."

My face felt tight, my lips pursing as I looked down at the bits of food on my plate.

"Your heartbeat is a mess too…"

Right, like me he could hear heartbeats. Great.

"I guess when you admit you have friends inside your head that were at one time more real than reality, you get a bit nervous," I mumbled, before laughing dryly. "You should be running the other way."

Jack shifted towards me, close enough that I could feel his thigh against mine.

He put a hand on mine. "I'm a chimera… I don't run from things," he said and squeezed my hand. "I told you, I kinda like you… you had a really difficult life in the greywastes and I know psychology enough to understand you might have some quirks but who cares? I have quirks."

I saw him watching me, but my eyes took me away from his gaze, I didn't move my hand though.

"Why me?" I found myself asking. "You're a prince who could have anyone... so why are you showing an interest in me?"

Jack's slender, long fingers gently stroked my rough, scarred hand. The contrast between the two of us had never been clearer as I watched the flawless tips touch me. Two boys who started out in the same steel mother. Then one was raised in luxury, and the other tossed into the greywastes with nothing but a hope and a prayer. How could we possible be so different? Yet the caps over my pointed teeth and the brown contacts in my eyes told me we were more similar than any arian or chimera out there.

"Because I don't think anyone cares less that I'm a prince than you," Jack said slowly. He gently lifted my hand and started tracing the spiral scars on my palm. "And I don't think anyone cares less about your past or your quirks, than me."

Jack raised my hand, before kissing my fingers slowly. My breath caught in my throat; my body froze but at the same time, it flushed with heat. "You have a deepness in your eyes that makes a thousand poems spring to my tongue. And a body that tells me I could paint you every day for the rest of my life and still be inspired. I might not know you well but..." He paused; his lips were so pink, so welcoming... "I feel like you're an old friend who managed to find his way home. How... strange is that?"

Like a switch had been flicked the heat in my body suddenly turned to, not ice, but guilt. And to confirm my own masochisms I found myself glancing up at him, and seeing his black eyes, so deep and full, staring at me.

Eyes that held warmth, and to further drive in that serrated dagger – trust.

I pulled my hand away and ran it down my face. I could feel his eyes burning into me.

"Jack... I need to tell you something..." I whispered. My heart jumped, and at the same time his did as well. "Please forgive me for this, but I can't be with you until you know."

Suddenly there was a crash outside the doors. It was such perfect timing that as I rose to my feet I swept the area for a camera, but there was none and I had always been able to hear electronics when I focused my hearing.

Jack got up too, looking nervously at me. I think he thought I had planned the crash as well, but as we both pushed the door open at the same time both our suspicions were dashed.

Because sitting behind one of the tables, surrounded by three other men – was Valentine.

Valen, dressed in a light green long coat smiled when he saw us. He looked like a piece of peppermint candy that had been left in the dish for too long.

"Jacky! What a surprise to see you here!" Valen said happily as the men surrounding him laughed. They were surrounded by half-drunk drinks but their appetizers hadn't come, they must not have been here for long.

Jack's pulse rose, I could feel the angry heat coming off of his body. He glared down Valen and the others before saying in a rather dangerous voice.

"This place is reserved for me and Sami," Jack spat. "Elish reserved it for us. Get out of here; you're not supposed to be here."

Valen scoffed and waved a hand, he was even wearing peppermint green fingerless gloves and pink nail polish. I was surprised he didn't have a skirt on with how much he liked dressing like a chick. "This restaurant is big enough for all of us and you have your private room. What's the big deal? Or did you not want us to hear the grunting through the thin walls?"

The other three laughed with Valen. One of them had oddly bright burgundy eyes, another one's eyes were silvery with flecks of blue, and finally a big one, whom I knew must be Felix, had moss green eyes trimmed with gold. All chimeras, every last one of them.

"We're just having a drink, Jack!" Felix grinned. He already looked drunk and the black-haired, skinny drug user who must be Ludo nodded, a joint tucked behind his ear. That man was smiling from ear to ear with a crazed glint in his silvery eyes that told me he was missing a few brain cells.

"Come join!" Ludo said with a lewd grin. "Stop being such a tight ass. We just wanna meet your beau."

I felt Jack's hand around my waist; he pulled me towards him in a protective way. "We're going to leave…" he said in a biting tone, but his heartbeat suggested he was nervous. The attitude only went skin deep.

A churn of anger moved in my stomach, both derived from Valen obviously trying to crash our date and the anxiety coming from Jack.

I took a step towards the group. Jack's hand immediately tightened trying to stop me but I broke free of his tendrils and walked up to the table.

I put my hands on the white tablecloth and smiled at the four of them. "Nice to meet you," I said to them. "I'm Sami, Jack's friend. We were having a wonderful evening before you four decided to pull something smart. Now… will you kindly leave this establishment – or are we going to have a problem?"

"Sami!" Jack gasped. He started to try and pull me away but I raised a hand above my shoulder to tell him to step back.

The four laughed and exchanged amused glances. But when I slammed the hand back down on the table they fell silent.

I leaned into them, feeling four pairs of eyes on me. All holding expressions of amusement and intrigue. Each chimera probably daring me to make a move, but little did they know they were staring right at their older, genetically superior brother.

"Did I stutter?" I whispered, dropping my voice. "Or are the stories about chimera hearing fabricated?"

Then Jack grabbed me and pulled me back, to my own shock my instincts snapped ahead of my reason, and with a snarl, I whirled around and shoved Jack away.

But when the boy stumbled back and fell into the table behind us the anger disappeared. I ran to him as he fell with a crash onto the ground, stammering an apology. Then I grabbed him from his underarm.

"Sorry, I'm sorry," I said hastily, ignoring the howls of laughter and the scraping of chairs. "Instinct. It's a touch thing… forgive me."

"Sami, you need to leave!" Jack suddenly cried. He looked over my shoulder and I saw his eyes widen, I could see flickers of movement in his pupil-less black eyes.

"Leave him alone. He's just a greywaster – he doesn't know our rules yet!" Jack yelled. I turned around and narrowed my eyes as I saw all four of them right behind me. Felix two heads taller than the other three, and Valen with his face twisted in an ugly sneer. They were staring me down like a group of hyenas who had just found a lone wolf near their kill.

Their threatening gazes knocked up against the half-built walls of my newly erected pride, and drew out of me the darkness that was the soul of every chimera. I was a Dekker and I was a chimera, and I'd be damned if I'd let these fucking toy dogs bare their teeth at me.

"I'll only warn you once," I growled, lowering my head and glaring at every single one of them. I twisted my lips back like a snarling dog, wishing I had my pointed teeth to show off. "You don't want to fuck with me."

Felix laughed, and I realized he had several scars on his face, suggesting he was a brute who had been in many fights. He shook his head like I had just told him the most amusing joke in the world, before retracting his fist and aimed to punch me in the face.

I ducked it as it swung, the motion of the swing throwing the brute off-balance. With Ludo, Valen, and Rio barking and laughing I swung my own fist and punched Felix in the windpipe.

The brute chimera, already off-balance fell forward, crashing into the table and breaking its legs. There was a loud snap of wood and he fell to the ground, their drinks spilling over his thick, muscular body.

"SAMI!" Jack shrieked. To my shock, he yanked me back right as Valen and Ludo went to grab me. I shoved Jack away a second time and punched Valen right in the face.

Valen was knocked off of his feet, but the moment his peppermint ass hit the ground Ludo and Rio had me. I snarled and tried to shove them away but there were too many hands over my body, hitting and tearing at my clothing, spitting curses and oaths as I tried to fight back and get any bit of flesh I could.

"Nero... Nero... the others are here they're fighting with Sami!" I heard Jack shriek. I was confused for a second before I realized he was on his remote phone. "Quick!"

Ludo punched me in the jaw, blindly I swung and hit something warm, then, like a leech to flesh, I grabbed it and yanked it towards me and bit it. Warm wetness was my reward, and even though I was on one knee getting blow after blow rained down on me, the smell of chimera blood was enough to flood me with adrenaline.

I pressed and heard a holler. It was Valen. I opened my eyes and saw I had the fleshy but muscular upper arm in my mouth. All of the other chimeras hitting me in the head trying to pry my mouth away from the bleeding, delicious piece of meat.

"Sami!" Jack screamed again. I saw his hand; he put it over my nose and pulled back. "Fucking stop it! You're going to make it worse! Just stop it and leave! Get the fuck out of here before Nero comes. Just go!"

Then a towering shadow behind Valen, Felix had gotten up. I looked up and immediately a growl reverberated in my throat as I saw his burning green eyes glaring down at me.

The last lucid thought was a fist connecting with my head, then everything became a blur.

CHAPTER 32

I GLARED INTO THE MIRROR AND SAW MY CRIMSON-red eyes staring back at me just as angry. My eyes matched the blood that had leaked through the bandage on my forehead.

With a growl I turned away from the bathroom mirror. I put in my contacts, stalked into the living room of my apartment and slipped on my leather winter boots. I had college and I decided I was well enough to go after missing several days. Though the wound on my forehead was forever bleeding through the bandage I was ready to face Jack and see what he had to say about what had happened a couple days ago.

Jan didn't say anything to me when I crossed the lobby, backpack on my back and an already lit cigarette between my lips. If the pissed off expression on my face wasn't proof enough I wasn't in the mood to be talked to, the bloody bandage on my forehead was.

I hid it with a panama hat and slipped into the brisk morning, seeing many Skyfallers around me making their way to their jobs or school classes. Everyone was bundled in clean jackets or expensive furs. I was surrounded by elites, people who would take one look at the old me and immediately recoil like they were smelling something awful. But little did they know – I was a chimera.

I was a fucking chimera, I was Sanguine Sasha Dekker.

And I was now sick and fucking tired of Valen not knowing who I was. And I was sick of Jack not knowing either.

I was going to tell him. I was going to tell Jack who I was today. He could keep a secret, and I couldn't keep this from him anymore.

I coughed, not realizing I had taken in a long inhale of my cigarette, enough to sear my lungs with the burning smoke. I blew it out quickly and picked up my pace, glancing at every black car I saw in hopes that it was Jack making his way to class. I knew he would stop to pick me up.

Unless he was pissed at me over what happened.

If so, he would understand when I told him who I was. No one would expect a chimera to take that sort of shit from his brothers. I had every right to defend myself.

My jaw locked, my taste buds filling with tangy nicotine as I broke the filter inside of my mouth. I bit the end off of it and spat it onto the road, and enjoyed the filter-less smoke burn my lungs and chest.

I fucking hated Valen, and the other three shits. The howling hyenas in their fucking pack. Even if I was a better fighter than them I couldn't go up against four, especially with that thick-necked brute.

What a shit night… though it wasn't like it had been going well before Valen's interruption. I hated myself.

With a stormy cloud over my head I stalked into CoS. I didn't have my first class, Fallocaust Survival Studies, with Jack but my next class, 4-point Science, was with him.

FSS passed by quickly even though I couldn't concentrate at all. The next thing I knew I was sitting down at my desk in my Science class. I knew I looked just as pissed off as I felt.

I was the only one in class at first but eventually the other students trickled in. Like was typical of me my heart jumped and fluttered every time someone came into the class with hair similar to Jack's but as the time ticked on… Jack didn't come.

Well, Perish was going to be mad at him for being late. Jack had told me that the red slips he had to get the teachers to sign were actually from Silas himself to make sure he was attending classes. He was a chronic absentee.

Then I heard the bell. I opened up my textbook to the page that was written on the white board and kept an eye on the door as Perish started his lecture.

But still no Jack…

The class continued. Perish talked to us about protein strands and genetic compounds – still no Jack.

I frowned and felt myself start to become nervous. What if he had been absent the entire week? With this in mind I decided to speak to

Perish after class. He was a chimera and he would know. On top of that since he wasn't a dick like Elish he might actually tell me.

After class I packed my things, looking longingly at the empty seat beside me. I put on my backpack and walked up to the teacher's desk Perish was sitting in front of.

Perish looked up from his laptop and gave me a big smile. "I heard you got into a fight. How are you doing Sang... Sami."

I stared at him, a bit taken aback. "You... know who I am?"

Perish laughed and nodded before closing the lid on his laptop. He spun around on his chair until he was facing me and crossed his arms. "Yes, don't ask me how though. Family secrets. But of course I recognize you. Are you feeling okay? Any problems with that head? Our intelligent and science chimeras have an extremely fragile skull but the stealths' heads are as hard as rock."

"Ah..." I ran my fingernails over my covered arms. The scar tissue made it hard to feel any pain so I really had to dig in. "Where's Jack? I've been out for a few days and I expected him in class... I really need to talk to him."

The room seemed to grow colder when I saw Perish's face darken. He sighed and started drumming his fingers together.

"Poor Jack..." he said slowly. "Got into a fight with Valen the day after the restaurant incident. Valen has been such a difficult chimera. So many failed enhancements, including an important one. He's not treated well. Jack's in the infirmary in Alegria with a broken arm and a punctured lung. I think he will be back next week. Yes, next week, I think."

"What!" I exclaimed. Perish hissed and held his arms out to try and shush me, but the anger was starting to crawl up my body like cockroaches. And though Crow might be gone that didn't stop the black haze from infiltrating my head. "Valen beat up Jack?"

Perish's face went pale. His lower lip became a victim of his tooth as he started to look nervous. "Yes..." he said slowly, his eyes going in all directions but my face. "But Silas has told us we cannot get involved in other chimeras power struggles. The second generation has to sort it out themselves and form their own hierarchy.

Our own hierarchy? What sort of bullshit was that? That didn't sound like Silas at all. Silas would never make us fight like that. Silas loved all of us and wanted to keep us safe.

But Silas wasn't here right now and he wouldn't be here for over three months.

"I'm going to go see Jack," I said darkly. At this admission Perish started to look faint. He put his head into his hands and groaned.

"I don't care what the family thinks," I spat. "I'm tired of that pink little shit picking on Jack and acting like a bully. Someone has to knock that fuck down a few pegs."

"Sang… Sami…" Perish said, lifting his head up from his hands.

"No," I said lowly, the adrenaline starting to push more anger up to the surface. "I'm done with this. I'm done with Valen. Jack could be my boyfriend soon and I'm not going to let that asshole hurt him."

Perish paused, and I saw his brow furrow, then after a few moments he nodded. "Okay…" He nodded more vigorously. "You're right. Just be careful, okay?"

I scoffed and re-adjusted my backpack. "I'm not the one who is going to have to be careful."

And with that I left the classroom.

I got two puzzled looks from the thiens guarding the entrance to Alegria. Though I didn't have the time or the patience to explain to them my altered appearance. They didn't stop me from entering the lobby and that was good enough for me.

Kirrel though wasn't as hospitable.

"No," he said firmly. I had come face-to-face with him in the hallway leading to the infirmary. The doctor, a former sengil as I had learned from King Silas, was holding a clipboard and giving me a warning look. He was dressed in his usual lab coat, with a stethoscope slung around his neck.

"I want to see Jack," I said firmly. "I know the drill, I know who I have to be, just let me see him."

Kirrel gave me a narrowed look. "Why?"

I gritted my teeth, and looked behind Kirrel's shoulder. "Because I want to? I…" I dropped my voice. "I live here. I can walk around Alegria as I see fit, I don't need to tell you why."

Maybe that wasn't the right thing to say but I had been pushing down a lot of anger since learning that Valen had beaten up Jack. The fact that the doctor was preventing me from seeing Jack wasn't doing my emotions any favours.

Just as I suspected Kirrel's narrow look quickly turned rather flat. Nonchalantly he stepped aside and crossed his arms. "I never thought I would say this, but I liked the snarling monster under the bed, at least he wasn't snippy."

I sighed and shook my head. "I'm sorry… okay? I'm just… my head is too full of other things. No doubt you heard what went on at the restaurant. May I please go and see Jack?"

Kirrel blinked, his cross expression turning rather surprised. "Alright, go ahead. You'll have to answer to Elish not me."

That was fine. I wasn't afraid of that asshole either. I walked past Kirrel and peeked my head into the infirmary. The same one I had woken up in when I had been taken from Jasper's basement.

"Hey!" I said pretending to be happy. Jack was bruised and bandaged, laying in the exact same hospital bed I had been laying in. He was reading a book and looked deep in concentration.

And to show that indeed he had been concentrating Jack jumped at the sound of my voice.

I had expected him to smile back and greet me but instead his face paled and his black eyes widened in shock. He put the book down quickly and pulled himself up into the sitting position.

"Sami? W-what are you doing here? You – you're not allowed to be in here!" Jack stammered. He looked behind him as if expecting a dozen thien guards to come charging in to pull me away from him. "How did you even get in?"

I stared at him for a second, feeling my mouth twist into knots. "I… ah…" I stuttered before another white lie slipped into my head. "Elish let me."

Jack gave me a look of disbelief before he nodded slowly. "Okay…" Then he smiled and seemed to shake the suspicion from his head. "Sorry, it's just… you're the last person I expected to see here. I'm – I'll be okay to come to class soon, just getting a lung inflated." Jack patted his chest which was covered in a thin grey hospital blanket. I saw his arm was also in a small cast. "How are you? You should ask Kirrel to re-bandage your head. Are you feeling okay? I was worried about you."

My face darkened as did my mood. I pulled up a chair and sat down in it. "It's not me you have to worry about. Perish said Valen attacked you the day after our date. Is this true?"

And as quickly as it came the smile faded, it was instead replaced with pursed lips and a nervous sound that I could hear reverberating inside of his throat. It was like his body was physically trying to stop him from answering my question.

"It's just chimera politics…" Jack's voice was full of nervousness and caution. I saw his Adam's apple go up and down as he swallowed. "Really… it's our family, things like this happen. He was just angry about what happened at the restaurant. I got my licks and it's over now."

And I'm a part of this family…

"How often does he do this?" I asked Jack.

Another swallow, and a nervous laugh. "Sami… you're new to Skyfall. You need to understand this is something strictly between our family. You… I appreciate the concern, I really do, but you can't get involved in chimera politics."

"How often does he do this?" I asked again, my voice starting to turn cold. "Answer me."

Jack took in my words like I had physically threatened him. His gaze brought with it a smog of heaviness to the room, but I welcomed the descending mood with open arms. Because I knew he was feeling the same apprehension and I didn't want him comfortable enough to tell me to shut up.

With a twist of the blankets in his hands he said in a subdued voice, "All – all the time."

Jack stared at his hands. "It never ends, Sami. He's angry about Silas and the family rejecting him and I'm his target. I'm his punching bag, his and the other three. That's… that's life."

"Not anymore," I growled.

"Sami… please…" Jack's voice went up a higher octave. "You'll get hurt… baby…"

I paused for a brief moment at him calling me baby, but if he thought that would stop me he was wrong. Instead it lit the fire inside of me that refused to let Valen hurt Jack anymore. Because that silver-haired man laying in the hospital bed was going to be my boyfriend, and I was going to kill anyone who dare hurt him.

I turned from Jack – and walked towards the door.

"Sami?" Jack screamed after me. I entered the hallway and eyed Kirrel in an opposite room that looked like a supply room. He was marking things off on his clipboard, his back to me.

I grabbed his jacket and wrenched him backwards, then spun him until he was facing me.

"What floor is Valen's?" I growled.

I was fully expecting resistance. I was expecting Kirrel to see how angry I was and tell me to piss off.

But instead the doctor's eyes widened, and I was witness to seeing every speck of colour drain from his face.

"Eighth," the former sengil whispered, before saying loudly. "I'm not telling you; get the hell out of here. I was nice enough to let you visit in the first place."

I smirked and patted his cheek, before dropping him and turning around. As Jack called after me, unable to move from the machines he was hooked up to, I went to the elevator still waiting for me, and pressed floor eight.

The elevator doors separated and I knew right away this floor belonged to teenagers. It was painted lime green with a black ceiling and purple-hued track lighting. The ceiling and walls were also completely covered in paint that the purple lights seemed to make glow.

I pushed past my desire to examine the weird glowing hallway better and stalked down towards the double doors. Every floor in Alegria had identical layouts, or at least the ones that I had been on so far.

I pushed the doors open so hard they slammed against the door stop embedded in the walls, making a loud crashing noise.

Immediately I spotted the pink-eyed little fuck on the couch, with an out of it Ludo underneath him with his shirt off. As Valen sprung to his feet I saw I was about ten minutes from interrupting something, but it looked like they had only gotten as far as making out.

An angry and annoyed sneer crossed Valen's face before his eyes widened in surprise. Though whether it was him realizing who I was, or him seeing the insane anger behind my colour contacts I didn't know.

"What the fuck are you doing here?" Valen spat quickly buttoning a green and blue button-down. His pink hair was falling over his flushed face, and I could see a bulge in his corduroys. It was his eyes that amused me the most though, they were bright and staring, as if he had assessed the situation in front of him and found if amusing.

We'll see how fucking amusing I was after I was through with him.

Without a word I stalked up to Valen and grabbed his partially buttoned shirt. He gasped from surprise as I wrenched him up towards me, and stared him down face-to-face.

"You beat up my boyfriend for the last time, my friend," I said lowly, ignoring Ludo swearing in a slurred voice. It was Valen who I had in my sights and the drug-fiend chimera looked too out of it to do anything. "Do you understand me?"

Valen's eyes narrowed. He tried to push me away but I shook his body until his hands dropped. Instead, to show his defiance, my brother turned his cheek away from me and raised the corner of his mouth in smirk dripping with taunt.

"Do you know who I am?" Valen asked. He seemed to sing those words in a way that told me they were not strangers to his lips. "Or is the rumour that all greywaster rats are retarded, true?"

Oh, a challenge? I liked this.

I smiled thinly and started twisting the collar of his shirt. In response Valen raised his chin and defiantly fixed his eyes on mine. He wasn't backing down, and the thought of having a challenge intrigued me.

"You're brothers aren't here to protect you, my friend," I said, feeling more like Crow in this moment than I ever had before. "It's just you, me, and dessert." I moved my eyes off to the side, towards where I had heard Ludo.

Valen snorted, though my mind exploded like a comet on impact as I saw the faint flicker of apprehension. "What do you want, *waster*? Me to start crying and blubbering? Please, I am–"

I backhanded him across the face with my free hand, the smack echoed throughout the room. Valen gasped and looked at me, his eyes staring in surprise at my actions.

In case he missed it, I backhanded him again before dropping him onto the ground. He almost got his footing right but he ended up stumbling and falling to the floor. The pink-eyed idiot looked shocked, like a spoiled little kid the first time someone gave him his first well-deserved spanking.

"If I hear about you messing with my boyfriend again–" I whispered. I got down on my knees and reached out to touch Valen's face. He jerked it away of course, his lips pursed as if trying to hold back the tantrum bubbling inside of him.

" –I will fucking destroy you. Do you understand me, Valentine?"

He was shaking with rage as he stood; his entire body was trembling like a dog left out in the cold. I enjoyed every emotion I could feel radiate off of him, to the point where I could taste it.

"Enjoy your last days on earth… you scum sucking…"

I backhanded him again; the force of my blow flew him backwards.

He hit the carpeted floor on his back and this time I didn't let him get up.

In a fluid movement, I quickly jumped on top of him and straddled him, pinning him underneath my weight. The pink chimera, now with a bleeding nose, looked up at me shocked and angry; his eyes two blazing pink roses, injecting as much baseless aggression into me as they could. But I wasn't afraid. I was done being dominated by cowards.

I wasn't chained to the wall this time. I wasn't helpless anymore.

I was a chimera, and not only was I better than the Skyfallers, better than the greywasters…

I was better than every single second generation as well.

Valen's eyes blazed, but my attention was deflected as I heard a door slamming behind him. I looked up and saw Felix and Rio running in from the backrooms of the apartment, Ludo the tattletale trailing behind.

They ripped me off of Valen and immediately I started thrashing and pulling, trying to grab anything willing to bleed for me. I hated these blunt, useless teeth in my mouth but even if I was fully armed I couldn't find anything to clamp onto.

We weren't in a restaurant this time and Jack wasn't here to stop me. I wouldn't hold back. I was quite tired of not being a chimera.

"PIN HIM!" Valen suddenly screamed. He was on his feet with a stream of blood running down his nose and dripping onto the carpet. "Fuck him in his tight bitch ass! You think you can screw with a chimera? Strip him down! Rape the little prick and pass him around like the whore I'll make him into."

"Yeah!" Ludo said, before letting out a high and manic laugh. "I bet he'll fucking squeal. I haven't had a squealer in weeks. Oh, baby, I bet you'll cum for daddy, eh?"

My throat tightened but I refused to show the tremor of terror vibrating through my body. I wouldn't show any fear, I wouldn't give him that.

I was thrown to the floor. I clenched my teeth tight, my mind a racing motor that offered me no way of getting out of this situation. Only my self-derisive thoughts were clear enough to read, and they were telling me I was a fucking idiot for waltzing into an apartment floor full of chimera teenagers.

Then a hard impact on my back, right on my spine. I grunted and tried to sit up but I felt the chimeras' hands on me, pinning me down. They were talking quickly amongst each other, laughing and pawing at my body. I growled and yelled at them, struggling and twisting my body to try and get away from their claws.

When I felt one of them slip a hand down my pants and grab my dick and testicles, I lost my mind.

Calling on every shred of strength I had, I reared up. I put my hands underneath me and tried to push myself up to my hands and knees, but like they were waiting for an easier access point I felt a hand on the front of my jeans and with an expert-like movement they unbuttoned them and pulled them down to my bent knees.

Then a finger roughly pushed against my hole before tearing past the dry friction and ripping into me.

I screamed at them, but in the middle of my screaming I felt another finger get roughly pushed into me. Pain ripped through my backside and it only accentuated when the chimera started roughly finger fucking me.

Then, to my horror, my body froze, and the breath got sucked out of my lungs.

All of a sudden I couldn't move.

His fingers were roughly ripping themselves in and out of me, their jeering and taunting assaulting my ears. I was surrounded by this pack of animals but I couldn't move.

Suddenly I was back in the basement with Jasper behind me. It was like my mind was reverting back to being eight years old and even though my brain was shrieking I couldn't move.

Oh god... I can't move – I can't move. Internally I was screaming, my eight-year-old self shrieking at me to move, to stand up, to run and fight. But I was paralyzed. As the infiltrator shoved a third finger inside of me and roughly pushed them deeper in me I only stared forward, tense and coiled but absolutely still.

"He's quiet..." I heard Felix say, he sounded disappointed. He was beside me; I think it was Ludo's fingers inside of me, grinding and digging deep inside my ass. "He's not pleading. It's not fun when he ain't pleading."

Move, Sanguine – for the love of fuck – move. Don't let them do this to you again.

Ludo laughed behind me. I felt him remove his fingers before I heard him spit. I felt wetness against my hole and his pants unzip.

"I'll make him scream once he feels my cock," he growled. "He's been raped before. I know that disconnected look. That's so fucking hot.

Who raped you, Sami? Was it your daddy? Did Daddy fuck you? If you wanna call me daddy it's okay."

Someone smacked my head, short small smacks like someone flicking their finger against your earlobe. Short jabs to enrage a pissed off animal but I remained frozen.

The brute chimera chuckled and I saw his finger in front of my nose. He tickled it before reaching down to stroke my chin.

"He ain't a fighter, is he? Poor little—"

You know what happened next.

Felix shouted as I clamped down on his finger, and even though my teeth were blunt I still had the improved jaw strength that all stealth chimeras had. I pressed down on the index finger and when he tried to wrench it out of my mouth I quickly clipped my teeth together and ripped it right from its socket.

Gleefully I watched as Felix yanked his hand away, a ribbon of tendon left behind to fall from my mouth like ribbon taffy. I growled with my prize, and as I felt knock after knock rain down on my head, I smiled.

Then he picked up my head by the hair and slammed me down onto the floor. Voices behind me, laughing ones, but a moment later more hands came to my mouth to try and retrieve the finger. I put it into my mouth and locked my jaw, and in response I was pulled to my feet.

My vision focused on Valen, his eyes still an inferno of pink fire, behind him Felix was pressing a red towel against his wound.

Valen's fists were clenched, and as I smiled at him, the brute's thick finger between my teeth, he shook with rage and started punching me in the face as Rio and Ludo held me back.

"SAMI!" a hysterical voice sounded behind the chaos. Valen's eyes shot past me and I saw them narrow.

"Valen let him go!" Jack screamed. I craned my head just in time to see Jack run into the apartment. He pushed the other two chimeras away from me.

"He has Felix's fucking finger!" Valen snarled. "He's not going until I stick my cock in his ass. Get the fuck out of here or I'll be fucking you next, Jacky."

Jack paused. I saw a wash of fear come over his face, but to my surprise when he looked at me I saw his expression change.

"Spit it the fuck out!" Jack yelled at me, his eyes glistening. "Give it back. What the fuck – what the fuck are you doing here?"

I looked at him, shocked. I had fully expected him to be sympathetic, or at least to stand up for himself.

Angrily I turned away from him and spat the finger at Valen. I shoved my arms away from the two chimeras holding me back and pulled up my pants.

But when I turned around Jack was right in front of me, to further hammer in the confusing attitude Jack had he pushed me hard in the chest, almost knocking me off of my feet.

"I told you no!" Jack screamed hysterically, tears now running down his face. "You can't fucking come in here and do this to a chimera! We're princes, you're just an arian. They can kill you!" Jack's face was going red; his chest was rising up and down like he was having trouble breathing.

"You can die for this. They can kill you for this, Sami!"

"No they fucking can't!" I suddenly snapped, and in my own anger I pushed him back. "I can fucking defend myself, you asshole. I don't need you, *you* fucking need *me*. They were about to fucking rape me!"

"What the fuck did you expect? You shouldn't even be here!" Jack yelled back. "We can do whatever the fuck we want to arians and you just served yourself up on a fucking platter! You went to their apartment and fucking threatened them first didn't you? Are you fucking insane!?"

Jack pushed me towards the door, Valen and the others laughing behind us. "Just get out. Get out before they fucking kill you. Just get out of here, Sami. I don't want to see you anymore. I don't want you around. It's over!"

My eyes widened. I turned around and looked at him shocked. But when I saw the fury and desperation on his face, and behind him the chimeras laughing, the shock turned into anger. I felt like hitting him; I wanted to smack him right across the face for how he was treating me.

"Fine!" I snapped back and shoved him away. "Fuck you. They're all right about you, you are fucking weak. Fuck you. Enjoy being their bitch."

I walked out the door, the loud taunting and laughing behind me, and headed towards the elevators.

CHAPTER 33

THE STORE OWNER STOOD BEHIND THE COUNTER, giving me stricken looks every time I roughly slammed an item I decided I didn't want back down onto the counter. She didn't dare comment on anything I was doing though. I had already handed her my black card and even if no one else knew I was a chimera… she at least did.

I looked at a handheld Game Boy before slamming it down too. "Don't you have the updated ones? The ones with the colour screens?" I snapped. "Or is this shit all you have?"

Television was starting to become boring. I couldn't sit and watch TV without needing to do something with my hands. I was starting to become bored in my apartment.

"Um…" the lady store clerk stammered; she gripped the side of the counter hard. "We have merchants constantly coming in from the greywastes. We can put a special order in for you, Prince Sanguine."

Yeah, see? I'm a fucking prince. I'm getting fucking sick and tired of people not treating me to my damn status. If Valen knew who I was he would've been pissing his pink fucking panties but no… no one knew.

I lost Jack – I lost the guy I had really liked. Who was going to be my boyfriend. All because I couldn't be a chimera and that fuckhead couldn't defend himself.

I paid for the items I did decide I wanted, including a Sega Gamegear, and stalked out of the electronics shop.

Well over a month since the incident with Jack and I hadn't been able to snap out of my angry and aggressive mood.

College had been painful and aggravating. Jack now sat in the front of the class, completely ignoring me. I had made and lost my first friend in my first month of school and every time my mind reminded me of that fact my mood plummeted. Though it wasn't self-hatred anymore. A lot of my self-hatred had left when I had told Crow to leave me alone. Now every ounce of it was directed at Valen and to a lesser extent: Jack.

Why? Because Jack was a chimera, not only that but a stealth chimera. We had been engineered for better than this and the fact that he was actively letting Valen bully him filled me with rage. Not to mention the furious reality that he'd had the balls to yell at *me* for protecting him. It was like Jack enjoyed being the fucking victim and that was like a piece of steel being dug into an abscessed tooth. It was a personal insult to me.

But could I do anything about it?

"I don't want to hide anymore!" I had said angrily to Elish over a week ago.

I slammed my hand against his office desk. I was in a private meeting inside of his office at the college, with Mantis standing in silence in the corner of the room.

Elish had given me a dismissive look. "I thought you enjoyed being a normal arian?"

I seethed and started pacing around his office. "No, I don't. I want them to know who I am," I said. "I'm a damn prince. I'm Sanguine Dekker. I'm a fucking danger to every single one of them and I'm tired of those fucking dirty pieces of shit not realizing that!"

Elish smiled, his amusement made an angry noise climb to my lips. "Well, it took awhile but you're finally acquiring the chimera-ego. Oh, how far you've come."

"Then let me!" I said, whirling around. "Let me be Sanguine! I want to wipe that smug-fucking smile off of Valen's face, and Felix, Rio, and Ludo while I'm at it."

I growled when Elish shook his head no. "King Silas will be awake in two months, and really, that isn't that long. Once King Silas is awake and he has seen your... progress, I'm certain he will arrange for you to start being integrated into the family."

"Why not now?" I challenged. "Why not show him once he wakes up that I'm just fine?"

Elish's smile turned into a smirk. A smirk just brimming with derisiveness. "Sanguine, you certainly are *not* fine. In fact, you're bordering on arrogant. Why haven't you made up with Jack yet? I have given you more than a few opportunities to apologize."

"Apologize!" I said incredulously. "He fucking told me to fuck off when I was trying to defend him, then when they tried to fuck me *he* told me to fuck off. He broke it off not me, why should I apologize? Isn't this what the second generation is supposed to do? Fight and maim until one of us reaches the top?"

"And from the sounds of the report you were the one dominated."

"Because I couldn't be a chimera!" I exploded. Elish's words stung on every sensitive nerve I had. "If I was Sanguine I would've been able to act like a damn chimera. Jack… now Jack hates me."

"Jack's outburst was solely out of fear for your safety."

"Since I'm just a stupid greywaster to him… problem is I'm not."

"Perception is reality. Jack wants you safe. That's the only reason why he's distanced himself from you."

"Valen is the one who needs to be safe," I snarled, slamming my hand down on Elish's desk. "That pink-eyed little shit is the one who is going to need protection, not me."

"Valen has a lot of protection. He has a gang of several men who follow him around like little groupies to a member of a boy band, plus his three chimera brothers who are his best friends," Elish responded casually. He tented his hands over his desk and looked up at me. "But you're missing the point. Chimera or not, prince or not. Jack sees you as nothing but an arian greywaster who happened to come into some luck. He's protecting you by freezing you out of his life. And chances are he will do so until Valen isn't a threat to you anymore."

"Valen is no threat!" I exclaimed, but as I shouted that Elish's words started to soak through the anger that had coated me like a thick film.

Elish seemed to sense this, he said nothing back, only continued to tent his hands.

"I'm tired of pretending…" I said slowly. "I'm ready."

"You're not ready, all you want is to dominate and punish Valen for humiliating you."

I swallowed the growl that trailed behind Elish's words. "He didn't humiliate me. I'm just ready to be Sanguine."

Elish was quiet, but Mantis behind us spoke.

"Are you sure it is Sanguine that you want to be?" Mantis asked.

"Because from your anger and attitude I would say you're more eager to become Crow."

"Crow's gone," I said darkly. "I told him to get lost in the janitor's closet over two months ago and I haven't seen him since."

"Or perhaps he realized that you were past obeying direct commands," Mantis commented.

My eyes narrowed, I turned around to face him. "He's gone."

Mantis tilted his head to the side, in a way that showed me he wasn't buying my answer.

"I think Crow and Barry ordered you around because you were a scared little boy in need of guidance. Now you're a teenager rebelling against the only authority he's ever had. But I would suspect this demon lurking underneath your surface cannot be expelled by mere yelling, Sanguine. I would be wary just who you're giving control to right now."

"No one!" I snapped at Mantis. "The only person who controls me is me. Crow's fucking gone, just like Barry."

"All I'm saying is be cautious," Mantis said. He picked up a mug of tea that had been cooling beside a windowsill and took a sip. "Crow isn't a physical person. He's the embodiment of all the pain and misery you went through in the greywastes. He can take many forms and can influence you in other ways, besides just yelling at you. Be wary, he seems smarter than your average chimera delusion."

I grunted and turned away from the psychologist. He wasn't even a chimera, though he was immortal. What did he know?

"Even if you're ready to be Sanguine, the order still stands," Elish said. "And though the second generation may be snarling and scrapping for shreds of authority the first generation has established theirs long ago. I'm the king and Silas's second-in-command, then Nero, then Garrett. And that is all that is important to you right now, Sanguine. I suggest you try and make up with Jack and try to rekindle the romance, rather than focus all your energies on being angry at not being *ohhh'd* and *aww'd* over for being a chimera. The need for attention and praise for being in the Dekker family is rather unflattering and it's an ugly colour on Valen. I suggest you do not pick up any habits as such. Silas would be extremely disappointed if he woke up to you being a petulant ego-maniac."

"I am none of those things," I said coolly.

Elish spread his hands. "Then what is the issue here?"

My face darkened as I stalked down the street. We were in the rainy season now and raindrops were starting to fall onto the dry pavement. It was cold out and Nero had told me we might be getting snow soon. It snowed sometimes at Jasper's farm but I had always hated the snow. Not because I didn't enjoy it but because I almost froze to death on many occasions in the winter and I just had a bad association with it now.

I would enjoy this winter though. I would embrace it and love it because I was a chimera and I wasn't afraid of anyone, anything, or any weather. I didn't have to pay for heat at Skylanding anyway so why the fuck should I be scared? Fuck it, fuck everyone!

I kicked a forgotten plastic bottle and watched it bounce across the sidewalk before landing right beside a mailbox. I kicked the mailbox as I walked by it for no other reason than because my mood was so foul.

They should be embracing the fact that I wasn't a coward anymore. They should be happy I wasn't hiding under the bed, throwing up from gorging on too much food, or going psychotic when Crow came. But my family seemed content letting me be Sami the greywaster and I was frustrated and angry with that.

I pushed open the glass doors of Skylanding, and looked towards Jan who was watching television on a small TV. He was used to seeing me now so he only smiled; the fear never left his eyes though.

"Get me Kass," I said to him. "Tell him I want pub food, greasy shit. Bring me leftovers for Jett too and I want a bottle of vodka with it."

Jan nodded and immediately got onto his phone. I took the elevator to my floor and locked my apartment door behind me.

"Brraaappp!"

My almost full-grown kitten came bounding towards me, his yellow eyes bright and his pupils wide. I picked him up, and because no one was there to see me, I smiled and rolled my eyes.

"It's hard to be in a bad mood with you, knuckle-head," I said and carried him towards the kitchen. He purred and stayed in my arms watching me intently as I opened the fridge and pulled out a stick of dried rat pepperoni. It would tide me over until Kass came to my apartment with my orders. It would have to satiate Jett as well. He always had dried kibble for him but he had more bad habits than I did. And he was about as eager to correct those bad habits as I was.

We sat down with our pepperoni and I turned on the Gamegear and plugged it in. There was only one battery factory in the factory towns and they were expensive as all hell. Since normal arians couldn't afford them, juice suckers such as Gamegears or boom boxes were altered so they could only be played by being plugged in. Game Boys were okay though but I didn't want an old one I wanted a coloured Game Boy advance.

I turned on Sonic and threw a piece of pepperoni for the cat. Sonic helped cheer up my mood somewhat but I was still annoyed at everything. I was looking forward to having some vodka to numb it, and Kass to keep around until I was tired of looking at him.

I settled in with the heat cranked up and my colour contacts out of my eyes. I was used to them now but if I kept them in for longer than five or six hours my eyes started to become itchy and irritated. So it was a relief once I was able to come home and kick back.

There was a knock on the door which I knew was Kass. I unlocked the several deadbolts I had and opened it up.

Kass gave me a smile before handing me the food. I noticed he had something colourful and rubber in his hand.

With an amused laugh from the housekeeper he put what I realized was a rubber clown mask over his head. "*Woooo!!* I'm gonna eat your dick!"

I rolled my eyes. It was a freaky enough-looking mask. The clown had wide staring eyes though the pupils were cut out so you could see, and a lip-sticked mouth wide open and grinning through pointed teeth. The face itself was white, but the rings around the eyes were blue and it had red fuzzy hair embedded into the scalp.

"IT is on the movie network tonight. You wanna watch?" Kass asked. "I knew you'd say yes so I bought this old Halloween mask. If there's shit that survives the Fallocaust perfectly it's fucking rubber Halloween masks."

I shook my head with a smirk. I took the bag from him and motioned him to come in. "I saw it was queued. Men in Black is on after in case you don't feel like going home," I said to him.

"Sure, I got nothing better to do," Kass said with a shrug. He brought the vodka to the coffee table before I heard the tinkling of glasses coming from the kitchen. I threw the mask onto the table and sat down.

"How fun do you want your drink?" Kass called.

That was our code word to how much liquor I wanted in it. Since Jack fucked off Kass had been my only friend to come and visit me besides Nero, so we were starting to have our own language. "Normal fun. It might change as the night goes on though. I'm just pissed today."

"You've been pissed for the past six weeks," Kass replied, before making a kissing noise at Jett. I heard my kitten give him a half-meow, half-purr before scrambling across the kitchen for a thrown piece of meat. Jett liked Kass and I liked Kass as well. He wasn't a part of the chimera family and once he had gotten used to my natural appearance he treated me normally.

"Jack's still ignoring me," I said irritated. "And I'm still ticked that Elish won't let me be Sanguine."

Kass brought me my newspaper-wrapped food, showing a slick of grease soaking through the newsprint like any good pub food. All of our pub food either came wrapped in newspaper or if you could afford the deposit: plastic containers.

I unwrapped the newspaper and started reading it as I devoured my burger, chocked full of shredded bosen meat, cheese, and bacon. The pub staff were well-trained, chimeras came to that bar often and we always got the best food. No rat meat for me and being a boy raised on jerky I fully appreciated it.

Though because I was in hiding I was forbidden from going in there flaunting my black card so Kass did the work for me. Technically I could get into trouble for buying the Gamegear but if Elish had that much time on his hands to find out it was me, he needed a hobby.

"*Irontowers Rebels Still Refusing Comment on Child-Sexslave scandal*?" I read the newspaper headline out loud and chuckled. I grabbed a fry before popping it into my mouth. "Why do they think being quiet will do anything? It's just going to incriminate them more."

Kass leaned over. He motioned to steal a fry but I gave him a growl. Though after seeing him retract his hand like he was touching caustic acid, I pushed a small pile towards him. I could always make him go get more so what did I care?

"That was pretty clever for you to think up. Though don't you think that might've fuelled them shooting down Silas's plane?" Kass asked. I had told him all of the details about what was going on with Silas and the family. I had no one else to tell and he knew he would be in my next sandwich if he dared betray me.

"Probably…" I said but narrowed my eyes. "I still think it was Elish though."

Every time I brought up Elish being behind these things Kass gave an animated shudder. Like the name alone brought a winter chill into the room. I could relate, that man was a brick of ice and as cold as a comet.

Though that being said, I still respected him. Why did I respect him even though I believed he was behind King Silas's plane being shot down? Because if I dared show hostility towards him, I knew he had the tools to have me killed, and me dying was an acceptable casualty if he had King Silas in his sights.

I might be just a greywaster and just a teenager… but I wasn't stupid. Elish was king right now, and it would be incredibly easy for him to kill me and suffer the fallout from Silas once he woke.

So I was normal towards him. Nothing special… just normal.

"You know… before you came here it was really obvious to us lowly civilians that King Silas and Elish would eventually become involved. I mean it's just too perfect," Kass said.

I sniffed airily. "Silas likes me, and Elish is jealous."

My eyes burned into Kass's as he chuckled. He stopped as soon as he saw I was glaring at him.

Kass grabbed two fries and shook his head, then he reached down to the side table and grabbed the ketchup. "Your family is just something else, but I kind of understand. Actually I probably don't but maybe that's the point."

"Probably," I said and I continued reading the paper. "I hope Silas finally decides there is enough public support to finally bomb Irontowers. I'm getting tired of them being around."

"Do you really think the chimeras will bomb them?" Kass asked. "Do they even know which part of the city they're in? Irontowers is fucking huge."

Yes, they have plants. But I didn't tell Kass this. Instead I shook my head no. "I'm not a part of that chimera faction. That's all Nero, not me."

I took the remote and switched it over to the movie channel, just as the movie about the murdering clown was starting. "Why are people so afraid of clowns?" I shook my head. "There's a lot more scarier things going on in the greywastes than men with face paint."

"Nero hasn't told you anything though?" Kass said, watching me as I leaned against the couch and popped the last bite of my sandwich into my mouth.

I shook my head. "Nah, we just bullshit then eventually after he's had a couple drinks he just wants to talk about sex," I said with my mouth full of food. I swallowed it. "Which basically consists of me saying 'No, I haven't fucked anyone yet. No, I haven't touched myself yet. And no, you can't take your pants off.'"

Kass laughed, I heard him hit his knee. "I still can't believe you've never even played with yourself. Buddy, you're almost twenty. I'm surprised you haven't exploded."

"Uh huh," I sighed. I was tired of this topic. "I think I'm never going to do it just to frustrate and annoy every single one of you."

"You know…" Kass said lightly. "Maybe if you made yourself cum, or just fucked someone for a few hours… you wouldn't so uptight."

"I'm not uptight!" I snapped, before grabbing the bottle of vodka. I saw Kass smirk at this but I decided to take a drink of vodka as appose to bashing Kass on the head.

"Do you have any real reason?"

I stiffened. I gave Kass a warning look before slowly shaking my head. In response Kass swallowed and nodding back then turned his attention towards the TV.

After IT was over and Men in Black came on I picked up my pack of cigarettes resting beside me and pinched the tip with my fingers. A red ember exploded and I took in a deep inhale.

"Can you light other things on fire besides cigarettes?" Kass asked beside me.

I kept the smoke in my lungs, and as I exhaled the smoke I reached my hand over and touched Kass's bare arm.

My friend yelped before recoiling, a red patch the size of my finger starting to form and swell. Kass swore at me under his breath and pressed his glass of vodka and ChiCola against it.

"Can you make like… your hands burst into flames?"

Wouldn't that be something to see? I smirked and shook my head. "No, but according to Silas we can alter the temperature. We can also draw out an electric current too, but I don't know how to do that, just the burning one."

I thought for a second about another altered sensation I had heard about from Nero and debated the intelligence of telling this to Kass, but he had never come onto me so I decided it would be fine.

"There is another one…" I said slowly.

To my surprise Kass's eyes lit up and I saw his lips curl into an impish grin. "The slave touch?"

One of my eyebrows rose. "That's what it's called?"

Kass's grin only widened and he nodded vigorously. "Because whoever the chimera does it to, is their slave for life. Willingly... because it's supposed to be fucking mind blowing."

"Hm." I looked down at my hands and wiggled them. "Obviously I don't know what one. Nero just said it's like vibrating static and in the right places..."

"Knee-trembling, prolonged orgasms that will bring you to your knees," Kass said with a dreamy sigh. "Too bad I'm too ugly to be a cicaro, too strong-willed to be a sengil, and too dirty to even be Skylander."

I ran my hands over my arm and tried to alter my burning touch into something else but there wasn't much use of it. I only succeeded in singing my arm hair; the smell was interesting.

"Okay, I want to try something..." Kass leaned down and picked up a carrier bag he usually packed around. I watched him root through it and to my utter perplexity he pulled out a yellow container with a blue cap.

"Is that lighter fluid?" I blinked. "You carry around... *lighter fluid*?"

"Oh be quiet, chimera," Kass said. He grabbed my hand and held it palm up towards him. "Davers picked up a part-time job lighting the barrels in the indoor shelter for the feral cats down at the seawalk. Sometimes on the way to clean here I light them for him since it's on the way. You chimeras are cat-obsessed so I'm sure you have no smart remarks for that."

I let him rub some of the lighter fluid on my fingers before he retracted his hand and nodded at me. "Okay, flame on, good buddy."

I gave my fingers another wiggle just for show before focusing whatever it was in my body that made this happen. Sure enough, to my and Kass's amusement, my fingertips burst into small orange flames.

And to my surprise it didn't burn me. I gave Kass a quizzical look before reaching my hand out towards his shirt to singe him. Kass jumped back with a laugh before hovering his own hand above my fingertips.

"Doesn't it hurt?" Kass asked.

I shook my head and eased the energy out of my fingertips to quell the flames.

And *then* it started to burn me. I yelped to Kass's laughing amusement and started shaking my hand back and forth. Once the flames were extinguished I put the burning tips into my mouth, tasting not only seared flesh but the sour, cold taste of lighter fluid as well.

"Once I turn off the flame-on, they start to burn though," I said after popping the tips out of my mouth. Kass got up and walked towards the kitchen and I heard the tap run. "I should talk to Perish one day and see if he can design me a way to throw fireballs or something equally awesome."

Kass handed me a glass of ice-cold water and sat down. "Well, chimeras are supposed to be weapons too, right? I'm surprised he hasn't thought of something like that already."

"Second generation is the experimental batch apparently," I told him. "They range from partial success which I guess would be me and Jack, to utter failure which would be Mr. Valentine."

"Valen..." Kass muttered. His oval-shaped face became hard, and absentmindedly he scratched his prickly facial hair. It looked like he was attempting to grow a beard but he was bad at it. "Fucking Valen and his bromance club. He was at the bar when I was there, you know? Flaunting his shit."

"Valen is a piece of shit," I said. "I'm going to knock out his teeth if I ever catch him without his chimera brothers. He's a miserable fucking shit."

"Everyone knows that. Jack has a good reputation in Skyfall, so do the silver twins, and Rio. Ludo is a druggy but he's friendly too, Felix is a shitfuck though. Ceph is feared because of what he and Nero do, but everyone knows Valen is the black sheep. Do you know what he did in that fucking pub man?" Kass shook his head. "He goes into the pubs, him and his goons pick out the three hottest guys, gay or not, and they take them into the abandoned buildings near Cormorant and rape the fuck outta them."

I could feel the blood drain from my face. Kass seemed shocked by this; he gave me a questionable look.

"H-he rapes them?" I stammered. Valen and the other chimeras had definitely tried that with me, but I assumed it was drawn from their anger of me storming into their apartment. "Innocent people? Not just... not just ones that might –" I knew it was the wrong way of saying it but I didn't know how else to say it. "– might deserve it?"

Kass stared at me for several more seconds before his lips pursed. Then to my anger he burst out laughing.

"You sound surprised!" Kass laughed waving me off. "A chimera rapes innocent people? Of course, every single one of you do. I bet even Jack has. That's a well-known fact of life here."

Like my blood had been ignited with the same lighter fluid still stinging my hands, I angrily rose to my feet and felt my teeth creak as I clenched my jaw. Immediately Kass recoiled away, his eyes wide and staring, and his laughter gone with the night's mood.

"My family doesn't do shit like that," I snapped. "Whatever you heard isn't true, and I never want that shit to come out of your mouth again. My family doesn't do that to innocent people."

Kass held up his hands but to my anger I saw the slight curl of a smirk on his face. Bravery fuelled by alcohol but it might be the last vein of bravery he ever felt.

"You've seriously been sheltered, lied to, or both, Sanguine. It's common knowledge here that your family can pick up and fuck any man they want, willing or not. Davers has been by Garrett just last year, and Chelsey's brother got nailed by Nero and Ceph at–"

I raised my hand and hit Kass right across the face, as hard as I possibly could. The housekeeper's head snapped backwards.

My entire body was shaking with rage; the dark essence that I had once attributed to Crow was soaking into me and coating my entire body. I could feel it slowly snake up my limbs, my chest, my neck, before pooling behind my eyes. I could hear an audible roar from the blood rushing through my head, and as it joined with the darkness my eyesight started to dim.

"Nero is my best friend," I said, my tone dropping. "He knows me; he would never do anything like that."

Kass quickly scrambled to his feet, with a quickened speed he walked past me and grabbed his jacket. "Bro… you're my friend… I…" He put his shoes on. "You've been sheltered."

"I – have – not!" I whirled around and screamed. "All of that shit is rumours, rumours you fucking peasants have started. My family doesn't do shit like that."

Kass turned around, looking angry. "And why the fuck would I lie? Ask anyone, Sanguine. Anyone. You've been in that family for no time at all. I was born and raised in Nyx. I've seen it happen, I've seen it accepted and ignored too. That's life under the royal Dekker family."

"Get the fuck out of here," I said lowly. "You're the one who has been lied to. Silas would never let that happen. He's a good person and a good king."

Kass started to laugh, until I picked up my tumbler of vodka and flung it at his head. He dodged it just in time and made a beeline for the door.

"Silas is a fucking tyrant, your entire family is," Kass said coolly. "You were different which is why I like you, but I'm already seeing you turn into one of them, just from your new attitude."

"You can't talk to me like that. I'm a–"

"A fucking chimera – I know," Kass snapped. "We all know. Okay? We all have to walk around in groups and run for our lives every time a chimera's shadow meets ours. We all live in fear... because *you're a chimera*, and we're just your family's fucking pawns. Good night, Sanguine."

The door slammed, just as another glass shattered against the wall.

I whirled around and stared at the dark brown curtains that were closed over my sliding glass door, so much rage was sweeping through me I felt like either screaming, pulling out every strand of my hair, or both. Instead I did the only thing I could think of... I picked up my remote phone and dialled Nero.

After several rings it picked up.

"What is it, puppy?" Nero answered. He sounded drunk and I could hear Ceph in the background chuckling.

"Is it true?" I shrieked, unable to control the volume of my voice. I felt my teeth clench and it took every ounce of restraint inside of my trembling body not to throw the phone too. Everything inside of me felt alive with electricity, small but strong sparks of lightning that seared and exploded my muscles and blood.

"W-what?" Nero said. I heard rustling. "What's true?"

"You... YOU! Have... have you ever raped someone? Has the family? Is this what this entire fucking family is about?" I screamed. "Is it?"

There was silence on the other end. Dead – full – silence.

"Puppy..."

"IS IT!" I shouted into the phone, my voice cracking not only under the volume, but under the weight of the realization.

"Sanguine..." Nero said slowly, his words slurred. "This isn't a conversation for the phone. This is shit Silas has to tell you about."

Silas has to tell me about? I felt dizzy, then a thud as I fell down to my knees. "I told you what Jasper fucking did to me, you were sympathetic.

Are you fucking telling me you do the same fucking thing?"

"FUCK NO!" Nero said angrily. "I'd never touch a fucking kid, you moronic shit. Ever!"

"I'm nineteen!" I screamed. "So it fucking started to become okay in the eyes of this fucking family as soon as I turned fifteen? Is that what you're saying?"

"NO!" Nero shouted back. "Stop cornering me. I'm not fucking smart enough to calm you down and I'm fuckin' drunk as fuck. I don't know fancy words like the others. I can't explain it properly just… you're a chimera, so no one can touch you, shithead. It never stopped being bad, kid or adult."

My jaw locked. Unable to stem the rage coursing through me I screamed from anger and gripped the phone in my hand. "You're all a bunch of fucking hypocrites!" I yelled. "And liars, a bunch of fucking liars! I'm – I'm… telling… I'm… does Silas know about this?"

More silence on the other end.

"Pup… I'm not going to pay for the lies Silas has told you. He wanted to shelter you from a lot of things until you were ready. Look he's healing fast…"

"Just shut up!" I tried not to scream but my voice was wobbly. "Just… leave me alone for a while."

I dropped the phone onto the ground, it hit the carpet hard and the battery popped out of its casing. I watched it bounce over and hit the side of the coffee table before becoming still.

He's not going to pay for the lies Silas has told me? I stared at the remote phone and the disconnected battery and for a moment all I could do was breathe.

So was that the reality then? Kass had been right? Silas had been sheltering me from how this family really functioned? We were all a bunch of fucking rapists or something and that was supposed to be okay?

I looked around my empty apartment, stunned. Everything inside of this place suddenly seemed dirty. It seemed contaminated, filthy like my body felt after Jasper had been on top of me. A dirty apartment bought with dirty money from a family of tyrants that I belonged to.

I was a chimera – and just an hour ago I had never been more proud of that fact.

Now?

Now I think I just wanted to be the boy in the basement again. At least my world was small back then; at least I knew who I was... Sami. Not even Samuel Landon Fallon... just Sami the celldweller.

I got to my feet and continued to look around the apartment. I never knew things could look so different. My eyesight hadn't changed but... everything else had.

My eyes fell on the yellow bottle with the blue cap. I picked up the lighter fluid and popped the cap off.

With no expression on my face, and no methods to my madness I squeezed the bottle over the coffee table and the carpet, before moving to the couch and the side chair. Then I squeezed the sour-smelling liquid onto the walls and finally emptied the rest onto the curtains.

This would be when Crow murmurs ideas in my head. This would be the time when madness takes over so I can be shocked over my actions later... but it was only me. Tonight... it was only me.

I didn't want to be a chimera. They can give me schooling, training, love, and family... but I refused to be a part of a family that was full of people only slightly better than the man rotting in a cell in the Dead Islands. I would rather rot in a basement, than rule with the man who lived upstairs.

My lips pursed as my eyes took in the apartment, the smell of butane crawling up my nostrils and clawing inside of my brain. I didn't want to admit that I was more hurt than angry. Hurt because Nero had said they all knew what had happened to me, and yet it seemed like they were no different. The family was full of tyrants and liars, and Silas was obviously aware enough of that fact to lie to me.

What a bunch of hypocrites.

I walked into my bedroom and picked up Jett napping on my bed. He was small enough for me to fit him into my book bag, and beside him I put Barry. The only two things in this world I cared about.

Then I walked into the living room, pocketed the remains of the lighter fluid, and not knowing why, I picked up the clown mask too.

Then I leaned down and touched the slick of oily liquid soaking into the couch –

– and I lit it on fire.

"S-Sami?"

I looked over, half-aware and half-caring. I was walking through the lobby towards the door to outside, pulling the caps off of my teeth one by one and slipping them into my pocket. I had gotten the front ones off in the elevator; the back ones I knew would be trickier.

But I would only need the front ones off.

Kass was staring at me. He was speaking with Jan, who was at his usual spot behind his desk.

"Kass…" I said. I walked over to him and handed him my bag, just as it started to move. I then reached in and pulled out another tooth. I put it in my pocket and ran my tongue along the naturally pointed teeth underneath the caps. It felt like I was greeting old friends. "Take care of my cat, alright?"

Kass blinked, but when he saw the bag move he quickly took it before opening it up. Jett's head popped out, his ears were pressed back and his pupils dilated but he was okay.

I pulled Barry out, who was sitting beside Jett and held him close to me. "Okay?"

Kass gave me a confused and cautious look. "Sanguine… you look really… unstable. I think you should call one of your brothers."

I already did…

"Will you look after Jett?" I repeated, not realizing how robotic my voice sounded until Kass had pointed out my state. Every movement I had had since I grabbed that lighter fluid had been from the hands of some puppet master. I felt like a marionette on strings and yet I knew the master was myself and only myself. I had no Crow to goad me on, no Barry to smile at me through pointed teeth. It was me and only me.

My only honest friend nodded slowly and lightly put a hand on my shoulder. "Of course, dude. Where are you going?"

Suddenly alarms starting blaring around us. As Kass and Jan started swearing, I pushed Jett's head back into the bag and slipped my last front tooth cap into my pocket.

"I'm going to go kill some rapists." I pulled the clown mask over my face, and with Barry tucked underneath my arm, I walked out of the apartment building.

"Sanguine!" Kass called over the alarms ringing in all of our ears. "Sanguine… fucking be careful."

"My apartment's on fire," I called to him, and walked through the glass doors of Skylanding, probably for the last time.

The night was cold and the hot breath coming through the mask was visible in the dim LCD lights. It was late but there were some people still wandering around. All of them giving me a single look before disappearing into the shadows and alleys. They were smart. Like how an insect displays bright colours to warn you that it was dangerous, my mask held the same warning.

I clawed bigger holes into the clown mask for eyes as I crossed through an alley of an old antique shop. It was a shortcut to the pub, the pub that I had sent Kass to get food.

The pub that Kass had said he'd seen Valen and since this was a weekend I knew the little pink shit wouldn't be sleeping early for school. If I was lucky I would see him sitting in a booth with his gang, and if I wasn't…

If I wasn't I would be taking the elevator to the eighth floor.

And there I would grab him and there I would hold him… and there I would squeeze his neck until I saw the blood stain the perfect whites of his eyes. Like a flower coming into bloom I bet it the red would look quite beautiful next to the pink.

I wonder what it would taste like.

For a moment I closed my eyes, and for just a moment – I wished for Crow to be here with me. I had Barry underneath one arm, but he was just a bear… just a bear with a song inside of him.

Sanguine, Sanguine.
Give me your heart to do.

And what was I?

My eyes narrowed as I emerged from the alley and into the car-less street, the streetlights shining overhead and illuminating the sign that said 'Popkin's Pub'.

I didn't give a fuck who I was anymore.

My boots clicked as I stepped onto the curb of the sidewalk, the tinted windows showing me different faces separated by the dim candles on the tables. Immediately when I pushed open the swinging wooden doors I was greeted by the low buzzing of voices, the smell of beer and greasy food, and fucking John Denver *'Thank God I'm a Country Boy'* blasting on the speakers.

The bar went dead silent.

"Life ain't a nothing but a funny, funny riddle… thank god I'm a country boy."

Almost silent.

"Who knows Valen Dekker?" I asked, my voice booming loudly over the acoustics of the room.

A sea of faces stared at me, white ones, dark ones, female and male, all of them with their eyes wide and their bodies frozen. Not a single one of them moved, not the patrons or the staff still holding trays of drinks.

"Who knows Valentine Dekker?" I asked again, raising my voice. I wondered if they could see my teeth through the horrifying-looking clown mask, though the mask itself held its own rows of sharp teeth.

My eyes immediately took me to the first signs of movement. I saw a round-faced bearded man wearing a black apron and a name tag, shift from one leg to another. Immediately I could see a glisten of sweat on his brow that reflected against the dim lighting.

I started walking towards him, still holding Barry in one arm. As I approached he shrunk back, his face creased in a permanent expression of both horror and shock. He quickly moved behind a table, the only thing separating the two of us.

"I don't need to give you a description, bar man," I said lowly. "Where's the pink chimera?"

The man let out a wheeze and wiped his mouth with his hand. "Those chimeras will kill you, you – you don't go fucking with chimeras, arian. You–"

There was a collective gasp and several screams as I pushed the table out of the way. It went crashing into another smaller table sending both to the ground. I closed the two feet of distance and grabbed onto his apron.

I slid my mask up over my face. And when the man saw my eyes and bared teeth he gasped and looked at me with the same terror that I had been seeing since I could remember.

"Do I look like an arian to you?" I whispered.

Suddenly I heard the door open behind me. I jerked my head towards the noise, slipping the mask back over my face.

"Stop them!" I snarled, my red eyes sweeping the room. And when every shocked patron stayed frozen in their stasis I growled and threw the bearded man down onto the ground.

"I said STOP THEM!" I screamed. I grabbed a bottle of alcohol and flung it at the door, catching one of the men on the leg. I snatched another bottle just as several men jumped to their feet and ran out the door after them.

And like lemmings, as soon as one got up the others followed. Soon every man, and some of the women, were running outside, then moments later the sounds of fighting.

I exited the pub to see several men holding back the three patrons who had been trying to escape.

The three men struggled, giving me angry looks. I knew just by looking at them that they were a part of Valen's groupies. All dressed in bright colours, flaunting dyed hair and arrogant attitudes.

"Who the fuck are you?" one of them said as he tried to yank his arm free. "Who the fuck do you even think you fucking are? Valen will fucking kill you."

I unscrewed the bottle of alcohol, a silver full moon on the black label. I dumped it over the man's head and onto the other two's heads as well. A string of curse words and threats fell from their mouths but the men holding them back didn't ease their grip.

"The next time Valen comes into this bar…" I said, raising my voice. The cold, dead night air seemed to amplify my words even better than the inside of the building. "Tell him that if he ever rapes another man again. I will burn him alive, and I will fuck his smoking corpse. You tell Valentine Dekker… that Sami Fallon said this."

"Sami Fallon?" one of them snorted. He looked at me, pretty little thing with dyed blue hair and badly shaped eyebrows. "The college kid who screams at himself? Who got his ass kicked at Red King and at Alegria? You don't learn do you? He'll rape you into a bloody, shredded heap."

I smirked and held my hand up to his cheek. He jerked it away with a sneer. Yes, he certainly was pretty. I wonder what he would look like with a few more colours on his face.

So I smiled, and then I gently patted his cheek. "Then I accept his challenge."

A puff of blue and purple fire erupted from my hand and quickly swept its flames through the man's face. He screamed, a high-pitched, desperate shriek that tickled and caressed the insides of my ears. Immediately the men holding him dropped him, just as I turned around and swept the other two's faces with my hands, leaving a trail of beautiful blue flames behind me like my hand was a paintbrush.

The entire street erupted into chaos, the three young men screaming and shrieking for their lives, and the ones watching the spectacle giving out cries of shock and fear. I left them all behind me as I walked down the dimly-lit street; the cold, crisp night cooling my burning face underneath the clown mask.

BOOK 3

The Chaos Of A Damaged Mind

CHAPTER 34

"YOU NEED TO WORK NOW?" NERO COMMENTED airily, a blue-embered cigarette in one hand and a pipe in the other. He was laying on Elish's bed, naked and exposed, as his blond brother laid beside him with a laptop balanced on his stomach.

"Yes, I've already wasted enough time this evening," Elish said curtly. He glanced up as Garrett walked out of the bathroom wearing a shining silk robe. "Put that away, it's mine."

"I think I look spiffy," Garrett said evening out the crimson folds. "Do kids still say spiffy? Rio made fun of me for saying spiffy last week."

"Not for about three hundred years," Elish mumbled, typing something into his laptop. "I'm sure if you say it during a few speeches you can bring it back."

Elish held onto the laptop as Garrett jumped onto the bed, landing on his side and bouncing several times before falling still. Elish rolled his eyes and shook his head. "Stay still. I need to get these stupid budgets set by tonight or else no one is getting funding this year."

Nero snorted beside him. He leaned his head onto Elish's shoulder, and as soon as Garrett saw what Nero was doing he did the same. Both brothers watched Elish typing on the laptop, punching numbers into a long complicated grid.

"Let's play Insanaquarium instead!" Garrett said after several minutes of silence. "Come on! It's a fun game."

"No," Elish said irritably.

Nero chuckled and put a hand on Elish's waist, before, with a coy smile, he started to move it down to Elish's groin. "We made you cum like five times and you're still so cranky. What about one more? Come on. I'll take the front, Gare and his talented tongue can take the back."

Elish shook his head. "I'd rather the both of you just go to sleep so I can get my work done. If you're appetites aren't satiated you can go and harass my sengil."

"Loren?" Nero snorted. "The reason you've been summoning both of us so often is because you've been breaking that poor kid's backside. You really miss Silas that much?"

"It's not often he's gone for this long," Elish replied. He brought up the aquarium game and shifted the laptop over so Garrett could play on it. "It's strange not having him around. He's the patriarch of the family after all."

"I don't miss him," Garrett said darkly. "He can be gone for five more months. I will never forgive him for killing Tom. I loved Tom."

"You love every sengil you have," Elish said, raising his shoulder in a futile attempt to get Nero to lift his chin up off of it, though he was unsuccessful. "Now you'll have to wait years to get a new one. We have too many chimeras and not enough sengils to go around."

Garrett made a noise and shook his head. "We should just start enslaving the second generation. Felix has been a complete rude and arrogant ass since he's reached puberty. I thought it would fade in time but he's getting worse. Not to mention Valen and Ludo – oh don't get me started on Ludo."

Then Garrett smiled. "At least Sanguine is doing well, though your plans for him and Jack didn't seem to work out."

"He sucks at matchmaking, eh?" Nero chuckled. "Come here, Sanguine. Come here, Jack. Okay, now if I put you two unstable fucks together surely you'll fall in love and I can have Kingy all to myself."

"Mmhm," Elish said.

"Oh don't play us for retards it's fucking obvious that's what you're trying to do. Didn't work out too well, eh?" Nero continued through a string of laughter. "You should've at least tried to wait until Sanguine stopped talking to himself and gouging holes in his skin before you tried to steer him away from Silas and towards Jack."

A silence fell on the room like someone had draped them with a thick blanket, the only sound coming from the beeps and chirps of the laptop.

"We're your brothers, man. You can admit it," Nero said aloofly, shaking Elish's thigh with his hand. "Everyone knows you love Silas."

"Silas is only treating Sanguine so kindly because he feels guilty," Elish said, there was an edge to his voice that threatened to cut the very air in half. "I was merely making sure he wasn't confusing his guilt for infatuation."

Both Nero and Garrett exchanged amused looks, but it was Garrett who spoke their mutual thoughts aloud. "*Merely* making sure Silas did exactly what you wanted?"

Elish was silent, and at his silence Garrett and Nero laughed some more. Then, at the same time, they kissed Elish's cheek, making the blond chimera's face scrunch in annoyance.

"The sengil usually goes to sleep after relations."

"Crying probably," Nero quipped. "Well, you might've lost out on hooking Sanguine up with Jack but at least you got the puppy out from under the bed. He is doing pretty well considering what Jasper was doing to him."

Garrett's smile immediately turned into a frown. "That poor boy. Can you imagine? He was Drake's age when he took him to that basement. It's just awful, no wonder Silas feels so guilty. Especially after you had him only months before, Nero."

Nero's smile also disappeared as well. He sighed and put his arms behind his head. "Don't fucking get me started. I'm still pissed off about it. I fucking had him. I had him and Silas just said… fuck it."

"Silas had no emotional attachment to the boy," Elish responded, his voice getting slightly defensive. "If Sanguine seemed to be doing well, why would Silas change his mind? If anything it's your fault for taking him to the house near Melchai."

"Hey!" Nero said angrily. He rolled over onto his side and pointed his pipe at Elish. "The fucking town was about to raid his little home base and they would've killed him. Sure I put him near Jasper but it was either that or death. It wasn't like I knew he was there."

Elish shook his head, beside him Garrett raised his head up from Elish's shoulder.

"I sometimes think the poor boy would've been better off dead. He's so miserable and lost. I just want to hug him to death."

"Sanguine's a chimera," Elish said. "He'll be fine as long as people stop sabotaging his progress."

"But he's been doing well in college right?" Garrett said.

Elish nodded. "He is doing well, yes. A good student and he is doing extra to try and make up for starting in the middle of a semester. He's quiet, unlike most of the others."

Nero sighed, and sparked a lighter he had laid next to him. He lit the pipe and started drawing into his lungs the burning hot contents. He held it in and passed it to Garrett before retracting Elish's sheets away from his bottom half.

Nero gently blew the smoke onto Elish's exposed penis before taking it into his mouth and giving the head a lick.

Elish momentarily shut his eyes. "Haven't you had enough?"

"One more… you know I pass out pretty quickly after I do ciovi, just give me one more to help the sandman."

"If you must…" Elish heard the laptop close beside him and Garrett setting it on the side table. Not too soon after Garrett started kissing Elish's chest.

Nero stretched out backwards on the bed and with a curl of his finger he motioned Garrett over. Garrett grinned and grabbed Nero's thigh and eased his leg back and put his mouth over the brute chimera's dick. Then, with a moan from Garrett's lips, he felt Elish's fingers start to ease themselves into his backside.

Nero ran his tongue along the base of Elish's dick, and roughly grabbed onto Garrett's hair before slowly thrusting his hips into his brother's mouth. "You know I got Sanguine's first handjob. Did I ever tell you that story?"

"Several times," Elish murmured before he himself pushed Nero's mouth back down over his stiff member. But as soon as he let go Nero slowly retracted his mouth, before he broke the seal with a pop.

"His cock was so hard. I knew if I even brushed a hand against it it would've cum right then and there. It was rock-fucking-solid, so swollen, and the precum… oh man," Nero groaned before giving the head a generous lick with his tongue. He stroked it a few times before flicking his tongue against the head. "I tell you… so close. So – fucking – close, my body twitched to jump on him because I knew…" Nero let out a gasp as Garrett inserted three fingers at once into his ass. He grabbed onto his knee and pulled his leg back to give Garrett more room. "I knew as soon as he felt my mouth he wouldn't let me… *ah*… stop."

"You should've fucked him," Elish said opening one eye. His fingers still moving in and out of Garrett, though during the conversation another finger had found its way inside of him. "You have my permission... no, you have my urging. Fuck him, let him fuck you, taunt him with fifteen-year-old boys still pure. I don't care. Just don't let him be a virgin when Silas wakes up."

Nero groaned and glanced up at Elish. "You devious fuck. You're going to pit my want, nay, my *need* to see that boy cum for the first time against the fact that I know you only want me to spoil him so Silas can't get to him first?"

"Yes, I am," Elish said closing his eyes again. His fingertips were starting to dig into Nero's neck. "You have the king's permission. Didn't you say he called you upset earlier? You can play best friend supporter. Hell, I'll even let you drug him."

"Fuck, you get so fucking kinky when you're getting laid. Jesus fuck, don't you just love Elish in bed, Gare? I love his naughty mouth." Nero grinned. "And tomorrow morning he's gonna be the same ol' cold-hearted, stick-up-the-ass asshole we love."

"Just shut up and finish," was Elish's response.

Several minutes in, as the intensity grew, all three of them heard a faint knocking on the entrance to Elish's apartment. Nero raised his head but Elish immediately shoved his face back into his groin. With a faint grunt and a push of his hips he started to cum into Nero's suctioned mouth. Immediately Nero groaned, and Elish opened his eyes to see cum spurting from Nero's own cock, being caught in Garrett's mouth. Elish's hand slid down and he batted Garrett's hand away as he rapidly drew him to his peak.

"Who could that even be?" Elish said with a furrowed brow, moving his hand away from Garrett as the chimera started to reach his peak. He checked his wrist watch. "It's three in the morning."

"Perhaps one of the second generation wants to join in the party?" Nero panted, his brow flushed and glistening with sweat. "I'm getting kind of tired though... *fuck*. I barely shot at all, I'm outta cum."

"Master Elish?" a sleepy voice suddenly called; the sengil knocked lightly on the door. "It's Lady Ellis."

The three of them froze, and immediately Elish closed the laptop lid. All of them got up off of the bed, and without waiting to be commanded of it, Garrett took off the red robe and handed it to Elish. He grabbed an older cream-coloured robe instead.

"I need all three of you out here now," Ellis's voice called from the living room. "This is important... very important."

"So important it can't wait until morning? Jesus christ, sissy," Nero said with a grunt, sliding his tan cargo pants over his underwear. Though that was dressed enough for Nero. He opened the bedroom door and walked out, Elish and Garrett following.

"Of everyone in the family it has to be the Boner Killer," Nero said with a huff. "Seriously, *anyone* else and I would've been happy. It just had to be the one without a dick."

Though the brute chimera paused when he saw the serious expression on his sister's face. He glanced to each side, at Elish in his silk red robe and Garrett in the cream-coloured one, and back to Ellis. "What happened...?" Nero said slowly.

"Sanguine torched his apartment tonight..."

The silence that descended on the room was immediately broken by Nero's vicious swearing.

Ellis continued, "He then went to Popkin's demanding for anyone who knows Valen to come forward. Three of Valen's friends were found and restrained... then he lit them on fire and now – and now we have no idea where he is."

"Valentine?" Garrett said surprised. "Why him?"

"We talked to Kirrel and he says it's because of Valen bullying Jack. Valen got Sanguine into his apartment and apparently Sanguine almost got himself killed. I'm not sure what happened tonight but Sanguine snapped it seems," Ellis said. "The apartment's couch and chair need to be replaced and the walls and carpet touched up but besides that the sengils can clean it."

Ellis shifted her weight; her face holding a great deal of stress. "He was wearing a clown mask, Elish. And he was holding that half-rotten bear. His face was covered at least. No one knows it was a chimera." She shook her head. "I think – I think we're losing him again. It sounds like he's completely gone off the deep end. I don't know what happened but something made him snap."

"What about the cat?" Elish suddenly asked. Everyone gave Elish a confused look, obviously not expecting Elish's first question to be about the state of an animal.

"Sanguine's mental state depends on whether he saved the cat before he left," Elish said coldly, looking annoyed at their confused looks. "If he left the cat to die... we have an even bigger problem. If the cat is with him, it means he hasn't completely lost himself."

"Funny you should ask..." Ellis glanced behind her. "You can come in, Kass."

Everyone's attention turned to the ajar door leading to Elish's hallway. A moment later an extremely nervous-looking young man, with an oval-shaped face and short brown hair came in holding a messenger bag.

"As some of you might know this is Sanguine's friend and housekeeper. I haven't had that much time to talk to him. I came here right away. But he has Sanguine's cat and he was the last person to see him before he left to torch Valen's friends," Ellis explained as the young man slowly walked into the apartment.

"Loren... put the cat in your room," Elish said, taking the bag from Kass before addressing the scared housekeeper. "Did Sanguine give you him or did you rescue him from the fire?"

"He threw me out after a fight and after he torched the apartment he walked down to the lobby and handed me Jett," Kass said. He seemed hesitant to give the bag to Loren but he didn't raise any objections. "He looked really unstable, really shaken up." Kass's expression darkened. "Um, I don't know the right protocol for this... can I speak freely or am I going to be tossed into Stadium if I do?"

"You have my permission," Elish responded, his arms crossed over his red robe.

"He has a really warped view of his new family, and the wool is starting to be pulled back. He thought you guys were you know... not... um." Kass coughed and after a moment of choosing his words carefully he seemed to settle on the least offensive. "Dangerous and above the law."

"Interesting opinion, housekeeper," Elish said darkly, but when Kass started sputtering apologies and excuses he raised a hand. "I will spare you the backtracking. We're not idiots and we all know what you mean. What happened to start this?"

Kass shrugged and shifted his weight. "Everything was going good but we started getting on the topic of Valen and his habit of taking bar patrons into abandon buildings to... have relations with." Kass's ears started to redden; he took in a long inhale. "And it bled into how it's rather common knowledge that *some of you* like to roam the streets and do the same. Sanguine flipped out, denying that ever happened and..." The housekeeper gave a nervous laugh. "And I... I obviously, um, thought that was a rather naïve thing to believe."

"Indeed," Elish said coolly; Kass shrunk down even more. The look on his face suggested he would rather be drowning in the greysea than standing in front of four chimeras. "And he–"

"Oh… fuck," Nero suddenly spoke up. His eyes widened and he gave a nervous laugh. "Yeah, Elish. He called me a few hours ago. It was right before you called me over. I was drunk as fuck partying with Ceph. I don't –" Nero held up his hands as Elish glared at him. "You knew I was drunk when you called, bro. You told me to take some Intoxone and get upstairs. I fucking forgot, shit I've still forgotten. He sounded kinda upset though."

"And you don't know what he was upset about? You forgot all of this?" Elish hissed. He looked at Kass before pointing to the door. "You may leave. Tell no one about this meeting. I don't need to tell you what will happen to arians with loose lips."

Kass looked towards the door then back at the chimeras. "Could I help look for him or something? I've really gotten to know him and I'm worried."

"No, get out," Elish said before turning his back to the housekeeper. But as he turned away he saw that Garrett's eyes were bright and full of wonder. Elish glared at the expression and tried to mentally warn him not to voice what was going through his –

"I want him!" Garrett suddenly said, clasping his hands. Elish sighed. "I need a new sengil. I want him. Can I have him?"

Behind Elish Kass's mouth dropped open, before the housekeeper raised his hands and gave a weak laugh. "You gotta be fucking kidding me."

Elish gave Garrett a flat look. "You're only looking for a rebound sengil after Silas murdered Tom. You can get a new one when they age in several years."

Garrett's mouth downturned. "I'm lonely."

"Guys…" Ellis interjected. She was standing by the door looking impatient. "I'm going to the pub, are you coming or is arguing about enslaving arians more important than the brother we all had a hand in messing up?"

"I had no hand in…" Elish paused before waving a hand at Garrett. "Do what you want just have him checked for diseases before you mount him. Ellis, we will meet you down there. I need to change into something acceptable first." His eyes then travelled to Kass who was standing there looking stunned and in shock.

He didn't have a sengil build. He looked like a street rat who happened to find a job in Skyland. But it would be Garrett's reputation that would suffer for having a gutter rat for a sengil, not Elish's.

Elish put a hand on the boy's shoulder and pushed him towards Garrett. "This counts as a birthday present. Enjoy your last moments of freedom, sengil."

The night was cold on Elish's skin, and the breath from his mouth visible, though the vapour was mixed in with the blue-embered cigarette he had between his lips. He was standing outside of Popkin's bar analyzing the burn marks on the ground.

"Where are the three?" Elish asked, taking a pair of white leather gloves out of his grey overcoat. He put them over his hands before running his finger over the burn mark.

Ellis stepped into view and watched as her brother brought his now black-stained fingertips up to his nose. His brow then furrowed and he wiped the fingertips onto his pants.

"In the hospital, their faces are badly burned. They're in a medically induced coma," Ellis explained. "What was it?"

"I thought it was lighter fluid like what he used to torch the apartment but this is moonshine," Elish explained. There was a scraping noise as he dragged his foot along the char marks, seeing several blackened shreds of skin flying up into the air. "It matches the bartender's story, all of it. We won't interrogate the three then."

"So, we…?"

"We see no reason to waste medical supplies on disfigured men. Their lives will be nothing but pain, isolation, and misery and we're still relying too much on scavenged medical supplies for me to want to waste them on men who will contribute nothing to society but being freaks. Kill them and give their bodies to the sengils for food," Elish replied, his eyes still carefully picking apart Sanguine's murder scene.

"What do we tell Valen?"

"I don't care what you tell Valen. Tell him they were executed, exiled, or the truth. I cannot suffer that little shit's attitude for long, so whatever you do just do not send the imbecile to me," Elish said. He glanced over and saw Garrett chatting happily to a terrified-looking Kass. The young housekeeper still hadn't gotten over the shock that in a single evening he had gone from being a free arian to a sengil.

"He's only like this because Silas, and to a lesser extent, the family, has rejected him," Garrett said defensively, turning from his conversation with Kass.

Elish ignored his sister nodding beside him. Ellis crossed her arms over her thien uniform. "Maybe if Valen felt like he belonged somewhere he wouldn't feel like he has to dominate and bully every–"

"I'm running Skyfall I don't need to hear about teenage angst," Elish responded sharply. "I don't think we're going to get anything more out of this scene. Give Mr. Mullins an acceptable cheque for the damage to his tables and make sure he keeps silent about what happened. Has he seen Sanguine before?"

Ellis shook her head. "No, but like I said he was close enough to Sanguine that he knows he's a chimera, the patrons don't though. Mr. Mullins has family in the military and he knows what happens to people who talk… but if Sanguine strikes again…"

The street fell into silence; only the light clicking of Garrett's boots walking around the crime scene could be heard.

"If he strikes again tell me immediately," Elish said.

Suddenly there was a loud crash behind the group. Elish turned around and faced a four-storey abandoned building, with half the windows boarded up and the other half missing entirely. As his eyes narrowed a second crash, this one sounding like sheet metal being dropped at a high distance, met their ears.

"Sanguine," Elish said lowly. He started walking towards the boarded up metal door but Nero put a hand on his shoulder.

"Bro, Sanguine's a stealth chimera… he wouldn't make noise. The kiddo's pissed enough to lay a trap though. I'll go in," Nero said in a low whisper. "He's a shadow, Elish. You, Gare, and Perish designed him that way."

Elish looked back at the tall building, made of grey brick with off-white plaster crumbling between sections. He tried to look inside but his night vision made everything inside a shade of blue, it was impossible to discern shapes.

"We both will," Elish said. "Garrett, keep your new partner close and if you wish to keep him longer than an hour make sure he doesn't follow, even if it is Sanguine." Without another word the two brothers crossed the empty, paved street and climbed up the half-flight of stairs towards the barred metal door.

There was a screeching sound as Nero pulled the nailed board out of the door frame. He tossed it down the steps and kicked the door open.

The brute chimera coughed into his hand as several large pieces of crumbling brick came off of the upper frame, then motioned Elish to follow him.

"Sangy?" Nero called his booming voice bouncing off of the interior walls. "A – pup – pup – pup – *puppy*!"

"Must you?" Elish said irritably.

"He likes it, reminds him of when he was little," Nero said defensively. "Would you prefer *here kitty kitty*?"

"I'd prefer you to act like an adult," Elish responded, his boots crunching against the dirty floor. He looked around the abandoned building, an old warehouse full of rows and rows of rusted machinery and the remains of vagrant camps before the monarchy banished the homeless to Moros and Cypress.

There was nothing worthwhile here, nothing living.

The warehouse was open and exposed, the shelves of machinery sitting stagnant and useless, waiting with an almost lonely desperation for someone to remember it existed. Though the modern civilization that was Skyfall cared little for the skeletonized remains. There would be no repairing this building or its contents. In time it would be stripped of its innards and the forgotten artifacts of old sold for either scrap metal, or thrown into the ocean for the greysea to reclaim.

Elish looked around, seeing cobwebs flickering silver-blue in his night vision, every strand made to look twice its size with the dust of over two centuries of age. Though the stagnant dust was what interested Elish the most. It was all sitting still and undisturbed… which meant the noise had come from deeper inside the warehouse.

Elish followed Nero as the brute chimera walked through the small welcoming area of the warehouse and onto the main floor. To Elish's annoyance he started whistling a tune, dragging his finger along the rusted remains of a forklift.

Then another crash. Nero stopped whistling and motioned Elish over before pointing to a distant door that was wide open in a soundless scream. They walked down several grate steps onto the main floor of the building and started walking past machines.

"Sanguine?" Nero called loudly. "It's Nero, bud."

Then a small voice, not belonging to Sanguine at all.

"I'm stuck, Nero."

Elish's molars ground together and he gave Nero a withering look, obviously for screaming the name of a man Jack wasn't aware existed. He swallowed down the anger burning in his throat and responded curtly, "And how did we manage to get stuck, Jack?"

A sigh could be heard as the two walked up another set of grate steps and into the room they could hear the young chimera's voice in. When Nero saw him he let out a barking laugh, but Elish found himself having to force down even more derisive comments.

Jack was hanging upside down, with his red high top sneaker stuck between two metal joists. He was dangling like a piece of string, his leather jacket and his purple shirt where gravity had left them, covering his face and exposing his pale chest and stomach.

Nero walked over, and because he never could help himself, he started tickling Jack's stomach. Jack immediately squawked and started struggling. "Stop it! I could've broken my damn..." Jack laughed and started thrashing harder as Nero continued to dig his fingers in and tickle the chimera. "Stop it, asshole! I was looking for Sami Fallon. S-stop!"

"Nero!" Elish snapped. "Just get him down... did you see Sami enter in here?"

Nero grabbed Jack's leg, and when Elish had the boy's underarms in his grasp Nero pulled Jack's foot completely out of the shoe and lowered him to the ground.

Jack shook his head as Nero jumped up and un-wedged the shoe from the two joists. "No, I just wanted to explore and see if I saw any sign of him." Then Jack paused and gave them a confused look. "Who's Sanguine?"

"No one," Elish responded in a dangerous tone, a tone that told Jack he wouldn't humour anymore questions about it. "How do you know what Sami did?"

"Ellis called me," Jack said back, rubbing his foot before slipping it back into the shoe. "Asked me if I had seen Sami, and mentioned Popkin's but she was gone when I got here. What happened?"

Elish and Nero both exchanged glances, and because Nero had been around his brother since before he was born, Nero knew to shut up and let the smart one handle it. This was a perfect opportunity to manipulate Jack into feeling affection for Sanguine and the smart brother wouldn't let such a golden opportunity pass.

"A mixture of you ignoring the young man and his hatred for Valen, that's what happened," Elish responded, Nero gave a slight nod beside him but kept his silence. "And now we have a murderer on our hands and we don't know where to find him."

Jack looked up from tying his shoe. "Murderer? Ellis said they were–"

"They will be dead within the hour," Elish responded. "And because Sami once considered you his friend we will be needing your help to apprehend him."

The young chimera stood up and looked around the warehouse nervously. As they started to walk back out onto the street he ran his hand up and down his arm. "I really liked him, Master Elish. But he really hates Valen, and he wasn't afraid of chimeras. I had to distance myself to protect him – I feel so awful about it." Then a silence, followed by a submissive voice. "Why is Silas and the first generation so interested in him? May I ask that?"

"You just did," Elish said, they all started walking down the steps. "And no, you will not ask why, just know it is Silas's wishes to keep the boy safe."

Jack let out a long breath and waited at the bottom of the stairs for Elish and Nero. "What can I do to help? I feel guilty this has happened, Master Elish. He's just a greywaster and he has no idea the trouble he's going to be in for threatening Valen."

The three glanced towards Garrett, Kass, and Ellis talking quietly amongst themselves. Elish stopped before they got into earshot, or at least the earshot of the housekeeper-now-sengil.

"You're semester is going to be cut short," Elish said quietly. "You literally have forever to catch up on your studies. Sami is in Skyfall somewhere and most likely still in Skyland. You're going to be combing the pubs, local hangouts, any place you think he would occupy and find out where he is. You may bring a brother along but besides that the media must not catch wind of this."

Jack stood up a bit straighter and nodded. "I can do that. Sami's shy; he doesn't like large groups and most likely he's going to be staying in one place." But then he paused. "The family won't hurt him if I find him, will they?"

"No," Elish said. He took out another cigarette and lit it with his fingers, then spoke through the smoke. "Silas wants him safe. Sami's safety trumps Valen's. In no way are you to harm him or let Valen or the others harm him. Understood?"

The confusion on Jack's face was palatable. The silver-haired chimera tilted his head to the side before his black eyes narrowed to slits. "He's important... I can see that."

"I will not humour any more–"

"Who is he?"

"Jack." Elish's voice was heavy with warning. A warning that any other chimera would've heeded without question. But Jack's curiosities won out of his seemingly born-in fear of Elish.

"Does Silas want him as a sengil or something?"

Elish walked past Jack towards Ellis, Garrett, and Kass.

"I know he isn't a chimera... obviously. We have none with brown eyes and black hair... so is he a new cicaro? Someone he wanted to train...?"

Elish slowly turned around and this time Jack visibly shrunk down. Elish's eyes burned into him with the power of a violet sun, and three times the intensity.

Though no words left Elish's lips, none were needed. Jack was frozen in place, his mouth tight and his shoulders square. And there he stayed where Elish's frozen gaze had left him, not another question falling from his lips

CHAPTER 35

I STAYED IN THE BACK OF THE DEN; BARRY WAS sitting opposite of me with a glass of water between his grungy, matted paws. I had ordered the water for myself and when the young boy had brought me a piece of taffy-like black substance I had sent it back and told him again: water.

Water meant something else here apparently.

My eyes focused to behind Barry. It was a strange sight to behold, because it seemed on first glance that I was in a morgue of sorts, but it wasn't that at all.

The men behind me, outstretched like corpses, with grey skin and sharp bones exposed, were not dead, they were opiate addicts and this was an opiate den.

The den itself was filthy, completely covered in un-washed, rank-smelling blankets from wall to wall, and also on the dirty mattresses that held the addicts in their cradles like cadavers on slabs. This place was disgusting, but not as disgusting as the people who writhed inside.

I looked over at a man half-naked, a skeletal face and missing teeth, his lips blackened by the tar and his left eye missing. He was staring off into space was a smile on a mouth that seemed made for frowning. At that moment, as I watched him, a cockroach crawled onto a scraggly beard and danced along his lips as if hoping to find food for it to eat.

With a shake of my head I took a drink of my water and pulled my hoody back over my head. Underneath that hoody was a red baseball cap that I had managed to tuck my black hair back into.

I still had my colour contacts. And though I had lost several of my tooth caps, I had saved the important ones in my pockets; the ones that hid the front pointed fangs. It had been enough to get by; enough to not rouse suspicion as I hid from my former family and the chimeras I knew would be stalking my steps.

But I knew they would never look for me here, and though when I had first found and entered this rank, decrepit place I had told myself it was only because no chimera would step foot in it, there was another, more personal reason.

I took in a deep breath, filling my lungs with the smell of stale sweat, unwashed bodies, dirty blankets and fabric that had been soaked and re-dried many times, all mixed in with the slight scent of stagnant urine and insects.

It reminded me…

It reminded me of the basement.

The young boy, probably only sixteen, walked up to me. He had glassy eyes that were brown and he was boney and thin, with a dirty mop of brown hair that matched the dirt stained on his neck.

"Can I get you… something?" the boy asked quietly. He glanced behind him and I looked to see an old man with angular eyes giving me a glaring look, behind him were two little girls with the same eyes, must be his daughters.

I shook my head. "Water's fine."

The boy didn't move but I saw a nervous expression cross his face. He moved on the spot like he was uneasy, or perhaps he was just high. Though the brown, sticky stuff seemed to sedate them rather than make them jittery. Perhaps this kid was on meth; Jasper had always liked meth.

"Look, I don't want Giuseppe to get pissed at me. This is a business, mister. You need to order some drugs or… he's going to kick you out," the boy whispered, stuffing his hands into his pockets and glancing behind him again. I looked too and saw Giuseppe's slanted eyes glaring at me, the two daughters standing on either side glaring at me too.

At first anger flared in me and I wanted nothing more than to dig into my bag and fling my black card at him, but that wasn't something I could do anymore. One transaction from the Sanguine Sasha Dekker black card and I would have Nero barrelling in here and dragging me out by the neck.

Though I hadn't been completely stupid. As soon as I had burned those three Valen sympathizers I had gone to the bank and withdrawn a large amount of money in cash. I had used it to buy a black satchel and a wallet and that was where my cash was being kept.

I shrugged and leaned back in my chair. The boy looked relieved as I started to open my satchel to get a few smaller bills. "What do you have?" I really wasn't interested in trying drugs; I never had since dealing with Jasper. But the negative association I had with Jasper doing and creating meth had faded since coming here. I had no moral dilemma; I had just never been interested.

"Everything..." The boy turned around and nodded at Giuseppe. Giuseppe nodded back and disappeared behind a water-stained curtain, his daughters following behind. "Opium, heroin, meth, weeder, twinkle, cocaine, opiate pills, ciovi. We have hallucinogens, PCP, and ecstasy but you're not allowed to take them, or any of the other uppers, inside of the den. This area is allowed only for downers, since – since the uppers tend to want to start fights."

I lit a cigarette and suddenly the boy's eyes widened. "A Blueleaf? You're from Skyland?"

I gave him a questioning look and moved the cigarette to the side of my mouth so I could speak. "Am I not in Skyland?"

The boy's expression got even more bewildered. It looked like I was digging myself a hole. I had assumed I was still in Skyland but I had been wandering around for days now looking for a dark place to hide.

"No... you're in the Cypress District, and we're near the south wall that separates us from Moros," the boy replied. Well, that made sense; I had climbed over a few walls that had been blocking the path my mind had absentmindedly set out for me. I guess it was obvious the districts would be separated by walls. I had never been out of Skyland so I had had no idea.

The boy looked behind him again, as if making sure Giuseppe was out of earshot. "You better not let him see you smoking Blueleafs. If a Skylander is here it means he's hiding from the thiens or the Dekker's and your bounty is more important than a few dollars revenue."

Immediately I took the cigarette out of my mouth and pinched the flame. But as I did I realized this boy was doing me a favour, and I needed someone to do me favours right now. Kass had been my unofficial sengil and I could use someone knowledgeable of the area.

So I took my pack of Blueleaf cigarettes and pushed it towards him. "If anyone asks questions, tell me first. Especially your boss, capeeshy?"

The boy picked up the smokes and stuffed them into a pair of tan pants that were belted with an extension cord. He nodded and looked behind him again. "Sure, I guess I can do that. So... did you want some drugs then?"

I shrugged and nodded. "Yeah, opium I guess." And then I said something I never thought I would say. Ever.

"And bring me a few bags of meth... for later," I smirked, but when the boy turned around and headed towards the stained curtains Giuseppe had disappeared to, the smirk faded and I glanced over at Barry.

He didn't speak, talk to me, or advise me, but his black eyes still stared at me with an expression of sadness.

"Why not see what it was like for him?" I said defensively, dragging the water glass over to me. "He did it a lot; he made it in the farmhouse. I'm an adult; I don't need to fucking steer away from his drug like he has some weird control over me still. Jasper has no more control over me, just like Silas and Elish and all of them don't. I'm my own fucking man. Fuck that rapist, hypocrite family and fuck Jasper too."

Barry stared at me. I let out a frustrated grunt and turned his head away so he couldn't judge me anymore.

I crossed my arms and looked away, though after several moments I felt a spring of loneliness inside of me. I picked up Barry and hugged him to my chest, watching the man a few feet from me give a groan, before flicking a cockroach off of his face.

I squeezed Barry and with that another pang of loneliness. I missed my friends, I even missed Crow. When bad things like this happened and I found myself alone again... they had always been there for me. First Barry as a boy and then Crow as my black-clad, demon-eyed monster friend. They may have told me to do bad things sometimes but that didn't take away from the fact that no matter what – those two had always been there for me.

And I had let Barry kill himself after the first time Jasper had fucked me, and I had told Crow to piss off for warning me of the truth: that I deserved to be locked up, that I was incapable of functioning in society.

As much as I had wanted to be in denial that day, when I was new and in college and ready to take on the world as a chimera, or at least Sami Fallon the secret chimera, in the end the proof was all around me.

I couldn't function in society.

"Here you go," the young man came back. He placed four overstuffed bags of meth onto the covered patio table I had been sitting at, and then a smaller bag holding the black tarry stuff. "Fifty dollars for everything. I can take back some of the meth if the cost is too high."

I shook my head no and brought out a new fifty dollar bill. I slid it towards the kid, and when he had stuffed it inside of a worn fanny pack over his waist he dug deeper into the pack and pulled out a little red tube-like device.

"Pin-sized amount, stick it on the needle and click the back until you smell or see the heat, and then put your mouth over it and suck it up," the boy explained in a tone that suggested he was reading a script inside of his head. "One hit will do you for hours; feel free to lie down if you can find a spot. You're welcome to stay but after ten you have to pay five bucks to spend the night. Is that okay?"

"Yeah, I'm a quick learner…" I said, before giving him a nod. "What's your name?"

"Frank," the boy said with a smile, but when I laughed the smile turned into a frown. "What's wrong with Frank?"

I gave him a wave and started rolling off a piece of the brown tar. "Where I'm from all the cute little teenagers have cute little names. I think the family names them I'm not sure. Frank just seems like a thick-necked greywaster with a beard, not a twiggy little guy like yourself. Do you at least go by Frankie?"

He shook his head, not looking too pleased with my laughter over his name. "No, Giuseppe calls me *leng zai* sometimes which I think means something in his ancient language, but no just… well, just Frank."

I wasn't planning on calling a scraggly little kid Frank that was for sure. "I'm going to call you Mouse."

Mouse's frown deepened. "You're not really getting us off to a good start," he said flatly but with a loud sigh he shook his head. "But I've been called worse. What about you? What name do you have that I can make fun of?"

The thought of telling him my full name just to see the shock on his face was tempting, but I knew that really wasn't an option. Arians immediately obeyed me when they found out I was a chimera and since I was just another drug-seeker in a shitty den I knew he didn't owe me anything and had no reason to be friendly with me. I had to become his friend the old fashion way, without fear, intimidation, and class-status.

Though as I opened my mouth to tell him my name was Sami I

immediately closed it and realized I couldn't tell him that name either. Both of my names were now known to the family.

Mouse sat down and rested the side of his face into his hand. I didn't think the expression on his face could get any flatter but there it was. "Does it really take you that long to think of a fake name?" He laughed at the surprised expression on my face. "It's okay it's typical for a customer to use a fake name ... why don't I name you then? I'd like to name you nosey jackass, but I think you're kinda cute so how about I call you Pumpkin?"

Pumpkin? I glared at him, feeling rather matched. He seemed like a meek, quiet little mouse but the more he became comfortable with me the more I realized he had quite the sharp tongue.

"You'll not be calling me Pumpkin," I said flatly. When Mouse pulled out a pack of normal red-embered cigarettes I stole one from him and rested it beside my opium smoker. I had given him a pack of Blueleafs so I dared him to raise objections. "Anything but Pumpkin."

"Sure, whatever you say, Pumpkin." Mouse winked and nudged the opium smoker towards me. "After a hit of that you'll be agreeable to anything. Have a smoke and relax, I'm off of work soon so I'll join you in a bit if you're willing to share."

I saw nothing wrong with that. Mouse helped the loneliness that Barry the boy and Crow's absence brought. So I nodded and picked up the opiate smoker, and clicked the igniter button.

My entire body was warm, like a blanket of tepid water had been laid over top of me. I don't remember much of what happened after my first hit, only that I couldn't stop running my hands up and down my body, and that everything seemed amplified when I closed my eyes.

I was in a corner with Barry beside me. I could see his paw with its dirty, formerly cream-coloured paw pad. Since Barry was here I was okay.

Sometime during the first day Mouse had lain down beside me, and I had heard the click as he took his own hit from the opium pipe.

I remember when he started running his fingers up and down my arms and chest, and in response, I did the same to him. His eyes were bloodshot and distant, and his mouth slightly slacked. A faint glisten of sweat was on his brow and it made his unhealthy brown hair stick to it.

"Want to make out?"

I must've nodded because he kissed me after. I opened my own mouth and welcomed his lips, but when his hand travelled lower I had grabbed it and pulled it away. He had respected that and time was lost again with our lips joined and our hands running up and down the upper parts of our bodies. Never touching too low, I didn't want that feeling… I just wanted the pleasure that being caressed on this drug gave me.

It was a wonderful feeling, each gentle stroke leaving an illuminated trail of welcome sensations. I could see the bright path of his fingers even though my eyes were closed; they left an invisible trail that I could retrace on his skin.

Everything was haze after that, beautiful thick haze. Haze that stretched on for days, weeks, or maybe only minutes. Though I think it was a long time. Eventually though I saw a break in the fog and in that break I felt a cold hand on my forehead, followed by a wet cloth.

I smiled as it slowly stroked my cheek. I opened my eyes, they felt heavy and weighted down with sand, and looked at Mouse's face.

"Hey, Pumpkin, feeling good?" Mouse said quietly, behind him one of the girls was holding a blue plastic wash bucket. She was standing so completely still I thought she might be a statue. Her face was smooth and her eyes dark and cold, I reached out to touch them but she was too far away.

My head dropped, it hit the mattress and I could feel a loose spring digging into my neck. I winced and nodded slowly before squinting my eyes. As I came back into reality I realized they were raw and itchy. They felt like a bag of sand had been poured on them and I didn't know why.

"Good… we're fine now," Mouse said to the girl. She nodded and left my vision. I squinted again and rubbed my eyes.

"Don't rub your eyes," Mouse said. "You have an infection… I have no idea what but it's turned the colour parts of your eyes red. Just close your eyes. I took some of your money to find a doctor. I think you might be allergic to this stuff, I'm not sure."

What a weird… weird infection.

Then in my drug-induced delirium my eyes opened wider. I tried to sit up but the comforting, fuzzy warmth of the drug urged me back down onto the mattress. The water-stained pillow looked welcoming, still holding the shape of my head with Barry and my satchel only a few feet away.

"No… no doctor…" I mumbled. I rubbed my eyes and squinted them and, sure enough, I could only feel one contact in my eye. The same one that was irritated and raw. I closed my natural crimson eye and looked at Mouse. "I need an apartment... I need to... rent an apartment. I'll pay you to help me."

Mouse gave me a concerned look but after a moment he nodded. "Okay, I can help you with that but Giuseppe will kill me if he finds out. He's been enjoying running up your tab. Give me a couple hours to talk to some friends and I'll come back with a shack for you. Are you fucking sure you don't need a doctor? Seriously, blood-fucking-red, not the whites, dude, the like... the coloured parts."

"I'm sure, I'll be fine," I mumbled and laid my head back down onto the pillow. I grabbed Barry and squeezed him to my chest, and in my drugged-up state, I wished for nothing more than for my old friend to talk to me again. To be alive and tell me stories like in the old days.

Old days, when I was a kid. The happy times.

Happy times when I was in the greywastes and my own person, before I found out I belonged to this stupid family. Fucking jerks... how could they think raping anyone they wanted was okay? How could they see what Jasper did to me as wrong but it was laughed about when Valen or the others stalked and fucked anyone they wanted when they were bored?

Though as I said this my eyes opened again. Oddly after several days inside of this den, the shock of what my family did seemed numbed almost. The wound still stung but it was farther away than it used to be, to the point where my brain was telling me... that perhaps I had overreacted.

Had I? I closed my eyes again and saw Nero in my head. I missed Nero, and I missed Jack even though he hated me.

I missed King Silas especially... even though it was him who'd lied to me.

Well, whatever, the opium was more appealing than thinking about my stupid family or my even stupider life in the greywastes. So I closed my eyes, got comfortable with Barry and let the opium blanket take me away.

The next time I was roused I found myself completely dazed. My head felt like it had been sliced open, then someone with a giant scoop came and scooped up my brain, then replaced it with... with fuzzy foam but not like the mattress foam but like the puffy white cotton that I picked out of the Tylenol bottle but lots of it all squished together like... like someone had come with a giant scoop and brained my head and replaced the scoop with… with white cotton.

Like that.

Mouse looked at me and chuckled. I heard Giuseppe in the background.

"Leave him there. He's bringing a lot of money in for me."

Mouse lifted me up and helped steady me. "His eyes are getting worse. My sister is coming to look at him. You said yourself we can't have him die here and if he goes blind here eventually someone will kill him."

Giuseppe said something angrily in his language as he walked me towards the door. I looked down with only one eye open and made sure I was holding Barry and my black bag. I should probably give the bag a name. I always felt bad when things didn't have names. They were forgotten more easily that way, just like that couch that gets forgotten in the greywastes and then gets rained on and it's sad. Remember that?

I remembered that.

My brow wrinkled when I felt the cold air on me. It was a shock to my lungs but my nose had gotten used to the smell of unwashed bodies and opium smoke. I inhaled loudly and grinned before looking at Mouse.

"Smells nice outside, eh?"

Mouse shook his head. "You're paying me for this, just so you know. I'm charging you ten bucks a day to look after your Skyland ass."

"I could just make you a sengil, then I wouldn't have to pay you shit," I slurred, stumbling down the sidewalk. Most of the buildings surrounding me were dark and unlit, and others missing entire sections of wall so only the metal beams were sticking out. I could see the plastic hanging off of those beams.

I reached out to touch it but it was too far away. Instead I rubbed my arms.

"Only chimeras get sengils," Mouse said, laughing an amused laugh that lasted too long. "And only greywasters get slaves, though I think that's illegal now. We have a ton of underground slavery in Cypress and Moros though, but you'll have to enslave them first and I'm still young enough to fight you off, Pumpkin."

"Not when I was in my prime," I mumbled. I stepped off of the road as Mouse directed me across the street, then I stumbled on the curb but thankfully managed to keep my balance. "Hey, any news reports on me yet?"

Mouse's head shot to me. He blinked and raised an eyebrow, he looked like he was about to comment on something but instead he clamped it shut and took my arm. "We're almost to your new house. It's a bit of a pit but it's a nice size for three people."

He led me behind a single-storey building that had white writing painted onto the door, though it was too worn to see. He then disappeared into the alleyway and I heard chain-link fence start to get moved around. I wandered to the front of the building and looked inside, but saw nothing but garbage-covered concrete and in the distance a collapsed interior ceiling. Everything looked gutted, even the walls were gone, probably copper thieves or scavengers looking for things to sell.

It reminded me of the greywastes though, I kept looking in and smiled to myself as I imagined me being seven years old again, climbing into these buildings and searching for food and shelter. I knew I was looking at my childhood with rose-coloured glasses but, damn, at least shit was simple back then.

"Okay, I have my sister inside waiting for you; you're going to be living in our house. Her name's Julia," Mouse said, grabbing my arm and pulling me towards the alley. I said goodbye to the window with the faded writing and let him drag me wherever my new home was.

I sniffed and started opening my black satchel to get my opiate pipe. I grabbed it as I walked and was happy to see I could still get one more hit out of it.

"Here he is..." I heard Mouse say in a low whisper. "I don't know which one he is... I just know he is one."

"Then why the fuck do you have him!" a female voice hissed, another hand grabbed my arm and both of them walked me down a dirt path with flattened brown grass on either side. I looked up and saw a small home with boarded up windows, coated in chipped yellow paint and white trim along the window frame. It had a front porch too but the railing had fallen down at some point in time. It was nice though; there was even a rusted car in the yard for me to play in.

"Because Giuseppe isn't stupid. He was going to find out sooner or later..." Mouse hissed back. "Not to mention when he gets high... he lets shit slip. He's a bad liar when he's on opium."

"Who?" I said out loud. Oddly Mouse pushed the pipe into my mouth and lit the end of it. I saw a lady with long brown hair and the same eyes as Mouse; kind of buggy and with dark circles.

"Nothing, Pumpkin, take another hit," Mouse said calmly before addressing the female again.

"What's his name?" Julia asked. They both helped me inside the old house.

"I just call him Pumpkin and he calls me Mouse," Mouse replied as I looked around the small but cozy house. It smelled like the must that makes your skin itch, like the itch of pink insulation when you ran your hands along it. I didn't think a smell could itch but here I was.

I wandered into the kitchen which was a simple galley kitchen with old yellow cabinets, a checkered countertop and a worn wooden table that wobbled when I moved it with my hand. I was feeling dizzy from the opiate though so I sat down on a chair and faced the living room. The carpet was so many different shades of mustard yellow I wasn't sure which one was the real one; the lights giving off yellow glows didn't help either.

I think I would call this the yellow house.

"What's wrong with his eyes? I thought you said he just had an infection," Julia hissed to her brother as she dragged him out of the kitchen and into the dining room.

"His eyes are naturally red, he got a hold of some colour contacts," Mouse whispered, craning his head backwards to make sure the chimera wasn't listening. "They fell out while he was spending the last week high out of his mind."

"Why is he here!" Julia said putting a hand on her head. "You have a chimera, why, why do you have a chimera? What are we supposed to do with him?"

"I… I haven't thought that far ahead," Mouse admitted. "I was thinking of ransoming him out to Elish but then I realized–"

"That was a fucking suicide mission?" Julia snapped. "You need to give him to Elish, drop him off anonymously to a thien station and pray that they don't realize you had him. There is no good end to this, Frank. You need to separate yourself from him."

"I can't," Mouse said shaking his head. "He has a fucking bag full of money. I've been able to feed myself and you, and rent–"

Julia groaned. She put a hand on her head and brushed back her brown hair. "That's where you've been getting the money from. From him?"

Mouse nodded and pursed his lips. "The satchel is full of money, sis.

More money than we make in five years."

"Take it from him and we can leave... now." Julia took a step towards the living room but Mouse grabbed her arm.

"He's high, he isn't retarded. He'll know it's me when he sobers up and he'll kill both of us. He's stupid when he's stoned but once sober... you've fucking seen the chimeras as I have. Nero ripped the spine out of a convict just last Saturday," Mouse said grimly.

Julia leaned against a wooden dresser that was missing its top drawer. She had the distinct look of a woman who would rather be anywhere than where she was right now. "You got yourself into some shit, Frank."

But Mouse shook his head at this, though if that was from pure denial or actually disagreeing was anyone's guess. "No, I ran into luck. Look, he knows I'm skimming some money to take care of him and he's cool with it. So I'm not stealing from him. Why don't I just keep taking care of him and we can eat and pay our rent with it. He's happy and I'm happy..."

"And when they money runs out?" Julia challenged.

Mouse opened his mouth to respond but closed it. He sighed. "I told you I haven't had that much time to think. He'll get more, right? They have money..."

"They have black cards that can be traced which is why he has cash on him." She glanced back into the living room and saw the chimera sitting on a wooden chair staring at the living room, a string of drool dribbling down his stubbled face. The chimera was completely out of it, looking like someone who had escaped from a mental institution with how he was gripping that dirty teddy bear.

"I wonder why he's hiding?" Julia said slowly, feeling a small pull towards the obviously sick chimera. "I've never seen him on the news or in Stadium and King Silas is always showing off the new babies or brought in family members. Every Stadium for the last year has had Drake doing his little magic tricks or Kessler and Nero sword fighting."

Mouse looked too, his face adopting a similar expression. "He's nice... he's really nice and friendly. If he wasn't maybe I would have taken that money and ran. But... he's also kinda nuts. He talks to that bear like it's a talking person and he seems really... sad, I guess."

They were both silent, watching the chimera with sympathetic expressions.

"Maybe the family rejected him or something?" Mouse suggested. "Or they've been abusing him? Fuck, sis. I'll show you later but... his arms, legs, torso... all covered in scars, scars on top of scars. The Dekker's are so private about their lives, how do we know what it's like there?"

Julia's expression hardened. "It doesn't matter, Frank. He might be nice but Elish isn't and neither is Silas once he gets back. We have a chimera and no matter how nice he is – he isn't going to be the one sending us to Stadium."

"We need the money... we could afford heat this year instead of spending all day at the shelters," Mouse said slowly. "We could have heat and food... we could afford a shuttle to Eros and we can try and get jobs. Fuck, Julia... this is our chance. I might not have a good end game... but right now we have free money and all we have to do is keep him safely hidden and high out of his mind. We're not doing anything wrong; we're just doing exactly what a chimera is asking us to do. Isn't that the law?"

"You're grabbing at straws..."

"Isn't that the law? Do what a chimera says?"

Julia went silent, her eyes never leaving the red-eyed man. He was still staring into space, closing one eye but he was now closing the wrong eye. A single crimson ocular was staring at the turned off television, glassy and unfocused but still showing off his chimera status.

"He would be in more danger at Giuseppe's –" Julia said slowly, more to herself than her brother. "– wouldn't he?"

Mouse nodded. "And if he was high and in Cypress or Moros... he would've been robbed and raped, probably murdered. We're doing good here... it benefits him and it benefits us."

Julia still didn't look sure, but even though her eyes were full of fear and her stance rigid, she nodded her head. "Okay... as long as no one knows we have him... and we can keep him either drugged or sleeping. But what happens when the money runs out? We can't afford to keep him after."

"We'll sober him up and ask him," Mouse said with a half shoulder shrug. "We've been living day-to-day since we left Edgeview. Why are you stressing out about something months in the future? In three months it will be spring and we'll be better off anyway."

"This could get us killed..."

"Artemis was on the news saying we're heading towards a cold snap. We could get killed outside in the cold or raped in the shelters trying to keep warm. You know this is worth the risk."

Finally Julia nodded. Mouse smiled back and clapped her shoulder. "This is a good thing. We're doing a good thing for him too." Mouse then picked up a worn patchwork blanket lying on the back of a chair in the kitchen and walked towards the half-awake chimera.

CHAPTER 36

JACK GLANCED UP AT THE CLOSED DOOR OF HIS bedroom. He knew it was locked but every once in a while he just had to make sure no one could disturb him. It seemed his entire life he had been being disturbed, the first memory he had was trying to pin a black curtain over his crib because Apollo and Artemis were always watching him and giggling amongst themselves. The twins had each other but Jack always preferred his own quiet company, though since Artemis and Apollo were identical in almost every way, maybe it could be said they also preferred their own company.

Jack let out a small sigh, before smiling as Jett tried to bat the paintbrush out of his hand. The cat was already sporting a small dab of red paint above his eye, and Jack just knew by the end of the evening he would be a canvas himself.

He smiled and went back to his painting, ignoring the laughing and carrying on of his brothers in the living room.

At one point in time in this new world, green and blue paint was probably the most important of paints. People must have bought it in bucket loads to paint their pretty trees, blue oceans, and sapphire skies... but now it was grey paint that Jack was constantly running out of. It was only when he was doing portraits did he end up using those more vibrant colours.

Just then a high pitch laugh, belonging to Valen, sounded from the living room. Jack sighed again, feeling his lips press together. He wanted to put on his earphones and listen to his Mp3 player instead of their loud conversations, but he needed warning if one of them decided to bother Jack in his room. He would fry their faces if needed be, he wasn't in the mood tonight to deal with half-drunk chimeras even if it was only Valen and Rio coming to visit Artemis and Apollo.

Jack hated having roommates; they were the bane of his existence. Though until Jack proved himself to King Silas he was stuck having to live with at least two of his brothers. At least Silas had been nice enough to let him room with Apollo and Artemis who were usually fairly quiet. They kept to themselves as they had real jobs and were no longer attending school, but that being said they were social and enjoyed visiting with the family. Jack would rather be left alone; a cat or a dog for conversation was good enough.

"Aren't you?" Jack smiled waving the paintbrush for Jett to bat at. Their old family basset hound Bingo had passed away last year and it had left a hole in Jack's heart. He had loved that droopy dog with all of him. Jett was a bit frisky for Jack's taste but he would grow out of it like most cats did.

"And now… we try and add the red…" Jack murmured to himself. He gently covered his paint brush with the red paint he had painstakingly been mixing and started to colour in the red tricycle he had added to the painting.

It was of the greywastes, a crater that had at one point been a large lake. He had come across it exploring the Dead Islands with Felix and Rio and had been struck with how vast and deep it was. There had been so many treasures at the bottom of it; he had even found a small rusted anchor and a statue that was in fairly good condition.

The tricycle wasn't there though; Jack had added that from his own imagination. The greywastes were so grey and monotone; there was rarely any colour unless you came across a fresh carcass. Jack had contemplated adding the remains of a rat or perhaps a biigo, but had decided the contrast of adding a red tricycle would be the most beautiful. Adding something as innocent as a child's first bike made the dreary, cut-throat greywastes seem more humanized.

He had gotten the idea when he had been with Sami Fallon…

Jack sighed again, gently stroking the paintbrush over the outline he had already made.

Sami had been raised in the greywastes, though somehow he had gotten King Silas's attention enough for the king to want to bring him here. He was still every bit a greywaster though, Jack had been realizing this more and more each day.

And each incident…

Jack had been out all day looking for Sami, but it was difficult to get the bartenders and restaurant owners to talk to him. The word of what happened at Popkin's had spread as fast as the fire on Valen's friend's faces.

Another laugh outside of Jack's door.

No one had told Valen yet that his friends were dead. It was Elish's job and Elish would do it when he felt like it. Valen was rather uninformed about what was going on, all he cared about was finding Sami and a part of Jack wished that he would find him first just so he could get his face lacerated.

Everyone in Skyland was on alert now for Sami, and though several people had made offhanded comments about 'setting the little fucker straight' Jack and Ceph had both been extremely *persuasive* in letting it be known that Sami wouldn't be hurt. He was important to the king (though Jack still didn't know why) and he had to be held unharmed, perhaps just restrained a little.

Those had been Jack's exact words when he had been talking to Jenardo at the Jamaica Bake'Ah downtown, a popular place for the family. Ceph had had a grand laugh at the thought of someone being able to restrain a man who lit three people on fire but… Jack knew Sami's heart and he knew he was just upset. Sami didn't want to hurt people; he just… really didn't like Valen.

"I guess me trying to save him from the family's wrath kinda backfired, huh?" Jack said out loud, petting in between Jett's ears. "At least he saved you though. Elish says that's a good sign that Sami is just having a breakdown and hasn't completely lost his mind. I should still be out there looking for him but… no one will let me go out at night."

And at this thought Jack frowned. "Even though I know he wouldn't hurt me."

Jett looked at him before squinting his eyes, almost the same way Sami used to when he was smiling. That man had this way of smiling without showing his teeth that looked so adorable. It had made Jack's heart skip when he smiled like that in his apartment.

"Bah!" Jack hissed at himself before giving his head a shake. He tried to push the warmth away from his heart but whenever he thought of Sami it just filled right back up again. It was dangerous to let himself feel that way towards someone like Sami. Silas might like him but if Sami did something to Valen, like him or not, he would be put into Stadium or just executed outright.

No, I can't let my feelings for him grow... I have to protect him. He's such a fucking nice, innocent person. I can't let my family taint that. As if to show himself what he meant he dipped the tip of the red paintbrush into a glass of clean water and watched the red swirls start to disappear into the clear liquid. Soon it became a clouded pink, and after he washed his other brushes, the pink would turn a dreary brown.

Like everything else in my life right now...

Jack finished washing his brushes and put his painting away. His stomach was pleading with him for food but not enough to show his face to his brothers outside. They should all be leaving soon at least, unless Valen got drunk and decided it was the right time for an orgy.

So instead he shut the lights off and put on a movie to distract himself before bed, making mental plans on where he was going to search tomorrow, and as the night went on fantasizing about what he would say to Sami when he saw him. Though in his fantasies he was as smooth talking as Rio and as suave as Garrett, not the socially awkward, shy idiot he knew he was in real life.

Sometime during the night there was a small knock on his door. Jack's teeth clenched in vexation.

"What?" Jack said in the most unimpressed, annoyed voice he could muster.

"I tired out the twins, let me in, I need a few more rounds," Valen's drunk voice sounded from the other side of the door. The doorknob then rattled as he tried to get in.

"No, piss off," Jack said angrily. "I'm not touching you anymore, I fucking said that."

"Come on, shithead!" Valen said angrily, the doorknob rattled some more before he pounded a fist on the door. "Come on, let me in! I'll be quick, just give me that ass for a few minutes."

"Fuck off!" Jack snapped, throwing off the covers. He jumped out of bed and when he got to the door he slammed on it himself. "Piss off, I'm not touching you. You're a piece of shit, I fucking hate you. Fuck off. Do you understand me, Valentine?"

"Hey!" Valen snarled, now desperately trying to pull the locked door open. "You want me to tie you up again, freak? I know where the master key is and Silas isn't home, you little bitch." Then with another bang on the door, this one sounding like it was him kicking it, there was silence.

Then the distinct sound of the door leading to the hallway slam, and at this Jack's heart dropped.

He was going to get the master key, and since Valen was stronger than him he knew he was going to get fucked tonight.

A ball formed inside Jack's throat; he tried to swallow it down but it stayed there and grew, restricting his air and making his head swim. The last thing he needed was Valen fucking him again; he just wanted to be left alone. Why was that so much to ask?

And why am I such a coward about it? Jack thought to himself as he sat on the bed. He stared down at his hands and hated himself for seeing them both visibly shake.

Sami was right, the entire family was right… I'm just a coward.

Even when he was younger he was a coward, letting Ceph tease him and Apollo and Artemis outsmart him at every turn. Valen had been his friend when he was little but when Silas rejected him at fifteen he had changed into the prick he was now. Now Valen joined the entire family in their collective disappointment with him.

Not wanting to remain in the room to await Valen coming back with the master key, Jack got up and grabbed a set of clothes for the morning, then snuck out of the apartment and into the stairwell. It was a coward's move, but he expected little more from himself. So with the disappointment in himself growing he climbed the stairs and headed towards Elish's apartment.

He opened the door and slunk inside of the dark apartment. He stopped to listen, just to make sure Elish wasn't with one of his brothers, but when the apartment offered nothing but the low ear-itching buzzing of electronics he closed the door behind him and tiptoed over to Elish's room.

Jack loved and respected Elish, the entire family adored and feared him, and Jack knew he wouldn't mind the company. What he might mind though was being woken up in the middle of the night when he had to continue being king in the morning. So Jack quietly opened the door and looked inside.

Jack's heart jumped with relief when he saw Elish sleeping alone. Loren's bedroom door down the hallway was closed too which meant he hadn't woken up the sengil either.

"Jack?" Elish mumbled. Jack jumped under the sudden voice; he could feel the room get cold as he felt Elish's piercing gaze on him.

"What is it?" Elish said, his eyes black slits under the blue-hued darkness.

"I just wanted to get away from Valen," Jack said meekly. "I don't feel like fighting tonight and I want to be up early to keep looking for Sami. May I please sleep with you? Or at least the couch?"

Elish looked at him in a way that told Jack he was strongly debating throwing him out of the apartment, but he ended up relenting with a nod. "You may sleep in here."

Jack smiled faintly, feeling relieved. "Thank you, I know I'm supposed–"

Suddenly the door to the apartment opened. Jack whirled around and felt his heart drop as Valen scanned the room before his eyes focused on Jack.

"What are you doing here!? Come to get Kinny to guard you?" Valen laughed, his rosy eyes were glassy and his face flushed. Jack was confused for a moment before he realized Valen's tipsy mind must've sent him to Elish's apartment since he was technically king now, not Silas's.

Valen sauntered in with a grin on his face, before raising a hand and beckoning Jack with his finger. "Come to daddy, you're only making me want you more, Jacky."

"Valen?" Elish rose to his feet; he looked annoyed and angry. Jack backed away from the doorframe and let Elish walk past. "What the hell do you think you're doing in my apartment?"

Valen paused, looking surprised and confused at Elish being there, but a moment later his eyes hardened and a sneer appeared on his face.

"Silas says to stay out of the second generation's hierarchy," Valen snapped. The attitude made Jack's mouth drop open. No one spoke to Elish in this way but King Silas. What was wrong with him?

"I care little what–"

"Yeah, well he's still king and he says I can do whatever I want with these fucks," Valen snarled. "So butt out of my business."

Jack felt faint. He quickly got into the shadows, and far out of Elish's line of sight. He didn't know if it was the alcohol or what but he knew the remaining minutes of Valen's life could be counted on his fingers.

Sure enough, Elish flicked the lights on; Jack could see a flicker of hesitation in Valen's eyes.

"You dare speak to me like that?" Elish said in a cold, frozen tone. "You dare have the audacity to come into my apartment and insult me as such? Are you drunk or has your shit engineering crippled your brain to the point of retardation?"

As Jack's heart took off like a rocket, Valen's face fell. It was Valen's only weakness, an open wound that was forever being ripped back open and poisoned by the family. Valen's engineering and the failure of almost all of his enhancements. Elish, of course, knew this weakness and Jack's most respected brother was never one to hold back his verbal lacerations.

Though much of the family, Elish included, didn't know Valen was supposed to be the most advanced chimera out of all of them, an empath chimera. A chimera with King Silas's mental abilities plus something called aura reading. But like his hearing, endurance, and jaw strength it had never developed. Once Silas had realized his pipedream of creating an empath chimera had failed, he had forbidden Valen from mentioning it to anyone. The only ones who knew just how much of a failure Valen really was, was Silas, Perish, and Garrett. Jack had only found out on the day Silas had rejected Valen. He had confided in Jack through tears – the last time the pink chimera had ever opened up to anyone.

Elish didn't know, but because he was a man of many emotionally crushing words, he continued, his voice plunging into dark frigid waters. "For one of the biggest failures in our family you certainly have been making up for it by acting like an insufferable bitch. Unfortunately the family is tiring of turning a cheek to you constantly terrorizing the successful ones like Jack and Sa- *the others*. Acting like a shit doesn't equal gaining respect, Valentine. Perhaps if you spent more time on your personality and less time thinking bullying equals respect, Silas would've kept you as his cicaro."

Jack's facial expression might've been blank but inside he was screaming from happiness. It felt like his body was going to explode over the joy he could feel rapidly expand inside of him. And the joy wasn't only derived from someone in the family finally coming to his defence, a large part of it was seeing the gob smacked and crushed look on Valen's face.

"Silent now are we?" Elish said lowly, icicles hanging off of every deadly word. "Don't you have anything to say? You're rarely silent, why so quiet now?" Then Elish shook his head dismissively. "You've been getting away with your arrogance for far too long. Though I'm in charge now and no longer bound by Silas's foolish rules. Tell me, Valentine, do you know why Silas doesn't stop you?"

Of course Valen didn't answer back; he only stood frozen where Elish's words had left him, standing stunned like a virgin after a brutal raping.

"It's because he doesn't care about you," Elish said. "Silas is hard on Jack, on all of us, because he loves us and we are worthy of his attention and critique, but you? He doesn't give a fuck about you; he doesn't care enough about you to discipline you. And you do nothing to gain his favour acting like a bitch and a bully."

Then to further twist the knife practically embedded in Valen's chest, Elish turned his back on him. "Get out of here, and if I hear of any more bullying – your deepest nightmares will not come close to what I will personally do to you."

Jack thought that Valen would leave, turn around and run with his tail tucked in between his legs. But even the most abused and injured of dogs will still growl and snap moments before their death, and Valentine Dekker was no different. Holding onto the scraps of pride he never really had in the first place, the pink chimera gave an angry cry, before picking up a letter opener resting on the side table, and charging at Elish.

Without thinking Jack's mind snapped into action. He grabbed onto Valen's collar and yanked him back. The pink chimera stumbled backwards, before whirling around and raising the knife in the air to stab Jack in the neck.

Then Elish was there, towering behind Valen he grabbed the boy's hand and crushed it in his grip, the letter opener falling to the ground. Valen struggled, and swung his free hand, grazing Elish's jaw and leaving a thin streak of red in its trail.

The blond chimera's eyes blazed. He violently shoved Valen into the wall before grabbing the young chimera's neck and clenching it in between his large, vice-like hands.

Jack took a step back, his mouth open and gasping, trying to fill his anxious lungs with air as he saw the scene in front of him. Valen struggling and choking, his feet dangling off of the ground, and Elish, an inferno of white fire, staring down the boy with a disdain in his eyes that told Jack he wanted nothing more than to crush the boy's windpipe until the life faded from his eyes.

"You are doomed to live among gods, and die as a mortal with them looking on," Elish said, his voice so full of darkness it made Jack's blood turn to ice. "You are nothing but a scientific failure who is only alive by the mercy of your king and creator. It is time you learn your place, Valentine, and your place is licking the boots of your greaters."

Elish dropped Valen onto the ground. The young man fell into a heap, clutching his throat and massaging it to try and ease air back into his lungs.

"Kiss Jack's feet."

Jack's eyes shot to Elish's, though he couldn't keep his gaze. Elish's eyes were on fire, his flawless face as bright as a harvest moon and just as radiant. He was beautiful, a demigod in this greyworld, but in that beauty came danger, and no other times than now did Jack understand that.

"F-fuck off…" Valen said, though his snapping, arrogant tones were lost. His voice had dropped to a whimper, a meek shadow of its former self.

"Don't make me ask you twice," Elish growled. "You can either kiss the feet of your greater, or I will command him to dominate you in a more appropriate way. A way that you seem to enjoy."

Rape him? Jack looked down at the whimpering mass, Valen's pink hair unkempt and stuck to his sweaty face, his lip-gloss smeared and his black eyeliner dripping down his cheeks from tears Jack hadn't seen before. The man who had been bullying Jack for years was falling from his pedestal in full view of his victim and his king.

Could I do it? Jack's eyes travelled from Valen to the incandescent spectre that was Elish, and as he gazed upon the man with shining blond hair he felt a warm tension start to constrict inside of him. And with that not only did Jack know that he could; he knew that he wanted to.

The prospect of doing that to Valen, and to further tempt his fantasy, the prospect of doing it in front of Elish, was filling him with a desire he didn't know if he would be able to shake. Immediately his mind started injecting image after image into him. Of Elish holding the screaming Valen down as Jack penetrated him, and holding his arms back as he viciously fucked him harder and harder.

Oh, fuck, to hear him scream… would Elish fuck me after if I begged him?

Though as Valen gave one last sniff and started crawling towards Jack, those dreams were dashed. Though it was bittersweet, because Jack was now witnessing Valen on his knees, leaning down to kiss Jack's socked feet.

Jack swallowed hard, resisting the urge to kick Valen right in the face. After the abuse he had had to endure for the last several years he knew it was within his right to do so. But instead he stood still and watched with smug satisfaction as his bully submitted right in front of him.

"Good, you're learning your place," Elish said behind them. "You may stop, and you may stand up."

Valen quickly got to his feet, refusing to look at either of them. He only wiped his eyes, smearing his black eyeliner across his face, and stared at the floor.

"Just let me go," Valen mumbled, his arms slowly wrapping around his body, the letter opener lying forgotten beside his feet. "I got school tomorrow."

To the surprise of both Jack and Valen, Elish let out an amused chuckle. This time Valen did raise his head and look at Elish, though his eyes quickly shifted away.

"You will find an amusing surprise when you get to class," Elish said with a cruel smile. He leaned down and picked up the letter opener and casually twisted the point into his palm. Jack's entire body gave a small shudder under Elish's bemused tone. He knew what was coming, and he knew what it was going to do to Valen.

"Do you know that Sami killed three men at Popkin's?" Elish smirked.

Valen paused, for a moment it seemed that he wouldn't answer back, but after gathering himself once again he nodded. "Yeah, a lot of the family has been looking for him."

Elish twisted the letter opener into his hand, before taking a step towards Valen and slipping it back into Valen's. He closed Valen's hand over it and gave it a pat.

"He was in that bar looking for *you*, Valentine. The filthy greywaster you hate so much killed three of your little gang. Tyler, Randall, and Yuri. He lit their faces on fire and made it well-known that anyone who knew where you were, needed to tell him." Elish's smirk turned into a smile as Valen's face went pale. Jack could see his pupils retract.

"Sami killed them. Why don't you prove to the entire family that you really are a chimera… and do something about it?"

"What!" Jack suddenly cried, but with a glaring look from Elish he held his hand up over his mouth.

Valen looked down at the pen knife; he sniffed but that was his only reaction. No screams of rage, no shouts of despair, he only looked at the knife and nodded. "That's how I'm going to prove myself? You want me to kill Sami?"

Elish took a step back, leaving Valen standing alone with the knife in his hand, the dim lighting of the apartment making the small blade sparkle and shine as he turned it.

"I want you to prove to me that you're not the waste of resources I am convinced that you are," Elish said coldly. "A greywaster has killed three of your friends. What are you going to do about it? You've already disappointed the family enough by just being born a failure, I suggest not disappointing us further. We have embryos waiting to be implanted that hold five times your abilities, don't give us a reason to create a replacement sooner than necessary."

Valen's face fell; a despair flooded his eyes that made even Jack's hatred towards him weaken. He disliked being reminded just how bad Valen had it when compared to him. Valen was a bully and an asshole, but he was also a genetic failure. And his older brothers had never missed a chance to point that out to him.

"It's not my fault, you know?" Valen said weakly. "I didn't ask to be… to be born like this."

But though Jack's heart was showing signs of wear, Elish's was not. If anything the blond chimera's facial expressions hardened further.

"None of us asked to be born like this," Elish responded, before turning his back once again on Valen. "Now get out of my sight and don't blemish my vision until you've proven you're worthy of my gaze."

The door of Elish's bedroom shut, leaving both Valen and Jack to stare at the closed door as if expecting it to give them more answers, but there was only silence.

Valen sniffed; Jack turned to see him staring down at the pen knife. He felt tongue tied as his brother slipped it into his pocket, and without a word… left the apartment.

For a solid minute Jack just stood there stunned, not knowing if he should race after Valen to beg him not to hurt Sami, or race in front of him to find Sami to beg him not to kill Valen. He didn't know what he was supposed to do, or if there was anything in his power he could do.

Instead he opened up Elish's door, and found his blond brother lying on his back, his eyes closed.

"You can't let him hurt Sami…" Jack whispered, wondering if he was making his own deadly mistakes.

"You're a fool if you think Valen will be able to hurt that man," Elish said, his eyes still closed. "Sami is from the greywastes, he was burning boys like Valen alive when he was six."

Jack swallowed; his throat feeling like it was compacting tighter and tighter by the second. "So you're sending Valen to die?" he said, his voice cracking.

"I couldn't care less what happens to Valen," Elish replied coolly. "If he dies, so be it. If King Silas wakes up to him dead it will relieve him of the guilt of having to dispose of him himself. Valen has no purpose in this family, Jack. Silas doesn't want him as a cicaro and neither do I. Every chimera has their own purpose, even the female found her place as commissioner of the thiens. Valen, and several others, have no place within this family."

Jack's feelings towards Valen continued to soften, not enough for him to feel sorry for his brother, but enough to feel that Elish was being unreasonably harsh with Valen's potential fate. "But he's still… our family."

"He's replaceable," Elish said back. He opened one eye and, oddly, motioned Jack over to his bedside. Jack was hesitant but he obeyed, as he walked to the far side of the bed Elish continued. "If he was a nice person to have around, if he showed other skills and potential, we would've kept him. But as of right now he and the others are a blemish on our family and reputation."

"Others?"

"Ludo, Felix, and Rio have been testing the family's patience. We have made vast leaps during the last five years when it comes to chimera engineering – I would like nothing more than to see all four of them disposed of to make room for more improved versions."

Jack's eyebrows raised in surprise. He laid down beside Elish and turned onto his side. "It just seems kind of… cruel."

The corner of Elish's mouth rose "And through cruelty and careful selection Silas will weed out the chimeras unworthy of immortality and status, and in the end… our family will be a force to be reckoned with. The second generation is full of defects, of chimeras not worthy to walk amongst their better brothers. Time will take care of some of them, but others… I want gone sooner rather than later."

And Valen is one of them… I wonder who else he means. Jack frowned at this.

"Who am I?"

"To who?"

Jack was confused over that response. "What do you mean?"

"You are many things to different people, Jack," Elish responded. "Are you asking if you're worthy to be in the family?"

Jack nodded slowly.

"As of right now? No."

Jack felt his heart crush, the sting made him start to get up off of the bed. With a tightness in his chest he started walking towards the bedroom door.

"Only you can change that Jack," Elish called after him, his frozen words slicing Jack with the indifferent frost that was Elish through and through. "And it is time you change. The family has been patient with the lower, less successful of the second generation but that time is coming to an end. Silas grows tired of the chimeras who are not living up to their potential. I will only warn you once, because I still hold hope you can become the man we created you to be: change now and change quickly."

Jack stared at his hand grasping the door knob; he felt his eyes start to burn under the shame of his own cowardice. Never more than in that moment did he hate himself for what he had become – and never more had he wanted to change.

"I will," Jack said, though to his humiliation his voice cracked. "I'll change."

"Time is running out," Elish said back. There was something in the way that Elish said that that made the hair on Jack's neck prickle. "Jack Anubis – time is running out, and it may already be too late. Do not forget this conversation and do not forget my words. You will sleep on my couch tonight, good night."

A single tear dripped down Jack's face. He let it fall to the floor, the silence that fell on the room so prominent he heard it patter against his foot.

"I… I won't," Jack replied quietly, and without another word, he opened the door and left Elish's bedroom.

CHAPTER 37

I PLACED THE SMALL WHITE ROCK ONTO THE BURNT piece of tinfoil, my fingers trembling and stained yellow from smoking cigarette after cigarette. I centered the little piece of meth and popped the glass pipe into my mouth. Then with the glass firmly clenched between my teeth I focused my burning touch onto the bottom of the tinfoil and made it as hot as I could.

As the smoke rose from the tinfoil I sucked it through the pipe, and when my lungs were filled with burning hot, rancid-smelling smoke I put the blackened tinfoil down and got up.

Not too soon after I felt the intoxicating rush blast through my body, setting my blood aflame and exploding every organic fiber. It covered me in its energetic haze and soon I was pacing the entire house with my hands rapidly moving from my pockets, to wrapped around my chest, to picking at my face.

I walked to the boarded up window which I had partially pulled down and looked outside. There was a fresh layer of prints going down the worn path that led to the alleyway. The chain-link fence had permanently been pulled back to make room for Mouse and Julia coming in and out when they came home from work. The two of them lived with me, or maybe I lived with them. I never did ask.

I scratched my face and shook my head back and forth. I was happy to be awake after sleeping for a long time. That was the routine but I hated my sleeping days, because when I slept I missed things and when I missed things, things happened. Bad things happened that Mouse told me about, like rumours in Cypress about the Dekker family coming closer to finding me out so they could send me back to Jasper's.

Back to Jasper's… they had been working with him the entire time. I hadn't realized it at first but this drug had opened up my mind and had made me start to pick up on things I had previously ignored. It was mind blowing the first time I had smoked meth. I had never realized that Jasper had been spying on me this entire time, and that the family I had once belonged to had been letting him. My close-knit, royal family wasn't who I thought they had been, no not at all.

I walked into my bedroom and looked around at all of the newspaper bulletins I had put on the walls. All of them streaked with shining oil, and filling the room with the smell of pub grease and meth smoke. When I realized the messages in the newspapers I had started taping them to the walls. I knew if I just read them close enough, analyzed their words… I would be able to crack the code. They communicated with each other and with Jasper through the bulletin.

It made sense… fuck, I couldn't believe what I was seeing when I started putting it all together.

The family couldn't communicate directly with Jasper or else I would know. They knew I was smart, see? So they put in these hidden messages in the bulletins and wrapped the pub food in the bulletins and sent it off to the Dead Islands as Jasper's food.

I ran my finger along one of my most read articles. It was about King Silas waking up soon and how the family was organizing a party for him. I wrote down how many letters of which were in that article. How many A's, how many B's, and so on. Then I took those numbers and assigned them their own letters based on their number in the alphabet, except when they repeated then I assigned them twice, and used the remaining number for a new letter.

Like this… like this… see… there were fifty-eight N's in the article and N is the fourteenth letter in the alphabet, so in the main message to Jasper there was three N's which would equal forty-two so there would be a remaining sixteen. Sixteen was P's place in the alphabet so that code told me there was three N's and one P in the main message. I did this over and over again until I had the list of numbers and from that it was just anagram solving and I was great at anagrams because in Jasper's basement I had nothing better to do sometimes I made anagrams of everything just to pass the time.

The first message was telling Jasper they were closing in on me. I had some leftover letters but I saved those because they perfectly rolled over to the next bulletin which was telling Jasper that I was in Moros or Cypress. This had happened during my last stretch of doing meth and that was why I was so upset with crashing. I hated crashing. I wanted to stay awake and the meth urged me to stay awake. When I crashed I slept for days and days and I woke up with bottles around me full of piss just like in the basement and sometimes Mouse beside me doing opium. I didn't do opium anymore because it made me sluggish and I couldn't be sluggish right now with the family coming closer to finding me. Would they have Jasper with them? I think they would.

I couldn't believe they had been in on it the entire time.

They had tricked me, they were smart. I had always known my family was smart but this was complex. They were after me; all of them were after me…

I looked out the window, my hands shaking at my hips. I counted the footprints and made sure they were only Mouse and Julia's. I had made both of them cut off a tread inside of their boots so I could tell that it was only them. The monarchy-issued winter boots all had the same treads and I had to be certain they weren't sneaking in when I was sleeping during my downtime.

Even Jack was in on it. I thought he would become my boyfriend but I was wrong, he was a plant, a plant, a plant. I bet even Valen was a plant to distract me from knowing the truth.

It all made sense. It all made sense!

Hours later Mouse came home. Immediately I took the paper bag from him and started carefully peeling the bulletins away from the greasy food. He had suggested he could just bring me home the bulletin everyday but that was such a stupid idea it made me laugh. If he did that then the family would know I was figuring out their messages to each other and to Jasper. Not to mention they could then switch out the bulletin for another newspaper; a fake one that would feed me fake information. No, no, it had to be anonymously given to me and the best way of doing that was wrapped up in food.

I scraped the cheese away and took my notepad and pen from Mouse. I went into my room and started writing down how often each letter occurred and started trying to work everything out inside of my head.

Sometime the next evening I had my list of letters. I paced the house reading the numbers over and over again, before finding a clean space on the walls to help work them out. Behind me Julia was smoking a cigarette and watching Maury. I found myself distracted with it too. I always tried to avoid watching that show. If I watched more than five minutes I became too invested in finding out who the baby's daddy was. Nowadays we had DNA testing kits, or even better you just grew one in a steel mother. I knew where all of my DNA was from, I had seen my papers and I had seen the papers of others.

I reached into my mouth and pulled out one of the remaining caps on my teeth.

Julia suddenly screamed. I looked at her and saw her froggy-like eyes were wide.

"Jesus christ, Pumpkin, don't pull out your teeth!" Julia hollered, there was a clang of dishes and she ran over to me. She took the tooth from my hand but when she realized I wasn't bleeding her shock turned to confusion.

So I smiled at her so she could see the pointed tooth hiding behind the cap.

"You have teeth like Jack?" Julia said in an awed voice. She pulled my lip down and I grinned for her so she could see them.

"We were raised in the same tube," I said. "Though they sent me away. Sent me away as some sort of blood money to Jasper." I narrowed my eyes and started preparing myself another hit. "I'm starting to think he's king. I know if I keep checking eventually I'll catch them calling him king. There are just too many signs; why else would they obey him?"

My thoughts took me away from her. I walked to the window and looked outside. It was dark though so I could only see silver footprints in the snow. My night vision didn't work with light behind me, no matter how hard I tried.

I should go outside... I grabbed my black satchel and walked to the door and put a hand on it.

"Where are you going?" Julia was suddenly there. She put a hand over mine.

"Outside, check the prints..." I mumbled.

"Last time you went out we lost you for – for ten hours," Julia said cautiously. She grabbed my satchel where all of my remaining money was but I tightened my hand on it. "Why don't you at least leave the bag here?"

I shook my head. "No, my money. My mask is inside of there too. Barry would be lonely. I'll get him. Barry should come too."

I turned and walked into my bedroom. I picked up Barry and turned around, but when I did I saw that both Julia and Mouse were there standing in front of the doorway.

"Pumpkin, we both think you should stay inside…" Mouse said cautiously. He looked down at either the black bag or Barry I wasn't sure. "We – we saw Valen asking around for you at the bar. We overheard him saying that Jasper was in town too. We really think it's a good idea for you to stay put."

I stared at Mouse in shock. Immediately I whirled around and raised the pressboard that had been barred against my window.

"Turn off the lights!" I barked to Mouse, and a moment later everything went dark, though in that darkness the outlines of the things outside started to glow blue. I could make out a tall wooden fence in the backyard and the lights of several other houses.

I looked down at the snow but I didn't see any footprints, the snow was new and clean. I could see several prints of birds though.

Of birds…

"Turn on the lights…" I said. I dropped the canvas bag but I still had Barry in my grasp. Julia and Mouse stepped back as I walked past them. My free hand travelling up to my face; I started picking at the scabs.

"Are there crows outside? Do they come outside and walk around?" I demanded as I finished preparing my meth.

"Sure… Cypress is full of crows…" Mouse said slowly.

"Do they talk?"

"W-what?"

"Do they talk!" I whirled around and snapped. Mouse paled; he held up his hands as he shook his head.

"No, they don't. Crows don't talk."

Yes they do. "Crows talk and Barry talks," I said, raising Barry up in the air. "He used to talk to me all the time but he stopped. He stopped after Jasper fucked me for the first time when I was a kid. Shot himself right after, his brains splattered on the walls and he never talked to me again. He was gone after that and I don't know how I'm supposed to get him back."

I ignored both Julia and Mouse's jaws dropping and clutched Barry to my chest. I then checked each and every window to make sure there were no footprints I didn't recognize. The crow ones though; I didn't like the crow prints.

Because… I remember…

I remember that they used to be able to have cameras inside of their mouths. I remember that, all of that, yes. The crows were recording what was happening and they were going to tell the Legion. So did that mean the Legion was against Jasper? Maybe my only friend was Nero. No, no, I couldn't trust anyone.

I frowned as I looked at Barry. I put him on the table that faced the living room and made him sit up. Then I sat down on the wobbly chair and folded my arms on the table.

"I wish you still talked," I said to him with a sigh. "I wish you could talk back to me… like when I was little. I could really use someone I trusted right now, even if you were always telling me I was a demon-monkey."

Barry stared back at me; I could see light reflecting in his black eyes. They were only little beads but once they were the eyes of a real boy.

'I'm still here.'

My heart jumped into my throat. I looked around until I spotted Mouse and Julia eating quietly in the living room with Hocus Pocus on. When I knew they weren't listening I lowered my voice.

"Where did you go?" I whispered. He was speaking inside of my head; I couldn't see the boy at all. "Didn't you kill yourself?"

'I did… Jasper raping you made me sad, but you seem better now. I missed you, Sami.'

I started picking at my face again, more from nerves than anything. I looked at Mouse and Julia again before dropping my voice even lower.

"How can you be here then?" I asked. "You're just a voice… a…"

'My body died… but I can get a new one,' Barry whispered to me. *'Me and my friends, other stuffed animal friends that have been forgotten. We can come back… you know how to bring us back, Sami.'*

I did…

There was another pull of my heart, a pull that seemed to rip away at the muscle, exposing old wounds and old scars. My heart had been destroyed and stitched together so many times, but scars tore open easily. This one was raw and bleeding, and it was letting more loneliness in.

I looked down at my notebook, full of my anagrams, my numbers, and my drawings. The entire world was against me, everyone wanted to see me hurt, they wanted me back to fuck me, to abuse me, mistreat me. Everyone wanted to hurt me but there had been a few friends who had only wanted what was best for me.

And one of those was Barry, my Barry the boy, now just a voice inside of my head because Jasper had made him kill himself.

Fucking Jasper…

"Hey, Pumpkin, time for food!"

I looked up and saw Mouse holding a dinner plate with a hamburger cut into pieces and potato fries. I shook my head though because I wasn't hungry and picked up a pen instead.

"This shit again?" Mouse groaned, before turning around to face his sister. "You can tell Moros and Cypress are in shit because even the meth addicts there don't refuse food."

"It's your turn to feed him. I had to try and get him to eat when he was conked out for three days," Julia called from the couch. "I told you to pick up some of that liquid meal replacement shit."

"It's more expensive…" Mouse mumbled. There was a scrape of the chair before he pushed the plate near me. "Come on, you eat and I'll help you with your math problems. You're getting a couple numbers wrong; it might mess up your end anagram result."

I looked at him alarmed before glancing down at my writing, every corner of the book was covered in numbers and letters and in the upper-half corner, a drawing of a crow.

"Which ones?" I said hastily, swearing at myself for getting something wrong. "Show me!"

"Eat something first."

He reminded me of King Silas… but King Silas had always been telling me to not eat quickly. Some things were the complete opposite of how they were and other things…

I got up and walked towards the window before checking outside to make sure there were no more prints. Still no more prints, thankfully.

While I was looking out the window I could hear the other two whispering behind me. Whispering about feeding me and making sure I didn't die because someone had been looking for me. I didn't know why they told each other that because I knew they were looking for me.

But they put a lot of emphasis on *had*. Not sure why.

"He's been checking out the bars… asking about someone named…" Their voices dropped and I couldn't hear them anymore. I wasn't interested though, they'd told me people had been looking for me. I knew they were getting closer, closer and here I was without a friend in the world.

I could have my friends back though.

When I turned around again I saw the two of them talking quietly, my black bag now resting beside them. I walked over and picked up the bag and sat down on the couch with it.

They stopped talking and I watched television with them.

"I want a stuffed animal," I suddenly said.

There was silence around me, only the hum of the television.

"A… stuffed animal?" Mouse asked slowly.

I nodded. "One that doesn't have a home. One like the couch that gets rained on in the greywastes. I want stuffed animals, find me big stuffed animals. I want some friends for Barry."

Julia groaned but Mouse laughed. He seemed amused by the request but I was dead serious.

"Okay, man. If it makes you happy… I'll bring you home a couple," Mouse chuckled, before glancing over at his sister. "He's a simple chimera with simple needs, isn't he?"

"We're lucky he's from the greywastes… most of them look rather high maintenance," Julia said. "As long as you eat your damn food, Pumpkin!"

I scoffed and waved my hand but when I saw she was holding a fry I took it just to make her happy. "I used to eat until I threw up in my old life. Now I can't stand food. Oh how shit changes." Then I remembered something. "Mouse, you need to tell me where I've been mathing wrong. Help me math. I was in college once, you know. But that was only to control my thoughts and my actions. They wanted to keep a better eye on me. I think they knew I was about to figure them out. Figure out their plan."

I handed Mouse the notebook and the pen which I had tucked behind my ear at some point in time. Mouse only shook his head before bringing out an old paint-stained calculator he had in his pocket. Barry and I watched him do his calculations though occasionally I had to walk around and check the snow.

Lots of crow prints... lots of crow prints.

Strange.

"Crows do talk," I said, glancing behind my shoulder. Mouse and Julia were both ignoring me, which was typical, after a while they just ignored me or agreed with everything I said. They only stopped me from wandering outside because of the family being after me. "They say things to me."

"Okay, Pumpkin," Mouse said. "I think you've done enough meth today though. Maybe you should stop for the night."

"They say... *Go on get*! And *Hello, Sanguine*. They were brought here by King Silas for me because they were my friends at Jasper's..." I said, though as I spoke those words my mouth started to slow, because I was realizing something. "Do you think... no, they're not spies. They spied on Jasper so they're my friends. I don't think they have cameras in their mouths... I should check."

I started walking towards the door but Mouse stood up out of the corner of my eye. "Wait, Pumpkin. I finished your calculations; I don't know what to anagram it with. Why don't you go into your room and try and figure it out?"

Figure it out? I nodded and prepared myself another hit of meth. I brought all of my supplies into my room, Barry, my tinfoil, my glass pipe, my rocks, pen, and notebook; and I closed the door behind me to start trying to figure everything out.

I was glad I stopped smoking the opium. I was happy I found the meth. My mind was so open; everyone else was stupid but me. This had cleared all the fog and cobwebs out of my brain and now I knew what was really going on. It was amazing.

I sat down on the bed with my legs crossed; Barry was in front of me, staring at me once again with his shining black eyes. Still just a bear though, always just... always just a bear...

'That's up for you to decide – do you want me to come back, Sami?'

What kind of question is that? I missed Barry, and I missed Crow. Friends who told me to do bad things and told me to hurt myself were a hell of a lot better than the spies. At least these two were the devils that I knew, not the unknown forces outside my house.

"I'll bring you back…" I mumbled. I put my hand on Barry's head and gently petted it. "I need to hold onto the friends that I trust. Who else do I have?"

'No one, just me and Crow. We've been here from the beginning. Though you haven't been a very good friend to us.'

No, I really haven't.

"Pumpkin!" Mouse called. I heard the door open and close and the sound of him out of breath. It was raining away all of the snow but it was still a long walk from where he worked to where we were living. "I got you a fucking present, are you awake?"

I looked down at the notebook, a fresh clean page though it had the grooves and dents of the other pages I had filled with writing. My face was tight as I looked at my anagram code, one I had spent the last three or four days trying to sort through. What it was telling me was disturbing, but my family was disturbing so maybe I shouldn't be surprised after all.

I closed my notebook and slowly got up, my muscles ached but they still had a fire inside of them that told me to move and move a lot. Pace, walk, clean, talk. I liked to talk the most.

Several minutes later the door opened. I hadn't even realized that my body hadn't moved. I was still standing on my mattress staring at the notebook full of my writing and anagram solving. All my thoughts and my suspicions, about my family, about my life, about Jasper and the fact that I knew I was being watched.

Constantly watched.

I glanced over and smiled when I saw a giant rabbit stuffed animal with long legs and long arms. I grabbed it and held him out so I can examine him closely.

He looked worn and old, like he'd had a hard life. He was wearing purple overalls and a spotted shirt underneath. He also had Velcro on his paw pads though they were full of dirt and other small fibers; his paws didn't stick together.

"What's his name?" I asked eagerly. I put him beside Barry and stood back so I could admire them both together.

"Umm…" Mouse thought for a second. "Patches."

I nodded my approval, still smiling. "I like him, bring me more. Do you have more?"

Mouse nodded. "Yeah, I told Julia to go get you a couple more. You're fucking weird, you know that?" Mouse then tossed a few more baggies worth of meth. "We're going to be running out of money in a couple weeks, man. Do you have a way of getting more?"

I picked up one of the bags and took out a small white rock. I placed it inside of the pipe, a new pipe with a little bubble on the end for easier smoking. I lit the bottom of it with my pointer finger and started moving the rock around to get the smoke going.

When I exhaled I closed my eyes, then remembering what Mouse was asking me. I shook my head. "They're tracking me… I can't go out. They're watching me." I got up and looked out the window.

I took in a sharp inhale and swore, right outside the window I saw a large crow hopping around the slush.

As soon as it saw the stream of light hitting the white snow it turned its head and looked at me.

Red eyes.

I quickly let go of the board, it smacked against the window frame making several loose paint chips fall onto the sill. I shook my head before picking up both Barry and Patches.

"No, I can't go out…" I said, my head rapidly moving back and forth, the world spun around me. "I can't… how many crows did you see outside? Are they talking?"

Mouse looked alarmed. He let me rush past him as I checked the other windows, feeling the terror and paranoia start to infect my internal wounds further. How a wound that was already festering and rotting could get more fetid I wasn't sure, but it was leaking its putrid pus all inside of me.

More crows… I could see more crows.

I was in trouble, they had found me. The crows had found me.

"I just checked a few hours ago!" I exclaimed. "They found me? How long have the crows been here for?"

"Just… just this evening, they were surrounding the house when I got home," Mouse said behind me. His voice was small, and it felt almost held back by the caution I could feel swirling around him. "I ran back out and got you the rabbit kinda hoping it would keep you calm."

Angrily I slammed my hand against the window frame of the kitchen and kicked one of the wooden chairs, Mouse flinched. "They're closing in on me, aren't they?"

Mouse shook his head, before offering me a cigarette, one of the ones with silver smoke. I took it and lit it quickly but my mind was racing, speeding ahead of my logic too quickly. It couldn't catch up.

"Okay, it's time you start easing off of the meth, man," Mouse said slowly. "At least enough for you to go and get more money. We're going to be out in a few weeks and–"

"A few weeks is a few weeks away," I said, narrowing my eyes at a small gap in the boarded up kitchen window. I could see just a sliver of the white snow on the porch. "That's a long time away. A few weeks away. I can't go out; they're closing in on me."

I heard him sigh but I ignored it. I went back into my bedroom and sat down on my bed with Barry and Patches. They looked good together, so I put them together and decided that they would be boyfriends.

Yes, they could be boyfriends. I thought I was going to have a boyfriend at one point in time but that probably would never happen now. I would never have sex. I would never touch myself. I was going to be alone for the rest of my life.

Frowning I leaned against the wall and opened up my notebook. Once again I was reminded of the code I had successfully cracked. The newest communication between Jasper and the family. As I read it over and over I could feel the tight, constricting feeling come back to my chest.

I took another inhale of the cigarette and blew the smoke over the writing, reading it over and over again, and over, and over… and over.

It wasn't making sense like the others…

Frustrated, I snatched the newest bulletin and started reading it through, trying to double check my numbers but nothing was making sense. Mouse had even looked it over and he said the letters I had written down were correct, but there were too many leftover numbers too many…

"You forgot the photo caption," a female voice suddenly said.

I looked up shocked. I stared at Patches. "You're a girl?"

"Yes."

"Barry's straight?"

"You're the one that wanted us to be boyfriends not him."

That was true. They could be brother and sister then, just like Mouse and Julia.

"You're getting distracted, Sanguine. Check the photo caption. The picture of Elish's press conference about the state of the rebels, who are losing support and quickly. What does the caption say?"

I looked down at the photo and saw Elish, dressed in a white cape and sporting his usual stoic expression. He had Garrett and Ellis on both sides of him and the Skyfall flag was hanging down as a backdrop.

"Elish Dekker, standing king, condemns Irontowers Rebels keeping child slaves. 1,000 Legion units to sweep Irontowers and outskirts," I mumbled. I decided to see if Patches was onto something. I started writing the letters down on the next page, then brought out the paint-stained calculator Mouse had let me borrow.

There are more M's now... more S's, there are more vowels too. A lot more I's. I needed more I's. I started connecting the numbers and writing them down, until finally a message to me started to form.

But now there were too many words. So I started to do a trick I had learned, another alternate way they communicated. I took the letters that had a lot of multiples and started reducing them. Two N's became one unless there was a remainder and then I let that one stay. I reduced the letters down and down until I only had a couple of each. Some I put together and then deleted altogether as well.

It made more sense that way. This way I could –

Then like it had suddenly burst into flames I dropped the notebook onto the ground and recoiled my hands. I gasped and let out a cry, before holding my hand up to my mouth.

It was right in front of me, the words starting to take shape on the notepad and inside my head. The horror seemed to drain the blood from my face, and in its place a pit started to form.

"What does it say?" Barry asked.

"What does it say, Sami?"

"Sami, what does it say?"

"What – does – it – say?"

I let out another cry, before ripping the sheets off of my bed. I desperately started hanging the sheet across the window, pushing the fabric through the rusted nails sticking out of the mouldy pressboard. My arms were shaking, my entire body was trembling as the desperation pooled and boiled, adding to the horror and the pit now eating me inside out.

And as I tried to hang up the sheets, and then the blankets to block off my window, I once again glanced down at the notebook. Now seeing all of the other letters gone, all of my drawings and all of my work, only a single sentence remained.

'We're on to you, Sanguine.'

CHAPTER 38

"WE NEED TO MAKE THIS PUBLIC, ELISH," NERO pleaded. Ceph was beside him nodding his head with his arms crossed over his chest. "No one has seen him, there's been no trace. There's only so deep we can go before everyone starts asking questions anyway. You fucking have Jack, Apollo, Artemis, Felix, and Rio looking out for him and they don't even know he's a chimera. This is ridiculous!"

Elish was standing beside the wall-to-wall window of his apartment, gazing upon the steel scaffolds of a distant skyscraper that was in the middle of being repaired. He said nothing back, only brought a cup of hot tea to his lips.

"Jack is already asking way too many questions…" Nero said angrily. "I can't see why you think this shit is going to work, bro. You can't hide Sanguine's identity from the family and have us successfully find him. He's hiding."

"Or he's dead," Elish mumbled.

Suddenly Elish was pushed from behind, his tea cup spilling over his robe and his face smacking against the large window. A split second later Elish whirled around and backhanded Nero right across the face.

"I fucking killed Silas for abandoning Sanguine and I'll fucking kill you too!" Nero roared. He took a step towards Elish but before his boot could touch the ground Ceph grabbed him and held him back.

Elish glared at him angrily, before ripping his tea-stained shirt off of his chest; the white buttons flying and landing with a *plink* onto the floor. "Save your weak threats, Nero. I couldn't give a shit what the dumbest of all of us has to say. I have my orders and so do you." He flung the shirt at Loren who was hiding in the shadows of the apartment and stalked into his bedroom.

"Yeah? Well I don't give a flying fuck what your orders are," Nero called back, shoving Ceph away as his fiancé tried to keep him from following Elish into the bedroom. Nero stalked over to it and kicked the door open wider. "I'm telling Jack, I'm telling all of them. It's been two fucking months. He's been missing without a trace for almost two months, Elish. We've combed Skyland, Eros, Nyx; we've even scanned Moros and Cypress. For all I fucking know he's gone back into the greywastes."

"Silas will be awake any day now."

"Silas would've put Sanguine's safety over him wanting the kid to remain anonymous to the family," Nero snarled, his hand slamming against the door frame. The paintings on either side of him shook. "You're only using Silas's stupid fucking orders to put off finding Sanguine, because you want him dead. Just admit it, asshole. You want Sanguine fucking dead."

Elish stalked past him, his fingers buttoning up a clean white button-down. "I will hear none of it. I have my orders, as do you."

Nero's face was hard, showing a crystal clear window into his emotions. He stood there shaking as Elish took a fresh cup of tea from an equally distressed-looking Loren.

Ceph could see the corner of Nero's eyebrow twitch, and at this point he grabbed Loren by the shoulder and retreated into the shadows with the young sengil. He knew his fiancé well, and he knew that Nero's top was about to blow off.

"He's our brother and our search is a fucking joke," Nero said. "We need more than just four chimeras asking around bars. Sanguine deserves better."

"Sanguine will come home when he's done acting like an idiot," Elish said coldly. "When he decides to start acting like a chimera and not like a petulant teenager, he'll come back wagging his tail."

"This is so fucking stupid!" Nero yelled, there was another slam, this time the credenza beside Elish's bedroom took the brunt of the brute chimera's rage and, sure enough, as he slammed his hand down on it there was an audible *crack*. "Why is everyone expecting a kid who's been locked up in a basement getting raped every fucking day to act like an adult? You're the smart one, *King* Elish. Why am I the only one here that doesn't expect him to be fine? Not to mention the lies Silas has filled his head with, and you trying to shove him into a relationship with Jack. It's mind fucking everyone assumes that Sanguine is supposed to act okay. He isn't fucking okay and he needs the family right now."

Nero let out an angrily bellow as Elish waved him off before turning his back to him. The blond-chimera took another sip of his tea.

"It's none of your concern, Nero. I'm planning an invasion in Irontowers since Sanguine's suggestion has completely obliterated public opinion on the rebellion. I'm going to need you there to organize and launch it, you, Ellis, and Ceph. You'll be leaving tonight for Cardinalhall."

Elish turned around, and when Nero saw the sinister smirk plastered on his older brother's face, his chest turned to ice.

"You'll be bringing Jack along as well; actually... you will be bringing all of the chimeras currently searching for Sanguine. When the dog gets hungry, he'll come home. I'm disbanding our search."

The apartment fell into a dead silence; the only sound was Nero's quickened breathing and the almost tangible sound of the air being sucked out of a room. For what seemed like an eternity no one moved, and no one spoke.

"You can't do that," Nero whispered, his deep voice shattering the void that seemed to have descended on all of them.

Elish's purple eyes found Nero's, and when they both made eye contact, Elish smiled thinly.

"I just did. Do you want me to stay it again? I know you're rather slow."

"Do you think Silas is going to be happy when he comes back and finds out *your* future king is missing?" Nero replied coldly, taking a step towards Elish.

At the comment Elish's smile disappeared, but to Nero's grim surprise the smirk did not. "There is only one future king, Nero. And you're looking at him. Now get ready to depart for Cardinalhall. I'm tired of your whining over that red-eyed defect. The desperation to be the first one to stick your cock inside of him is tiresome and–"

Another push but this time Elish was ready. He quickly spun around and punched Nero right in the face.

With a bellowed roar Nero raised his own fist, and not holding back this time, he punched Elish as hard as he could.

Elish's head snapped back with a spray of blood and bone, hitting the window with a hard crack that made the entire frame rattle and protest; then the blond chimera fell to the ground in a heap of white.

Nero's shoulders heaved but as he looked down at his brother, he froze.

"Oh... shit..." Nero whispered. He glanced behind him and saw Ceph and Loren in the corner, staring at him with their eyes wide. Nero sucked in a breath and pursed his lips, before leaning down and checking Elish's pulse.

"Yeah... I – I killed him," Nero said in a thin voice. "I'm going to get fucking drowned for this..." The chimera turned back around, just as Loren made a mad dash for the door.

"Ceph!" Nero barked, but Ceph was already running after him. With a squeal and a scream Ceph grabbed the sengil and dragged him back into the apartment.

"Loren... Loren, we're not going to hurt you," Nero yelled, sprinting towards the shrieking sengil as he tried to smack and punch Ceph. "Look, you little fucker, I'm king now. I'm third-in-command and with Elish dead I'm king. Understand?"

"I'm loyal to Master Elish!" Loren yelled angrily. "And you just murdered him!"

Nero and Ceph both exchanged glances, their eyes seemingly having a conversation of their own. It took them both several moments before, with a nod, their gazes broke.

Ceph started dragging the screaming sengil to one of the backrooms and a moment later a door closed and locked. Though that did nothing but muffle the panicked sengil's screams, he could still be heard through the thick doors.

"We'll get Kinny to feed him... he's your sengil right now anyway," Ceph said as he walked over to Elish. A pool of blood was now soaking into the carpet, with several drying streams running down his pale face. "You're going to be in shit when Elish wakes up, hunny."

Nero wiped his face with his hands. He swore again and turned away from Elish, then let out a frustrated groan. "I wasn't trying to fucking kill him. I was just... pissed." He grabbed his phone, his brow starting to shine with sweat.

But then he paused. "If I'm king now..."

Ceph looked up at him and raised an eyebrow.

"I can... do what I need to do to find Sanguine, can't I?"

Ceph's eyes narrowed and he cautiously nodded. "Technically yes..."

However when a wan smile started to creep onto Nero's face, Ceph's own expression darkened. "Nuuky, you could get in a lot of shit if..."

"I think I'm going to get praised and promoted," Nero said, cutting Ceph off. "Silas loves Sanguine. This isn't about following orders; this shit is solely because Elish is jealous of Sanguine." As Nero said this he pulled out his remote phone, and ignoring the concerned and nervous expression on his fiancé's face, he dialled a number and held it to his ear.

"Yeah, Zhou... meeting at six in my office. It'll be an important one."

Ceph shook his head and stepped away, still hearing Loren shouting and yelling from behind the locked door. Though he was willowy and slight the kid certainly had a set of lungs on him.

As Nero gave his orders Ceph nudged Elish's side with his boot, and then, for no other reason than taking an opportunity – he kicked Elish in the head, twice.

"Okay, the meeting is scheduled... I love being king." Nero chuckled. He seemed like he had just found cloud nine and he was on his way to paradise. This did nothing to dampen the nervousness that Ceph was feeling though; Nero had never been one to fully think things through. He was famous for being impulsive and ignoring the eventual ramifications of his actions.

It had gotten him encased in concrete on more than one occasion, and every time he was brought out of that claustrophobic hellhole he promised and swore that he would be obedient. But promises made after months in that constricting, maddening hell were soon forgotten, and the old Nero would resurface.

"He's not that injured, Nero," Ceph said. He wiped his brow and realized he had started to sweat. "Two days maybe... will you be able to find Sangy in time?"

Nero paused as if to consider this, then to Ceph's horror he watched his fiancé walk up to Elish with a devious glint in his eye.

When Ceph saw Nero pull out his combat knife he swore and turned away, then the sound of a knife slashing skin filled his ears.

He closed his eyes and groaned, the irony smell of blood crawled up his nostrils. Usually a satisfying smell but today it brought nothing but nausea.

But there was nothing he could do. Even though it would be him suffering too when Nero was punished for this, he had to do what his Imperial Commander, his best friend, and his fiancé wanted.

So with a sigh Ceph turned around, seeing Nero wiping the blood off of his hands. He then looked down and saw Elish with a vertical slice down his chest, though no blood was leaking from his wounds, it was just a deep slice that showed in its crease a slight hint of white bone.

"I'm going to get into shit anyway, why not put it off and give myself some time to find Sangy?" Nero shrugged, getting on his phone again, though when he saw Ceph's disapproving face he made a noise and roughly put his arm around his fiancé. "It's fine, Cephy. I know I'll get into shit, but I'm immortal. What's important is finding Sanguine. Sanguine needs me, more than I don't need a sound beating. Anyway." Nero squeezed his partner to him and kissed his tense cheek. "I'm still pretty sure this is exactly what Silas would want me to do and if not... I'll take my licks. He'll be awake soon, possibly even before Elish wakes up."

The look Ceph gave Nero made him chuckle, it was so sad and pathetic, like a puppy after you yelled at it for shitting on the carpet. The brute chimera kissed his partner again, his spirits not being dampened at all. It was an odd thing to see, especially with Elish lying in a pool of his own blood.

Nero got on his remote phone and pressed several buttons.

"Yes, Jacky-whacks!" Nero said cheerfully when the call connected. "Come over to me and Cephy's apartment in an hour, we gotta talk to you about something. Bring Valen, alright?"

Nero's smile faded though; he looked at Ceph. "Valen's disappeared. Apparently Elish schooled him a couple weeks ago. Okay, Jack, bring yourself then."

When Nero got off of the phone Ceph was already at the double oak doors, more than eager to get out of Elish's apartment. Eventually one of them would have to move Elish to his bedroom, and after that dispatch the sengils to clean the mess and feed Loren now crying softly in the bedroom.

It was obvious and had been obvious since Elish had been killed that Ceph wasn't feeling the energetic, happy vibe that Nero was freely broadcasting, but as Nero smiled at him and strutted over with a bounce in his step, Ceph smiled.

"Just be careful, hun," Ceph said quietly. "I miss you when you're gone, you know?"

"I'm immortal, puppy... whatever happens to me isn't permanent. But Sanguine isn't immortal. I gotta do what's right since it's obvious I'm the only person who fucking will. I let the kid down when he needed me the most; I'll be fucked if I'll let that happen again. Support me?"

There was no question that he would; he would support Nero no matter what he wanted. He had loved that man since he was a kid, at first as a goofy big brother, and now as the man he had received permission to marry.

But he still sighed, and he still hesitated under Nero's gaze, but he managed a nod.

"Always, Nero. Always."

Then a throat cleared behind them.

Nero and Ceph both turned around and at the same time their mouths dropped open.

King Silas was standing in the hallway outside of the apartment with his arms crossed over his chest, Garrett behind him looking just as shocked as Nero and Ceph.

"K-kingy!" Nero said happily, though there was a nervous catch to his voice. He plastered on a fake smile before deliberately stepping in Silas's view of the dead and mutilated Elish who was laying just several feet behind him. "You're up! I missed you bunches."

Nero took a step towards Silas and held out his arms to give him a hug, but the stone-cold expression on Silas's face stopped him dead in his tracks.

King Silas's emerald green eyes flickered past Nero to the dead Elish lying on his back on the floor, a pool of red soaking the carpet around him, making his hair strawberry blond. Without a word the king walked past Nero, his movements gliding and his shoes making no sound as they approached his first born.

Silas kneeled down, the silver cape he had clasped around his neck getting blood on the clean trim. He put a hand to the red welt on Elish's grey face, before slowly brushing the tips of his fingers against the carved knife-marks Nero had just made.

"You murdered your brother, and you macerated his flesh to prolong his resurrection?" The cold, sharp tones of Silas's voice made Ceph swallow, but Nero only stood there frozen.

He had no expression on his face, but every chimera could hear his heart. It was like a giant knocking on a hollow door, two deep brass tones that echoed in the living room and showed everyone listening that Nero knew he was in dire trouble.

Though as the Imperial Commander stood behind Silas, he seemed to realize that there were two paths in front of him. And though many of his younger brothers would choose the path of pleading for King Silas's forgiveness, Nero knew his king enough to know that he was not one to soften his heart to grovelling. No, the king knew only reason, and justification – this was no time to plead.

So with this in his head Nero walked towards Silas and Elish, leaving Ceph and Garrett with their nervous looks.

"Sanguine has been gone for two months," Nero said standing tall. "Elish has only sent Jack, Rio, Artemis, and Felix to try and find him and they don't even know Sanguine is a chimera so I doubt they're searching that hard. And I just learned from Elish he is disbanding the search saying Sanguine will come home when he feels like it."

Nero felt a flicker of hope when Silas retracted his hand which had been brushing against Elish's neck.

"Garrett has briefed me on what happened with Sanguine," Silas said, rising to his feet and taking a towel from Kinny who had wandered in during their exchange. "Two months he has been gone and no word?"

Nero nodded, feeling that it was safe he put a hand on Silas's back and gently led him towards the couch. They all sat down but a moment later a shrill scream of Nero's name came from the bedroom.

Silas and Garrett both looked towards the bedroom before Nero's mouth twisted to the side. "Kinny, let Loren out and tell him to shut the fuck up because Silas is here. Get Silas some food and some drugs. Okay, Kingy?"

Silas glared at him before pushing the towel into Nero's hand. "You think you're off the hook, Nero? You murdered Elish in cold blood, and you think I will let that go?"

Once again everyone froze in their places, Nero included. He was hoping he was off the hook but the burning anger in his king's eyes told him he wasn't going to be that lucky.

"You would rather me let him disband the search for Sanguine?" Nero asked, his own eyes narrowed. "I did what I thought you would want, which is to put in every effort we have to find him. Elish was only fucking doing this because he's jealous of–"

"Enough." Silas's raised voice broke the heavy tension in the room like a rock to a window. "Even if he was about to make that mistake that does not give you the right to kill him. If I let my chimeras kill their brothers whenever they disagree with him I will have my entire family wiped out within the month."

Nero's teeth ground together and he felt his temperature start to rise. "That's fucking bullshit!" Nero snapped. "Sanguine could be fucking dead and once again you don't give a shit?"

"This isn't about Sanguine," Silas said coldly. He walked up to Nero until they were almost nose to nose and glared into Nero's indigo eyes. "This is about you thinking you can kill anyone who disagrees with you. Just like when you murdered me after my decision to leave Sanguine in the greywastes. This has been an ongoing problem with you Nero Sebastian and it seems even being in concrete for several months hasn't taught you obedience."

"I'm doing what's right! Because you don't give a fuck about him. No one does!" Nero yelled. He threw the bloody towel against the wall in anger, a visible vein bulging in his forehead. "I'm the only one who fucking cares about him. The only one who loves him."

"This – is – not – about – Sanguine!" Silas's tone dropped. It was a known fact amongst the chimeras that when Silas got angry, he didn't raise his voice, on the contrary it dropped to frigid dark tones, ones that made even the bravest of them quake in their boots. "I will find him in the ways I see fit. You need to understand that you are not in control, you are not king, you don't get to kill your brothers when they do something you don't like. Whether it be disagreeing about military orders or Sanguine. Obviously my methods of discipline mean nothing on you."

Then Silas looked past Nero, to Ceph who was standing beside Garrett, his face pale and his hands nervously kneading together.

Nero's fiancé wasn't stupid, as soon as Silas's eyes fell on him his own widened. Immediately he looked away and ran a hand nervously over his short auburn hair before going back to squeezing and kneading his hands.

"Garrett, Ceph will be held in the pool until Elish wakes up," Silas said lowly. As soon as those words left his lips Nero yelled his name, but without even flinching Silas continued. "When Elish wakes up, you may take him out. Twice a day, morning and after dinner you will bring him out of the water while Nero is there, and he may gaze upon him."

"YOU FUCK!" Ceph suddenly yelled, though his green eyes were on

Nero not Silas. "You motherfucker! I told you you were making a fucking mistake! You fucking asshole, thanks a lot! Fucking thanks a lot, you fucking shit! Fuck you!"

"It wasn't his fucking fault!" Nero bellowed. He tried to hold back his temper, knowing that was what got him in this situation in the first place, but he could practically feel the anger bursting through his skin. "He didn't do shit! Fucking come on, Silas! Please!"

But like Nero had deduced before, his pleading fell on deaf ears. Silas looked at Garrett and nodded, before turning back to Nero.

Over the swearing and yelling from Ceph, Silas put a hand on Nero's muscular shoulder and gave it a pat. "I didn't just give him to you from the goodness of my own heart, Nero. He will be used as I see fit when I feel you need a reminder of your place. Now, are you going to sit with me so we can discuss Sanguine? Or do you want to watch Garrett tie the weights to his chest?"

Nero watched helplessly as Ceph turned away from him, his shoulders already shaking. Within the hour he would have hundred pound weights tied to his body and then he would be submerged in cold water with only a thin breathing tube in his mouth. A tube that would only allow enough air to keep him from dying, and just barely.

The chasm, as it was called, was originally created by Silas and Elish to train the chimeras to control their own heartbeat. It was done by making the breathing tube not only small, but it was designed to contract if one was trying to suck too much air out of it. The person could only get a sufficient amount of air in his lungs if he remained calm and gradually drew the air into his chest.

Though this was easier said than done, especially once the darkness set in and the mania. It was a struggle to remain calm when you were surrounded by dark cold water with only your thoughts to keep you company. Usually when one was locked up and the madness set in they were free to yell and scream as they see fit, but not in the chasm. You were forced to remain still, remain in a state of suspended animation, with your mind constantly demanding for you to take a deep breath.

It was maddening... so maddening. I would rather be encased in concrete than put in the chasm. And now I just condemned my fiancé to days and days of this.

"Cephy..." Nero choked. "I'm sorry."

Ceph didn't turn around, but in a small act of pride he squared his shoulders and walked out of the apartment, his head held high but his hands still trembling under the reality of what he was about to endure.

The door closed. Nero stood there until Silas's presence could be felt beside him. He looked down and saw the king smiling at him.

"Now that that's taken care of, come sit and do some drugs with me, love. We need to make ourselves a plan on how we're going to find Sanguine." The light and deceptively tender touch on Nero's shoulder made his skin tighten, and though it lit his fuse once again the dynamite it could detonate had already been reduced to a black burn mark on the floor.

"Okay…" Nero whispered, watching the last place he had seen Ceph. He made himself a familiar promise to control his temper next time, but this time something felt different.

He finally found my Achilles' heel… Nero said to himself. *I'm such a fucking idiot…*

"I have a meeting with Zhou at six," Nero said to Silas, sitting down and grabbing the sniffer that Kinny had already laid out. Without waiting for Silas to give him the okay he iced three lines and rolled it to Silas. "I want the entire legion looking for him."

Silas shook his head no. "No legion. We need them to bomb those fucking rebels. Thiens and the family only. I'll be telling Jack who Sanguine is tomorrow. Whisper not a word of it when he comes to collect Elish." Silas glanced at his watch. "The second generation can go looking and some thiens as well."

Nero stiffened; his muscles started tensing one by one.

Caringly Silas brushed a hand over Nero's short black hair, and smiled kindly at him. "You try hard, love, and I dislike punishing you so. Do control that temper for your master, yes? I see you already getting angry again."

"We need as many people as possible…"

"We need the media and the rebels not knowing about this, and having hundreds of people looking for him will only frighten him," Silas countered. "This is a family matter and it will be kept as such."

A family matter which would've never had to be dealt with if you didn't lie to Sanguine and try to convince him you weren't a maniac, Nero thought bitterly to himself, but he decided to keep the vinegar away from the raw wound, so he only nodded.

"Smile, Nero," Silas said. "You've received your punishment now everything is as it should be. I've been dead for four months – smile."

Nero stared at the finished lines of powder, now just dusty remains like a road in the greywastes half-covered in ash.

"SMILE, NERO!" Silas suddenly screamed. His tone holding such an uncharacteristic tone to it the Imperial Commander actually jumped from the surprise.

Nero forced his lips up and looked at the king to show him he was smiling. The king glared back, before picking up the blue sniffer. Wordlessly he leaned down and took the four lines Kinny had laid out on the marble coffee table.

"Everything is just fine," Silas said under his breath. "It'll be fine."

Nero stared at his king, the fine hairs on the back of his neck rising. A sudden unease washed over him that made him shift away from Silas. He had been too distracted by the simultaneous events of the last hour to notice anything unusual with his king.

But now that Nero watched him…

Silas wiped his nose and gently placed the sniffer down. "We'll just be happy, that's all. We didn't need… I didn't need…"

Nero stared at him, wishing that Elish wasn't dead behind the couch they were both sitting on. He would've been able to handle this, even Garrett was better at this than he was.

"Are – you okay?" Nero asked, forcing his voice to a light more supportive level.

The king didn't look up. He only sat on the couch with his elbows on his knees, his nostril flexing as he sniffed the drugs up to his septum. Eventually though, after a solid minute had passed, he nodded.

"Just be happy, Nero. Perhaps I just–" Silas's eyes flickered up to Nero's and the king himself smiled. "Perhaps just seeing my family happy will be enough for now. I just want my family happy."

Nero couldn't understand his odd response. "Did something happen while you were at the lab with Perish?"

Even in his inner turmoil the king's movements were graceful, a silk ribbon being drawn over smooth marble. Even if the act itself was only Silas brushing his strands of golden hair over dark-circled eyes.

"A lot happened, love," Silas said in a deceptively calm tone. "And I had four months trapped inside my own crystal fire to think about it."

"Kingy…" Nero said pushing back the terror that was braiding up his spine. He felt like he was in a horror movie, trapped in the murder house with the main character. "What happened?"

"As you know Baby Adler died in the plane crash, love," Silas responded.

Nero nodded; he had been the one to put the six month old fetus's corpse into a small bag. "But what you didn't know is that… half of Sky's brain matter was with me. I only have a finite number of tries until… until his brain matter his gone. I have enough for perhaps five more graphs. If I don't figure out how to make a born immortal – my dreams of resurrecting Sky will die just like that infant."

Nero let out a sympathetic breath and stood up. He sat down beside Silas, and even though Ceph's scathing words echoed in his brain, he put his arm around him.

Sky had been a name he had been hearing since he was young. A born immortal like Silas but one who had figured out how to kill himself, apparently because he had fallen into madness and had become a terrible person.

Like Silas had said there was a limited amount of brain matter that remained of Sky. And unfortunately using Silas's or Perish's was out of the question. The born immortal's brain wasn't identical, even the twin's. They realized that after creating the first generation of chimeras. All three born immortal's brains worked differently and responded differently to manipulation. Tests to try and create a clone of Sky would have to be done with Sky's own DNA.

"I'm sorry, Siley-pie," Nero said. "That's shit luck… we'll bomb the fuck outta the rebels and get some good revenge on them. I'll rape a couple just for you."

Silas's expression was dull and dead, but he managed to nod. "Yes… I want the Legion inside of them. I want to know just how they knew I would be in that plane. We have planes going in and out of the greywastes all the time – how did they know I was on that one? I need answers, Nero. I need to know if we have a turncoat in the Legion."

"Okay," Nero said, talking about the Legion and not his fiancé made him feel better. It made him feel more centered in this hour of chaos.

Nero felt himself able to push down the feelings regarding his fiancé, and instead stepped into his shoes as Imperial Commander. "I'll talk to Zhou. You'll send the family to find Sangy… I'll organize an attack on Irontowers. I know you love him, unlike Elish. I'll–" Nero smiled for Silas when the king glanced up at him. "I'll put my puppy's fate in your hands."

"He'll come home when he realizes I'm awake," Silas responded. "We have a strong bond... I do love that man."

Both of them looked up as they saw Loren coming into the living room, Jack behind him looking bewildered at both Silas being awake and Elish dead behind them.

Silas smiled at them, before leaning into Nero as the brute chimera squeezed him to his side. "Everything will be fine, and we'll all be happy. I'll be fine with the family I have and... when the technology is there – I will have my Sky. My beautiful... Sky."

CHAPTER 39

MY LIPS WERE CHAPPED, PEELING... WHEN I RAN MY tongue along them I felt rough mountains underneath that tasted like copper if I left my tongue on it for too long. When this happened I would break the scab and enjoy the taste inside of my mouth. I liked the taste of blood, that in itself would never change.

Surrounding me were stuffed animals, all of them in a row with the walls behind them full of newspaper clippings and the writing I wanted to have easier access to. It was like its own wallpaper now, writing stapled to the brittle drywall and bulletins patching up the holes made in the walls. I was surrounded by these things and surrounded by the smells I had been accustomed to in the basement.

I loved my stuffed animals. I had teddy bears, two cats, a penguin, a dog, a panda, and Patches my rabbit. They kept me company but sometimes they yelled and screamed at me.

My hands picked at another one of my scabs. I felt a dull pain that turned to a sting when my finger brushed open the bleeding wound. Thinking of the times the stuffed animals screamed made me nervous and guilty.

It made me guilty because they were trapped inside of themselves, condemned to being stuffed animals again. They wanted to be real like Barry had been before he died. They wanted to be real boys and real girls but I didn't know how to free them.

Barry was still trapped inside of a bear – so dearly did I want to see that grinning face and those black slate eyes, black eyes like Jack had.

But I didn't know how to free them, so they screamed and they screamed, a constant assault on my brain.

'Help us, Sami. It's dark and it's cold; it smells like stale piss and blood. It smells like Jasper's cum. We're trapped inside of these bodies and all we want is to escape.'

'You escaped but you left us behind, you left us to get fucked by Jasper.'

That wasn't true; they had never been in the basement. But they yelled it anyway and all I could do was watch their expressionless faces staring at me and watching me sleep. Watching me like sentries, like my dead friends in the shanty town had watched me.

I liked it when they watched me.

'Sami? Come on, look at me!' Patches suddenly said angrily. I looked at her noticing her voice was different. *'Sami?'*

I stared before I realized it wasn't her talking at all. So my eyes took me to the door and I saw Julia standing, the light of the hallway behind her making her brown hair glisten. Though not shining locks smelling like soap, her hair was shining from grease and I could see it on her face as well.

"What?" I mumbled. I was hunched over my notebook, writing. I was dressed in lots of clothes and they all smelled bad. My hair was messed up and my face was rough as my lips. I had picked and picked at my skin and my face and now I left spots of blood wherever I went. It was even on the walls, blood speckles on the walls where my writing was and my drawings and the newspapers I collected.

They were coming for me – they were all coming for me and I would have to leave soon. This was concluded through bouts of panic and anxiety, through spouts of yelling and ranting that usually ended with me tearing down the papers I had stapled to my walls.

Soon the walls would shake and the hands would slither down the windowsill like a snake. They would grab me and pull me through and throw me in the basement with Jasper. My stuffed animals would watch with their blank faces like Barry watched me. Barry would be by my head with *Daisy Daisy* playing, his music box drowning out Jasper's moaning.

"We're out of money – you need to get more, Pumpkin," Julia said. When she was angry she called me Sami. I don't know when she learned my name but sometime during my time here she started injecting my birth name into her nagging. Women loved to nag.

"Get out of here," I whirled around and snapped. "I'm not going out; there are crows all over the yard! I need protection. I can't go anywhere until my friends get their bodies back!"

Julia made a noise. I saw her kneel down in front of me. "Pumpkin... you're already dressed and ready. We need to go to the bank. We're fucking out of food and you're going to be out of meth tomorrow. We need to go, now."

I looked past her at my friends lined up against the wall, watching everything that was going on.

If I only knew how they could rise up and eat Julia alive, eat Mouse alive too. Everything would be well if I only knew how. They would stop screaming at me then too.

My eyes fell to the notebook, pages and pages of my writing. As I looked I realized there was blood on the pages, my hands had been bleeding from writing so much. The entire side of my palm was raw, stinging, and painful.

"Sami!" Julia suddenly slapped my face.

"Don't touch me!" I snarled as I glared her down.

Julia's eyes widened. She got up quickly, her heartbeat revving like an engine, and quickly left the room, shutting the door behind her.

I stared at the door, a brown door not white like at Jasper's, and heard her yelling at Mouse.

'You need to leave soon,' Barry said, his voice was small and weak. Barry needed strength; he was weak from being shot in the head. He had the strength to speak though, the others could only moan and scream.

Pleading, pleading, always pleading.

I frowned and shook my head. "They'll see me... my contacts are gone and the caps in my teeth are gone too. The family will find me. I just know they have Jasper looking now too." Then another prick in my heart, this one bleeding more doubt into my already anxious mind. "And you're too weak, Barry. If I take you out in the cold you'll die again. I can't handle that."

I ignored the crashing and the yelling outside my bedroom door. Julia and Mouse fought a lot, over me usually. Sometimes I heard my real name, Sanguine, but that didn't alarm me. There were so many other things to worry about.

Julia and Mouse had stopped bringing me bulletins too. Not until I get them more money – it was all about money for them, they didn't care that

I had to hide from the family and Jasper. They didn't care that I was stumped as to how I could bring my stuffed animal friends out of their bodies and make them real.

The thought of being surrounded by them made me smile. With Barry beside me, maybe he would be my age now, and Patches and the others. I would not only have protection... but I could go outside too.

I prepared another rock of meth and filled my room with the white smoke. I was halfway through my rock when Mouse rattled my door knob. He shouted some things at Julia while he had the knob turned, then finally pushed it open.

"Pumpkin..." Mouse said in a subdued voice, but it had a definite edge. His face was covered in sores like mine, except he didn't shave, Julia shaved me. His stringy hair was all greasy like Julia's too and his white shirt a dingy brown. "We're taking you to the bank tomorrow morning, if you keep saying no... you need to leave."

"The... the crows are watching me," I said, "and Barry is too weak. I can't carry my other friends either. I can't go outside, you said yourself so many times it's dangerous. It's dangerous. You don't even let me read bulletins anymore, I can't go out!" As I said this my voice rose and as it did Mouse shrunk down.

He looked nervous but his voice was still hard. "We have you dressed in winter cloths and we have sunglasses. You either go with us or you get out. I'm sorry but we can't afford to keep you and your money is gone."

I stared at him. He'd been getting mean over the last couple weeks. The less money we had the more mean him and Julia got.

'They aren't your friends,' Barry said in a grave voice. I looked at him and made his ears wiggle back and forth with my fingers. *'They're turning against you. What if they were lying the entire time and it's safe to go out?'*

I shook my head at him, but the seed of unease had been planted long ago, perhaps that was what Barry was nurturing. He knew I was starting to get nervous being here; he knew I had to leave soon too.

Mouse made an angry noise, then in a flash Barry disappeared from my grasp. I looked up and jumped to my feet, but I stumbled backwards and hit the board-covered window.

"When you fucking get money, you can get Barry back," Mouse snapped. "We shouldn't have let you have so much meth, you're a fucking lunatic. Fucking stupid chimera. Just get off your ass and go to the fucking bank and get money. Then we can continue to rot here like the low lives we all are. It isn't fucking complicated, Sanguine."

I stared at him; his angry voice and biting words striking me dumb for a second. Julia just hit me and now Mouse was yelling at me?

Were they turning against me?

I looked behind my shoulder at my stuffed animal friends, standing with the backdrop of stapled pieces of paper that made up my wall. They looked like a shrine, an offering to a faceless god. All lined up in a row with the wallpaper of ramblings. Their black eyes reflecting the single light I had above me, hanging like a noose from a black cord.

Then Mouse hit me, then he hit me again. The last one knocked me off-balance and I landed on the mattress, the back of my head smacking against the frame of the window.

I squinted, stars and sunbursts exploding in front of my eyes, sparkling around Mouse as he stood in front of me, Julia behind him. Both of their buggy eyes were filled with anger, brown eyes matching the rough scabs on their gaunt faces.

"You're going to agree now to go tomorrow, or we're throwing you out," Mouse said angrily. "We can't fucking afford to feed you. We don't have all of Skyfall's money in our bank accounts. Got it, chimera?"

Mouse threw Barry back at me. I heard a clunk as the beads that made his eyes knocked against the wall. Automatically I picked him up and clutched him to my chest, momentarily mute over the chaos that had suddenly found its way to my quiet room.

"Fucking retard," Mouse said furiously. "I've done so much for you – we both have. You have no fucking idea how much money we could get for you."

"I told you we should've told the rebels we had a chimera," Julia's voice sounded as I checked to make sure Barry was okay. I kissed his nose and smelled him; he smelled like the basement. I liked that. He was my –

"SAMI!" Mouse screamed.

"OKAY!" I shouted back, holding Barry close to me. "Okay, I'll go tomorrow. Okay, okay. I'll go..." I swallowed, feeling like I was seven years old again. "I need bags to carry my friends. And also make sure the crows don't see me... make sure the family doesn't – doesn't see me."

"No one is looking for you, Sanguine," Mouse snapped. "We've had the silver-haired fuck sniffing around two bars and he hasn't been seen in weeks. No one is watching you, it's the fucking meth. Now shut the fuck up and stay in your fucking room. I'm sick and tired of being the babysitter of a literal retard."

Mouse dug into his pockets and threw a pill onto the mattress. "This is Intoxone for meth, take this and detox yourself. You're too fucked up on meth and even when you do get money... we're putting you back on opiates."

I looked down at the pill, a small red pill with an M on it. I had heard of these pills before, but... "The meth opens my mind," I said to him weakly. "It makes me smart; it makes me see what has really been–"

The door slammed and they were gone, not even listening to what I was saying. A moment later I heard Mouse through the closed door.

"If the rebels knew chimeras were this fucking weak and retarded they would've invaded Skyfall long ago."

"Well, Sanguine agreed to get us the money. If you're that frustrated we can take the money and try and get in contact..."

The voices faded into the white noise. I sat on my bed with my legs crossed, my chin resting on Barry's head. I sniffed, not even the meth was making Mouse and Julia's anger fade from my mind.

I picked up the almost empty baggy and looked at the two remaining rocks.

Then a spur of anger went through me. I tossed the baggy across the room and in defiance of my own mind telling me to heat up another rock; I popped the red pill into my mouth and chewed it. A bitter, acidic taste coated my mouth which made my face pucker but I swallowed the remnants down my throat.

My mind told me not to, it yelled and screamed at me that the insider information I had been infiltrating would be harder to crack once the meth was out of my system, but a stronger voice was telling me I had to take a break from the drugs. It was a darker voice, a soothing voice, it almost sounded like Crow but – he was gone.

I listened to him and ignored the pull to make myself throw up the pill and cook the meth, then I laid down on my bed and stared at my paper-covered walls.

'Sami... Saaammi.' Their voices were low, moaning susurrations that came from lips sewn shut. They were muffled and desperate, their hands outstretched and reaching for me. They were begging me to free them, begging me to rip their bodies apart to expose the person inside.

I had been hearing their voices since they had been brought to me, and I had to free them. I had to free them. I needed the help, and I needed the protection.

My eyes felt like two bags of wet sand but as soon as I opened the heavy lids I felt myself unable to close them. In a way it seemed like my eyes had never closed; they had been open the entire time staring at the numbers, the papers, the images in my mind.

Maybe my eyes itched because I hadn't blinked in so long – though if they only knew the realizations I had come to while I was staring off into space they wouldn't have blinked either.

The problem I had been trying to crack while I was lying in that bed had been solved. I knew what I had to do not only to protect myself from my family, but from Jasper.

I sat up in bed; the light was still dangling above my head, swaying back and forth in the stagnant and pungent room. It coated my black-eyed friends in a soft, yellow glow.

I smiled at them, and Barry smiled back. Then I rose to my feet, my muscles aching from being stationary for so long, and stuffed Barry into my satchel. I put him beside the old clown mask, hearing the several tooth caps I still had rattling around the thick denim cloth.

Then I walked out of the bedroom and into the hallway with the living room in front of me. The kitchen was behind that with its boarded windows with shreds of curtain still sticking out between the boards. Blue curtains.

I put the satchel in front of the door but grabbed Barry and slipped on my shoes. The living room was dark; all of the electronics had been shut off to conserve power. The only light that was on was the one in my bedroom, shining yellow in the darkness but it was nothing but a sunburst in my eyes. I shut off the light and picked up half of my stuffed animals, juggling them in my arms until I could fit six of them. That was half, I had thirteen in total.

Snoring reached my ears, a faint rumbling that told me I was the only one conscious in this house. The lights were unconscious, the electronics sleeping; tonight it was just me, just me and my friends.

Silently I walked to Mouse's bedroom. I opened the door and let it open wide. I looked inside and saw Mouse sleeping with his blankets pulled tight over him. His brown hair was spread across his dirty pillowcase; the white fabric and splayed-out brown hair making it look like he had gotten shot in the head.

For several moments I only stood and watched him, remembering the first time I had laid eyes on Mouse. He was a friend at the opiate den, who got me drugs and warned me that Giuseppe was going to try and keep me there to make money off of me. I remember the gaunt skeletons of the men laying on the soiled blankets, how they looked like survivors of war with their unhealthy, filthy skin and their hollow, vacant eyes. I would have been like them eventually, or perhaps not – my family would have found me in time.

Mouse, Mouse… your real name is Frank but I called you Mouse.

I laid my stuffed animals in front of the doorway, facing Mouse's bed. Then I went back to my bedroom and grabbed my other stuffed animals. I laid each one in the doorway, facing Mouse. I wanted them to watch.

I always did like the audience.

When everyone was in their seats I walked back to the kitchen.

I grabbed a knife, a long knife. One that Mouse had used to cut our sandwiches in half. It still had mustard on the tips of it. Julia had always been bad at washing things.

I picked up Barry, who was sitting at the front of the crowd, because he had been there first. I hugged him to my chest, excited about what I was doing for my friends, and for him too.

Because I think I knew my Barry would come back when I was done.

With a smile, and his song echoing in my head I wound his butt and held the winder. Then I set him down in front of the others and I let the dial go.

And he sang his song, a song I hadn't heard in so long.

Daisy, Daisy
Give me your heart to do.

Mouse jumped under his blankets, but the several thick comforters made it hard for him to move. He took one look at me, standing in the doorway, and his prominent eyes opened so wide he really did look like a Mouse.

"Sanguine…" Mouse gasped. He tried to shift out of his blankets, but it was too late. I was too quick, I was too fast. I was –

– half-crazy, all for the love of you.
It won't be a stylish marriage,
I can't afford a carriage,

I straddled him and pressed my knees against his shoulders, pinning his arms down. Then I raised the knife with a smile and twisted it back and forth in a taunting manner.

I could feel the adrenaline speeding through my veins leaving in its wake such a tense feeling I felt the tightness in my jeans come back. I grinned in spite of myself, and as Mouse gasped and sputtered I snatched his chin and wrenched it back, exposing the dirty center of his neck, and pressed the cold blade against the skin.

But you'll look so sweet,
Upon a seat,

Mouse screamed when I started to saw through his skin. I pressed his chin back as far as I could to make the neck tight, but as the blade drew back and forth towards his windpipe, I found myself able to press back farther and farther.

"PUMPKIN! NO! NO!" Mouse shrieked.

I watched his eyes but, so I wouldn't be seen as selfish, I turned his head towards the door so my friends could see. By now his neck had a large gap in it, and his screaming had been reduced to nothing but pleas, spits, and hacks, every cough bringing a spray of blood onto the grey-blue blankets and the fitted sheet that was only done up on three corners.

Of a bicycle built for two.

I pressed down on his face as he coughed, and held the knife tighter. I stuck the tip into his windpipe and dug it in hard, trying to find the sweet spot. I put some weight behind it before giving it a hard jerk and, sure enough, with a groan and a rush of heat, a pressurized stream of blood shot from his neck and sprayed across the room, coating my friends and leaving a mosaic pattern on the dingy carpet.

Satisfied and content, I watched Mouse die; his eyes bugged out, showing more white than colour. They were staring like a fish out of water and his mouth was opening and closing like one too. Open and closed, open and closed. A fish needed water but he needed air; I could hear the whistle-like wheezing from his exposed windpipe.

There was so much blood – it was everywhere. It was streaming down and coating the sheets, it flowed like a river.

It was so pretty! I wished Crow was here to see it.

When Mouse's mouth had stopped gasping, I yanked his hair back and continued slicing.

"SAMI!" a horrified shriek pierced my ears, threatening to take with it my pleasant mood just from the sheer ear-splitting sound. I looked up and saw a black figure in the doorway, its arms out like it was a monster but they were shaking with fear.

She was stepping all over my friends like she was Godzilla; her bare feet kicking them all around like she didn't care that they were in the middle of a show.

Then she ran.

Immediately I jumped off of Mouse's corpse and pursued her, the bloody knife in my hand and tuffs of Mouse's hair in the other.

She was sobbing, wearing a pink tank top and Hello Kitty pajama pants. She was running towards the door, screaming and screaming. She tried to open the door to outside but it was locked, dead bolted locked. Another scream broke through before she turned around and looked at me, her large eyes wide like her brother's had been and holding the same insanity inducing fear.

"Pumpkin, no!" Julia sobbed. She dropped to her knees, shaking her head back and forth. "Please don't kill me, please. Please, Pumpkin, I don't want to die."

I wiped the knife with my sweatshirt sleeve and looked down at the red stains it was leaving on the thick fabric. Her sobbing was disruptive to the quiet milieu I had been enjoying. She was like a harpy screaming through the hallowed woods, breaking my much coveted silence.

I needed her anyway. I had use for both of them – everyone had their use in the world and she would be much better off with what I was going to do to her.

"Christ, Pumpkin…" Julia sobbed. I saw she was looking at my pants. I looked down too and saw my penis had become hard, my jeans outlining an obvious bulge in my crotch area. "What are you going to do to me?"

I smiled, and her face dissolved before disappearing into her hands. I knelt down in front of her and stroked her shoulder gently.

"I'm going to help my friends," I whispered nicely. "You can come too. Everyone can come, Julia. Even Mouse."

Then, in a swift movement, I drove the knife into her neck, right below the ear. The strength of the blow making her fall to her side and onto the floor, cries of shock sputtering from her lips. I held the knife firm and kept it in its place, pinning the side of her face down to the floor like I was spearing a fish.

She screamed and thrashed but only for a second, then her hands fell and her entire body started shaking. As she died I saw a wet patch form on her backside, and the smell of urine mixed in with blood.

I slowly and methodically twisted the knife imbedded in her neck, and was amused to see her arm twitch and jump from whatever nerve I had hit.

I looked behind me and laughed from happiness when I saw three of my stuffed animal friends had been able to see this show. I pulled the knife and stepped back so they could see. My boots stepping in the growing pool of red that was spilling from her wound like a forgotten bathroom tap.

Well, now it was time to get to work.

I grabbed Julia by her greasy hair, the same as I had done for Mouse before I was interrupted. I sliced through her neck and separated it from her body. It was easier than when I was a child. The spine was always the hardest part but if you stick the tip in between the vertebrae and wedge them apart you can twist the knife and use that as leverage to separate them fully. Once that's done it really is just slicing through tendons which can be tough but if you have a sharp knife you'll be okay.

I laid Julia's severed head beside my collection of friends and finished the job with Mouse's head.

I stepped back and admired them together. I always thought it was weird how different humans looked once their heads were cut off. Their facial features seemed to change, but I could still tell who they were.

I walked into Julia's room afterwards and found her sewing kit. I took out the thick strips of leather, and with my knife in hand, I kneeled in front of Julia and Mouse.

Patches would be first, and the other one would be my penguin who I named Sir because he was wearing a little tuxedo. They would be my first friends and my main sentries, the others I would put in a bag and take with me.

I picked up my knife, with the strips of leather beside me – and I went to work.

It was eleven at night. The sun long concealed behind the mountains, not to be seen until the frozen hours of the morning. It was cold outside, and the smoky fog that surrounded me only made it appear colder.

I had never seen fog before. Only in movies had I seen the silver blanket rise from the ocean to wrap itself around the cities it had snuck into. It was ominous and beautiful, with its own unique smell that tasted like winter itself. I liked it and welcomed it, for it felt as if the world itself was trying to hide the dark transgressions that had gone on in the house behind me.

No… it wasn't the fog trying to hide the horrors from the world. As I stepped outside, fearing nothing now, I realized the fog was a gift from the universe to hide me from the family I ran from. All of this was created for me, a thank you for the terrors I myself had gone through.

I had been patient and this was my reward.

Yes, I had been patient, though in truth I had a lot of work to do. I didn't want to go outside in the daylight; darkness had to be my cover because it was in that same darkness that I had always felt safe. Night was my friend, fog was my friend. Tonight I was surrounded by friends.

I patted my satchel that had Barry the bear's head sticking out of it, and slid the clown mask over my face.

Sir giggled beside me. I looked down at him and lifted the mask up.

"What do you find so funny?" I said with a smirk.

Sir shrugged. A little boy with yellow eyes sporting a tuxedo. One who loved to skip around instead of walking. "You look silly in that mask."

"I think I look mighty fine!" I protested sliding it back over my face. I looked behind me and saw Patches. She was wearing her overalls and spotted long-sleeved shirt. She had beautiful blond curls, and her voice was soft and gentle; she even had red ribbons in her hair. I loved her already like a little sister. I would take care of that one.

"Are you ready too, missus?" I said to her.

She nodded but didn't speak. Soft spoken and silent, I liked them like that.

I opened the door of the house and gave the entire area one last sweep of my eyes. Immediately the smell of gasoline and blood penetrated my nostrils, the sickeningly sweet and alluring scent soothed my heart and made my mouth water.

I picked apart every last inch of the derelict house before looking down and seeing the trail of gasoline-soaked rags that led to the doorway. There would be someone in Cypress angry that his gas was stolen but I'm sure he would get over it. It could have been a lot worse for him.

Confident that everything was in place I left the door partially ajar. Then I leaned down and touched the rags with my hand.

In an instant a burst of flame erupted from my hand and, like a ravenous, starved dog, it ate the fuel before venomously following the trail of rags in search for more. Satisfied at the flame and its path I closed the door and picked up the bulging pack that held my remaining animal friends.

Then I looked down at the bodies of my two new friends; new because I had repaired them and made them brand-new.

I picked up Sir's animal body first and smiled at the severed head of Mouse that I had sewn onto the stuffed penguin's body. He didn't smile back though, his lips were turning black and his eyes were staring off into nothing.

Once I found a new place to live I would wash him, wash the blood off of his tux he had on, then perhaps I would sew his face into a smile. Maybe weights onto his body too since his head was so heavy it was always upsetting the balance of his body. Well, it didn't matter either way, Sir the boy was here and so was Patches, my plan had worked out quite well.

"Well," I said, picking up the body of the rabbit which now had Julia's head sewed onto where the original rabbit's head had been. "Let's go then. We need to find a new home before the sun rises, then once we're all settled in I can make everyone else into little boys and girls too. Wouldn't we like that?"

"Yeah!" Sir said happily. He skipped ahead, his little legs springing him up to the air. Patches followed him, holding a little dolly in her right hand. They sprinted off into the night, the sounds of children playing echoing off of the alley's walls.

Barry laughed beside me and put an arm around my waist.

He was taller now, the same age as me. He had sparse facial hair, but he still had the little bear ears that stuck out of his head. Everything else had changed, even his voice had changed. It had gotten deeper like mine, and more gravelly.

He also had red eyes now.

Barry kissed my cheek before giving it a pat. I smiled back at him, feeling better in this moment than I had in months.

"I sure missed you, Sami," he said in his raspy but smooth voice. "Come, let's find us a new home."

The smell of smoke joined my nose already full of the enticing aroma of blood and gasoline. I heard a low roar behind me as I walked down the dirt path and towards the alleyway.

I so badly wanted to stay for the fire. I quite liked fire. But I had places to be and I knew – there were a lot of infernos on the horizon.

"Yes, *mihi*," I said to him, smiling wide with my mouth closed, the world becoming smaller as my eyes squinted under my smile. "Let's find us a new home."

CHAPTER 40

JACK WRUNG THE WASH CLOTH INTO THE BUCKET, the large and almost entirely empty room filling with the orchestra of trickling water as the rosy drops rained down onto the pink-tinted water below.

He squeezed out the remaining water before, with careful and trained hands, he gently started washing the alabaster body that was stretched out on the makeshift slab below him.

One day they promised him a skyscraper of his own, but for now Jack would've settled for a better equipped room to prepare the dead for resurrection. This room was more of a hospital morgue, with white walls, a grey linoleum floor faded from being washed over and over again, and metal slabs cold to the touch and squeaky wheels. On top of that the cleaning chemicals made his skin irritated, and even the heavy fragrance of soap wasn't enough to kill the sterile smell in the air.

Jack let out a breath not realizing he had been holding it. He had learned the ins and outs of this job since he was assigned it two years ago, but it was always tense when he had his boss looking over his shoulder.

As if on cue, a flawless hand with long, slender fingers and well-manicured nails, came into his vision and took the cloth from him in a gentle but firm touch. A moment later Silas appeared beside him where he started cleaning one of the long lacerations on Elish's chest.

"Pat it dry afterwards, love," Silas said, his voice kind but still holding in its tone dominance, like a hammer wrapped in linen. Jack had been brought to his knees many times under that voice, and today was no different.

Why was he here? Jack took a deep breath, but the tight restriction in his throat made his breath shudder; as if his lungs were trying to prevent it from leaving. *He hasn't watched me do this since I had stopped apprenticing him...*

With this thought the tremble came back to his hands. Though he pushed it down as ridiculous paranoia and instead started patting dry the healing wounds on Elish's chest, feeling his oldest brother's skin warm under his touch.

Jack smiled at this and placed a hand over Elish's chest. He could feel his heart beating strong underneath the closing wound on his chest.

Despite his fear he took Silas's hand and laid it on Elish's chest as well.

"Now... how long do you think it will be, Jack?" Silas asked. The king, of course, knew, but it was another part of Jack's job to memorize the times it took for his immortal brothers to resurrect.

Silas was the slowest, then Nero, Elish, and Garrett resurrected the fastest. Though Garrett always took longer to grow limbs, so if you wanted him to be gone for longer just remove fingers. Nero though grew limbs fast and Elish always recovered from head wounds quickly...

Jack's eyes flickered over to a black leather-bound notebook that he had. The one that held all of his well-written notes and instructions. It had silver writing on the front that was a language of his favourite book in the world, Quenyan from Lord of the Rings. He had learned that language from Elish when he was in his early teens and Elish had learned it from Silas. Just a pet hobby, it wasn't like anyone spoke it. It looked beautiful written though.

Quickly Jack tried to do the calculations in his head. He took a moment before speaking with confidence. "I think he will be awake tonight. The muscle has healed over and almost all of the fat layer has healed as well. Since he's breathing soundly and his heartbeat is strong it means his head wound is completely healed also."

Jack looked at Silas, eager but nervous for his response. He would either get that faint smile or the king's face would harden in disappointment, and if he was in a foul mood, he would get verbally berated or worse, hit.

The relief Jack felt when he saw Silas smile was painted on his face, and when Silas patted his hand with a nod he had to resist jumping into the king's arms. Instead he held himself back and beamed instead.

When Elish was washed and dried they wheeled the metal slab he was laying on to the elevator for pickup. The elevator was too small for the metal slab; he would be carried up by Nero once he came back from a meeting with Ellis.

Jack pressed the button for Silas's floor, trying to enjoy his king spending time with him. They had spent a lot of time together when Jack was younger, but since he had started college and his duties as the Grim Reaper of the family, and since Silas had been busy with his own kingly duties, it didn't happen as often as Jack would like.

He still summons me for sex every couple of weeks and I love our conversations after we're both basking in the afterglow, but still – this is different.

And I treasure it more since… since…

I have been so scared for Sami. Jack's face became tight and tense; he stared down at his shoes as the despair and worry washed over him again. The same thing that happened to him every time he was reminded that his friend was missing, and the family was actively searching for him. Jack had been tearing apart every district in Skyfall but no one had seen his tormented friend. Elish had given him leave to use all of the family's resources to try and find him. Elish had been so kind and helpful, and yet – nothing.

The guilt over what had happened overwhelmed him to the point where he cried at night from worry. So many things he should've done different, Sami missing for over two months had been the sole result of all of Jack's mistakes.

I had only pushed him away because he would've gotten himself killed attacking Valen and my other brothers, Jack said to himself. *What else could I have done? I did it to protect him… I did it because he was just a greywaster and my brothers' soulless monsters. They wouldn't hesitate to rape and murder Sami just for the sheer thrill of it. Not to mention the thrill of being able to hurt me.*

Jack's fists clenched as the anger started to trickle down. Anger over this was a new feeling, before he had met Sami Fallon he rarely got angry at his brothers' abuses. But since he had spent time with that mad greywaster he had found his confidence, he had found his pride. If an orphan greywaster who had so many issues could stand up to four chimeras, why couldn't he?

"What are you thinking of, lovely boy?" Silas murmured. Jack's tense body relaxed as the king gently stroked his neck. "Don't lie now; what is making your beautiful face scowl?"

Jack sighed and tilted his head towards his king's touch. He didn't think he could lie even if he wanted to, though he seemed to be getting better at lying.

"I'm worried about Sami," Jack replied honestly. "I made a lot of mistakes with him and I feel responsible for making him run off. I'm also responsible for him killing Valen's friends. It was all because I was trying to protect him from the family."

The elevator doors opened, Jack stepped back to let Silas exit the elevator first, then followed him down the decorated hallway towards his top-level skyscraper apartment.

"Yes, Nero told me all about it," Silas replied. "You wanted to date Sami, did you not?"

Silas turned around and Jack was shocked to see a flicker of hostility in his eyes, enough to make him stop in his tracks. Though as soon as Silas saw the surprise in Jack's face the hostility disappeared and a smile took its place.

"Y-yes," Jack said with a nod so faint he wasn't sure if he had actually nodded. He kept walking and they both entered the apartment.

"Did he seem happy with you? Did he act of himself?" Silas asked.

Kinny, who had been obviously taking a break from his sengil duties because he was sitting on the couch eating potato fries, jumped to his feet and rushed towards Silas, a smudge of cheese on the corner of his mouth. It was obvious the sengil wasn't expecting them to be back so quickly.

"Yes, it seems so. He has a lot of quirks, but I found them endearing," Jack said back, handing Kinny his coat. The confusion over this brothers', and, to a larger extent, the king's interest in Sami, once again flooring him. "I – I like him, King Silas."

Then Jack cleared his throat. "I was wishing once he's found… that I could ask your permission to take him as my boyfriend."

Silas's head snapped towards him. Jack stared back in shock as the king's green eyes seemed to cut him down right on the spot. The hostility coming back with vengeance that no conjured smile could erase.

"Date him?" Silas said, his voice as cold as ice yet it seared Jack's mind like the fires of hell. "You want to date him?"

Jack stared back, unable to move, the hairs on his arms prickling and raising on quickly erupting goose bumps. Even Kinny had frozen in place, both their jackets draped over his now shaking arms. The both of them stood in fear, equal spectators but what show it was they were watching seemed lost on both of them.

None of this made sense…

"Silas… Master…" Jack whispered. He rubbed his nose from sheer nerves and looked at Kinny for support, though all he caught was a blur of black and blue, the sengil already halfway to the kitchen.

Then, like the incident had never happened, Silas's smile returned. He reached a hand up and gently stroked Jack's face, ignoring the fearful, stricken look of his black-eyed chimera. He dismissed it to the void like it had never happened in the first place.

"Yes…" Silas murmured with a nod. "Perhaps that would be best for now. I would destroy him with the state I am in now. Yes, yes, I know enough to know that…" Silas's tone dropped though his rambling words kept falling from his mouth. "Once I'm back – once I've accepted it… perhaps then."

Jack stared, confused and worried. Silas wasn't one to mumble and ramble, only when he was in an emotionally dire state. Usually when something had gone wrong in Kreig with Perish's research. Was that it? Was that why Silas seemed so…

Wait a moment.

Did King Silas like Sami? Was – was that what it had been all along?

The thought made Jack's mouth drop open, and suddenly everything started to make sense. Everything from Silas's invested interest in Sami, to the first generation being so involved in Sami's life as well.

"K-King Silas…" Jack stuttered.

Awareness suddenly seemed to click back to Silas's eyes. He looked at Jack, as if forgetting he was even there, before Jack saw his jaw tighten.

"Get me some tea," Silas said sharply, before uncharacteristically he snapped at Jack, "Now!"

Jack nodded so quickly and rapidly he felt dizzy. He almost ran out of the living room and into Silas's large kitchen. He spotted Kinny, pale-faced and grave, leaning against the stove which held a steaming kettle.

Then Jack heard the familiar sound of the doors leading to the hallway opening. He peeked out and saw Nero, Garrett, and Ellis walk in. Though usually Jack would walk out to greet them, their expressions were all grim and that alone made Jack stay silent.

"Okay…" Jack heard Nero say, not waiting for Silas to greet him. "We got issues, Kingy. We have bad issues."

Jack tucked himself into the best blind spot he had and watched the four of them with fascination.

"What is it?" Silas asked, his voice was back to its normal silken tones, as if the slight manic moment Jack had witnessed had been nothing but a phantom. Though it was so unlike Silas to act as such perhaps it hadn't happened at all.

"Missing people and murders… and lots of them," Ellis said, her purple-blue eyes seemed aflame, and she kept shifting from one foot to another. "We have two people missing from Cypress, entirely missing, and a headless corpse that was discovered last night in Nyx, the northern area which borders Cypress. To top it off…" Ellis sucked in a breath and shifted her weight again. "There was a house fire in Cypress four days ago. We thought nothing of it but a thien noticed crows picking at the wreckage, and we found two headless corpses still smouldering in the remains."

"Crows…" Silas murmured. Ellis nodded Silas.

"You can guess which ones, Father. The half-crow half-ravens – *his* crows," Ellis replied. "The bodies belonged to a brother and sister. Frank and Julia Gallenski. We asked around and we got a rather interesting report from where Frank worked… an opiate den run by Giuseppe Xianwu. He – he says Frank ran off with a new, and rich, customer, who came in with a lot of money."

Then Ellis paused, her chest rose as she took in a deep breath. "Several people reported seeing a man wearing a rubber Halloween mask the morning of the fire, a clown to be exact. He was carrying a stuffed bear in his arms."

Jack held a hand up to his mouth to stifle the gasp. There was no mistaking who Ellis was talking about. Sami was in Cypress? But he had spent two weeks asking around there and there was no sign.

And not to mention – did they think Sami was killing people? Not Sami… he would never kill someone, or at least… he wouldn't kill someone innocent.

Would he?

"He's killing because he's upset…" Silas said. "All of my loves fall back on that when they're in emotional turmoil. Why he wants their heads though… I am not sure."

"We need to find him, Dad," Ellis said frustrated. "The Underground Free Media has picked up the story and since Elish is dead he wasn't able to send word to squash it. Nero couldn't get to them in time. The newspaper is blaming it on a chimera, and since they're right I don't know what to say back. Sanguine is getting sicker and sicker, something has to give and–"

Chimera?

Sanguine?

Jack stared at Silas, his hand slipping from his mouth and falling to his side with a slap. The sound of it made all four of them turn towards Jack, just as the silver-haired chimera fell to his knees. He put both of his hands over his mouth and looked up at the four in absolute shock.

"Shit... you didn't tell me he was fucking here!" Ellis swore. She turned from the four of them, a chain of expletives falling from her mouth.

Jack tried to talk, he tried to say something but all that came out was string after string of nonsensical stammering. Even when Nero came over and pulled him to his feet, all he could do was stare at Silas. His mind jamming, the gears inside of his head seemingly rusted to the point where nothing was moving, nothing was processing. He was struck dumb and in that moment, unable to even stand.

"It's... it's okay, puppy," Nero said, holding his entire weight. "Just breathe..."

"C-chimera?" Jack stammered, his voice now stuck at an octave so high he sounded like a meowing kitten. "C-chimera? Sami? Sami?"

Jack took in a deep breath before, unable to stop himself, he shrieked it. "SAMI IS A CHIMERA?"

"Pup... it's okay," Nero said soothingly, but the roaring behind Jack's eyes paid no attention to Nero's calm voice. In an instant the rusted gears of his mind started to rev, spinning faster and faster. Every bit of information started flooding to him to the point where he didn't know if he was going to go crazy, pass out, or throw up on the floor.

Jack shook his head back and forth. He didn't even realize he was hyperventilating until the stars starting to cluster to the corner of his vision. He shook his head rapidly at Nero, before his legs once again gave out from under him.

How the fuck... oh, no, no... fuck no. Are they serious? Is this reality?

Sami is a chimera? He was a chimera all along?

Oh fuck. It makes perfect sense.

The family's involvement; Silas's interest in him. Of course he wasn't some greywaster Silas wanted to date, you fucking imbecile. He's a chimera, your brother.

"Of course he is!" Jack screamed, more at himself than the others. Garrett was there now helping hold him up. "Of course he fucking is!"

Jack burst out laughing, his entire body shaking from sheer stress and anxiety, but not five seconds later he started to cough, and five seconds after that… he threw up on the floor.

"Why…" Jack hacked, a string of spit falling onto the floor. "Why the fuck was this kept from me!?" Every word Jack spoke only became louder and shriller. "Why didn't anyone tell me this!?"

Jack swayed again, he started to feel faint.

"Hold him up…" Silas's voice suddenly sounded.

"Silas, don't be mean to him – he really loves the guy. Please, Kingy."

"I have no intention, now hold him up."

Jack looked up, vomit dripping down his mouth; his world swirling around in dizzy anxiety. His mind kept boiling in its confusion, every few seconds brushing on the terror this realization brought before spinning off in a different direction. He was so confused in that moment he still didn't know what to do with himself. Everything seemed a thousand miles away, all but the bright beacon in his mind that kept screaming at him:

SAMI IS A CHIMERA!

Jack groaned, then felt a hand on his chin. It was lifted until he was face-to-face with King Silas.

"Everything will be fine, my lovely Grim," Silas said soothingly. He smiled kindly and framed Jack's face with his hands. "Relax… take in a deep breath. We have important matters to discuss, lovely Jack. And we don't have time to deal with your shattering world. So hush for your master, and breathe in and out with me."

Jack whimpered, but he felt better under the caring touch of his master. So he nodded and tried to take in a rattling breath.

As he did he felt a rush of calm wash over him, like he was taking a hit of the finest opiate powder. It was coming from Silas's hands and, sure enough, as Jack looked into the king's eyes he saw the brilliant green emeralds turn black for several seconds.

The calming touch of King Silas was an ability unique to him, though they had tried to inject these strange abilities into Valen without success. It was an ability that tweaked your very brain, soothing the open wounds of whatever was causing you inner chaos and healing them with his gentle white light. It was unbelievable the power the king had, and something Jack had only witnessed a handful of times.

King Silas had ended the world, and started the Fallocaust and it was during times like these that Jack understood why the world should fear him. He was the most powerful man in the world, with a touch that could tame even the wildest of beasts.

The calmness covered Jack like a thick canvas and embraced him in its warmth. He could feel the anxiety get siphoned out of him in a way that reminded Jack of an infected wound, hot and ready to burst, finally being lanced and drained.

"Now breathe out…" Silas whispered calmly, his hand still gently caressing Jack's cheek. Jack nodded and obeyed, breathing out what felt like an intangible mountain of anxiety and terror.

"There we go, your heartbeat is slowing, your blood pressure is falling… does my love feel better?" Silas whispered.

Jack opened his eyes, though in reality his eyes had never been shut, only the awareness came back to him. He nodded to Silas, seeing his king standing in his glory behind him. Though a split second later a trickle of blood ran down his nose.

Though he still felt dizzy, Jack raised a hand and gently wiped away the blood.

"You'll sit with us in the living room," Silas said calmly. He looked behind him and nodded to Nero and Garrett. They both released their hold on Jack, slowly to make sure he could stand on his own. "Any questions you have may be asked, but planning is more important. Come now."

Jack nodded dumbly, the questions still surging through his mind like a thousand people trying to rush through a single door, but the calming touch of Silas gave Jack the tools to be patient. He felt like Silas had wrapped him in a protective blanket. The anxiety was still there, and the shock of his realization, but it was far away from his mind, far enough for him to be able to function through the meeting.

Sami was a chimera… Sami was a chimera…

I will do as Silas asks and breakdown about this later – right now I need to bring… I need to bring…

I need to bring my boyfriend home.

Jack's lips tightened and though shock and fear had reigned supreme over his emotions just moments ago, he was surprised and proud of himself to feel a new swell of bravery and determination go through him. He felt empowered to help his new brother. He felt responsible for him even more so now. A new attachment to this strange man had rapidly started to form inside of him, and a protectiveness that Jack knew would grow like a thousand scattered seeds.

Yes, Jack nodded as he sat down on the living room couch. *I'm going to bring my boyfriend home.*

You're my boyfriend, and my brother. I now understand this attraction I've always felt towards you, and now – I won't try and push it away.

I'll find you, and I will love you through your madness. I promise you, Sami. I will love you as I know you had once loved me.

"We need to bring him home," Jack said, gratefully taking the cup of tea from Kinny. He warmed his hands on it, his entire body was shaking from the sheer emotional impact of the news he had learned.

"You know we will," Nero said. Jack felt a warm hand on his knee and a caring rub. Nero had always been the perfect older brother. Even though he was almost forty he still acted like a kid himself most of the time. "I met him when he was only seven, and it was me, Ceph, and Silas that took him out of that dude's basement."

Jack felt a pull on his lips. A sadness filled his heart as he remembered the tidbits of personal information that Sami had given him when they had their date. "He told me... he told me about that. How long was he held captive for?"

Nero and Ellis exchanged glances before, oddly, they looked at Silas nervously. They looked like they both wanted to speak but as the silence sunk into the room Jack realized they were both waiting for Silas to answer.

"Eleven years," the king finally said after several moments had passed. "He was kidnapped by a meth addict who tortured him and abused him. He got him shortly after Nero and Ellis found him and let him stay in a small two-storey house we have in the greywastes. When I first met Sanguine he was terrified of everything and would hide under the bed most days. It took a lot of work to get him to even go outside... and the food hoarding." Silas smiled at the memory. "He hoarded food like a little squirrel, but he was so... endearing and sweet. I enjoyed watching him discover the joys of life for the first time."

"S-Sanguine?" Jack's voice faltered under the realization. "His name isn't really Sami?"

All four of them shook their heads. "Sami was the name his adoptive mother gave him; she died when he was one. He called himself Sanguine when we found him but Elish gave him the alias Sami Fallon when he sent him to college," Silas explained. "He is my Sanguine Sasha Dekker. He shared a steel mother with you Jack."

Silas leaned over and opened a drawer of his marble coffee table. Jack's eyes widened when he saw a photograph on the top of the pile. He took it from Silas and started to feel his breathing get shallow when he saw who it was.

It was Sami, but his eyes were blood-red, and the large smile he had on his face showed off pointed shark-like teeth. The same type of teeth that Jack had.

He has teeth like mine? He's – he's so much like me.

He's stunning.

"My *crucio* was so shy over his appearance, and Nero tells me he was happy to wear dental caps and coloured contacts. He was making grand strides before I was killed," Silas explained. His voice was still full of pride, like he was showing off a kid who just got accepted into a premier college. "Was he excited to go to school, Nero? Did Elish and Mantis treat him well?"

The photo shook under Jack's trembling hands. All of this was too much for him and he wanted nothing more than to run to his apartment and sit in complete sensor-depleting darkness for a while. The pit of nausea seemed to feed on these new realizations. It absorbed and consumed the shock that each hammer blow made and used it to grow and expand.

Jack closed his eyes and took in a deep breath in an attempt to calm himself. He opened them to the smiling photo of Sanguine, and felt his heart shudder as he gazed at his brother's face.

No… my boyfriend… my boyfriend.

Jack put the photo down and his cup of tea as well. He then slowly wiped his hands down his face before resting his elbows on his knees and burying his face into his hands. He stayed there with his eyes closed, and tried to use the manufactured darkness to calm his mind down and center himself.

With his face covered by his hands he stayed completely still, and listened in on the conversation going on between Silas, and Jack's other siblings.

"No, but we do need to make Oniks aware of what's happening," Jack heard Silas say. Jack had said nothing during this conversation; he was content retreating back into his head and hiding there until he was needed. He had so much on his mind at that moment he barely knew what to do with himself.

"We already have, and we're injecting someone new in to try and weed out the turncoat," Nero commented, his mouth full of some sort of snack that Kinny had brought. "We have all of that taken care of and the invasion is scheduled for five days from now. Just focus on Sangy, leave the rebels up to me, puka. Are you sure you don't want some of our legion trackers? We have the clothing we found him in and that stuff is fucking rank with his smell."

"Actually… I don't think I want him to be found quite yet."

Jack's head shot up. He looked surprised at Silas and saw that he wasn't alone. All three of Jack's brothers and Ellis were giving Silas shocked and confused looks.

Silas, of course, didn't care. The king, who was nibbling on the end of a chocolate wafer, with a blue-embered cigarette in his other hand, was staring at the photo of Sanguine that Jack had put down.

He put the cigarette into his mouth and moved the photo until it was facing him. He then took an inhale of the cigarette and gently blew it across the smiling face of Sanguine.

"I think Sanguine's murders are the perfect distraction right now from our planned invasion," Silas said, before nodding to himself like what ideas he had forming inside of his head were indeed the right ones. "We already have the media on this don't we, Ellis?"

Ellis nodded. "That's why we came as quickly as we could. The UFM is all over this saying it's a chimera and Haden at the SNN says we're going to have to either make a statement or let them run stories about it or the public is going to start to either try and get a hold of the UFM or think we're hiding something."

"We don't give a fuck what the media –" Nero paused as Silas raised a hand.

"Like it or not the media needs something," Silas said with a frown. "I don't like it either but I refuse to muzzle the media in Skyfall. That's what happened before the Fallocaust and the people revolted like you wouldn't believe. We need them to believe they have free media and that means printing things that might not put us in the best light. If we let the occasional bit of bad publicity slip it means we'll have liberty to stop the actual damaging stories."

"But, Silas, forgive me but… *this is pretty damn damaging*," Nero protested, though his words were small and submissive. Ceph was still in the chasm and he knew a single toe out of line would condemn his fiancé to even longer in his watery darkness.

"If it's a chimera, yes…" Silas said. "But Sami isn't a chimera. They have no proof that this was done by a chimera it could be any sort of mad man or serial killer. Nero, tell your contacts to run the story but I want it heavily implied that this isn't the work of a chimera. The rest will write itself. We've had serial killers in Skyfall before and I've seen more than enough of them before the Fallocaust. The people love a good active serial killer and the media will eat it up like candy. This will distract them from the invasion and that is what we want right now. Yes," Silas said and nodded again. "This is a brilliant plan."

"But Silas…" Jack said worried. "Sanguine – Sanguine needs to come home."

Silas gave him a warm smile, but it didn't help the fear that had already cannibalized Jack's other feelings. If anything the king's deceptive smile fuelled the anxious feelings.

"Sanguine needs to do what chimeras do, love," Silas said, his voice was gentle but it was deceptive, like a wasp hiding inside a rose. "He needs to kill and make himself feel better. Perhaps when he's killed a few people it will be easier for me to explain to him the nature of the chimera. The very reason he ran away was because I left out some of our family's… more darker facets. No, Sanguine will be fine and he'll come home when he's ready. Until then the family will make use of his bloodthirst."

Make use of his bloodthirst? More like make use of the misery he's in! "That's bullshit!" Jack suddenly yelled, surprised more than the others at his sudden outburst. "He's in turmoil right now! He needs to come home!"

"Jack!" Ellis and Nero both snapped at the same time.

"NO!" Jack rose to his feet, feeling the corners of his eyes burn. "He needs help; he needs his family not to be used to push that stupid rebel agenda! This is a load of shit. I thought you coming back would mean we'd find him, not the fucking opposite!"

Though the rage he was feeling was clinging to his bones like a tight glove, Jack still shrunk down when Silas rose to his feet. And when the king's green eyes burned into him Jack took a step back, and nervously crossed his arms over his chest.

"You will not raise your voice to me in my own home, Jack Anubis." The room around Jack seemed to get darker as King Silas's cold voice enveloped him. A tone that sucked the light out of the room like it was a black hole.

"I'm – I'm sorry," Jack whispered. He nervously wiped his nose and stared at the floor, feeling like a small ant in the presence of a great dragon. A small useless insect that only survived being around the powerful being because he was too small to be noticed.

"Look at me," Silas said coldly.

It was the last thing Jack wanted to do. He wanted nothing else but to turn tail and run as the dark voice creeped into his ears and seeped into his brain. Jack's body seemed to scream at him to get as far away from Silas as he could, but fleeing was never an option, even though that was the prey's only instinct.

So Jack lifted his chin and looked at him.

"You may look for him, and only you," Silas said slowly, "and if he injures or kills you. I will feel no guilt."

A flood of relief and gratitude overwhelmed the silver-haired chimera. The feeling was such a contrast from the terror he had just experienced his mind temporarily stalled from confusion. All he could do was nod dumbly at this king.

Then a sudden knock on the double oak doors. Jack sighed with relief and quickly sat down, his heart pounding and his brain aching from the constant barrage of anxiety and stress.

Kinny skittered towards the door but the moment he opened it he was pushed out of the way. The sengil stumbled back with his eyes wide with surprise as Ludo and Felix walked in, both of their faces stony.

Silas, who was already edging a foul mood from Jack's outburst, gave them both a narrow look. "Did Mantis not warn you during your therapy not to approach me with this again?"

Nero got up and sat down beside Jack, before nudging him with his elbow. "Watch, this is gonna be good."

"You have the family out looking for some greywaster retard and you won't let any of us look for Valen!?" Ludo threw his hands up into the air before letting them fall to his side with a smack. His silver eyes looked like a moon rising over lavender hills, the permanent circles under his eyes never more prominent than when he was upset.

"Don't pester me with him." Silas's eyes flashed dangerously. "And don't you dare speak to me in that tone. I'm growing tired of snippy teenagers trying their teeth on me."

"He's your creation!" Felix interjected. He stood over a foot taller than King Silas and twice as thick, but even the brute chimera looked like a shadow under the king's piercing glare. "Come on, King Silas. I know you fucking hate him but he's just a fucking kid."

"Felix!" Nero shot up and quickly got between Silas and Felix. He took a step towards the brute chimera until he was nose-to-nose. "You will stand down and speak to your king with respect."

"No, it's alright, Nero." Silas put a hand on Nero's shoulder and gently directed him away from Felix's face. "Let the child throw his tantrum. It's amusing to see just how quickly my creations fall into insubordination with my four month absence."

Silas stepped in Nero's spot and, like Nero had done, he stood right in front of Felix, though unlike Nero he had to look up at the brute. "Both your attitudes are quite amusing. Tell me, Felix, what makes you think you can speak to your king so? And in front of your older brothers, your sister, and Jack? Does that defective specimen mean that much to you? I thought you had a boyfriend, hm?"

Felix's eyes shifted over to Ludo, who wasn't standing nearly as tall as he was a moment previous. Ludo didn't look back; he seemed to be second guessing whatever their plan had been.

"I mean no disrespect, Master," Felix said slowly, his chest visibly shrunk as he let out what looked like a tense breath. "We're both confused as to why you're sending so many chimeras out to find that Sami person… when your own chimera is missing."

"Sami is a better person than that shit eater will ever be," Jack snipped. He glanced up at Felix and Ludo before taking another verbal bite. "You'll be seeing a lot of him, and with how Sami is hell-bent on killing Valen, you've probably seen the last of that – oh what did you call him, King Silas?" Jack's own eyes flashed as Felix and Ludo's widened in anger. "Oh yes: *defective specimen*."

"You shut the fuck up you motherfucking faggot," Felix suddenly snapped. Then, in one fluid motion, nothing but a blur to the others, Felix reached into his pocket and flung a pocket knife at Jack.

And though it was sheathed, it was still a made out of metal. The objected flew past Silas's head, past the coffee table, and towards Jack's face.

Jack ducked, the projectile coming so close to his head he could feel the air tickle his ear. And though it missed Jack it didn't miss the large mirror hanging up on one of the support beams of the apartment. It hit the middle of the black-framed mirror and with a loud crash it shattered and fell to the ground.

The shock that Jack felt was quickly replaced by blazing anger, with a scream of rage he drew on the wellspring of confidence that had been growing since he had met Sami – and lunged at Felix.

Then, drawing on those same instincts, the ones Jack felt imprinted on his genetics and his being, he opened my mouth and clamped down on Felix's jaw and right ear. He held his hand to Felix's head and clenched it like he was a cat pinning down a bird, and with all his strength, with all of his might, he bit and clawed. And when he could feel bits of Felix's flesh inside of his mouth he devoured it and sunk his pointed teeth back into the hot and bleeding wound, desperate for more.

Then Nero grabbed him and started pulling him back. Jack clamped his teeth together, and when he grabbed hold of Felix's ear, he didn't let go.

Felix yelled and howled as Jack snapped his head back, Felix's ear firmly clamped in his jaws. He only dropped it when screaming and spitting threats became more important that holding the ear between his teeth.

Everything around him, audible and visual, had become a blur, everything but Felix who was grabbing his face and staring at Jack in surprise, ribbons of red falling down where his ear used to be, before becoming gems on the carpet below.

Jack didn't stop – he couldn't. In his rage he spat threat after threat, swearing on anything and everything the danger they would be in if they ever threatened him or Sanguine again. As he shouted he could feel a burning inside of him, a different one than before. It was like he had stumbled upon an untapped oil well, and someone had had the misfortune of throwing a match down the hole.

Something is snapping inside of me – something is changing.

Jack tried to wrench himself free of Nero, ravenous to taste the blood that was leaking from Felix's face. He wanted it so badly his mouth watered, and something else… something else was happening.

He was getting aroused by it.

Surprisingly Nero laughed, and his grip became a hug, then there was a kiss on Jack's cheek which seemed to draw Jack down to earth. As he descended down from whatever cloud of madness he had stepped onto he heard Ellis's booming voice followed by the quick exits of Ludo and Felix. Ellis left with them, her face red with anger and her fists clenched.

"He works! He works, Silas!" Nero laughed kissing Jack again. The silver-haired chimera felt a low rumbling in his throat and he realized he was growling like a tom cat who had just spotted another male in his territory.

"We got two stealths!" Nero raved, shaking Jack back and forth. "He just needed to fall in love, that's all! Aww, I'm so proud of him, look at his cute little face all growly."

Silas was beside the snarling chimera. As soon as Jack felt Silas's cold hand brush his cheek the growl left his throat. He swallowed as the sanity started to trickle back, and tried to catch his breath.

"He does… finally. Look at him," Silas said in a hushed voice. He drew Jack's soft cheek towards his face. "I was worried we had failed with you, but no. Just hear the blood rushing through your veins. You finally stood up for yourself, and for your family."

Then Silas smiled, not the dark smile that held behind it a thousand nefarious thoughts and plans, but a genuinely happy one.

"You've become a chimera today, Jack Anubis," Silas whispered. He leaned in and gently pressed his lips up against Jack's. "You have truly become a chimera and a Dekker. Welcome to the family, love. Today you have made your king proud."

Jack's body filled with pride, he wanted to dive into Silas's arms, no… he wanted to take him to the bedroom and ride him to his peak again and again. But strangely that seemed like something the old Jack would do, the immature teenager, not the new chimera he was seeing finally break out of his cocoon.

So instead he stood tall and proud, but still smiling as Silas stroked his cheek.

The king then leaned in and kissed him again, his time separating Jack's lips with his own and slipping his tongue into his mouth.

Then, with a low groan, Silas pushed his hands down Jack's pants and grabbed his stiff penis.

Nero kept his hold on Jack and watched; Jack could hear his brother's breath quicken as he watched Silas draw the hard member out of Jack's jeans.

"I have a wonderful plan…" Silas said in a seductive voice. His fingers gently traced the slit before he drummed the pads of his fingers against the tip of Jack's dick. Jack started to feel lightheaded under the building pressure of his king's touch.

"I want you to not only help find Sanguine…" Silas said. "I want you to give the media something to write about. I want you to find your king some abandoned buildings… and I want you to burn them to the ground. And if a few Cypressians or Morosians happen to be in there at the same time… so be it."

Jack stared at Silas but said nothing, the alluring and seductive pleasure doing its work on the chimera's mind. He found it surprising that he felt no inner objection to Silas's order, on the contrary, the thought excited him.

Feeling his approval Silas nodded. He wrapped his hand around Jack's penis and gently tugged the head. A moan fell from Jack's lips soon after.

"My Sanguine seems to love starting fires." Silas leaned in and whispered into Jack's ear; the heat of his breath touching Jack's neck drove him wild. "So set his world on fire, Jack. Create an inferno – that not even Sanguine's psychosis can resist."

Jack nodded, and at his nod Silas turned his touch to the seductive pleasuring static that made a slave of every man who felt it. Jack let out a high pitch moan and started grinding his dick into Silas's hand.

"Good boy," Silas said, then his eyes flickered to Nero, then to Garrett. "Let's welcome Jack to our family the proper way, shall we? Today he sits at the top of his generation – and I do want to see just how well he fucks now."

CHAPTER 41

"HAVE A GOOD NIGHT, CROWS," I SAID HAPPILY TO my crow friends as I walked inside of the abandoned office building.

"Good night, Sanguine."

"Got any food?" "Come here, crow."

I smiled through the cigarette locked between my lips and gently closed the door. My crow friends always knew where to find me. It hadn't taken them long to find my newest home. They were loyal beyond belief, and I loved them for it.

I walked down the concrete steps one by one, descending into the darkness with a severed head swinging from my right hand. The blue ember of the cigarette hanging out of my mouth was nothing but a white orb in my vision, brightening and blinding me every time I inhaled the soothing smoke.

The temperature seemed to drop a degree with every step but soon I would be warm. I had responsibilities now to keep my friends comfortable so I had bought a heater with the money I had stolen from my corpses' wallets. They had no need for them anyway, I had even asked as I watched the life fade from their horror-stricken eyes.

I flicked the ash from the cigarette and felt my boots hit the dirty floor; they scraped and scratched as I made my way through the narrow hall, crumbling grey brick on either side of me. The hallway was so close together I couldn't stretch out my arms without brushing the musty brick, it was closed in, tight, restricting, claustrophobic – it was home.

Yes, this was my home, and never more than now did I feel safe in this basement that I had claimed as my lair.

I pushed the door open and walked inside. Immediately a rush of heat hit my face, and my vision temporarily went white as my eyes adjusted to the yellow halogen lights that I had bought last month.

"Sanguine's back!" Sir said, his tenor voice happy and jovial.

I squinted and opened my eyes, while my vision focused I saw my little friend Sir jumping up and down. My other friend Noodles was beside him also jumping up and down. He had cat ears on his head, orange ones that matched his orange striped hair. He reminded me of Drake but he spoke in an English accent – not sure why.

"Did you bring us something, Sanguine?" Teddy, Barry's younger brother took the bag from me and looked inside. To my left Barry took the head from me and sat it down on the floor. As I handed the kids the bag I glanced down at him and saw he was holding a new stuffed animal, a mouse. "I got a head and found that stuffed mouse. We'll use the head to bring Fingles back and I'll go out tomorrow night. What do you think we should name him?"

Barry held up the severed head, strings of tendons and veins hanging off of the stump like the arms of an octopus, though the red ribbons reminded me of pasta more than anything else. My friend held him up by his ears and gave him the once over.

"I'm not sure. Did anyone see you?" Barry asked cautiously. I heard the kids' squeal over the snack cakes I had got them and I went to the heater to crank it up. I was siphoning electricity from the store beside this building. They hadn't noticed the plug and I had made sure it was hidden. Anyway, if they found out I was borrowing their electricity I would make sure they didn't mind.

I had my ways.

The kids were distracted with the snack cakes in my black bag so I grabbed the head, a long skewer, a strip of leather, and a knife. I sat down on a mattress I had bought secondhand and started carefully cutting Fingles's old head off. There was always that guilt there, cutting off their heads, but it was worth it once they became real. Fingles was my last cat and he was Noodle's brother except he was gray with a white mask on his face and white paws.

The person I had killed had red hair and green eyes; I think he was in his early twenties. Unlike a lot of the men I killed he had fought me, I was sporting a welt on my shoulder from where he got me with a brick.

I sucked on my teeth and felt a large bit of skin in my mouth. I chewed on it and swallowed then continued to stitch his head onto Fingles's body. Then, getting a great idea, I wound Barry the bear's butt and made him sing the Daisy song as I worked.

Of course my friends loved it. They laughed and hollered and chased each other around as the song echoed through the warm and welcoming basement. It was about twice the size of my living room apartment but not as clean. The floor still left black marks on my feet when I walked around barefoot no matter how many times I swept. There was also dusty boxes in the corners, stacked one on top of each other, the cardboard so fragile it was slowly collapsing under the higher up boxes' weight. A few nights ago Fingles and Noodles were horsing around. One of them made a box fall onto the ground. I had sprung to my feet, my heart slamming in my chest like an unwanted visitor banging on your door. I yelled at those two until my throat was sore, but apologized for it in the morning.

When I was finished I admired my handiwork and picked up Fingles and walked him to a side room that was through a metal door. It was where the other repaired stuffies were.

The smell of pungent rot mixed in with the smell of decaying buildings hit my face like an invisible wall. I pushed through it and held the door open with a loose brick and smiled at my friends hanging from their hooks.

Sir, Patches, Noodles, and Fingles were hanging off of contraptions that I'd made myself. They were coat hooks dangling from ropes I had tied to the ceiling joists. I hooked them through a hole I'd made in their scalps and made it so their feet were touching the ground. Little stuffed animal feets and paws, so adorable and cute but most now stained with brown and buzzing with fat flies.

I had to make these contraptions for them. Since their heads were so much heavier than their bodies this helped them see what was going on. Though I knew they couldn't see; I had set them free.

I brushed my hands carefully over each head, some with faces red and purple just starting to form the first beads of putrid-smelling liquid, others like Sir and Patches now green and grey; their eyes eaten by rats and their mouths slacked open and full of wiggling maggots.

I wished the maggots and rats hadn't come but that was life and I had accepted it. They had chewed a lot of their faces though and some of the fabric. I could see the maggots wiggling around in the synthetic cotton, wiggling back and forth like squirmy wormies.

"This is Fingles," I said to them, and grabbed onto a hook I had already prepared. I poked my tongue out of the corner of my mouth as I stuck the hook through the thick skin of Fingles's scalp, and when it poked out the other end I slowly retracted my hands to make sure he would stay.

Fingles didn't move. He stayed still and his white paws just barely touched the ground. He looked like centaur kind of. It would've been interesting if they had come back to life that way.

"He'll be here to keep you all company," I said to them, patting Fingles's red hair. He would become real to me the next morning, that's how it usually worked.

The bodies of my friends didn't answer back and I knew they wouldn't. They had been set free and were eating snack cakes in the main area of the basement.

When I was finished I pushed the heads aside gently and went deeper into the second room. The smell of rot became almost unbearably strong on my nostrils, to the point where I could feel vomit in my throat. I was no longer used to the stench of decay, even though I lived in it as a child.

I approached the back of the room and was greeted by the previous victims' bodies. They were also hanging on hooks, though these ones were meat hooks hanging off of rusted chains. I had been eating my prisoners though the meat had been turning. Thankfully I had a new man for us to consume. Before I had brought the head I had carried the man's leg down here and what I could carve from his ass cheeks and face cheeks. I stashed it in the back where it was coldest, my mouth watering over the anticipation of what he would taste like.

In Alegria we still ate arian meat, but it was previously carved up and cooked. That was okay but there was something about carving off your dinner from a cold, dead corpse that made my throat tighten and my brain light up like a flare. It was something that I had deeply missed.

Oh if only I could go back to the greywastes and live how I used to. I missed that, and now that I was older –I knew I would rule that greywaste. Me and Barry, we would become kings in our own right.

That night I ate dinner with my friends and watched them put on shows for me. We had no television down here but I did have a Game Boy and some books I had found. Mostly though I found myself watching my friends, sometimes for hours and hours. They loved to entertain me and act out scenes from my books or movies I had watched. I enjoyed that. I enjoyed them.

There was no meth down here and no opium and since I had chewed that red pill that Human Mouse had given me I had no desire to smoke meth or do any other drugs besides a weed joint I had found on one of my victims. I realized as the days went on that the meth had been fuelling my paranoia of my family.

I still knew they were out there, but I no longer suspected my crows of being spies, or that they knew where I was. Though the meth had opened up my mind to a lot of things I had been oblivious to, I was able to sort the realities from the fantasies.

As I laid down to sleep that night I wondered if Jasper had come to the same realization when he was off of meth. I wonder if he realized the Legion was never after him.

Or that the night the legionary came, when we were burying Cooper – that they had been looking for me.

If I'd listened to Crow and sat up in that grave – I would've been found that very night.

"When do you think it will be spring?" Barry asked the next day. I had been preparing to go outside to find a head for the new mouse stuffed animal. His name was Ralph, named after a book I had loved when I was younger.

"A couple months I think. Not soon enough," I said back. I picked up my clown mask and tucked it halfway into my jeans. I wouldn't be bringing my satchel until I had made my kill, it would only get in the way.

"When you wear t-shirts everyone's going to see the ugly scars on your body," Barry said. When I looked at him he grinned; he was sitting in a pile of gnawed-on bones. I had eaten a lot last night, that man had tasted good.

I ran my hands up and down my arms. "Jack didn't mind them…"

"Jack probably thinks you're dead," Barry said nonchalantly. He picked up a bone, with red meat still clinging to the joints. He twirled it around and put the end of it in his mouth. I saw a flash of pointed teeth as he gnawed on it and sucked the marrow out of a broken tip. "You're such an ugly little fuck. The older you get the uglier you get."

My lips pursed. I turned away from Barry, a dark smog descending on my previously decent mood. It was funny how easily I forgot how Barry was. How he was always pushing me to –

"You should cut yourself."

I whirled around. "You should shut the fuck up," I snapped at him. The kids scurried away at the booming sound of my voice, made only louder by the gutted ceiling above us. They hid behind the boxes and even behind the metal door where the bodies were kept. They hated it when I yelled but I was already getting sick and tired of Barry always putting me down.

"You can stay here tonight while I go out hunting." I booted Barry the bear over towards the bed and walked through the door towards the narrow hallway. "And if you keep this up I'm replacing you with Noodles. I'm a damn chimera and I don't need to take this shit."

"No, you're a meth addict. You're Jasper," Barry's snarling, his taunting voice called after me. "Crazy fucking meth-addicted Jasper. You hang out with kids too. Do you let them watch when you grind your cock against your pillow at night?"

His words struck me like a physical blow. I stood there stunned and silent, feeling the light get sucked out of the room.

I turned around slowly.

"D-don't ever... say that again," I whispered to him, but as my eyes scanned the entire room... I realized he was gone. All of them were gone; the room was entirely empty save for the faint buzzing of flies and the hum of the space heater.

I turned my back on the empty room and closed the door. Like I had stepped from one world into the other the cold darkness hit my burning face, and cooled it in its frozen embrace. Immediately I felt relief in the pitch black, and because I craved the anonymity of night I closed my eyes as I walked down the hallway, and while I walked I stretched my hands out and let my fingers run over the rough, crumbling brick.

Then, unexpected to even me, I suddenly let out a loud, agonizing scream. A thousand feelings suddenly burst from my brain like a skewered abscess and sprayed its pus across my entire body. Unable to contain the overflowing emotions ravaging me inside and out, I turned to the only blunt object I had in my range.

I punched the brick with my fists, letting scream after scream roll from my lips unabashed and uncontrolled. The ferocity of my emotions throwing me into temporary insanity, urging me to get out as much rage as I could through both physical force and my maddened screaming.

I didn't know which straw broke my back, I just knew they had been collecting for a long time now. Whether it was Barry's poisoned words or just the desperation and loneliness I had been pushing down I didn't know. The only lucid thought inside of my head was that I had to get some of that pent up rage out or else I was afraid I would physically burst.

The last angry scream erupted. I felt the ground against my legs as I collapsed onto my knees.

I stayed there in silence for several minutes before I pounded on the brick one more time, and rose to my feet.

With my teeth clenched and the rage boiling my blood I stalked down the narrow hallway, filling the stairwell with noise as I stomped up the stairs towards the surface. No thoughts inside of my head but finding someone alone so I could punish them for the pain that had been collecting inside of my body since the day I crawled under the porch of Sunshine House.

I slammed the door of the abandoned office building. Two people a half-block down the street looked at me but they were females and I wasn't interested in killing women. I wanted someone who would fight back, I wanted a brawl. Someone who would get a couple hits in and make me feel some pain. Maybe I wouldn't even kill someone tonight; maybe I'd pick a fight and just let them beat me to death.

My eyes closed, and my jaw gave a jolt from the pressure of my pointed teeth clenching too tight. My entire jaw was locked in place like a closed bear trap and I wouldn't be surprised if I broke teeth tonight.

There was something going on inside of me. Something was building, like a cancerous tumour that fed on my misery. A cancer that had always been there but had now grown to the point where my body could no longer sustain it. I swear I could feel it pressing against my skin, so much pressure I knew it was going to rip out of me. There was so much tension, so many taut wires wrapped around my body. I could hear the low twanging whine as they became tighter and tighter.

Tighter and tighter… they were going to snap. I knew they were going to snap.

Cypress stretched out in front of me. A poor district that was on par with the slums of Moros when it came to poverty, drug abuse, and everything else you would expect to find in this skid row of Skyfall. It was a sad and depressed place to be and the buildings only reflected the despondent atmosphere that seemed to encapsulate this district.

Almost none of the buildings had been repaired, most everything had been left as it was for time to slowly pick away. Skyland was constantly under renovation and the upper-class district of Eros as well. Nyx got what Skyland and Eros didn't want but Moros and Cypress were left to fight over the materials they could salvage in the other districts' shit.

But I was comfortable here; it reminded me of the greywastes I had left behind. Tall, dark buildings that stuck out like fractured bones, all of them missing their windows and some even stripped of their siding like nature had stripped their pride. There was nothing left in the world for them but to wait for time to bring them to their knees, then they themselves would be cannibalized to repair the buildings around them.

Like how we ate each other in the greywastes. The dead always had their uses and the rats and croaches could make their homes in what remained.

That's all life is, waiting for your comrade to die so you can consume and grow stronger from his corpse. And you always knew that comrade was waiting to do the same to you.

There were many people in my life I was waiting to consume. I wonder what a chimera would taste like. I bet we tasted better than the malnourished greywasters I had eaten, and the starving Cypressians and Morosians I had killed and devoured. I had tasted a Nyxian just several days ago – the marbling on his flesh had been nice, melted wonderfully when I cooked myself a steak on top of the hotplate I had bought.

A jolt of pain ripped through my jaw from clenching it too hard. I flicked the butt of the cigarette onto the deserted streets and watched the blue fireworks explode from the still burning ember, before dying on the cold ground.

Immediately I lit another one and walked past one of the tallest buildings in Cypress. It was an empty shell, dark grey with black stains dripping from its windows like tears. The only colour, the only light it had was mismatched spray-paint. Declarations from Cypresses's gangs or the occasional mural of wanna-be artists trying to add some colour to this monotone dystopia.

My head turned at a scratching sound, but all it was was a stray cat pawing at a cardboard box. I nodded at it but it was feral, so all I got was a stricken look for my efforts, then dilated pupils as he noticed the crows following behind me.

And at this inner mention of my friends the lead crow landed on my shoulder. His claws scraped against the leather of my jacket before he settled.

"Hello, Sanguine."

A smirk found its way to my face, even though inside the tension was continuing to strangle me alive. I appreciated the greeting but the night was too silent to disrupt it with my voice. I carried on towards the foreshore in hopes to find some stragglers in the ocean-front park. A drunk personal may be more willing to brawl with me and if he was surrounded by friends all the better.

Several cigarettes were killed as I weaved through the abandoned buildings and alleyways full of garbage and dozens of scavenging animals. The deeper I went into Cypress the less people I saw.

Suddenly though I heard a sound. It was a male voice but it was faint, which meant it had to be far away considering the silence of the night on top of my chimera hearing. I paused and shooed the crow off of my shoulder so its heartbeat wouldn't disrupt my hearing. Then I craned my ears and focused every sense into my hearing, even going as far as to close my eyes.

The voice continued. My brow furrowed as I realized it was a protesting, almost pleading voice; and there was another one as well, though I couldn't hear it properly. The higher tenor of the male's voice was louder, this second voice held deeper tones.

I sprinted to the edge of a sidewalk and kept myself in the shadows of the abandoned and boarded up shops that the sidewalk edged. I extinguished my lit cigarette and put it back into my tin before following the mysterious sounds that had piqued my interest.

The closer I got the more I started piecing together just what I was listening to. The two people were walking together, but one of them obviously didn't want to be with the other. He was pleading and sniffing and several times I heard scuffing like he was being forced to walk with the other one.

The other one was another male, his voice was cold and biting but it had a slight slur on it that suggested he was under the influence of something. Whenever the first one complained he hissed sharply, most likely telling him to shut up.

When I got close enough to the two that I could make out their footsteps, I slipped my clown mask over my face and fingered the knife that was sheathed on my belt. The crows behind me seemed to sense my need for silence as well, there was not a single word from them, just faint rustling of feathers and the sounds of their claws scraping against the lamp posts and awnings when they landed.

"Let me go…"

"That isn't going to happen," the man said, another scuffling noise as the younger one stumbled. Then I heard the sound of a rusted door opening, I could hear it scraping against the dirty floor.

"Go in."

"I'm not going in there!" the younger one choked. "Fucking let me go. I'm not going in there with you."

The man laughed. My eyes narrowed at the sound of this laugh; there was something about it that was familiar. I had heard it before.

I sprinted to a four-way split in the road and turned a corner. I pressed my back against a phone booth and held my breath as I saw the glowing blue figures on the other side of the street.

One was cowering down, his arms crossed tightly over his chest. The other was a man with a backwards baseball hat, taller than the kid and dressed in newer clothes. He was holding the door open, his other hand pulling on the kid's shoulder.

The two disappeared into the building and the door slammed behind them. I didn't move though, I was still analyzing that voice, trying to figure out just who it belonged to. I didn't think I recognized the man but he was far away and my chimera night vision wasn't nearly as developed as my daylight vision. His face had been distorted under the blue glow.

I knew that person – how did I know that person?

Then a piercing scream sounded, its shrill desperation amplified by the empty building. It was quickly followed by an out of breath sob, and worse still – a gasp like he had just been punched.

Then it hit me, it hit me with such obviousness I felt like a fool. A naïve fool with his mind too focused on his angst to realize that there was only one explanation as to why someone would be taking a young man into an abandoned building.

My brain kicked into gear. I ran across the road, feeling the flames once cooled by the midnight walk start to gather fuel under the boy's agonizing screams. Now falling into a rhythm that made the taut binds snap back around my chest.

"*Ah- ah – ah – ahhh! Fucking take it out!*" He gagged on his breath before he said something I knew I would never forget.

"*I'm only thirteen, I'm fucking only thirteen.*" – He let out another scream mixed in with a choking sob.

"Then what the fuck were you doing at an adult bar? Fucking liar."

My entire body was shaking with rage; red was seeping into my vision, bathing the metal door in front of me in a bloodied haze. The pressure inside of my body was pressing against my skin like a balloon was inflating in me. Something was going to give, something was going to snap. I wasn't going to exit this door the same person who was now swinging it open, it was impossible.

The metal door slammed against the side of the building. I saw him.

And I immediately recognized him.

Ludo looked up at me with an expression of shock and anger. He had his pants unzipped and open, pressed against the bare ass of the young man on his hands and knees. The kid's arms were crossed in front of him and his face buried in the center. Something that I myself had done many times when Jasper was fucking me. Covering my face in shame, inhaling my own recycled breath, counting the thrusts as they slowly quickened, waiting for the grunt and the disgusting wetness that remained inside of you for hours after.

"What the fuck!" Ludo snarled, his cock still inside of his victim. "Get the fuck out of here."

Then it seemed Ludo noticed just what was standing inside of the doorway. He paused and I saw a look of perplexity cross his face as he stared at this masked spectre, before it was replaced by nervous unease.

"I fucking said… get out," the chimera said, his voice losing the snarling dominance it had had just seconds before.

I slowly shook my head back and forth before I started taking deliberately gradual steps towards him. The clicking of my boots echoed off of the high ceiling; they broke the silence with such an intensity it sounded like gunfire.

Ludo pulled his cock out of the boy, before quickly tucking the deflating flesh back inside of his pants. The boy, also afraid, scrambled away and out of my line of sight.

As Ludo was tucking himself back into his pants I took out another cigarette and stuck it into my mouth. Then, as the chimera watched me, now matching my steps as he walked backwards, I brought my fingers up to the unlit cigarette… and lit it with my heated tough.

A visible look of relief washed over Ludo's face. He laughed and wiped his hand down his face. "You scared the shit out of me… I didn't recognize you with that mask. Okay, you got me, who is it?"

I shook my head again and took an inhale of my cigarette. I blew it towards Ludo and continued to walk towards him.

The corner of Ludo's mouth rose in a smirk, and he took another step back. The apprehension was creeping back to his face.

"Come on… you're going to make me guess?"

I nodded.

Ludo gave out an uneasy laugh; he glanced behind him, most likely trying to spot an exit, and there was one, but the inside of this building was an open floor. He knew he would have to turn and run, and he knew since I was a chimera also – that I could most likely outrun him.

"Okay… y-you're Jack?" Ludo said, his hands were fidgeting, he kept wiping his nose. "Jack finally g-growing some balls?"

I shook my head.

Ludo swallowed, and looked behind him again. His backwards steps were getting faster and his heartbeat as almost as loud as my footsteps.

"You're too tall to be – be King Silas," Ludo laughed nervously. "Apollo and Artemis would – would never…"

Ludo suddenly stopped and held up his hands in the *'you got me'* posture. "Okay, I'm done; you're scaring the shit out of me. You got me, fine. I'll give you a congratulatory blowjob. Who is it?"

He didn't move as I closed the last several feet of distance, but I could tell from the thrashing of his heartbeat that he was in a panic. Every step I took only accelerated the anxiety that I knew was eating him alive. He didn't want me near him, and yet his trust in the family was strong enough for him to stay still and let me approach.

Ludo smiled nervously when I stopped in front of him, but when I got close enough for him to see I wasn't one of his brothers the smile suddenly disappeared from his face.

His mouth dropped open and he stood, frozen, as I slowly raised my hand and grabbed the top of my mask. I realized with perverse joy that his night vision made him unable to see that my eyes were red.

But the chimera night vision wouldn't spare him from my other genetic enhancement.

"Who – who are you?" Ludo whispered, taking a step back.

I pulled the mask off, my crimson eyes squinting as I gave him a friendly closed-mouth smile back.

Ludo stared. "Fucking Sami Fallon? What the fuck…?"

I laughed and raised my hand. I pressed it against his cheek, and as I slowly stroked it.

Then I grinned, showing off every one of my pointed teeth. "Not quite, *mihi*."

Ludo's eyes widened; his mouth opened as if he wanted to scream, but instead nothing but stammering and spitting made it past his tongue.

Ludo wrenched himself away from my hand, taking two quick steps back – before he turned and ran.

I tucked my clown mask into my jeans and took a long inhale of my blue-embered cigarette, watching Ludo run across the open floor, his boots slapping against the concrete and his breathing laboured.

When he was almost at the door I nonchalantly flicked the cigarette off into the darkness, and started to run after him.

Or else it would be too easy, of course.

I ran through the open door and out into the cold night, the air brisk and biting, but even though I was scantily dressed in a thin leather jacket and black jeans, I wasn't cold at all.

My eyes took me to the dark figure running down the sidewalk. He glanced behind his shoulder and I heard the low moan when he realized I was pursuing him. I picked up my pace as he turned a corner but as I rounded the same corner I realized he was another one of Silas's failed chimeras. He was already slowing down, and the wheezing gasps of his breath told me the chase was going to be the equivalent of a wolf hunting a hamster.

"Get the fuck away from me!" Ludo screamed through gasps. He turned around before stumbling forward. He steadied himself on a telephone pole. I could see the whites of his eyes, shining brilliant in my night vision, making it appear as if the waning moon had gotten lost in the dark streets of Cypress. "I'm going right to Silas, you fucking psycho. C-chimera or…" Ludo gave up on whatever he was trying to say when he realized I was still running towards him. He ran to the left and disappeared into an alleyway half blocked by a rusted out pickup truck.

Then I heard a slam. My eyes narrowed and I quickly covered the distance to where he was. I realized he had decided to hide rather than run. Smart for someone who couldn't run a mile without collapsing, but foolish since he knew I was a chimera.

My mouth flooded with anticipation of killing him in that building. I felt a twinge in my cheek, the same trigger that seemed to happen whenever one imagined eating delicious food. I was going to devour his flesh raw, and if he was still there when I was finished I was going to bring some for the kid Ludo had been in the middle of raping.

I opened the door and walked inside, but was immediately greeted by the sour aroma of gasoline. There were other rusted cars around so I coped it up to it being leftover fuel and walked down the grate ramp that led to the main floor of the building. An open building with grated catwalks above me and high ceilings filled with pipes and long chains.

"Ludo? Oh, Ludo!" I sang with a smile, seeing rows of thick metal shelving, most holding old car tires and auto parts. This place was full of areas one could hide in, and rusted, cobweb covered industrial machines he could climb. Well, this may be fun after all.

I smirked to myself, feeling so alive in this moment, so unhinged and free, I kind of felt like singing.

"*Ludo, Ludo, give me your heart to eat,*" I sang as I walked down the middle of the floor, craning my ears as I finished the first line of the Daisy song to listen for his pounding heart. "*I'm so excited; I just can't wait to taste your meat…*"

I heard a hammering thrum tickle my ear canal. I paused and listened, before my eyes shot to the far left hand corner of the room. There was a large machine, half dismantled, in the corner of that room. I immediately noticed the dust was disturbed around it. I could see a hand print on one of the metal rungs.

"*It will be a painful send off. I'll chew your fucking face off. I'll eat you alive, leave you for the flies – and no one will miss you,*" I sang with a grin. I got out my knife and deliberately let it hit the side of a stack of car doors and laughed when I heard his pulse jump.

Then he made a break for it.

Ludo shot out from behind the machine like a cockroach once you turned the lights on. I saw a flash of absolute terror on his face when he saw how close I was, but he didn't stop; he made a break for the door.

I jumped up onto the roof of a nearby car and used it as leverage to jump onto a double stack of cars to my right. I quickly climbed to the top, the rust peeling off in my hands, and without stopping, I leapt off of them – and onto Ludo's back.

Ludo screamed as he slammed, face up, onto the floor. Not just a scream of fear, but an absolute terror-filled shriek. It was so loud it broke his voice and only stopped when he had expended every ounce of air in his lungs.

The chimera screamed and writhed, twisted and contorted as I sat on his stomach, straddling him with a grin on my face that was nothing compared to the overwhelming joy I was feeling. The tightness, the cancerous pressure inside of me was slowly being let out of my body. I could already feel my entire body relax. I didn't feel as coiled, I didn't feel as stressed.

My god – I felt alive. It was like I had been a main character who had gotten stuck in the wrong book, only now did I realize that this was where I belonged. I was doing what I had been born to do.

I was alive. I was alive.

Ludo sobbed, tears and snot running down his face. He was sputtering and stammering pleas to me, nonsensical ramblings peppered with desperate promises. They were rapidly falling from his mouth like he was hoping that if he threw enough against the wall, one of them would stick.

But there was no point. There was no empathy inside of me, there was no sympathy. I sat down on his chest and grinned at him, a thousand thoughts coursing through my mind, but not one of them involved letting him go.

I petted his cheek. I liked the sensation, so I drew up my other hand and framed his face. Unable to stop myself I leaned down and kissed him.

Ludo's sob made his mouth open. I took advantage of it and slipped my tongue into his mouth, almost wishing for him to bite it just so my own blood could lace his cries.

I groaned and moved my hips, uncaring that my cock was rock hard and throbbing. I ground it into him as I kissed him, feeling a well of pleasure pooling inside of me.

My breath got short. I drew my lips away. Ludo gasped for breath. I kissed lower until I got to his neck, and slowly ran my tongue along the side.

I inhaled and took in the scent of sweat and fear. I kissed his Adam's apple, my hips still grinding into him.

Then I bit.

Ludo's neck stretched out as he screamed, I used that opportunity to open my mouth and fully clamp it around his neck. My mouth closed around the soft center and I felt my teeth puncture the flesh, then a moment later – hot blood gushed into my mouth.

Chimera blood... we did taste different. And like I had taken my first hit of my own special drug I knew this was the beginning of a most wonderful addiction.

And there was a lot of blood. I had severed an artery. I closed my lips around the wound but it was too much to drink. I let it spill over my mouth, the heat of the blood making steam rise up into the air.

Ludo grabbed onto my jacket and weakly tried to pull me away, but my mind wasn't aware of it. All it was concentrated on was the blood, the blood, the chimera blood.

My eyes closed at some point in time, shutting off as many senses as I could so I could focus solely on this addictive feeling.

It was overwhelming, like a valve had been turned, releasing the pressure and the constricting madness that had reigned over my mind for so long. It was as if the thousands of weights that had been steadily added to my body were finally being lifted off. And something told me that if I let go of Ludo's neck I would surely float away.

I was as light as air, nothing could stop me. The pressure was fading – and fading.

Though some of it remained. In the throes of this overwhelming pressure I realized my hips were still grinding against Ludo's now dead body. My penis was so hard and burning inside of my jeans. It wanted release; it wanted to experience what my mind was experiencing. The same build-up of tension, followed by the ecstasy that came with the sudden release.

He was dead, he wouldn't fight back – I could do it – no one would know.

My hand slipped down and I grabbed onto the front of Ludo's pants.

"Sami! Oh my god… oh my god, Sami," a voice suddenly sounded.

My jaw unlocked from Ludo's mouth. I opened my eyes to see an open gash dead center of Ludo's neck, the blood trickling down though the pulse was gone. At first I thought I had imagined the voice.

"Sami!" Jack gasped.

I turned around and stared in absolute shock.

Jack was standing behind me, with a gas can in his hand.

For more than just a few moments we stared at each other, our eyes locked and our bodies frozen like a switch that controlled the flow of time had been turned off. What was going through his head I didn't know, but my own mind was aflame with a sexual lust I had never felt so strongly.

And as I stared at him, his narrow face, full lips, large eyes that were the only true black in my night vision, I found my feet taking me to him. As I approached him he didn't move; the shock of discovering me over our dead brother's body still leaving him where he stood.

Without a word, without an uttered sound, with only the hammering beatings of our heart echoing in this soundless room, I put my hand to his cheek and kissed him on the lips.

Jack didn't push away, and I don't know what I would do if he did, because the heat I was feeling inside of my body was stronger than my own free will. It was uncontrollable, a tight burning and begged for the same release I had gotten when I had murdered Ludo. A booming, screaming voice inside of my head that commanded the same pleasure, the same liberation of pressure, and told me there would be no getting out of it this time.

I was almost twenty years old, I had put it off long enough, and if I didn't get my release from this man whose lips were locked on mine, I didn't want to see what would happen.

Jack's mouth opened, I slipped my tongue into his mouth before I roughly grabbed his ass. He stumbled backwards until his back hit a stack of wooden pallets, I pinned him with my body and pushed his groin into mine, our mouths open, our tongues weaving in and out of each others, and my rock hard dick grinding against his groin.

The gas can he had been carrying dropped to the ground with a clang, the sound seemed to awaken my sense of smell and I realized the pallets I had pinned him against were soaked in gasoline. And not only that – I was starting to smell smoke.

Jack read my thoughts. He broke our kiss, his rapid breathing hot against my neck. "We need to leave… I lit the upstairs offices on fire."

I kissed his neck; the pleasure burning me alive only grew at his words. "We're not leaving," I growled. So desperately did I want to bite that neck, draw a flow of blood for me to taste. I enjoyed the taste of Ludo, the taste of chimera.

"I have a car right outside the building," Jack said breathlessly. He let out a groan, and in response I grabbed his hand and pushed it behind his head. I framed him with my body and continued finding his lips as he tried to turn away from me to speak.

"Sami…" Jack whispered as I unbuttoned his pants and slipped my hands down the back of them. "Stop. We need to leave."

"We're not leaving," I said again, even though the smoke was starting to descend on us. I pulled his jeans down and moved my hand forward. I took the hardening dick into my hands and drew his boxer briefs down with the other.

Jack swore and he closed his eyes tight. I smiled now that he was unable to see my teeth, and pulled my own pants and underwear down. I leaned in and gave his neck a generous lick, then I grabbed his leg and when he didn't try and stop me, I locked my arm over it, then his other leg. I pushed him against the pallets, holding him completely off of the ground and ground my hard cock against his ass.

"Sami…" Jack said again. "Sami… put me down."

I pressed it against his hole and smiled. "Position it," I growled and jerked my hips into him. The head of my cock was pressing against his hole, and if I had the free hands I would have grabbed it and pushed it into him until I broke through. He was a chimera, he would love the fucking pain and I knew it.

Jack let out a cry as I put more weight into my aimless pushes. I saw his pointed teeth clench. "The fucking –" Jack groaned, then his hand was drawn to his face. He started licking and getting saliva on his fingers. "– The fucking building his going to burn down." He opened his eyes and looked up, his lips pursed but finally he swore and shook his head.

My mind exploded with lust and desire when Jack grabbed my dick, and forcefully, directed me into the right spot. Lubed with his spit he squeezed the burning head in a way that told me he was trying to inflict pain into me, frustration I presumed, then he adjusted himself so his bottom half was easier for me to access.

"There you go, chimera." Jack narrowed his eyes as mine widened. "I should know better than to tell a chimera who just murdered someone, no."

I stared at him, and at my shocked expression Jack's narrow eyes glared further. He then pulled on my dick and dug his thumbnail into the base. "Now you're shocked? Shocked about what, Sanguine? If you wanted to keep hiding your identity so well don't let me stick my tongue in your mouth, though I found out days ago anyway. Now shut up and fuck me before we both burn with that piece of shit in the corner."

My hands were shaking from desire, no, my entire body was trembling. I wanted to say so much back to him but my primal instincts had taken over my body. Instead of continuing to be shocked over the fact that Jack knew who I was, I pushed my hips, and with his hand directing the throbbing piece of flesh between my legs, I felt the head break into him.

I gasped, the tensioned pleasure overwhelming me. I sunk myself to the hilt and drew Jack closer to me, hearing his heavy breathing almost in tandem with our racing hearts.

Below I felt him grip me, as if his body was trying to consume my own. It was tight; the heat of my own cock mixing in with the taut inferno that was the inside of him burning me alive. I felt like the flames above us had already started to eat us both. It made me dizzy, it made my mind swim and swirl with lust and desire.

But just being inside of him wasn't enough, it wasn't enough for the voices in my head that demanded release. They commanded more, demanded it to the point where the screaming lust was drowning out the cries spilling from Jack's lips.

My hips started to thrust slowly, going in and out of the tight, constricting opening that seemed eager to take me in deep. With every drive of my hips I heard Jack's faint cry, and as my mind demanded more and more, I started to go faster.

Jack clawed my shoulders and started to shift his legs, I grabbed them harder to keep him from unbalancing me and dove myself faster into him. The chimera writhing in my hold let out a gasp and dug his fingernails into my skin, and to my shock he roughly drew them down my neck, leaving a burning sting behind.

It only made my desire increase. I moaned and shifted him up higher, seeing his pale, white knee bent over my arm shake back and forth as I fucked him. It was shrouded though, and I realized the smoke had come to devour or bodies. But there wasn't a care in the world, on the contrary, I welcomed the flames around me.

"S-Sanguine... slow..." Jack cried and raked his fingernails against my back. He shut his eyes tight and I saw those white teeth lock together, then his head stretch to the side showing off the neck, milky white and perfect. I leaned down and kissed it and continued my speed. There was no ounce of self-control inside of me that would let me slow down. I needed the release, I needed the release.

The pallets shook, sawdust fell on us, Jack continued to cry out and writhe, pinned between the pallets and my body. Occasionally looking down at our joined bodies, before closing his eyes and swearing between gasping moans.

"Sanguine!" Jack finally cried, this time he grabbed my hair and wrenched my head up. Our eyes locked, I saw sweat coating his head, his mouth open to help him breathe. "I need a break, put me down. I'm bleeding."

I looked at him for a second, the voice in my mind growling at me to not only continue, but to speed up. To make him scream, thrash, make him take it even though he was asking me to stop. It wanted me to cum to him pinned underneath my body, crying and begging at me to take it out, to stop.

But I didn't listen to it. I nodded and slowly eased it out of him, seeing a sheen of blood on the shaft and gathering underneath the rim of my head. I put Jack down and picked up the gas can, and turned from him.

"What – what are you doing?" he asked behind me, completely breathless. I could smell his blood on me, and on him. It mixed in well with Ludo's blood, the gasoline, and the smoke… the smoke.

I looked up and smiled as I saw the black smoke pouring out of a door on the second-storey, the offices Jack had been telling me about. It had almost blacked out the entire ceiling and was slowly thickening around us, slowly sucking the fresh air out of the old building and replacing it with life-snatching, oily black smoke.

"I like fire," I said as I turned around and grinned at Jack. Then I turned away and started dousing Ludo with the gasoline. "They all like fire, Crow especially. It almost makes you want to sing, eh?" I laughed and poured the last stream of the gasoline right into Ludo's silvery eyes.

"*Ludo, Ludo, give me your body please. I'll light you on fire, after I coat you in gasolineeee!*" I held up my hand and wiggled my gas soaked fingers. I turned around again, grinning wide at Jack. I just wanted to make sure he was watching.

I still loved being watched.

"Sanguine…" Jack looked at me, a look of fear and worry crossing that beautiful, beautiful face.

"*You made the wrong enemy, you really shouldn't'a fucked with me. Now you're dead, I'll fuck your head, and no one will miss youuu*!" I focused my thermal touch and watched as my hand burst into flames, then with a chuckle and Jack's panicked screaming behind me, I lowered my hand and ignited the body.

"SANGUNE!" Jack cried as the gasoline on Ludo's body exploded. I was thrown back, a bright, blinding yellow light searing my eyeballs, and the intense heat burning my body. I landed hard on my back and heard Jack behind me. Shouting something before he started patting my hand with his pants.

I sat up and smiled again as I saw Ludo's body burn. The intense pain in my hand only adding to my jovial mood.

"Sanguine… you're sick…" Jack said hastily. "Fuck, I didn't realize you were this out of your fucking mind. Sanguine – Sanguine, we need to go home. You need to get help."

I grabbed onto Jack's shirt and brought him in for a kiss. He indulged me for only a moment before he drew himself away. "Sanguine, get up. Please, please, I'm not fucking around we have to leave–"

My head shook back and forth and I smirked at the worried, horrified look on his face. Then I pushed him down to the floor, and got onto my knees; the cold concrete a sharp contrast to the burning flames in front of me.

"Sanguine, no! Not – here!" Jack said panicked, but he didn't stop me from grabbing both of his legs and pulling them back. I leaned into him, pressed my mouth against those trembling full lips, feeling them peel from the heat of the flames.

I looked up from our kiss, and saw Ludo's blackened face in front of me. His silver eyes now bubbling and boiling in their sockets, and his cheeks burning away to show rows of perfect teeth. The smell was incredible, the painful heat indescribable, the front row view I had of his corpse being eaten by the flames added its own gasoline to the roaring inferno inside of my body. The one that knew – I wasn't going to stop.

Jack cried out as I penetrated him. He grabbed my back with his claws and dug into them with what I knew was all his strength. As soon as I was inside of him my hips started thrusting hard, with no break, with no slow build-up, I fucked him hard and fed on his gasping cries as he shredded my skin with his nails.

And as I fucked him… I watched Ludo burn. I smelled Ludo burn. I took into me and devoured the beautiful scene playing out. It was almost too much for me, for my body and my mind, so many different sensations ravaging me all at once. So many satiated demons and yet the demon pinning this man to the ground wouldn't be satisfied until I released him from my body.

And the tension gathering inside of me was telling me that I was getting close.

I didn't know what to expect. I didn't know how it was supposed to happen. I drew on the image I had of Nero. How I stroked him off and watched his body writhe and twist. How his face tensed and his eyes closed; how he gripped the sheets and moaned as I ran my hand over his dick faster and faster. Channelling my experience with him I leaned further into Jack, taking his legs with me and exposing more of his ass to me. I positioned myself over him, so my cock could get as deep into him as I could get, and started a quick, intense rhythm.

Unable to control myself I started to moan with every exhale. At first my mind screamed at me to slow down as the tension got almost unbearable, telling me that if I pushed for much longer something was going to happen and to my inexperienced mind that wasn't a good thing. But I knew I had to push past it, I had to break that barrier and throw my body into what would be my first orgasm.

I closed my eyes, though the red of the flames still seeped into my vision, and I thrusted. When my body was urging me to stop, to stop building up the tension, I pushed my mind past it and continued, letting the groans spill and the cries echo through the burning building. I thrusted, and I thrusted through the pressure.

Then the binds snapped.

Suddenly I let out a loud cry, the pressure I had been pushing through reaching a critical point. With a wave of intense, mind-snapping tension, I cried out and slammed my hips against Jack's body. The pleasure was almost too much to bear. It started as a slow, drawn-out compression but as I pushed through it amplified, doubling in size, then tripling until it became so overwhelming I collapsed on top of Jack, my hips still thrusting as I came inside of him.

My mind was swimming, it was a haze. I was lost in the feeling as it rolled through me again and again, every time I thought the orgasm was going to subside another wave claimed me, urging me to jolt my hips to ease it along.

Then finally it subsided. I groaned into this heaving, sweaty body I had pinned onto the cold concrete and forced myself to sit up. As soon as I got up Jack scrambled out from under me, leaving me on my knees.

I brought my hand down to my sensitive, still hard dick, and touched it. I looked down at the stiff, blood-streaked member and watched the last spurt of cum shoot out of it, leaving a milky white streak on my trembling hand. The first time I had ever seen my own cum.

I rubbed it in between my fingers and glanced over at Ludo. I could see his skull now.

"Sami..." I felt cloth get pushed onto my lap. "You got what you wanted – we need to leave now." His voice was oddly soft and coaxing. I was expecting him to be angry but he was the opposite. He was speaking to me in such sweet tones I felt like this grisly scene in front of me was nothing but a hallucination. There was no room for such love-filled, soothing words. I was no cat hiding under the bed with its owner coaxing it with treats. I was the demon watching the body of my brother get reduced to blackened flesh and bones.

He was getting shrouded by black smoke.

Oh, there it was. I smelled the air, nodded and stood up. *There was that heavy, toxic-smelling smoke. There was the smell of burning flesh and treated wood.*

"Everything's on fire," I stated. I looked at Jack and saw the top of his head, he was kneeling on one knee.

He picked up my leg and put my foot through my pants. "We should've left long ago," I said.

"I know," Jack said in a low voice. My other leg went through my pants and he hoisted them up and buttoned them. "We need to leave. Sanguine... don't let go of my hand. Do you promise me?" Jack's hands framed my face, he made me look at him. "You're extremely sick, Sami. Promise you won't try and pull away from where I am leading you."

"Where are we going?" Just as I said that the upper level, where the grated catwalk above us was leading to, collapsed, raining blackened, burning wood and debris down to the floor with a deafening crash. Jack pulled my arm harder and urged me to sprint.

"Home, Sanguine – we're going home."

CHAPTER 42

NOT ONCE DID JACK LET GO OF THAT HAND UNTIL they were safe inside of the car Jack had driven into Cypress. And once Sanguine was safe inside the vehicle he drove and drove fast.

Though several times Sanguine asked him to stop when they got near what Jack realized was the abandoned building he was staying in, he only drove the car faster, keeping a hand on the automatic locks in case Sanguine tried to unlock the door and jump out.

Jack's heart was racing, the blood was soaking through his pants, and his skin was sore and burning, but Jack kept driving and he didn't stop.

Though when he got Sanguine inside the lobby of Alegria he found himself pausing.

He had never seen Sanguine in the light, not his true form.

Sanguine's red eyes looked around like he only partially knew where he was. Two deep crimson eyes that seemed unfocused but yet aware. He was scanning the lobby with a scowl, confused as to where he was and probably wondering why he was here.

"The family found me," Sanguine announced, though he looked to the left, opposite as to where Jack was, like he was speaking to someone else. "Tell the others I won't be home for a while, but I'll be back. Will you feed them for me?"

Sanguine stared to the left, though where he was looking had nothing there but a ceramic pot holding an apple tree sapling.

"Thank you, Barry," Sanguine then said, then he turned to Jack. "Okay, I'm ready to see him."

Jack tried to force a smile onto his face, but he seemed paralyzed with worry. Not just worry about Sanguine's mental state but the worry about the ramifications of Sanguine killing Ludo.

Plus the fact I let him fuck me. As Jack led Sanguine to the elevator a jolt of pain ripped up his backside. Every step was uncomfortable and he could feel the blood and possibly semen soaking into his jeans. *Though that is the one thing I might've done right. He got his release and afterwards he listened to me. Typical god damn chimera.*

As Jack stared at the elevator doors closing he felt a shudder go through him. His memories brought him back to that heated scene in the abandoned building. Though it was painful and at times rather scary – the energy that had been radiating off of Sanguine as he fucked him had been intoxicating.

It wasn't casual sex, it wasn't making love, it was downright fucking – and I might have enjoyed it more than my tempered mind is willing to admit.

Jack glanced to his side and almost smiled in spite of the heavy situation. Sanguine's face was glaring at the elevator doors, though it wasn't a scary glare full of malice and hatred, but more of a scowl like he was unimpressed with something.

Jack squeezed Sanguine's hand and this time he was able to smile. "Silas will be overjoyed to see you, Sanguine. He missed you a lot, the entire family has missed you."

"Is Jasper going to be there?" Sanguine asked. He scowled further. "I need to prepare myself if he is."

"Jasper?" Jack said slowly. He racked his memories to try and bring up who he was. Had Sanguine told him during their brief friendship? Before Jack's fear of Sanguine getting killed by Jack's brothers forced him to sever whatever it was they had been building?

Another mistake. Why didn't Silas tell me who Sanguine was before he was killed?

Sanguine looked over at Jack, his red eyes turning grave. "The man who kept me prisoner, who fucked me since I was eight. You know who he is. You guys let him fuck me to – to punish me. You were all… in on it. Were you – in on… it? I don't–"

Jack put a hand over his mouth as the words stumbled from Sanguine's lips. He stared at Sanguine in shock as his brother tried to find his words. He was tripping over the most horrible of accusations, like he had a loaded gun in his hand and he didn't realize he was repeatedly pulling the trigger.

"No… that was… the meth fucking with my brain." The furrow in Sanguine's brow deepened. He looked sad and confused. "I don't know what's real anymore, do I?"

"Sami…" Jack whimpered, feeling an overwhelming sense of sympathy for Sanguine, and a new sense of understanding. Suddenly Sanguine's problems, all of the problems Jack had seen inside of him, made perfect sense.

"Yes?" Sanguine answered. The elevator finally stopped and opened, revealing the decorated halls of King Silas's floor.

"Your family loves you…" Jack whispered. "I… I love you. Jasper isn't here. Silas might've already killed him for all I know. None of the family had anything to do with him – with him keeping you prisoner."

"You love me?" Sanguine stepped out of the hallway, following Jack's lead. "I thought you hated me?"

Jack let out a guilty breath and shook his head. "I was trying to protect you. I thought you were just a rather naïve greywaster not… not my brother. Everything's changed now, things can be different for us if you want."

There was no time for Sanguine to answer back, halfway to the entrance to Silas's apartment the double oak doors swung open.

King Silas's smiled when he saw Sanguine, but when he saw the injuries on the two of them the smile darkened.

"And what did you do to my Sanguine?" Silas said in a tone that made Jack's chest quake with anxiety. He hadn't been expecting that reaction at all, though as Jack's mind did spirals trying to figure out what to say he wondered to himself just what he had been expecting.

"I… I didn't do anything to him, King Silas," Jack stammered as he squeezed Sanguine's hand. "I found him when I was burning the old automotive building – I brought him home because… because, Master, he's sick."

"He's not sick, my beautiful creation was only letting off some steam," Silas said airily. With a smile he walked up to Sanguine but frowned when he saw the hesitation in Sanguine's eyes.

"Why are you looking at me like that?" Silas asked slowly. "Aren't you happy to see me? It's been months since we last saw each other."

Sanguine didn't answer but his body language told its own story. The red-eyed chimera was tense and his face scowling, and he had a look in his eyes that suggested he was talking to the voices that Jack knew Sanguine heard in his head.

"I don't want to do that," Sanguine suddenly said.

Silas, who had been raising his hand to touch Sanguine's face stopped. At the same time Perish, only wearing nightclothes (his shirt was on backwards which suggested Silas had summoned him for the evening), appeared behind the small party.

"No, I can't... not here, there are too many of them here," Sanguine said and this time he shook his head. "I don't even know if this is real life."

Silas stared at Sanguine, and behind him Perish approached cautiously, his body cowering.

"Master... you didn't tell me he was this bad," Perish said in a rapid voice. "You told me he only mumbled to himself. Why didn't you tell me he was hallucinating?"

"I told you enough," Silas snapped. "I don't need you on me about his problems, Elish was bad enough. He was fine when I was killed and he will fucking be fine now. He just needs some time with me."

"He's hallucinating..." Perish dropped his voice even lower, in front of the two of them Sanguine continued his conversation with this hallucinations. "This isn't... Silas, this isn't normal chimera problems like you told me. This is critically worse."

"No... it's not," Silas said flatly. "And I know what you're suggesting and you will not bring voice to it. You saw him during his classes, yes? Wasn't he normal then?"

"The first day he attended school... he got anxiety and left and I overheard him yelling and screaming at things in a janitor's closet," Jack spoke up, though his voice was timid and cracking under the weight of his own fear. He knew very well that he was cornering Silas right now, with the help of Perish, the smartest chimera ever created. "He had his normal moments but there were times... when I knew something was deathly wrong with him. King Silas... he did something horrible in that factory..."

"What's going on here?" Everyone but Sanguine turned around and saw Elish stepping out of the elevator doors. When he eyed Sanguine his face became cold. "So it's true then? The dog has come home?"

Nausea started bubbling in Jack's stomach, and in that churning pit he could feel a deep sense of dread. He could almost see a clock on Sanguine's face, slowly ticking down to what Jack knew would be an explosive event.

"King Silas... this is too much for him," Jack whispered as Elish approached. "Please, you have no idea the long night he's had. Let me take him inside."

Silas glanced at Elish, his own facial expression equally matching the cold glower on Elish's. There was no mistaking Elish had inherited it from him.

"Yes, go... feed him," Silas said. "Get out of his way if he gets violent."

Jack took Sanguine by the hand and led him inside. Kinny was still asleep so Jack led Sanguine into the kitchen and started bringing out tinfoil-wrapped plates of food.

"How do you feel?" Jack asked him, trying to ignore the steadily raised voices that Jack knew was only going to escalate.

Sanguine watched him before letting out a slow breath. "One minute I'm here and I understand what's going on... and then... my friends come and start telling me conflicting things. They're reminding me that the family is bad, that – that you guys had been working with Jasper. There was a point just several weeks ago when I was sure that was right and then... and then I get a hold of reality and I know that's not true."

"We would never ever work with him, Sanguine," Jack said, trying to force strength into his words so Sanguine would believe them. "That was your mind playing tricks on you. We've been looking for you to bring you home after you got upset over things you've learned, and possibly for me... rejecting our friendship."

Suddenly Sanguine's eyes widened. He looked at Jack with a shocked expression. "That's right. You know who I am now don't you?" Then he put a hand up to his mouth. "I fucking killed Ludo. I killed Ludo."

"Shhh!" Jack held out his hands and looked behind him, but though Silas, Elish, and Perish had moved their escalating argument over to the sitting room they didn't hear Sanguine's admission. "We're not telling them what happened, okay? Not right now anyway. Don't even tell them we had sex."

Sanguine's face fell, then he stumbled back until he hit the kitchen counter. His hand covered his mouth again, but the stunned expression on his face still shone through.

"Did I rape you?"

"NO!" Jack said loudly. He rapidly shook his head back and forth. "No, no, fuck no and if you ever ask that again I will hit you. We just both got caught up in the moment." Or Sanguine had gotten caught up in the moment but Jack wasn't about to admit that.

Sanguine shifted uncomfortably; he rubbed a savage scratch mark on his neck. "My neck and back are scratched to hell…"

"That's normal for chimeras," Jack said hastily. Because though he had done that to try and inflict the same pain in Sanguine that Sanguine had been inflicting in him, he could never tell him that.

Or admit that at several points in time he had been begging Sanguine to stop because he had been in so much pain, and had even been afraid for his life.

Sanguine would never know.

Never.

"He's fine! Everyone is fine, everyone is happy!" Silas suddenly snapped from the other room. Both Jack and Sanguine looked over to see Silas, with a look on his face that made Jack take a step back.

The scene spoke for itself. Silas was standing up, his eyes blazing and his posture rigid. Both Elish and Perish were side by side facing Silas, their arms defiantly crossed over their chests and their own eyes cold and unwavering. They both seemed determined to finally get Silas to admit something was wrong with Sanguine. Something that went deeper than just the ramifications of being kept in a basement for so many years.

Silas suddenly looked at Sanguine, and when he saw him Silas smiled and clasped his hands together. An odd, almost crazed and desperate look in his eyes.

"Aren't you, love?" Silas's voice dripped honey as he approached Sanguine. Sanguine put his hands on the counter top behind him and looked at the tiled kitchen floor.

The room fell silent but not still. Behind Silas, Elish and Perish walked behind their king, both with equally stormy faces.

Sanguine looked at the king, then at Elish, Perish, and finally Jack.

"King Silas…" Sanguine said. "I did some terrible things tonight."

Silas only smiled though, before laying a caring hand on Sanguine's cheek. He stroked the prickly skin softly before saying, in the same sweet voice, "You're speaking normally, you're not lashing out. You're better than I've ever seen you, love. You've made me so proud."

"People in real psychosis don't act crazy twenty-four-seven, Master," Perish said. "This isn't normal chimera–"

"Enough!" Silas whirled around and snapped. "Let him speak, Perish."

"No…" Sanguine shook his head, and gripped the edge of the counters hard. "He's right… I – Silas, I killed Ludo tonight. I almost raped Jack. I need help." Jack's heart broke as Sanguine's face crumbled into agony. "I don't know what's real and what's inside of my mind. I cut the heads off of two Cypressians who took care of me, I sewed their heads to stuffed animals. I did it with several more people and I saw my friends come to life, Silas I saw them." Sanguine looked up at Silas, his red eyes starting to glisten. "For all I know tomorrow I will fully believe whatever delusions my mind projects to me. My times of sanity are getting fewer and far between. Silas – help me. Please help me before it's too late."

It was like the air got sucked out of the room. Everyone stood still, frozen in their places. Everyone but Silas who had retracted his hand from Sanguine's trembling cheek.

"All – all chimeras kill," Silas said in a confident and soothing voice. "I'm not cross you killed Ludo, sweet one. My lovely chimeras are pre-dispose to violence. It's fine. Does it make you understand some of the things that made you angry at me before? The things that made you run aw-"

"STOP!" Sanguine suddenly cried. With a frustrated scream he pushed Silas hard.

The king stumbled back and was caught by both Perish and Elish. He stared at Sanguine in shock as Sanguine slammed his fist against the granite countertop.

"Why can't you accept I need help!" Sanguine cried. "How can you possibly… possibly think I'm okay? I'm not okay!" he screamed. Tears sprung to Jack's eyes as he watched his brother and friend breakdown in front of him. "Are you that much of a selfish asshole that you'll let your own guilt over Jasper keeping me prisoner overshadow the fact that I'm fucking pleading for help? How can you be that selfish? How can you be that stubborn!"

"I might be fine now. I might be fine for months but this keeps happening and it keeps getting worse. Something is wrong inside of my head and it seems everyone in this fucking family has accepted this but you," Sanguine yelled.

"Don't say it," Silas whispered. His face had turned ashen, behind him Elish and Perish both gripped Silas's shoulder in a way that suggested they wanted to make sure he couldn't flee from what Sanguine was threatening to say.

Sanguine's eyes widened, but it was no look of surprise. He looked livid. "You knew all along didn't you?"

"Don't say it," Silas whispered again; he started shaking his head back and forth. "It never happened, so don't even give the delusion light."

"Delusion?" Sanguine said incredulously. He took a dangerous step towards Silas, who had now refused to make eye contact with him.

It was a strange and terrifying sight for Jack to take in. The black-haired chimera, his grey face a mask of solid stone, and his red eyes blazing like two burning cigarettes, slowly approaching the King Who Ended the World like he was Satan himself calling on him to finally answer for his crimes.

Silas wanted to create a demon – and he had indeed succeeded.

"You think... what Jasper did to me... was a *delusion*?" Sanguine's voice dropped to such a low level Jack's chest seemed to vibrate and rock under the rasping tones. "You think I imagined him raping me several days after he tricked me into coming to his farm? You think him locking me in that piss-smelling, dark basement with nothing but my own desperate loneliness, until I almost wanted him to come fuck me just so I had some human-fucking-contact, someone to talk to... was a delusion? Three times a week, Silas, sometimes four. The only break I got was when I started becoming a man and that was only because he brought in other boys. Two of them you have now. Tell me you never asked Juni and Levi just why they were there?" Sanguine snarled.

Silas kept looking to his side, his eyes glaring suns and his lips welded shut. Like the others the king seemed frozen by Sanguine's leaded words.

"You let this happen to me, you let a six-year-old boy fend for himself in the greywastes because you wanted what? This? Is this what you wanted?" Sanguine continued, his face now dangerously close to King Silas's. He kept moving his face as if trying to force eye contact, but Silas refused. "Is this your ideal end result? Admit it to me, Silas. Admit that you know what Jasper was doing to me in there. And admit you let your own creation fall into the hands of some depraved pedophile."

Sanguine took a step back. "And then you can admit that you expect him to be absolutely fine with a few lies and some new clothes."

Silas's eyes remained glaring and focused as Sanguine's last words hung heavy on the toxic thick air. They lingered on everyone's ears until they were drowned out by the sounds of five racing heartbeats.

Then those same eyes shot to Sanguine, and they did not soften, nor did they look away when Sanguine glared right back at him.

"You're not only an insane defect, you're a compulsive liar," Silas said coldly. "You're full of shit like an attention-starved teenager. You fucking delusional lia-"

Sanguine let out a loud, gut-wrenching bellow and lunged at Silas. Elish snatched the king and pushed him into Perish's arms before grabbing the insane chimera and pulled him back.

"Fuck you!" Sanguine screamed, tears running down his face. "You inhuman monster! How the fuck can you say that? How can your own feelings, your own stubborn denial, be more important than admitting it? ADMIT IT!"

"You're a fucking liar!" Silas screamed back, the crazed glint in his eye matched only by Sanguine's. "It never fucking happened, you attention whore! You fucking attention whore!"

"Elish, get them out of here!" Perish shouted. "He's about to blow. I can feel it gathering. Get them out of here, now!"

"He needs to fucking accept it so the god damn boy can move on!" Elish suddenly, and uncharacteristically, yelled at Perish.

"They're both still mortal and if he fills this room with radiation the roof will blow off of this skyscraper!" Perish yelled back, holding Silas tight in his arms as the king shouted and screamed cruel and biting insults at Sanguine. "Get them out of here. I need to take him outside. I'll take him outside; I'll take him outside."

Elish's teeth clenched as Perish started dragging the king, seemingly in his own insane psychosis, towards the sliding glass doors.

He turned to Jack, and pushed Sanguine towards him. The chimera had stopped thrashing and trying to get to King Silas; he seemed to have gone back to his stunned state. "Get out of the building, take Sanguine some place safe and wait for us there. He's your responsibility. Keep your boyfriend safe."

My boyfriend? Feeling an overwhelming new sense of responsibility Jack nodded. He took Sanguine's hand and when Sanguine didn't fight him or dig his feet in he quickly took him towards the door.

Back outside... Jack's eyes stung as they both got into the elevator, but he pushed back the tears and stood tall, gripping his boyfriend's hand so tightly he was afraid he would snap Sanguine's bones. *Back outside where we just were… I didn't expect this to go so badly.*

"Sami?" Jack whispered as the elevator started to descend. He was half-expecting to hear an explosion above him. He had heard terrifying stories about what sestic radiation could do, and though chimeras were immune to the radiation itself, they weren't immune to explosions. "Sami, are you okay?"

Sanguine only stared forward, saying nothing back. And though he was in an almost catatonic state, he was suggestible and followed orders. So Jack saved the many questions he had burning his lips and led Sanguine to the car he had just parked beside Alegria.

"I want to go to my basement…" Sanguine said when they were both in the vehicle. "Where my friends are, in Cypress. Take me there."

Jack's hands gripped the wheel. He had been heading to Sanguine's old apartment, now with a fresh coat of paint and new furniture. But though he badly wanted to bring Sanguine there he knew what was more important right now was putting Sanguine some place he mentally felt safe.

So with a nod he turned left at the next intersection, and headed towards the dark shadows in the distance, the low-class district of Cypress.

Following Sanguine's directions Jack pulled into an old building with broken and boarded up windows and a lean to the structure that made Jack nervous. He parked the car in an alley, fully expecting it to be stripped of any sellable material by daylight and followed his new boyfriend through an echoing, dusty interior that made him sneeze several times.

And then the descent. Jack could hear his pulse pick up when Sanguine turned a corner and directed him towards a flight of stairs leading into darkness. A hole that seemed to come out of nowhere, surrounded by a railing painted with chipping white paint and half-collapsed on the left hand side.

Sanguine stood in front of the stairwell and rested a hand on the railing. In front of him was a wall with a corkboard covered in dust, and a filing cabinet missing two of its sliding doors. To his left was stacks of chairs and to his right, desks and lamps. Everything was coated in grey dust and gravely plaster from the ceilings and the walls. There was also insulation everywhere too and an intense, undesirable smell of dried, rotting wood and must. It was a horrible place for anyone to be.

Then the realization; one that made Jack smile.

"This building reminds you of home doesn't it?" Jack whispered. His boots crunched against the plaster as he walked up to Sanguine, and throwing caution to the wind, he put a hand on Sanguine's shoulder. When Sanguine's heartbeat didn't pick up or his body tense, Jack rubbed it gently.

Sanguine slowly nodded, then he ran his hand over the railing, paint chips sprang up behind him like a rooster tail following an outboard motor. He then looked at his hand, now streaked with white paint and dirt.

"I miss home," Sanguine said slowly. He rubbed his fingers together, making dust fall down to the floor below them. "This is kind of home. My friends are here... my friends who... believe me, and love me anyway."

"Sanguine..." Jack said, a little more sharply than he meant to. He squeezed Sanguine's hand and walked up to him until they were side by side. "Everyone believes you, even Silas. He's just ravaged with guilt because he knows he's responsible. Elish is with him and he'll probably call Mantis – they'll both speak with him. Silas listens to those two; they're his counsel."

Sanguine stared down the dark stairwell before, without a word spoken, he started to descend to the basement. And though Jack's heart was beating its anxiety over following Sanguine down these stairs that seemed fitting for a horror movie, he did.

Sanguine stretched a hand out as they walked and let his nails scrape against the rough brick, the sound grating on Jack's ears like nails on a chalkboard. The further down Sanguine led Jack the more the fine hairs on the back of his neck creeped up.

Then in the distance, down the long hallway, he saw light leaking in from a closed door, and though the temperature was frigid he could feel hints of warmth against his skin.

"Let me go in first," Sanguine said quietly. "I need to tell them you're here."

Jack was confused for a moment before he remembered the conversation he had heard Sanguine have with his imaginary friend Barry. Telling the person to feed the others while he was gone.

Nervously Jack stayed behind as Sanguine let go of his hand and pushed the door open.

"Hello, friends," Sanguine said, his voice was dead and emotionless. "Did Barry feed you?"

Jack waited behind the closed door, and it was there he started to smell the distinct stench of rot. His heartbeat sped up anticipating just what he was going to see when that door opened.

"Good... I have a friend here. I need privacy with him. You will need to spend the night in the storage room with your bodies. But I will come back and get you, I promise."

He's so sweet... even in his madness he's the sweetest chimera I know. Jack felt his heart break for Sanguine. The pain he knew Sanguine was going through was so intense it physically hurt his heart. So badly did Jack want to snatch the pain away from him and push it into himself.

Never more than now did he realize he was falling in love with this mad man.

The door opened and Sanguine's shadowed face appeared. "Okay, you can come in... they're gone."

Jack smiled at him, and Sanguine nodded back and stepped away from the door as he opened it for him.

When Jack stepped in though his smile faded.

The basement he had been staying in was... something not even a rat should be allowed to live in. There were stacks of dusty, half-rotten boxes, crates, old blankets, and what looked like decaying bones in the corner giving off a horrible stink. The walls had chunks of brick missing and the mortar was worn to the point where the bricks were sitting bare on top of each other. The place looked like it could fall down at any minute.

And his bed... Sanguine had an old double mattress in the corner with blankets that Jack could smell from where he was standing. Like everything in this place they stunk of stale water and dirt, and Jack could see several stains of multiple colours.

Jack stepped into the open area. The only redeeming thing in the dungeon-like room was the fact that it was warm and lit. There was a heater in the center of the room connected to an extension cord, and two lamps with halogen bulbs. Then behind it beside a metal door was a hot plate with a dirty pot and frying pan on each element.

"It's a lot better than the basement at Jasper's," Sanguine said in a voice full of shame. "And the shanty town too. And it's safe and... and far away from everyone."

"It's your safe spot, it's wonderful," Jack whispered. He slipped his hand into Sanguine's again and squeezed it. "We can stay here until you feel safe enough to come live with me."

Sanguine looked down at his and Jack's hands, with the light fully illuminating him Jack realized he looked incredibly worn out and tired. "Live with you?"

Jack nodded slowly and since the room they were in was sweltering hot he started to take off Sanguine's torn clothes, wincing and chastising himself when he saw the vicious claw marks on Sanguine's back and neck. Though the reminder of the intense sex they had experienced earlier that evening made Jack's backside give a painful throb.

When Sanguine's shirt was off he gently led him to the mattress, trying to hide the wrinkle in his nose as the smell became more pungent. He knew his nose would get used to it and the least of his concerns should be what the mattress smelled like.

"Lay down," Jack whispered.

Sanguine hesitated. "I don't think we should…" His words trailed away as he saw Jack shake his head.

"We're not, we're going to sleep that's all, Sanguine," Jack said to him in a low but soothing voice. "Lay down with me." He walked over to the two halogen lights and turned them off. When he turned back around Sanguine was laying in bed, staring almost blankly at the ceiling.

Jack took off his own tattered shirt and laid down on his side, and when he didn't tense up, Jack pulled Sanguine into his arms and held his burning body against his own. The skin-on-skin contact making Jack feel more connected to Sanguine than what had happening in the abandoned building.

"Sanguine?" Jack whispered. He closed his eyes and felt Sanguine's hair on his cheek.

"Yeah?" Sanguine said back.

"Will you be my boyfriend?"

Jack's pulse quickened at the same time Sanguine's did. He felt Sanguine shift until he was on his side facing Jack.

"You don't know what you're getting into," Sanguine said, then he paused. "Actually… you do. Why then?"

Jack's stomach prickled like he had just swallowed a thousand small needles. For a moment his mouth felt glued shut, but as the seconds passed the anxiety turned into a solemn determination. One that told him now was the time to tell him how he felt.

"Because I think I love you."

Sanguine's heart jumped. Jack slid his hand, which had been laying against Sanguine's side, over to his chest and felt his heart pound against his palm.

"You love me?" Sanguine sounded confused. It made a small smile creep to Jack's face, and when he opened his eyes to see the Sanguine's perplexed look, it only widened.

Jack nodded. "I do. I love you. I want to help you. I want to be near you, beside you. I want us to – to spend the rest of our lives side by side, facing this… crazy family together."

Sanguine's eyes looked into Jack's before they diverted away. "I have nothing to offer you but pain, drama, and possibly physical injury."

"I don't care, stop being so… self-deprecating," Jack said lowly. "Just… just say yes so I can start taking care of you. So I can start…" Jack smiled again. "So I can start having a say when I make you do things for your own good."

Jack's heart soared when Sanguine returned the smile. "That's really it, isn't it? You want to be my boyfriend so you can start bossing me around?"

Jack's eyes raised to the ceiling. "I assure you I have no idea what you're–" Jack gasped when Sanguine reached up and pinched his cheek hard. In retaliation he smacked Sanguine's chest, and when Sanguine laughter filled the room Jack put his arm around his neck and drew him in for a kiss.

Their lips locked together, and Jack felt Sanguine's hand gently slip down the small of his back. They stayed together, their mouths slowly moving to take each other in, before breaking apart.

Jack could feel Sanguine's warm breath on his lips; he slowly opened his eyes to see his chimera brother staring back at him. He looked almost lost, but at the same time he looked as if he had found something he had been searching for for years.

"I think I love you too…" Sanguine whispered. "I think… that's what I'm feeling."

"What does it feel like?"

Sanguine was quiet for a moment, but his brow furrowed suggesting he was trying to decipher what was going on inside of him.

"Warm, electric, kinda fuzzy and… incredibly scary, nauseas, and I keep having to remind myself that… you do know I'm completely out of my mind half the time," Sanguine responded after several moments. "You do know... you do know this lucidity isn't going to last? The next stressor that triggers it..."

"You have me now to help calm you down," Jack said. He leaned in and kissed Sanguine's lips gently. "Elish and Mantis will handle Silas, and soon everyone will get the help they need and we can all be a happy family. I promise."

"It won't be that simple..." Sanguine said with a sigh. "If I agree to be your boyfriend, you need to promise me something. And you must promise you won't promise me unless you plan on doing it."

Jack didn't like the sound of this, but he nodded anyway and gently started stroking Sanguine's prickly cheek, his face just as burning hot as the rest of his body. The chimera seemed to radiate heat, which was a stark contrast to the cold skin that most of his brothers had, himself included.

"Promise me that when I go into that state... you'll leave," Sanguine said slowly. "Swear on my life, Jack. I'm not in control. I almost raped you in that building and you saw what I did to Ludo. Promise me if you see that come out of me – you'll get as far away from me as you can."

The room fell back into silence, though the emotions racing through Jack's body seemed to have their own voice. They were telling Jack that there was no way he could leave Sanguine alone when he was in the crazed state he had discovered him in, but at the same time – he also knew what Sanguine needed to hear.

"I promise," Jack said with a nod. "I will, but I know what gets you into those states – all we have to do is keep you calm and feeling safe, and you'll be fine."

Sanguine let out a sigh of relief, and for a brief moment, he closed his eyes. "I'm just happy that I know what's going on with me. That I'm aware enough to know that this is happening. At first I thought it was the drugs I was smoking with Mouse and Julia but now I know – this is a deeper issue inside of my brain. The meth had only amplified it, added fuel to the delusions. You're right in saying... we just need to keep me calm."

Meth? Jack bit his lip to keep him from shouting that out loud. Meth made even the most level-headed of people paranoid. It would ravage someone like Sanguine.

But that wasn't the time or place to chastise him about it. Instead Jack kept stroking Sanguine's cheek, trying to cool it with his own cold touch. "Accepting it is a big thing. I know Mantis will be happy you have awareness." Then he gently pinched Sanguine's cheek and shook it. "Now make it official… come on, I want to hear you say it."

Sanguine drew him in for another kiss, this one parting Jack's lips gently. They kissed deeply, each taste of Sanguine's mouth lighting a small flame inside of his chest.

"We can be boyfriends," Sanguine whispered after their lips separated. "Until madness do we part."

CHAPTER 43

SILAS REACHED HIS HAND OUT OF THE OPEN CAR door and Elish took it gently. He helped the king out of the black car before sweeping the area with his purple eyes, making sure he could spot the three thiens they had accompanying them as they walked around the slum district of Moros.

Behind him Nero stood with his fiancé Ceph, and their younger brother Felix who had a white bandage covering the side of his head. All three of them stern of face and firm of stance, but dressed entirely in casual clothes. The only indication there was that they were of higher status than the Morosians around them were the assault rifles strapped to their backs.

Even Silas and Elish were dressed in normal arian attire. Elish in a black trench coat and a brimmed hat, and King Silas in a black leather jacket and blue jeans. There was no mistaking that they were trying to blend in, though with how the Morosians were stopping to stare at who they knew was their king, it was obvious that anyone paying attention would see that they were amongst royalty.

"We're sticking out like sore thumbs," Elish mumbled. He put a hand on the small of Silas's back and directed Silas towards the slanted, garbage-strewn sidewalk. "We should've just summoned the boys and made up an excuse."

Silas shook his head, and as he glanced up at the cloudless blue sky above them it was obvious that the king was in mental turmoil. His large green eyes were rimmed with black bags, his face was gaunt and paler than usual. Even his stance told a story of sleepless nights and mental baggage. King Silas was not in a good state.

"I want to see how they live. I want to see how they're fairing," Silas whispered. He allowed Elish's hand to stay on his back and the two of them walked down the dirty streets of Moros, Nero in front of them and Ceph and Felix guarding them from behind.

"You care about how Ares and Siris are doing and yet you haven't said a word about Valen and Ludo both missing," Felix suddenly said coldly. A moment later there was a heavy thud as Ceph smacked him upside the head.

"Not another word, subordinate," Ceph growled, and at the same time Elish whirled around to give the dark-haired brute chimera a searing gaze. A gaze that no doubt would have been a physical blow if they weren't in public where appearances had to be kept.

Felix's eyes narrowed; he looked away with a soured look on his face, though no more words slipped from his mouth.

And to only accentuate the uncharacteristically defeated mood that King Silas was in, he only kept walking. No scathing remarks, no verbal beat downs, no mind destroying punishment like what would be expected from the king. It seemed like all he was able to do in that moment was put one foot in front of the other.

"Moros is a lot safer than the greywastes, Silas," Elish reassured. "Perhaps Moros would be a fairer place to drop off chimeras we wish to grow up with a harder nose."

"Perhaps…" Silas whispered. They turned a corner and were greeted with a single lane road with abandoned cars, stripped of everything but their frames, half on the sidewalk. The buildings on this road were in particularly worse shape, even for Moros. Most had their roofs caved in and several had been completely gutted, only charred skeleton roofs remaining and metal beams that stuck out of the wreckage like the dead trees of the greywastes.

Elish's nose curled as they walked by a man sitting beside a dirty cart. He was selling half-rotten vegetables and what looked like newspaper wrapped leftovers he must've scavenged from the dumpsters of the local pubs and restaurants.

The man looked up at the party and his gaunt eyes widened. Immediately he got down on his knees and bowed as Silas walked past. Silas gave him a nod and kept on walking.

"I wonder if they buy their food from him?" Silas said out loud when the man was behind them. "How long have they been out of Edgeview?"

"They wander in when they get hungry, and we've instructed the house nurses to give them food if they ask nicely. But they do not make them stay," Elish replied as he started looking more closely at the buildings, no doubt trying to spot the twin boys they were seeking. "They're eleven years old now."

Silas let out a small sigh and nodded. "They'll be men soon... though with how my other brute chimeras have grown they probably already weigh more than me." The king looked around and when he spotted a shadow in a broken window, he smiled for the first time in days. "I think I see one. Go ahead, Nero."

Nero took off a backpack he was wearing and placed it with a thunk on top of a stripped Ford truck, covered in spray-paint and regular house paint, with a nest of cloth and fur inside that suggested it was some animal's nest. He opened up the bag and took out several tin cans of food.

Then, almost methodically he handed a can opener to Ceph and one of the cans, before picking up the other one and tapping the top of the tin with his fingernails.

"Kitties!" Nero sang, making Elish put a hand to his head and groan. Unable to witness the scene, Elish walked away and distracted himself with staring through the shattered windows of an old movie store.

But when he heard Silas laugh he turned around and shook his head at the king, a smirk appearing on his cold, stoic face. "You know he makes a mockery out of years of chimera research by calling them like cats?" Elish said, though his unimpressed expression lightened when he saw the first hints of his old king come back.

"They come to it, don't they?" Nero responded as he walked around the middle of the empty street, still tapping the can. He gave out a loud whistle before turning to Silas. "I started doing it when they were just little guys, five I think, and it's just kinda our thing now."

"No one else is around to hear us anyway," Silas said, his eyes were looking intently where he had last seen one of the twins. "I hear them coming down the stairs..."

Sure enough, as all five pairs of eyes turned towards an open door leading into a wooden building, a boy with short black hair poked his head through the door.

"Nero!" the boy exclaimed. He stuck his tongue out like a happy dog and started running towards the group. Several seconds later an identical boy burst out of the same doorway and also started running towards them.

They were unique-looking children, as all brute children were. Though they were only eleven years old they were only a head shorter than Silas, and didn't have the normal willowy build that most young boys did. They were thick and burly, with muscles already visible through their torn shirts.

Both the boys skidded to a stop as soon as they got close to Nero, but as soon as they stopped running they started bouncing around instead.

"Did you bring us Chef Boyardee!?" one of them asked excitedly. At the mention of what was most likely their favourite food the other one let out a squeal, and started doing a strange half-wiggle, half-bouncing dance.

Elish stared at them before once again putting his hand to his face, groaning, and turning away from the scene.

Though like when Nero was calling the twins like cats Silas smiled and even laughed when the two boys started hollering and whooping when Nero handed them both cans of ravioli.

"Siris – Siris – Siris –" the boy who had to have been Ares said as he patted his brother on the shoulder. When Siris, who now had his face in the ravioli can, looked over at him Ares raised his can and grinned.

Siris, knowing what his brother wanted, grinned back. Then at the exact same time they raised their cans and clinked them against one another while saying, quite enthusiastically, "Cheers!" Before tipping their heads back, mouths wide open like baby birds, letting several of the little raviolis fall into their mouths.

Silas was smiling, Nero and Ceph laughing at the two boys' antics. They let the twins eat their food in peace and Silas watched both Nero and Ceph start bringing out cans of food, vitamins, ChiCola, and movies for the boys to bring back to the apartment they both lived alone in.

"Okay you little shits, you've had some food. You need to say hello to King Silas and Master Elish," Nero said after the kids had downed half of their food. They had orange sauce streaked all over their faces and their hands, Ares even had a bit of pasta on his chin. "Do it like I taught you."

The twins put their cans down on top of the Ford truck and saluted King Silas, their grinning faces turning stern, though both of their lips were twitching to keep from smiling. "Nice to meet your acquaintance, King Silas and Master Elish," they both said in unison.

Silas smiled and nodded at the two twins. "They bring so much humour and joy with them, even though they have been raised in such desolation. How can these two boys be so happy—" Silas looked over at Felix who was scowling at the scene in front of him. "And the ones we have raised underfoot, with every privilege in the world, turn into such unappreciative pieces of shit."

Felix's lips pursed but he said nothing back.

"It's not all bad, Kingy," Nero said reassuringly. "Jack's doing a turn around, Apollo and Artemis are like your perfect little prodigies, and Sangy will be fine eventually. It's just… the remainders we need to work on."

"Say our names if you're going to insult us," Felix said. "Me, Valen, Rio, and Ludo. Two of which are missing and I'm sure Rio will go missing soon as well."

"Watch your fucking mouth, Felix," Nero barked. "If you want to get respect, earn it. You don't default get respect just because you're a fucking chimera. No matter how many arians and greywasters you bully into fearing you."

"Chimeras are so awesome," Ares's could be heard whispering to his brother.

"I know!" Siris whispered back.

"I would be more willing to earn it if two of my best friends weren't missing with the family giving not a single shit," Felix snapped. His dark green eyes shot to Silas, and when the king made direct eye contact with him they narrowed in such a hostile manner Nero's teeth grated against one another.

"You better do something about this, asshole," Felix threatened. "Or else—"

There was an angry bellow and the swing of a fist. It connected hard against Felix's head, throwing the brute chimera off balance and making him tumble towards the ground.

Ceph stood over him, his chest heaving, behind him Silas stared forward, his eyes an inferno and his face void of all expression. The look he was giving Felix was so caustic, everyone but Ceph took a step back.

But to all of their surprise Silas said nothing. The distant, depressed look on his face came back, sending away the jovial contentment the twins had brought.

"Wait in the car, Felix," Silas said in a dead tone. "We'll be leaving soon."

The shock was apparent on all of their faces, but it was most prominent on Elish's. The blond chimera looked absolutely taken aback at Silas's nulled emotions. Silas seemed to have extinguished the fuse that Felix had lit on him, snuffing out the flame with nothing but a disinterested look. He didn't seem to care anymore, or have the energy and drive to discipline something that, in most cases, would've led to the chimera in question being beaten within an inch of his life. This alarmed Elish to extent, and made a chill come to his chest.

Felix must've picked up on this vulnerability, like any chimera, brute especially, they could sniff out weakness in anyone chimera or arian. It was in the brute makeup to take advantage of frailty and exploit it to their own advantage. Felix was young, hotheaded, and still testing his teeth on the authority figures of the family. This was typical for a chimera teenager but unlike when the others tried to assert their dominance – Silas didn't seem to have it in him lately to rain the hammer of Thor down on the rebellious.

He had been too defeated since the incident regarding Sanguine coming home. Silas had been quiet and distant since the event several days ago, and it was only getting worse. The first smile Silas had had since the chaos had been this very visit with the twins Ares and Siris.

"That one's a big fuck," Ares suddenly piped up. "You should send him to Stadium. If you do can we watch?"

Though in normal circumstances everyone would have at least cracked a smile at the young boy's comment, the mood had quickly turned toxic.

Silas put a hand on the boy's head and patted it. His eyes seemingly unfocused and his gaze distant. "Yes, love."

"How long until we can join the army?" Siris asked. He had his entire hand wedged inside of the can now; he turned it back and forth like a corkscrew until it was covered with sauce, then proceeded to lick it.

"That's... what you told them?" Silas asked Nero in a quiet voice. Nero nodded.

Silas stepped onto the sidewalk and looked ahead at Felix's turned back as he headed back to the vehicle. "When you're fifteen, loves. Only three and a half more years."

"That's too bad. I wanna kick that big fuck's ass," Siris remarked with an orange-mouthed smile. "Thank you for the food and toys, King Silas, and Master Elish, and Imperial Commander Nero, and Commander Ceph, and big fuckface whatever-his-name-is. Will you come say hi on Skyday like last year?"

"So well-behaved," Silas murmured. "Elish these boys are faring well. Look at them."

Elish knew why Silas spoke those words and he knew what was going on inside of his king's head. The two snarling dogs, one called denial and one called reality. Silas was a stubborn man, but Elish also knew he was intelligent and reasonable. He knew King Silas would accept what Jasper had done to Sanguine – but it would be when his mind was ready to handle the guilt.

"We will all come and bring you two presents for Skyday."

The boys hollered and celebrated, then the king gave them each a pat on the head. "Take care of yourselves and eat well. If anyone picks on you – tell the precinct."

The twins laughed at this. "We do the pickin', King Silas," Siris said.

No one spoke when they got back in the black car. Felix was in a foul mood and he did nothing to hide it. He was staring out the window with an angry expression on his face, wedged against the window with only Ceph keeping him from the death glares of Nero.

"Home then, love?" Elish asked as they pulled onto the main road, the one that would lead them through the concrete fence that separated Moros from Nyx.

To everyone's surprise Silas shook his head, his dead eyes downcast.

"Where would you like to go then?" Elish asked in a kind voice.

Elish's words lingered on the air before becoming lost in the steady rumbling of the car motor. Abandoned buildings passing them by, and the occasional surprised face of a Morosian. No doubt wondering why a car, let alone a royal car, was soiling itself being driven around their slums.

And in this time Silas didn't speak; he continued to stare out the window his face blank and his body slouched. The sadness that had taken hold of him ever since the night Sanguine came home, almost visible in front of the five.

"We're going to the Dead Islands," Silas said finally, in a dark, eerily cold tone. "We're going to see Jasper."

Elish's hand tightened on the wheel. It wasn't his place to tell Silas no, especially when Felix was in the car with him. The brute had already smelled Silas's weakness and for Elish to question Silas's decision in front of him would only accentuate it. Silas would deal with Felix's attitude when he was feeling better and not until then.

"Silas... let me come in with you," Nero said in the back seat. "I... I need to come with you."

No, Elish said to himself. *I need to come with him. I need to be there when he talks to Jasper. I need to be there when he can no longer run from the truth. And when his world crumbles and the guilt brings him to his knees... it will be my arms that will shelter him.*

Not Sanguine's.

Mine.

"I will be speaking with him alone, but everyone in this vehicle will be accompanying me to the island," Silas responded, and though Nero's jaw clenched he said nothing back.

Elish looked into the rear-view mirror and made eye contact with Nero. He nodded slowly at his youngest brother. "Call us a Falconer. We'll leave for the Dead Islands immediately."

Silas's lost expression didn't change even when all five of them boarded the Falconer. With Ceph flying the plane and Felix in the co-pilot's seat, it was just Silas, Elish, and Nero in the back.

"Please, let me go in there with you," Nero said slowly, sitting beside Silas and putting his arm around his king. Elish was on Silas's other side, being silent support. Nero's approach had always been direct, Elish preferred being a rock rather than the reassuring friend.

Silas glared at Nero as the brute chimera squeezed his body, small in comparison to Nero's, against his side. "I must do this alone, and though I know you think you have some say considering you've been a part of this since the beginning – I assure you, you do not."

Nero sighed and let Silas go. He wiped his face with his hands before shaking his head. "Yeah, I know. I know, Silas," Nero said in frustration. He got up and walked towards the window.

Taking the opportunity Elish put his own arm around Silas and drew him close, even going as far as to wrap his cloak partially around his king's body.

"Well, I hope you get what you need out of him," Nero said acidly. "So we can solve this, get Sanguine home and move on."

"I want no further talk of Sanguine." Silas's face turned stormy; Nero had no idea how much his words had contaminated that raw wound. "Are you not leaving tomorrow for Cardinalhall anyway? Is there not an invasion the day after tomorrow?"

"There is," Nero's tone dropped. "A great fucking inconvenience. I've been waiting years for you to let me invade Irontowers and now I want nothing more than to stay home so I can be there when Sanguine comes home."

"You'll be far away from it," Silas said. "I think you've gotten too close to the boy anyway. You have an unhealthy attachment to him, one I haven't seen even in your fiancé."

"I was the first family member who gave a shit about his well-being," Nero said coolly, and though he didn't turn around from the window of the Falconer, Silas could see his eyes glaring at him in the window's reflection. "It's always been me and him. And in the end, years from now, I bet it will still fucking be me and him. Because I trust that little shit and he trusts me. We have a bond and you can't–" Nero's eyes shifted to the cockpit, where Ceph was, and as if remembering what he had to lose by the words he was about to speak, he shifted uncomfortably before mumbling an apology.

Silas continued to glare at him. "It seems giving you a fiancé has worked. Even the remedial chimera is starting to learn to shut his mouth."

Elish smirked; Nero could see it, Silas could not.

"Yeah, I'm sorry," Nero mumbled. "Forgive me."

"You're forgiven, lovely boy," Silas said back and let out a tense breath. "Are we close?"

"Yeah," Nero said back. "We're almost there. Did you just want me to wait in the plane or something?"

"No." Silas leaned a head on Elish's shoulder. "Why don't you go take Felix and Ceph to the lion pens and see if there are any cubs we can take home for a couple days. Drake's birthday is next week and he can show it off to his friends."

"Jorvik was mentioning he's put the carracats into the lions' pens as well. They get along great," Nero said, he was gazing out the window with a troubled look on his face. There was no doubt that lions and carracats were the last thing on his mind. "The island is getting full though, we're going to have to budget another facility or start releasing more breeding pairs into the greywastes."

"Perish has been on me for that for quite a while," Silas responded. There was a slight jolt before the engine motor switched to a lower octave, then everyone felt the odd nauseas pull as the plane started to descend onto the island below. This island was called Cortes, but the entire string of islands that littered the west coast of the greywastes were referred to as the Dead Islands.

Some islands were for military bases, some for scientific research and experiments, more than several held large animal sanctuaries that were open to the public for elite vacations. One was even kept in pristine condition because Silas had lived there as a child.

The one they were landing on was one of the islands used for scientific research, but it also was used during the rare times that King Silas wanted to keep a prisoner alive for an extended period of time. Something that almost never happened considering most lawbreakers went to Stadium, or were executed on the spot. Skyfall had no jails because Silas didn't believe in lawbreakers taking resources out of the mouths of those in need. Those who committed serious crimes like rape, murder, or arson were sent to Stadium and those who had been caught for lesser crimes were sentenced to hard labour where they had to pay back their debt with sweat and blood. And if you were a repeat offender, three strikes to be exact, you were labelled a genetic dead-end and you were sterilized, petty crime or not.

And after that? There was no fourth strike, it was as simple as that.

The plane touched down. Nero pulled the Falconer door open and stepped out. He raised a hand for Silas to grab and helped his king down from the plane.

"I don't need an escort," Silas said to Nero. "Elish, you may wait outside the facility for me. The others can go and see the lions."

"Yes, Master," Elish and Nero said at the same time. Without another word the king walked ahead, a large single-storey base painted grey and surrounded by a large concrete fence in front of him. It looked like a military base, with guard towers stationed on all four corners but oddly the grass was brilliant green and there were grazing animals surrounding the cold, sterile building. It was a strange sight for anyone seeing it for the first time, but to King Silas it was just another place to be.

"Nero?" Elish said under his breath. He was looking ahead at Silas, watching his king who had his shoulders slumped over and his fists clenched. Unlike his usual stealthy movements, ones that always reminded Elish of a spectre or a ghost, Silas was stalking towards the entrance of the building.

"What?" Nero said. He turned towards the plane as the sound of boots scraping metal was heard. Ceph and Felix undoubtedly getting some food for the lions.

"The motor on the plane sounded off when we were descending," Elish replied, just as Felix and Ceph hopped out; Felix was carrying a white grocery bag that smelled of dried meat. "I think Ceph should stay behind and check it out."

"Aww, come on!" Ceph said annoyed, but when he looked to Nero he saw that his fiancé's eyes were locked with Elish's. "You're not going to make me stay, are you? I want to see the fucking lions!"

Nero and Elish continued their silent conversation, before Nero nodded. "No, he's right, Cephy. Stay behind and check the oil and all of that bullshit. I can't imagine Silas being long with Jasper. I don't think he has much to say to him anyway." He looked at Felix who had a piece of the rat jerky in his mouth. "Alright, let's go."

"Bullshit," Ceph mumbled, and there was a clank from him kicking the metal side of the Falconer, but he knew better than to raise too much of a fuss. Ceph jumped back into the storage area of the plane and started opening up crates.

Everyone who Silas passed bowed to him, some of them even getting on one knee when they saw the expression on King Silas's face. A king without his smirking grace was a strange and terrifying sight. The men and women who worked underneath the iron fist of the Monarchy knew Silas as only the assured, confident deity that he was; to see him with such a blank, staring look on his face was enough to set even the higher-ranking military officials off-balance.

And since saying anything about it was far out of the realm of reality, they only bowed before slipping out of the staring gaze of their king. Wondering to themselves, as they had been for months, just who this bedraggled man being kept in such maximum security was, and why he had been allowed to live unlike the hundreds of men and women each year who fell onto the sword of Stadium Night.

Silas approached two young men standing guard near a single metal door, both holding carbines against their chest. They were dressed in identical legionary uniforms and combat armour, newly pressed and clean without a hint of dust or wear. There was no mistaking the difference between the legionaries in the greywastes and the ones who worked in the military facilities on the Dead Islands, you only had to go as far as the condition of their uniforms.

The two stepped away from the metal door, their eyes were fixed forward in a confident stare, but their heartbeats sold out their true emotions.

"Leave," Silas said to them and, like their boots had been coated in soap, the two immediately slid away from the doors and disappeared into an adjacent room.

Silas allowed himself a single breath, and as he held it in his lungs he craned his ears to listen for any electronics that could be recording around him. Almost every Dekker-controlled facility had cameras inside of them but this was not one of them. Silas didn't want what was going to happen to be recorded; he wanted it lost in the flow of time and perhaps one day – forgotten.

With a slow exhale the king put a hand on the metal lever imbedded in the door, and pushed it open. He walked in and immediately saw the man in his fifties sitting on a plastic chair in front of a plain grey table, the kind you would see in a school.

He looked better than when Silas had first lay eyes on him, which was more of a testament to how he had been living in the greywastes than how he had been treated here. When they found him his hair was greasy and knotted, his face that of a walking skeleton, with most of his teeth missing and his skin so dirty it was dyed brown and grey.

And though he was only allowed a cold shower once a week and a once-a-day meal of rice and corn, it seemed to have been a step up from his previous living conditions. His skin was back to being white, his long dark hair now pulled back in a ponytail, and his gaunt face healthier.

Silas felt a burst of anger go through him, because though the man held bruises on his face, and on closer inspection, he was missing all but a single finger and thumb on both of his hands, he had obviously been taken care of too well. Not nearly a big enough punishment for a man who had tortured a chimera for eleven years.

But as Jasper looked up at him, Silas realized the healthy appearance wasn't because of his guards taking too good of care of him, it was because he had been off of meth for the better part of a year now.

"And how different is life now that you're no longer poisoning your brain with meth?" Silas asked in a low voice. He sat down on the other end of the table in a plastic chair that had been brought in for him.

Jasper kept looking at him, his body full of tension but his breathing was steadier than Silas had expected. He wasn't a terrified shell like Silas had assumed he would be, though obviously beaten down he hadn't slipped into any sort of terrorized psychosis. Silas wanted to be disappointed at this but it would make things easier in the long run.

"Say what you will about meth – but in the end the Legion *was* after me," Jasper said in a raspy voice. "Though I never realized just what for." As Silas stared back at him the side of his mouth rose in a smirk. "Never in a million years would I have thought…"

"That you kidnapped one of my princes?" Silas said back.

"Princes…" Jasper seemed amused by the word. "The only man who would have a harder time believing that the boy was a prince would be the boy himself." He tapped a single finger against the table and shook his head. "So much hypocrisy these days."

King Silas's eyes narrowed, refusing to acknowledge the surprise at how different this was going than expected. He hadn't seen Jasper since the night they had rescued Sanguine from the basement. He had expected the same screaming madman, covered in lice and fleas.

"Hypocrisy?" Silas answered back coolly.

"I know why you're here," Jasper said back. "You're here to arrange my death most likely, for what I did to a *chimera*, as he's called. I have no idea why you've kept me alive for this long to be honest. When I went to the Skyfall harbour in my younger years I heard nothing but the stringent laws in Skyfall. And here I am still alive after everything I did to your… *prince*."

"I'm not here to arrange your death," Silas answered back in the same dead voice he had acquired since the night Sanguine had tried to come home. "It is not my place to kill you, it's Sanguine's and he's not ready yet."

"Sanguine…" Like when his mouth seemed to play with the word *prince* Jasper also seemed amused by this. "He called himself that as he got older, and the friends he spoke to called him that too." Jasper then smiled, his finger still tapping against the table. "I miss him some days. He was – entertaining. He gave good reactions, and when you're all alone, with every day the same as the next, you just love the reactions you can get out of people."

"I know the type," Silas said. "How long until he started developing those imaginary friends?"

Silas watched Jasper as he said those words, focusing his hearing and every other enhanced sense he had to try and determine if he was going to get any of the information he wanted out of Jasper. The man who had kept Sanguine prisoner had little to lose now, and he was either going to talk to Silas and answer his questions or flip him off and ask to be returned to his cell.

Though from what Silas had already been able to gather Jasper seemed open to talking to him, and he seemed to want to speak more. Most likely it wasn't often that he had someone to talk to, and if he had been found with three other people it meant he had been lonely.

This was something Silas could play with, until he got the information he needed.

"He had them when I met him," Jasper responded. "He was a really fucked up kid, naïve as all fuck in the beginning..." Then to Silas's anger Jasper laughed dryly. "Though the older he got... oh fuck did he ever turn into a demon. I would have let him go once he started sprouting hair but I knew the moment I unclipped that collar those fucked up teeth would be around my neck. Plus I knew he would take my little boys, and I still had use for them."

Silas's insides turned to ice, but he didn't show it on his face. He kept staring forward, a red haze threatening to creep into his eyes – he pushed it down with every ounce of control he had.

"Sprouting hair?" Silas's tone dropped, he felt the air start to get sucked out of his lungs, the room around him seemed to be getting smaller and smaller.

Jasper looked at him again, the same derisive smirk on his face. "Yeah, at thirteen he start getting those soft little pubes, then his cock and balls started to grow. That sweet squealing little voice deepened and all of a sudden – I was fucking a man."

The words hit Silas like a plane had crashed into the building, and this time he wasn't able to hide it on his face. He stared, in a state of frozen shock, at Jasper, and when the man saw the dumbstruck expression he chuckled.

"Too graphic for the king who ended the entire world?" Jasper said amused. "You personally actually follow the Rule of Fifteen? You're missing out if you haven't had a screaming eight-year-old pinned underneath you. I suggest you try it."

"Eight?" Silas uttered under his breath, then said to himself. "He was... telling the truth?"

Jasper snorted, his fingers tapping still against the table. "Telling the truth? What sort of bullshit is that? The guards beat me for it regularly." Jasper held up his hands and wiggled the one finger and thumb he still had on each. "Nero's been instructing them to take a digit each month from my fingers or toes. I lost my teeth trying to tell him about the night I took your damn prince's virginity." Then, as Silas still sat stunned, Jasper got up and pulled the dirty pair of sweatpants he was dressed in, over his groin.

There was nothing there but a badly healed purple scar surrounded by patches of oily black public hair. Everything else seemed to have been violently hacked away

"And I got this when I told him how I fucked Juni and Levi in front of him." Jasper's voice dropped. Then he pushed the table towards Silas in anger, a loud scraping sound echoed off of the walls. "And still you hypocritical fucks won't kill me."

Silas didn't move; he still seemed stunned and welded into place. Jasper let out an angry bellow and slammed his palms down on the table. "What the fuck is it going to take? I raped your little prince when he was eight years old; he didn't even know what was happening to him or what sex was. He cried for Nero every night until he lost hope and started acting like a lunatic instead. Don't tell me he hasn't said this to you?" Jasper snapped. "Or is he even still alive? Because if you're not here to kill me then why are you here? To tell me he's dead? Or maybe you're here to ask me to take him back since he's a fucked up, schizophrenic, worthless nut job."

Jasper pushed the table again, this time hitting Silas as he sat quietly. He seemed frustrated with the state the king was in; even though Jasper didn't know the king, he seemed to know something extremely unusual was going on with the king of the grey world.

Jasper let out an angry bellow; he raised the table and dropped it. "He would go into the same state. Dead to the world staring at the walls for days. Did a big bad man fuck you too?"

"Answer me, king!" Jasper yelled. "I'm taunting you, King Silas. I'm disrespecting you. What the fuck is it going to take for one of you, big scary chimeras to finally kill me? KILL ME!" Another slam from Jasper's hand.

"You know what, *My Liege*." Jasper's tone dropped. "You should be thanking me. Because that naïve, idiot boy wouldn't have lasted to twenty if I hadn't kept him in that basement. He was so cripplingly lonely he would've gone with anyone who smiled at him. I kept him alive for you, King Silas. I did your fucking dirty work for you and all I wanted in return was somewhere to keep my cock warm. You and this bullshit family couldn't have cared where that little fuck-up ended up if you thought leaving a kid who looked like a monster out in the greywastes was a good idea. You bunch of spoiled, pampered little rich fucks. You have no idea how bad it is out there do you?"

Jasper pushed the table again. "ANSWER ME!" he screamed.

The door opened behind him. "Get back!" Elish's voice suddenly barked.

Jasper gave Elish a heated glare, before lifting up the table and throwing it off balance. It crashed onto its side as Elish pulled Silas out of the room.

"Silence him," Elish said to the two legionary who were standing in the hallway. They both nodded, and with Jasper screaming in the room behind him Elish took Silas and started walking with him down the hallway.

Though they didn't head out the door like one would expect. Elish took Silas through two metal doors and down another hall. He then pulled him into an empty room with a single bed in the corner and closed the door.

Elish locked the door; he turned around just in time to see Silas drop to his knees, a look of utter agony on his face. Elish rushed over to him and reached out a caring hand, but like he was father time as soon as his fingers touched Silas's cheek the king seemed to age fifty years, then his face crumpled. With a gut-wrenching sob King Silas broke down in front of his oldest chimera, his most trusted advisor and counsel, and openly wept.

Without hesitation Elish took Silas into his arms and held him tight. He drew his cloak over the king and started to quietly soothe him.

As Silas sobbed into him Elish's eyes glanced around the empty room. He knew cameras were not welcome in this area of the Cortes base but he had to be sure. King Silas rarely broke down but when he did he shattered, and with the rebels active and some of the second generation rebellious and losing respect for Silas's vulnerable mood, if anyone saw the king in this state the consequences could be dire.

But they were alone, and since the room Elish held his king in was soundproof he knew no ears would hear the king's heartbreaking wails. Silas had to breakdown in silence, away from those who would take advantage of the weakness, and Elish's arms was the safest place for that to happen.

For I am the man he trusts the most, Elish said to himself as he gently rocked Silas back and forth, still making shushing noises as he did. *Sanguine holds no candle to what I can do for the king. Perhaps I was worried for no reason; he could never be the rock to Silas that I am. It won't be long, soon I will be king next to him.*

When Silas's sobbing started to die down, Elish gently started to stroke Silas's back, rubbing it in small circles as he continued to rock him back and forth. He could feel his king's pounding heart start to slow, and his body, tightly wound from stress begin to relax.

"I'm tired, Elish," Silas suddenly whimpered. The voice of one of the oldest men alive in the world was weak and small. A shadow of the slippery, confident tones Elish and his brothers were used to hearing. "I'm so tired."

"I know, love," Elish said back to him, and he squeezed Silas tight against him. "For someone like you, who carries the weight of the world, I can only imagine what storms are ravaging your head right now. A normal man would've driven himself to insanity."

Silas sniffed but besides a small shudder he said nothing back.

"Blow your nose, that's always made you feel better after," Elish whispered to him. Silas's sobbing had been reduced to shudders and chokes. He shifted Silas slightly before reaching into his robes and handing him a small red kerchief.

Silas blew his nose and wiped his eyes, a miserable look on his face. "I hate doing this in front of you," he said weakly. "I shouldn't show weakness to anyone, in front of you most of all."

"Nonsense," Elish responded, taking the kerchief from him. "Even the King of the Fallocaust needs a shoulder to cry on and a pair of arms to break down in. If not me, who?"

Silas was silent for a moment. "I know, love." His lower lip quivered and Elish picked up the kerchief again. He gently dabbed the tears still slipping down Silas's flushed cheeks.

"I know this breakdown isn't solely because of your confirmation regarding Sanguine," Elish said as gently as he could. He knew he was treading on a field full of landmines; if he was going to continue to be his king's one and only confidant he had to walk slowly and carefully. "Tell me what happened. Tell me what makes my king feel so tired?"

Silas sighed and closed his eyes. "When I was with Perish, taking care of baby Adler. Not only did I have to look at my Sky every day, hear his voice through Perish, feel his body hot against my own when I was intimate with him... I had to see the little baby in that glass tube look more and more like him every day." Elish watched Silas's eyes squeeze tighter like he was in physical pain "I was surrounded by my Sky, his essence, and I made the mistake of not only growing attached to that baby – but also the hope that this time it may work. That this time we might've successfully cloned the love of my life."

Since Silas's eyes were closed Elish's own eyes narrowed and his face became cold. There was no question how he felt about Silas's long dead boyfriend. A boyfriend who was no dream man, but a tyrant who was emotionally, physically, and mentally abusive to Elish's king. Though time had seemed to have given Silas a pair of rose-coloured glasses. Silas saw nothing of the abuse he had endured under Sky's iron fist, he only saw the good – what little there had been.

The stories Perish has told me makes my blood boil. I only wish I had been alive to beat that man into a bloodied pulp. It was a good thing the tyrant killed himself.

"It didn't work though," Silas continued, unaware of the mental poison running through Elish's head. "Once again I'm back at square one and worse yet – Sky's brain matter was nowhere to be found. The suitcase was never recovered and Nero says it must've been incinerated. I lost so much of his brain matter, now there is less of a chance of cloning him."

Good. Elish tightened his grip on Silas.

"I just wanted everything to be fine when I got back, but then I wake up and my Sanguine–" Elish felt Silas fidget and tense under his protective hold. "Sanguine is missing, terrorized by his own madness, the madness I brought onto him."

"No, love... it wasn't–"

Silas's eyes opened, cold and glaring, and Elish stopped talking.

"Everything wrong with that man is my fault. I feel such agony when I'm around him, so much guilt. Look at the shit I said to him, look at how weak I've become under this stress. I'm falling apart and I'm king, Elish, I cannot fall apart," Silas's face tensed in self-derision. He shook his head stiffly; he looked livid with himself. "I cannot fall apart right now, Elish," he said again.

"Perhaps you should take a few months leave," Elish suggested. "Spend some time in one of the vacation blocks in the greywastes or perhaps spend some time in your old hometown. Take a vacation and let me be king. I'll handle Irontowers, I'll handle Sanguine…"

Elish stopped when he saw Silas's face darken, a caustic sneer appeared, quickly sweeping away the weakness that had been so fleeting.

"No… I cannot pass off my problems like some sort of child," Silas said in a tone that reflected the expression on his face. As his tone and body language shifted, the king rose off of Elish's lap. "I cannot let you clean up the mess I made. I have to be involved, I have to fix this." Silas turned from Elish and clasped his hands behind his back. "I need to stop whining. I need to stop blaming myself and fix this."

"Master…" Elish said, his voice cooled but still kind. "You said yourself you are tired, you need a break from all of this. You may be a born immortal and the most powerful man on earth – but, love, even gods take rest. Let me take the burden for now."

"No, all of this has happened because I've been complacent," Silas said staring at the white brick wall in front of him. "Because I have been too kind." He turned around, Elish saw the green fire start to return to his king's eyes. "I have let too many people walk all over me for too long. And you know what, golden boy?"

Elish remained silent for a moment, before forcing his tone to remain kind. "What, Master?"

Silas's eyes flashed dangerously. He reached into his pocket and pulled out his cigarette tin, he brought a cigarette to his lips before lighting it with the tips of his fingers.

"I'm about fucking done being nice," he said, every word seemingly dripping acid. "I'm done being a whining bitch about this. I'm done being tired; I'm done fucking crying. And I'm done letting those failures of chimeras walk all over me. Ludo is dead, Valen is gone – who remains?" Like someone had replaced the sobbing king Elish held so close to him with a completely different copy, Silas pushed the metal door open and stalked out of it. His robes flowing swiftly behind him and a trail of silver cigarette smoke.

Elish stood in the doorway for a moment and admired his king walking so swiftly and confidently down the hallway. Though the dark corners of his mind were annoyed he wouldn't be able to be king like he had wanted; there was the swell of pride he felt by seeing Silas pull himself out of the toxic swamp he had created for himself.

King Silas had his moments of weakness, but they were few and far between, and they never lasted. After he had himself a breakdown and got it out of his system, my phoenix always rose from the ashes better than before.

And more dangerous than before.

One day we will rule this world together – one day I will be king beside you.

"The ones remain… Artemis and Apollo, Cepherus, Rio, Felix, Jack, and Sanguine," Elish responded. "Ludo has been confirmed dead. Nero and Ceph retrieved his burned bones from the building we had directed Jack to burn."

Silas nodded and roughly pushed open two metal doors. He walked through the hallway where Jasper was still being kept and passed the two guards Elish had dismissed earlier.

"Open the door," Silas said to the two guards. "Open the door and leave us."

Elish crossed his arms and smiled an amused smile inside of his head. Jasper was about to meet an entirely different king, and Elish was quite looking forward to how this was going to play out.

Without hesitation the male guard to the left opened the door, and after an exchanged nervous glance with his work partner, the two of them quickly walked down the hallway, the same direction that Elish and Silas had come in, and disappeared through the metal doors.

"You're back?" Jasper snarling voice sounded. "Sami used to stare like an idiot for days. You –" Suddenly a strangled choke cut off the man's scathing words. Elish quickly walked into the room and bore witness to an astounding sight.

Silas was standing in front of a struggling Jasper. The king's face was as cold and blank as the arctic tundra but his eyes were two infernos of black fire.

And not only that – energy was emanating off of the king, an almost visible wave of swirling darkness that seemed to hold no colour, on the contrary it seemed to suck the light from the room. It was an incredible sight to behold, one that made Elish stop in his tracks and stare in awe.

Jasper on the other hand appeared to be in pain. The greywaster was grasping his head with both hands, his fingers turning white from the intensity of his own strength. His eyes had rolled back into his head and his entire body was trembling like someone had started shaking him.

No expression graced the king's face as he stood in front of the writhing, screaming man. He seemed to watch Jasper with an indifferent yet burning expression on his face. There was no smile of enjoyment, no sinister laugh or even a scathing last remark. Elish watched with continued awe as Silas seemed to destroy the man right in front of him.

Elish had seen his king do it before, but it was rare – and as a trickle of blood fell down Silas's nose, Elish was reminded why.

Silas had incredible mental powers but they came at a price. If he did them for longer than the short period his mind allotted him; he died under the stress of his own abilities.

But King Silas didn't seem to care. As Jasper screamed, his hands now tearing out his long dark hair, Silas's eyes only narrowed further, followed by another almost tangible pulse of energy.

Then the man became silent, his hands dropped and his body became limp. And when Silas lowered his hands Jasper collapsed onto the ground, his eyes glazed over and his mouth open and slacked.

Silas looked down at the man before nudging him with his foot. Elish walked over and dabbed the king's nose with his kerchief.

Silas jerked his head away from Elish's touch, the energy still not dissipating even though Jasper, still alive, was nothing but a twitching heap on the ground. The king turned from Elish, and without a word, he walked out of the room.

Elish shadowing his footsteps, wondering just what his king had planned now. The mind of Silas Dekker was a fascinating one indeed, a wonderful and yet scary thing to behold.

It was almost like he was a mental shapeshifter

Yes, Elish said to himself. *He's like a mental shapeshifter.*

The king confidently swept past the legionaries who had gathered out of curiosity to see what all the noise was. All of the uniform-clad men and women were watching their king in awed respect. For some of them this may have been the first time they had laid eyes on King Silas in person.

"Would you like me to call Nero to prepare the plane?" Elish asked. He stepped outside of the base with King Silas still two paces ahead of him, and followed him down the paved strip of road which led all the way to the harbour; green grass and grazing animals surrounding them. The Falconer was parked in a parking lot just beyond the concrete walls.

"No," Silas answered back. The mental shapeshifter's tone was as confident as Elish had ever seen it. He felt a jolt of intrigue despite of his usually placid emotions.

"Are they feeding the lions?" Silas asked.

"Yes," Elish replied, a smirk started to crawl onto his face, "Nero and Felix are."

The king nodded and took a narrow side path that cut through the green field. Several grazing deer and a horse looking up at them as Silas and Elish walked past them. In the distance they could both see chain-link fences and as they got closer the sound of Nero and Felix laughing.

The two brute chimeras were standing over a wooden shelf that wrapped around the chain-link fence. The two of them were hanging off of it with a white bucket beside them full of various human body parts. Below them ten large lions were hovering around, looking up at the two chimeras with their tails flicking back and forth. The lions had blood stained on their muzzles and were standing over chewed bones with meat and skin still hanging off.

Nero looked over at Silas and Elish and immediately his smile disappeared. Felix who was standing beside him had a different reaction. Though his smile also vanished upon the realization that the king was watching, it wasn't replaced by concern like Nero, the soured look he had on the plane returned.

"Are we leaving, Kingy?" Nero asked, dropping a strip of flesh he was holding back into the bucket. Both his and Felix's hands were streaked with blood from picking up the flesh inside of the buckets.

Then to everyone's shock – Silas smiled.

"Why would we leave, amor?" Silas said through his smile. He casually flicked his blond hair back and held out his hand to Elish. Elish helped him walk up the stairs and onto the wooden walkway Nero and Felix were standing on. "You're not done feeding my lions."

Nero's eyes nervously shot to Elish, but if he thought his brother would offer him any reassurances he was sadly mistaken. Like Silas, Elish had also seemed to snap back into his norm. The soothing words and affection had been left back in the room inside of the base.

Nero forced his face to smile. He picked up the chunk of meat he had just dropped back into the bucket. Below him several lions chirped, their nails scraping against the concrete slab that stretched out several feet until the grass took it over.

"Oh, I cannot get my hands dirty, lovely," Silas whispered to him. He reached out a hand and gently stroked Nero's muscled arm. He traced his fingers over the large bicep and eyed the flesh that seemed to be from a similar area on the human they had been feeding the lions.

"Why don't you give it to Felix?"

Nero's expression dropped; his pupils retracted making the blacks almost drown inside of the indigo irises. He turned around and looked at Felix, who had turned several shades paler.

"Give the meat to Felix, *bellua*," Silas purred, using Nero's own special pet name. Something that Nero and the other chimeras knew could either be a reassurance of their own safety or a condemnation.

Nero's Adam's apple bobbed as he swallowed hard. He did as he was directed and handed the piece of flesh to Felix. The young chimera took it with a steady but cautious hand before turning around and throwing the meat into the lions' pen.

In an instant the heavy tranquility was broken up by the sounds of vicious fighting. Like their alley cat comrades the lions snarled and screamed at each other, claws and fur flying as they fought over the small chunk of meat.

"Hand him another one," Silas commanded. "Look how hungry they are. My poor babies, so many lions and so little food to go around."

Nero picked up a foot and calve, shreds of flesh and snares of veins hanging off of it and resting cold against Nero's skin. He once again handed it to Felix who was looking more nervous than ever.

"What is… this?" Felix said lowly. "I'm not playing this fucking game with you, Silas."

But Silas only smiled at him, before tightening his jacket around him. It was a warm day, winter was leaving, but there was a certain chill on the air – an uneasy bite that everyone could feel stinging against their skin.

"Throw the meat over the edge, Felix. Feed my lions. There are too many of them – and if they're not well fed – they will start to consume one another," Silas said in a voice dripping sweetness. He raised a hand and swept it over the lions' den. "They're hungry, my lovely little brute. Feed them."

"Fine…" Felix mumbled. He turned to the front of the chain-link fence and tossed the leg down. Once again the pen echoed with the sounds of snarling, roaring cats as they argued and fought over who would get the piece of meat. It was a worse fight this time, a smaller male got a hold of the leg infuriating the large dominant male. The alpha, with a thick black mane, advanced on the smaller male, his tail high in the air and his front paws shaking the ground as he charged him. The smaller male shrunk down with a snarl, cornering himself in a corner of the pen.

And as Felix watched the commotion right below his feet, Silas's eyes locked with Nero's. They burned into his, emerald slaying indigo again and again, before he nodded at Nero and said in a low voice:

"Do it."

Without a moment's hesitation Nero whirled around and grabbed Felix, one hand on his underarm and the other one grabbing his belt. Before the dark-haired, brute chimera had time to defend himself, or utter a single pleading word, he was thrown over the fence and into the lions' den below.

The screaming rang across the yard like the ringing chapel bells, and as Silas walked to the edge of the chain-link fence and gazed down at the grisly scene below, a new, demonic smile appeared on his face. One that made even Elish's heart jump.

Silas took in the scene, Felix on his back struggling and screaming as the lions tore at him with both claws and teeth. His eyes were wide open, the whites showing through the glistening red blood pouring from the deep lacerations on his face. Though soon, like his pale skin, the white was covered, until nothing but deep reds and soon the various shades of his innards could be seen.

"Silas!" Felix managed to shriek, his voice garbled and gurgling as the lions yanked him around like a child's ragdoll. He looked up at Silas for a fraction of a second and locked eyes with him. "Master!" he screamed.

"Goodbye, lovely boy. Sorry it didn't work out," Silas called with a loving smile, before he wrapped his arms around Nero's thick bicep. He squeezed it tight and hung off of Nero's arm, Felix's screams fading away as the lions fought over his body, before the screams stopped altogether.

"I will not miss him," Silas said, stroking Nero's arm lovingly, "but oh was he ever a beautiful specimen."

Silas kissed his hand and gently laid it on top of the chain-link fence. Felix now in several pieces, his remains firmly in the jaws of several lions who were taking him to different areas of the pen. "Come now, loves, we're going home." Then he looked at Elish with the same content grin. "And when we get home, I will find my Sanguine and I will make sure the rest of his immortal life is spent in happiness." Silas ignored the frown on

Elish's face, and still hanging off of Nero's arm, they turned their backs to Felix and walked down the wooden stairs. "And once he is home safe, love, I want Ares and Siris home. They make me smile and laugh and I think our family needs some lightness."

"Yes, Master," Elish said with a nod. He reached out and affectionately stroked Silas's shoulder. "The family does need a cleansing, I commend you for your decision."

"Yes, things are about to change within our family, for the better." Silas's smile darkened.

It was silent save for a whistle on Silas's lips. When they finally approached the plane they could all see Ceph. He was standing with an oiled rag in his hand and his head deep into the plane's engine.

Silas broke away from Nero's arm and started waving his finger back and forth like he had a tune stuck in his head. "Ceph, my love, what's wrong with our plane?"

As Silas walked ahead, Elish heard Nero let out a long, tense breath. When the king was far enough away Nero took Elish's hand and silently squeezed it.

"How did you know?" Nero whispered, his voice barely audible even to chimera hearing.

"I knew he was heading towards a meltdown. I know his mind," Elish said in the same quiet voice. His purple eyes watching Silas as he spoke happily to Ceph.

"And I knew if the mood took him – Ceph would be down there with Felix," Elish continued.

Nero swallowed and nodded, and with a quick glance to make sure Silas wasn't looking, he gave Elish a quick, but emotional, hug.

"Thank you, brother," Nero whispered. He broke away before Silas or Ceph could see him. "I owe you."

"I know," Elish replied, "and I won't forget it." His eyes flickered back towards the plane. "Let's go home."

CHAPTER 44

I WOKE UP TO SOMEONE POKING ME IN THE NOSE. I opened my eyes and saw Barry staring down at me with a mischievous grin on his face and his bear ears wiggling back and forth like he was excited about something.

"Morning…" I yawned and stretched out my limbs, the sounds of my bones and joints popping filled the underground room I had made my lair.

Then a smile came to my face. I turned my head to say good morning to Jack but it disappeared when I saw his side of the bed was empty, though the imprint of his head was still on the pillow. Unable to help myself I grabbed the pillow and smelled it; I could smell his hair and his body. It made my chest shudder and fill.

"I bet he had enough and ran," Barry taunted, his voice getting raspy as the days went on. He sat down and wrapped his arms around his legs before he started rocking himself back and forth. "Jack and Sam went up the hill to fetch themselves some meat. Jack fell down and Sanguine frowned and they both ate each other's fucking faces."

"That doesn't even rhyme, idiot." I yawned and got up before stretching again, the warm air from the heater keeping my body warm. As my ears adjusted to the sounds of the room I heard my other little friends playing behind the stacks of boxes. I liked their laughter reverberating off of the walls, it made things happy. "He's gone to get us some food, just like he did yesterday and the day before."

I rubbed my eyes and as I dressed myself. Jack and I were both the same size except I was taller and lankier than he was. I wore the shirt he wore yesterday and buttoned it, then zipped up my old pair of black pants.

"Nah, I'm sure he's fucked off and ran." Barry lit a cigarette and stretched out on the bed before putting his hands behind his head. He looked at me and grinned through the cigarette. I leaned down and took it from him and went to get myself a glass of water.

"I don't think so, not this time," I said.

I couldn't help the shake inside of my chest when I remembered the last night we had had together. We had been making out almost non-stop over the last three days. The next morning after I had killed Ludo we had both woke up with a fire inside of us. Though we had never gotten further than kissing and touching each other; I just wasn't ready for something like that. It was different doing it when the bloodlust and madness was coursing through me, but when I was normal it still made me nervous and anxious. Jack had understood that but he had been taking full advantage of my lips and I of his.

It had been an intense couple of days, though Barry and my other friends had been starting to get annoyed that I hadn't been paying attention to them. And I also hadn't been able to go out and create any new friends, the new mouse still needed a body.

"He will," Barry said in a singy voice. I shook my head and drank a ladle full of water, we had a plastic bucket full of water and a ladle for dipping. We would get something better eventually but this was good enough.

"You do know you can't handle friends let alone a boyfriend, right?" Barry chuckled.

"I seem to be doing well with my boyfriend so far," I said wiping my mouth. The word boyfriend still made my body shudder like the word itself was a live wire. I'd had a boyfriend for going on four days now. It was an exciting prospect and it was making me feel like I was king of the world.

I had a boyfriend! I had a boyfriend and not only that, my boyfriend was Jack. My chimera brother, who not only knew who I was but he also knew me. He knew me and the shit I had done and what had happened to me – and he still wanted to be around me.

Who would have thought that would happen to me?

"Sami?" a small female voice sounded behind me. I turned around and saw Patches looking up at me, her hair ribbons were blue today, they matched her eyes.

"Yes, little lady?" I responded.

"You haven't brought us anyone new to play with for days now," she said with a pout. She started swinging her dolly back and forth. I noticed behind her the others were gathered together, their eyes fixed on the both of us. It was almost like she had picked the smallest straw and she was the one that had to confront me.

"Ralph our mousey is still trapped inside." Patches lowered her voice and as she swung the dolly it turned into the mouse I had rescued. "And we can hear him screaming. Can you hear him screaming?" Patches walked up to me and held up the mouse.

I leaned down so my ear was against the mouse and tried to listen.

My entire body spasmed in shock as an ear-piercing scream sounded from the stuffed animal. It was so intense it ripped through my mind and caused me physical pain. Out of reflex I jumped back and dropped the ladle onto the ground.

Patches didn't move or react to the noise. She only stared at me with grave eyes, the mouse still being held out by her tiny little hands.

"He's suffering," she whispered and clutched the mouse to her chest. "Why are you letting him suffer, Sami?"

"Yeah," Sir spoke up. Fingles was beside him, his nose twitching invisible whiskers. "Why is making out with Jack more important than freeing your friends? Why is he suddenly more important than us?"

"Yeah!" The others exchanged glances of confirmation. They nodded at each other, several of them started to look angry. "Why is he more important than us? You're just like Jasper. Gross touching makes people turn evil. Evil! And BAD! You're going to have sex with him!"

"No, it doesn't! And I'm not!" I snapped back at them, but the guilt was welling inside of me. Maybe I had been a bad friend. I had just been having so much fun with Jack. Didn't I deserve some happiness?

"Yes, it does," Barry said behind me. I turned and saw that he was standing; he had another cigarette in his mouth. He was starting to look differently which I found odd. His black eyes were starting to have flecks of red in them, and his curly hair was starting to straighten and turn black. "Sex turns people into things. They're right, Sami. You've been shoving them into the back room and ignoring them so you can kiss Jack. We've been there for you since the beginning and now since you have him we're not needed?"

"I deserve some time to be happy…"

Patches pushed the stuffed mouse into my hand and patted it. "Ralph deserve to be happy too. He's trapped inside and he's suffering. If Nero and Silas were like you, they would've left you alone and suffering in the basement. Even they were better people than you."

"What a shitty friend," Moose said. He had been my sheep dog. "Enjoy fucking Jack. Pervert."

Their words were like a spear through my chest. I found myself too stunned and hurt to answer them back. I could only stare at them as their twinkling eyes glared back. Angry eyes. Ones that held in them a disappointment and hatred I had seen one too many times in both my youth and adulthood.

"Sanguine?"

I jumped and gasped from shock as I felt a hand on my shoulder. I whirled around with my heart giving a thrash, but a moment later there was a swell of relief when I saw the face of my new boyfriend.

Though Jack's expression was troubled; I could see two lines on his forehead from him scowling so much. "What are they saying to you, baby?"

I turned away from them. Jack put a hand around my waist and walked me towards a patio table with two plastic chairs. We had brought them down during Jack's first full day here. I sat down on one and Jack pulled the other one beside me. He placed two brown paper bags in front of us, the bottoms shining with grease.

"Nothing…" I mumbled, though my friends had successfully soured my mood.

"Sanguine…" Jack rested a hand over mine and squeezed it. "Come on, boyfriend. Are they yelling at you? Or telling you to do things to yourself?"

I shrugged.

"Why don't you put them into the back room and I'll get us out our food."

I turned as I heard my friends give out howls and cries at Jack's suggestion.

'He's always putting us away!'
'He doesn't fucking care about us anymore.'
'He made us just to abandon us!'

Barry laughed. I looked to him and saw he was lying on the mattress with a comic book in his hand, his cigarette still pressed between his lips.

"They don't like being put away," I said as I looked towards the closed shut metal door. Jack hadn't seen what was behind that door yet, though he kept asking to see. "They scream at me when I put them away. They want to be free."

My words were swallowed by my friends constant howling. I clenched my teeth and for a moment I closed my eyes tight. Their voices sounded like battering rams, constantly throwing themselves against my brain even at the expense of their own bodies. It was a constant barrage when they were unhappy, hit after hit until visible cracks were apparent on both my inner mind and their bodies.

"Shut up!" I whirled around and snapped. They screamed and shrunk back, some even holding their hands over their own heads as if expecting me to strike them. Watching them do that filled my mouth with acid. It was what I looked like when I was afraid of Jasper striking me. The realization made me sick.

"Sanguine..." Jack said in a voice full of concern. "What are they telling you to do? Please tell me – are they telling you to hurt yourself?"

I shook my head and heard Jack let out a relieved breath, but a moment later his heartbeat gave another start.

"Are they... telling you to hurt me?"

My head shook again. "I'd never hurt you... I love you."

Soft lips kissed my hand, and his heart jumped at my words. "I love you too, Sanguine. I want to help silence them. You're so happy and joyful when they're locked away. What can we do to quiet them again? Until you're ready to come home with me."

Home? This was my home... I didn't want to go back to Alegria. I didn't want to see Silas ever again. Silas had made it clear exactly what he thought of me. I was nothing but a lying whore to him, someone who, in his mind, had made all of this up.

Jack had said Silas knew, he was just saying he didn't to protect himself but I didn't care.

There was a rustling of paper, Jack brought out two plastic containers. Each one had a hamburger in it and potato fries, and even a small section for the red ketchup and mayonnaise. I hadn't been hungry before but the wonderful scent of real bosen meat made my mouth fill with saliva.

"They want me to kill again," I said as I stared down at the patio table, once white but now every patterned groove was crusted with black. "The mouse is screaming inside of his body. He's screaming at me to free him – I heard him myself. Everyone is unhappy. I put them away too often. They say I'm ignoring them because I have you now."

Jack paused. His eyes hardened as he took the top off of one of the plastic containers. "We'll eat our food now… and after… will you answer some questions for me?"

I shrugged and took half of the hamburger out of the container. "I guess, if it doesn't make them angry." I took a bite out of my hamburger, my friends had stopped screaming at me but they were whispering now. I hated it when they whispered because it was like a background radio was playing. I didn't like listening to this one though, as soon as they knew I was trying to listen in on their conversations their voices suddenly rose and got harsh.

And then the screaming would start all over again.

As I ate Jack decided to fill the empty, tension-filled air with his own adventures outside. He told me which pub he got the food from and some of the rumours that had been going on. He told me that sometime soon, though he didn't know when, there was going to be an invasion in Irontowers. He said no one knew the exact date so the rebels wouldn't know when it was. I responded back by telling him what my suggestion had been to Nero and Silas for a way for the family to sway public support for the rebels and he praised me for helping.

"I love Nero a lot," Jack said after he had swallowed his food. He still ate so politely, at least I was getting better with my manners. I no longer talked with my mouth full. "He's always been a fun older brother to have. Elish is as well, he's strict and cold, but he's reliable and calm in the face of our chaotic family." Jack smiled at me warmly. "Garrett is just a big softy and he's had a hard time fitting in because he's just so un-chimera. I've only seen him go into 'chimera-mode' maybe twice, for the most part he's just a normal fun guy."

I grabbed a fry and bit it in two. "It seems like the first generation turned out alright." I paused and tried to block out my friends whose voices were starting to rise. "But the second generation seems to have a lot of issues. Silas always seemed frustrated with you guys, and Elish – especially Elish."

Jack's mouth downturned. He swirled one of his fries around in the ketchup. "Once Elish and Garrett started getting into genetic engineering they started developing the technology to make even better chimeras. So, excited to try out the new technology, they created a bunch of us: you, me, Apollo, Artemis, Valen, Felix, Ludo, Ceph, Rio, and Perish. Though Apollo, Artemis, Ceph, and Perish were created before us but we still consider them second gen. I think I mentioned that before. Anyway..." Jack let out a breath. "There still seems to be a lot of bugs in the coding they used for some of us. Me and you seem to be okay genetically, all of our enhancements took, same with Apollo and Artemis, Ceph and Perish. But Valen's genetics are a complete mess, Ludo barely developed any enhancements and had tons of mental problems, and Felix seems to have processing issues, so he gets angry a lot and has little impulse control. Whereas the first generation seems perfect –" Jack shrugged. "A lot of the chimeras Silas took pains in raising have turned out to be disappointments and failures." Then he shrunk down. "Even those whose genetics worked out perfectly seem to be failures as well."

I shrunk down with him. "I know I'm a failure," I said. "You're not... you're perfect."

He rubbed my hand and patted it before picking up his hamburger again. "I'm not perfect but thank you, you're so sweet. I think some of the family sees me as a failure because I don't have that cruel streak in me and I don't go crazy and lash out – well I didn't anyway." A half-smile appeared on his face. "I kinda snapped when Felix was insulting you. I kinda tore one of his ears off."

I stopped chewing and stared at him blankly. "You tore Felix's ear off?" I quickly swallowed and blinked, feeling rather perplexed.

Jack's eyes turned up to the ceiling. I laughed and drew him in for a kiss. It was hard to kiss him because we were both smiling though so I decided to act like a goof and I licked his cheek.

This got a giggle out of him and he kissed the corner of my mouth. "I love you. Did I tell you that today?"

"I love you more." I kissed him back. "Or at least I think that's what this feeling is..." I scowled a bit and Jack pulled away from me. "I don't think I even know what being in love feels like. Maybe that isn't it at all?"

Jack laughed at my scowling face and patted it. "Just don't think about it too much. I don't know either, maybe no one does? All that matters is you feel good and you're relaxed."

Suddenly Barry appeared behind Jack; he was towering over him with a wide grin. His pointed teeth showing, the top and bottom row perfectly folded into each other like weaved fingers. "You're not capable of loving anything," Barry taunted. "You'll just hurt him like you hurt everyone else. You loved King Silas and now he thinks you're just a lying whore. *Lying whore, lying whore!*" As Barry sang I jerked my face away from Jack and snatched the plastic container of food. As I got up Jack put his hand up to stop me but I stalked away towards the darker corners of the room. Barry singing and singing, his voice steadily getting louder and more piercing.

"What's wrong?" Jack called after me.

'Lying whore, lying whore!'

"He needs to shut up!" I snarled. I heard Barry laugh behind me, his taunting voice felt like sandpaper scraping over my ear drums.

I put the plastic container down and picked up an old mantle clock that we had found in one of the cardboard boxes. I turned around and when I saw Barry giving me that stupid grin I clenched my teeth hard, and with all of my strength, I threw it right at his head.

I heard Jack yell, and right before it hit him Barry ducked. Though as his attention was diverted away from me I picked up the hotplate I had been cooking my food on and flung it at him too.

This one did hit. As Jack grabbed my arm I watched Barry's face snap back and he was thrown backwards. He landed hard on the ground and I laughed at him as Jack pulled me back.

"Now shut up!" I yelled at him. Though as he shut up my other friends started to scream over what I had done. Instead of Barry's taunting chant I was now assaulted by my small friends crying and shrieking, hollering over the fact I had injured Barry.

It was too much, it was too overwhelming.

"Shut up! All of you!" I screamed. I tried to wrench my arm away from Jack but he wouldn't let go. "All of you, just go to your room! Leave me alone!"

"Sami's just like Jasper! Sami's just like Jasper!" they all chanted in unison, their small yet booming voices were assaulting against my brain, and the contents of their words poisoned me. I found myself screaming from frustration and my hands went to my head. As I crumbled under the sensory overload I started tearing at my hair.

"Sanguine... Sanguine..." Jack whispered. "It's okay, close your eyes." I felt something push against my lips, it was Xanax. He had picked them up for me a few days ago. I took the pills and chewed them and closed my eyes like he asked. The voices wouldn't stop though and the darkness only seemed to give them physical form.

"They aren't going to stop," I screamed. "They won't stop until I do what they fucking ask. They're only my friends until they want something. Just like Crow!" Fuck, just like Crow.

It was Crow all over again. Yelling and yelling until I did what he said. Constantly harassing me until I obeyed him and only then would he be my friend again. Only then would he be quiet.

"What are they asking you to do, hun?" Jack whispered. He started making shushing noises while he rubbed my back.

"They want me to go and kill someone... so I can make the mouse real. They hate me because I haven't made the stupid mouse real," I said to Jack. "The stuffed animals... they want to become real and until I make them real they're in agony. They're trapped in darkness, confinement, like I was at Jasper's. I can't let that happen to them, Jack. You don't know how it fucking feels!"

"Shhh, shhh," Jack said soothingly. "So... you're saying that your friends are constantly yelling at you because you haven't gone out to kill someone?"

I nodded.

"And how does killing someone make the stuffed animals real, hunny?"

I got up. Jack tried to stop me but I took his hand to urge him to get up as well. "I'll show you," I said, and the voices started to die down as I led Jack towards the metal door in the back of the room. The one I had asked him not to go into.

Jack held my hand but he seemed hesitant. "What – what are you showing me?"

"How they become real," I said back. "How I make them real. This is where I lock them when I need my time with you. They go back to their physical bodies, well, except Barry. Barry has always been real so he's always been intact."

"In – tact?" Jack said nervously. "What do you mean...?"

I pulled the handle on the door and shoved it open.

Hanging from the ropes I had tied to the support beams hung my friends, their human heads still sewn onto their stuffed animal bodies. All of them were now green and grey and leaking fluid which now stained the concrete below them in dark puddles. Their eyes had all been eaten by rats now, and the maggots had infested their flesh, and the old maggots were now buzzing flies around the corpses. Their stuffed parts were rancid and smelling as well. Their colourful fur, some purple, blue, greens, others browns and whites, all had been stained a putrid brown, but I could still see some of their colours.

I beamed at them, my lovely friends with their little paws and little suits and admired them like one would admire a beautiful piece of art. Mouse and Julia looked the most beautiful, their skin and flesh had started to slide off of their faces, their yellow-stained skulls now peeking through the slippery meat.

I turned to Jack with a smile, and saw him staring forward with his eyes wide open as was his mouth. He looked so in shock that when a fly landed on his face he didn't even blink.

Jack's mouth opened and closed like his mind was commanding him to speak but his mouth was unable to form words. He seemed to have become a statue in my doorway, unmoving and lost.

"That's…" I saw Jack's throat constrict, before a funny look appeared on his face.

"Sanguine, that's beautiful."

Now it was my turn to be shocked. I looked at him like he had just grown five heads.

"Really?"

Jack nodded and took a step over to them. He put his hands on his knees and looked down. "It's like art. The most… grisly, twisted art I have ever seen. When I get home I'm going to paint this for us. We'll hang it in our living room. I wish I could paint it now… you're an artist and I bet you didn't even realize it."

I shrugged, feeling heat come to my face, his flattery was making me feel embarrassed. "Thank you… I never thought you would like it… or understand."

Jack nodded. "I do understand. You sewed their heads to the stuffed animals and after that… they become real to you, don't they?"

"Yeah," I whispered. "I have others I haven't created yet… I didn't feel like I needed to once I met you. You're my boyfriend now, and that makes you my best friend too."

He put an arm around me and pulled me close to him. "You only have one stuffed animal left?"

I nodded and since the smell was horrendous, I turned away from the metal room and closed it. Then Jack and I went to back to the main part of the house. "Just the mouse, his name is Ralph."

I leaned down to pick up the small mouse but the moment I touched it a scream tore through my head. Immediately I retracted my hand, my jaw clenching as the gut-wrenching sound echoed around me. It was a horrible noise, a scream I knew I had heard somewhere but my brain refused to tell me where.

"Do you think the voices will stop yelling at you… if you make him alive?" Jack picked up the mouse and held him with both hands. Obviously he was unable to hear the screaming.

"That's what they want…" I said. I sat back down with the food and Jack followed me, still holding the mouse in his hand. "That's what Barry wants."

Jack put the mouse down beside Barry who sat on the foot of the bed Jack and I shared.

"Well… why don't we?" Jack said slowly. He looked up at me and I could see the hesitation on his face. I knew he wasn't sure if he was saying the right thing. "If it will stop them from bothering you. I mean… it's just one more person right?"

"I guess…" The mouse was sitting beside Barry, a little grey mouse with pink paws and feet and whiskers too. It was an old mouse but he looked new next to Barry. Barry had been through a lot in our years together, he was old and worn and his stuffing was warped in some places.

I still loved him a lot though; I think Barry the physical bear wasn't the same as Barry the boy. My bear would never say such cruel things to me.

"You would be okay with that?" I asked

Jack picked up Barry and brought him over to our table. He set him down beside our food and sat down himself. "Anything we can do to give you some peace. We're chimeras, we're princes. We're allowed to kill whoever we want."

I was silent after he spoke. I finished my food and he finished his, Barry the bear looming over both of us with the kind black eyes that the friend inside of my head never had. In the distance my little friends played with one another, though every once in a while I could hear them whispering to each other that I would be putting them away soon.

And that I was a bad friend, who didn't even care that the mouse was in pain. That and many other insults, it seemed just like before the friends in my head were starting to become enemies.

I looked at Barry the boy, sitting on the bed with his cigarette, and saw his black outfit. Though it was changing too – the black fabric had a sheen on it, it was almost like – it was starting to grow feathers.

He was starting to become someone else too.

"Okay," I agreed after our food was finished. Jack had been sitting politely watching me eat, a napkin crushed in one of his hands.

My boyfriend smiled at me and started putting all of our trash into one of the bags, and set aside the plastic containers so we could get the deposit back. As he rose he kissed my forehead and petted my hair back.

"We'll have fun. I'd love to see my chimera in action."

I wasn't sure how much truth was behind those words.

That evening found me in Jack's arms again. We were lying in bed together, our shirts forgotten on the floor but our pants and shoes still on. Jack was half on me, his fingers rubbing and teasing my nipple and his tongue joined with mine in our mouths.

Jack broke his lips away from mine. I closed my eyes and stifled a groan when I felt his mouth on my nipple. I leaned back and enjoyed it, before it started feeling uncomfortably good.

"Okay…" I gasped and immediately he removed his mouth. Then with a smile he gently blew air onto my erect nipple, the wet from his mouth making it sting with cold.

"When are you going to take me again," Jack said in a growled voice. He bit the corner of his lip and took my nipple between his fingers again. He pinched it, which only made the tightness worse. He was having a wonderful time finding and then exploiting all of my sensitive places.

I frowned but he only smiled back and joined our lips again. I could smell the lust radiating off of him, it was usually at this point in time that I started trying to cool things down between us. We could only make out for so long before he started needing more, something I couldn't give to him right now.

I pulled away. "I don't know if I can ever do it when I'm not… in that crazy state," I said to him. I started to get up and Jack took the hint and slid off of me. "It really makes me uncomfortable."

Jack got up with me. "I understand – you just drive me crazy," he said with a mischievous smile, we both started putting our shirts back on. "I just want to be closer to you and be intimate. What we did in the abandoned house was fun and all, but it wasn't intimate at all. I want to make love to you and with you."

My ears burned. I mumbled an apology and started looking around for my tin of cigarettes.

Jack laughed. I felt him behind me, before he put his arms around my waist and kissed my neck. "I love you, you're such a silly muffin. Especially when I make you nervous."

I grunted at him. "I don't think you're taking my mental issues seriously. I'm not putting off sex because I'm being silly or a *muffin* as you call it. It's because I'm dangerous and the last time I fell into that state I almost raped you, after I murdered our brother. I even showed you the severed heads in my room and you say it's beautiful?" I turned around and gave him an exasperated look as I put a cigarette into my mouth. "Something tells me you're not taking this seriously."

"That's not true at all." Jack sounded offended at my words. "I'm just doing everything I can to keep you calm and keep you relaxed. When you're calm, as you said, you don't switch into that state. You know what calms chimeras down? Sex, sex and killing things." Jack picked up one of my knives and shoved it into my bag, then he pushed the bag into my arms. "And off we go to kill things." He stalked past me.

"Just…" I lit the cigarette and started following him towards the door, grabbing Barry on the way. "Be careful. Remember what I told you – if I start to go squirrely you promised you would run."

"I'm not defenceless," Jack said, and as if to show how not defenceless he was he showed me his own set of pointed teeth. "I ripped off Felix's ear, remember? I can handle you. You're not even that strong."

I glared at him as we both started walking down the cold hallway. The door behind us shut and after a few moments my eyes started to adjust to the darkness.

"I am so," I said back. "When I'm mad at least."

"Well, we'll never know… we won't let you get mad," Jack responded. "We'll keep everything calm until we can eventually go home."

"You're so patient it's sickening," I grumbled. Jack turned around at this and gave me a smug smile. I rolled my eyes.

We got to the rickety old stairs that led to the ground level of the old building. I hadn't been up here in four days. I wouldn't say I was happy to be out of my safe basement but it was nice to get some fresh air. It was cold out but my long sleeve shirt was enough to keep me warm.

Jack waited for me at the top of the stairs, but as I climbed the last two steps I noticed he was frowning. And as I reached the top I realized why.

"Something smells rotten…" Jack spoke both of our mutual thoughts out loud. Something did smell rotten; an animal or something had died near here.

"Maybe a radrat?" I said cautiously. Jack and I both started walking to the main entrance of the building, our steps cautious and our eyes and ears peeled for anything out of the ordinary.

Then I saw them.

I froze in place before letting out a stifled cry. I ran over to the front of the office building and got down on my knees in front of them.

Five of my crows were in the front of the building, all of them embedded on wooden spikes that had been hammered into the floorboards. The spikes had been jabbed through their chests and their wings had been sewn into the next crow's wings in some sort of demonic circle. They had been set up as some sort of display.

And as I stared in shock I realized that's exactly how they had been set up: on display for me to find.

"Oh shit…" Jack whispered behind me. His silhouette appeared beside me before a hand reached out to gently touch their cold bodies. "Who the fuck did this…?"

I let out a small cry and brushed my hand against the middle crows head. Two dull red eyes stared at me, its mouth open as if it was trying to speak. Their bodies were stiff but as I touched their skin I felt movement. I pulled my hand away realizing that underneath their skin were probably hundreds of maggots.

"Sami…" Jack said under his breath. He put his arm around me and squeezed me to him.

"You were just up this morning…" I stammered. "They must've killed them days ago if – if maggots have hatched. I… I don't understand. Who… could've…"

"Do you think you might've snuck out when I was sleep–"

"I didn't do this!" I suddenly screamed. Jack immediately pulled away. I let out a sob and put my hand over my mouth. "I would never hurt them – I love them."

"I know, I know…" Jack said hastily. "I just… who the fuck could it have been, love? Someone who knows where you are at least…"

Someone knew where I was. Someone wanted to send me a message. But who?

"Did... did anyone follow you when you were out getting food for us?" I asked.

Jack helped me to my feet, rubbing my side caringly as we both looked down at my dead crows. It almost looked like they had been crucified – like I had been at Sunshine House.

"I don't think so..." Jack said. We both looked towards the wide open door, seeing the dark streets ahead of us, void of any light but the silvers of the moon. "But I didn't really check... I mean, no one seemed to care I was just picking up food."

"We'll bury them when we get home..." My tone started to shift, Jack could tell because his hand soon found mine. "And I'm going to be guarding this place tonight after. I'll find out who did this." As I walked into the empty street I was relieved to hear the familiar sound of claws against metal. I looked up and saw half a dozen of my crows standing on a street lamp. I smiled at them, there was no words to explain the relief I felt that the mystery person wasn't able to kill all of them.

One of them flew down and with a flap of wings he landed on my shoulder. It was the lead crow; he had always been the bravest.

I got a piece of tact out of my pocket and fed him.

"Go on get!" the crow called, and above them one said, *'Got any food?'*

Jack smiled with me and we started walking down the road. Sure to their personality my crow friends started to follow me, always loyal and always waiting for me.

"King Silas brought them from Jasper's farm, he says they're actually half-raven," I explained to Jack as we started walking down the street. I was looking in all of the alleyways we passed for any sign of life. I wasn't picky tonight, any man or woman with breath in their lungs was going to be my target. "I went outside for the first time because of them. I spent a lot of time hiding under the bed."

"I bet that was cute," Jack said and squeezed my hand. The guy really seemed to like hand holding. "Silas was really patient with you, huh?"

My mouth twitched at this. "It was all a lie. He painted a pretty false picture of who he was."

"No, he is like that..." Jack said, though he didn't even know how nice Silas was, just some of the stories I had told him. "He's just... he's kind of sociopathic most of the time, but sometimes he has these times of intense empathy and caring. It's just that it doesn't happen often… he's a wonderful king though. I love him a lot, even with his faults."

There really wasn't much for me to say about this so I just grunted. Jack squeezed my hand and we continued walking.

It was a beautiful night out, the sky was clear and we could see the stars twinkling above us. The air was fresh and clean as well, and I could smell the ocean which was only a few blocks away. I would like to go there one day, perhaps see some of the boats that travelled from the harbour over to the factory towns. Maybe I would visit one of those one day too.

Jack and I walked together for the next two hours. The two of us taking whatever street we decided we wanted to take and several alleyways too. We didn't see a soul though but as the air above ground cleared my head I realized that wasn't important. My friends screaming at me in the basement seemed far away when I was on the surface with Jack. Their demands were distant and only a harsh whisper, and even that was quickly dismissed by Jack's voice.

"Maybe we could try and find a way… to get rid of them?" Jack said when I told him what was on my mind.

Get rid of them? "I couldn't do that…" I said, feeling bad that I was even entertaining the thought. "They're just kids."

Jack fell silent. I could see him out of the corner of my eye. His hair looked so beautiful in the night, like the moonlight itself had fallen from the sky only to weave itself into the strands of his hair. And his eyes… those eyes captured me every time they made contact with my own.

"But… they're not real," Jack said slowly.

"They're real to me," I said defensively, "and they scream at me all the same. How can you say they're not real when I hear them constantly?"

Jack's lips vanished into his mouth as he seemed to consider this. "Okay… but maybe once we go home we can start looking into medication to stop the voices?"

The way he worded it made me sound like a crazy person, but then again I was a crazy person. So maybe he –

Suddenly there was an incredibly loud, thunderous bang behind us. We both whirled around as the ground below us shook, almost throwing us off balance.

We watched in shock as an explosion sent a spray of dirt and material up into the air. It seemed to touch the very heavens before fiery debris started raining down below us like asteroids falling to earth. Large chunks of building landing with heavy thuds, all of the pieces smoking and smouldering with toxic black smoke.

As we stood stunned, we both saw a black object appear in the sky, a trail of smoke behind it. Then a low whistling sound pierced our ears as it started to fall down to the ground.

When it landed there was a second rumbling explosion, this one close enough for us to see the red and orange flames peeking through the oily smoke.

"That's from a rocket launcher. Someone's fucking bombing Cypress!" Jack screamed over the noise. He pulled on my arm and we both ran down the street.

"The rebels?" I asked, looking behind my shoulder.

"Yeah, they have rocket launchers, this I know," Jack called hastily. He pulled out his remote phone and turned it on. "I think... Sanguine, I fucking think they bombed the building your basement is in."

"What!" I stopped dead in my tracks and turned around. I put my hand on my satchel to make sure I had Barry with me but still I felt a jolt of fear go through my heart. "My friends are down there! I need to get them." I started to run towards the explosion.

"SANGUINE!" Jack screamed. "NO! Sanguine, they're not real!" I heard him start to follow me but my mind was too focused on getting my friends out of there. They might torment me and yell at me but I couldn't fucking leave them. They were just kids! They were kids like I was.

Jack screamed after me but all I could do was run, my mind was going in a thousand directions but the only one I could focus on was straight ahead of me, into the heart of the explosion.

What was I doing? Sanguine, they aren't real, they aren't real.

And then I heard them screaming.

All of a sudden an onslaught of agonizing shrieks filled my ears. The sounds of my kids burning alive. They sounded like Pauly and Gabe when I lit them on fire; they sounded like me when Gill nailed me to the wooden planks.

And as I got closer, as the smoke filled my lungs, a new scream echoed. One that was drown out by the other ones at first, but the closer I got the more it rang inside of my head.

This scream I knew; this scream had been embedded in my bones for the past twelve years.

It was the scream that was my own – the first night Jasper fucked me.

"I'm coming!" I screamed out loud. "Shut up, I'm coming!"

I coughed, my lungs filling with smoke, and I heard Jack coughing behind me. As I ran through the quickly gathering smoke I yelled at Jack to turn back, but I couldn't slow down enough to know if he did or not.

I looked to my left to see another black object shoot across the sky. It landed a block away from us and another thundering explosion rolled through me. I turned the opposite direction from the exploding missile and cut through an alleyway, my building was just across the street. I would be in and out in… in…

I skidded to a halt, so quickly I felt a large impact and a grunt behind me as Jack crashed into my back.

I couldn't believe what I saw.

Valen was standing in front of my building, with two other men dressed in camo. These two men were holding assault rifles in their hands, ready to shoot whatever was going to emerge from the door. The apartment building, two structures away, was on fire, casting a shimmering glow of orange and red like an inferno of borealis.

It was obvious what was going on in front of me. Valen and these two men were waiting for Jack and I to burst out of the building then they planned on shooting us like smoked-out scavers.

"Get the one on the right, I'm going left," I growled at Jack. "We'll kill them first then get Valen."

I was expecting Jack to voice his disagreeance; I was expecting him to grab onto me and beg me to go back to Skyland with him, but he didn't.

"Okay," Jack said in such a low, gravely register it temporarily silenced the screaming voices in my head. "Go for their necks and stay away from the assault rifles."

I nodded, and as I started to run towards the man on the left a growl erupted in my throat. And over the low rumbling of the infernos around us I could hear Jack growling as well.

We were chimeras, the most advanced chimeras created to date. We were genetically engineered to be killing machines. We were barely human.

I jumped onto the one on the left, and as I felt the heat of the burning building hot against my neck and face, I slammed him down on the ground. I heard the other one beside me hit the pavement with a scream and as I bit the man's neck the sound of Valen shouting from surprise.

I tore a chunk out of his neck before grabbing a fistful of his hair. I repeatedly smashed his face against the concrete, feeling sick satisfaction every time I felt a bone crunch on impact.

I didn't stop until his face was nothing but a bloodied mess; then turned to see how Jack was fairing.

Lust shot through me as I witnessed Jack on his hands and knees, his teeth flashing as he chewed through the dead man's neck. Blood was spraying through his mouth, painting the streets in a red that shone and shimmered from the fires around us. The reward of our efforts tantalized my nostrils, the insatiable smell of blood mixed in with the tangible aroma of burning buildings. It was such an arousing sensation I felt the tight strands start to weave themselves around my body.

Then another missile, and another rumbling impact. Jack and I both looked towards the noise to see the side of a large skyscraper explode. This one dangerously close to the harbour, which meant it was most likely full of people.

I looked to Jack and saw the fire reflecting in his eyes, his face held shock but it was an odd expression with the blood running down his mouth and neck. He looked like a demon interrupted during a feast, glancing around in stricken surprise to see what had disturbed his meal.

But Jack's eyes weren't fixed on me; he was looking past me. Then he started crawling over the corpse on all fours, those demonic black eyes fixed on nothing else but the unfortunate fool he had in his sights.

I looked too, and when I spotted this prey Jack had zeroed in on, I smiled. I smiled and I rose to my feet, and with a grin and my boyfriend by my side – I started to chase after the fleeing figure, nothing but a silhouette in the descending black smoke.

Valen looked behind him, his eyes widened, I could see the whites of them. It was like throwing fuel on the fire that had already ignited in my veins. He was scared, and the fact that I was seeing fear in those usually cocksure pink eyes...

Oh I wanted to make him scream.

"Stay the fuck away from me!" Valen screamed as he ran past the building the rebels had bombed. He turned left on a dime and ran down an adjacent street, his pink hair flying behind him and his exhausted breath so loud I could hear it perfectly.

We caught up to him easily.

I grabbed his jacket with a laugh and yanked him backwards. Jack caught him in his arms and put him in a headlock. But Valen was stronger than I gave him credit for. He jerked forward, taking Jack with him and when my boyfriend's feet lifted up off of the ground he was flung over Valen's head, landing on the concrete.

In the commotion I ran up to Valen and punched him right in the face. He stumbled back and looked up in shock, and as his mouth opened to scream at me, I kicked him in the shoulder, making him stumble back and fall to the ground.

"Who were those men you were with?" I said with an open mouth grin.

The look Valen gave me was one of pure horror. He started shuffling backwards.

"Don't tell me you betrayed the family and joined up with some rebels?" I smirked.

Valen gasped and jumped to his feet. He turned and started to run again.

Adrenaline coursed through me, and it pooled in all of the wrong places. I quickly caught up to him and pushed him back onto the ground.

Valen's head smacked up against the concrete, blood started to drip from his nose. This time though I jumped onto his fallen body and as the bloodlust claimed me and branded me as its own, I found that my control was starting to leave me.

A black vale descended on my vision, cloaking everything in front of me in a fog that seemed hot inside of my mind. I had felt this feeling before, and I had embraced it before. The same tense, beautiful constriction like the day I had killed Ludo, the day I had fucked Jack.

I didn't fear this feeling, nor did I push it away. And as Valen started shrieking, pure, unhinged, terrifying shrieking, my lust exploded.

And I started pulling off his pants.

The back of my mind was screaming at me, literally screaming at me to stop, but the black vale pushed it back until it was nothing but a pleading whimper. There was no going back, my body and my brain commanded me to pursue this feeling, to chase it to the end and find the dangerous lust at the end of this fucked up rainbow.

Though as I pulled Valen's cargo pants off of his body, exposing tight blue underwear I saw Jack's feet at Valen's head. I looked up, fully expecting for his horrified look to rip the dark shroud from my eyes –

– but instead all I saw was my reflection smiling back at me, a wide grin, dripping derisiveness and the same lust that had taken the reins of my mind.

Something flashed in Jack's hand. My boyfriend got down on his knees, Valen's head now trapped between his thighs. He leaned down and with an uncaring slash he cut Valen's underwear off of him, and in the process, cut Valen's skin with it.

"Fuck him, Sanguine," Jack growled at me, and when he made eye contact my chest burned from the lust in his eyes. This uncontrollable, starved lust that held a promise in it that Jack had just as many layers as I did.

"Do it, I'll hold him down."

I stared at him for a second, before a grin was cut into my mouth. I reached down and ripped Valen's bloody underwear off of him and unbuttoned my pants.

What was happening to me? I knew, and Jack knew too. We were both willing spectators to the madness that had sunk into both of our bodies. We were chimeras, but we had also been victims all of our lives. Being beaten down, humiliated, and treated like dirt by those stronger than us, taller than us, and those who outnumbered us.

We were chimeras, and tonight – we would both mutually find out just what that meant.

Just what that entitled.

And just what the consequences would be.

I unzipped my pants and next I pulled down my underwear. Jack, who was now pinning Valen's arms back with his knees, stared at my hard cock with a desire in him that told me he ached for what the oncoming minutes would bring.

Valen was screaming. Oh was he ever screaming. He was adding his chorus to the perfect orchestra of senses, each one bringing their own beautiful music to this symphony that played in my ears. The smell of blood and fear, the feeling of heat and the cold air against my cock, the sounds of screaming mixed in with the snapping of burning buildings and finally… my own pounding heart as I grabbed Valen's leg and pushed it into Jack's awaiting hands.

"No… no, no, no!" Valen screamed and struggled, lifting his ass up off of the ground and trying to twist it away from the burning cock I had in my hand. I cared nothing for his pleas and spat on my hand before mixing the saliva with the blood now smudging against smooth testicles that were tucked tight against his skin. He couldn't be more flaccid, though a part of me wanted to make him cum just for his own humiliation.

"Ready, Jacky?" I grinned holding Valen's other leg back. The chimera was essentially pinned, he couldn't move and as he started sobbing and gagging I knew he realized there was no escaping what was coming next.

"Do it!" Jack urged with a sickness in his eyes. "Do it."

I winked at him before reaching down and giving Valen's clammy cheek a stroke. Then I positioned myself over the sweet spot. "Now scream for me, Valentine."

And he did.

Oh, did he ever.

As I roughly penetrated Valen, his panicked, shrill screaming echoed off of the buildings, adding to the roaring flames around us. I grinned and looked into his pink eyes as I viciously shoved myself up to the hilt, before, without pause, I started to roughly fuck him.

Jack let out a low, sensual groan. I looked down and saw him take his cock out and start to stroke it right over Valen's screaming face. I watched it intently, fucking Valen with all my strength, enjoying the tight friction of his un-lubed ass.

And was it ever tight. I groaned and pushed his legs back further. I looked down and saw that I had already torn him, probably on penetration. It did nothing but make the tight binds inside of me constrict further, and with every taut string another intense wave of pleasure rushed through me.

But though it felt wonderful, I was getting the most turned on by his screaming, his screaming and the fires surrounding me. Deep in my trace I couldn't see the inferno quickly consuming the buildings but I could smell the black smoke ravaging my lungs. It was perfect, this scene was perfect, another painting for my Jack to paint, another fantasy for me to imagine deep at night. I found my hips in automation, thrusting and thrusting into this screaming prey, and with that I lost myself in my own madness. Pushing into him with no end in sight.

I was only woken from my trance by Jack. His moaning had quickened. He was rapidly stroking himself. His eyes focused on my cock penetrating this screaming, writhing creature we would both have a turn in dominating. Those black eyes were glassy and full, dripping lust and a want that told me he needed a turn next.

I smiled and leaned into him, slowing my pace, and when he realized my intentions he slowed down his stroking and we locked our lips together. Immediately my tongue met his and we kissed deeply as Valen choked on his own blood and saliva.

I didn't like his screaming slowing down, I didn't like when I could only hear ragged breathing. So I jerked my hips and smiled through the sharp cry followed by a desperate sob.

Then I leaned down and took Jack's cock into my mouth. It was rock hard, hot with his own blood rushing through it. The defined head was swollen and it twitched as it rested against my tongue. I created a suction and gave it a generous lick, and was rewarded for my efforts with a loud cry and a warm spurt inside of my mouth.

I let the first shot of cum coat my tongue, before taking out his cock and milking the shaft so the rest of it spilled onto Valen's face. The chimera's pink eyes, horrified and in a state of catatonia, became alive again as the cum shot from Jack's cock and onto him. I took this opportunity to immediately resume my intense pace, and in return he opened his mouth to scream.

Jack grabbed his cock and laid the tip on Valen's lips, another spurt wetted his lips and mouth, making the pink-eyed chimera scream again. And to both of our pleasure, we saw ourselves a tear.

"Cum, Sanguine," Jack urged. He was out of breath from his orgasm but his hands started stroking his cock almost immediately after the last spurt of cum shot out of him. "Cum, baby. Fucking cum inside of him. Do it.

'Do it. Do it, Sanguine.'

That raspy dry voice – he almost sounded like Barry but no... he sounded like someone else I had once known.

I grinned and locked lips with Jack again. Then I looked down at my blood-soaked cock, red now smudged all over Valen's ass and pubic hair. His pubes were pink too. So those Skytech pills turned the hair colours everywhere, eh?

With Jack egging me on, I fucked Valen hard, making the kid's screams ring throughout the street. I looked around just once, and was mesmerized to see several of the buildings on fire. Every time I had fucked someone it had been underneath fire – I liked that.

Then a loud shriek, one of a higher octave like the ringing squeal of a rabbit caught in the jaws of a beast. I looked down and saw Valen's eyes wide open and his mouth too, scream and scream rolling from lips coated in Jack's cum.

Then oddly – he fell silent.

I smirked at this, remembering with cruel indifference how I fell silent when I was raped. The fact that this didn't make me stop immediately a window into the ferocious, manic state I had fallen into.

Silent and still, I laughed and watched Valen. Jack's taunting echoing, though his face was getting shrouded in black. Yes, there was smoke all around us, thick smoke.

Still I laughed and as I found myself crawling to my peak I grabbed Valen's chin and clenched it.

But when I leaned down to kiss it I paused and stared in perplexity.

His eyes had gone black.

How… odd.

I laughed. "Jack… look, he–"

Suddenly, like the entire world had ceased to exist, everything around me became black. My senses left me one by one like they had been stolen out from under my nose. The smell of the fire and smoke left, the roaring inferno left, my pleasure of fucking Valen left – it was all gone, and nothing remained. Like I had been killed and thrown into limbo I found myself floating in blackness, not a single shred of awareness coming to me. It was like someone had turned a switch off on my mind.

When I came to, I was in hell.

I opened my eyes and immediately saw Jack laying beside me. His face was turned away from me but he was laying with his pants still down. He wasn't moving.

I rolled to my side and groaned, my head pounding and my lungs screaming from the toxic smoke I had inhaled. The smoke was impossibly thick now, and so full of ash it stained the bare skin of my groin.

My pants were still off…

With my head filled with fog and pain I pulled up my pants. I looked around in a daze before crawling over to Jack to shake him awake.

I reached a hand out and laid it on his shoulder, but as soon as my skin touched his I retracted it like he had become electrified.

I stared in shock, the sound getting sucked out of the world around me.

Jack was cold.

I touched his cheek and felt my heart wrench. His cheek was frozen, his eyes half-open but unseeing. He was laying there still.

He was dead. Jack was dead.

"SANGUINE!?" I heard a deep voice scream. I recognized it as Nero, but my eyes only stared at my dead boyfriend. Thinking with false hope that if I only waited he would gasp and become awake. Thinking with a thousand delusions that it was impossible for him to be dead. How could he be dead? What killed him?

Valen? How could he...

A sob broke my lips and I struggled to my feet.

"SANGUINE? JACK?" Nero screamed. "WHERE THE FUCK ARE YOU?" He was out of breath; he was running closer and closer.

I took a step back, my hand over my mouth, tears burning my eyes as I saw, in full view, Jack laying on the pavement as still as where death had lay him. I kept stepping backwards, away from him, away from the burning buildings My skin was blistering, my lungs screaming, but still the only sensation in my head was the horror and guilt of what I had let happen.

I didn't know how. I didn't know what he did. All I know is that Valen had taken back his power, and he had killed Jack.

"SANGY!?"

I looked to my left but when I saw the silhouette of Nero coming closer I didn't run into his arms like I thought I would. I didn't come crying to my best friend like I would have when I was a kid. Instead, with a thousand awful emotions eating me alive, I turned and ran into the nearest building I could find. Unable to face Nero when he discovered the dead corpse of our brother.

Another sob broke my lips. I ran through the smoke-filled building, the lobby around me almost invisible. I turned down the first door I saw and ran down a hallway.

"Sami..." a weak voice groaned. My head snapped to the left, into an empty room.

It was Sir...

Half of his face was blackened, just an eye white in his socket staring at me. His tux had been charred away and he was so burnt he was on his knees. He was crawling towards me, he was crawling towards me!

"Sami... you left. You left!" Sir whimpered.

I gasped and turned to flee away from him, but as I turned I saw Patches. On her hands and knees with her blue ribbons hanging off scorched hair.

"Sami... help," she cried. I could see red flesh peeking through the charred mess that was her arms. Her back was both a marble of yellow and black. I could see it start to split open in front of me.

Oh god, she was crying. She was crying.

I turned and ran down the opposite hallway, as I got farther away from them I could hear them pleading. They were pleading with me, begging me to pick them up. Pick them up like Nana used to pick me up. Hold them in my arms as they died. Oh god, I could hear their voices ringing in my head.

I cried out and opened the first door I saw. It was a flight of stairs. I climbed up the stairs, desperate to get away from them. Get away from the fucking voices.

What had I done? What the fuck had I done?

A loud crash underneath my feet, one that made the stairs rumble. I looked up and hoped for the roof to come crashing down on me. I didn't want to be here, I didn't want to be in this.

Oh god... what had I done?

I should've never left Jasper's. He had been right. Fuck, he had been right. I was supposed to be a monster. I was never supposed to be let loose on the world. Look what I had done. I had killed my boyfriend. I had killed my Jack. I had killed my friends.

I climbed up set after set of stairs, tears streaming down my cheeks and dropping into the dry and dusty floor. I wanted to stop and cling to the hot railing until I died but for some reason I just kept climbing.

When I pushed the door open to the roof I was sobbing uncontrollably. I collapsed onto the ground, the cold air a relief to only my lungs. I grabbed onto the door handle and cried like a lost child.

"I give up!" I suddenly sobbed, my screaming lungs making me double over in hacking coughs. I let out a loud cry and slammed my fist onto the hot tarmac. "I fucking give up! I'm done. I'm done..." I shook my head and leaned over until my forehead touched the roof. Despair rushing through me, pooling in my heart and filling me with its poison.

I had hung on when I had to flee from Sunshine House. I had hung on when I was run out of town after town, and when Cory tried to kill me. I had fucking hung on when Jasper had kept me prisoner, raped me at eight.

I had hung on – I hadn't quit. I hadn't given up.

I had kept going. I had kept breathing.

But now, today, in this moment –

"I'M FUCKING DONE!" I screamed and slammed my hand again against the roof.

My poor Sami, a raspy voice sounded. One that was so full of derision and smugness it made me scream from rage. *My poor lost Sami*

"FUCK OFF!" I screamed and looked up at Barry. My old friend was standing over me.

But as I looked at him I realized it wasn't Barry anymore. The changes I had been seeing on my friend had fully taken effect. Barry's ears were gone, his hair was now black and shiny. His eyes were two burning red coals that squinted from his closed mouth smile.

No… it wasn't Barry.

It was Crow.

It had always been Crow.

Unable to look at him I turned away and took a stumbling step away from him. I choked and coughed from the smoke burning my lungs and started to walk.

"Sami…"

"SHUT UP!" I cried. I whirled around to face my old friend but as I looked at where I had seen him I realized that he was gone. Another voice had said that.

My agony shot into me as I saw someone I never thought I would see again.

"Nana?" I whimpered.

Nan was standing in front of me. She was wearing a blue kerchief over her crinkly black hair. She was smiling at me, a kind, motherly smile that she had held for me so often at Sunshine House.

"Oh my Sami," she whispered. She opened her arms. "Come here."

"Nanny?" I staggered to my feet and started walking towards her. "Nana, can I come home yet?"

Nan nodded as she smiled. I kept walking towards her but even though I walked towards her I still couldn't get closer to her. I didn't care though. I would eventually get to her; I would eventually find my Nana.

"Come here, Sami," she urged me. Her arms open and welcoming. "My sweet Sami. My sweet, sweet Sami. You can come home."

"Nana…" I said again as I stumbled towards her, ignoring the fires around me, and the stinging in my eyes. "Nana. I missed you."

"Just one more step," Nan said. "One more step to Nana."

I smiled and nodded. I felt my foot step up on a ledge. I stood on the ledge for a second and opened my arms for Nan to take me into hers. For her to hold me, protect me, protect me… protect me…

I took another step as I felt my name screamed behind me. I took a step forward… but instead of falling into Nan's arms – I only fell.

I closed my eyes as the wind started rushing all around me.

I was falling.

I was falling.

But it was okay.

Nana was there.

BOOK 4

My Life After The Madness

*Deep in my madness, he had heard my pleas.
A boy locked in darkness, loneliness, and naivety.
Isolated from others, chased from his home.
He went looking for a friend, and far did he roam.
The boy was captured, tortured, raped, and abused.
But he had his Crow beside him, to give up he refused.
Eventually he was rescued, but that Crow remained.
No longer a friend, but beast with madness ingrained
And though I ran and I ran, in a desperate attempt to be free.
I realized I could not out run him.
For this Crow had become me.*

CHAPTER 45

ELISH PICKED UP JACK AND HELD THE LIMP BOY IN his arms. His face was grave but firm, sweat beading down his face as several buildings burned around him. He looked behind him, where he had last seen Nero, pursuing the man he was sure had killed Jack.

Or had he?

"There are no fatal wounds on him…" Silas said confused. He lay a hand on Jack's mouth and made his touch cold. There was too much noise around him to listen to the boy's heartbeat – if he even had one.

"No… there isn't," Elish responded, his eyes narrowing. "This is quite the puzzle. I would suggest the rebels have gotten a hold of some biological weapon but here we stand."

"Indeed… here we stand," Silas murmured, but then his eyes widened. "Elish…" He quickly retracted his hand. "He's still alive. It's his thermal abilities – the cold must be his body automatically reacting to the heat." Silas lay his ear against Jack's chest and nodded to himself. "He won't be alive for long, but he breathes…" Then Silas glanced above, at the smouldering building above them. "Nero needs to hurry, before it's too late."

Elish seemed surprised at this. "Too late for what? Surely…"

Silas's lips tightened, his emerald eyes two fire pits that reflected the inferno around them. It was almost unbearable, but they had both made their bodies cold so it was tolerable for the moment.

"Sanguine loves him… his pants were off, Elish. Whatever happened to them it happened while they were intimate. I've already ruined

Sanguine in many ways. My first step towards repairing what I ruined will be to not let him lose Jack. I'm going to make Jack immortal... if it isn't too late," Silas said, resting a hand on Jack's forehead. "Take him to Perish, lovely. I'd rather him do the surgery but if I don't make it back in time to use my brain matter, use his and perform the surgery yourself."

"He's only twenty..." Elish said slowly but Silas held up a hand to silence him.

Then suddenly there was a sickening thunk behind them. They both whirled around to see what the noise was, and at the same time both their jaws dropped.

Silas let out a gasping scream and ran towards the heap of black shrouded in the smoke. Elish followed, Jack still being held in his arms.

"No... NO!" Silas screamed. "NO!"

As Elish got closer and saw the mangled body of Sanguine his heart jumped. And though for the rest of his immortal life he would swear to Silas it had jumped in horror – in truth it was from happiness and hope.

Hope that Sanguine, laying with his head cracked open like a ripe melon – was dead.

"NERO!" Silas screamed. He jumped up and started pulling Jack from Elish's grasp. "DROP HIM!" the king screamed. "Drop him and bring Sanguine to Perish. NOW! NOW, ELISH!"

Elish looked down, Sanguine's skull visibly split from the horrific hairline crack in his head. The boy's eyes were half-open but they saw nothing and reflected nothing. The boy... surely...

"He's dead, Silas," Elish said as he lay Jack onto the hot concrete, behind him a loud crash as a distant building fell to its knees. An eruption of smoke rose to the air, filled with fire and debris like an exploding volcano. "Silas, I'm sorry, love. He's dead."

Silas turned and shoved Elish hard. "NOW! NOW!" he shrieked, completely unhinged and full of desperate madness. "GO!" Then the king let out a cry and fell to his knees. "GO! RUN!" Silas commanded.

"Silas – he's dead!" Elish snapped. "Let him be at peace, you tortured the boy enough!" He had to stall Silas. Even stalling him for a minute could mean the difference.

The difference between spending an eternity with Sanguine and having the man just be a bad memory. A memory of the red-eyed defect who threatened to take his place as king beside King Silas.

I will not let that happen – I will be king. It's my right, it's my place.

Not his.

Then Nero burst out of the smoking door, but he spared no glances to Silas and Elish. Without asking permission Nero picked up the mangled remains of Sanguine, the young chimera like a broken ragdoll in his arms, before turning and running towards where the car was parked. Sanguine's satchel with that disgusting bear still dangling off of his corpse.

Elish's teeth gritted; he mentally sent out a prayer to the universe that the boy was indeed dead and this could all be resolved in the easiest of ways. But it was Sanguine he wished dead; he had been seeing something salvageable in Jack, and he did not wish the boy to die too.

Elish picked up Jack, and with Silas's shadow in front of him, running after Nero – he ran too.

Nero had his hand on Sanguine's head, trying to hold the boy's fractured skull together. A groan fell from his lips as he tried without success to keep the two splits to stay open, every time he withdrew pressure the two fractures of skull burst open, revealing a hint of the pink brains underneath.

The entire car smelled of blood and smoke, the rear-view mirror a testament to the hell that they had left behind.

Elish looked at the smoke they were leaving behind. *The fires are near the harbour – we will lose buildings but the harbour and parkland that separates Cypress from the other districts may be our saving grace. Let the slums burn – as long as it crosses no borders. The districts that matter will be fine.*

Ceph, who had been driving, had remained silent after calling Perish on his remote phone. Perish was in town, luckily, and he was ready.

He would be waiting with a suicide pill for Silas, then after the king was dead his brain tissue would be extracted and surgically implanted into Sanguine and Jack.

Elish hid the smirk as he watched Nero, with tears rolling down his face, try to keep Sanguine's head from splitting back open.

The boy is surely dead...

After what was probably an eternity to Silas but a fraction of a second to Elish, the party burst through the door of the surgery floor, a room above the hospital wing Kirrel was in charge of. Perish was waiting, scrubbed in and in scrubs. Silas ran to him and Perish gave him the suicide pill but Silas shook his head.

"Get the saw, now," Silas said hastily as he laid down on the operating table.

"You need to die first, Master!" Perish said in his usual quickened tone.

"There isn't time!" This surprised even Elish, but it also filled his heart with unease. Silas was desperate to have Sanguine become immortal. What if this experience only bound him further to Sanguine? What if Sanguine's love for Jack mattered not now that the king had come face-to-face with the possibility of losing that deranged lunatic?

As the sounds of the saw filled the room Elish's face darkened. He watched with a poisoned look as Nero lay Sanguine down on the operating table beside Silas. Perish holding the buzzing saw in his hand with Silas staring at the ceiling. A determined and fearless look on his face that held a window into the bravery that the King of the World had.

"Hold his hand," Nero barked to Elish. Elish's teeth ground but his legs brought him to Silas's side. He shielded Silas's eyes with one hand and grasped the king's hand with the other. He squeezed it tight and watched as Perish lowered the buzzing handheld saw down onto Silas's hairline.

The sound of the saw changed octave, and Silas's hand clenched Elish's in a grip that threatened to break Elish's hand. And as the skin and soon, bone, started to fly through the air, pricking and stinging Elish's face, the king didn't scream. His teeth only locked together, his lips peeling back as he grimaced. Elish admired him in that moment.

As a mercy Perish kept cutting an inch into Silas's brain matter, the hot meat flew onto Elish's face, stinging his eyes and blinding him temporarily, but it did its job – Silas's hand went limp and his face relaxed.

Elish nodded at Perish and Perish, with a tooth biting down on his lip, made another several quick saws until a triangle of skull was cut out of Silas's head.

"Garrett is going to assist," Nero suddenly said. He put a hand on Elish's shoulder. "He's waiting outside. I need to take care of this Cypress stuff and you need to come with me. You're king now."

Elish gave him a cooled look as he wiped the blood and brain matter off of his face with his sleeve. "I'm more experienced with medicine than him. I'm staying."

"No, you're not." Nero's eyes flashed as he said this. "You're coming with me, and don't make me embarrass you by saying why I want you to come with me. We have to help Ellis evacuate Cypress. Let's go."

This was the last thing that Elish wanted but he got up anyway. If Nero knew his preference for Sanguine dying the king would undoubtedly blame him if Sanguine did indeed die. If Sanguine died it would be a strategic move for him to be Silas's support system and if Nero ruined that with whispers of Elish botching the surgery, he could lose his king forever.

So, begrudgingly, Elish left the surgery floor and he and Nero headed towards the Skyland military base.

It wasn't until the early morning that Elish, Nero, and Ceph made it back to Alegria. All three of them were exhausted, in foul moods, and Ceph was even laying his head on Nero's shoulder, his green eyes glazed and slowly closing.

Nero looked outside, the hellfires of Cypress still burning in the distance. They had several fire trucks on hand for fires but once the firemen got to the other side of the Cypress walls it was obvious that half of the district would be uninhabitable.

Though it could've been worse and Elish knew it could have been worse – it could've been a district that actually mattered.

Which was curious to Elish.

"Why Cypress?" Elish murmured more to himself than Nero. "Why one of the poorest, filthiest districts? Perhaps because the rocket launchers would be obviously seen in a more populated district? Still though..."

Nero didn't move and for more than several moments he didn't speak either. The brute chimera's mind was with Sanguine; Elish couldn't say the same.

"We'll find out," Nero finally responded. "There will be nothing holding me back this time. Public opinion or not. In two days half of the greywaste legion will be at the Augustus Military Base, and we will find every single one of those fucks."

Yes, the plan had been hammered out to every last detail. Nero and General Zhou and General Taylor had been pouring over a map of the city, lists of available legionary, weapons, and talking to their top strategists over the invasion that was coming. The rebels were going to be crushed once and for all. All that they were waiting on now were the planes and vehicles that would be piling in to the greywastes military base. Ones that would be full of legionary waiting to have a hand at killing something.

But still... why Cypress?

Elish's face hardened as he remembered picking up Jack. The boy had seemed dead but there hadn't been a visible wound on him. Surely the missile couldn't have stunned him that much. Jack in all respects had been dead.

The car pulled up in front of Alegria and everyone filed out. Ceph half-asleep and Nero looking just as soured and troubled as Elish was himself.

"Look, Eli, I appreciate you saving Ceph and I realize you have my nuts in your hand for that, but I gotta be honest... if Sanguine's dead –" Nero said in a voice full of warning. "– and I see a smirk on your fucking face..."

"I'll try and internalize my leaps of joy," Elish said coldly as the car door slammed. "I would think someone like you, who had seen Sanguine at his absolute worst, would see it as a mercy for the boy to finally be out of pain."

Nero sighed and shook his head. "I feel bad for you, bro. You can't love for shit, or show compassion for shit. Your life must suck big time to not feel a damn thing."

"Somehow I live," Elish snipped back. He held his chin up high as the legionaries keeping guard of Alegria opened the doors for them, "and my life is just fine, thank you."

Nero snorted; this brazen act made Elish's mouth purse but he didn't take the bait he knew Nero was going to dangle in front of him. Instead he kept reminding himself that all of his problems may be over, and it would be he laughing as Nero wept for the red-eyed chimera.

"You know why Silas will never take you as his partner?" Nero suddenly said.

Elish almost stopped; he almost turned around and struck Nero for even shedding light on the desire only the first generation of chimeras knew of. Elish's darkest secret, and darkest desire.

"Because you're a fucking stone-hearted sociopath. Even when you're loving towards him I can see it on your face, it's forced. Silas wants someone real. Silas wants a partner who's a real person... not this fucking robot that you are." Nero's tone dropped as Elish walked further away from him. "And the fact that you wish your own brother ill, that poor fucking kid who was raised in a hell your silver-spooned mouth could never imagine in his nightmares, just proves it."

"I'm not having this conversation with you now," was Elish's response. He stepped into the elevator and was tempted to order Nero and Ceph to take the stairs to give him some peace. "You're over-emotional due to last night's events. I suggest not taking it out on me."

Elish closed his eyes in exasperation as Nero let out a frustrated noise.

"What happened to you!?" Nero suddenly exploded. "When you were a teenager you were our little ball of emotion. You clung to King Silas like he was your security blanket. What the fuck happened, Eli? What happened to make you turn into such a dick?"

"I grew up," Elish said. "You should do the same, especially since you'll have a husband soon to watch out for. Funny, you were never this emotional as a child or a teenager. Love has really weakened you."

"Love isn't weakness," Nero said, annunciating every syllable in hopes that they would stick into Elish's brain. "And you know what? One day you're going to fall in love, and I'm going to laugh my ass off as I see it happen. We all will. One day, Eli. You're going to fall head over fucking heels and maybe then you'll stop acting like such a fucking dick."

"I don't think so," Elish said back, then he paused. And to his own surprise he felt the need to defend himself further. Though he would never admit that his brother's scathing words had got to him. "I love King Silas, and it has not changed me."

It seemed like Nero was ready for this response. "Do you really love him, Eli? Do you love him because he's a king and your master, or do you love him for being Silas Dekker?"

Elish was silent.

"Because if you loved him as a partner should love a partner, you wouldn't be secretly hoping that the man Silas is ravaged with guilt over failing, is dead. Knowing that it will fucking destroy Silas if Sanguine dies. Loving someone is wanting the best for them, even when it might not be what is best for you. Chew on that for a while, bro."

The elevator stopped, and Elish stepped out without further comment. Though he was privy to Ceph's whispered words as Elish walked down the hallway.

"And they call you the dumb one." And then the sound of a kissed cheek.

The smell of antiseptic and blood was heavy in the air when Elish walked into the surgery room. He looked around the open floor, full of stainless steel equipment, beeping machines, and covered hospital beds and spotted Perish sleeping on one of the beds.

As he approached the scientist he glanced at the three sheet-draped bodies and resisted the urge to start uncovering each one. He so dearly wanted to unwrap their bodies like Skyday presents, in hopes to receive the only thing he had on his list: the greying, decomposing body of Sanguine.

Because, though Nero's words did echo through Elish, he couldn't help what he felt, and what he wanted.

And what Elish wanted was Sanguine Dekker dead and out of his king's heart permanently.

Elish was the oldest out of all of them physically, he was thirty-three and had been the last chimera to become immortal as far as the first generation went. And in being the oldest he felt a responsibility for his king's wellbeing, and he was firm in his belief that he knew what was best for Silas more than the king himself did.

And the best thing for Silas was for Sanguine to be dead and gone. Yes, Silas would be sad, he would grieve, but eventually the failure of a chimera would be nothing but a memory. A wound to eventually scar and fade away.

I know what's best for Silas, not Nero. Silas doesn't need a partner in the ways that Nero is suggesting. He needs someone who knows what he's doing, someone who won't let emotions control logic and reasoning.

And I'm the only one in this damn family who has those skills.

"Elish..." Nero's choked voice sounded behind Elish. "They're covered... why are they covered?" Nero sounded so unlike himself. Elish's brute brother, a man who usually was every inch an Imperial General, made Elish uneasy. Perhaps that was just another one of many reasons why Elish disliked Sanguine. He didn't like how his brothers, his king, even his sister, all seemed enamoured with the boy. It was odd, they had never shown this much emotion or patience when it came to the other second generation. They had all been with Elish in his disappointment with how most of the second gen had turned out.

"Silas is covered too, it says nothing," Elish replied flatly, but in truth he was also wondering just what it meant. And as he pondered this he also came to the realization that he himself had been delaying checking to see if Sanguine and Jack had survived the surgery.

Nero walked up to one of the covered sheets. He took in a deep breath, his face pained. And he slowly drew the sheet down. A mop of silver hair appeared, then the paled face of Jack Dekker.

Nero lay a hand on his forehead, and immediately his lips pursed. He looked at Ceph and smiled. "He's warm." Nero's voice cracked; he let out a long sigh and patted Jack's cheek. "Not just warm – he's hot. Well, that's our very first second generation immortal… let's see if we have another one."

Ceph grabbed onto Nero's shoulder and squeezed it hard. All three of them walked over to the sheet-draped body that they knew was Sanguine just from the height of the body. Elish felt his chest tense and his hands clench at his sides, but he refused his face from making any expression but his usual stoic look.

Nero grabbed the sheet and gently pulled it back. Underneath the white cloth was the grey, gaunt face of Sanguine, his mouth partially open as were his eyes, his skull hastily stapled together.

Nero's hands were trembling as he reached out and gently laid his hand on Sanguine's cheek.

And he burst out laughing.

Elish narrowed his eyes, a twinge of pain rippled up his jaw as Nero let out a loud whoop and took Ceph into his burly arms. Behind him Perish jumped in his bed over the unexpected noise, his icy-blue eyes darting around wildly from shock.

"He's alive, bitch!" Nero hollered. He lifted Ceph up off of the ground and even though the brute was almost two hundred and seventy-five pounds of muscles Nero twirled him around like he was twirling Drake.

"He's hot as fuck! They're alive!" Nero yelled through his laughter. "They're alive, puppy! Holy fuck. Oh my god, Silas is going to piss himself!"

Nero stopped, the corners of his eyes glistening with tears. He looked over at Elish and grinned. "I don't care that you're pissed. I really don't. I don't give a shit because you know he fucking deserves happiness. You fucking know it."

Elish shook his head slowly, feeling a coldness wash over him that coated him from his head to his feet. And in that moment he wanted to be anywhere else but in that room. "Silas will wake soon and you are more than capable of handling the invasion. I'll be taking on Perish's research in Kreig until I am summoned back. Loren will be accompanying me."

Nero threw his hands up into the air and let them drop. "Come on, asshole. You can't be that pissed that Sanguine is immortal. Stop being such a bitch."

"I'm taking my leave," Elish said crisply and started heading towards the door.

"You know, if you loved Silas like you say you do, you would want to be there when we tell him Sanguine survived. You'd want to see the happy look on his face," Nero called back.

Elish said nothing back.

Nero watched him go with a soured and angry look, but a moment later he seemed to remember just what he had been celebrating. The grin returned and he took Ceph back into his arms with a joyful bellow.

He kissed Ceph's cheek before turning to Perish. "It went well then? Everything went well?"

Perish nodded; he was smiling just as wide as Nero and Ceph, though his unfocused eyes were looking everywhere but into Nero's. "Yes, yes, it went very well. Garrett left to go to sleep, he was exhausted. We stapled Sanguine's head and..." Perish walked over and pulled the rest of the sheet off of Sanguine's body.

To both Nero and Ceph's surprise Sanguine's skin was painfully raw and lobster red and in some places even blistering. His pubic hair had been scraped away as well, and to Nero's horror, the skin on his penis and testicles peeled away to the meat.

"What the..." Nero's temperature started to raise and Perish could tell. The scientist held out his hands as Nero gave him a dangerous look.

"It was Garrett's idea. Since Sanguine's body is so full of scars, we decided to coat his body in an acid-type solution and scrap the skin away and remove some skin altogether. Sanguine will take longer to wake up but when he does... his entire body will be healed and new." Perish beamed and patted Sanguine's head gently. "He'll be a brand-new chimera, to start his new life." Perish clasped his hands and started rubbing them together, one of his many nervous ticks. "I think Master will be pleased at this decision. Poor Sanguine had so much scar tissue inside of his rectum from being raped by that man. I'm glad Master never had sex with him; he would've been horrified once he was inside of him. Poor Sanguine had been savaged but it's okay, we made him all better. This will make King Silas pleased with me. He was angry at me over disagreeing with him when Sanguine came back and said those things, but this will make him happy."

The thought of Sanguine's body finally being void of those scars brought the smile back to Nero's face. He reached down and pinched Sanguine's cheeks before giving them a pat. "You did good, Perish. The king won't forget this. If Elish is going to go pout in Kreig I hope Silas lets you stay for a while. You're a lot easier to get along with than that icy bitch."

Perish grinned and rolled back and forth on the balls of his feet. "Thank you, Nero. I'm just happy to make Master happy and the family. I would love to stay."

"Why don't you go get some sleep." Nero pulled back the last sheet and with Ceph's help he picked King Silas up and slung the boiling hot king over his shoulder. "I'll bring Kingy to my apartment since he'll wake up first and he can decide where to put our shark-teeth twins. Take a couple days off, Per. Go fuck whoever you want. I want at least three sengils or cicaros in your bed every night polishing your cock until further notice."

Perish looked at Nero and blinked; he looked absolutely perplexed yet mesmerized at the prospect. Nero had to laugh at this. He turned around and nodded for Ceph to follow him to the doors outside. "And I'm going to be fucking you once we get home. Everyone's fucking tonight. Come on, Cephy. We got some celebratin' to do."

CHAPTER 46

IT WAS LIKE I HAD BEEN IN A DREAM, A LUCID DREAM but there were no images dancing around in my head like most dreams. Instead I only saw a white fire that seemed to be both hot and cold at the same time. It was a welcoming fire and it felt odd against my skin, like I was continuously being coated in a liquid ribbon of silk.

Every time I gained a shred of inner thought I found myself curious about what was happening to me. Sometimes I had concluded to myself that I was indeed dead and this was my oblivion, but other times I had convinced myself I was in some sort of coma and eventually I would wake up. Though most of the time I had no comprehensible thoughts, I just floated in these flames and waited for something to happen.

Then, when several lifetimes had past, I started to hear different sensations. At first it was the sounds you could hear from sewer pipes, the sound of water rushing through something narrow. I didn't know what that was until the drumming rhythm of my heartbeat started to sound, and it was then I realized I had been hearing the blood starting to rush through my veins again.

Finally the opal flames that had been a blanket around my body started to become red before they disappeared completely. Only the crimson remained and with that sensation the feeling of warmth against my face. I think it was the sunshine.

I opened my eyes but immediately closed them again as a sharp sting of pain ripped like I was being stabbed in the eyes. I wasn't used to the sun it seemed, the light hurt.

I rolled over, away from where the light was coming from and grimaced. My limbs were stiff and frozen, every muscle ached like I hadn't used them in months. It wasn't even this bad when I was in the basement. I paced a lot while I was down there.

After a few minutes of trying to get my hazy mind back, I opened my eyes again. I squinted them and looked around the room and realized that I recognized where this location was. I was back inside of my bedroom in Alegria, inside of King Silas's apartment.

Wait. I frowned. Why was I here? Where had I been before? The last thing I remember…

I tried to wrack my brains and come up with my last memory but everything was just a haze of black. I was in that abandoned building with Jack and then… nothing. Had Silas come for me? Had he put me in a coma?

I sat up but to my absolute perplexity I heard a tinkle of a bell. I looked down and realized a small red string had been tied around my wrist. I looked up to where the string went and found a little bell that was attached to the bed post. Almost like…

Almost like someone wanted to know when I woke up.

I rubbed my eyes, confused but feeling strangely good. I yawned and scratched my hair, hoping that I would be able to see Jack soon. I wanted to know what had happened and why I was here

"Lovely…"

I jumped and looked towards the door. Without even hearing him approach I saw King Silas standing in the doorway with a soft smile on his face. He looked well, and was dressed in a casual black button-down and new blue jeans, and he seemed happy to see me.

"Hi…" I mumbled. I started flexing my hands to try and get the muscles to stop aching. I didn't understand why everything was so stiff and sore. "So you caught me, eh?"

Surprisingly Silas laughed softly. He glided into the room and sat down on the bed beside me. He reached a hand over and gently stroked my cheek with a caring, gentle touch.

"Caught you? No, my crucio, but I understand your confusion. You don't remember anything do you?" Silas asked softly. His hand traced down my cheek, then he rubbed my neck, before murmuring. "Beautiful."

I let him touch me for a moment, but then I remembered what had happened the last time I had seen him. At the memory of his scathing words to me I jerked away and felt myself tense.

"You seem rather affectionate," I said in a bitter voice; I looked directly into his eyes. "Am I not just a lying whore to you, King Silas?"

Silas retracted his hand and winced as if my words held an actual stinger to them. He put his hand down and we fell into a collective silence.

"Sanguine," Silas said slowly. "I am not a man to apologize often, nor am I a man who takes joy in admitting when he has handled something badly." He returned my confused look with a faint smile. "But I handled what happened to you badly because of my own guilt and denial, and being your king things should've been done differently. I'm sorry, lovely, for my words, and most of all: I'm sorry for the previous twenty years. I failed you as your king. I should've been protecting you and I didn't."

He seemed genuine. I had seen many different faces of this man, but something told me that he was being truthful to me. It wasn't much, his words still festered in me like an untreated wound and it would take a while for it to become clean, but it was a start.

"Thank you," I said, watching as his hand reached down and gently took my own. Silas's hands had always been so soft and slender, yet they were hands that had done such horrible things.

"You have had a hard life and unfortunately I failed in making your time here as carefree and enjoyable as I wanted," Silas continued. "But I would like that to change. I'm going to make up for everything you experienced, and I want to start today."

"What starts today?" I said slowly.

"Freedom, *crucio*," Silas said patting my hand. "You're going to get some privileges that my second generation do not have. I'm doing this because… I want to put what would make you happy above what would make me happy."

His smile faded, but the stroking of my hand did not. "You love Jack, don't you?"

I stared at him before I nodded. I wanted to ask him where Jack was, but I decided to wait.

Silas nodded too, though this seemed to sadden him in a way. "I'm going to give you permission to be partners with whomever you want, which is a grand privilege in this family. Not only that, love, I'm going to allow you two to get your own apartment. If you wish to continue with college you may, or you two can start your assigned jobs. If you do not wish to date Jack, you may have any of my creations or an arian of your choosing. You don't have to make the decision now, and you can change your partner at any time. This will be your privilege."

I was taken aback by his words; I knew what I was being given was a great gift. And though I was confused as to where I was, where Jack was, or what had happened for me to get here, I was still excited at what he was saying to me.

"Thank you," I said, and as I smiled he smiled wider. "I do want to be with Jack. I want to be a part of this family…"

"And you will be. We will have a coming out party for you, love. To introduce you to the family, introduce you to Skyfall, and have it well-known your status." Silas smiled wryly. "Do you know why you woke up in your old bedroom, love? Do you have any memories over what happened to you?"

I shook my head. "Not the slightest clue."

The expression on the king's face told me he was happy with this. He got up and tugged on my hand, encouraging me to follow him.

I wasn't sure if I would be able to but I knew I would have to get out of bed eventually. So with his help I put both feet on the ground and tried to stand erect.

My face tensed in pain and it took every ounce of energy and balance not to fall. I grunted and started trying to stretch my legs.

"Jack and Kinny have been taking turns exercising your legs," Silas explained, noticing I was struggling. "Or else you would be a lot worse. You have been asleep for almost two months, sweet boy."

Two months? The realization almost made me fall back onto the bed. "How so?" I said alarmed. I looked behind me at my messed up bed and saw that there was no IV, no nothing to keep me alive. "How is that even possible?"

Silas smirked and gently led me towards a full length mirror that stood near my dresser. When I entered my own vision I saw I was dressed in nothing but black boxer briefs. I was almost entirely naked, my hair was longer too but my face had some colour to it. Though I –

I froze. I ignored Silas's laugh at my stunned expression and took a step closer to the mirror.

My scars… my… my body…

I held out my arms and looked at them, stunned. They were brand-new, the skin soft and flawless. I used to have scar tissue that caked my arms like pink plaster, rough, ugly marks that raised up like mountains in some places from being cut again and again.

Then I looked down at my stomach, it was clean of any scars, of any of my own masochistic abuse, and below it my pubic hair was clean and freshly trimmed. No huge chunks of scar tissue peeking through the black strands from me cutting my own genitals from pure inner hatred. Everything was new…

Silas reached a hand out and gently drew down my boxers, my flaccid penis poked out and he held it in his hands. "New as well, love. New skin, the same with your bottom, inside and out. It's all new, Sanguine. Any physical reminders of your past are gone, you're a brand-new person."

Silas tucked my penis back into my boxer briefs and slowly ran his hand up the curve of my side. I couldn't stop staring at myself, at my new body.

Then my eyes started to burn. I held a hand up to my face to shield Silas from my emotions and turned from the mirror.

Never in my life had I been new, never had I felt anything more than an ugly, scar-riddled monster. The only time I had been close to feeling like a normal arian was when I had put on the brown colour contacts and the teeth caps.

But now? As the tears slipped down my cheek and onto my soft hand I had to pull my hand back and examine this new body once again. I realized as I breathed in and out that physically I felt better too. My lungs seemed clearer, and though my muscles screamed from not being used, I still felt stronger.

I felt like a whole new person… even…

Even the voices weren't screaming at me.

When I felt Silas's hand on my shoulder, I turned around and threw my arms around him. Unable to hold it back I felt several hot tears slip from my eyes and onto his shoulder. I sniffed them back and squeezed him tight.

My king… the king I had thought I had lost, but it looks like he had just been hiding. In that moment I loved King Silas so much my heart overflowed with appreciation for him. I made a promise then I would follow this man for the rest of my life, through the good and the bad.

"How did you do this?" I choked as he squeezed me back. "Was t-this Skytech medicine?"

Silas pulled away from me, but his hands were resting on my shoulders. He shook his head before saying two words I knew I would never forget.

"You're immortal."

My mind jammed, the gears stopped turning and I seemed to fall into my own stunned stasis. I stared at Silas with an astounded look as I tried to gather my mind which had seemed to have scattered all over the place.

"Immortal?" I stammered. I started to feel dizzy, a heat that had first started pooling inside of my head seemed to overflow and start trickling down my body. I found myself stumbling back and with the same lighthearted laugh Silas led me to the bed to sit down.

"You made me immortal?" I rasped.

Silas sat down beside me; I felt his lips press against my cheek. "The rebels bombed Cypress, love. Cypress has been evacuated and stands abandoned, its residents are now in Moros. You were caught in the flames, you and Jack. The two of you were so near death… you especially. Your skull had been split in half."

I looked at him alarmed but he held out a hand as if to physically stop the emotion that was about to burst from my lips.

"Jack is just fine. I made him immortal too. I made him immortal for solely you," Silas explained kindly. "We don't know what happened leading to the events, but you must've found Jack dead and in your own misery you jumped off of the building. Nero, myself, and Elish were there and we carried you two back to Perish. I was dispatched so they could use my own brain matter and they made my two stealth beauties immortal. The very first second generation to receive this gift. Another thing we shall be celebrating at your party."

This was all too much for me. I shook my head in awe before slowly wiping my hands down my face. Silas seemed to see I was feeling overwhelmed. He got up and I heard him call to Kinny to get me something to drink.

"This is really a lot to take in," I said when Silas came back holding some berry juice. I took a long drink of it but made a face from it being so sour, or perhaps my taste buds were oversensitive. "I don't know if I should be happy or horrified I'll never die…" I looked down at the glass. "I have a lot of issues. You know that."

"It's nothing we can't fix," Silas said. I could smell something mint and I realized he had a cup of tea in his hands. "I think now that your body is healed, and you have a boyfriend for companionship – we will be seeing improvements from you." Then he paused for a moment. "And that... you know now some of the quirks our lovely family has."

A lump formed in my throat at this. I had been out of it for so long that certain memories seemed distant and hazy, but I remembered enough the reason why I initially ran away in the first place.

"You know, love," Silas began. "I knew when you first came into our family, terrified, unstable, a veritable madman... that you would not be able to handle how our family functioned. You must understand that, yes?"

I nodded. I did understand that now.

"What you needed was stability, patience, and a belief that we were as normal and plutonic as we could be. I don't think it was a mistake, the mistake was that the rebels shot down my plane and I was gone for four months," Silas explained in the patience voice he used with me. "I would have slowly introduced you to the more transgressive aspects of this family when I felt you were ready, and when you started showing the tendencies towards them that all chimeras have."

"Instead I showed those same tendencies and fell into psychosis again," I mumbled.

Silas took a sip of his tea and nodded at me to drink. "All of the things you did, love. Killing Ludo, killing those men and women in Cypress, it's all a part of growing up. You hated Valen and his chimera group for raping arians but it is just who they are. You must understand, love." Silas smiled. "We're above the parasites. They are ours to do what we will. Yes, a moral person may not like it, and if you dislike it, don't do it. But we're royalty, Sanguine. We have all the power in the world and sometimes, especially a teenager trying out this power, may use it to oppress others."

I frowned, but the frown wasn't because of his words. It was because I had little to say in defence of the arians because I myself had done exactly what I had condemned the other chimeras for. I had murdered, tortured... I had even almost raped Jack. Yes, I remember that now. Though he had told me adamantly he was a willing participant.

My brow furrowed. Something was nagging me, a tickle inside of my inner ear. A small inclination that I had done much worse but I couldn't put my finger on what. It was lost in the haze of the events leading up to me becoming immortal.

"When you were in the greywastes, the greywasters mistreated you, hated you for being different, chased you from towns, and that man..."

Silas frowned as his voice trailed, but he then picked it back up again. "Here, Sanguine, your differences are not only celebrated within the family, they will draw out fear and respect from the parasites below us. Embrace it, you're better than them and for that you mustn't feel guilty. You are a prince, and one of your king's most treasured and beloved. It's time you embrace royalty, embrace that you're better than them." Silas caressed my cheek. "And don't feel cross when your brothers do the same. It's our nature as chimeras, lovely. And you're well past being stable enough to accept our families more transgressive natures, yes?"

I understood what he was saying, and though the guilt was still there over what I had done to the ones like Mouse and Julia, it wasn't as potent as it had been before. "But you won't ignore the fact I do have mental problems?" I asked. "The ones that aren't from being a chimera? I still need help with that, with the psychosis. You understand that I have issues still?"

Silas nodded. "I do, love. I do. Which is why I'm letting you be with Jack, so you can heal. But I don't think you will have any more issues."

"Really?" I asked.

"Yes, love. I think you falling in and out of psychosis due to stress or other triggers is a problem we'll no longer have to face." Silas rose and held out his hand for me to take it. I did and we both started walking down the hallway and into the living room. I saw Kinny ironing some clothes. I think they may be for me. "If you're still terrorized by the voices, or by Crow, you'll tell me right away, or if I'm out of Skyfall you'll tell Perish." Then he paused and gave me a serious look. "Only the two of us though, am I understood, Sanguine? If you see any of them you will tell only Perish or myself. We will fix you then."

"I understand, Master." The amount of relief I felt over his words overwhelmed my already taxed and fatigued mind. Silas was finally taking my problems seriously and seemed willing to help me sort through them.

Silas rested his tea cup down with a small clink and picked up the clothes Kinny had been ironing. I watched him walk over, and in the background Kinny took a load of laundry and disappeared out the double doors.

"You're so perfect," Silas murmured as he sat down on the microfiber couch beside me. Unable to resist touching me he started stroking my bare arm. This time though he made his touch warm and almost electric, like he had a field of static around him.

"I never thought I would be." I held up my arms again and still couldn't believe the flawless, alabaster skin that was now my own. Then I flushed a bit. "And inside too?" I knew I was scarred and ruined internally. I never really explored down there but I could feel it and occasionally it would bleed.

Silas nodded. "You're a virgin again in all respects." This notion jarred me, but also made me flush further. Because as Silas said this his hand travelled to my flat stomach, he traced my faint abs before trailing it down further.

What surprised me most of all about Silas's wandering touch was that I no longer felt the spasm of horror or tension when he or anyone else touched me when I wasn't in that manic state. I was completely lucid and yet... I didn't flinch away.

There was something different inside of me, something had changed inside of my head during my resurrection. I don't think I was afraid of intimacy anymore. I actually think I was no longer afraid of a lot of things.

What had happened inside of my brain? Had resurrecting really repaired some of the damage I knew I'd had? I didn't know but the prospect was fascinating and intriguing.

And showing that he could tell the difference too, Silas's hand didn't retract, nor did I see hesitation on his face. Instead I felt his heart skip, before he leaned in and gently pressed his lips against mine.

Feeling almost intoxicated over the lack of fear, I parted my lips and welcomed his, then I slipped my own hand to the small of his back and drew him close to me. He took my signal and I felt his weight on my body. I fell back on the couch and soon he was on top of me, our mouths open and our tongues greeting each other after what had been months and months of separation.

I had missed my king's lips, and though I longed for Jack's as well I was understanding how my wonderfully odd family functioned. To love my king as I loved him took nothing away from my feelings for Jack. I understood this, and I embraced it. There was no guilt inside of me as I felt his slender, firm body on top of mine but, then again, there never had been.

Though my body was full of warm pleasure, I felt a spasm when Silas pulled my black boxer briefs off of me. It wasn't nervousness or fear, just that jolt that anyone got when they realized something was about to go further.

Silas tossed my underwear onto the floor and gave me a coy grin. Playfully he twirled a finger through my trimmed pubic hair and walked two of his fingers up my trail of hair that led to my navel. "Should I be so bold to admit I am loving this relaxed side of you?" Silas said with a smug look. The corner of my mouth raised, I was equally enjoying this playful mood he was in. "I had no plans to be intimate with my beautiful creation and yet…" He leaned down and I let out a shocked groan as he pressed his tongue against the head of my dick, hardening quickly under his attention. "I find I am unable to help myself."

My mind was going wild over not only his advances, but the way my mind and body was reacting to it. I felt completely high with just adrenaline over not being afraid. I never realized it but the most potent drug I had ever had was feeling fearless. I had never felt fearless when I wasn't also deep into my own psychosis.

I shuddered as he put his mouth over my dick and started lavishing attention on the crown. The harmony of soft sucking and the multiplying breaths inside of my chest the only sounds around us. I separated my legs further for him and watched his head going up and down just slightly over my groin. It was blowing my mind in so many different ways, and the pleasure I was feeling over his mouth was unbelievable.

Silas removed his mouth with a suctioned pop and looked at me with that same smug smile. My now fully hard dick, without a single scar on it, standing erect with the defined head pink and glistening from Silas's mouth, firmly held in his hand like he was wielding a sword. "Is this your first blowjob? Or did my Jack get to you first?"

I shook my head. "He never did. This is my first… kinda like you were my first kiss too."

I knew this would make Silas happy and, sure enough, the smug smirk only broadened. He kissed the tip of my penis before his pink tongue poked out. He stiffened his tongue to a point and ran it up and down the slit before putting it back into his mouth. After several minutes of sucking he pulled it away and started stroking me with his hand.

"But you fucked him, yes?" Silas asked. My dick disappeared back into his mouth.

I closed my eyes as the pleasure intensified and nodded. "In the psychosis I did fuck him, it wasn't intimate at all though. Just that…

bloodlust, that need for release. It was after I killed Ludo, his body was only several feet away."

"Mm, I wish I could have been there to steal your first penetration of a man. Usually once my creations turn fifteen I take them for myself and let them take me. It is my right as your king to have your first time…" Silas said. "But I forgive you. I know chimera bloodlust, I just wish it was me this beautiful cock penetrated."

Cold air hit the head of my dick as he once again removed his mouth. Though after several moments of missing his touch I opened my eyes to see what he was doing. They widened when I saw that he had already taken his blue jeans off and was pulling a pair of matching black boxer briefs down his slender thighs.

"Let's fulfill your king's wish." Silas leaned down and kissed me. He tugged on my cock now throbbing with anticipation. "Sit up on the couch, love."

I never moved so quickly. I sat up on the couch, naked and full of tension and heat. Silas opened up a drawer in the coffee table and with a crack, he opened a bottle of lube and squeezed the bottle onto my cock. The oil immediately liquefied on the head from the heat. I rubbed it in as Silas prepared himself, and then the king climbed on top of me.

He grabbed my cock and I felt my head rest up against the tight opening, burning with heat and twitching from want. My mind reeled with desire as I saw Silas bite the corner of his lips with his teeth, and with his eyes locked with mine, I felt pressure on my cock, overwhelming, tight, pleasurable pressure. Then, with a gasp from his lips and a cry that drove me even wilder, he broke through and lowered himself onto me.

He was so beautiful; he had once been a normal person but he looked like a god in front of me. Wavy golden hair that shone without sunlight, a porcelain face that was narrow, yet full, and two large eyes that seemed to have stolen the green that was once so abundant in the world.

I wanted him, every inch of him. And not only that, I wanted him with Jack right beside me. I wanted me and my boyfriend to tag team this beautiful demigod, and make him make all sorts of noises.

I watched intently as Silas sunk my cock into him, all the way in until my testicles touched his backside. He closed those emerald eyes and leaned his forehead against mine, then, with a groan drawn from us in unison, he started moving himself up and down.

It felt amazing, and though it had felt equally amazing with Jack there was something different about doing it in a lucid state. I could feel his emotions more, I could feel the pleasure more. I was so in tune and in sync with his body it was like I was having sex for the first time all over again.

Though with this new body, and this new, repaired mind – perhaps I was.

"You're so perfect; your body is perfect, as you always should've been," Silas said through groans in rhythm with his movements. He lifted his forehead off of mine and put a hand on my shoulder. He leaned away from my body, his hips still rising up and down. I glanced down and felt a rush as I saw his cock standing erect, and below that thick and long dick I saw my own penetrating him; it turned me on so much I took Silas's shaft in my hand and started stroking it.

"And we have eternity together, love. Does that make you happy?" Silas asked. He looked down with me and we watched our connected bodies. No longer able to help myself my hips started to thrust.

"It does," I answered back. I pulled Silas close to me, and the king fell into my arms. I held him tight against my body and started thrusting into him. In response he groaned, an unhinged sound that drew me closer to my peak. I started to thrust inside of him faster. "I thought once I would be scared of being immortal, since my life was so horrible, but now…" I groaned. "I think I'm kind of excited."

Silas didn't answer; he only positioned himself over me so I had a better angle to thrust into him. But it wasn't enough, I needed more room, more space…

I shifted off of the couch, Silas still on my lap. The king gave me one confused look but he didn't try and scramble away from my touch. He trusted me enough to let me lift him up, temporarily disconnecting our bodies… and lay him on top of the marble coffee table.

Silas gasped as I laid him down, but I knew it was from the cold rock rather than the surprise. This coffee table was sturdy for a reason, surely he must've used it before.

I grinned and kissed his neck. Silas pulled his legs back and at his invitation I positioned myself and slowly penetrated him. My teeth clenched over the feeling. Oh, did I ever love this feeling. I closed my eyes, the power of being in control over King Silas's body and our intimacy intoxicating me. Embracing this control I had over him, I started thrusting my hips into his backside, further falling deep into this state as each thrust gifted me a sharp moan of pleasure from Silas.

This, this I liked. I liked being in control; I enjoyed this sort of sex. Being the bottom partner might take some getting used to but I could do this all day and all night to every one of my brothers. Oh, yes. I would like that.

I sucked on Silas's neck as I continued to pound him, the coffee table shaking back and forth. I even heard something drop onto the carpet but I didn't care. I continued my rhythm and I didn't slow down, Silas's sharp, sensual moaning gracing my eardrums and forever tightening those binds I knew were about to burst.

Though Silas beat me to it. His moans started to become closer together, and I could even feel his ass tightening and twitching as it grasped my cock like a constricted fist. I sped up my thrusts and found his lips. I kept pushing, even when the tightness started to become unbearable I kept at my speed. I remembered what it took to reach orgasm when I had been fucking Jack, I had to thrust through the tension and then I'd get my reward.

"Ah, fuck!" Silas suddenly cried, then he let out a loud, unhinged moan followed by another one. His body writhed underneath mine and his hands grabbed my back, not only that I could feel his hole start to spasm and tighten, gripping my cock hard and plunging me to my own peak.

I let out a cry as the tension reached its critical point, fireworks exploding all throughout my body, lighting my blood on fire and shooting the flames to every corner of my shaking frame. I pushed and pushed through each wave of the orgasm, every thrust I made becoming easier as my cum filled the king.

The orgasm was intense and, like the first one, the waves of pleasure kept coming, one after another like aftershocks after an earthquake.

When it was finally over I collapsed onto his body, sweaty and exhausted from the intense climax. I stayed there for several moments before I slowly pulled out of him and fell onto my knees in front of the coffee table.

Silas let out a long and satisfied breath before sitting up in front of me, cum dripping down his toned stomach, and stuck into his blond pubic hair. He looked at me, also sweaty and exhausted, and that beautiful smirk appeared on his face again. The king seemed to glow, there was an almost invisible aura around him; he radiated pleasant feelings and contentment. It drew me to him like a moth to a flickering flame.

"We're going to have ourselves a wonderful life," he said simply. He pressed his lips against my clammy forehead but soon found my lips again. We kissed passionately and then the king rose to his feet. "Come now, love. Let's shower and get ourselves a nice meal. My sweetness hasn't eaten anything proper in almost two months."

I smiled at him, feeling more content than I had felt in a very long time. I followed him into his bedroom, knowing I would follow this man wherever he wanted me to go.

CHAPTER 47

SILAS TUGGED ON THE COLLAR OF MY SHIRT AND smiled at me. "Your heart is racing, such a silly thing you are. You're nervous about seeing Jack, aren't you?"

I blushed and looked down at his hands. He was buttoning my red button-down and was holding a leather vest in his hand. I already had on black trousers and shining leather shoes. I looked quite handsome and black and red were my favourite colour combinations.

"Maybe a little," I admitted. "Enough to make me want to look nice for him."

Behind me Kinny ran a brush through my hair, even though he had been messing with my hair all afternoon now. The sengil had enjoyed primping me and styling me to his standards. I think he was enjoying that I was no longer hiding under the bed in my own filth. I had no more qualms about the sengil making me look nice, after all he and all the sengils were well-trained in chimera grooming.

"You look perfect," Silas said. He stepped back and nodded at me. "Perfection. I will be going to Kreig to visit Elish for a few days, see if he's done pouting yet. Feel free to summon Kinny if you two want a third partner."

The red already on my cheeks deepened, of course Silas enjoyed this. He had been teasing me all morning but I loved it. He loved this side of me he was seeing and I felt the same about his lighthearted attitude. It seemed to be a golden age in the chimera family right now.

"I hope you're going to tell him you're letting me date Jack," I said, because though I was smug that Elish was angry I was now immortal, I still respected the man. He was another immortal brother that I was going to be spending a long time with. Now wasn't the time to make eternal enemies. "That will make him feel better about me being immortal."

"Perhaps," Silas said. He handed me the vest to put on. "Elish will be fine. I know my golden boy more than he knows himself. It's cute when he gets insecure about his place in the family and with me. Sometimes it's fun to exploit it as well." As Silas said this he patted my cheek playfully. "But he has no need to worry, as you don't. You're my most favourite out of our second generation which makes you my fifth-in-command. Elish, Garrett, Nero, and you. Just think, lovely, if all four of us are dispatched or out of Skyfall you get to be king."

A devious grin crossed my face which Silas laughed at. He zipped up my vest and straightened it. "I shudder to think of what you would do with Skyfall, lovely. Okay, let's head out and see Jack. He's eager to show you your new apartment."

I grabbed Barry as I headed out the door. My satchel had to be thrown out because it was burnt and smelled like rot and smoke, but Barry had survived. Silas had even let Kinny wash him carefully and he smelled wonderful now. I could even see his cream paw pads which had been almost the same colour as his matted fur previously.

I hugged Barry to me. He was just a bear now, and if becoming immortal had really repaired my brain – I think he would always remain a bear.

I was okay with that. It was time for me to join this world, and this family. My world had suited me when I was still recovering mentally from being Jasper's prisoner, but I didn't need them anymore. It was sad, and I did feel an ache in my heart, but I was twenty now and an immortal chimera. It was time for me to say goodbye to them.

"What floor is it?" I asked.

"There are twenty-seven usable floors in this skyscraper. Mine is the twenty-seventh, Elish's the twenty-sixth, Garrett's is the twenty-fifth, Nero and Ceph the twenty-fourth. Naturally since my love has quickly risen up the ranks, you get the twenty-third floor. If you wish you can be assigned a sengil as well. We have two of them who will be of age soon, if Garrett behaves and is allowed to keep Kass he will have no need for a new one so they can be assigned to you and Jack and most likely Apollo and Artemis. You haven't met them, no?"

Kass? *My* Kass? I decided not to ask that question, I could ask Jack later. The prospect that he had become Garrett's sengil baffled me though.

"No, I haven't," I replied. "But Jack talked about them, they're intelligence chimeras right?"

Silas nodded. "That's right. Brilliant and well-behaved twins. Silvery-white hair, violet eyes, and handsome yet soft features. They are drawn from Elish's DNA and my own, with a bit of Perish's thrown in there for balance. Never had a single problem with those lovely boys. I will be making more from their strands in the future." He pinched my arm. "And you too, since you've turned out to be so strong. Would you like a little chimera brother like you?"

"Like from me?"

Silas nodded. "You turned out to be incredibly endurant. We will be using your DNA for future projects, Jack's as well. The wonderful thing about our chimera project is the more successful chimeras we raise the broader we can make the gene pool."

"What chimeras made up me?" I asked.

The elevator stopped and we slowly started walking down the hallway. It had clearly just been renovated; it was painted a dark grey with black trim and there were recessed lights above us with black borders around them.

"Nero of course." Silas smiled, though this surprised me. "Some of Garrett but Nero mostly, but you have a lot of engineered DNA in you. DNA that comes from none of our chimeras, it's strands that our science team created that gave you things like your sharp teeth and red eyes. Like I said eventually we won't need to manufacture the DNA as much. From now on if we wish to have chimeras with pointed teeth we can just isolate the gene inside of you or Jack and implant it in the embryo. It would lead to a higher success rate, it took us years to successfully create you and Jack."

He spoke in such a casual way it was like he was expecting me to understand what all of these things meant, but when he glanced over at me he laughed. "Sorry, love. I know it's confusing. Though you're as intelligent as they come you'll never be able to understand genetics, and scientific research like your intelligence or science brothers. Just know, it's fascinating and I would love to show you Kreig one day. Perish is working on an actual machine with a user-friendly interface to make chimeras. Where you can select everything from eye colour, penis size, height, intelligence, just from accessing a program!"

"The Chimera-Maker 5000," I smirked, and inside I beamed as Silas laughed again and playfully squeezed my bicep. He was in a great mood. I just loved it. When Silas was angry the air darkened around him, but when he was happy it was like the Fallocaust had never happened and the world was still greens and blues.

Silas knocked on the door though he didn't get past rapping his knuckles against the wood three times before it opened. I think Jack had been waiting by the door for us to arrive.

My boyfriend, looking better than ever, looked at me for a single moment before his large black eyes started to glisten. He tried his hardest to say something but all that came out was a whimper, then he threw his arms around me and squeezed me tight to him.

"I'm back," I said, not knowing what else to say to him.

He whimpered again. "I've known you would be waking up for almost two months now. I bathed you, exercised you, I slept beside you when Silas would let me… but for some reason I never thought I would hear your voice again," Jack said in a voice high with emotion. "I missed you, Sami."

I kissed his cheek and gently pulled him away from me. I tucked a strand of his stray silver hair behind his ears and smiled at him. "It's just Sanguine now, love. I think it's time for Sami to be laid to rest. I'm not him anymore."

There was an odd look that crossed Jack's face, it disappeared quickly but I saw it. It was an expression of sadness. Perhaps he was looking into my words too much. I never meant I was a different person now, I had always been Sanguine inside of my own head. I just wanted to put my past behind me and move on with my life, and that meant asking to just be called by my real name.

And in truth, Jack was one of the only people left who had called me Sami.

"Okay, Sanguine. Old habits die hard though," Jack said with a smile. Then he looked to King Silas. "Can I get you anything to eat or drink, Master? Or perhaps a cigarette or some powder?"

Silas walked ahead of us into the living room. "Some powder would be wonderful, Jack. I supposed since we no longer have to worry about Sanguine becoming addicted to opiates he's allowed to have some. Oh, what a beautiful apartment, lovely boy. Sanguine, come look at what your boyfriend did. He is certainly our decorator and artist in the family. You get that from me you know, the artistic part anyway. I used to draw and write books to excess in my younger years."

I took off my boots and looked around the living room as Jack and Silas walked towards two couches chatting happily with each other. The apartment was well-decorated and nice-looking to say the least. It was painted in the same dark greys as the hallway, with black trim on the walls and windows. There were deep red curtains too that covered the wall-to-wall picture windows that all of Alegria's apartments had, and many black shelves that held the most interesting sculptures and trinkets.

Also a lot of antique-looking things. There was a wooden cabinet with designs going up the sides and inside of it was full of DVDs and electronics, but also a black stone statue of a panther and a newer one that looked like a carracat. Beside it was a wood bookshelf full of books, the shelves inside of it black and white marble. My new place looked expensive.

"Look at that. Nero managed to recover you some marble for a coffee table? Perfect." I heard Silas comment. "Almost all of us have marble coffee tables, Sanguine. It doesn't scratch the surface when my chimeras decide to cut their drugs." I looked over and, sure enough, there was a coffee table with the same black and white marble, sitting on top of metal cast iron legs. Two black microfiber couches surrounded it and a recliner chair with a laptop tray behind, all of this centered around a large flat panel television with game systems tucked into a black entertainment center.

"This looks like it cost… a lot," I said in awe. I glanced over at the kitchen, partially closed off by a half-wall, and saw it was full of stainless steel appliances and the fridge even had a cold water tap like King Silas's had. The countertops were also marble and there was even a little counter island in the center. This place looked brand-new.

"It did!" Silas laughed. "But you're my fifth-in-command. Your apartment should speak of your status, my prince. Just wait until you see what I got you for your welcoming party, it will double as a birthday present. This apartment we're saying is a Skyday present to keep the jealousy down. Though Apollo and Artemis have never been the jealous type."

I smirked at this. "I can't wait to show Valen, fucking rub his nose in it. Felix and Rio too."

Jack's head jerked back to look at me; his expression noticeably changing. Silas's didn't though. The king sat down on the microfiber couch and picked up what looked like Jack's black card, the edges of it crusted with white powder.

"You didn't... ask him yet?" Jack asked submissively. He took my hand and brought me to the couch.

"Ask what?" I asked as we both sat down.

No one interrupted the king though as he leaned down and took in some powder into each nostril. He rubbed his nose and passed the sniffer, which looked like a cut up pink pixie stick, to me.

"He obviously doesn't remember, Jack. Though I suppose it would make his day." A devilish smirk graced Silas's face as I took the sniffer from him. He pushed the silver tray the powder had been sitting on towards me and encouraged me to do some. I had only done opium but I gathered it would be the same feeling. So I indulged myself and passed the pink straw to Jack in a way that reminded me of the blunt passing I used to do with Mouse and Julia. A life that seemed to have taken place on a distant planet.

"Valen is missing," Silas said casually. My eyes widened from surprise, and Silas seemed to drink this in. He loved watching people's reactions to news.

"He ran away from home while I was resurrecting but we had reports here or there of him, but since the rocket launcher attack on Cypress there hasn't been a single sighting. We're going to declare him dead soon. We're assuming he was hiding out in Cypress and got caught up in the missiles. So it looks like all of the chimeras I had been not overly happy with are now dead, what a wonderful coincidence," Silas said the last part in a rather singy voice.

"Valen is gone?" I repeated those words to myself. "Wow..." I watched as Jack plugged one nostril and inhaled a line of off-grey powder. "It seems like I woke up in a dream, in a perfect world. I'm immortal. Valen is gone. I get to live with my boyfriend, and I'm back on great terms with my king." Then I glanced up at the ceiling. "And Elish has buggered off too."

Silas laughed. "Hit him for me, Jack. He mustn't say such things!"

I grinned as Jack smacked me on the shoulder but he was smiling too. "I'll admit, everything is so much nicer now that certain chimeras are gone from the world. Felix is dead too, Sanguine. He had an accident on the islands. Rio was just a tag-a-long, he's working at Skytech right now and he never did anything overly wrong did he, Master?"

Silas shook his head before leaning back and putting his hands behind his head. He looked relaxed, content. "No, as you said he was no ringleader, or even a leader. He will not be made immortal but we do need his mind for Skytech's future goals. I will never make the mistake of producing so many chimeras at once. With each generation we will breed smarter and more obedient chimeras, and those who don't pass the test… will be killed. I feel no guilt over it anymore. I created my loves and I can kill them as I please."

Jack and I both nodded, and I know we were thinking the same thing. We were already immortal so if King Silas was going to become harder on the future generations of chimeras… well, he could go right ahead.

After some back-and-forths and a few more laughs Silas got up and gave us both hugs as he got ready to leave.

"You two be good. I won't be gone for long and I will be back in time for Sanguine's party. Garrett is planning it of course, and he is king until I return. Nero will be busy cleaning up the last remnants of the rebels, Sanguine, but I'm sure he will make time to see you. He missed you as well, and in a few months he and Ceph will be married too."

"Is there anything you would like us to do while you're gone, King Silas?" Jack asked, holding the door open for him.

"Keep him relaxed and content, that's what you must do, Jack," Silas said sternly. "Tell me if he goes into psychosis. Sanguine, if you start seeing any hallucinations you are to tell Perish immediately. Remember what we talked about before. This is an order from your king, am I understood?"

I nodded. With Elish gone the only other sciencey-smart chimera that was of proper age was Perish. I think Garrett was just intelligence. So I guess it would make sense that he would want to know if I started to slip again.

"Good." Silas gave me a kiss and then kissed Jack. "Have lots of sex and enjoy yourselves. If you feel the need you can kill whomever you wish but stay away from your remaining brothers. We wouldn't want to cull too many of them. Chimeras are a complete pain to raise. Goodbye, babies. Behave now."

"Goodbye, King Silas, have a nice trip," I said, and after Jack said goodbye as well the door closed and we were alone.

Jack almost knocked me off of my feet when he threw his arms around me once again. He held me tight in his grip to the point where I could feel my rib cage creaking inside of my chest. I didn't voice my displeasure though. Though I had missed Jack too, I had been lost in the white flames of resurrection and had only occasionally been conscious. Jack had been awake and waiting for me to wake up as well for almost two months.

So I squeezed him back and slowly rocked him back and forth when I started to hear the whimpering come back. From what I knew of him Jack rarely cried; he just seemed to edge the cusp of tears through whimpering and glistening eyes.

When Jack pulled away he framed my face with his hands and looked at me. I could see my reflection in those onyx gems, so full of love and relief. He stared at me, like he was searching my eyes for someone or something.

"You really are my Sanguine?" Jack whimpered. Then he nodded as if he was confirming it to himself. "You are, I see you are. I was just so worried – I was afraid that your brain would heal to the point where you weren't my baby anymore. But you are, you're my Sami."

I wanted to correct him again but out of everyone in my family he had got to know me on a personal level, more than even King Silas did. He got to know Sami before he even knew I was Sanguine, so perhaps I would let him call me it... sometimes.

"I am me, of course I am," I said with a shake of my head. I was amused he would be worried about something so stupid. "I've never felt better. I feel like a new man; I fucking am a new man, look at me." My red shirt was long sleeve so I pushed back the cuffs and showed him my arms. "Inside and out."

Jack nodded and gently touched my arms. "I know, Silas told me what they did to your skin and... inside of you. You were resurrecting for longer than I thought you would... you were kept in Perish's operating floor for quite a while." He frowned at this but he shook it off and walked to the kitchen. "I have lots of food... and I talked to Jiro. He's Apollo's boyfriend and also is in charge of what TV shows and movies are on our channels. He's playing your favourite movies on channel thirteen. He also says if we give him a list he can start working on our own special channel! Only the top chimeras have gotten that privilege."

I put Barry on the windowsill so he could look outside and started walking back towards the couch. Then I spotted someone unexpected napping on a tall black and grey cat tree.

"Jett!" I exclaimed. I picked up Jett who was hot from the sun beaming down on his black fur and held him in my arms. He looked around sleepily but after a pet on the head he settled in and started to purr. "You've been taking care of the little bastard? Thank you. He's huge now!"

Jack beamed and walked over to us. He scratched Jett behind the ears, and the cat squinted his eyes and raised his head. Jett was in cat heaven.

"He has such a great personality. I was thinking we could get another one to keep him company. I thought we would get Dave for a while but Elish took him too. The tell-tale sign that he's planning on being gone for a long time." Jack said. "It would have to be another kitten. Old tame cats are so hard to find, quite the opposite before the Fallocaust Silas says. Maybe we could get a specific breed? Though I do love black ones."

"That would be nice, let's do that," I said. I had missed a lot of Jett growing up when I had run away from the family, it would be wonderful to add another kitten to the apartment. "How long do you think Elish will be gone for?"

"Sometimes he's gone for months and months," Jack said, letting Jett go back onto his perch. "I think he's solely working on cloning right now." Jack shrugged at this and I followed him back into the kitchen. "There is this secret project they call Chimera X that Perish and Elish take turns trying to figure out. A side project when the family isn't creating new chimeras. Silas never tells us much about it, it's really personal. But I'm guessing if Elish succeeds he would get into Silas's good books and well…"

"Elish is in love with Silas so that's what he wants," I mumbled. I grabbed a plate of white cookies that were half-covered in tin foil and took a bite out of one. "I don't know why Elish doesn't go out and say he wants to be partners with Silas."

Jack laughed at this, hard. I gave him a quizzical look as my boyfriend started taking the lids off of various containers full of delicious-looking food.

"Elish admit he has feelings for someone? Never. I don't think it's physically possible for Elish to admit he loves someone, even King Silas. I don't even know if he should… Silas has never had a boyfriend before, he's always just had us… every one of us are kind of his boyfriend in a way. I mean he treats us all like boyfriends," Jack said. He got a knife and started cutting out pieces of lasagna, my mouth started to water at this.

"That's true," I replied, "but you would think Silas would eventually want someone just for him, right?" I shifted. "I thought it was going to be me for a while. I think Elish did too which is why he hated me so much. He even told me Silas would eventually destroy me when he caught Silas cuddling up to me in bed." I paused. "I guess he was right."

Jack looked up, I saw him frown. "Elish thought Silas was going to choose you?"

I nodded. "I was flattered. I like being special to him. I really love our king. I think I understand him differently than the others and he talks to me on a different level than the others too. Maybe that's why Elish felt so threatened."

"Huh," Jack sniffed, before he roughly stabbed the lasagna with the knife, a little harder than necessary. "Interesting."

All I could do was watch as Jack mangled the poor pan of lasagna. He roughly sliced it down the middle, filling the kitchen with the *tink tink tink* sound of the knife tip hitting the metal pan.

"Are you… okay?" I asked slowly. "Silas and I just have a special bond that's all. He really did a lot for me when I first came here. And you should be happy we've patched things up. It'll make our lives easier if the king is happy with us, right?"

"I'm fine," Jack said crisply. "And yes, you're right, it will."

One of my eyebrows raised. I had watched enough romance movies to know that when someone says they're fine, it means you're about to get your head bitten off.

Then I thought of it further and realized I had seen this reaction before, pretty much every single one of the chimeras got jealous when they saw how patient and kind King Silas had been towards me. It took me seeing how King Silas usually was to understand why it ruffled their feathers so much. Silas and I had a close bond though, maybe I was able to nurture that bond between us because I didn't have any pre-conceived concepts of him. He had treated me well when I was at my worst, scared, terrorized, and too afraid to even come out from under the bed, and we had forged a tight bond between us. One that still continued to this day.

And to my surprise I found a spark of annoyance that Jack was going to be yet another chimera to be jealous and angry over my bond with the king. He was my boyfriend now, and he and the entire family were constantly telling me how our love for the king was different than our love for our partners.

I let out an irritated sigh. "Maybe if all of you didn't walk around Silas like you're walking on egg shells and treat him like a person you guys would get along better with him."

Jack's lips disappeared into his mouth. I took a step back since he was still holding the knife in his hand.

"You don't need to be all jealous and weird over how nice he treats me," I said annoyed. "You're just like Elish."

And slam went the knife, down on the marble counter with a loud clack.

"I'm not jealous that Silas treats you nicely," Jack snapped, his black eyes a blaze and his body tensed. "I'm jealous because you… I'm jealous of Silas, okay?" He turned away from me slammed one of the plates of food into the microwave, the kitchen filling with the sounds of crashing plates. I stood there, surprised as he flung the door shut and started pushing buttons.

Then his shoulders slumped. "You talk about him and your eyes brighten, your heartbeat picks up…" Jack's hand dropped from the buttons as the microwave turned on. "I'm just feeling insecure because… I feel like I'm your runner-up prize. Your spare because… because Silas doesn't want you as his partner."

I smiled and shook my head, though his back was to me. I walked up behind him and put my arms around him and squeezed his back to my stomach. "You're so stupid," I said with a smile. "Are you serious? I just woke up a few days ago, I've only seen you for an hour, and you're already feeling insecure and jealous?"

"I can tell you love him," Jack said quietly. "And it really hit me when you commented that Elish could tell as well. It's obvious to the entire family that you two have a strong connection that none of us do. And though they're all jealous of you – I'm jealous of Silas. I want that with you. I want you to look at me like I saw you look at him earlier."

I kissed his neck, and heard a small sigh escape his lips. "Well, I won't start off our relationship by bullshitting you, Jack." When Jack tried to pull away I only pulled him closer. "Do you want me to be honest or do you want me to just tell you what you want to hear?"

Another sigh before, he nodded. "Okay… go ahead."

"Silas was with me constantly when I first came here. And yeah, he was patient, caring, loving, and attentive. He helped me with homework and defended me against Elish. Of course I love him for that. He was the first man to show me some genuine compassion. I didn't know he didn't do that for you guys. So I would be lying if I said I wasn't welded to that man. I love him because he's Silas, not because he's some scary master-king." Then I kissed him again. "But you said yourself, he isn't looking for a partner and he has given me permission to date you, and I want you." Another kiss on his neck, I started to feel him relax. "You're my boyfriend and he's my master, and the same goes for you too." I nipped the area I had kissed and started stroking his stomach. "You can't expect my feelings for you to develop that quickly, we just started dating and for most of our relationship I was in psychosis. I know you want things to move fast, with the *I love yous* and all of that but… come on, Jack-love, it'll take time. We're pretty much starting our life together today."

Jack was silent until eventually the microwave beeped. He pushed the microwave door open and I withdrew my hands, then smiled as he turned around. Though he was frowning at me.

"You're right…" he said, and let out a long sad sigh. "I guess I just want you to love me as much as I love you. But I know that's unreasonable, you've been mentally sick for most of the time I've known you, and I feel protective when it comes to you. I guess I'm just pathetic and I need reassurance. Maybe I'm still scared being immortal might've changed you. I'm scared that now that you're not the Sami I stayed with down in that abandoned building's basement, your feelings towards me might change. You know… since you don't need me anymore."

The lines on Jack's forehead deepened as he frowned. I clucked and shook my head. I was so amused and enchanted with this new needy side of my boyfriend. I found it endearing though. I loved seeing his shortcomings and his need for reassurance. I didn't mind giving it to him, he had done the same for me many times. "You have such stupid worries," I said playfully. "I'm still Sami. I'm just better than anything Sami could've ever been. Unless you want me to be sad and miserable so you can take care of me, we'll be just fine."

He smiled at this and nodded. "I know… I just needed to hear it." He took the hot plate of food out with his bare hands and put it on the kitchen island. "It's a lot of emotions for one day, I know I'm acting like a teenage girl with all these worries."

"Kinda," I remarked. I got a scathing look for that, he tossed me an oven mitt and I used it to carry the hot plate into the dining room.

"Just promise me... I'll always be your number one, right?" Jack asked behind me. "I'm... I'm more important that Silas? I mean... I know he's our master but...but... you know what I mean."

I did know what he meant. Though I loved Silas and I would do anything for my king. My boyfriend was my boyfriend; he was my partner and the man I would wake up to every morning.

"I do, and you will be. Don't worry," I said smiling. "You'll always have my heart."

"Did you get the chicken nuggets?" I hissed as Jack sat down with a paper bag full of food. I looked over my shoulder and scanned the busy restaurant around us. We were in a converted fast-food restaurant, a chain made by Dek'ko called VanCouvers. It served hamburgers, fries, and all the food you would expect in the pre-Fallocaust fast food restaurants and it tasted great too.

"I did," Jack said with a giggle. He scanned the occupied red metal chairs most of them situated around tan tables and sat down beside me. He immediately grabbed a plastic container from the aromatic bag and opened it up. The restaurant was full of the low murmurs of conversations, occasionally interrupted by the beeping machines that made the salty yet delicious food. It seemed that everyone was preoccupied.

Immediately my mouth salivated over the salty smell of meat. I popped one in my mouth but as the hot food burned my tongue I spat it back out and started to blow on it. Playing hot potato with the chunk of food to keep the oil from singeing my fingers.

Jack grabbed a nugget too and bit it in half. He picked out a small piece of breaded meat from his mouth and reached for my jacket.

"Blow on it first," I said under my breath.

"I made my touch cold, it's already cooled down. Come on, I want to see!" Jack kept giggling like a kid, it was adorable. "*Pss, pss!* Are you hungry?"

A little pink nose poked out of my jacket, and her small nostrils flexed as she smelled the nugget. Jack *aww'd* as the little tabby female's face started moving towards the piece of nugget, her green eyes vivid and staring intently at the food.

Then another nose, this one grey, quickly followed by a solid grey face with a single wisp of white on his muzzle. Yes, we got two. We couldn't help ourselves, there were only two kittens left and we both agreed without much resistance that we couldn't let one of them stay behind all alone. They would've been lonely!

I laughed and felt my heart fill as Jack let out a squeal. He looked around the busy restaurant again before breaking off another piece of nugget for them. No one had noticed the kittens yet but we had a few looks from people who either recognized Jack, or noticed my red eyes. I wasn't sure which.

We got our food to go, and were waiting for a car to pick us up and take us back to Alegria. We had decided to walk to the pet store on our own since it was such a beautiful spring day and I wanted to see my crows, but, true to our personalities, we didn't think it through that we might not want to walk the entire six blocks back home with kittens in tow. Especially since the Skyland cars would freak them out.

"They're purring!" I said gleefully. I scratched the little grey one on the head with one finger but he was more interested in the food than his new owner. "Their personalities are wonderful." I tried to discourage the kittens from coming out of my jacket by putting them closer to the food, they had been sleeping and we probably should've let them continue to sleep, but we just had to look at them.

"Excuse me…"

Jack and I both looked up to see a lady with brown skin standing over us. She had a fake smile on her face and a rolled up paper in one of her hands. She was dressed in a blue skirt and a red top, and was obviously an elite from not only her clothing but the fancy leather purse she was carrying.

"What?" Jack said. He pushed on the tabby girl's head until she ducked back inside my jacket and I started zipping my jacket closed.

"I was wondering… when King Silas was going to make the official announcement over… our new prince," the lady said in a cheerful voice. I didn't like it though, it seemed fake, but that being said everyone gave us fake smiles, mostly because they were scared of us.

Jack grabbed our paper bag of food and glanced towards the windows, most likely looking to see if our ride was there.

"What new prince?" Jack's eyes narrowed.

The lady looked over at me, still keeping the plastic smile. "Well, there has been quite a few articles written about a Sanguine Dekker. And several photos too, and as our royal family must know the UFM has been writing about it as well…"

Jack got up and grabbed my arm, by now half the restaurant was watching this exchange, and I could see out of the corner of my eye several people quickly leaving the restaurant. Probably afraid that shit was about to go down.

"And how would you know what the Underground Free Media has been reporting?" Jack asked coolly. He extended his arm and twitched his hand, requesting the rolled up paper that the lady was holding. The lady handed it over without hesitation, though Jack's words made her heartbeat rise.

"It's rather easy to get…" she said hastily, her red lips moved to the side of her mouth. "My apologies. We are all rather excited to meet the newest members of the family. King Silas is usually eager to reveal new chimeras to his subjects."

"Indeed…" Jack mumbled. He glanced down at the paper and his brow furrowed. "Silas will release the information when he sees fit. If you value your life I would steer away from the lies that the UFM spreads. Especially since their sympathies regarding Imperial Commander Nero invading Irontowers are an obvious window into their bias reporting. The UFM is nothing but anti-chimera propaganda by a few pathetic and unappreciative fools who apparently see nothing wrong with pimping out children. Remember that King Silas saved your ancestors from the wars and gave you shelter from the sestic radiation."

The lady bowed her head. "I meant no disrespect, Prince Jack. I only bring it up as an encouragement to clear up any misconceptions the UFM may be reporting. You and Prince Sanguine have a wonderful day. And congratulations on the new little kittens. They're lucky beyond words."

Jack, still with his hand on my arm, directed me outside.

"She had a video camera in her purse," Jack mumbled as the warm sun hit our faces. He glanced behind him and took me to an awning that was shading the front of an electronics store. "Or else I would've wiped that smile off of her face." Jack pulled me into an alleyway before bringing out his remote phone. He put it to his ear, his eyes still darting around, mine were too. Why would she be recording us?

"Most likely she's a reporter," Jack said under his breath when I asked him that very question, "or she's working for the UFM, either way Ellis needs to know. And I'm going to get her to drop us off a copy of this month's UFM newspaper just so we can see what they're saying about you. It's the start of a new month now, I think a new copy might be out already or out soon."

I was quiet as he spoke on the phone, my arms around my stomach to hold the kittens up, but they were being still. I peeked down my jacket and saw that they were falling asleep all intertwined into each other.

Then my attention was diverted to the sound of a car. Sure enough, a black car with tinted windows pulled up, making my crows hop around and several of them take flight. I tapped Jack's shoulder and we both got inside, Jack still speaking to our sister on the remote phone.

"Alegria," I told the driver. I was eager to get the kittens home but I was more eager to see what Ellis had to say about this nosey reporter. Why would she be recording us? Perhaps it wasn't common knowledge that chimeras could hear the humming whine of electronics if we focused our hearing, or maybe she thought the noise of the restaurant would block it out.

He was on the telephone for the entire drive. Giving Ellis a detailed description of the brown-skinned woman including her outfit, and a play-by-play of her questions and enquiries. By the time he put the remote phone down we were walking down our grey hallway towards the double doors leading to our new apartment.

"Ellis says she's not a rebel; she thinks she's just a nosey reporter for the bulletin wanting a bonus on getting some stills of you," Jack said finally. I opened the doors and walked in, still cupping the warm and fuzzy little bodies napping inside of my jacket. "But Ellis has dispatched thiens to bring her into the precinct for questioning either way. But with Nero destroying the rebels while you were resurrecting, and the fallout from that, she's calling King Silas right now to see if he wants to allow her to run the story. Jack and Sanguine adopting fuzzy kittens would actually make a wonderful story right now," my boyfriend explained. "If we can be an adorable new couple and get media attention for it, it might be beneficial to the family and it's not like we care, right?"

I shrugged as I sat down on the couch with the kittens. "Whatever is best for the family, I guess. Bring the paper over I want to look at it though. Is Ellis sending over a UFM newspaper?"

Jack nodded. "She's sending someone over with a paper right now. Just don't get mad when you read it, they can get quite nasty."

My stomach started to move so I unzipped my black nylon jacket. I slipped down so I was slouched on my back and revealed the two little balls of fluff on my stomach.

Jack coo'd at the kittens as he sat down beside me. To my joy he laid on his side and nestled into my arms as we watched the kittens look around with half-asleep eyes. They seemed happy on my stomach, the two of them snuggled up next to each other.

I put my arm around Jack and watched as he brought up a folded newspaper, the one that the reporter lady had been carrying with her.

Jack chuckled and pointed to an article at the bottom left-hand corner, right underneath the main article which was something that required a huge picture of Garrett and another business man in front of an impressive-looking building.

"*Mystery Prince Sanguine spotted with Prince Jack outside of Skytech Pharmacy, fuelling speculations of a secret relationship.*" Jack read with a smile. He kissed my cheek and nuzzled my neck with his nose. "Those cameras are everywhere, that was only three days ago that we made that pharmacy trip."

Indeed it was, my first time being outside since I resurrected. I had been immortal for an entire week now. "Like you said, at least it's positive stuff. Anything bad about us in there?"

Jack shook his head and started turning the pages. "No, we control this newspaper, or well, the men and women in charge of it are under our control. A lot of this is just what's new in Skyfall or who's to be sent to Stadium, boring economy stuff, business stuff, things that only Elish and Garrett would find interesting. Plus they've been keeping everyone updated with what happened after Cypress was bombed."

I was quiet for a moment, and though he couldn't tell I was wondering if I should give a voice to what was on my mind. I didn't know if I wanted to go there but... perhaps it was time to ask.

"What did happen after Cypress was bombed?" I asked him. "I don't remember anything..."

Jack laid his head on my shoulder. "What's the last thing you remember?" He put a hand up my shirt but it wasn't to start something; that was clear when he wiggled his fingers underneath the fabric, making the female tabby rear up and pounce on my chest.

"Us being inside the basement... I remember being upset because Barry and the kids were starting to torment me again," I said. It was hard to remember that day, not only because it was fuzzy but it was hard to remember how sick I was in the head. I was in absolute mental turmoil and thinking about it brought a cold chill up my spine. I never wanted to go back to being that person.

Jack looked relieved at this which made me suspicious. "Why?" I asked slowly, flinching as the grey kitten sunk his sharp little claws into my neck. I tried to blow hair on his face but he had suddenly become enchanted with my almost chin length hair. "What do you remember?"

"That's about it…" Jack said in a tone that made me skeptical. "That and a lot of flames… *a lo*t of flames." He frowned and snuggled himself even more into me. "We both almost died. I don't know what I would do without you. My life seems so boring before you came. Isn't everything so perfect now, at least? I never want it to change. I just want us to be happy forever."

"Me too… I could use a mental break," I said. "I can't believe the hallucinations and the voices are gone. I thought Crow and Barry were too much a part of me to ever disappear for good. It seems… too good to be true, you know?"

We both watched as the grey kitten got brave and jumped up off of my stomach. His sister followed him and soon they were sniffing around the coffee table exploring their new home.

Jack, with his hand still up my shirt, stroked my stomach gently. "It does, but it is true. Your brain healed and now you can just be Sanguine. We can find out everything about Sanguine together." He kissed me on the cheek before turning my lips towards his. We both kissed, long and drawn-out until our lips parted. When he broke away Jack brushed a hand over my nipple and slowly started to rub it. "I can paint, and you can try painting too, or learn to play an instrument, or maybe learn to cook…" He stroked my pec with the ball of his finger until it started to become hard. "There's a lot of things you can learn… a lot of things I can teach you."

The corner of my mouth rose in a half-smile. "Don't get all dirty on me now, boyfriend – the kittens are watching."

Jack burst out laughing, his ears going red. I let out a yelp as he pinched my nipple as punishment for breaking the seductive mood he had been trying so hard to cultivate. I grinned at him before drawing him in for another kiss. I really was starting to fall for this boy of mine.

Then a loud knock on the door. Jack and I both scrambled to our feet.

"It'll be nice when we can get a sengil to answer the door for us," I commented, walking across the plush grey carpet towards the door to the outside hallway. "Just think of how easier life will be."

I opened the door fully expecting it to be a sengil or a thien with the UFM, only to see a flash of black before I was snapped up and constricted in a tight almost bone-breaking embrace, like a deer who just got attacked by an anaconda.

It took me a moment before I recognized those burly arms. I snorted a laugh as Nero spun me around with a gruff bellow, the world around me becoming a dizzy blur. I always forgot how much I missed having Nero around until he barrelled himself back into my life.

"My immortal boy!" Nero exclaimed. He dropped me but as soon as he saw my grinning face he took me into his arms again and crushed me against him. "My fucking immortal little bitch! Oh, fuck me, Sangy. It's been a long fucking two months but I don't give a shit… look at you!" Nero grabbed my nylon jacket and literally pulled it off of me, a black t-shirt on underneath. He then snatched my arms and shook them before yanking my shirt up so he could see my stomach. Then he kept raising my shirt until I gave up and took it off.

"Fuck, just new… fucking new, every inch of you. Fuck me, I can't believe it." He shook his head before clapping me hard on the back and pushing me to his side. I looked towards Jack in a half-serious attempt to garner some help from him but he was too busy beaming at the two of us.

"I'm so happy you two are immortal. I just hope he does my Cephy next. If he makes Ceph immortal my entire life will be perfect, fucking perfect." Nero let out a loud sigh before sticking his tongue out of the corner of his mouth. Then he reached down and started trying to grab the front of my jeans. My reflexes had me quickly jumping back though with a laugh.

"Come on, bitch! You gotta show me the goods! It's no fair I only get to see your junk when it was all skinned and horrific. Jacky-whacks, you break in this beauty yet?" Nero said as I continued to hop away from his busy hand.

Jack blushed. "No, not since he's been immortal."

"That's right," Nero said with a nod. "You fucked him after you diced up Ludo, right? How was your first cum? Pretty nice, eh?"

"F-first cum?" I groaned as Jack said this in a stammering shocked voice. "You… Sanguine?! What's he saying?"

"Watch…" Nero whispered to Jack. "Watch how red his ears get."

I sat down on the couch and put a throw pillow over my face. "I hate the both of you."

"He never... you never?" Jack stuttered, still not believing what Nero was implying. "Really?"

"When you hate your body, and your body belongs to someone else... you don't really want to explore it too much, Jack. On the contrary, you want to cut it, abuse it, and feel as much pain as you can because you hate yourself inside and out," I said in a low tone. "Can we just not humiliate me with it?"

An awkward silence fell all around me. I knew I had brought their giggle-fest to a dark place but the reality was what it was. My body had belonged to Jasper and I had hated that very body. I had the scars to prove it.

I felt weight on both ends of me and Nero's burly arms reach around me. "Sorry, peaches. I got caught up. I'm just hyper to see you again, you know I love you bunches. I'm sorry I brought up that shit."

I sighed and pulled the pillow away. I gave Nero a half-smile. "It's alright, I understand. It's good that you're here. We just had something interesting happen at the VanCouver's a few blocks away."

To my surprise Nero reached into his jacket and pulled out what looked like the bulletin but it was printed on regular paper. It was only two pieces of paper with print on both sides and it was held together by a single staple.

"Ellis sent me over since this is pretty sensitive information. I wasn't doing anything and Ceph is taking care of the rebel shit. I wanted to see you anyway." Nero handed me the paper and I felt Jack shift closer to me. "They're pissed... and they have every right to be pissed. We invaded their home and bombed quite a few buildings. Unfortunately a lot of them escaped into the sewers below but we have no fucking clue where they went. We think they went underground or are hiding in one of the pre-Fallocaust barricade buildings were we wouldn't see their lights and shit," Nero explained. "We found ammo, weapons, a couple greywasters they were keeping prisoner for food and sexcapades, but not nearly enough to justify their huge presence over the past several years. We're picking apart Irontowers and the surrounding location but we're sure they have another base we don't know about."

"We're hoping that this means they've disbanded," Jack said, then when Nero snorted he added. "Nero doesn't think so, neither does King Silas but who knows? Perish is planning on releasing some of his new radanimals into Irontowers as well. We have young carracats in need of new homes and urson and deacons, plus a whole island full of big deer, biigo, long horses, and wild bosen for them to eat."

Nero nodded. I scanned over the UFM article he had in his hand and immediately felt angry at some of the articles I was seeing. Everything from claiming Silas was the father of Ellis's son Knight (ew), Silas purposely eliminating the straight population and skewing the number of female births (which was also bullshit, that was happening in the greywastes too where it was pretty much lawless and untouched by the monarchy), to Silas poisoning the Morosians and Cypressians and even – my lips pursed – an article claiming Silas was the one keeping child sex slaves. Retribution for my idea so many months ago.

"That topic gets written about regularly," Nero said when he noticed the look on my face. "No one believes it, not after those staged photos. Those kids had a ball doing it. We even let Juni keep the whip we planted near them."

"I still don't like it…" I mumbled folding up the UFM and handing it to Jack. I didn't want to read any more of that garbage. "If we have an insider on the UFM why don't we just crush it once and for all?"

"Actually Silas is starting to agree with you," Nero said. "He used to be adamant about not controlling the media too much because of what happened before the Fallocaust. Apparently that was when things really started going to shit. But he's starting to lean more towards your opinion recently. With those buildings in Cypress being bombed and the amount of money that's going to cost the crown, plus this long drawn-out battle with the rebels and needing public opinion – I think Silas is going to snap soon and start going dictator again."

"Dictator?" I asked, and Nero nodded.

"When we were teenagers we had a huge problem with rebels and uprisings. Silas had been trying to rule with the people in mind, giving them what they wanted, caring and shit. Then one day he was just done and he went fucking iron fist on Skyfall. Every rebel was killed, the up risers were killed, half of the men Silas had running Skyfall were killed. It got easier once the first gen was old enough to take some of the burden off of his shoulders and since then, with our help, Silas has relaxed a bit. But with his stress over the second generation, you, plus the rebels, I wouldn't be surprised if he snaps again. He kinda goes crazy every few decades and I was hoping we could avoid this decade's snap. Doubt it now though, but maybe with you and Jack okay, the rebels taken care of for now, Valen assumed dead and Ludo and Felix dead – he'll relax a bit more."

"He seemed okay; he seemed really happy when I saw him," I said. I was surprised at Nero's words, but I guess I only knew Silas as Silas, not so much the king of Skyfall and the greywastes. I knew he had to be a different person as soon as he left Alegria.

"Silas is about a billion people in one, peachy," Nero said. He leaned down and scooped up the grey kitten and sat him down on his lap facing him. Then he started making his paws swing around like he was dancing. "He might make sweet sweet love to you, then he leaves Alegria and tortures informants for hours, poking out eyes, ripping off fingernails and raping their grown sons in front of them. Then he'll come back to have a Transformers tea party with Drake. He's kinda nuts like that, Silas isn't just one person."

"No, he's one person, he's just complex," I said in his defence. "He's the oldest man in the world, of course he's going to be a bit… more extreme in some parts."

Nero chuckled at this; he continued to make the kitten's paws wave around, all by gently controlling the kitten's paws via its underarms with his fingers. The kitten was perplexed but he wasn't making a move to get off of Nero's lap. "Yep, totally see why Elish hates you and Jack's heart is racing right now. So did Silas sink his little claws into you? Have you bounced around with just Jack or did Silas break in that brand-spanking new backside?"

I turned my hearing and, sure enough, Jack's heart was a motor. I let out a long sigh at Nero's wonderful timing. This was the worst possible time for me to tell Nero that Silas and I had indeed had sex, not too long after I had woken up – and I had been the one on top.

Jack wasn't going to like this.

"Yeah… Silas and I have… already slept together, during the two days in between when I woke up and when I moved down here," I said slowly.

"And how did you like it?" Nero said eagerly. "Was he gentle? I would've been. Sucks though since you promised me I'd get to top you first."

The speed of Jack's heart picked up. I was glad he didn't have the lasagna knife in his hand. I decided to try and stem the flow of hurt on Jack's end but I wasn't sure if this news would make things worse or better. "I was on top," I said. "I haven't... taken it, yet." Jack and I hadn't even gone past making out since I moved in here, though we were sleeping in the same bed.

Nero whistled. I looked over at Jack to give him a submissive smile and saw that my boyfriend's eyes were fixed forward. He had picked up the female kitten and was petting her so hard her eyes kept stretching back to the whites. I took the kitten away from him.

"So I still have a shot, huh?" Nero grinned. "But I know Mr. About-to-fucking-kill over there won't let me."

Jack's eyes seemed to snap out of their trance, he looked at Nero and shook his head. "I'm sorry... Nero can I get you something to drink? We have Dilaudid powder too." Jack got up quickly and started walking towards the kitchen.

"Sure, pup," Nero said. He looked amused by Jack's reaction and I knew my brother enough to know he would show no mercy. "Root beer and I'll indulge in some dilly powder. I've been working around the clock, I'll hang with you two for a few hours." Nero scratched my head affectionately. "I missed my little ankle-biter."

CHAPTER 48

THE NEXT FIVE DAYS PASSED BY QUICKLY AND NOT once did I leave the apartment for anything. I just hung out with my boyfriend, watched television, tried out some of our new video games, and watched the new kittens prance around and play with their big brother.

Though Jett had been alarmed at the little fuzz balls invading his territory as soon as he realized he could play with them they became best friends. Luckily Jett was just over a year old so he still was playful and not as set in his ways as older cats seemed to be. We had even caught all three of them napping just yesterday.

Jett ran past me as I used the lint roller over my black leather vest, behind him Lydia the tabby female followed with her little tail straight up in the air. Yes, I named the female kitten after my adoptive mother, there wasn't any female names I could think of and Jack had wanted to name her Jenny which I thought wasn't a suitable name for a cat. We just called her Lydi though.

The male we had been calling Mouse, an homage to my friend in Cypress that I had killed in my psychosis. I thought it would also fit since, well, he was a cat and that added a bit of humour to it. Plus he was grey, so Mouse fit.

Jack appeared behind me with a coy smile. I narrowed my eyes suspiciously at him when I noticed he was holding a small black gift box in his hand.

"I thought you would look cute in this." Jack handed me the box and took the lint roller from me. He was dressed in a silver vest with real sterling silver buttons, underneath was a black silk shirt, then black dress pants and shoes polished to shining. I was dressed in the same outfit but with my leather vest and a black silk shirt with wine-red cuffs. We could fit into each other's clothes, though I could use an extra inch on the pants, but it was good enough for us to get away with it. One of the big pluses of having a chimera brother as a boyfriend.

I opened the top off of the box and grinned. Inside was a red bowtie. I had never worn a bowtie before.

"Thank you, sweet heart, I think I'll look nice in it," I said.

Jack took the bow out and started tying it to my neck. I glanced at myself into the mirror as he tied it and nodded to myself. I did look rather dapper now. I was going to make a great first impression to the chimeras I hadn't formerly met yet.

"You look so handsome," Jack gushed. He took my hand and we started heading out the door. The floor we were going to was number eleven. I had never been to this floor in Alegria but apparently it was just a big room with several private rooms off to the side. It was specifically for our parties and get-togethers. We had family dinners every Sunday apparently and I guessed that since tonight was my introduction to the family Jack and I would be attending them now.

"You do too," I said back squeezing his hand. He still had his obsessive handholding issue, but like him cuddling me to death in bed and always needing to have me in his line of sight, I was getting used to it.

My insides were churning with excitement over this party. I wasn't nervous even though I knew there was going to be a lot of people there. My social anxiety had dissipated over the last year and now I didn't even get nervous in large crowds. One by one my quirks and hang-ups had been eliminated, and though I should be modest about it, in truth – I was fucking proud of myself.

The elevator opened to the sounds of faint rock music and light conversation. Jack and I walked, hand-in-hand, down a decorated hallway, complete with painted pictures and statues and a persian rug on the floor and walked towards the open doors.

We walked in and I smiled at the scene. About twenty or so chimeras and a handful of sengils were all mingling around round tables draped with white tablecloths. The lighting was dim and welcoming and the aroma of food as intoxicating as the liquor I could see being served by a sengil. The atmosphere was pleasant but electric, with the rock music I had heard earlier coming from a sound system that was placed beside two large tables of covered food. It looked like this room was supposed to be much bigger though, there were two black curtains covering the front and off to the left. The one at the front was partially open though, I saw what looked like a makeshift stage hiding behind it.

"Not here! No!"

I blinked as Garrett came out of nowhere and grabbed my arm, quickly he pulled me into a dark corner of the party room and then through a door I hadn't even seen. I blinked from confusion, Jack trailing behind me.

"Didn't you get my message? You can't just waltz in, how is that an entrance?" Garrett chastised as we walked through a room that was full of spare chairs, tables, and lots of boxes. "You need to stay in here, silly boy. Silas is going to call on you as soon as he speaks with our brothers, then you're going to strut out there and show our family just who this new favourite is."

"We didn't get a memo…" Jack said defensively, he still had my hand even though Garrett's tugging of my arm was making it hard for him to keep hold.

Garrett's brow knitted. "I was sure I had called… well, I may have been drunk and imagined it. No worries, no one saw you." Garrett pulled me through another set of doors and from this room I could see a portion of the stage. "You can watch Silas speak from here. Jack, come with me. Sanguine, it won't be long Silas just gave me his five minute warning. Stay, and don't let anyone see you! I want this to be perfect."

I watched helplessly as Jack was dragged away, my boyfriend giving me a look that made it obvious that he wanted to stay. Though when he disappeared and I was left alone in this storage room I remembered that Garrett had been the one to plan my party. He had probably obsessed over every detail and he seemed like the type to go into crazy-mode if things didn't go as planned.

King Silas ruled the world, Garrett ruled party planning.

I chuckled at my own joke, then pulled up one of the spare chairs and watched the stage.

Not long after I heard a change in the buzzing of voices, which I knew were the chimeras greeting King Silas. The nervous flutter in my gut grew and soon I was pacing the back room I had been ushered to, unable to sit still or settle down. I wasn't afraid of anything but in the same hand – I really didn't know what the fuck to expect.

"Lovely!" Silas's voice rang out like a ringing bell. I turned around and saw my king beaming at me with Garrett beside him. Silas was dressed nicely in a dark blue dress shirt, black pants and a black robe that was clasped under his neck with a silver ornament that shone in the dim lighting. His wavy hair was parted to the side and his ears adorned with beautiful gems of red, green, and blue.

"Hello, Master," I said giving him a bow. We embraced.

"Did you miss me? Don't you look handsome today. I saw Jack skulking by the door to this room. He really doesn't like to leave you alone, does he?" Silas chuckled. "No matter. Let's get the boring stuff over with so we can have some fun, hm?" Silas gave me a wink, though there was a certain glint in his eye that I found alluring. "Alright, Garrett. Make my introduction, they're going to start without us if we make them wait longer."

"Nothing wrong with that!" Garrett said cheerfully. He seemed to skip towards the door to the stage, everyone seemed happy and excited. Tonight was going well so far.

Silas's hand rested on my shoulder; he patted it affectionately. "I have a surprise for you, love. A wonderful surprise that just came off of the plane with me."

A surprise? I looked at him unable to hide the intrigue and confusion. "What is it?"

Silas smiled, his hand still rubbing my shoulder. "You'll love it. I think… it is a long time coming."

I stared at him, the excitement going off like fireworks in my gut was quickly being replaced by apprehension. But I trusted my king, and I knew he would never do anything to hurt me. So I brought no voice to my unease and instead directed my attention towards Garrett. As the curtains drew the lights of the room shone down on him like the sun itself had found its way into this building.

"Gentlemen, let's get this started, yes?" Garrett said, his words were met with cheering. I could specifically hear Nero and Ceph's cheers in the crowd. "Good. As you know tonight's family gathering is for a specific reason. We're gathered here today to welcome our newest brother into the family. One who has already gotten into enough trouble to be made immortal. Our brother, oldest stealth chimera, and fifth-in-command, and, of course, King Silas's newest little favourite which pisses me off but whatever..." The crowd laughed, and Silas and I did as well. Garrett grinned at this. That man sure seemed to love attention.

"But he is our brother and we will love him all the same. Shame we can't kill him for taking our king's attention, but *cest la vie*, eh?" More laughter. "Though before we bring out Sanguine our king has some words, and a few announcements to make. So without further ado – your king, master, and our saviour of the world, King Silas Dekker."

Silas gave my shoulder one last pat before he walked out onto the stage, his robe flowing behind him and his golden hair flashing in the light. The entire crowd was clapping and whooping as soon as he made his appearance on stage, and I was clapping as well.

"Hello, lovelies," Silas said happily, a large smile on his face. "Before we get to the fun things, and yes, we will get to that, I do have some announcements to make. It looks like we have everyone of age in this room, which is wonderful."

Silas cleared his throat, and immediately the entire room fell silent. I walked up to the doorway and leaned against it, not enough for my family to see me but enough that I could watch everything that was going on.

"As some of you may have heard we have lost several family members in the recent months," Silas started, his tone dropped and as quickly as it came the light atmosphere in the room seemed to shift as well. "The first one I would like to bring attention to is the death of Felix Region Dekker. It has been told to the family that Felix died during an unfortunate accident in the Dead Islands and nothing more."

Silas's face darkened; he clasped his hands behind his back and I saw his emerald eyes sweep the room. "This is false," he said. "I killed him."

My mouth dropped open, but besides my own quickened heart I heard nothing from the audience, just a stone-cold, dead silence.

"I fed him to our lions as he screamed for mercy," Silas continued in the same cold tone. "I watched his limbs get pulled off one-by-one and then I turned my back on him." Silas started to slowly pace the stage, his eyes hardened granite. "Elish also sent Valentine on a fool's mission to kill my Sanguine while Sanguine was ill and living in Cypress, knowing full well it would result in his death. He was acting on my own disappointment with a few of our second generations of chimeras. He did well and I praised him for it. And on top of that, my lovely Sanguine killed Ludo, which indeed saved me the inconvenience of killing him myself, which I would have done. The last one, Valen, hasn't been seen in months and tonight I am declaring him dead. That is three of my failed chimeras who have been put to death, and a fourth." Silas's eyes flickered to a spot where I knew Rio must be. "That has only been spared by my own mercy, though he will never be given the gift of immortality."

Silas's words seemed to hang in the heavy air, but a moment later it was broken up by a small voice.

"T-thank you for your mercy, King Silas," I heard Rio say weakly.

"I have been more than patient with my second generation of chimeras, but this golden age has now ended," Silas said as he paced back and forth. "From now on, and with future generations of chimeras, I will tolerate no disobedience, no relentless bullying. I will tolerate absolutely nothing but loyalty from my creations. Because let it be known –" Silas stopped and faced the audience again. The hairs on the back of my neck started to creep up. "– you are replaceable. Every single one of you. Even the immortal chimeras, so do not think the first generation and Jack and Sanguine are spared. There will be punishment for my disobedient immortals, a punishment as some of you already know – days, months, and even years encased in concrete, with nothing but a hole for air and if it fancies me in that moment – a hole so I can hear your screaming. If you disobey me, if you *piss me off* – you will be condemned to live inside this concrete tomb until your body dies from dehydration, only to resurrect in the same black coffin. If you betray me and I wish to not lay eyes on you ever again – I will create a clone of you, and replace you without so much of a thought, am I understood, lovelies?"

Silence – a dead, heavy silence like Silas's words had sucked the life giving air out of the room.

Then a low murmur, almost entirely said at once.

"Yes, King Silas," they said, and I found myself murmuring it too.

Silas smiled at this and clasped his hands together. "Though my remaining creations are so obedient. Apollo and Artemis, you make me proud every day, Cepherus, you're turning out to be quite the success, and my Jack has made exceptional strides towards reaching his potential – and my Sanguine–" My chest tightened with nerves as Silas looked at me, his eyes fixing on mine. "My beautiful Sanguine, you have made me the most proud. Sanguine Sasha Dekker, come out and meet the family."

After you just threatened to kill or entrap the entire family in concrete? I swallowed down the boulder in my throat and walked towards the stage. My legs felt like jelly but also like I was floating at the same time. If Silas was listening to my heart he would hear it attempting to rip out of my chest. I swear I could hear my ribs creak under the pressure.

I walked to Silas, and probably to try and defuse the tension in the air, Garrett gave a whoop and started clapping, soon everyone followed suit and I got my first ever round of applause.

Silas held up a hand and the applause stopped. "Sanguine was raised an orphan in the greywastes. It has taken him almost a year to become strong enough to be welcomed into this family, but he has surpassed his difficulties and has become a rather impressive chimera," Silas said as he laid a hand on the small of my back. I looked at the audience, nothing but rows of eyes, some of them reflecting in the dim lighting and others not. I couldn't make out their faces or who was who, but they were all staring at me and King Silas. "He is my fifth-in-command and he has earned that place in our family. You will all accept him as your brother and love him as I do."

I smiled awkwardly, not knowing what else to do.

"Sanguine's time in the greywastes was troubled. He came to Skyfall a broken man, driven to psychosis and insanity due to intense mistreatment and abuse, not only at the hands of the parasitic greywasters but at the hands of a man not worthy to even gaze upon my Sanguine." As Silas said these words my stomach clenched and started to twist into tight knots, a nervous heat started to rise, starting at the back of my head and slowly moving to my ears and face. I didn't like where this was going, and I wracked my brains trying to find a way to stop him from saying further who Jasper was and what he had done to me.

Surely Silas wouldn't say it in front of the entire family…

"This man kidnapped Sanguine when he was eight years old and held him for eleven years in a rotting basement, void of fresh air, sunlight, proper food, and freedom."

My heart sank to my knees, and I think I knew what was next.

"This man, named Jasper, started raping Sanguine at eight years old and it continued until Nero found and freed him at nineteen."

I dropped to my knees, my hand over my face. The dimly lit room around me, a buzz with voices, swirled around like I was on a rollercoaster. I couldn't breathe; I couldn't move.

"Why are you telling them this?" I rasped, though my voice was muffled by my hands.

But Silas didn't care. Though I heard the sound of a scuffle in the audience. It was Jack, I was sure it was someone stopping Jack from coming to comfort me, to take me away from this.

"Jasper has been being kept prisoner on the Dead Islands," Silas's booming voice grated against this festering wound in my soul that he had just ripped open. I winced from his words, my hands now shaking as they clasped my mouth. I was still on my knees, the room was still spinning, I was sure I was going to throw up.

"He has been confined and still allowed to live – until today."

I looked up at Silas in shock, and saw the king with the light shining on him, look back down at me. A dangerous smile spread on his face that hinted to an inner plan that I couldn't discern. He put a hand on my head and petted my hair. "Bring him out, Kessler."

Bring… him out?

A scream ripped through this torment that was physically weighing on my shoulders. I found my head rising and my hand falling from my mouth as a strong-looking chimera in a high-ranking legion uniform appeared in the doorway, leading a scrawny man with a burlap sack over his head.

"No…" I shook my head back and forth, my eyes fixed on the man being led towards me. "I don't… I don't want to see him… I don't want to see him…" I scrambled to my feet but all I was able to do was shuffle backwards, my head shaking back and forth.

"I don't want to see him. I don't want to see him," I kept saying as he came closer and closer to me. The room was full of talking, the heartbeats slamming against my ear drums to join the blood rushing behind my eyes. The dizziness intensified and my empty stomach gnawed at me as if my body was attempting to eat itself alive to spare me this horror that was now stepping onto the stage.

The memories of when I was locked in that basement were all coming back to me. Memories I had locked away, stuffed down and hidden. Memories I had just started to forget. Jasper's meth binges, painting the crows on the walls, watching him fuck Juni, Levi, Lyle.

And Cooper… I had killed Cooper to spare him.

I pushed my hand over my mouth to stifle the cry as these memories ravaged me. It felt like Jasper was fucking me all over again. I didn't want to go back there. Why was he doing this to me? Why was be putting me back in the basement?

"SILAS!" Jack screamed, but he didn't even manage Silas's full name before someone muffled his voice. I just sat there on my knees, my back pressed against the back of the stage, shaking my head back and forth.

Kessler roughly pushed Jasper onto the stage. My captor stumbled but he didn't fall. He was dressed in a grey jump suit, his hands were shackled. But it was him. I had memorized every inch of that body during my imprisonment with him. I knew the hands that used to hit me; I knew the chest I stared at when I was little, then as I grew up I looked at his collarbone, his neck, and then his face. I knew that skinny, meth-ravaged body, and I knew the face underneath that bag.

"And here he stands," Silas said darkly, his voice plunging back into those dark and dangerous tones; tones that were not only sharp, but laced with a lethal poison. "Here stands the man who raped and held captive a prince, my chimera."

Silas looked behind him, and when he saw me cowering against the wall I saw his eyes narrow in anger. "Get up, Sanguine."

I shook my head.

"GET UP!" Silas snarled. "You are no child cowering in the corner anymore, Sanguine. You are a chimera, you are powerful!"

I shook my head. "Just kill him already, don't make me rip open these wounds, Master – I just – I just healed them. I was just starting to become okay. He's not worth the trouble, just kill him and be done with it."

I expected him to laugh at me, that seemed to be the state he was in. A cruel state that cared nothing for what I was going through, he only wanted what was best for him. The man who was a thousand people in one body as Nero had said.

Perhaps Nero had been right.

Instead though Silas didn't smile. With Jasper being held towards the audience by Kessler Silas turned his back to me and looked towards the crowd.

"Many of you have seen my Sanguine at his most powerful. When he gives in to a different personality that he calls Crow, when he gives up control to these voices he becomes a chimera to be reckoned with. He killed Ludo under this psychosis, and murdered quite a few Skyfall residents as well in the most morbid of fashions. All to appease the voices in his head, the personalities he submits to," Silas said.

I sniffed and looked up at him, feeling my heart crush inside of me. I wanted the caring Silas, the attentive king that I knew was in there somewhere.

Did Silas have his own voices he was slave to?

But I – I had defeated mine. When I had resurrected – they had all gone away. I had been healed.

"Now the trouble with Sanguine listening to this psychotic side of him, was that he became uncontrollable. He became a raving, rabid monster without restraint who could kill friend and foe alike, and not only that – my Sanguine was miserable. My creation was taunted and tormented by these voices to the point of madness, and as his king, I couldn't bear to see him in such a state." Silas started pacing again. I watched him, my breathing starting to quicken to the point of hyperventilating.

"And yet when he listened to Crow…" Silas turned to me. "He was beautiful – oh was he ever a force to be reckoned with. Look at him now… look at how weak he is when faced with his past. He's happy without the voices, yes, I do love seeing him happy." Silas started walking towards me, a horrible smile on his face. "But then again… I also love seeing his beautiful – alluring – madness."

Silas leaned down. I pursed my lips and looked away from him; he raised a hand and took my cheek and turned me to him.

"Why not have the best of both worlds, lovely?" Silas purred. He leaned in and kissed my trembling lips slowly, then rose back to his feet.

"In Silas's Fallocaust." Silas raised his voice as I sat on my knees, feeling lost, confused, and scared. "We can have the best of both worlds can't we?" Silas started walking towards the stage, and, oddly, several chimeras started pounding on the tables.

"Can't we?" Silas said louder as more chimeras started joining in to the rhythmic drum beats, one beat after another, getting louder and louder until the room echoed with its tribal noise.

"CAN'T WE!" Silas yelled. He spread his arms out in a welcoming gesture and the pounding quickened. I found my hands covering my ears, and the first shots of what I knew was going to be an anxiety attack.

"YES – WE – CAN!" I heard my brothers yell in unison. "YES – WE – CAN!"

Silas laughed. When he turned around I saw he had a small device in his hand. He held it in his left hand and grinned at me.

"I agree."

Silas pushed the button.

Immediately my neck snapped back as an electric current ripped through my brain. I screamed and tried to grab my head but the electricity had welded my limbs to the floor. Instead I closed my eyes, feeling the current course through my body, it was so strong I could feel it in my teeth.

It was painful, it hurt so much I screamed again, but on the heels of that scream I could see a dark cloak start to descend on my head, a dark cloak that was covered in black feathers. It covered my brain and seemed to focus the electricity inside of it. In a way it was even comforting, it was warm, inviting. It was… alive.

Pulsating.

Moving.

It was… talking.

Daisy, Daisy… give me your heart to do.

"SAMI?" Barry's voice rang out like a chorus. "SAMI! Kill Jasper. Kill Jasper."

"Kill Jasper, Sami."

"SAMI!" The voice started to change, it started to become lower, gravelly and dry. *"Sanguine… Sanguine, my mihi, my mihi. Kill him, or will you cut yourself again? Or will you jump from another building again after raping Valen bloody?"*

"Why are you standing there scared? My mihi, my Daisy Daisy – why won't you give in to me?"

I opened my eyes and looked around the stage, the sounds were muffled but I could see them still. It was odd, the sounds were images, auras almost, rippling and surrounding the room.

Then I saw him inside of my head.

Crow was indeed back.

Silas had control. He could throw me back into psychosis at his whim.

He had done something to my brain while I was resurrecting.

What had he done to me?

My gaze turned to my Crow. He was standing tall and confident with his close-mouthed smile. He was dressed identical to me, all the way down to the red bowtie. His hair was down to his jaw line and as black as a crow's wing; his face pale and healthy and his burning red eyes squinted and bright.

I looked like him.

Crow had started out as a boy with fuzzy bear ears, brown hair and black eyes, he called himself Barry. Then as I got older he had slowly started to change, each transformation suited to the person I needed him to be. Perhaps I had been my best friend all along?

Was that it?

I slowly rose to my feet, my mind quickly darkening, like Silas's button had pressed an off switch; it was fading into the abyss, so fast, I couldn't grab hold of it again. I couldn't reach it.

The psychosis was back, Crow was back.
I was back.

And the sounds of the room came rushing back to me with a force that threatened to knock me off of my feet. The pounding of dozens of fists against tables matching the beating of my heart, the heavy and electric atmosphere of the room that cradled and exploited these mind numbing noises, the intangible feeling of excitement, intoxicating and aromatic.

And the smell of fear.

My eyes turned to the skinny man standing hunched over, behind held by Kessler in a firm grip. He was on display to the audience like slave set up for auction to slavers, with many pairs of glowing eyes drinking in this play they had been treated to. I saw their movements, their pounding fists and as I rose to my feet the sounds sped up, and when I smiled the entire room exploded in excited noises. They were like starved dogs when their master came to feed them, my brothers were animals, eager and excited to see just what kind of food I had brought them.

Well, I had never been one to disappoint.

I did love an audience.

"Take off his hood," I demanded, my voice was raspy, it was dry. I didn't sound like me but there wasn't a fiber in my being that didn't enjoy that fact. My body was soaking in this wonderful feeling of confidence and power and though I was well-aware that this was brought on by something that Silas had done to me – I didn't give a fuck.

Kessler, a young chimera legionary that had a square face, a thick neck, and short dark hair looked at me, and smirked. He raised a hand and ripped off the hood that had been covering Jasper's head.

And when I saw that man, the man who had kept me prisoner for over eleven years, raping me, abusing me, torturing me, my smile only widened, then, unable to contain my amusement…

I laughed.

I laughed because I never realized how small and pathetic he was. A man who had once been so scary, this big imposing person who brought terror and misery on his heels, was now... was now...

Human.

Jasper's hazel eyes widened when he saw me, his face gaunt and grey but from imprisonment rather than meth. His half-open mouth showed me no teeth, and from the scars he had on his face and arms I could only imagine what they had done to him.

I walked up to him, my eyes fixed on him and the closed-mouth smile on my face. He didn't move or shrink down, but his heart was banging like the drum-like thuds of my brothers' fists.

The first thing I did, with the dark cloak masking and hiding all of my anxiety and fear, was backhand him. Then, as his head snapped back, a stream of blood shooting from his nose, I hit him again; the crowd behind me cheering and banging harder.

Then I held up a hand, and the crowd became silent, all but a slight thrum of their hands against the tables.

"Hello, Jasper," I said to him, my eyes squinting from the same smile I had learned from watching Crow.

"Sami," Jasper said simply. He looked at me so intently, like he couldn't believe who was standing in front of him. "Or is it Sanguine now? What are you calling yourself today?"

"No," I said casually, the banging and hollering in front of me starting to becoming drowned out as I spoke to Jasper. "It has always been Sanguine. They implant our names into our brains when they're creating us. Did you know that?" I asked. "Did you ever stop and think that perhaps – you were keeping a chimera prisoner?"

"I didn't care what you were," Jasper replied with a bravery that defied his racing heart. "You were young and stupid. You could've had three heads and scales and I would've still fucked you. All I cared about was a tight little ass and a small cock for me to look at."

Chairs scraped in front of me, brothers enraged by his words, but I held up a hand again and didn't let the smile disappear from my face. Indeed I didn't mind this bravery; he knew he was going to die tonight, and that no amount of begging would spare him from his fate.

"Yes, we both thought I was nothing but a mutation, a side effect of the sestic radiation that made me look like this," I murmured with a shake of my head. "What did you think when they told you I was a chimera? That I was royalty?"

"I was proud of myself for being able to fuck a prince." Jasper smirked. "I destroyed a prince and made him nothing but an insane nutcase. What's there not to be proud of? Sure, you'll kill me tonight... but it is what it is. I left scars on you that immortality will never heal. Do you think of me when they fuck you?" Jasper jerked his head towards the audience. "Or the king? Do I flash through your vision?" He chuckled. "You're still just a pathetic little eight-year-old boy, eager to make a friend, just waiting for the next man to control you, whether it be me... or that blond fuck in the corner. The only thing you're good for is sucking cock and going crazy."

The audience was angry, fast talking and more chairs scraping. The pounding had stopped but I hadn't even realized it, the entire room had turned from electric with anticipation to caustic anger.

I brought my hand up and patted Jasper's shoulder. Then I turned to King Silas who was standing at the opposite end of the stage.

The king had no expression on his face, but I did notice he was standing beside a table. One I hadn't noticed before. As I turned from Jasper and walked towards the table I saw that a spread of weapons had been laid out on it. Hunting knives, scalpels, forceps, guns, bottles of liquids with labels anywhere from gasoline, acid, and mercury, and even a chainsaw.

"Choose your poison, amor," Silas said to me, and when he looked at me he smiled. "Whatever you want."

I picked up a few bottles, and ran my fingers over several of the daggers. "Actually, Silas. I would like you to do something for me..." I leaned in and whispered something into Silas's ear, and with a smile, the king hopped off of the stage, and with everyone looking on in surprise, he walked out of the room.

I turned around with a bottle in one hand and a long narrow dagger in the other. The room so quiet that my boots echoed off of the ceiling, *click clack click clack*. I walked up to Jasper who was glaring at me, though I saw the hints of apprehension in his eyes.

"Nero," I called. "Come up here and help Kessler."

Nero was there before I even finished my sentence. He appeared behind Kessler and held a hand on Jasper's shoulder.

"Hold open his mouth," I commanded.

Nero grabbed into Jasper's jaw and squeezed it, though Jasper was clenching his toothless jaw closed. Kessler held him tight as my former captor struggled, making muffled grunts as he fought with Nero's strong fingers.

I sighed and shook my head. I batted Nero's hand away and pushed my fingers into the small gap between Jasper's gums that Nero had been able to make. I wiggled them in until I was deep enough into his mouth to grab hold of his lower jaw …

… then with all my strength I pulled it forward then yanked it down, hearing bones popping and snapping as I wrenched his jaw from his skull.

Jasper's muffled screaming filled the room, and the slow thrumming of fists started to pick up. The jaw bone was now loose and flimsy in my hand, so I pulled it down further, watching with satisfaction as the skin started to bulge and pulse from the dislocated jawbone pushing forward like a hinge.

But it worked, his mouth was open!

"Wonderful! Now do you have anything smart to say?" I said with a laugh. I glanced up as I started to unscrew the bottle.

Jasper stared at me, his mouth gaping open and his toothless gums giving off a rank and disgusting smell. I could hear a wheezing sound coming from him and perhaps a gurgling, but no words.

"Nothing?" I said cheerfully. "Nothing at all? How fortunate, because I also have nothing more to say to you." I nodded at Nero who seemed to get an idea of what I wanted to do. He grabbed Jasper's head and tilted it back, Jasper's mouth stretched open like a ghost in a horror movie.

And now he started to struggle. Kessler and Nero held him firmly in their grasp, the excitement of my actions breathing new life into the stunned crowd of brothers in front of me. I waved my hand to encourage them and as I tilted the bottle of gasoline towards Jasper's mouth their pounding started up again.

The first trickle went into his mouth, filling my nose with the wonderful aroma of gasoline. I tipped the bottle back further and soon a steady stream of yellow liquid started to pour into Jasper's mouth and down his throat.

Jasper gagged, his eyes rolling around in their sockets. I saw a bubble of gasoline come back up as he tried to throw up, but besides a stream that dribbled down his chin gravity kept the rest down. I winked at Nero as my best friend grinned at me and waved around the long dagger I had picked up.

Then, past Jasper choking and moaning, I saw a figure in the open door way, a man with two smaller figures on either side of him.

"Bring them here, love," I called to Silas as I doused the dagger with the rest of the gasoline. "No need to be afraid, boys. If you can be brave you can do something you'll never forget."

As they walked closer I took a step away from Jasper, the gasoline-soaked dagger in my hand. I watched as the two smaller figures stepped into the dim lighting; my two little friends, Juni and Levi. Both of them at least half a foot taller, dressed in crisp sengil outfits, combed and brushed hair, and rather shocked faces.

Levi nervously clung to Silas's leg, but Juni's face brightened. He ran from Silas, jumped onto the stage, and dove into my arms.

"I missed you, why didn't you come visit me?" Juni said with a smile. He looked up at me with adoring eyes.

I patted his head and looked to Jasper. "I'll visit you all the time now, mihi. But first, we have something we need to take care of."

Juni looked at Jasper and I was amazed that the boy showed no fear towards him. Though Levi was still welded to Silas's leg, the boy, even though he was older than Juni, wasn't moving, but that was alright, I only needed one of them for what I wanted done. Levi watching was good enough.

"He's still alive?" Juni said flatly. I heard several chuckles come from the crowd and I laughed too.

I handed Juni the long knife and walked him over to Jasper, red foam was now bubbling from his loose jaw, dripping down his boney chin and trailing down his neck. He was groaning, but the pain I knew he was feeling was keeping him still, his thrashing had been reduced to nothing more than a twitching writhe.

"Not for long, little one," I said to him. I lifted up Jasper's shirt and pointed to where I knew his stomach was. "I want you to stab Jasper, right here, right where my finger is."

Juni nodded with a grin and stepped forward, but I raised my hand and he stopped.

"Just one more thing," I said with a smirk. I reached down and touched the long knife. "Now do it quickly before it burns you." I focused my altered touch on the tip of my finger, and as soon as it became hot the entire blade of the knife erupted into an almost invisible blue flame. I quickly stepped back and nodded at him.

Juni, still grinning, took the knife and without a word he retracted his arm and plunged the knife into Jasper's stomach.

The explosion knocked us both off of our feet.

I stumbled back but I didn't fall. I turned my face away from the spray of blood and gasoline and was temporarily dazzled by the sensory overload, both sight, smell, and sound. There were sounds all around me, cheering, Juni's high-pitched laughter, and the gurgling wheezing of Jasper taking his last breaths.

Then hands on my shoulders. I was steadied, enough for me to look towards where Jasper had been being held.

My former captor was on the floor, a gaping hole in his stomach that was aflame with blue and orange fire, entrails were littered around him, spirals of intestines and organs of various shades of red and pink, all of this on top of an ever growing pool of blood and the rainbow gleam of gasoline.

Juni was keeled over laughing, his small body covered in red blood; he had it coated over his entire face as he jumped up and down in glee. Nero and Kessler were behind Jasper with two matching grins, clapping their hands to the rhythm of the drum beats.

I watched Jasper. I watched the man with his eyes wide and staring, his dislocated jaw open and sucking in his last breaths. I watched him with tense eyes and was there to witness his last breath. I watched him until he was dead.

Jasper was dead.

"Good job, mihi," praised Crow, though I knew it was only my own voice praising me. He was no longer a separate person, at Silas's whim I would become the uncontrollable demon that would undoubtedly respond to his every command. He would control the voices inside of my head, and as such he would control me.

"I didn't even have to yell at you this time. I will enjoy the times that our master lets us free from our cages," Crow mused. *"I did miss you, mihi."*

Silas walked up to me with the remote in his hand. I looked down and saw him flick the switch to off with his thumb. And with that simple act, I felt the odd dark cloak lift from my brain, and with that every single sensation in the room came back.

I gasped and felt my knees weaken, but the arms behind me steadied me. Like I had walked in front of a train the emotions of what had just happened hit me.

"What did you do to me!" I snarled. I tried to yank my arms away from the person holding me but he wouldn't let me, perhaps he knew I couldn't stand on my own. "What the fuck did you put into my brain?" In an instant the comfortable acceptance of Silas's manipulation of my brain was gone, as Sanguine came forth and Crow faded into the darkness I realized just how much my king had betrayed me.

Silas smiled sweetly at me. "Would you prefer to go in and out of your psychosis without warning? With the risk of hurting Jack? Or your mortal brothers? Drake, or even young Juni?"

I was quiet, my lips pursed and the anger igniting the already heated blood in my veins.

"There is no cure for your madness, Sanguine," Silas explained. Behind him I saw Nero lift up Jasper, Jasper's smoking guts from the cavity in his stomach and slipping down Nero's jacket. Sengils were already cleaning up the mess. "I could either leave you as is, or control it for you."

"By a fucking remote?" I snapped. "So you can have control over my fucking brain from now on? Why not just shut it off for good?"

Silas, still smiling, patted my cheek. "Because you are mine, love, and I have uses for that psychosis. You are my chimera for the rest of eternity, and when I feel it so, you will join my side as my bodyguard. You are my beloved fifth-in-command, my prince. And as your master it is my right to control you."

I growled at him, but Silas's hand still tenderly stroked my cheek. "Is it not worth having a peaceful mind, love? Would you rather I take the implant out and you can be taunted by the voices inside of your head? The hallucinations? I have given you a gift, crucio, a wonderful gift. I would appreciate a thank you. Don't forget everything I have done for you, and the chimera I have given you to love." Silas looked behind me and I realized the person holding me the entire time had been Jack.

The growl in my throat disappeared, and the words I had heard Silas speak echoed in my head. The threat to all of us that we were not outside of his punishment just because we were immortal. Though I had seen and had loved Silas as the patient and loving king, he was a thousand personalities in one, and I had to be cautious of all of them. Not only for my own safety, I had to take care of Jack now too.

And taking care of Jack and keeping him safe was my top priority. I had to push down my own feelings of betrayal and my own loss of control – and let Silas do what he wants with me.

So I nodded, and with Jack squeezing my shoulder I got down on one knee and held his hand to my lips. I kissed it and looked up at him.

"My apologies, my king," I said to him. "I was running on emotion over what has just happened. I'm sorry."

Silas nodded his approval and motioned for me to rise. Then he put an arm around me and turned us towards the crowd. The dozens of chimera eyes stared at us, the smell of blood, burnt flesh, and gasoline heavy in the air.

"Sanguine Sasha Dekker," Silas said in a proud voice. "Welcome to the family." Then pulled me to his side and beamed at the crowd. "Let's eat! But leave room for Jasper." I felt a kiss on my cheek. "My lovely will get the choice cuts."

CHAPTER 49

I SPEARED A FORKFUL OF MEAT AND LOOKED AT Jack. He was dipping his meat in a rich gravy that had been spilling out of his mashed potatoes like an overflowing volcano.

"Okay," Jack said with a dry laugh. "One… two… three…"

We both popped the meat into our mouths at once and chewed, my pointed teeth shredding the meat easily in my mouth, which was good because barbequed Jasper was kind of tough.

"Not bad, a bit stringy," I said picking a fiber out of my front teeth. "Jasper would do better in a slow cooker I think."

My boyfriend laughed and nuzzled my neck. Around us our brothers were enjoying their food, the buzzing talking filling the room and mixing pleasantly with the aroma of cooked meat and alcohol. The stage I had been on was still lit, but instead of me being on display for the masses to drink in, there was only Jasper's cooked leg on display surrounded by platters of already shredded meat. That on top of the buffet-style metal dishes that were situated beside the sound system. It was quite a feast.

"You're feeling okay, baby, are you sure?" Jack asked for the fifth time since I had been allowed to sit down with him. King Silas was sitting with Elish, and though I couldn't hear the conversation he was having with him it was making Silas beam like a bulb. Elish seemed relaxed as well, and Perish who was also sitting at their table.

"I am," I said with a nod. Though I was only okay because the continuing party around me had been numbing the more traumatizing parts of my welcoming party. If there was one thing I had learned about traumatic experiences it was that you didn't realize how much they fucked you up until after. At the time your only goal was to push through them.

And though Silas's implant inside of my mind kept sending shocks of anxiety through me I had resolved myself to the reality that there was little I could do. If he had asked me beforehand I would've been okay with it, I think. It was that he had to make a show of it that bothered me. Silas seemed to love entertaining his audience just as much as I had.

As it stood, Silas shouldn't have reason to turn off the implant that was allowing me to live a normal life, so I should be okay. If he wanted to use it to get obedience out of me, so be it, I didn't plan on doing anything to make him mad. I loved my king, I was loyal to him, so why should I worry?

Anyway, I had a lot to celebrate – as I said this I speared another piece of Jasper meat and popped it into my mouth – I was eating my captor after force-feeding him gasoline and blowing him up. Not to mention the fact that I was now fully welcomed into this family after almost a year of being in Skyfall. Everything was just fine.

Jack beamed at me. I swallowed my food and kissed him on the lips. With Jack beside me, well, there wasn't much to be upset about. The door on my past seemed to finally be closed.

Eventually my brothers and I had eaten our fill. The sengils came and took away our plates away and, oddly, the entire tables too. Then to further my confusion Kinny came over to us and handed us a bag.

"Are you staying?" Jack asked in an amused voice, one that made me give him a suspicious look.

Kinny bit his lip but soon a smile appeared on his face. "The dominant chimeras outnumber the submissive ones, Master Jack. Most of the chimera-owned sengils will be joining."

"Joining what?" I asked confused. Kinny put a hand over his mouth and giggled before scampering away.

I looked at Jack only to find that he was blushing too. He peeked into the bag, the tips of his ears reddening and handed me a small green piece of plastic. I looked at it and saw it was something called Listerine strips.

I cocked an eyebrow at Jack.

"Silas is strict about us having clean mouths for this, especially since we just ate. He hates bad breath; he's so silly…" Jack took the container from me and cracked it open, inside was a thin strip of green that smelled minty. He took one out and handed it to me and took one for himself.

Following his lead I put it on the roof of my mouth.

"Clean mouths for what?" I asked, my mouth filling with an overpowering minty taste.

Jack nodded towards the stage and I looked. Jasper's remains had been wheeled away and in place the sengils were setting up... a bed?

Then an odd shuffling sound. I looked towards it as Jack giggled and saw more sengils drawing back the black curtain that had been covering the other half of this large room. Behind it was... one giant bed, about five king size beds all pressed up against one another, almost wall to wall. On these blanket-covered beds were sex toys, whips, lots of bottles of lubricant...

"Oh my god, you have to be kidding me?" I exclaimed. "Why didn't you warn me... is this with all of us? Are you serious?"

Jack seemed to be enjoying this, he was grinning from ear to ear. "This usually happens during our big parties, but you don't have to join in, hunny. You can just watch or even wait until Silas is distracted and leave. You know how our family is, we're–" He thought for a moment before smirking. "– reinforcing family bonds."

"By having an orgy!?" I exclaimed. I heard several laughs coming from different tables, one I recognized as Ceph and one as Garrett. Nosey fucks.

Jack shrugged playfully and kissed me again. "They're fun, baby. You'll have a great time, just stick near me. No one is going to make you do anything you don't want to do and, like I said... we can both leave if you really don't think you're ready."

I groaned and buried my face into my hands. "We haven't even had proper sex yet since I woke up... why are you okay with this?"

"Because I want you to feel comfortable with our family," Jack explained He put a hand on mine and rubbed it. Behind him sengils were handing out the bags, I hadn't even looked to see what else was in them but Nero was taking out a bag of white powder. "Us making love in our own bed is a lot different than a family gathering, you know this by now."

My lips pursed and I shook my head. I didn't know how I felt about the casual but electric feeling in the air was starting to get to me. Perhaps this might be something interesting to... watch at least.

This family was strange. They had sex with each other to, as I had been told many times before, reinforce bonds and feel close to each other, and they seemed to be able to completely separate it from their feelings for their partners. In a normal relationship this just wouldn't happen, or at least what my version of a relationship had always been. Nero having sex with Silas, or any one of us, didn't seem to affect Ceph at all, it was just something that was accepted without thought.

I looked at Jack who was watching the sengils set up the bed on the stage, he was vibrating with excitement. This was the same boyfriend who got livid when he realized my close bond with King Silas, the same reaction I had gotten from Elish.

Then it hit me.

"You and Elish got jealous of my connection with Silas because it was based on emotion, on something deeper than just sex. It wasn't about sex, because until recently Silas and I had never slept together," I said to Jack. "Which is also why Elish was so angry when he caught Silas snuggled up to me, asleep in my arms. He also knew we hadn't had sex, it was purely our strong emotional attachment to each other." I scowled as the wool got drawn back from my eyes, suddenly how this family worked was making sense to me. "This right now, is just sex, and sure, we're reinforcing bonds but it's family bonds not relationship ones. That's why you're okay with this, but yet if Silas and I cuddled on the couch spilling our feelings to each other you and Elish would probably murder each of us, am I right?"

Jack nodded, looking proud that I had finally got it. "That's right! See, we can have some fun tonight." He took the paper bag and peeked inside of it. "Wow, we get MDMA tonight and ressin! The MDMA will make us all feel warm and fuzzy, it makes touch feel awesome too. The ressin will make us, well, you'll see – want to try some?"

I shook my head, though I could see similar bags on the few remaining tables and chimeras already cutting them with their black cards. I recognized all of them, I think Kessler, Apollo, and Artemis had been the only two I hadn't met yet. I could see the twins sitting next to each other, laughing and talking and touching each other affectionately as well. At the same table was a young man with spiky black hair and a smaller man with blond hair with dyed blue tips dressed in a sengil uniform. I didn't count them but I'd guess there were about twenty of us, sengils included. This was going to be interesting.

Then, without an announcement or anything like that, Silas walked on stage with Kessler walking behind him. Silas was now wearing nothing but a black silk robe and Kessler too. As soon as they entered the lights on the stage dimmed further.

Kessler sat down on the bed and shifted himself backwards. I looked around at the chimeras to see that Garrett was already on the giant bed to the left of me with none other than Kass, both of them making out, their shirts off and their pants unbuttoned. Everyone else was watching Kessler and Silas, some with white powder rimming their nostrils and others having their clothing removed by their brothers.

I looked back to Kessler and Silas and saw Silas's robe off, his slender body glowing in the warm halogen lights. Kessler was lying down on his back with Silas on his hands and knees over him, his dick semi-hard and being played with in Kessler's hands.

"Kessler just turned fifteen last month," Jack whispered in my ear. I felt his hand rest on my thigh and start to creep towards my groin. "He had his own initiation party, you missed watching him lose his virginity."

Wow. I felt a twitch in my pants at the thought of seeing someone lose their virginity for the first time. "And it… was in front of everyone?"

Silas was now kissing Kessler's neck, I saw his tongue licking the side before travelling down to his collarbone. Kessler was running his hands through Silas's wavy blond hair, his legs spreading further with anticipation.

"Yeah," Jack said. I felt my pants loosen, he had undone one of the buttons. "Though it's in a different room, a private room for the two of them but there are two-way mirrors for the family to watch. It's quite… hot." Jack's head disappeared. I watched him get down on his hands and knees in front of me. I lifted my backside up off of the chair and let him draw my pants off of me, followed by my underwear. At first I felt shy and self-conscious over being exposed to the entire family, but then I looked to my left and saw Elish. Cold-hearted, impassive Elish. He had his shirt off and his pants down and red-haired Kinny was on his hands and knees with his head bobbing up and down.

Well, fuck it, if Elish could do this in front of our family – I could.

And it looked like I didn't have a choice. A moment later, with my eyes still on Elish and Kinny, I felt Jack's warm tongue wrap around the head of my dick. Then when I turned back to Silas and Kessler, I saw Silas now flipped backwards on Kessler. Kessler was licking the king's hole and Silas was going up and down on his dick.

I groaned, feeling my ears burn so hot they physically hurt, my senses were getting overloaded by everything I was seeing and this thing had barely started. I felt like my mind was going to melt.

I watched, in utter ecstasy, as Silas and Kessler worked on each other. Silas's dick was now rigid, Kessler behind him devouring Silas's ass as the king stroked and licked Kessler's dick. I never thought watching other people do stuff like this would be hot but I was already feeling the temperature rise in my body, and the heat that started on my ears was beginning to pool inside of my head.

A chair scraped beside me. I looked towards it and smirked as Nero, completely naked, pulled up a chair, Ceph also naked was beside him. Nero got up and Ceph sat down without a word and he pulled me in for a kiss. I was startled by the abruptness of this, I didn't know Ceph as well as Nero, but I let him and when he opened his mouth I welcomed his tongue.

Though as we kissed passionately I felt Jack withdraw his mouth, only to put it back onto my cock a moment later. I looked down and my eyes widened when I realized Nero now had my dick half in his mouth, his eyes closed and his hands now gently rubbing my balls.

"Nero!" I said in shock.

They, of course, laughed at me. Nero looked up at me and winked, before the rest of my dick started disappearing into his mouth, until I could feel the head sliding down his throat. The feeling was amazing, there wasn't a centimetre of my shaft in view, just trimmed pubic hair and Nero's shit-eater grin.

And as Nero worked me over I saw my dirty little boyfriend with Ceph's overly large dick in his mouth. And Ceph giving me a smug little grin as if wondering if I was going to make a deal out of it. To prove to him and Jack that I was a game player I grabbed Ceph again and kissed him.

"Ah-hah, there we go!" Nero said after he withdrew his mouth. He grabbed my cock and made it wiggle back and forth, before he gave it a few slaps against my thigh. I put a hand over my forehead and swore at the sensation.

Then Nero got up and slapped his hands together like he was clearing dust. Then he made the 'get up' motion to me. I obliged but a moment later I wish I didn't. Nero picked me up, slung me over his back and started marching me towards the bed.

"Oh, Nero found his prize!" I heard Perish laugh. He came into view with Apollo sitting on his lap. Both of them naked, and yep, Perish's cock deep into Apollo's ass. Perish, my college professor, waved at me, his unfocused eyes bright and his smile wide.

I rolled my eyes at him before saying a loud *ouch* as Nero laid a hard slap on my bare ass. Perish laughed at this, and even Elish, who was only a foot away from him still being blown by Kinny, had a smirk for me.

This family – is so weird.

I glared at Jack as I was carted towards the giant bed against my will. He had jumped on Ceph's back and was being piggybacked behind me. He looked positively euphoric right now which made me happy.

Then, with a yelp, Nero threw me down onto the bed. I bounced several times before landing on my back. I quickly sat up before Nero could pin me down and gave him a mock glaring look.

Nero reached over and grabbed a baggy of powder. As he tapped some onto his fist Jack was thrown down beside me, and Ceph was quickly on him, unbuttoning his shirt and helping him out of his pants.

"Snort this," Nero said as he pushed his fist into my line of site, a lump of powder was on top of it. "It's MDMA and some ressin, it'll make you able to go all night and you'll feel great. It's perfect for the nerves too if you're nervous about what I'm about to do to you."

What he's about to do to me… oh boy. I leaned down and plugged one nostril and took the powder. Then immediately gasped as my nose and the back of my throat started to burn badly. As I rubbed my nose and coughed Nero took off my shoes and socks until I was completely naked in front of him.

"I was thinking it would be Jack's right to be my first… since he's my boyfriend," I said to him, though deep down I was nervous about what I knew he was wanting to do to me.

But as soon as that thought entered my head, my thoughts went back to just several hours ago when I had killed Jasper. His taunting words to me, that I would think of him whenever a man fucked me, I wanted to prove him wrong.

"Fuck that!" Nero exclaimed. "I put my dibbs on you, fuckhead, don't you dare cheat me out of my reward. Do you realize how patient I've been?" He looked towards Jack who was on his back, Ceph licking and sucking his left nipple, Jack's leg already pulled back and allowing Ceph's hard penis to grind against his. "I was the first man Sanguine ever jerked off. We did it when he moved into his new apartment. He opened that robe for me and I saw that fucking hard-as-rock cock aching for release, precum just oozing off of it, never touched, never once allowed to cum. And you know what he did after he made me cum?" His made a face before saying in a mocking tone that I gathered was supposed to be my voice. *"I'm going to have a shower and wait.* And I let him, Jacky, I said okay. I respected him, Jacky. Me, Nero Sebastian Dekker."

Jack's black eyes widened like someone had just told him Silas had taken a wife. "Seriously?" He looked at me for confirmation and I nodded. Jack looked absolutely taken aback by this news.

"Wow, good job, Nero!" Jack said before he smiled. "I don't mind if Sanguine doesn't. I want our first time to be just the two of us, a little more intimate than this. You have my blessing, Master Nero."

Nero hissed his victory, before claiming his reward by locking his lips with mine. "What do you say, puppy?" He pulled away. "I'll seriously stop if you want, you know I will."

I shook my head back and forth and smirked at him. "I always kinda knew it would be you. You and I… we got something between us that goes back further than anyone here." I kissed him, before reaching down and taking his over-sized, thick dick into my hands and lightly squeezed it. "So this is my thank you… for never giving up on finding me. I love you."

"Aww," Nero said. I saw blush come to his cheeks. "You just gotta turn this into a lovey thing. Fuck, I love you too, Sangy. I'm so fucking proud of you." He grabbed onto my leg and pulled it back. I heard a crack of the lube bottle which was in Ceph's hand and felt Nero's fiancé start to prep the both of us. Soon after, Nero's fingers slipped inside of me and gently started to move in and out.

After several minutes of finger play, our lips once again locked, he held my left leg back. I positioned his dick to the right spot, and with our lips still joined, I felt the pressure of him trying to enter me.

Soon though I broke away, I clenched my teeth and swore through them as the pressure quickly turned into pain. I felt more lube get drizzled over my ass and Nero's dick, and tried to rub it onto his head as he pushed against my tight hole.

Jack's hand slipped into mine and I squeezed it hard, my other hand was digging my fingers into Nero's back as the brute chimera pushed hard.

When the head popped in I let out a gasping cry, the burning didn't dissipate, it only got more intense. I remembered the first time I had had this happen to me, the unbelievable amount of pain, but I forbid my mind from lifting the dark shroud that was shielding me from that memory. This was no time to remember my past, and thankfully, my mind – or perhaps the implant – respected that.

Nero pushed himself in further, and as his prominent head got away from the tight opening and deeper inside of me, where there was a bit more space, the pain lessened. But it was a false sense of relief, as soon as his length sunk into me the tight burning feeling came back with vengeance. And though Nero was groaning, I was writhing under him from being so uncomfortable and in pain.

"Take it out… it's too big for him," Jack said his voice full of apprehension, but I shook my head. I wasn't going to be a wimp about this. I knew not only Jack and Ceph were watching us, and if Nero took it out, and even worse, got off of me, the entire family would laugh, especially when they saw the look of pain on my face.

"I'm fine," I gasped, putting a hand up to my face. I bit down on my finger and tried to distract myself with that pain. Nero's tongue gathered the blood from my sharp teeth, leading me to sink my fingernails into his back in an attempt to try and pay him back for the pain he was causing me.

Nero slowly withdrew himself, before sinking it back in, he did this several times, me trying to stifle the cries and him the moans; then he started picking up his speed.

Beside me I heard a soft cry from Jack. I opened my eyes and saw Ceph in the same position Nero was in, his dick already penetrating my boyfriend. Jack's hands were pulling his legs back almost up to his neck, giving me a full, unobstructed view of Ceph's cock thrusting inside of him.

It was hot; I was surprised with how hot it was to see Ceph fucking my boyfriend.

I wanted to keep looking, but instead I turned all of my attention to Nero, who had been eagerly kissing my neck as he took his time with each drawn-out thrust.

Then Nero put one hand on either side of my head, my legs locked over his arms. He positioned himself for the long haul and when he was satisfied with where he was he started sharply thrusting inside of me.

But the pain was starting to disappear. I could feel an influx of cozy pleasure start to coat my body like a fuzzy blanket, gripping me tight in its hold and sending wave after wave of good feelings all through me. I was confused at first until I remembered the MDMA that Nero had made me snort, mixed in with the sex drug ressin. It was not only relaxing my mind, but my body too, and as my tight muscles started to loosen like someone unwinding the peg on a guitar string, I started to enjoy the feeling of Nero inside of me.

"There we go, puppy," Nero whispered, his breath hot against my ear. He must've felt my body start to loosen. "Relax and let it take you. Close your eyes and enjoy it."

"Mmhmm…" I smiled, and he kissed that smile and continued with his sharp, well-aimed thrusts; his large cock easily sliding in and out of me, the smell of lube and the sounds of moaning chimeras and sengils becoming a beautiful symphony to my ears. In just several minutes I had gone from tensed and in pain, to relaxed and floating around everyone in the room.

I closed my eyes and let it take me, Nero's dick hitting a pleasurable spot inside of me that I never knew I had. Every time the rim of his head brushed against it I felt a pleasurable pressure inside of me that made me shift myself down so he would hit it better.

Nero's heavy breathing and our mutual moans sung all around me, they drowned me in their song and moved inside of my brain like lizards wading in thick mud. It was all condensed into one continual rhythm, thrusting, moaning, pressure.

I liked it, yeah, it was good. There wasn't a single shred of apprehension or fear inside of me and with that realization I fully accepted the implant that Silas had put in my brain. If this could be my life now, I would take it. Let Silas have Crow when he needed him, if it meant I would be able to finally enjoy my life, free of my mental illness.

Someone patted my cheek, I tried to open my eyes but I realized they were already open. So I focused them instead and saw Nero with an amused smile.

"You're really high, eh?" Nero said. He had rainbowy aura around him, it was hovering over him like the heat waves off of a hot car. Everything was shimmery, it was so beautiful I kind of wanted to touch it. I wonder what it would taste like – I bet it would taste nice, like sugar and rainbows.

I nodded and we kissed again, though I broke our lips when he gave me a hard thrust. I moaned, and he pressed my legs back further until he had lifted my ass off of the bed. Then in that position he picked up his speed and started roughly plunging into me, hard pounds that added a smacking sound to the chorus of moans and cries. I glanced down at his muscular body and saw his short pubic hair and the shaft of his thick cock. No blood at all, just an insurmountable amount of pressure and pleasure.

Then I got my lucidity enough to see that we had become a popular sight. I looked to my left and saw Garrett, Kinny, Perish, and Loren. Perish had Garrett on his hands and knees and Loren was on his back underneath Garrett. He was sucking him off and Garrett was reciprocating. The sengil's stiff cock was glistening with saliva as Garrett devoured him. On his knees watching the three was Kinny who had his eyes on me, his hands swiftly moving on his dick, surrounded by a thatch of flaming red hair.

And to my left, Silas was on his back getting fucked by Elish. Kessler was behind Apollo and Apollo was making out with Silas. The whole family seemed weaved together, fitting into one another like puzzle pieces.

"This is nuts," I mumbled to Jack who had his knee so far up it was almost touching his ear. Ceph was kissing Jack's neck, his muscular body enveloping and consuming him. Artemis was kneeling in between Jack and I, watching both of us get fucked by the brutes.

I hadn't seen much of Artemis before, and in my high state I felt like making a connection with him.

"Hi, Artemis," I said through my out of breath moans. I lifted up a hand and waved at him.

Artemis turned his head towards me, sweaty silver-white hair stuck to his face and framing his purple eyes, his pupils were huge. He was just as high as I was. He was pretty fucking handsome, he had Silas's eyes but Elish's facial structure.

"Hey, Sanguine." Artemis grinned, before his eyes flickered up to Nero. Nero was picking up speed, his moans and grunts getting closer and closer together. He was close, though I hadn't even been paying attention to my own cock.

I looked up and saw I was hard, and the pink head was dripping pre-cum. I took it into my hand to stroke it but no sooner had I done that did Artemis's hand bat mine away. He took my cock into his hand and started finishing me off, just as Nero let out a cry and started deeply pushing into me.

Artemis picked up his pace; Nero was still pressing my knees back, sucking in ragged breaths as his hips gave me several last thrusts. As soon as he lifted himself onto his knees Artemis leaned down, and took my cock into his mouth.

That was it for me, Nero hitting that spot inside of me had been building me up, and it only took several generous licks and strokes of Artemis's talent mouth and hand before, with a cry, I started to cum.

Like starved dogs the cum was fought over. I watched as the pleasure ripped through me like an electric shock as Artemis put his mouth over the head to catch the spurts of creamy white semen, only to have Nero grab my dick from him to catch the next. A string of cum shot onto his face before the head disappeared into his mouth, and when Artemis came to claim the last of it, Nero put a burly hand on his face and pushed him away. If I wasn't in the middle of orgasming I would've laughed at that.

Nero gave up my dick after my orgasm subsided and gave it to Artemis to clean up the rest. Then, sensing his brother needed help, I saw Apollo crawl over with a grin. He took Nero's place and I watched him separated my cheeks and started licking Nero's cum out of my ass. The pleasure of this was overwhelming, I threw my head back and swore, then got an even further wave of shock when Artemis straddled me and took my dick into his hand. I was surprised to see that not only was I still hard, but I was immediately ready to go again.

I needed my own supply of this ressin, I quite liked it.

Artemis sunk it in with a grin that matched the one of his identical twin brother, and with a smirk back I closed my eyes and felt the pressure, followed by the release of tension as my cock broke into him.

Jack giggled, I could recognize that giggle anywhere. I opened one eye and looked at him and saw that he had his chin resting on his crossed arms. He had his ass up in the air, with King Silas behind him, his green eyes locked on my body as he slammed himself into my boyfriend. It seemed like I was just blinking but with how everyone was switching positions I think time was going by faster than I thought.

"You're so fucking high, baby," Jack said playfully. He was glowing with sweat and I could see wet spots of cum underneath him. "Your pupils are huge, I can barely see any red." Jack let out a sharp cry as Silas picked up his pace. I just loved how his silver hair shook back and forth with Silas's movements, like his entire body was dancing to a choreographed song.

"I can't even see yours," I laughed. I grabbed onto Artemis's back and pulled him onto me. The silver-haired twin let out a soft moan and started licking and nipping my neck, his hips still moving back and forth. I could feel cum already in his ass, dripping down onto my testicles. It was quickly being devoured by a tongue though as his brother pursued every loose drop.

Jack smiled at me; he looked high out of his fucking mind. We all were, every chimera and sengil I could see had dilated pupils, their guards completely down and any inhibitions they had gone with the white powder encrusted on their nostrils, even Elish.

Fuck... I looked and saw Elish. He was on Nero now, thrusting into the brute chimera who was on his side with one leg bent at the knee and being held back in his hand. Elish's face was tensed in concentration, kneeled over Nero with a hand on the mattress to support him. Nero was staring at the various sexual acts taking place in front of him, his eyes glassy and glazed over.

I guess this was my family. Tomorrow we would go back to our jobs, our duties, and commitments. Tomorrow we would go back to addressing our greaters as Master and each other as brothers. We would run Skytech, Dek'ko, the college, the greywastes, and Skyfall, with stoic faces, unwielding eyes, and a powerful iron fist. We would go back to subtly manipulating each other, trying to outsmart one another to win favours with our king or brothers we wanted to impress. We would all go back to our day-to-day routines as the great and feared chimeras of Skyfall.

We were kings, princes, imperial generals... but right now, we were just family, brothers, and lovers.

And tonight I truly became a part of this crazy family of mine.

I could never be more happy.

CHAPTER 50

I WOKE UP FROM WHAT SEEMED LIKE A HUNDRED year sleep. There was bits of gunk crusted in my eyes, and as I tried to breathe I realized it was plugging my nose too. Everything seemed gunked shut and as I rubbed my eyes and freed them from their crusty prison I could feel the same crap all over my face and the prickly beginnings of my facial hair.

I tried to shift over to my side but as soon as I moved I winced. My body felt like it had been tenderized by a meat hammer.

Then, as my mind came back to me, I remembered that it pretty much had been.

For the entire damn night.

My eyes opened. I looked over and was immediately greeted by two dull black eyes, staring at me with a look so flat and miserable if I could manage it I would've smiled. My poor Jack looked as pathetic as I felt. He had the covers pulled up to his chin and his silver hair was sticking out in all directions, it looked like sometime during the night he had lost an earring as well.

"Kill me," Jack mumbled weakly, then he pulled the covers up further. "No... get me drugs, then kill me."

"No, you need to kill me first." I yawned before, despite of the pain, I chuckled. "That would work now wouldn't it?" I weakly grabbed my pillow and playfully pushed it against Jack's face as if to smother him.

Jack snorted and grabbed my pillow, he threw it weakly back at me and I stuffed it back under my head. "I feel horrible, every time the family does this I swear I'll take it easy next time. Then Nero and Ceph come with their monster cocks and I'm back to needing a wheelchair for a week."

"I still like my killing ourselves idea." I yawned again, feeling my jaw pop.

"Silas, Elish, Nero, and Garrett do that," Jack explained, his voice still rather pathetic and frail. "Since they have to run Skyfall. Technically we could, but I guess they wanted us to suffer this time." Then both our attention was turned to a looming figure in the doorway.

"But at least that means you get to borrow one of their sengils," Kinny said with a smile, though the poor boy looked just as tired as we did. "I prepared you two some Dilaudid powder. I thought I would see if you were hung-over before I offered some food. I wasn't sure if you wanted a light meal, a heavy one, or none at all."

"We need one of these permanently," I mumbled to Jack, then turned to address Kinny. "I'm not hung-over at all I just feel like I got hit by a truck. Meat, eggs, bread, and put cheese on all of it. What about you, babe?"

Jack nodded. "And coffee, Kinny. Lots of coffee… feel free to wait an hour or three to put the order in. We'll drag out asses to the living room once the food arrives."

"Speak for yourself," I said, and pulled the covers over my face.

Two hours later the sengil summoned us for our breakfast, though when I slagged my ass into the living room and saw the clock I realized it was five in the afternoon. This didn't surprise me though, I lost track of time but I gathered none of us made it back to our apartments until the sun had already risen.

"What's the last thing you remember?" I said to Jack. I was sitting on the couch and he had his head on my lap, I was lightly playing with his hair as we watched a marathon of Futurama. None of us had the energy to change the channel so we were watching Nero's TV channel.

"Elish fucking you."

I looked down at him and narrowed my eyes. "Don't even joke about that."

Jack stared up at me with an innocent look on his face. His colour had come back after a good meal, lots of coffee, and a healthy dose of opiates. Though he was about to look like a battered wife if he kept joking about Elish and I having sex.

"It's true," Jack said, he seemed amused at my denial. "You two were last and we all watched since, well, it was quite the sight to see. I was in the middle of Loren and Garrett, then everything kind of faded into darkness. I don't even know how we got home."

My mouth curled at the thought of Elish on top of me. Sure I respected Elish but… fuck, not enough to sleep with him. Jack laughed lightly and puckered his lips for me to kiss but I shook my head and pinched his nose instead.

We didn't move that much for the next several hours, and after watching poor Kinny try to clean our apartment we invited him to sit and watch television with us. The sengil obliged without hesitation and sat down with bowls of potato chips, some of which were appropriated by the kittens and Jett. I never would've figured that kittens would like potato chips but there you go.

Never more than today was I glad to be a chimera, there was no job for me to go to and no Skyfall for me to run. I would have to enjoy this time in my life before Silas saddled me with a job. Though at least I could just kill myself and be all fresh and new for the morning. There were so many perks to being immortal.

I loved this family – everything was just fucking wonderful.

Then the television started to flicker, the image of Bender became scrambled and distorted before Futurama disappeared entirely, replaced by a blue screen.

"What the fuck?" Jack said annoyed. "Kinny, go hit the receiver."

Kinny got up with a grunt and walked up to our entertainment center. He smacked his palm against the top of the black receiver before reaching over to wiggle the wires. Though nothing was working, a blue screen taunted Kinny's efforts.

Jack made an annoyed noise and changed the channel, but that channel was blue too, as he surfed through all of Skyfall's channels we were dismayed to see that every channel on the television had gone offline.

I sighed. "Maybe there was a power outage or something?"

Jack shrugged and lifted himself off of my lap, he smacked the remote against his knuckles. "I hope nothing is wrong with the satellite. It might take Skytech months to find another satellite signal for us to use." Then he got up. "I'm going to call Silas and see if he knows what's up."

"No." I shook my head. "He must already know. When peoples'

television goes out they get really pissed off really quickly. He'll just get mad at us."

My boyfriend stopped and nodded. "You're right... we have some movies we can watch at least. I don't have the mental energy for video games. What about *Seven*? That movie is pretty good, have you–"

All of our attention was drawn back to the television when the blue on the screen suddenly changed. It showed a room that was draped in black curtains with a wooden stool in the center. It... it looked like it was a live feed from the video quality.

Then to my shock a figure with washed out pink hair and blond roots appeared on the screen, and sat down on the stool.

Valen.

Valentine Dekker looked rough. Not only was his faded pink hair knotted and messy, but his face was grey and gaunt, and his usual sparkling pink eyes were dull and surrounded by thick black circles. He looked horrible, but why was he on the television? Where was he? Why wasn't he dead?

"Valen..." I heard Jack whisper. I stood up and took my place beside him as we watched Valen adjust the camera so it was focused right on him.

"This is a message for King Silas Dekker," Valen said to the camera. "My former king and my former master. Yes, after constant abuse and rejection by my family I have come to the decision to renounce my status as prince and as a Dekker. I have joined the rebellion and will not rest until the Dekker's are out of power and Skyfall is liberated. The human race was free before the Fallocaust and it will be free now."

"Shit..." I swore, my insides started to boil with anger as that smug-fuck little shit stared into the camera. I wanted to jump right through it and strangle him. Who the fuck did he think he was?

"I know what you're thinking, King Silas," Valen continued. "Why the fuck should you care? I'm nothing but a failure to you, nothing but a rejected science experiment. I'm worthless to you and because your scientists failed to produce what you wanted I'm condemned to life as a dog to be kicked and eventually put down. Especially now since Sanguine Dekker decided to slither his mentally-handicapped self into my life. The fact that you see that retard as a success and me as a failure is the worst insult of all, and as such, I feel no guilt as to what I'm about to do. You deserve it, you deserve it for how you've treated me."

Jack's heartbeat spiked and so did mine. Valen then left the view of the camera and I could see him talking to someone off of the screen. Jack and I both didn't say anything, but, knowing he needed it in that moment, I slipped my hand into his.

Then Valen came back and, oddly, he was holding a briefcase in his hand. He sat down on the stool and a smile curled his lips. Without a word he clicked the two locks on the briefcase and opened it – then pulled out small clear cylinders.

"What the hell are those?" I said confused. Each cylinder, with a black cap and a white label, held inside of it a small white piece of organic matter.

"I don't know…" Jack whispered, his head shook back and forth. "But Valen seems to know."

"You know what these are, King Silas." Valen's eyes flickered up to the camera, a dangerous half-smile on his face as he waved one of the cylinders back and forth in front of the camera. Then surprisingly… he dropped one onto the ground. There was a crash of breaking glass and the camera panning down to the broken container, the organic matter in the center, surrounded by the clear fluid it had been floating in.

"There are seven left, and every day I will break one more. You will deliver Sanguine Dekker for three bottles, Jack Dekker for the two, and a truck full of ammo and weapons for the remaining two. You will deliver me Sanguine and Jack first by tomorrow evening at the Wal-Mart entrance in Irontowers. If I see any surgical scars on them, showing me that you've made them immortal beforehand, I'll break every single fucking glass." Valen snapped the lid of the briefcase shut and handed it to someone off screen. "There will be no bombings of Skyfall since you obviously don't give a shit about your people, so this is a direct attack against you. I'm not fucking around, you wanted the second generation to become true chimeras, well here is your wish, *my liege*. Good evening."

The screen went back to blue for a split second, before the channel Jack had switched to came back. Neither of us spoke for a moment, we just stared at the screens, dumbfounded.

"At least… we're already immortal," Jack said slowly. He had his other hand covering his mouth as he stared at the screen in shock.

I nodded slowly. "Let's go to Silas's apartment and see if he's there. Valen was acting like he knew that those cylinders were important to Silas. We might… we might just have to go in there and get them for him." I pulled on Jack's hand and the two of us headed towards the elevator, Kinny behind us.

"I can't believe he's still alive," Jack said as we waited for the elevator. I squeezed his hand supportively, his heartbeat was a mess. "Though there never was proof that he was dead." His face darkened and his eyes flashed dangerously. "And he joined the fucking rebels." He looked at me. "We're going to kill him, the two of us. We'll make that clear to Silas."

I smiled, feeling more than just a little turned on by that lethal expression on his face. I really loved it when he acted all chimera in front of me. There would be nothing more I'd love to do than hunt down and kill Valen with my boyfriend. We were a virulent team and I was itching to prove that to the family.

"We will, it'll be fun, especially since we can't die." I winked at him.

The elevator doors opened, but the elevator wasn't empty. Elish was standing with an annoyed and angry look on his face.

"Why couldn't you walk up the four flights, you lazy imbeciles!" he snapped, obviously pissed the elevator had stopped for us. "Get in already. King Silas is going to be beside himself with anger." Then he looked at Kinny, his already threatening purple eyes seemed to burst into flames. "You – stay behind if you value your life."

Kinny didn't need to be told twice, he nodded and sprinted back to the apartment as the doors closed on the three of us.

"What's in those vials?" Jack asked as the elevator started to climb the last three levels.

"Something extremely important," Elish responded in a tone covered in ice. "More important than all of our lives. Prepare yourselves, the king is going to be out of his mind with emotion. He will be different than what you're used to; handle it like chimera adults or I will break your skulls."

"Yes, Master Elish," Jack and I both said. As the elevator stopped and the doors opened I reflected on the previous night when every single one of us was naked and in each other's arms. Even Elish and I if Jack's smirking admission was indeed correct. What I had deduced that night had come to pass, lovers for our family gatherings, but the next morning we stepped back into our shoes and became brothers, masters, and submissives again.

Elish walked ahead of us, when he rested a hand against the door he glared at the two of us. "Let me go in first, stay in the shadows where you two belong, am I understood?"

"Yes, Master Elish," Jack and I said again, and Elish opened the one of the double oak doors and glided in.

"DID YOU SEE THAT!?" I heard Silas scream. My face fell. King Silas sounded like he was in absolute agony, he sounded like his heart was getting ripped out of his chest.

Immediately I headed towards the door, Jack tried to grab my arm but I jerked it away. Silas had dealt with me at my worst, it was time for me to repay him for his patience and kindness.

I walked into the apartment to Silas in a horrible state. His face was twisted in extreme anguish, his hands clutching his hair; he was pacing with wide and staring eyes as Elish stood beside the support beam that separated the living room and one of his sitting rooms.

"We will get it back," Elish said calmly. "You heard Valen, he wants Sanguine and Jack dead and we can give him just that."

"He broke one already," Silas yelled, his voice seemed to start off as normal but by the end of his sentence he was screaming again. "He broke one… he broke one already. Did Nero really recover Adler's corpse? Tell me they don't have him too, promise me!"

Elish held his hands out to Silas, trying to calm him down. "I saw the baby's corpse, love, the baby did indeed die. We're guessing that perhaps you threw the briefcase out of the plane after it was hit in an attempt to save Sky's brain matter. The rebels must've seen it and retrieved it."

Sky's brain matter? I stopped several feet away from the door and turned around to Jack. "Brain matter?" I whispered to him.

Jack held onto my arm and we both turned our attention back to Silas.

"I'll murder that little shit. I will kill him slowly!" Silas screamed, his eyes seemed to glow green like they had been coated in uranium. "I should've drowned that little bitch as soon as Garrett confirmed his enhancement had failed. I swear on Sky's grave I will never put up with failed chimeras ever again!"

Silas let out a choke, before he stumbled forward. Elish caught him and the king completely broke down. He clenched his jaw, his eyes wide from inconsolable pain, but the king didn't cry, he seemed so insane with emotions that no tears were coming, there was just inhuman, uncontrollable pain and sadness.

"I want my Sky back," Silas screamed, though he seemed to snarl this at the same time. His hands clenched Elish's robes and tore at it. "I want him back, Elish. I have to have him back. I can't do this. I have to have him back." Silas kept repeating this like a mad man. "I need to have him back. I need to have him back."

He wants Sky back? But who was Sky? Was he a chimera that Silas had loved or someone before the chimeras were even created?

It didn't matter, whoever Sky was his brain matter was inside those bottles. My master need those vials to make him happy and I was going to get them for him. I couldn't stand by and see him like this, it filled me with such an anger that I was helpless standing here. And I was no longer helpless.

I grabbed Jack's shoulder as Silas's agonizing cries filled the room. I turned him to me.

"Can you fly a Falconer?" I asked him.

Jack looked shocked at Silas's reactions, but he managed a nod.

I gave one more passing glance at Silas, his face stricken like he had shell-shock, his eyes seemed twice the size as they usually were, or perhaps it was the whites that were showing. Either way it was a jarring sight, it was like I was looking at a monster and yet, a fragile being at the same time; one I felt compelled to comfort. This man had ended the world; he had seen the terrors of the last world war. He was strong, but as I looked at that terrorized face I realized that behind those emerald eyes lay a deep and terrible pain.

A rage swept through me, but the rage wasn't directed at Silas. It was a rage for the injustice I was seeing play out in front of me, because my king had been through enough in his long life and he didn't need this. He didn't need something so important to him, to his past, taken away.

Silas had told me last night when he had turned off that remote control, he had said that one day I would be his bodyguard. And I didn't need to be in psychosis to do this job, I would get the vials back for him. I would bring them to him and be the person to put that smirk back on his face.

I loved my master, I owed him everything, my freedom, my sound mind. I was bound to him and he was to me, no matter how much Elish and Jack hated it.

"Let's go," I said to him.

Jack nodded. We turned from the gut-wrenching scene in front of us and headed for the stairwell. Though I was confused when Jack started going down the stairs instead of up to where Silas kept the family's personal Falconer.

"We need guns," Jack said simply when I inquired about this. "Nero has guns, lots of them. We'll sneak into his apartment and grab some assault rifles, ammo belts, grenades, maybe some knives."

"I like the sounds of this," I said. The empathy I felt for Silas and the excitement of going to Irontowers to kill Valen was creating the perfect chemical reaction inside of me. I could feel the adrenaline bubbling and churning and it was starting to make my head light.

"We don't even have to worry about dying," I chuckled as we started on the last flight of stairs until Nero's floor. "Sometimes I forget the reality of that. I still can't believe I'm never going to die."

"I try not to think about it; when I think about the reality of living for eternity it makes my stomach fill with butterflies," Jack said as he picked up his pace. Though our boot steps were barely registering on the high ceilings of the stairwell, we were both trying to be quiet. Perhaps we were mutually afraid that Elish would bark at us to get our asses back to Silas's apartment; no doubt he wouldn't approve of us barging into Irontowers but I didn't want to waste time planning. Valen had already shown he was willing to smash those vials.

The two of us entered onto Nero's floor, and without knocking, I quietly twisted the door handle and peeked inside. When I couldn't see anything or hear anything I motioned for Jack to follow me and tiptoed inside.

Nero's place looked exactly what you would expect Nero's place to look like. Purple walls and grey carpet, black leather couches and chairs, a giant television and sound system, movie posters and hot guys with their cocks hanging out on the walls, but hilariously enough some of them were posted next to framed paintings of people in Victorian outfits and groups of people in scenery, paintings that looked like they had been stolen from a museum.

Then I spotted it, a large metal gun rack with a glass front, ten assault rifles on display and underneath the rack, a table littered with miscellaneous ammo, pistols, knives, grenades, and… sex toys.

Yeah, this was Nero and Ceph's apartment alright.

I walked inside.

"Come to steal my guns, eh?"

Jack and I both jumped. We saw Nero with his arms crossed, leaning against the door frame of his bedroom. Ceph was grinning beside them.

I sighed, they were both naked and Nero's cock and public hair were glistening with lube. Didn't they get enough last night?

"Did you hear Valen's television announcement?" I asked. Since Nero knew why we were here I made a beeline for his guns and ammo and started putting on a holster for around my chest.

"Yep, we did, we were just finishing up before we called a chimera meeting. You two aren't going alone, immortal or not," Nero said as he started putting on a pair of green cargo pants. "Wait for the meeting."

I shook my head. "No, we're going now. Valen wants the two of us anyway so what's the meeting going to be about? We're going anyway. Those vials…"

"… hold Sky's brain matter, I know," Nero said as he belted his pants. "Si's flipping out isn't he?"

I nodded, handing the same type of holster to Jack. "Who's Sky? Why is he so devastated over Valen having those vials?"

"Sky was Silas's boyfriend before the war," Nero explained. "He was madly in love with him and he's been trying to clone an exact copy of him, but Sky had some special shit going on and it's proven to be real difficult for the smart chimeras to do. The brain matter gets eaten up as he attempts to make a Sky baby so this brain matter is extremely valuable to him. You're going to get major favours with him if you do manage to recover it." Nero started buttoning up Ceph's jacket for him. I turned around to ask Nero more questions when I saw a look cross over his face as he looked at his fiancé.

Then Nero stopped, he looked at me with his face lined in a deep scowl. "Lots of fucking favours… Silas would worship the feet of whoever brought that brain matter back to him."

I started sheathing knives to my belt, including my favourite long dagger I recognized from killing Jasper last night, it was blackened. "Yeah, I'm not fucking doing it to get his praises, Nero. I'm doing it because it's the right thing to do."

"Yeah…" Nero's voice trailed. "You're fucking noble like that…"

I looked Jack up and down, he looked sexy as hell. He had an assault rifle on his back and an ammo belt, and several knives on his belt and two grenades in his pockets. He was armed and ready and so was I.

I turned around to leave, but found myself almost running into Nero.

My brother and friend pushed past me and started handing Ceph weapons.

"What are you doing?" I blinked.

"Turn the Falconer on and get ready," Nero instructed. "That's an order. We're going with you."

"What!" I exclaimed. "You? Why? We can do this shit ourselves."

Nero shook his head. "I need to come to do the trade-off anyway. Valen's obviously taking you so someone needs to get the five ransom vials. We're going, we'll break you out after, and when we get the briefcase we're going to say Ceph got it back."

"Why…?" I said slowly.

Nero looked at me, a rare look of heavy emotion on his face. His lip pursed and he glanced at Ceph who was zipping up a bullet proof vest.

"Because if Ceph brings Silas that briefcase… I think that'll be what it takes for him to make Ceph immortal." Nero's voice softened. "He's… made no mention of making him immortal, Sanguine. I'm… afraid he has no plans to do it." For the second time today my heart started to clench, another stoic and strong family member of mine was showing emotion that was complete opposite of their personalities. "I can't lose him, Sangy. I can't watch him grow old and die… I love the little fucker."

"Aww, Nuuky…" Ceph whispered.

I guess that was it then. There was no way I wasn't going to let Nero do what he needed to do to make Ceph immortal. If there was someone out there that I owed more to than Silas, it was Nero.

"Okay… we'll warm up the plane," I said with a nod and a faint smile. Then, without another word, Jack and I both headed towards the door.

CHAPTER 51

I LOOKED OUT THE WINDOW OF THE FALCONER AND saw the impressive city of Irontowers below. It was large and had many tall buildings. Some broken and crumbling with piles of grey debris at their feet, others fully intact to the point where I was sure people could live inside of them. It had several skyscrapers as well, all of them standing tall though they held streaks of black stain that made the broken windows look like they were crying.

The roads were an interesting sight as well. Some of the paved roads were cleared off, though you could see the hairline cracks through them. Others held bumper to bumper cars; all of them rusted shells that stained the ground below them brown. These cars were packed like sardines on the main road and the double-laned road leading out onto the highway, people desperately trying to escape the bombs though it looked like a lot of them were unsuccessful. From an aerial point of view it looked fascinating, it was like the universe had pressed pause on their lives. Time continued to flow forward but the lives of these people had been snuffed right out.

And made everything grey… just like my greywastes, my home, Irontowers was nothing but a marble collage of greys, blacks, whites, and the occasional streak of rusted brown from the cars. It was a dizzying sight to see all of these buildings below my feet, hundreds of them and miles and miles of cracked road, and soon I would be stepping down on this pavement. My first time back in the greywastes in almost a year.

"We're touching down," Ceph called from the cockpit.

Jack looked down at the city, and I was proud to see that my boyfriend's face held no looks of worry or concern. Jack stared down at the grey, broken buildings with an underlining energy about him that told me he was excited. But why wouldn't he be? We were immortal and no matter what we would come home. Even if we had to take a few weeks to resurrect from our injuries.

"What's on your mind, love?" I asked him. There was a shake around us as the Falconer's engine switched and the wings adjusted. These planes could land vertically; they were one of the last military planes made before Silas started the Fallocaust, and Silas owned every one of them that the Legion had been able to recover.

Irontowers reflected in Jack's eyes as the plane started to lower, the large Wal-Mart in plain view which was surrounded by a parking lot. Though as I inspected our destination I saw scorch marks on the ground and charred buildings, I had thought it was just normal wear from my aerial view but I realized it was from the legionary invasion I had missed during my first resurrection.

"I'm surprised at myself…" Jack said with a thin smile. "Because I really am becoming a chimera. I'm not scared at all; I'm excited. Immortality really is something else. The only thing I'm worried about is that if we have to resurrect for months… we'll miss the kittens growing up and they may not remember we're their owners."

His face split into a smile as he said this, as if he knew it would make me laugh and, sure enough, it did. I kissed him and lightly stroked the back of his neck tenderly. "We'll not only come back to our kittens, we'll be the ones to make Ceph immortal."

Nero whooped from the cockpit. Jack and I laughed again and exchanged another kiss. It wasn't long after that the plane touched down on a street about a quarter block away from the Wal-Mart. It was in another parking lot surrounded by smaller single-storey structures; it wasn't completely hidden but it was harder to get at from the main road which was packed with cars. So whereas we could leave in a whim, it would take a long time for their military vehicles to get to us if we were being pursued.

Armed to the teeth and Ceph in full combat armour and a helmet, the four of us started walking down the street towards the Wal-Mart in front of us. The lighter mood the four of us seemed to have had left as soon as that door had opened though. We were quiet and on guard, four pairs of eyes scanning and going over every exposed window in case we were being watched.

This place smelled like the city Nero and I had been in together, the ones with the celldwellers. It had the same musty and stale smell to it that just smelled like home to me. Though smelling my old home didn't fill me with warmth, it immediately put me on guard and switched my mind right back into survival mode.

"No electronics…" I mumbled under my breath, the quiet whisper that all chimeras used when they wanted only our advanced hearing to be able to pick up our words.

"No animals either," Nero mumbled back. "Perish has been releasing F4 carracats steadily here with the game animals, urson and deacons too. He's been releasing them on the north side though, perhaps they haven't made it this far yet. Or else the rebels have been shooting them." Nero looked ahead, the Wal-Mart was quickly coming closer. I could see a barricade of sandbags and brick in front of the large building, and more freshly plastered brick which made up the front. They had been repairing this place to be a fort from the looks of it, but this was confusing. Why would they build their base in a place where they knew the chimeras could find them? Perhaps they thought since they had Valen we would be more careful about where our bullets went – if so they were idiots.

"You two are going to go quietly," Nero instructed. Our feet had just hit the thinner pavement of the parking lot, the entire stretch of road so cracked and broken it resembled the bottom of a dry lake bed. There were even tuffs of yellow and, surprisingly green, grass poking out as well. Though I would bet the radiation was weaker here since we were so close to the radiation-free Skyfall and factory towns. "We'll bring the five vials back to King Silas just so we know we have those ones safe. If you have the opportunity or you see they're not as strong as you think – shoot and bite your way out and light a fire for us to find you. You have a day to get this done before the family comes to get you. How's that sound?"

I exchanged glances with Jack and we both nodded. "We can do that," Jack said.

There was silence after that but the silence wasn't for long. As we passed an old shopping cart corral we saw the first signs of life emerge from the Wal-Mart. Two men dressed in military camo with a red and green band around their arms and large guns on their backs. They propped the doors open with bricks and a moment later, Valen walked out.

I heard an odd sound and glanced over. I realized that Jack was grinding his molars back and forth; he was glaring dangerously at Valen. I could practically see the chimera state coming to his black, pupil-less eyes. He looked dangerous; I loved it.

Valen spotted us, but surprisingly he immediately turned away, his arms crossed over his chest and his head hung low. This was the complete opposite reaction I had thought I'd see. Maybe Valen was only brave when he had a video camera separating him from his family.

What a fucking coward. We would shove a stick up his ass like a skewered pig and roast his body over the bonfire we'd make to signal the family. The entire Dekker clan could celebrate Silas getting those vials back with a big meal, maybe we'd even celebrate Silas announcing he was going to make Ceph immortal.

"Stay right where you are!" a booming voice suddenly sounded. The four of us looked over at a burly man with short blond hair. His face was creased in a sneer and he was ugly as fuck.

Not just that... I looked closer and realized that the entire right-hand side of his face had been burned and healed; it was covered in bumpy skin that looked like dried dough, much like mine had been before I'd become immortal. He was even missing his right eye which was clouded over and milky in its socket. He looked like one of the bad guys I'd see in the GI Joe comics I used to read as a child.

"We have Sanguine and Jack, we're not here for small talk," Nero called back, his voice dripping hatred. "Send the pink fuck over with the five vials. I want to see they're okay."

Valen, still huddled in on himself, looked up and immediately shrunk back. The little shithead looked absolutely terrified, just seeing him radiate such weakness turned my stomach. He was like a little mouse in the presence of cats, only around until one of them got hungry. He didn't belong with these rebels, that much was sure.

The man turned to Valen and nodded his head towards us. "Valen is going to come over and handcuff the two mutants. If you make a move to kill him, we'll destroy the vials and we'll kill Valen for good measure too. Jack will go first and Valen will bring you the two vials, then Sanguine will come next and Valen will bring you the three. Then get the hell out of here until you have our military weapons and ammo for the remaining two."

My brow furrowed at this and I saw Nero was scowling as well. Valen certainly didn't seem that popular amongst the rebels but he definitely wasn't a prisoner. He had no binds on him or anything plus he had his own gun. Maybe he was just low on the rebel totem pole.

"Alright," Nero said, making sure to hide his confusion in his voice. My friend and brother was in Imperial General mode, and it was a fascinating thing to see. All of us had our roles and duties, and leading the entire legion army was his and Ceph's.

Valen came over with a pair of handcuffs in his hand, strong-looking ones with links twice the thickness as regular handcuffs. He looked just as dishevelled and gaunt as he did on the camera, except he seemed even smaller now. I had always seen Valen dressed in bright colours to make himself stand out, purple vests, pink jeans, neon green shirts, I never realized it until I saw him in drab green and brown camo just how small and insignificant he was.

It looked like all Valen had been trying to do was stand out so the family… or someone… would notice him.

And as I looked at the sad and defeated expression on Valen's face, I felt a dangerous feeling inside of me, I think I felt bad for him.

My teeth locked and I shook it out of my head.

Valen stood in front of me, and as soon as he saw I was looking at him his face twisted into a sneer and his shoulders squared themselves. A weak attempt to try and make himself appear strong and in control but it was written on his face. The little fuckhead was terrified about this exchange; if he thought I was dumb enough to not see that he was a retard.

"Put your hands out," Valen said in a voice trying so hard to be authoritative and threatening. It was like when Mouse, my kitten, puffed himself up to try and appear threatening. In his head he was as big as an elephant, but to everyone else he was just something to laugh at.

"Are they keeping you prisoner?" I asked him in the whispered chimera tone.

But Valen didn't answer me back, he put the cold cuffs over my wrists and started tightening them.

"He can't hear you, his chimera hearing never developed. He's actually half-deaf, Silas busted one of his ear drums," Jack murmured to me. "You know he isn't anyway, he has a gun."

Valen dropped my handcuffed hands and looked up at me, before looking at everyone else in the group.

"I practically fucking raised you, your fucking crib was in my closet,"

Nero said darkly. "I bottle fed you, you unappreciative little bitch. How could you do this to your–"

Suddenly Nero's eyes glazed over and his mouth stopped moving in mid-sentence, next was Ceph and, to my horror, Jack's eyes rolled back in his head, though everyone still remained standing.

I whirled around to attack Valen but when I looked at him I saw his eyes had turned from pink to black.

Then a moment of recall that hit me with so much force it seemed to have its own physical weight. I had seen his eyes turn black before, and right before a strange dark vale enveloped my mind, I saw something in my memories.

Valen on the ground screaming, blood running down his nose, his face full of terror. It was hot, fire was reflecting in his eyes and it was burning my body. Yes, his body, it was hot and sweaty underneath my own. He was tight, I could feel his hole tighten around… around…

I was… having sex with him?

No, he must be putting things inside my head or something. I wouldn't do that, not after what has happened to me.

Then the cloak wrapped itself around my brain and everything became clouded and hazy. I was walking though, I knew I was walking. One foot in front of the other with my brothers on either side of me. We were all walking like robots, Valen in front of us with his head bowed.

What was happening? Was Valen doing this? The feeling inside of me was almost identical to the strange shrouded sensation that I got when Silas had flicked the switch on that remote. This feeling was stronger though, whereas the psychosis was suggestions, screaming demands, this was like someone was controlling my movements like a puppet master. All four of us were under this control.

But then…

It was gone.

The vale lifted while I was walking down a homemade hallway. It was made up of stacks of sandbags piled a foot higher than my head with boardwalks made of two-by-fours that stretched across the gaps. Everything was lit with bluelamps, casting a cold glow and haunting shadows on the barricades that surrounded us.

The first thing I wanted to do was grab Valen and break his neck but as I walked I saw several men with assault rifles, also in the rebel camo. So I decided to play along; I had Ceph to worry about.

Jack was to my right, his movements stiff and sluggish, his mouth slacked like he was completely out of it and gone. I walked like he did and also made my mouth loose, and kept on following Valen through this maze.

It was dark inside of here. I could smell sour must and the distinct aroma of a fire that was burning chemically-treated wood. Sure enough, in the distance I could see a haze of smoke and a stream of light for the smoke to escape. It looked like they had just started settling in, from the compact look of the sandbags and the dust collected around them I think these barricades had been made before the Fallocaust.

"Is the demon-looking one fully under your control?" One-eye asked. Valen nodded, and One-eye continued, "I want to get his DNA before he goes with the others." I stayed still as the leader turned my face towards his and pulled my upper lip. He whistled at my teeth before raising a hand and slapping me across the face.

Inside of me I was boiling alive, but I didn't flinch and I didn't move.

With a rough yank he pulled me down a different barricade maze and into an open room with a sandy linoleum floor. It was only a room because it had been closed in with the store shelving and more sandbags.

I immediately saw a woman with blond hair and green eyes. She was cutting open what looked like a severed biigo head with a scalpel.

"Oniks… we got him," One-eye said, and immediately my heart jumped. I had heard that name before, she was the undercover agent for the family. I gave an internal sigh of relief as the woman rose to her feet and walked over to me.

"He's conked right out…" she mumbled. One-eye laughed and gave me a slap upside the head.

"Sure is," he said. "Check out the teeth on him, and those eyes. If we can hack into their system again and collect more of their chimera research perhaps one day we can make one of those for the Crimstones to use. An entire army, eh, my dear?"

Oniks's eyes narrowed, obviously not too keen on being called *my dear*. She lifted up my lip like One-eye had done and shook her head in amazement. "If Valen wasn't masking his brain those teeth would be around our necks. I can't believe this worked, Valen is indispensable."

How was Valen doing this?

"Not just Valen." One-eye laughed dryly. "Your informant on the inside is twice as valuable as he is. If he didn't tip us off about the king flying overhead on that Falconer we would've never gotten a hold of such a priceless thing to ransom. Who would've known the king would be that obsessed over brain matter."

Inside my heart dropped to my stomach, but I didn't have time to process the information. It took every bit of restraint inside of me not to flinch as Oniks stabbed my arm with a long needle, so deep inside that I could feel it scraping against the bone.

And she didn't stop there, she moved the needle around in my skin until blood rushed into a vial attached to the top of the needle. When she was done she withdrew the needle and nodded to One-eye.

"Murphy can do the rest, he says he wants a day with this one and the others before we can kill them. We're going to tie a few rocks to Nero's neck and dump him in the sewers to drown until they find him," Oniks said as she held the shining red blood up to the light. "Take him back to Valen. I don't trust his abilities when he's so far away and I don't want to fucking be near this one if he snaps out of it."

No more words were exchanged. One-eye walked me down the maze of sandbags into what might've been the manager of this store's office by the metal desk and the look of the place. Though now it had been transformed into a dungeon-like prison. There were shackles and chains on the walls and half of it was enclosed in the same sandbag barricade. The wall to the left had been blown open as well but I couldn't see what was on the other side, it was too dark.

I saw Valen sitting on a chair, a rag held up to his nose; he looked weary. To my right, as I walked into the room, I saw Ceph, Nero, and then Jack who was standing beside the doorway. All of them looking like mindless drones.

"Can I have some food? Using the abilities takes a lot out of me..." Valen said in a weak voice. He wiped his nose and I saw a streak of red on his finger, just like when I had seen his eyes go black in that flashback.

Why didn't I know Valen could do this? Did any of the chimeras know? Did Silas?

"There's some ramen packs in the bathroom."

"You said... I could have some of Kimroy."

I heard a smacking sound before a person stumbled and fell, it wasn't Valen though – the one-eyed man had kicked Jack.

It took everything I had not to whirl around and attack that man, but I didn't. I kept the blank look on my face as Jack slowly got up, dirt covering his front and a large scrape on his face. He rose to his feet, still inside the vale, and stood beside a filing cabinet.

"Deal with it. Go tie them up in case your trick fails. Oniks already collected his blood." Then the sound of boots scraping against sandy ground but no more words were exchanged. I heard Valen sigh and more scraping boots that faded as he walked further away.

I looked around at my brothers. All three of them were standing like statues, staring into oblivion with dull expressions on their faces. As I watched them I was dismayed to see that our guns had been taken away while I had been in that temporary disconnection, all I had was the long knife I'd used to kill Jasper strapped to my ankle.

And I'm cuffed... I sighed and tested the chains. It looked like we were both deep inside of this building. If Ceph wasn't with us we could make a break for it even if we did get shot, but that was out of the question unless we were going to sacrifice Ceph.

So even though I was conscious – I wasn't sure what I could do about it at this moment. If Valen was some worshipped member of these rebels, or Crimstones as One-eye called them, I could hold him ransom, but it looked like he was still lower than dirt.

Valen came back into the room with a hot plate, a kettle sloshing with water, and a Cup-a-Soup ramen cup. He sniffed, looking miserable, and put the kettle on the hot plate. Then he pulled up a chair and put his sleeve against his bloody nose.

Not too long after I saw a tear drip down his cheek, before he buried his face into his hands and started to cry softly to himself. He cried and cried until the kettle started to boil, then, with shaking hands, he filled up his soup cup and curled up on the chair. His face was red and his lips trembling.

Then he looked at the four of us and wiped his eyes. As if we were an afterthought he got up and walked towards me. He grasped my handcuffed hand and picked up one of the shackles.

I pulled my hand back. Valen jumped and gasped, and when he looked up at me I saw his pupils retract like a wilting pink flower. He knew I was aware now – and he looked terrified.

But I had no madness for him, and no threats.

"You don't want to do this do you?" I said to him in a level tone.

Valen stepped back and I saw the black cloak his eyes, but I found myself able to actually push the vale away from my mind with ease. I wasn't sure how, or why I could do it but the others couldn't, all I knew is that I was immune to this power Valen now had.

I shook my head. Valen stepped back again, the pink coming back to his irises, then he turned to make a break for the door.

"Get me some ramen... I'll eat with you," I said, then I decided to call his bluff. "Or else I'll uncloak Nero, Ceph, and Jack's mind and I'll let them handle you."

Valen skidded to a halt, his heartbeat was revving like someone was flooring a gas pedal on an engine in neutral. I saw his hand clench the frame of the door before he turned around.

"How?" he asked, his voice just as weak and defeated as he himself looked.

"I have my ways," I said to him. "Now get me one of those Cup-a-Soup things. I'm hungry and it looks like we have a lot to talk about." He stepped back as I moved towards the hot plate. I pulled up a chair that had been collecting dust in the corner and sat down. "Go on, go." I nodded towards the door.

Valen just stared at me, the confusion was so palatable on him I could taste it. I enjoyed seeing him confused, in a way I myself was confused over how I was handling this, it was uncharacteristic for me to be this calm when faced with such dire circumstances. My darker, more derisive half told me I was just being cocky since I was immortal, but the nicer side of me told me I was growing up and I recognized that if I played my cards right – we could get everyone out of here safely.

I couldn't risk Ceph... I'd never be able to look Nero in the eye if I got Ceph killed, after all of this was my idea.

Valen came back with another of the styrofoam noodle cups and filled it with hot water. The entire time he was giving me nervous glances as if he expected me to attack him. He was used to dealing with chimeras of course, and I was used to acting like one, but I was seeing too many chinks in this kid's armour not to try the civil and safer approach.

When the second noodle cup was filled and had a fork resting on it, he handed me the fork he had been carrying around and his cup which had been simmering long enough for it to be done. This interested me, he was feeding me first even though he had told the one-eyed guy that he was hungry. What was with this kid?

I opened up the cup and stirred around the noodles. I had found a twelve case of these once when I was little and ate like a king for a week.

Even though there was next to no nutrients in them they were pretty fucking good. I took a few bites and eyed the kid who was just staring at his shoes.

"Are they keeping you prisoner?" I asked him.

Valen shook his head. "I went with them willingly, when I was gone for weeks trying to find and kill you I met them in a bar." He let out a long sigh. "I hung out with them and learned Silas was awake. Then I learned that not only was the family looking for you, that once again no one gave a shit where Valen was, no one cared about me once again. Story of my life."

"You've always been a pretentious, snobby little shit to me, maybe you're part of the reason they don't give a shit about you," I said, completely forgetting I wasn't trying to piss off the guy who had me in handcuffs and my friends and boyfriend under his mental control. "My first day of college when I ran into you you immediately treated me like dirt and started flaunting your chimera status like some sort of pampered prince."

Valen's mouth downturned. "When someone with no control over anything, no power over anything, and a family that hates them, has a chance to bully some dumb arian below them – you run with it," Valen explained dully. "Or at least that's what Mantis always told me. I didn't know you were a fucking chimera. You were just some dirty greywaster that was getting more attention from Jack and the family than me."

I mulled this over for a moment and ate a few more forkfuls of noodles. "I could see why that would piss you off, but was that really enough to betray the family?"

Valen's fuchsia eyes glared at me. "Don't flatter yourself, it wasn't you that made me do this. It's an entire lifetime of Silas's constant abuse, constant reminding that I didn't develop correctly, that I was a failed chimera. I was supposed to be his cicaro, did you know that? I was supposed to have one of the most honourable positions in the family – but he never gave me a chance. And when Silas started treating me like garbage, Elish followed, and after Elish the entire family started treating me like the lowest of the low. Do you have any idea what it's like to be hated because you were born wrong? To have your family hate you because of something you can't help?"

This struck me. I paused, and lowered my fork. "Actually, I do," I said to him. "I was a red-eyed, pointed tooth monster in the greywastes. I got crucified, burned, chased out of towns because of how I looked. I know what it's like to be punished for something you didn't have any control over."

Valen sniffed and picked up his styrofoam cup and peeled off the lid. "Then you came to Skyfall and now the entire family is kissing your ass. And what do I get?" Valen swept a hand around the room. "I thought joining the rebels would be my chance to take control of my life, but in the end I'm still treated like shit and if I step a foot back in Skyfall Silas will kill me in an instant." His lips pursed. "I don't even have a single friend there anymore. I read the bulletin this morning… the death announcements for Felix and Ludo, that on top of you killing my other three friends… I'm all alone." Then his expression got hard. "I have nothing left to live for but to take as many of you fucks down with me as I can."

"But wait…" I said. I glanced behind Valen at Nero, Ceph, and Jack. All three standing like mannequins staring into nothing with dead eyes. "How did you do that shit then?"

Valen didn't even look up, he just twirled his noodles around on his fork. He stared at them for a second before dropping the fork back into the steaming up. "I guess trauma was the key to unlocking my empath abilities because… I was able to finally do it… while you were raping me."

There was a clunk as I dropped the almost empty cup of food. My blood turned to ice as his words sunk into me but I found myself desperately shaking my head.

"I… I didn't do that…" I said slowly. I started to feel nauseas.

Valen laughed dryly. "I guess you wouldn't remember. I shut your brain off and Jack's while he was holding me down for you. You went limp, still inside of me, I had to pull you out and push you off of me. The buildings were burning from the rebels' missiles, and I left you two there, hoping you would burn in the inferno. I guess I wasn't that–"

"I didn't rape you," I stammered, my words coming too quickly as the sick feeling rotted my gut. "I've – I've been raped hundreds of times. I wouldn't… I'd never–"

I put my hand over my mouth, the emotion over this reality overwhelming me. "I'm… I'm sorry."

Valen shrugged; he took another bite of his food. "I'm worthless, Sam. I deserved it and worse. I was standing outside of your underground lair with a couple rebels with guns wanting to shoot you two when you fled the smoke. I'm not going to lie and play the victim, I'm too far into this shit to care what you think of me. I should be thanking you for making me discover my abilities."

I took a moment just staring at the wall, feeling disgusted with myself. Valen's justification did nothing to quell the sick feeling inside of me. If I was that angry I should've just killed him, not raped him. Even in psychosis that…

I thought back to when I had killed Ludo, how close I had been to fucking his corpse just because the psychosis had made me feel so sexually aggressive – who was I kidding? It was me to do that.

"Silas fixed my psychosis… kind of," I said to Valen. I don't know why I felt compelled to say that, I just felt like I should say something. "So that won't happen anymore…" Then I thought of something. "If your abilities work though – why didn't you come home? Silas would be happy to hear that enhancement took wouldn't he?"

"It's already too late, I smashed that vial," Valen said bitterly. "If I didn't I knew I'd get my head cut off by these *Crimstones* since no one would pay a ransom for me. And why should I go back?" He slammed his fork down again, his pale and unhealthy face creased with anger. "Silas would only like me because of my empath abilities, he still wouldn't give a shit about me. So fuck him, fuck the monarch, fuck Elish, and the entire family."

He ate the last several bites of his food before he threw the container behind the tipped over office desk. He looked absolutely miserable but in a way he reminded me of a child who ran away from home but had absolutely no idea what he was supposed to do once he left his backyard. This kid had no survival skills at all, but he had a mental power inside of him that seemed to rival Silas's. That could be a dangerous combination especially in the hands of the rebels. Valen was easily manipulated it seemed, and I knew this, but, oddly… what I was about to say next wasn't manipulation.

Because even though I had hated him while I was Sami Fallon, fucked in the head, insecure, and dealing with extreme mental issues – now that I was Sanguine Dekker, a confident, immortal chimera who knew his place in the family and felt secure in his life – I emphasized with him, I understood him, and I felt bad for him.

He reminded me of me when I was a lost eight-year-old, and I knew the dangers of a kid going off with the first older man who told you he wanted to be friends.

"I think we would've been good friends if we met each other under different circumstances," I said to him with a half-smile. "I think we would've been close, don't you think?"

Valen's troubled eyes seemed to soften, his lips disappeared inside of his mouth.

"Maybe," he replied. "It's too late now though, what's done is done."

I shook my head. "It's not. I have pull with Silas, me and him... we're close. Why don't you sneak us out of here and we can go home."

Valen looked hopeful for a moment before his doubt came back to him. "You're lying to me. You just want me to take off those cuffs and you'll kill me."

"I don't need cuffs to kill you, I'm made out of weapons," I said to him. "You know as well as I do the family is going to come and break us out."

"They – they won't risk killing you and Jack..."

"Jack and I were made immortal the night after Cypress was hit with that rocket launcher," I said, and when Valen gave me a suspicious look I pulled up my jacket, showing off my clean, blemish-free arms. "You have a lot to lose, Valen. Your best chance is to give Silas that briefcase and come home with us. Since your empath abilities have been discovered, you have a good chance of getting through this. Just... come home."

"To what?" Valen mumbled. "My friends are dead, the rest of the family fucking hates me..."

"I'll be your friend."

My heart threatened to break when Valen looked up at me. Because I saw in his eyes the same look I knew must've been my own every time a man had told me he wanted to be my friend. I saw hope, I saw relief that I would no longer have to be alone, and I saw caution – because I had been betrayed so many times by wolves in sheep's clothing.

And like me, the hope of finally having someone to talk to, of finally having some to trust, won out over years of being betrayed and burned.

Just like when I had gone with Jasper, even though my entire life was deciding to trust someone and then being betrayed by them. I saw myself in those pink eyes so much I could feel a burning behind my own.

Because I wasn't Jasper. I had gone from being the boy desperately wanting a friend, to being the one that could be that very friend.

I wasn't Jasper, I was Sanguine.

Valen's first real friend.

I held my shackled hand out, and hesitating at first, Valen took it. I pulled him up and rose with him.

"Come on, let's go home," I said to him.

And Valen nodded.

CHAPTER 52

AFTER VALEN TOOK OFF MY CUFFS, THE TWO OF US looked towards the other three who hadn't moved an inch. In the first test of his loyalty I stood back and crossed my arms, before nodding towards them.

Valen let out a pensive sigh. His shining pink eyes looked past me before narrowing slightly. I saw them turn black as he focused whatever strange ability he had been born with.

Then I heard several gasps, before the sounds of all three of them collapsing onto the ground. Though no sooner had they hit the dirty floor did they scramble to their feet.

"Good work, Sangy," Nero growled, his twilight-coloured eyes narrowing dangerously. "You're good at manipulating that little bitch." He took a step forward but Jack jumped in front of him and lunged for Valen.

"NO!" I snapped at them. I grabbed Jack and shoved him backwards right into Ceph who was trying to get to his feet. I spread out my arms and glared at them. "It wasn't manipulation, nothing I said was false. He's going home with us and that's an order." Then my eyes flashed at Nero, the only man who technically outranked me. "You need to do this for me Nero. Valen is coming home with us."

Nero's face was the embodiment of rage but I didn't stand down. I glared at him and I didn't flinch nor did I blink.

The brute chimera let out a frustrated, but muffled, bellow before whirling around and laying a punch onto the brick. "Fine!" he snapped, then he turned around. "I'll go with this but I will not back you up when Silas gets a hold of him."

"Deal," I said, before turning to my boyfriend.

Jack's expression matched Nero, though I saw a mixture of hurt. I put a hand on his shoulder and squeezed the tense skin. "A life of rejection affects everyone differently, love. Please, all I'm asking is a chance. Will you trust me?"

Jack burned me with his eyes, before I saw him look past me. I turned and saw Valen staring at the ground again, making no move to run from the three chimeras chomping at the bit to rip him limb from limb.

"I'm sorry, Jack," Valen said simply. "Can we get out of here now?"

Suddenly the ground underneath our feet started to shake, immediately followed by a loud and thunderous bang that rattled the teeth inside my head. I looked up just in time to see plaster and debris rain down on us from the ceiling, like a god above us had slammed its hand down on the roof.

"Let's go!" I barked. I pushed Jack out of the door and grabbed Valen, but surprisingly he pushed me away. "Wait!" Valen said hastily. He ran to the tipped over office desk and grabbed something.

The briefcase.

I immediately took it from him and pushed Valen out of the door, just as another explosion rocked the building, this time bringing on its heels the deafening crashing of something collapsing. My heart dropped at the deafening noise, I tried to mentally calculate where we should go next but all I could do in that moment was get everyone out of this office.

We rushed out of the makeshift prison we had been kept in and into the main part of the Wal-Mart, though we could barely see anything over the stacks of sandbags that acted like mazes throughout the structure. Though we didn't need to see the destruction that the explosions were bringing, as we ran down the maze a stream of light illuminated the path in front of us. When I turned around to check its source I saw that in the far right-hand side of the building there was a gaping hole in the roof. It was late in the evening but it was also spring, I think the daylight would stay for a few more hours, we had that going for us at least.

Another explosion. I coughed and heard the others around me hacking as dust rose up all around us; only four feet away from Valen a large air vent came crashing down, taking out one of the bluelamps and draping itself over the sandbag walls.

"Valen, what way out?" I yelled to him. I had his arm in my grasp, I didn't trust the others to not try and leave him behind. I wasn't going to leave him behind.

Valen looked around, his eyes wide. "We can't go to the front, that's where they'll all be…" Then he looked to the right, where the gap in the roof was. "Our best bet to escape undetected is to go through the connecting mall. The Wal-Mart is a part of a larger mall, there are a lot of exits in the main area but…" He hesitated. "The rebels have been capturing Perish's radanimals."

"But they're in cages?" Nero asked. He was already pushing Ceph over one of the sandbag barricades. I grabbed Jack, Nero took him and started helping him over them as well.

"The stores in the mall have those metal security curtains, they're behind those," Valen yelled. "They're –" There was a loud crack and a sandbag burst beside me. Before I even saw where it was coming from Valen pulled his assault rifle from its holder and soon the entire area was full of the sound of gunfire.

"Go, your turn," Nero yelled over the noise. I saw the rebel Valen was shooting go down in a spray of blood and more sand, so I grabbed the kid and pushed him ahead of me. Ceph grabbed Valen by the jacket and pulled him over, and, knowing that Nero's rank and pride would never allow him to go before me, I quickly climbed up the sandbag barricade and jumped to the other side, more ceiling debris and dust falling around us as explosions sounded in the distance in a way that felt like the apocalypse was happening again. Whoever it was they were bombing Irontowers again, and this building seemed to be their favourite target.

Nero's boots slammed down onto the ground behind me. I scanned the area, but before I could get a proper feel for my surroundings, Valen was waving us to follow him. With his hair coated in dust and dirt he started navigating through the ceiling material towards what I realized was a huge opening. Sure enough, to Valen's word, through the opening I could see rows of closed off shops and a second-storey with an escalator almost impossible to access because of debris. The second-storey resembled the first but it was full of shoddy barricades and even several abandoned vehicles.

The mall was in horrible shape and the hole in the ceiling illuminating the state of this building did it no favours. The shops were all closed with the metal security cages like Valen had said but even they looked flimsy and patched together. It was just dust and junk in every direction, some even stacked on top of each other to bar off what looked like blown out walls. Scars from a distant past but nothing had been given the opportunity to heal.

I sprinted ahead of Valen, my boots kicking fluffs of insulation that further added to the thick dust around us, the fine particles were clogging my lungs making each cough feel like I had swallowed sharp shards of glass.

"This ceiling is going to fucking collapse on us," I turned around and called to the others. They looked almost unrecognizable in the heavy dust. "Valen... where's an exit?"

Before Valen could answer us several gunshots rang out towards the main floor we had just come from. I looked into the heavy dust but saw nothing. I ran up to Valen and Jack and grabbed Valen's assault rifle. I rubbed my finger against the trigger and ground my teeth as I tried to pick out any movement, but it looked like the person was shooting blind, just as we had been.

But I was wrong, more gunshots snapped the heavy air in retaliation. I grinned and grabbed Jack's shoulder. "That's our family, they're coming to get us."

"We can't go through the front to get to them, this place is a maze even without the dust," Jack said, coughing into his hand. I spotted Nero and Ceph behind Jack, Nero was trying to wipe the dust off of Ceph's face.

We all turned to Valen. The pink-haired chimera was looking around with a panicked expression on his face, but looking to the chimera with the weakest eyesight wasn't going to get us out of here. I handed the assault rifle back to Valen and ran ahead of the group and into the dust, towards where I had seen several open hallways which might lead to an exit for us. I was having to go by memory though, the slight visibility we had only minutes ago had been reduced to nothing. It was like we were in a dust storm in the middle of the desert, even my eyes were becoming irritated and sore.

I held out my hands and after several steps they rested against a metal security cage.

I looked inside to see if anything was residing in it, or if there was a fire exit we could perhaps use.

Suddenly there was a flash of black. I stumbled back and almost fell as an extremely large irradiated bear called an urson slammed its paws against the security cage, making it rattle with such intensity I thought it was going to fall right on top of me. I scrambled away, knowing that getting the fuck out of its sight was what was best for our survival. So with my hand on the wall I sprinted through the dust until I felt the gap I was looking for.

Though as I turned to call the others a flurry of gunshots assaulted my ears. These ones so close I could see the sparking fire from the guns, more than one. This wasn't Nero shooting at something, someone had found us.

"Nero?" I called before doubling over coughing. I took another step when, just thinking this couldn't get worse than it was, I was thrown off of my feet by another explosion.

And this one was close – this one was really close.

Dust and chunks of plaster rained down on me. I threw my hands over my head and mouth and closed my eyes as I felt the ceiling debris hit my body. I swore and tried to look to where the group was but all I saw was grey.

"Jack?" I coughed. I knew he was immortal but I had to get to him. I crawled through the now knee-high piles of debris, hearing more gunshots – more gunshots.

Then a scream – a scream that didn't belong to my group. I looked up just in time to see a rebel fall to the ground, his eyes wide with horror and blood pouring from his eyes and ears. He was dead before he even landed on the ground.

Valen's work.

Another scream. I saw a silhouette in front of me but it disappeared. I managed to raise myself to standing but as I walked my left leg buckled underneath me. I looked down but saw nothing, though I could feel the blood start to soak into my socks.

More gunfire, and some debris from the ceiling falling onto my chest. I kept walking towards the shadows, my ears filling with a roaring noise as the sounds around me drowned out and claimed every single one of my senses.

Then a new sound… one that made me whirl around and stare at its source with my mouth open in shock. I screamed the word fuck louder than I had ever screamed it before as I heard the metal security cage fall to the ground.

And a large black figure come barrelling out and into the dust.

"Nero!" I screamed. I turned and ran towards the silhouettes, panic coursing through me. Rebels we could handle, we could do rebels, but I had seen urson before in the greywastes and you didn't fuck with those things. They were the size of grizzly bears before the Fallocaust and ten times as angry. The radiation had driven them and all radanimals into insanity and they never missed a chance to take their rage out on anything they came across.

"NERO, URSON! GET CEPH AND VALEN OFF THE GROUND!" I yelled as loud as I could, hoping my voice would carry over the chaos.

Suddenly behind me I heard a gut-wrenching scream. I ran towards it but a hand pulled me back. I turned and saw a ghost, someone completely covered from head to toe in dust, except he had a heavy fountain of blood running from his nose and mouth.

"Jack… found an exit…" Valen choked on his own blood, his hands were trembling. "He's going to get the family. He's out."

"You go too!" I yelled. I started backing up as I saw the shadow of the bear tossing someone around like he weighed nothing, guns were going off all around me. I swear these rebels had us surrounded, it felt like they were everywhere and yet I couldn't see any of them.

"They'll kill me, I don't even have the briefcase, you do!" Valen said, his voice shrill. He looked ahead where the bear was and his eyes widened. "Nero has my gun… Nero has my fucking… we – we have no guns."

"Sangy!" Ceph suddenly came barrelling towards us; he was out of breath and his head was bleeding. He grabbed me and started pulling me away from the urson. "The exit Jack just went through caved in as soon as he opened the door but he got out. We're going to the second level and we're going to find a window to jump from." Ceph turned around and I saw his face drop as he spotted the urson, though he didn't say anything. He pushed the two of us ahead of him, a large combat knife in his right hand.

Seeing that knife reminded me of the one I had. As I saw the outline of the escalator in the distance I reached down and pulled out the long narrow dagger I had sheathed on my ankle and let Valen go ahead of me. Though this made my walking up the slippery steps all the more harder, the briefcase was still in one hand and now my knife was in the other.

"How many rebels are back there?" I yelled, my voice drowned out by the gunfire, and the falling debris around us.

"Dozens," Ceph yelled back. "Nero's shot, he wouldn't let me stay, he's taking care of them, that stupid fuck… fucking faster, Valentine!" Ceph snapped, though it wasn't his fault, the escalator was uneven and hard to navigate with the junk it was clogged with, every step we took was loose and unbalanced and crap kept falling down the steep steps as we dislodged it.

Valen got to the top and looked around, blood dripping down his face and landing on the covered floors. He turned to wait for me but my foot was slowing me down, with every step more and more pain was shooting through me and though I could tough out the pain, the weakness in that leg was still there. Blood had pooled in my boot too, it squished with every step; I knew there was a lot of it.

Finally I got to the second level. I turned around to help Ceph, but for a brief moment the breath left my chest and I froze.

Behind Ceph was the urson, its milky white eyes glowing against the backdrop of dust. But as it moved towards Ceph I could see just how gigantic it was. It looked even bigger than it had in the cage and it was rapidly closing in on Ceph.

"Faster!" I screamed at him. I ran down and grabbed his jacket and pulled him. I could hear the urson's ragged huffs as it climbed the stairs

Ceph looked behind him and swore. The two of us ran up the rest of the steps, my heart exploding from the adrenaline boiling in my chest. The primal fear that claimed every man when he had become prey momentarily made me stop, but it was fleeting, the next thing I knew I was shoving Ceph towards Valen and blocking the escalator from the giant beast sliding and scraping up the steps; its small eyes wild on its large muscular face.

It stared at me before it reared up on its hind legs and roared. Rows and rows of yellowed and broken teeth contrasting against the hazy dust, I could see blistered and pus-filled sores inside of its mouth, and on its face too, crusting its skin in dull yellow that covered the patchy, scabby fur that was spread sporadically throughout its body. It was a terrifying creature, covered in muscles that flexed and rippled on its black skin, but it was still suffering from the radiation like every Fallocaust animal.

I kept my stance, trying to make myself as tall as possible, and felt a growl inside of my throat. I threw the briefcase down beside a tipped over planter pot and clenched the knife hard in my hand. The beast snorted at me and took another step, long black claws the size of my fingers scraping against the rubber stairs.

"Get Valen and go," I yelled to the two I knew were behind me. "I'm immortal and this is an order. GO!"

Ceph gave out a frustrated yell but I knew he was going to obey me.

Then there was a loud explosion of gunfire, so close to me it stung my ears. I thought that it had hit me but suddenly the urson let out a bellowed cry before shooting towards me in a desperate attempt to get away from the bullets. I jumped back, trying to get out of its way, but it charged right into me, knocking me off of my feet and throwing me backwards into a pile of jagged debris. I felt a sickening snap in my leg.

I'll never forget what happened next.

I looked up and saw the urson charging towards Ceph, Valen behind him. Valen got thrown backwards but Ceph was too taken by surprise to move. The brute chimera stared at the giant bear as it charged towards him. Then, in its madness, it reared up and pushed Ceph down, sending him crashing to the ground. With the combat armour hanging loosely off of him he tried to rise, only to have the bear take his head into his jaws and fling him like a ragdoll.

"CEPH!" I screamed. I scrambled to my feet but fell, pain ripping through my leg and my side. I screamed his name again and saw Valen running towards the bear, nothing in his hand but one of the ceramic planter pots.

Valen smashed the urson's head with the pot as the bear tore and ripped at Ceph's body.

The urson turned around, drool dripping off of its thick, scabby muzzle. And Valen, in all of his bravery, didn't move. He stayed still and even stepped closer, trying to distract the urson from Ceph who was now laying still.

I tried to get up again but when I failed for a second time I looked down to see what was stopping me. My heart sank when I saw the white of my leg bone poking out of the top of my boot, compound fracture, but… but I could still walk. I grabbed the bone and tried to shove it back into place but the pain almost made me pass out. Instead I started crawling towards the two of them.

"Sangy? Ceph?" Nero's voice knocked against the chaos inside of my head, but I was too focused on Valen and Ceph to answer. I crawled towards them, the knife in my hand, not knowing what I could do just knowing I couldn't watch them both be killed.

The bear reared up again and roared, Valen slowly backing up with his hands outstretched. I yelled at him to get back, to run, but he stayed in front of the seven-foot tall beast with the urson stepping closer and closer.

Then I realized – Valen was controlling it.

Sure enough, as I crawled closer I saw Valen's eyes had turned black again. Blood now flowing freely down his nose, mouth, and to my horror – his eyes. He continued to step backwards as the bear obediently followed him, its head lowered and its mouth open and oozing drool.

Then Valen's head snapped towards the metal railing of the second level, specifically to a gap in the railing that had been taken out in the explosion. The bear looked too and even though my mind was overwhelmed with a thousand screaming emotions I watched in awe as the urson ran towards the broken railing, and threw itself off of it, a loud crash sounded not soon after.

Valen collapsed onto his knees, just as Nero got to the top of the escalator steps.

He ran to me, he was bleeding from the neck and from the arms, bullet holes littered his black combat armour. I looked at him and saw the shock on his eyes.

"It got Ceph," I gasped and started hacking so hard blood sprinkled the dust. "It got Ceph, fucking help him." I pointed to Ceph and felt a lurch in my heart when I realized he still hadn't moved.

Nero's head snapped towards where I was pointing. He let out a bellowed scream and ran towards his fallen fiancé. I tried to crawl towards Nero as he dropped to his knees and picked up Ceph's head.

A pit formed in my stomach when I saw how Ceph's neck was moving, limp and loose like it was made of rubber – his neck had been broken.

"No... no... no..." Nero cried, shaking his head back and forth. I had never heard him so desperate, his voice so thin. It gave me the strength to pull myself to my feet and stumbled over to him on one leg.

I walked past Valen who was trying to roll onto his stomach, and kneeled beside Nero. I looked down at Ceph and when I saw his eyes half-open, like small pockets of green forest against the grey dust. I knew he was already dead.

I put my hand on Nero's shoulder. My best friend was sniffing, stifling chokes as he stroked Ceph's chalky hair back. I saw his teardrops fall onto Ceph like rain; Ceph's face almost unrecognizable in the dust. I found myself wiping the debris away with my sleeve.

"I'm sorry," I whispered to Nero. "He – he died protecting us, all of us."

Nero cried out; he leaned his head down until his forehead was touching Ceph's. He slowly shook his head back, more tears falling onto the brute chimera's face. Ceph looked so different now, he wasn't meant to be quiet, he wasn't meant to be still. Ceph was born to be loud and obnoxious, yet in his soul, he was friendly, charismatic – and one of the funniest men I knew.

"Cephy…" Nero whispered. He kissed Ceph's forehead, his eyes closed tight. "I love you."

As I heard a noise I looked over and saw Valen. His face was covered in blood, mixed in with the dust it formed thick cakes of pink on his face. He kneeled down in front of Ceph and put a hand on his head.

"Don't touch him!" Nero suddenly bellowed, the entire mall echoing his words. In the distance there was more crashing as the building collapsed around us, but I knew we weren't moving. "This is your fault, you little cunt!" Nero screamed, agony soaking into every word. He was trembling so hard underneath my hand I wondered what was keeping him from attacking Valen right now.

Valen looked up at Nero, his pink eyes wide and his own hands trembling on Ceph's head.

"I can still see his aura…" Valen said to him. "He's dying – but he can still hear you."

Nero's chin tightened; his lower lip started to tremble. He looked down at Ceph and patted his cheek. The sadness in Nero's eyes tore me. I felt so desperate, so helpless. There was nothing I could do but bear witness to another heartbreaking sight that I knew would haunt my dreams.

"Cephy… Cephy?" Nero choked. He pursed his lips and shook his head. "I love you, puppy, do you know that? I–" I watched as Nero's eyes widened, before he looked at me. I was confused to see hope and desperation on his face. "Where's the briefcase?" he asked.

I pointed behind us to where I had laid the briefcase, right beside the escalator. Nero jumped up and got it. He flicked the two locks on it and, to further my confusion and the worry I had for my best friend's mental state, he let out a choked laugh and picked up one of the vials of Sky's brain matter.

Nero looked at me, his face crumpled in agony. "We have to try…" he choked, before running his hands down his face, leaving a streak of pink skin framed by the dust. "Sky was a born immortal, Sanguine. It's… it's such a fucking long shot. We can make him immortal. I… I think I know enough…" Then his eyes shot to Valen. "You need to help me drag him into one of these shops, we need as much protection as we can."

My mouth dropped open, I wanted to feel hope but all I felt was doubt. A part of me wanted to tell Nero that this was too big of a long shot. I didn't know a lot about the immortal surgery but I knew Perish did them, a scientist and a doctor. Not only did I think this wasn't going to work – but it was going to use up some of the brain matter Silas coveted so much.

"Sanguine – please," Nero choked, sensing my hesitation. "I love him like I've never loved anyone before. Please, let me at least try."

I looked at him and saw the pain in his face, then looked down at Ceph, pools of red blood now mixing in with the dust, plaster, and shards of wood and metal. He already looked dead, nothing but a broken shell whose spirit had left long ago.

But I knew I couldn't let Nero down now, not after everything we had been through, everything he had done for me.

I nodded at him. Then Valen, as if waiting for my okay, got up and grabbed Ceph's arms. Nero gave me the briefcase, minus one bottle, and took Ceph's legs

Nero and Valen dragged Ceph across the walking area of the mall and into one of the open stores. I hobbled behind but fell down several times, unable to put any weight on my leg. I was starting to have doubts whether I would be able to get Valen out of this alive with how the building was crumbling around us, and now that we had to do surgery on Ceph those doubts were amplified.

Nero leaned down in front of Ceph and kissed his lips for what might've been the last time, and as I grabbed the long and narrow knife I had tucked back into my pants I heard him whisper to him.

"This is going to hurt, peaches, and I'm sorry, but it's the only way. I love you, hold on, for as long as you can, sweetness – hold on." Nero took in a deep breath. I extended my hand to offer him the knife. Nero took it, reached over and took Valen's and then got out his own.

He stabbed the first knife right into Ceph's skull, followed by the second several inches away, and then the third. He stabbed them with such precision they were able to make a triangle in the back of Ceph's skull. I heard Valen groan but I was fascinated with it.

Nero then wrenched the knives back and forth, sweat beading down his forehead and his mouth open to accommodate his heavy, ragged breathing. He pulled two of the knives out and with the last one, my knife, he wrenched it up and popped out the piece of skull. Underneath, framed with the blood leaking from Ceph's scalp, was the pink, wrinkled mass that was his brain.

"The brain piece is connected by a thin wire, take it out gently or it'll die, don't disconnect it from the lid of the bottle." Nero handed me the bottle of Sky's brain piece, all of us ignoring a thunderous explosion that sounded like it was coming from the front of the Wal-Mart.

I opened the bottle and saw the thin, almost invisible wire that connected the piece to the black lid of the bottle. I had originally thought these vials were just in normal bottles but on closer inspection I saw the thick lid held a little mechanism and button battery inside.

Nero took the lid from me, and with his tongue poking out of the side of his mouth, gently slid my long, thin knife deep into Ceph's brain, before twisting it to make a small gap.

"Hold the knife," Nero instructed. I quickly held it steady for him.

Without a word, he slid the piece of brain into Ceph's own brain. Then, as I held the knife that was wedging the space in Ceph's brain open, Nero pushed his finger into the opening and slid the now bare wire out of his brain. Nero took out his finger and tried to pinch the space shut.

Then Nero took the knife from me and gently shaved off a piece of Ceph's brain, a small pink area right beside a thick blue blood vessel. He picked up the little chunk and skewered it onto the wire, and handed it back to me. Knowing what he was doing, I screwed the replacement brain piece back into the bottle and put it into the briefcase. I closed the briefcase lid and locked it, then took a deep breath not even realizing I had been holding it.

Nero sniffed, and let out a stifled cry. He put the piece of skull back into its place before he completely broke down.

I put my arm around him and held him as he cried, patting his back and trying my best to reassure him. I didn't know if this was going to work; I didn't even know if he had done it right, I just knew my friend needed me right now, and I would never let that man down.

"NERO? SANGUINE?"

Nero and I both looked up and towards the exit to the store we had found shelter in. We saw nothing but the outlines of objects but Silas's voice was clear, even over the crumbling building.

Nero shot to his feet. "He can't see us," he said, his voice full of fear. "I have to hide with him, in case… in case it worked." He looked around. "Go and tell him you couldn't find me after I went looking for Ceph." Then his eyes fell on Valen. "Keep this secret and we're good, me and you, for everything."

I felt Valen's arms help me to my feet before he said in a weak voice, "If Silas doesn't kill me first." The young chimera looked into the haze and swallowed hard. Though as we walked out of the store and towards the voice, it felt like he was holding onto me for protection more than he was helping me walk.

With the briefcase in my hand we started walking towards Silas, who was still yelling our names. It sounded like he was deeper into the mall, which gave me hope that perhaps they had found an exit.

When I felt like we were far enough away that Silas wouldn't be able to discover Nero I answered back. "SILAS?" I called. "We're over here!"

A shadow stopped and then sneezed, but it was an animal sneeze. I felt Valen tense up beside me as it came bounding over, but immediately I could tell it was friendly. It was a large cat with spots, though its spots were barely visible in the smoke and dust.

"Pickles… hey," Valen said weakly, but suddenly he took in a sharp breath and clung to me harder.

Silas walked through the smoke, when he spotted me he looked relieved, but the relief turned to soured anger when he saw Valen.

"Wait… wait!" I called. I held out my arms to protect Valen as Silas's eyes narrowed. His teeth locked and, to my horror, I saw the same blackness I had seen in Valen's eyes, appear on Silas's, then behind me a sharp scream.

"NO!" I hollered. I grabbed Silas by his shoulders and started shaking him to snap him out of it, behind me I heard a thunk as Valen dropped to the ground. Silas's eyes remained fixed on Valen so I did the only thing I could think of: I hit Silas.

Silas's head snapped back, but it worked, the green came back to his eyes but immediately they seemed to burst into flames. I didn't care though, I was so tired, so fucking mentally exhausted, my leg was broken, and for all I knew Nero was holding the corpse of his fiancé with the faint, miniscule hope that he had made him immortal.

"I have the briefcase," I said quickly. I knew this was the most important thing to him. "Valen got it back." As Silas's eyes started focusing on Valen again I framed the king's face with my hands and made him look at me. "The building is about to go down. I can't explain it all to you, but Valen is coming home. Silas, his empath abilities work, he works. He's–"

With an angry snarl Silas smacked me right across the face, without Valen to steady me I fell to the ground hard, my broken leg screaming with pain.

Silas walked over to Valen who was laying on the ground, the inferno in his eyes crystal clear even in the smoke and dust. I could feel a terrible anger inside of him, one that made Valen start to shake and whimper.

Then Valen let out a scream, the young chimera grabbed his head and clenched his hair, curling up like a dead insect and shrieking like his entire body was on fire. I couldn't see Silas's face but as he stood, towering over the boy, I knew the depthless black had come back to his eyes.

"Silas!" I yelled as I tried to get to my feet. I reached over to try and feel for anything that could help me stand and, to my relief, I felt something solid. I managed to stand up and take a step – then I tackled Silas to the ground.

We both fell, and I pinned him down with my arms. Silas glared up at me, his face was without expression but the anger radiating off of him was so potent it seemed painted on his entire body.

"He is nothing but a product of the environment *you* put him in!" I yelled. "Just like I was. You treated him like shit for something he couldn't help, just like the life you forced me to experience. This isn't his fault, you made him this way now except responsibility!" I cried, slamming his shoulders down onto the ground. "He wants to come home. He's sorry and we have the fucking briefcase, Sky's brain matter is in those vials we have all of them." I took a deep breath, my lungs filling with dust.

Silas's expression changed, it was like he had only started hearing me now.

"You have Sky's brain matter?" Silas whispered.

I nodded. "We were able to recover all of the vials, all seven. Without Valen, they would've been lost. He made a mistake. You know above everyone else how much I hated that boy but I understand him now. He's

– he's just like I was…" I loosened my grip on Silas's shoulders. "And I would've given anything to have a friend during those times."

When I saw the shift in King Silas's face I breathed a cautious sigh of relief. I crawled off of Silas, and the king rose, then walked over to the crumpled Valen.

"Get up," Silas demanded.

Valen looked up, fresh blood on his face and his body shaking violently. He struggled but managed to rise to his feet, and though I expected Silas to speak to him, instead the king turned his back on Valen and looked at me.

"He will forever be at the bottom of this family's hierarchy, and no one will ever know he is an empath, ever," Silas said, his eyes narrowing dangerously. "And he will forever be your responsibility. Actually –" Silas turned around and faced Valen, the boy shrunk down at what I knew was a scathing look. "– I believe he will be the first chimera sengil, your sengil. You can kiss the feet of the chimeras you hated so much, until you're too old and ugly for them to want you."

Silas was trying to be cruel but I was too relieved at the fact that he was letting Valen live to care.

I nodded at the king. "I will take him as my sengil, J-Jack and I will."

Silas didn't look happy; he once again turned his back to Valen and started walking towards the far end of the mall. As he disappeared into the dust Valen took my arm again, and started helping me walk.

"Thank you," Valen whispered, though he looked defeated. "Though I have a feeling I will one day regret being spared."

Silas started calling for Nero as the two of us followed him, Pickles running ahead. I could see Silas's cape swaying back and forth as the king walked gracefully into the dust, the briefcase held firmly in his hand.

"We all have those days, Valen," I said to him as I stared at my beautiful, yet dangerous, king. I swallowed down the lump in my throat and pushed myself onward.

"And we always will."

CHAPTER 53

I TOOK IN A DEEP BREATH, FEELING ABSOLUTELY stupid for feeling nervous about something like this. Given what the last year of my life involved you would think something like this would be easy – it wasn't though, I felt like I was going to throw up.

Oh god, what if I threw up? I groaned and walked towards the mirror as my brothers all buzzed around behind me, no one looking as nervous as I felt.

I stood in front of the full length mirror and adjusted the stupid rose and little white flowers I had in my pocket. Garrett called them boutonnieres. I bet he knew all of the dumb names for wedding things. I suppose it did make me look nice though, nice enough to do several poses in front of the mirror. It wasn't often I saw myself in a suit; I did look pretty handsome, it had even been fitted for me. It was a black suit with a silky blue blouse underneath, but even though I had begged and begged Garrett he wouldn't let me wear my red bowtie.

There was a flash of silver and black behind me, then something smacked my backside. I turned around with a glaring look and saw Jack, pretending that it wasn't him. I paid him back with an equally hard smack on his ass, making my boyfriend yelp and laugh.

"Okay, everyone ready?" I turned around and saw Garrett with Kass standing beside him. Garrett looked stressed to the max, enough to have white powder underneath his nose. Kass didn't look much better, my poor friend was caring a binder in one arm and a timetable in the other. He looked like he wanted to jump out of one of the windows behind us.

"Yes…" everyone called, most using a tone that hinted to them wanting to be anywhere else but here, especially Elish who had his arms crossed in passive-aggressive defiance.

"Good!" Garrett clapped his hands together, then his face dropped in shock. I didn't know why until I saw a flicker of movement to my left. I laughed as I saw Drake throwing one of the wedding rings up into the air and catching it, little Knight, Ellis's son, giggling as he watched.

Quietly Elish snatched the ring in mid-air, and without even saying a single word, only giving the boy a cold glare, he handed it back. Drake took it back with cautious fingers.

"Thank you, Elish," Garrett said with a smile, then turned back to us. "Okay, Elish and Sanguine, you're the best men." He looked at his watch and his mouth started to move as he counted down. As soon as he looked up at us the music started, a piece that our most musically talented brother Artemis had written. Garrett's smile widened and he stepped aside and gracefully waved the ring bearers, Drake and Knight, towards the doors. Then two (exactly two) minutes later – Elish and myself.

Elish walked ahead and I kept pace with him, together we opened the doors and faced the hall in front of us. All of the wedding guests quieted down when they saw me and Elish.

Everyone from chimeras to elites, to Nero's top legionaries were in attendance, all of them sitting down on refurbished church pews the legionaries had recovered from the greywastes. There were at least two hundred people in attendance, all to witness the Imperial General and his second-in-command, get married.

I looked ahead and smiled as I saw Nero. He was standing at the end of the walkway with a grin so wide it lit up the entire hall. He was dressed to the nines in the same style of black and blue, except he was sporting a pair of black combat boots. And just to further save his Imperial General pride, he had a loaded SN Scar assault rifle on his back, an early wedding present from his future husband.

Past Nero I saw King Silas, radiating just as much happiness as Nero was. He was dressed similar to Elish, in a blue silk shirt but instead of a suit he had on a magnificent black robe embroidered with blue and green patterns. He looked more like a sorcerer than a king, but those two never missed a chance to look mystical.

"Stop smiling you look like an idiot," Elish muttered beside me as we slowly walked down the hall.

"Stop frowning you look like a dick," I muttered back. Elish let out an irritated sigh and we kept walking towards Nero and Silas.

Nero winked at me when we got to the end of the hall, as his best man I took my place beside him and watched the other chimeras walk down the carpeted walkway behind me. Nero's top General, General Zhou and Garrett, then Jack and Ellis (we couldn't walk together since I was best man and Garrett refused to allow it).

Finally Ceph appeared in the archway. His auburn hair longer now, and curling at the edges, and his brilliant green eyes bright and full of life. My best friend's fiancé had the same look on his face that he had when Nero and him stepped off of the Falconer after vanishing for two days after the bombing of Irontowers.

Why Ceph was so happy after being trapped inside a collapsed building so long was anyone's guess. I smirked and looked up at the ceiling, trying to proclaim my innocence even though I was only speaking inside of my own head.

Unable to help himself, Nero walked towards Ceph and met him halfway down the aisle. He held out his hand and Ceph took it with a half-smirk. Nero leaned in and kissed his cheek and the two of them walked the rest of the way together.

The ceremony started, and as Silas spoke about Nero and Ceph's youth and a few stories, I stood beside Jack and found his hand. I squeezed it.

Jack squeezed it back, we had barely left each other's side in the month since we had escaped from Irontowers. It had been difficult at first since we were now sharing a space with Valen but slowly we had all been finding our normal routines.

"I love you," I said to him under my breath. Like everyone in the family besides me, Valen, Nero, and Ceph, Jack didn't know the truth behind what had happened after he'd escaped from the mall. I felt guilty about it, but the less people that knew the better.

"I love you," Jack said back, then he tugged on my hand. "That will be us one day."

I snorted, a little too loud so I tried to mask it into a cough. "Not for another twenty years."

Jack grinned and kissed my cheek. We both turned our attention to Silas as they started getting down to the vows, and when the *I do's* were exchanged and rings placed on each other's fingers, Silas turned to the crowd and announced Nero and Ceph as married. The first chimera besides Ellis to get married in our family.

Nero got what he had always wanted. Ceph was immortal, and he would have him forever.

Though this thought brought an unease to me, because I knew that one day Silas would find out about what we had done to Ceph. That we had used a piece of Sky's brain matter to make Ceph immortal. The consequences for that act would be extreme, I knew this, Nero knew this, and so did Ceph… but… what choice did we have? That was a worry for another time, right now I think all of us deserved to be happy. I knew I was looking forward to some peace and quiet, with my boyfriend by my side.

After the ceremony the celebration moved to the same floor I had faced Jasper on. The non-chimeras had their own celebration in a hall down the street and the chimera family settled in to a night of drinking, drugs, and a hell of a lot of food. Though I noticed that the left-hand side of this room had all of the beds removed now, so it wasn't going to be one of *those* nights.

Valen took a drink of his cream soda and vodka, his hair now back to its natural blond and his clothing choice a little less loud. Jack had told me that Valen's bright colours made him angry, like flashing red in front of a bull, so I had asked Valen to tone it down and dress more normally. My new sengil wasn't happy about it but, well, he was my sengil so he had to do whatever the hell I told him to do.

"How are the headaches?" I asked him. I watched Jack dancing with Artemis, already a little tipsy though I had decided to stave off of the alcohol. I was nursing a rum and ChiCola and that was good enough for me.

"Manageable," Valen said with a shrug. "The opiates are helping. Funny, I always forget that opiates are actually pain killers too." He chuckled at this and so did I, then he let out a breath and looked around. "I… never thought I would be back here."

"I didn't think you would be either," I said to him. Or that I would want him back, but in truth, once Valen had been pardoned and accepted back into the family he had been improving. He had gotten more mature and perhaps a little more sure of himself, even though he had been demoted to sengil. The family treated him differently now too, though they didn't show him more respect they didn't berate him or ignore him.

"Do you know what you're going to do if Silas ever finds out?" Valen asked. The king was chatting happily with Garrett, a drink in one hand and a cigarette in the other.

I shook my head. "No idea, I think we're hoping he decides to make Ceph immortal on his own and we can just... go with it. Or else..." I thought for a minute. "Fake it? I don't know, Val. I don't want to think about it right now."

Valen nodded and took another drink. "Fair enough... we'll think of something, all three of us." Valen gave me another smile. He seemed to glow every time he mentioned our four-way pact. I think being included in a family secret made him feel like he belonged.

Poor little fucker had just wanted to belong somewhere. I wished I was mature enough to see that when I met him but I had been pretty fucked up myself.

Then a shadow appeared to my right. I looked up and saw Elish with a drink in his hand, looking down at the two of us. A smirk on his face that I didn't trust in the least.

I looked back at him and motioned to an empty seat. "All danced out?"

Elish gave me a cold look and I tried not to laugh at my own quip. The thought of Elish dancing with the others (to rock music no less) was an amusing mental image.

"Valentine..." Elish said in a tone that was like ice melting over a hot blade. "Loren is drunk and making a fool out of himself, please take him to his bedroom and see that he stays there."

Valen raised an eyebrow as he got up. "Do you mean... see that he stays there or..." Valen smirked. *"See that he stays there."* Valen's smirk turned into a grin.

Elish gave him a frosted glare though I laughed. Valen didn't wait for the answer he knew would never come, he turned and left to find Elish's drunk sengil.

I lit a cigarette and took another drink, I blew the smoke out of my mouth and watched as Elish reached into his pocket.

He pulled out one of the brain matter vials – and rested it on top of the table.

As I stared at it, knowing the blood was draining from my face. Elish spoke, "I thought I would come to you before I came to King Silas with this – rather disturbing – discovery I made when I was testing his vials for contaminates."

A part of me wanted to brush it off and play dumb, but I knew it was already too late for that. He had seen the expression on my face.

Not this – not so soon.

"Tell me, Sanguine, why is Ceph's brain matter in his vial?" Elish asked in a tone ripe with taunting. "Why is Sky's seventh vial missing? This is –" A nasty smirk crept onto Elish's face. "– quite the mystery."

I was silent, then I put my cigarette down in the ashtray. "He's your brother, Elish," I said, scanning his face for any hint that brotherly love would impact any of his decisions, but there was none. Elish was a cold, heartless sociopath and I knew there was no part of him that would be swayed by Nero's love for Ceph.

"Yes, but being my brother and a chimera does not mean he can do what he will–" Elish paused as if savouring the expression on my face, and the racing heart I wondered if he could hear over the music. "Nor does it mean he can make whomever he pleases immortal. You do realize when Silas finds out – he will encase Ceph in concrete, or worse."

My teeth clenched, the smirk on Elish's face became more prominent. I stared at that vial, Elish's slender, manicured fingers gently drumming the table beside it.

"He loves him," I said through my teeth.

"I care not."

"Of course you don't!" I snapped, feeling my heart clench as I saw Nero sitting on the edge of the stage with Ceph, talking happily with one another – Nero's arm was around Ceph's waist. He looked – he looked so in love.

"You don't even know what the fuck it is to fall in love," I said angrily to Elish. "You think you love Silas but I can tell you – you don't. You don't love Silas, you love the idea of Silas, you love the idea of being king, and one day you're going to fucking realize that. You're going to realize you're just a miserable emotionless monster incapable of loving anything."

Elish's smirk disappeared from his mouth. "You're not doing a good job of persuading me."

"Why bother?" I snapped, the emotion rising in my voice. "If you can come here on your brother's wedding day and taunt me with this." I flicked the vial towards him. "There is no persuading you. If you're that inhuman then go fucking tell Silas; you're just a fucking vampire that feeds on peoples' miserable reactions to your games and I'm not giving you shit."

Elish was silent, yet his face held no emotions. "Do not make me out to be the villain when it was you four who decided to lie to the king," he said in a dropped tone. "You four decided to use that brain piece without his consult, and believe me, Sanguine, if there is one thing you don't want to fuck around with when it comes to Silas – it's anything that has to do with Sky."

My blond brother grabbed the vial, his chair scraped as he started to rise. But as he was getting up something came to me, a memory that hit me like a rocket. Something that I had caught when I was being held in Irontowers, an exchange between One-eye and Oniks.

"And what would Silas say if he knew you were the one behind his plane being shot down?" I suddenly said. "You were their secret informant."

Elish froze.

I grabbed the chair he had just risen from and pulled it back out for him. Elish stared me down, his purple eyes blazing, and sat back onto the chair.

"We can make this easy," I said to him coolly. "You use up that vial when you go back to Kreig and no one knows, and I'll pretend I never heard Onik's admission. I think Silas finding out you were the one that started all of this, including what happened to me while he was dead for four months, might trump a single missing vial. Or you tell me?"

He kept his face placid but I saw his jaw flex as if he was clenching it. I didn't show it, but inside I was hollering my success. I wanted to jump up onto the table and just yell that I had outsmarted Elish.

"I think the last thing you want is for Silas to bring Sky back," I continued. "A Sky clone would replace you in a second, that and the fact that Silas would be dead for months and I would be left alone and under your control – you just couldn't resist the chance, could you?" I smirked and went further. "I bet you also arranged your chess pieces in a way that pitted the chimeras *you* found unworthy against each other. And I played right into your hand, didn't I?"

Elish's eyes narrowed. "You don't want me as an enemy, boy."

I shook my head. "No, I don't." I extended my hand to him. "Which is why I think we would make better allies. We both have secrets we want to keep hidden – so why don't we come to a mutual understanding that we can trust each other with them."

He stared at my hand like it was poison, then slowly, like every part of his pride was screaming at him not to, he took my hand and shook it.

"I suppose you are right, Sanguine," Elish said, firmly grasping my hand in his. Then he let it go and rose to his feet. "Enjoy your evening."

I smiled smugly as Elish left; his gliding, confident movements taking him directly towards King Silas. I watched him go, feeling so satisfied and proud of myself I felt like I was floating.

Then I saw Jack watch Elish leave. My boyfriend came walking over with a grin on his face. He pulled up a chair beside me but I shook my head. I pulled away from the table and patted my lap and in response Jack sat down on my lap and wrapped his arms around me.

"I love you," Jack said for the hundredth time this day and the millionth since we had been reunited after Irontowers. He nuzzled my neck and kissed it. "Make love to me tonight."

My face flushed; I put my arms around him and leaned my head against his. We hadn't had our first night together yet, we had been too busy adjusting to having Valen living with us now, that and the chaos of the wedding hadn't given us any free time.

Though tonight was a night to celebrate – for more than one reason now.

"Alright," I said with a relented sigh. "Tonight can be our night, just you and me."

Jack grinned and nuzzled me again. "I'm so happy with you; it was a long road but – we made it." He then stroked my hair back. "I don't like the fact that Silas can control your psychosis but… at least you don't need to suffer anymore. You can have peace and quiet now inside that poor mind."

I nodded and absentmindedly touched my head, wondering to myself just where the device was in my brain. "I haven't heard any voices. No sign of Crow, and Barry is just my bear again," I said. "I miss them but… it was time to join the real world, and my real family."

Jack sighed, a happy, content sigh. The two of us looked on at our family members. Some of them were dancing to the rock music, others, like Nero and Ceph, were sitting down sharing drinks and smokes, and everyone, except perhaps Elish, seemed to be enjoying themselves.

We were a family, and in no way were we the perfect family. We had our faults, our shortcomings; we did things differently than most families I had seen on TV. But we were close-knit and deeply joined with one another; we all shared a bond that went further than genetics, further than just being men living under one skyscraper roof.

I held Jack close to me and closed my eyes, taking in the loud music, the heavy smoke in the air, and the sounds of men laughing and having the time of their lives. I took it in and enjoyed it, reflecting back on how far I had come. I had come a long way from being a little baby hiding under a porch.

I had done it, I had survived.

And I had found a place where I belonged.

THE END

EPILOGUE

Twenty Years Later

I RAN UP THE STEPS TO THE FRONT OF ALEGRIA, AND even though the thiens would've questioned anyone bursting into the king's skyscraper with a desperate expression on their face, they did nothing to try and stop me. All they did was back away from me as I pushed open the doors and ran inside.

If it wasn't twenty-seven floors up I would've ran up the stairs to Silas's apartment, and with anxiety like broken glass inside of my chest, I felt like it. But I knew the elevator would be quicker, so I pressed the button, ignoring the inquisitive looks of Silas's bodyguards, and waited.

Was today the day? After twenty years would today be the day of reckoning for my best friend and his husband? It seemed like just yesterday I was watching Nero slip that ring onto Ceph's finger.

But the desperate phone call from Kinny, now retired as a sengil and acting as Alegria's personal physician, could only mean one thing. He said the only word that he could make sense of while tending to a hysterical Nero, was my name.

And I was the last man besides Elish and Ceph who knew our secret. My Valentine had passed away at twenty-four and until his last breath did he keep our darkest secret.

Finally after what seemed like an eternity, the elevator doors opened.

I took a step inside but paused. Lying on the elevator floor holding a bloodied jaw, was Drake.

"Drakey, are you okay?" I ran to him and kneeled down. I put a hand on his forehead and tilted his head back to get a better look at the swollen and quickly blackening jaw.

My brother gave a whimper; I could see blood drying in his curly blond hair. "Master is so mad," Drake said, his voice heavy with sadness. I brushed a hand over his jaw and winced – it was broken.

"Why did he hit you?" I whispered. I turned around and pressed the elevator button for floor twenty-seven.

Drake let out another whimper and held out his arms towards me like a child needing to be picked up. So as the elevator brought us to the floor of Silas's apartment and Drake's home, I held him and rubbed his back.

"Nero hitted me..." Drake said, then he sniffed. "I put a hand on Nero's shoulder for comforts – Nero got mad. He's in the bad place with – with Ceph."

I pulled back and looked at him. "The backroom?"

Drake nodded, his orange eyes full of tears.

Without another word I turned around and looked at the keypad of the elevator. I knew which room that was; it used to be Nero's apartment after Garrett moved into his own skyscraper and before Nero and Ceph moved into one of the Skyland mansions. It had been converted to what was now called the backroom, two flights of stairs that led from Silas's top floor apartment, past the second floor that used to be Elish's apartment, to a darkened room that had... that had...

The concrete tombs. The grave markers that cradled inside of their coffins immortal chimeras who had been condemned to spend their punishment in claustrophobic darkness. To live out their sentences, days, months, sometimes years, in sensory deprived nothing, with no water, no food. They would die, and resurrect inside their cocoons with only their insane thoughts to keep them company.

"Ceph's already been... he's already been encased?" I whispered.

When Drake nodded back at me my heart died inside of my chest. I looked behind me as the floor numbers steadily climbed, the sickness I felt rising with it.

I pushed floor twenty-five, the one that led to the back room.

"Get Kinny to look at your jaw..." I said to Drake with a gentle pat on his shoulder. "Stay away from Silas's apartment for now. Maybe go see Garrett?"

The elevator came to a halt. I rose and turned from my brother and pressed Kinny's hospital floor for Drake. Drake may be immortal and, as a cicaro, used to Silas's moods, but I would feel better to know at least one of my brothers was safe and far from this hell I was about to enter.

The next movements in my body were that of a robot, or perhaps a soldier who was walking into the heart of the warzone. I knew chances are I wouldn't be coming out of this alive. If Nero could hit Drake, our intellectually slow brother who had the mentality of a puppy rather than a chimera, I could only guess what he would do to me.

Someone who was there the day he made Ceph immortal – someone who, in all respects, was the one who got Ceph killed in the first place.

I took a deep breath, Nero's old hallway in front of me, and started walking towards the double oak doors. No longer leading to my brothers' bachelor pad, full of posters of naked men, dozens of gun racks, and every electronic on the planet; but now taking me to a dimly lit black panelled room with empty walls; the windows covered in a thick black curtain that let no light or fresh air through.

I pushed the doors open and stepped into a graveyard,

Darkness was all around me, the only thing breaking up the cold void were two squares of concrete in the back of the room standing like tombstones, an oriental rug underneath them.

And huddled beside one of the tombs, with his face buried into his drawn up knees, was my best friend. His shoulders were shaking and his breathing laboured. I could smell the agony on him, almost as pungent as the aroma of newly poured concrete.

"Nero..." I whispered, feeling my emotions crush under the weight of Nero's despair. My gaze rose from my friend to the concrete block Nero was leaning against, hardened but with visible blood smears, dents, and claw marks on the outside.

Ceph was in there... lighthearted, carefree Cepherus. Who had a talent of making anyone he encountered laugh, or at least have their day brightened. A chimera who was fiercely loyal and such a good brother, such a good person...

He didn't deserve this.

I walked towards Nero, the room seemingly getting colder with each step. I spared a glance and a fleeting moment of guilt for the other immortal, whose origins I was unsure of, and approached my friend.

"Nero?" I said again. I got down on my knees, my burly brother never looking so small. He seemed like a lost child in that moment, something that seemed alien on a visage that usually radiated smug self-assurance.

"Get the fuck out of my sight."

Immediately I stood back up, and took a step back. "N-Nero, it's Sanguine…" I stammered.

Nero raised his head and when his royal blue eyes locked on mine my heart jolted. The anger smouldering in his eyes, every ounce of it directed at me, was something I had never seen in him before. He was looking at me with such a focused hatred I felt like looking over my shoulder to see who he was really staring at.

"I should've left you in that fucking basement, you worthless piece of shit," Nero said, in an inhuman tone. "You fucking pedophile's slut. You- you fucking – you fucking…" Nero's lower lip pulled and I saw his eyes fill. As he carried on I watched his countenance breakdown in front of me. "You – if you…"

Nero let out a strangled sob; he put his hand over his mouth and let out a heartbreaking wail.

I got down on my knees and threw my arms around him. Nero clung to me, drew me to his chest and clutched me hard as he started to openly sob.

"I'm sorry," I whispered in his ear, though I was unsure if he'd be able to hear me over his own grief. "I'm sorry, Nero. I'll talk to Silas. I promise, I'll do all I can for him."

"He hates enclosed spaces!" Nero managed to scream as he broke down in my arms; he was trembling hard and hyperventilating. I had never seen him in such a state; it made me fear for his sanity. It made me fear for his future.

"He's claustrophobic. He – he hates enclosed fucking spaces!" Nero continued to yell. "He can't be in there. He'll go crazy; he's going to be scared – he'll go crazy!"

"Shh-shhh." My eyes closed tight but the tears were already slipping down my face. I didn't know if Ceph could hear us but I could only imagine what he was going through, only inches away from us. "I'll talk to Silas."

"SILAS!" Nero roared. He suddenly shoved me away and rose to his feet, his body heaving and his fists clenched so hard his veins were bulging out. I noticed then his hands were bloody and swollen. "I'll fucking kill him! I'll fucking kill him."

I jumped to my feet, and put my hands on Nero's chest to stop him. "No, you know that won't help." But what would help? "Tell me how did he find out? When did he find out?"

Nero's tear stained face crumpled; he shook his head. "He was fucking bound to find out, Ceph is supposed to be forty-four and though we gave him glasses and dyed his hair, kept him in Cardinalhall as much as we could. I don't know how Silas found out but he came back from the Kreig lab livid." Nero's teeth clenched. He whirled around and laid a hard punch to Ceph's concrete tomb. I realized now where the dents and blood streaks had come from.

"What happened to Silas in Kreig?" I asked. I didn't even try to stop Nero from punching the concrete, though even with his immaculate strength I knew he could never break through to free his husband.

"Sky," Nero said the name like it was a piece of shit on his tongue. "Always fucking Sky. I hope he used up the last of that fuckhead's brain matter so he can just fucking get over it already. I'm glad he's going to fucking be alone forever; he deserves it. I want him to have all the fucking misery in the world, fucking emotionless son of a bitch. Fuck Silas. He deserves to be alone forever and I told him that. I'm glad he's miserable."

Another wave of agony swept Nero's face. He turned from me and crossed his arms over Ceph's tomb before leaning his head into it. More desperate sobbing reached my ears.

"Sky?" I murmured before glancing over my shoulder. "I… Nero, I'm going to go talk to Silas." Silas and I had always been close and over the last twenty years we had kept our close bond. Silas spoke to me as a friend not just a master – if anyone was to get through to him…

Maybe… just maybe.

"He was screaming at Perish and beating on the sengil when I left him." Nero's tone was hostile and biting. "I hope he's miserable – I hope he's alone for the rest of his life. He's only taking Ceph away because he – he…" Nero let out another cry and lowered his head back into his arms. "He's going to go crazy in there, Sangy. Ceph – Ceph's going to go crazy in there."

Without another word, only a fleeting glance of sympathy, I left Nero and made my way back to the elevator.

Quietly I rode up to the twenty-seventh floor, Nero's agonizing screams ringing in my ears and planting poison inside of my heart that I knew would quicken. There were images and sounds that lived in my head that I'd never been able to forget, ones that came forth in the form of vivid nightmares. Even at the age of forty I still woke up screaming, drenched in a cold sweat. Jack always beside me reassuring me that I wasn't back in

Jasper's basement.

Jack and I had been together for twenty years now.

A part of me wanted him beside me for this, but a stronger part was glad he was back in our skyscraper away from this sea of chaos I was so freely wading in.

The door opened and like I had walked into a torture chamber, I was greeted with the sound of painful screaming and the snarling, rapid voice that I immediately recognized as Silas's.

I ran into Silas's apartment and when I saw Silas with a whip in his hand, viciously beating on Perish, I didn't stop running.

"Silas!" I yelled. Perish was on the ground, his body covered in split open, bleeding lacerations; he was missing an eye and as I ripped the whip out of Silas's hand I realized he had huge chunks of skin and flesh missing.

The reason was obvious when I looked down at the whip and saw it was embedded with blood-covered razor blades, some still holding bits of lacerated skin.

Then something else caught my eye. I looked to my left and my mouth dropped open. Silas's sengil, a young man of eighteen named Dakota, was lying on his back in a pool of blood. His torso had been mangled; his stomach holding a gaping slash with a string of intestine that looked like it had been caught in one of the whip's razors. It was stretched several feet across the carpet, leaving a bloodied shadow underneath it.

"What the fuck?" I screamed. I dropped the whip and took Silas by the shoulders, a vacant yet demonic look on his face. "What the fuck is wrong with you?" I shook him, hearing the sound of shuffling as Perish scrambled away from him.

The devil stared back at me, his face pale and his lips thin. He locked those demonic eyes with mine before, to my shock; he raised his hand and punched me right across the face. The force of the blow knocked me off of my feet and I fell to the ground hard.

Out of the corner of my eye I saw the razor blade-imbedded whip move. I managed one more cry of Silas's name before I felt the first overwhelming stinging pain rip its way up my back, immediately followed by the snap of the whip before a second rained down on me.

"Silas, STOP!" I screamed. I tried to scramble away but a third hit me. This time I could feel and hear the skin getting ripped off of my back, followed by the coldness as the air hit what I knew was my bleeding exposed muscle. "Silas!"

"I will kill every single one of you!" Silas suddenly cried, though his tone held none of the hatred that his words implied. Silas sounded devastated, desperate, and as full of agony as Nero. "All of you! You're nothing, you'll never be him! None of you will ever hold a candle to him! You're done; I will encase your mutated bodies in concrete, you fucking failures!" He shrieked the last part so loudly his voice broke under the strain, and at the same time another vicious strike hit my back, this one withdrawing with the feeling of two pieces of Velcro being split apart.

"Who? Sky?" I cried back. Quickly I rose to my feet, just in time to dodge another crack of the whip. My own skin and blood raining down on me as the long strip of leather snapped the air.

Silas's eyes, wide and holding in their emerald oculars black flames, stared at me. His face speckled with blood and meat, and his blue shirt stained purple. He looked like a serial killer in the throes of his finale, though in all respects perhaps he was.

Something was wrong with my king – something that went further than Ceph. I was realizing as I stared at this mad immortal that Ceph was perhaps a victim of Silas's state, not the cause.

"What does this have to do with Sky?" I held out my hands in a pleading posture, trying to remember what I used to do when Silas was angry. It had been so long since he had been this out of control. This was always handled by Elish out of sight, but Elish was in Kreig – he was supposed to have been with Perish trying to create…

I looked over at Perish who was dying, only his remaining eye showing a colour besides red. He was staring at me as he held his neck, his throat gurgling while the blood filled his lungs.

"What happened in the lab?" Of course, it was always something to do with Sky. Every time I had seen my king in this state of insanity it had to do with that damn boyfriend; the man that the entire family despised, even if we'd never met him.

"Get out of here!" Silas screamed, clenching the whip hard in his hand. He choked and his face tightened. "All of you… all of you just leave me. Every one of you have been nothing but a disappointment from the start. Insane, damaged creatures. No more, no more chimeras." The whip slipped out of his hand. "I almost had it… I almost cracked the code, Sanguine. But it's gone – we only have three more pieces left, three more pieces of Sky's matter until it's done. I'll never have him again."

I watched him, analyzing him. He had started showing the first hairline crack in this insanity but I could never know if that would make it safe to approach. Silas was my friend, my master, and I loved him – but I didn't have the same pull on him as Elish did. Silas, whether he admitted it or not, saw Elish as a rock that even he could lean on. I was not that rock.

"You still have three though, Master," I said cautiously. "What about young Lycos? In several years time he will be old enough to start working on the chimera code, just as you created him for." The little boy was seven years old now and living with Silas's top non-chimera scientist and his husband. He had been made to be the best scientist there was, specifically to create chimeras and, as those closest to Silas knew, to create Sky's clone.

I ducked as Silas picked up a nearby statue and flung it at me. I heard it smash into a credenza behind me, near where Perish had been hiding.

"So he can fail again with my last three pieces?" Silas snarled. "It would've been four. I would've had four if one of them wasn't wasted on fucking Ceph. I would've had five if that pink-eyed little defect didn't drop one! If he wasn't dead I would make him immortal just to fucking kill him all over again!"

My teeth locked, not only at the mention of Ceph but at him bringing up Valen. Valen had been my boyfriend for two years before he died. I had temporarily left Jack to take care of him when I had learned Valen was going to die from his empath abilities, to give my neglected, depressed sengil and friend the best years of his life before he passed on.

And I had done just that.

But I had to swallow down Silas's hateful comment. This wasn't about my dead boyfriend, this was about saving Ceph. Though the prospect of reaching Silas and calming him down enough to free Nero's husband seemed impossible at this point.

"But because of Valen we were able to retrieve the remaining seven," I said calmly to Silas. "If it wasn't for Valen we would've assumed the suitcase was–"

I ducked as another statue flew past my head.

"Get out of here," Silas yelled. "Get all your damn brothers and that bitch failure of a daughter and get the fuck out of my city." Then his jaw clenched and he paused. "And bring their partners here. Every one of them, and I want Ellis's failure kids as well. Bring them here."

My eyes widened, there was no questioning why Silas wanted the chimera partners here – he was going to fucking kill them. There was no question in my mind of that fact.

Because if Silas couldn't have Sky – why should they have their life partners?

I had to do something, but what? Yes, Silas was insane with rage but he would eventually calm down, wouldn't he? The only issue with this was who would lay dead in his wake before he regained his usual confident nature.

What had been me pleading for Ceph's release was quickly turning into me talking the king out of kicking us out of Skyfall and murdering our partners.

"And you can bring Jack here too."

My mouth went dry, my gaze turned from the door to Silas's face.

He glared back at me, the blood of me, Perish, and the dead sengil staining his pale skin. Why it hadn't started boiling on his face from the sheer anger that was radiating off of him I didn't know.

"Silas…" I whispered. I took a cautious step towards him. "Love, I know you feel betrayed by Nero; I know you're upset about the brain matter running low…" Another cautious step, Silas's body tightening with my approach. "But sending us away and killing our partners isn't the solution. Let us help–"

In a flash another strike was dealt across my face.

"ENOUGH!" I suddenly yelled. I don't know if it was just me tired of being abused by him, the blood loss from the gouges on my back or that I had reached the end of my rope, but no matter the consequences I was tired of being his punching bag. "You're being unreasonable and you're being a fucking tyrant, Silas Dekker. Calm the fuck down and act like a king and not a fucking dictator!" I whirled around to face Perish. "Get to Kinny and make sure Drake's okay."

Perish stared at me, his pupil a small pinpricks against his icy blue eye. His gaze shifted behind me to Silas. Then he nodded hastily before rising and fleeing towards the double doors.

When they shut behind me I turned to Silas, who was staring blankly at the spot where Perish had been.

"It's just us," I said to him. I took another step closer and, without him noticing, I kicked the dropped whip away from his reach. "Talk to me."

"Get away from me," Silas whispered, his eyes still focused yet they looked like they were seeing things not in this world. "All of you – get the fuck out of my city. I never want to see you failures again. I will rape and murder your damn partners and I will spit on their graves."

I shook my head and lightly put a hand on his shoulder. Taking this brief moment of calmness in his insane rage, I gently directed him into my arms. "I know you will, love."

"I hate you," Silas said, though he didn't move away from me as I put my arms around him and held him to my chest. "I hate you so much."

"I know." I started to rock him. "But we love you anyway."

"Do you know how close Elish and Perish were?" Silas whispered. "I held him in my arms, Sanguine. His name was Adler and I held him in my arms. I fed him a bottle."

Because he couldn't see me I closed my eyes in relief. I think the worst of it was over. My brothers would never know how close their partners had come to being executed one by one, or suffering the same fate as Nero's husband right underneath my feet.

"What happened to him, love?" I asked.

Silas was silent for a moment. "I wanted to know for sure he was a born immortal – so I smothered him. I woke up the next morning to Elish telling me he was cold and stiff. I saw his little body in a black body bag." Silas's arms tightened around my waist, though his touch was like fire against my whip and razor wounds. "I had to know though."

I patted his back. "But why couldn't you just create a non-immortal clone of Sky and make him immortal yourself, love?"

Silas shook his head. "I don't want someone who looks like Sky. I want Sky. And a chimera with Sky's features is not my Sky. My Sky was powerful, a demon to be feared. A man who held more powers than all of you and me combined. He was evil, an emotionless sociopath but in the same thread… funny, charismatic, intelligent, loving when it was just us."

Silas pulled away and I saw wetness in the corners of his eyes. "I want a born immortal of my Sky – why is that so much to ask? Why…" Silas's face suddenly crumbled. "Why haven't I gotten over him, Sanguine?"

Oh my god, he was confiding in me. This prospect both intrigued and horrified me. I was dancing with the devil right now, and I knew I had to tread carefully.

"I have over a dozen chimeras…" Silas whispered. "And yet I've never felt more alone. I can have any of you in my bed, in my arms… and here I am feeling like I'm in an empty room, screaming at the top of my lungs for someone to… hear me."

Because that is what you wanted, you always kept us at arm's length. You made yourself a master and us the pets, the only person you ever confided in was Elish, and Elish…

Elish's feelings towards Silas had changed over the last twenty years, and not for the better.

"Why don't you create a chimera to be your partner? If only until Lycos creates your Chimera X," I suggested, rubbing his shoulders in a loving manner. I was trying my best to be supportive but the blood I could feel dripping down my back was a testament to my deteriorating physical state. I was going to have to dispatch myself tonight, this I knew.

"You're my slaves not my partners," Silas said bitterly. "That chimera would only get too big for his place and cause problems. Just like Elish."

My eyes widened at that remark, but I decided to steer away from that landmine. "Well, you need someone, King Silas. You cannot carry the weight of this world on your own shoulders, and if you insist on it not being one of us – at least have someone you can actually confide in, someone who you don't need to grow concerned of judging you."

"There is no one," Silas whispered. "You all can carry on with your perfect fucking lives that I gave to you. With your damn boyfriends and husbands, loving them more than you could ever love me."

"Don't say that," I said sharply. "We love you more than–"

Suddenly there was a loud slam. Both of our attention drew to the oak door that had suddenly swung open, and to my horror Nero, looking absolutely insane, walked through.

"Let him out…" Nero said, his tone low and threatening and his eyes red from crying. "Let him out, Silas."

Silas stiffened beside me. "I said all I want to say to you, Nero. Get the fuck out of my apartment and get the fuck out of my city. You're all banned from Skyfall, like the fucking failures you are. Get out."

Shit. I had been hoping the brief talk I'd had with Silas would quell this insane notion he'd gotten in his head, and perhaps I had but Nero's presence had destroyed that.

"Nero…" I said slowly. I stood in front of Silas and held out my arms. "You must leave now. You're not going to do anything to help this."

Nero, his eyes like that of a crazed bull, remained fixed on the king. "Let him out," he said again. "Let him out or I will break him out of there with your fucking skull, Silas."

Silas stepped in front of me, I could see his eyes narrow. "Another word out of you and his encasement will be permanent, Nero. Now get the fuck out–"

Nero let out a roar and charged towards Silas.

I jumped back in front of the king and when Nero put his hands on me to shove me away; I skidded behind him and jumped on his back. I put one arm underneath his neck and pulled it back, and squeezed.

"Stand down, Nero!" I yelled as he tried to throw me off of him. I held onto him tight but he was thrashing and swinging me around like I had just jumped on the back of a wild horse. "I know you're upset but…" Suddenly Nero's arm was behind his head. A new jolt of pain ripped through me as Nero grabbed a handful of my hair and viciously yanked me forward. I held on as tight as I could, hearing my scalp start to rip off from my skull, before the pain and pressure temporarily dazed me. As my arm loosened from behind me, Nero threw me over his shoulder and I landed on top of a side table with a crash, the table breaking under my weight.

I groaned and tried to rise.

"HE'S CLAUSTRAPHOBIC!" I could hear Nero scream. "He'll go fucking crazy in there!" Nero let out a sob. "Put me in there, I did this, it was my idea. Put me in there!"

As I got to my feet I saw Silas walking past him towards the credenza, Perish's blood still soaked into the carpet.

"I don't give a shit; he can go mad in there," Silas said bitterly. "It's about time for another cleansing, and I'm looking forward to seeing the horror on your faces as I execute your partners one by one. You fucking failures." He opened up the credenza drawer. "And with Kessler now leading the Legion – I see no reason to have your shadow taint mine."

"How about we encase you in concrete?" Nero said lowly. "How about we put you away instead? This fucking entire city would run just the same without you. We already do everything for you anyway. You're the worthless one not us and everyone knows it, from Elish to Drake. You're just a crazy maniac that everyone hates. Which is why no one wants to be around you, which is why you have to force us to spend–"

Silas turned around, a revolver in his hand; he raised it with no more words and shot Nero in the head.

I didn't move as my friend stumbled back, a dark spot on his forehead that immediately started leaking blood, and I didn't flinch when Silas shot him again in the face, blowing off the side of his jaw.

Silas put the gun back into the credenza, the sounds of the gun blast making my ears throb.

"Leave, Sanguine," Silas said dully, the only sound besides the ringing inside of my ears was the light closing of the wooden door.

"Silas…" I said slowly.

I was alarmed to see the anger gone in his eyes, the passion and the fire that had been injecting hatred into me and the others since I had stepped foot in his apartment. He looked…

Done.

"Leave," Silas said again, still staring down at the shelf in the credenza, looking more sad and empty than I had ever seen him. He reminded me of – damn, he reminded me of how I looked.

My mind went back to my life before I had come to Skyfall and the tumultuous year that followed. I had seen that dead look on myself many times, and even with Ceph suffering below and Nero and the sengil dead around me, I felt more sadness and empathy for the king than I had ever experienced before, and not only that, I felt understanding and sympathy. Because even though he had done, and continued to do, terrible things, I knew why he did them.

When I was at the lowest point of my life, my king had coaxed me out from under the bed. He had loved me through my insanity and had taken care of and nurtured the seeds of trust in me he had planted. Silas had let me be with my boyfriend, the love of my life, for twenty years, and had even understood my request to date my own sengil when I had been told that Valentine was dying.

Here I stood in front of my king, and though he was just a king and a master to so many of our brothers – to me, Silas was more than that. I had seen the mask slip off of his face and had neither been horrified or scared of what I had seen. Because underneath the hatred, the jealousy, and the mania… I saw a man with a sense of humour, patience, kindness, and generosity.

I knew who Silas Sebastian Dekker really was.

And as I walked into the elevator and pressed the button for the lobby, I was reminded that, especially with Elish's growing resentment, I might just be the last man on earth who did know him.

The drive to me and Jack's skyscraper was the longest one I had ever had. In that twenty minutes I made many resolutions to myself, most of which made my heart hurt. But there was nothing more I could do, though I would tell them I was doing it to protect my family, and protect my family's partners, in truth I was doing it because I held inside of me a loyalty to Silas Dekker that rose higher than the love for my family.

I will never forget what Silas did for me when I was at my weakest, and seeing the state he was in now, I was going to do the same for my king.

And not only that... if I was close to Ceph... perhaps there was something I could do for him too. If only to help him keep his sanity.

My Jack, my little silver devil, was sitting on the couch with Jett on his lap. My first kitten, now a twenty-one-year-old elderly cat, was laying his head on Jack's leg, looking content.

"Is everything okay? You – you have blood all over your clothing, why are you wearing a jacket now? Are you hurt?" As soon as Jack saw my face his own paled; he gently shifted his leg away from Jett and stood up.

I could already feel my heart break to pieces, shard by shard they fell onto the floor, only to disappear into the darkened abyss that was below it. But I knew what I had to do, so I steeled myself, even if the burning in the back of my throat was telling me I was on the verge of my own breakdown.

I put a hand to his face, and in response he tilted his head towards my touch.

"I love you, and I will always love you, *diligo*," I said to him, and at this statement his eyes widened in surprise. "But it is time for me to repay my debt to Silas."

"W-what?" Jack whispered. His black eyes immediately filled, like a dark ocean on a moonless night. "What happened, Sanguine? Y-you can't be serious."

I framed his face with my hands and leaned in and kissed him; his lips trembled under mine. "I will come back for you, but for now... Silas needs me more than you do."

Jack pulled away; I was disheartened but not surprised to see his face change from sadness to anger. "Silas? Silas needs you? What the hell does he need you for? What are you saying?" Jack's voice started to rise. "He said you were free to date who you wanted so don't fucking give me that. Is he making you do this?"

I shook my head as I started to walk back to the door to the hallway; I hadn't even closed it. "No, he is not making me do this."

"Then why!" Jack demanded. "Why are you doing this if he's not making you?"

"I'll come back for you, one day," I said again, my throat tightened further. I swallowed hard though my resolve was quickly leaving me.

"Come back for me?" Jack suddenly screamed. "Like I'm some fucking side-whore waiting for his master to come back? Fuck you! Why are you doing this? Tell me! What happened there? You only said he had Ceph and fucking left. What the fuck happened?"

I can't tell you – another secret I've kept from you for years.

"Sanguine!" Jack screamed as I walked out of the door and back towards the elevator. "I've been your boyfriend for twenty years. You've never kept shit from me before so tell me – tell me what happened."

I pushed the button on the elevator and briefly closed my eyes, another deep breath filled my lungs but it felt like I was inhaling from inside a burning building.

"I need to be with him now; he's not in a good state. You know I owe him, and I mu-"

"You're not a fucking martyr!" Jack yelled, then I heard him sob. "Stop being a fucking martyr! You did the same shit with Valen when we found out he was dying. You go and sacrifice your happiness for others, and in turn you end up fucking me over as well. Don't do it this time; you owe Silas nothing! I'm your fucking boyfriend, Sanguine. When you go off and do these selfless missions of misery you end up screwing me as well. Just don't, not this time, Sanguine. Not this time."

"I owe him my life," I whispered, and not only did Silas's head flash through my vision, but Nero's did as well. If I could… if I did this… I could help Ceph. I knew I could. "My life belongs to them."

"NO IT DOESN'T!" Jack was hysterical; my eyes started to burn. The pain in his voice was too much to bear. "It's been twenty years; you've repaid your debts! Sanguine, you need to stop this self-sacrificing, you're your own person now. You don't owe them." As I walked through the doors he let out another strangled choke. "Sami, please!"

I stepped into the elevator and when I turned around Jack was on his knees in front of me, his hands clasped to his front. He was begging me.

I had to be strong. I had to be strong. I could do this and I had to do this. He would understand why one day. This wasn't about me, or him, this was about saving the family, saving Silas, and saving Ceph.

"I love you, don't do this to me. Don't do this to you. It's time for you to just be Sanguine and stop putting their happiness before yours – before ours," Jack pleaded. "Please, Sami."

My eyes closed; I could feel the tears slipping down my cheeks.

But I still opened them – and pressed the button for the lobby.

"I'm sorry," I whispered to him. Finally, unable to hold it back any longer I let out a sob and put my hand over my mouth. "I love you."

Jack, tears streaming down his face and his shoulders trembling, stared at me as the elevator doors closed. The last image I had of my boyfriend, before he became just my brother, was him on his knees, pleading at me to stay.

But I couldn't stay, and perhaps one day I could make him understand why.

Twenty minutes later found me walking the hallway back to Silas's apartment, though to me if felt like I was walking down the valleys of the shadow of death.

Though as that ancient passage said, I would fear no evil. To me Silas had never been evil, and because this was known deep in my heart I knew it was my responsibility to be the one to calm him. A task that no one in my large family could take on. The last man to walk side by side with the enigma that was Silas Dekker had been slowly turning his cheek to him in the last several years.

I stopped in front of the ajar door and held my head up high. For a moment my eyes closed and in the darkness I saw the face of my boyfriend, and in that same darkness I let him go, with only the faint comfort that we were both immortal, and one day my hand would once again find his. In these last remaining moments of my freedom I wished him well, and to show myself that, unlike Silas, I was not a jealous man, I even wished that he would find someone else until I could claim him as my partner once again.

Then after allowing myself my last moments of melancholy, I pushed it away with a deep inhale – and walked through the doors.

To my grim realization I saw that Silas hadn't moved at all. The tortured king was standing in front of the bloodstained credenza, staring with empty eyes at the drawer. Nero still dead only several feet from him, and the poor mutilated sengil as cold as the chills still sweeping my body.

Without a word I walked up to him. I rested a caring hand on his shoulder and rubbed it, but still Silas didn't move. I wondered with sadness just what was going on inside of that head, for I knew the more still I had been, the louder the tormenting voices inside my mind were.

I bet the voices that had once ravaged my head held no candle to the ones inside of Silas's.

The thought made me squeeze his shoulder, clammy and tense under my hand. "If you will let me, my king," I said quietly. "I would like to pledge my life to you."

Silas looked up from the credenza, my words seemingly breaking his hypnotic almost catatonic state. "What?" he said in a dead voice, one that held none of its former power.

"I would like to become your sengil. I want to devote my immortal life to your care and happiness until you no longer wish me around, if you will allow it."

Silas turned around and looked at me, the agony and sadness deeply painted on his face. In this moment, my terrible king seemed but a forgotten waif, a shell of the terror he once was.

"Why?" Silas whispered.

I gently grabbed his hand and squeezed it. "Because I love you." I kissed his hand gently. "More than I love Jack, and more than I love my freedom. Let me serve you, Master."

Intently I stared at him, tracing my eyes over each feature in his face, analyzing each movement, each strand of tension. Wanting to gauge every reaction to see if this is what he wanted, if my need to help him was truly something that he could see as beneficial. So badly did I want to help my king, to tend to him and take care of him body, mind, and spirit, to rebuild him as he did me, without judgement.

Elish had always had underhanded intentions when it came to loving Silas, whether he would admit it or not. And perhaps a part of me did as well, though my inner hope that I could help Ceph with his punishment was only a small part of my drive to help my king.

Ceph… claustrophobic Ceph. If Silas would let me back into his heart, and his home – I could help you. I have my ideas and my plans. As I healed Silas I can give you the tools to help you during the maddening monotony I know you're experiencing.

Everyone will benefit from this, and the only man who wouldn't – one day I would make him understand.

"Please, Silas. I love you more than any of them, this you know." My lips tenderly kissed his hand a second time. "So let me serve you. Let me be the one to be beside you."

The king watched me rub his hand, the expression on his face barren. The silence that overtook him coated both of us, and under that cloak the two of us stood in the reticence for over a minute.

I had almost given up and taken my idea as a failure, when I saw him nod.

"Okay," was all he said back.

<u>A Note from Quil</u>

Well that was definitely a difficult book to write for many reasons, the time that Sami spent at Jasper's especially. I wanted to tell Sami's whole story but was left with the issue of not wanting to go into great detail with the physical things that Jasper did to Sami. I know I'm not one to gloss over anything sexual in my books but quite frankly that goes out the window when dealing with young kids (obviously). You don't want to read about it and I don't want to write about it, but I think I got the point across without (as I said in the beginning of the book) glorifying it or embellishing it. In the end I think I did Sanguine justice and told his story in the best way I possibly could.

I wish this book could've gone on for longer though to be honest. There are a lot of things I wish I could've written about but, once again, book length held me back and the fact that there is just so much to tell! Don't worry though; this is what companion books are for.

I am planning on *at least* six books in the main Fallocaust Series and that means six companion books as well. Please remember that the first generation of immortals are ninety-one years old, Sanguine was seventy when the main series started. There is a huge expanse of time from where Severing Sanguine ends to when the main series begins. I can't stuff all of that into one companion book without selling all of my characters' stories short. So please, be patient! Their stories will all be told as the series goes on. No one will be forgotten about and it will eventually all weave together. Instant gratification won't be found in The Fallocaust Series but if you will be patient and let me tell the story how I feel it should be told – it will be fucking amazing.

Next on the list is polishing up The Gods' Games and I am still hoping to have it released summer or fall 2015. After that I will either be working on that book's companion book or moving on to Fallocaust Book 3. Please check out my website www.quilcarter.com for my 2015 to-do list and my current progress.

I would also like to thank Kristie and Mare for being my beta readers. You two are awesome, thank you for helping me with Severing Sanguine. And thank you to Christina for making the book covers to my physical books look awesome, for being a beta reader also, and for just being your crazy self.

And as usual for updates on book releases, to view excerpts, or to watch my continuing descent into madness, follow me on Twitter @Fallocaust, also find me on Facebook /quil.carter.

Thank you for continuing this journey with me.

Sincerely,

Quil Carter

Printed in Great Britain
by Amazon